PRAISE FOR

SONG OF THE NILE

"Selene has a fascinating history . . . Stephanie Dray has done a wonderful job bringing to life one of history's lesser-known women, weaving magic, intrigue, and historical characters into a must-read novel for fans of historical fiction." —*Night Owl Reviews*

"Author Stephanie Dray did a splendid job of re-creating Selene from vulnerable young woman to woman of great strength . . . Delicious prose, an exotic setting, and a heroine that will impress you with her unfailing courage and determination to reclaim what was once hers . . . historical women's fiction at its finest." —*History and Women*

LILY OF THE NILE

"Stephanie Dray's *Lily of the Nile* is a spectacular blend of history and unforgettable fiction . . . a fresh and vibrant story of family, loyalty, political games, and love. It's exquisitely written and left me begging for more. The only letdown was that it had to end."
—*San Francisco Book Review*

"In this account of the fate of Cleopatra's daughter in the household of Augustus Caesar, Dray reveals the same events we've seen in *Rome* and *I, Claudius* from a very different perspective, that of a teenage girl. Cleopatra Selene has unusual gifts and problems, but her struggle to understand herself and her destiny is universal. The glimpses of the cult of Isis leave one wanting to know more, and the story keeps you turning the pages until the end."
—Diana L. Paxson, author of *Marion Zimmer Bradley's Sword of Avalon*

continued . . .

"*Lily of the Nile* is graceful history infused with subtle magic and veiled ancient mysteries, at a time of immense flux and transition. Cleopatra Selene—regal, stoic, and indomitable daughter of the legendary Pharaoh-Queen Cleopatra—carries on the spirit of her mother, the goddess Isis, and the soul of Egypt itself into the lair of the conquering imperial enemy. Selene, whose skin speaks the words of queen and goddess in blood, channels the dynastic pride that is her birthright, and seals the fate of the Roman Empire. Meticulously researched, thoroughly believable, this is a different kind of book, and a true achievement."

—Vera Nazarian, two-time Nebula Award–nominated author of
Lords of Rainbow and *Mansfield Park and Mummies*

"With clear prose, careful research, vivid detail, and a dash of magic, Stephanie Dray brings true life to one of Egypt's most intriguing princesses."

—Susan Fraser King, bestselling and award-winning author of
Queen Hereafter and *Lady Macbeth*

Berkley Titles by Stephanie Dray

LILY OF THE NILE

SONG OF THE NILE

DAUGHTERS OF THE NILE

DAUGHTERS
of the
NILE

A NOVEL OF CLEOPATRA'S DAUGHTER

STEPHANIE DRAY

BERKLEY BOOKS, NEW YORK

THE BERKLEY PUBLISHING GROUP
Published by the Penguin Group
Penguin Group (USA) LLC
375 Hudson Street, New York, New York 10014

USA • Canada • UK • Ireland • Australia • New Zealand • India • South Africa • China

penguin.com

A Penguin Random House Company

DAUGHTERS OF THE NILE

This book is an original publication of The Berkley Publishing Group.

Berkley trade paperback ISBN: 978-0-425-25836-1

An application to register this book has been submitted to the Library of Congress.

PUBLISHING HISTORY
Berkley trade paperback edition / December 2013

PRINTED IN THE UNITED STATES OF AMERICA

10 9 8 7 6 5 4 3 2 1

Cover art by Alan Ayers.
Cover design by Judith Lagerman.
Interior text design by Kristin del Rosario.

*To my sister, Jennifer, a daughter of the Nile
without whom this journey would be unbearably lonely.*

Dear Reader,

I've adopted some conventions that bear explanation. To start with, I've embraced the most familiar spellings and naming conventions for historical figures. For example, I've used Mark Antony for Marcus Antonius, Octavian instead of Octavius or Octavianus, and Cleopatra instead of Kleopatra. I've also used English words for Latin concepts whenever possible. One instance is my adoption of the word *lady* when the word *domina* may have been more accurate. Another is *book* instead of *codex*. Moreover, I've addressed Augustus as the emperor throughout the novel even though our modern understanding of the word differs greatly from the traditional Roman concept of an imperator. I stand by this choice because of his nontraditional use of *imperator*—a title he held lawfully in 43 B.C. and should have relinquished that same year but did not.

I've tried to respect this work as a novel more than as a biography, and my choices and changes are explained in the author's note at the end of this book. My heroine's relatively uncritical acceptance of the idea that native peoples must be "civilized" is not an endorsement of the idea but a reflection of the historical attitude of the time. Moreover, I've unabashedly adopted the slant most favorable to Egypt, Selene, her family, and her religion; the biased perspective against Rome and Augustus reflects her views as I've imagined them, not my own.

ACKNOWLEDGEMENTS

First, my thanks go to my wonderful husband for his patience, love, and support. Next, to my family, for their enthusiasm and encouragement. Then to sharp-eyed critique partners Sheila Accongio, Christi Barth, Gabrielle Carolina, Eliza Knight, Kate Quinn, Vicky Alvear Shecter, Kristen Stappenbeck-Baker, Stephanie Thornton, and Becky Wilson.

Many thanks too, to one of my literary heroines, Margaret George, for taking the time to read this manuscript before it was polished. Thanks also go to my fellow historical authors, Sophie Perinot, for moral support, and Teralyn Rose Pilgrim for help with the Vestal Virgins. I'm grateful to Kristianne Scalese Buker for help with flowers, Ana Beniquez-Sabo for help with interesting research tips on the Garamantes, Rachel Blackmun for various pieces of advice on writing in the ancient world and to Christine Rovet for information on plowing.

I must again thank Duane W. Roller, professor emeritus of Greek and Latin at Ohio State University for generously answering questions and offering advice. Historian Lindsay Powell also talked me through theories on Agrippa, and his book on Drusus the Elder was invaluable to me. Nevertheless, any mistakes in this manuscript are mine and mine alone, and should not be ascribed to anyone who helped me.

Mindful that footnotes are distracting in historical fiction and that my sources are too numerous to cite here, I would, nonetheless, like to credit several. For information on architecture, I consulted the writings of Vitruvius. For calculating travel times, I consulted Scheidel, W. and

Meeks, E. (May 2, 2012). ORBIS: The Stanford Geospatial Network Model of the Roman World at http://orbis.stanford.edu. And for information on Carthaginian architecture, I cite the work of Mark Dienekes on Historum.com. In my study of the Ara Pacis, I owe a debt of gratitude to Wayne Andersen's *The Ara Pacis of Augustus and Mussolini.*

I am again indebted to other authors who have also tried to bring Selene's world to life, including Andrea Ashton, Alice Curtis Desmond, Michelle Moran, and Vicky Alvear Shecter. Additionally, I cite W. W. Tarn's scholarly paper titled "Alexander Helios and the Golden Age" as well as Duane W. Roller's *The World of Juba II and Kleopatra Selene,* Margaret George's *The Memoirs of Cleopatra,* and the splashy Hollywood film *Cleopatra,* starring Elizabeth Taylor.

However, it was Beatrice Chanler's 1934 novel *Cleopatra's Daughter: The Queen of Mauretania* that inspired me most. My work is heavily influenced by her ideas, imagery, and lofty prose. In particular, Ms. Chanler's book captured my imagination because of its unusual theory that Cleopatra Selene and her twin brother were religious symbols—a theory that I've extended into the fantastic.

In adopting and modernizing this theory by reimagining Isiac worship, I relied not just upon ancient sources and current scholarship but also upon the worship of Isis as it's currently practiced. M. Isadora Forrest's *Isis Magic* was invaluable on that count, as was Ms. Forrest herself, who kindly offered advice on rituals that Selene may have been familiar with. The calling prayer of Isis in this novel is her work. In seeking an authentic and educational vision of death that would illuminate the ancient mind, I turned to Normandi Ellis's moving translation of *The Egyptian Book of the Dead* for inspiration in crafting both Cleopatra's final thoughts and Selene's. While *The Egyptian Book of the Dead* is as old as civilization, Ms. Ellis's *Awakening Osiris* is one of the most beautiful translations ever written and helped me form the spiritual core of this series.

While it is always dangerous to speculate about the sexuality of historical figures, I was emboldened to envision an affair between Virgil and Marcellus in this series after reading *Virgil in the Renaissance* by David Scott Wilson-Okamura and Saara Lilja's *Homosexuality in Repub-*

lican and Augustan Rome. In this series, I've explored Selene's sexual morality through the lens of mythic Isiac fertility rites, which is rooted in Merlin Stone's fascinating book *When God Was a Woman*, itself inspired by the work of Robert Graves. While no record of Isiac mystery rites has survived, I drew upon the legend that Isis herself had served as a prostitute in Tyre. I was also mindful of Herodotus's claim that female adherents of goddess cults gave themselves to a stranger at least once in their lives—an idea echoed by Strabo. And, of course, I must express appreciation for *The Golden Ass: Being the Metamorphoses of Lucius Apuleius*, an Isiac work and the only Latin novel to survive in its entirety. I blended all this information with extant accounts of the Eleusinian Mysteries. And Josephus was invaluable with regard to all the story lines regarding Herod.

Insofar as this novel is about Augustus, I relied upon ancient historians Cassius Dio, Suetonius, and Tacitus, and I freely admit to having adopted the latter's most uncharitable views of Livia. When it came to reconstructing Berber culture as it may have existed in Selene's reign, I consulted Susan Raven's *Rome in Africa,* Paul MacKendrick's *The North African Stones Speak*, and *The Berbers* by Michael Brett and Elizabeth Fentress.

Additional inspiration was derived from Petronius, Mary Renault's work on Alexander the Great, and Elaine Fantham's work on Julia Augusti. For additional sources, please see my website at stephaniedray.com.

CHARACTERS

The Court of Augustus Caesar

AUGUSTUS CAESAR, or Octavian, Gaius Julius Caesar Octavianus, the Emperor of Rome

    JULIA, his daughter by his former wife Scribonia, and his only child

    AGRIPPA, his son-in-law and most powerful general
        Gaius, his son, the emperor's grandson and heir
        Lucius, his son, the emperor's grandson and heir
        Julilla, his daughter, the emperor's first granddaughter
        Agrippina, his daughter, the emperor's granddaughter
        Postumus, his son, the emperor's grandson

    LIVIA DRUSILLA, his wife, scion of a powerful noble family, the *Claudii*
        Tiberius, her oldest son by her former husband, the stepson of the emperor
            Vipsania, his wife, the daughter of Agrippa from a previous marriage
        Drusus, her youngest son by her former husband, the stepson of the emperor

    OCTAVIA, his long-suffering sister
        Marcella, her daughter by her first husband
        Iullus Antonius, her son-in-law, son of Mark Antony, husband of Marcella
        Antonia Major, her eldest daughter by Mark Antony
        Antonia Minor, her youngest daughter by Mark Antony, also called Minora, wife of Drusus

Germanicus, their eldest son, Livia's grandson
Livilla, their eldest daughter, Livia's grandson
Claudius, their youngest son, sickly and enfeebled, Livia's grandson

MAECENAS, his political adviser and overseer of imperial artistic programs
Terentilla, the beautiful wife of Maecenas and former mistress of Augustus

ANTONIUS MUSA, his renowned physician, a freedman of Mark Antony's

The Court of Cleopatra Selene & Juba II

CLEOPATRA SELENE, Queen of Mauretania, Daughter of Cleopatra VII of Egypt and Mark Antony

JUBA, her husband, the Berber-blooded King of Mauretania
Isidora, their daughter, the Princess of Mauretania
Tacfarinas, her childhood playmate, a Numidian tribesman
Ptolemy, their son, the Prince of Mauretania

PYTHODORIDA, her niece, ward of the queen

CHRYSSA, her Greek freedwoman, now a court minister
Maysar, her husband, a Berber tribal leader and royal adviser

TALA, her Berber attendant, sister of Maysar
Ziri, her son, later called Mazippa

CAPTAIN KABYLE, her Berber-born ship's captain

EUPHRONIUS/EUPHORBUS, her court physician, mage, and priest of Isis from Alexandria

CRINAGORAS OF MYTILENE, her court poet

MEMNON, her captain of the Macedonian guard from Alexandria

LADY LASTHENIA, her adviser, a Pythagorean scholar from Alexandria

MASTER GNAIOS, her father's famous gem cutter, now her court sculptor

LEONTEUS OF ARGOS, her court tragedian

CIRCE, a Greek *hetaera* turned grammarian and teacher at court

DAUGHTERS
OF THE
NILE

PART ONE

THE SOWING

One

I will never see my mother's Egypt again, I think. The closest I will
ever come to touching my native soil is bathing in the same sea of
green that caresses its shores. So each morning, I go down to the
water where the frothing waves tumble over themselves and the
brine-scented spray leaves salty kisses upon my cheeks. Squinting
into the brightness, I might imagine that the lighthouse gleaming
white in the harbor is a far-off vision of the Pharos of Alexandria.
But the breeze that sweeps over the forest of ships' masts reminds
me that this is my kingdom of Mauretania. This wind carries with
it no Song of the Nile, but the melodic voices of my Berber fisher-
men, singing as they haul in their nets.

Later, my skin tingling with dried salt water, I linger between
the billowing white curtains of my chambers in the palace. Standing
beside me, stirring a dark greenish-brown paste in a bowl, is Tala,
my chief attendant, the woman who nursed my daughter—the only
one I trust to care for my little princess. Together we watch my
women gather henna in my gardens. They squat with their colorful
skirts hitched up to their knees as they choose leaves for their baskets
and cut efficient swaths with sharp scythes.

As Tala stirs the paste, her silver bracelets and beaded earrings
jingle, outdone in their brilliance only by the indigo shawl draped
over her hair, the dye from which stains her skin blue at the creases.
"Best to harvest all the henna now before the winter rains come,"

she says. "By the time we finish making you beautiful for the king's visit, we'll have used all the henna we have left in the storeroom."

Though I've been married to the King of Mauretania for more than five years, our marriage is only by contract.

Tonight will be the first time I take him into my bed.

This I must do if I want a life of my own, an escape from the emperor who forced my parents to suicide and made me his war trophy. His possession. His mistress. The emperor will never believe that I do not belong to him unless he sees me as the true wife of another man. So if I will not make love to Augustus Caesar, I must make love to my husband.

Lavender perfume wafts up from the linens, and a shift of gossamer white drapes over the chest at the foot of my bed. Every beeswax candle in the palace has been brought to my chambers as if to turn my bed into a sacred altar. But the preparations make me uneasy. "Must we go to so much trouble? King Juba is, at heart, a practical man."

Tala tests the consistency of the henna paste between her fingers. "He is also a man preparing himself for you as a bridegroom. After his morning ride on his new stallion, he washed, sat in the steam room, and had himself rubbed down by a Nubian slave before calling for a barber. He's demanded a special dinner in your rooms and hasn't let a drop of wine touch his lips."

Warily, I ask, "How do you know this? Do you have spies in his chambers?"

Tala shrugs with insolent mirth. "If I reveal my sources, you'll think I'm easily replaced."

"What if I paid you extra to tell me?"

She grins. "Never haggle with a Berber, Queen Selene. You cannot win."

Tala is typical of my adopted people. Proud and resilient with a fierce sense of self. I've chosen to live amongst the Berbers and rule as their queen. I've *chosen*, I remind myself, to forsake my mother's throne in Egypt and make my life here with a man who is my husband but is also, in many ways, still a stranger to me.

In making myself ready for him, I allow the servants to pluck every hair on my body below my eyebrows. I linger in a bath of honey and almond milk. Then the slaves dry me with warm towels. They massage lavender oil into the muscles of my arms and legs until I'm so limp and lethargic that I quietly acquiesce to the painting of Berber patterns on my nude flesh.

I try to adopt the native customs of my kingdom whenever practicable. In this case the custom suits me, because Berber brides go to their husbands tattooed. As my husband is a Berber by blood, I hope it will please him.

While the henna sets, Tala urges me to play a game of Senet with her. I race my ivory cones against her ebony wheels until I emerge victorious, a thing from which I take great satisfaction because it's not in Tala's character to let me win. When it's finally time to scrape the dried henna from my body, she reassures me, "The color will change in time. The tattoo will deepen, just like the love between a husband and wife."

At this, I scowl. For though I'm the daughter of two famous lovers, I didn't marry for love. By the traditions of my family, I would have married my oldest brother, Caesarion, the King of Egypt. When the Romans murdered him and conquered Egypt, I should have wed my twin brother, Alexander Helios.

But when I came of age, the emperor wanted me for himself.

In Juba, the emperor found a man who was willing to pose as my husband. It was only as the spoils of war, as a reward for his loyalty, that I was given to this Berber king. In truth, I have many reasons to despise him—and not only because of our chaste wedding night and his willingness to surrender me into the emperor's bed. I am acutely aware that my husband has, in his own way, been partly responsible for every tragedy that has befallen my family and me.

And yet my resentment is tempered by the knowledge that I have betrayed him too. Tonight we must forget these betrayals, so I want to be done with these endless preparations for an act that has been more than five years in the waiting. "Let us not speak of the love between a husband and a wife, Tala. There's no need to fill my head with romantic notions. I'm no fearful virgin."

Never cowed by my imperious nature, she asks, "Then why are you sweating like one?"

She's right. In spite of the coolness of the autumnal evening, my nape is damp. Fortunately, I'm not compelled to answer her question because we're interrupted by the king's slaves, who beg admittance to deliver platters of food for our supper.

Tala makes them wait as she finishes dressing me. A touch of red ochre to my lips and I am left to recline upon cushions on the floor, where I will receive the king. Meanwhile, my husband stands awkwardly in the doorway with his slaves and our dinner.

King Juba is ten years my senior, and the years sit well on him. He's a man with a head of thick dark hair and high cheekbones. I've always liked the look of him, and I see that tonight he's resplendent in a purple tunic embroidered with pearls.

He is a handsome man; perhaps my duty will not be so unpleasant.

When we're alone, the king takes his place on cushions beside the low table. A flicker of lamplight shadows his eyes, so I cannot read his expression. I offer him first choice from the plate of lamb shank braised with quince and cinnamon, saying, "I hope I didn't make you wait so long that it's turned cold."

Juba cocks an eyebrow. "Do you refer to our meal or to your bed?"

I smile at his cutting joke, for it reminds me that the king can be witty. Tearing a piece of warm bread from the loaf, I use it to scoop up a little of the meat. The aromatic dish is delicious and I'm grateful that he's arranged for this private meal, as I'm uncertain I could bear with any dignity the ribald jests of our courtiers, who take an interest in our long-awaited reunion. It is already difficult enough to woo and be wooed without the eyes of others upon us.

"Will you have wine?" I ask.

The king shakes his head. "I had enough when we were apart."

It is, I think, his apology for the way I found him when I returned to Mauretania. He was abed in daylight, drunk to the point of illness. Nevertheless, I now fill his goblet near to overflowing, saying, "It's my opinion that tonight we should drink to excess. My parents formed the Society of Inimitable Livers . . . We should see whether it's possible to imitate them after all."

"As I remember it, the girl I married wasn't overly fond of wine or frivolity."

The girl he married was a fourteen-year-old captive too consumed with the fear of death to take pleasure in life. He has only known me as the emperor's caged bird, a prisoner of Rome and of my own ambition. All that has changed. It *must* change. I gulp from my own cup, then say, "I'm a woman of twenty years now—almost twenty-one. The girl you married is no more."

He leans back, eyeing me carefully. "So I'm married to a stranger."

"Aren't we all?"

Juba gestures like an athlete in the arena who has been felled by a well-dealt blow. Then he lifts his goblet. We toast in honor of something we do not name. We drink to fill the silence. My husband is a learned man who knows well how to pass the time in banter, but the weight of what we're about to do consumes our feeble attempts at lighthearted conversation. "Will you tell me what happened?" he finally asks when the wine has loosened his tongue. "Tell me why the emperor has sent you back to me."

Since I was a little girl, marched through the streets of Rome in chains behind a statue of my dead mother, Cleopatra, I have been the emperor's possession and obsession. Juba has always known it. What my husband wants to know now is why the emperor has finally released me. And I don't want to tell him. There are things that I *cannot* tell him. Things too painful to remember. Things he would never understand or believe. "Let it be enough to know that I'm done with Rome, and Augustus too."

Juba snorts. "Augustus could turn our kingdom into a Roman province with a snap of his fingers. He's our patron, Selene."

I do not need reminding. Everything my husband has ever done has been precisely calculated to please the emperor, and I hate this about him. It's also what I hate about myself, for I have done the same. The memory makes me drain my cup, then fill it again. Wine will make this night easier.

Come, Dionysus, and dull my senses.

"We owe Caesar our fealty," Juba continues, as if trying to talk himself out of touching me.

Perhaps he feels as if he needs his master's permission, which makes me insist, "We owe him nothing more than fealty. If he wishes, let him declare an end to the Roman Republic. Let him call himself King of Rome, the King of Kings. Let him rule the world from the Palatine Hill and settle the squabbles of all his client kingdoms. We can keep ourselves apart, here in Mauretania, and reign in peace."

Juba considers my words, staring at the rim of his cup. "It will be no simple thing. You're a Ptolemy, born to intrigue, drawn to the center of political power like a moth to flame . . ."

It irritates me that he uses my legacy as an accusation, when it's my prestigious bloodline that helped secure his throne. "You're the one who longs to return to Rome, not me."

I think he might deny it, but he wipes the corners of his mouth with a napkin and says, "I dreamed all my life of returning to Africa as a king, never realizing that it would be an honorable sort of exile. I pine for Rome because that is the only home I've ever known. But Mauretania is our kingdom now and it must become a home for us both."

His stark honesty softens me. He must sense it, for he offers me a hand and helps me to rise. My sweat-slicked palm slides through his grip and my cheeks flush. I've spent a lifetime masking my emotions, mastering my body down to the slightest tremble so as not to quail from the emperor's touch. But I cannot seem to cool my blood, which now runs hot with anticipation.

There can be no going back from this.

Juba seems as anxious as I am about the long-overdue consummation of our marriage, and when our eyes meet his voice becomes a hoarse whisper. "It doesn't have to be tonight."

He's wrong. It must be tonight, before the emperor thinks better of having let me go. It must be tonight, before I am again summoned to Rome to play another deadly political game. It must be tonight, before either of us loses our courage. So I tilt my face to him in invitation, sweeping my eyelashes low in the way I have learned excites a man. It has the desired effect. As if resolving an argument inside himself, Juba says, "Cleopatra's daughter, you *are* lovely." Then he catches sight of the pale henna designs on my skin and frowns. "But why must you come to me painted?"

Because I can never let you see me unmasked.

The henna is set. He cannot wipe the intricate designs away like he wiped my face clean of paint the night we were wed. These tattoos are, for a time, an indelible part of me. A barrier that he cannot breach. The only defense I have. "Tala said this is ornamentation for Berber brides."

"But you are no maiden bride," he replies, as if to shame me for having attracted the emperor's lust. "These patterns only remind me I'm not your first lover."

It would be easy to let my temper boil with offense, but I am guiltier than he knows. I carry a secret love for a man whose name I cannot say, so my tart reply is without real venom. "Yet I need no henna to remind me that your bejeweled *hetaera* still graces our court, well rewarded for having prostituted herself to you. She cannot be the only one . . ."

My husband takes in a breath as if in preparation for a bitter rejoinder, but then chuckles. "Only you would think that a relevant comparison. A wife has a duty of marital fidelity; a man may take pleasure where he likes."

It's pointless to argue, for in truth, I don't much care where my husband takes pleasure. I know what it is to feel the *true* stab of jealousy, one that bleeds your soul. I've drowned in misery and longing for the man I love. Juba is not that man. Nor is the emperor that man. That man, my true king, the other half of my soul, may be forever lost to me. And because I must swallow that bitter draught down with all the rest of it, I ask, "Must we speak of duty and dishonor?"

My husband brushes an errant strand of dark hair from my eyes. "I would have this night be about neither."

This night is about freedom. Perhaps, if I am honest with myself, curiosity too. I enjoy the way my husband looks at me now, heavy-lidded with years of unfulfilled desire. He's well in his cups and I must be too, for I speak with brazenness. "Do the tattoos trouble you so much, or will we make a son tonight?"

Experience has taught me that the desire for a son, an heir, and a legacy that reaches beyond the tomb can be a potent aphrodisiac. My husband is not immune. His pupils widen, the flickering lamp-light reflected in their dark depths, and he draws me closer, burying his nose in my hair, inhaling the lavender perfume with pleasure. With vague amusement he murmurs, "It may take more than just one night . . ."

But that is more than I am willing to promise. "No. We will need only one night to make our son. I need only open myself and invite my goddess into my body to make it come to pass. For I am a vessel of Isis and these things are in my gift."

Then I kiss him, lest he say anything to change my mind.

Two

THE KINGDOM OF MAURETANIA
SPRING 18 B.C.

IT is a month too early for my baby to be born. We hope my cramps are phantom pains that will subside, but they do not. Panting on my bed as we await the midwife, I wave Tala away. "I don't want to be painted again."

My Berber woman purses her lips. "Henna tattoos fight the evil that is drawn to childbirth."

She nearly died birthing her son, years ago, but surely I don't face such danger. I've inherited my notoriously fertile mother's wide birthing hips. My daughter was born healthy, and Isis has always watched over me. But the pain that pierces me now is so sharp it steals my breath.

At last, the midwife marches into my chambers with a contingent of slaves and servants who busy themselves in preparation, like an army on the eve of battle. At the head of their formation is Chryssa, my Greek freedwoman, fair hair piled atop her head in glistening ringlets, secured with expensive hairpins made of gold and sapphires. Though once she was a cowering slave, few hints of her former servitude remain, and she isn't hesitant to give orders in my presence. "Put the birthing chair by the window so she catches a breeze, and open the drapes. The queen likes to see the ocean."

In recent months, others have viewed my return to Mauretania with bewilderment. I am a Ptolemy, after all. The blood in my veins is the same Macedonian blood that thrummed through the veins of Alexander the Great. I am heir to the throne of Egypt. They wonder why I am here birthing a child for my Berber husband when I could be in Rome at the emperor's side, scheming to reclaim my mother's lost throne.

But Chryssa never wonders. Beneath her blousy *peplos* pinned with little gold brooches at each shoulder, she hides a tangle of pale, knotted scars—her keepsake from a flogging she received at the emperor's command. Chryssa knows better than anyone what manner of man the emperor is and why I fled from him to bear a son for my husband. She will never wonder. We need not even speak of it. And that it is why it is a comfort to have her near.

"Has anyone told the king?" she asks, critically inspecting the midwife's tools, linens, sea sponges, and pots of goose fat, olive oil, and sweet-smelling herbs.

"The king has yet to return from Spain," Tala replies.

"He should be here," my freedwoman snaps. "He is not the King of Spain!"

In this, she echoes my petty complaints. Here in Mauretania my husband is king. But in cities across the narrow strait in Spain, he has no royal authority. There he serves as a Roman magistrate, setting aside his crown to drape himself in a toga as the emperor's legate, sitting not upon a throne but upon a low folding curule chair—that strange little stool with curved legs that the Romans use as a sign of office.

My husband doesn't see this as an insult to his royal dignity nor does he resent it as yet another way in which Rome exploits his loyalty. To the contrary, my husband sees these unusual responsibilities as evidence of the emperor's faith in him. And so I find myself defending my husband in his absence. "It makes no difference if King Juba is here or away, and in any case, he had no cause to know the child would come so soon . . ."

Before I can say more, pain rips through me. I clutch my belly, groaning. The midwife examines me, her face grim. "It's too soon for the child."

Chryssa all but hisses. "We know it. Tell us what to do, woman. Or must I send for a civilized Greek physician?"

"He'll tell you the same thing," the midwife replies. "There's nothing to do but wait."

And so we wait. In the grips of agony, I feel sweat soak my hair and run down my back. Chryssa mops my brow with a cold cloth, murmuring a prayer to our goddess Isis that she may deliver me safely of a healthy child. Meanwhile, Tala again insists that I let her paint me, and I'm too pained to argue. She uses her henna paste to draw intricate symbols on my feet and ankles. When she reaches for my hands, however, I stop her, for they have been a canvas for symbols before.

I am Cleopatra's daughter. I am a sorceress. I have carried the words of my goddess on my outstretched palms, in vivid hieroglyphics that ran red with my own blood. I worry to submit my palms now to sacrilege. "What do the symbols mean?"

Tala looks up with impatience, using the same tone she uses to scold my little daughter. "On your feet, the symbols are protective talismans to keep evil from seeping up from the earth as you walk. Over your womb, a symbol of fertility. On your hands I would paint the stylized sun, to purify and protect you against your enemies. You know Egyptian magic, Majesty. But we Berbers have magic of our own."

When the first gushes of bloody water pool beneath me, I will gladly accept *any* magic to help my child. There shouldn't be so much pain. Surely there wasn't this much when my daughter was born. I would have remembered!

Tala wraps me in linens and I stifle the cries that threaten to tear from my throat. At length, an arrow of excruciating pain shoots through me. I scream and the voices of my attendants mingle into a dull, faraway roar.

I'm hoisted up onto the squat wooden birthing chair with its open bottom. Then the midwife waves a small clay pot of mint under my nose, and the bracing scent helps me make ready. Since the night I shared with the king, I've curled round my womb, cooing softly to the baby inside. I've dreamed of holding him safe and warm in my arms. To know my baby is struggling for life even now, before he has taken his first breath, fills me with a fierce determination.

This child will mark me as my own woman, no longer the emperor's plaything. This child will be the beginning of a new life that I've chosen in defiance of every expectation of me as Cleopatra's daughter. Even if my baby is tiny, I will see that he grows strong. I will safeguard him as Isis nursed her secret child in the marshy reeds of Egypt.

But first, I must give him breath.

"CHILDBED fever," someone says. And as I toss and turn upon sweat-soaked sheets, I'm filled with dread. Merciless *fever* has taken loved ones from me. I know to fear it. Fever ravages the body and the mind and it ravages me. My breasts leak and ache. My empty womb cramps and I cannot find my ease. I sleep too long. I shiver and burn by turns. My only comfort is the sound of a raspy cry, breathing ragged and desperate.

My son *does* breathe, and that is what matters.

After several nights—I do not know how many—I hear Chryssa murmuring prayers. I smell the burning sage she offers to our goddess. My Berber woman is there too, pressing a wooden talisman into my hand. It is the looped symbol, sacred to the native goddess Tanit. Narrowed only a little, it is also an *ankh*, the symbol most sacred to Isis. It is meant to protect my soul.

So they think I am dying . . .

Pharaohs journey to the West when they die, finding immortality with the setting sun. But I am not Pharaoh and Mauretania is already near the western edge of the living world. The world of the dead is very close now, just past the veil. I am not eager to reach beyond it, for I have fought for my life since I was a child. My survival has always been at the mercy of Augustus and his obsession with my mother, and then with me. All my life, I have charmed and reasoned and plotted to stay alive. But this illness cannot be charmed away or reasoned with or plotted against.

The luxurious room, with its wispy linen draperies and alabaster lamps, blurs white in my fevered eyes. Above my bed hangs a gilded circular frame carved with my proud Ptolemy Eagle. When I look up, he's no longer wooden but alive and glowing, spreading his wings. I blink and the bed netting that drapes from his jeweled talons turns to mist.

Then I see them. My lost loved ones. My regal mother wearing fat pearls and the amethyst ring that once was hers but is now my betrothal ring. My father is there too in his red cloak and crested parade helmet. My brothers, each one. Caesarion riding his horse, fitted out as the King of Egypt with a diadem of white ribbon in his hair, giving me a jaunty smile as only the son of Julius Caesar might. Our half brother Antyllus is at his side, his arms thrown open in generous welcome. There too is my little Philadelphus, ripe dates in one hand and a pair of dice in the other, his pudgy cheeks scrunched up in a smile.

I see them all sheltered by the iridescent wings of Isis. I want to go to them. I want to run to them. I want to clasp my mother round her perfumed neck and bury my face in her hair. I want to weep for the joy of our reunion upon my father's broad shoulder and feel the stubble of his chin scrape my cheek. I want to hold my brothers. Caesarion, and Antyllus, and Philadelphus, and . . .

"*Helios*," I moan from beneath the blankets where I shiver.

With his hair lit golden in the sun where he practices with his sword, he glances at me over one broad shoulder. That is how I know my eyes play me false. I *cannot* see Helios in the afterlife, for he is not there. Last of the Ptolemies, they call me. The only survivor. But I am not the only one. My twin brother escaped the emperor's clutches. They think he is dead, but he battles the Romans still, known only as an outlaw, Horus the Avenger. And yet, in my delirium, I see him in the afterworld.

Helios. My twin, my king, my beloved . . . he reaches one hand for me. The same hand I have been reaching for all my life. I long to take it. I long to rush into his strong arms, to be made whole again by his kiss, to love him and be loved by him. To beg his forgiveness, to stroke away every moment of separation between his skin and mine with fevered fingertips. I am desperate to go to him, but I cannot.

Last of the Ptolemies, they call me, but I am not the last.

I *won't* be the last.

I have a daughter, and when she was born, I swore to her that I would never leave her. I vowed never to leave her afraid and vulnerable the way my mother left me. Now I have a new baby son. He has not heard me make this promise to him, but I have already made it in my heart. I will never leave him. My mother surrendered to the venomous bite of an asp. My father fell upon his sharp sword. My brothers are dead or presumed to be. But life has always been my stubborn companion.

I *survive*. That is what I do.

"YOU'RE not meant for such an end as this, Cleopatra Selene."

Is it jackal-headed Anubis speaking, releasing me when he finds I am too tough a morsel to chew? I open my eyes to see not the death god but the mage at my bedside. This wise old man of Egypt is the only man, save the king, whom my guards would admit into my chambers. His name is Euphronius, but to escape the emperor's wrath, he masquerades at court as a physician by the name of Euphorbus Musa. I know the mage's secrets and he knows mine, for he has gifts of seeing I do not possess.

"How will I die?" I murmur. "Have you seen it in the Rivers of Time?"

My wizard presses a cool cloth to my brow. "You have years ahead of you, Majesty, and much left to do."

From my birth, much has been foretold. I was to be a divine child and a powerful queen. I was to bring about a Golden Age. I was to save my goddess too. I have failed at it all, save that I am queen. But if I am to fulfill any of the prophecies that attended my beginning, I think it will be easier to know how I will meet my end. Perhaps death will come to me in poison, offered to me by a false friend at the behest of my enemies. Perhaps it will be the edge of a knife's blade that slithers into my body to bear my soul away. Perhaps one day when I'm swimming, a strong current will drag me under and I will sink into blackness. Or perhaps it will be the venom of an asp, its fangs sunk deep into my flesh, bringing me to the gods like the serpent that killed my mother.

I think it will go better for me if I *know*.

"Tell me how I will die. I command you."

The old man only smiles, for he knows his disobedience will never result in punishment. He has been with me too long, or perhaps he has reached the age at which men no longer fear their monarchs. "Majesty, I can only tell you that yours will not be an ordinary death."

I awaken to the scent of roses. It is the season when blossoms are harvested to make wreaths for funerals, weddings, and festivals, so slaves have adorned my bedchamber in rose garlands. The whole palace teems with the perfume as I reach out for my son and they put him in my arms.

He is tiny and his skin is petal soft, pale like mine. I can see the blue veins beneath his skin. And I worry over a shallow indentation on his chin that I hope will become a dimple. My daughter hovers over us, watching her newborn brother sleep. I stare at them both, this daughter I didn't want and the son I shouldn't have had. And I love them fiercely. They are part of me, molded inside my body, brought into being like magic. They will be my legacy. The part of my family that lives on.

For nearly three hundred years the Ptolemies have thrived. It will not end with me.

With a lilt of excitement, my daughter says, "The king has returned from Spain, Mama. And he wants to see the baby."

My freedwoman frowns and I know what she is thinking. The baby is fragile yet. No one can say if he will live. Better to wait until little cheeks are flush with color lest a husband be tempted to order a sickly child be left on a hillside. Many babes have died at the command of their fathers, exposed to the elements, vulnerable to predators, at the mercy of the gods. This is what all my women are thinking, though they will not say it in front of my sweet daughter, Isidora.

And they dare not say it to me.

I draw my daughter close and kiss her fingertips. They are lightly sticky, as if she's recently visited the kitchens where the cook spoils her with honeycombs. My daughter has never known fear, and if I have my way, she never will. So, when she looks up at me with her unnerving blue gaze, I am decided. "Then we'll take the baby to the king."

My freedwoman frowns again. "Your fever has only just broken. You shouldn't be so soon out of bed, Majesty."

I do not want to admit that Chryssa speaks the truth, but as my servants dress me, I can barely stand upon my shaky legs. I feel bruised and battered inside. Worse, a glance in a polished mirror reflects back my image, deathly pale and stripped of vitality. Still, what I'm about to do, I need to do while I still have the courage for it.

Tala appears, her silver bracelets jingling together as she knocks lightly against the half-opened carved wooden door. "The king has called together the court to attend to him."

So we leave for the throne room, my sandaled feet shuffling slowly on the mosaic floors. My Macedonian guards snap to attention, their eyes lowered in deference. I am a tall woman, but I make myself stand taller, for I must preserve my reputation as a fertile young queen. My ability to bring forth life in this land is at the heart of the people's love for me. I cannot be seen as weak.

In an archway, I peer between shimmering draperies to see King Juba seated on his ivory throne chair—the one given to him by the Senate and people of Rome, along with a purple robe, ivory scepter, and golden crown. My husband's full lips turn down at the corners when he is pensive, and they are turned down now. He fidgets while our courtiers crowd the throne room.

Romans. Greeks. Egyptians. Berbers. Ours is a court of many languages and complexions. Knots of men stand together amidst the pillars, fanning themselves with palm fronds to fend off the afternoon heat while discussing the latest news from Rome. In the farthest corner, Lady Lasthenia instructs her students on some point of Pythagorean theory. Reclining upon a cushion in the presence of royalty as only our court poet is brave enough to do, Crinagoras sees me beneath the archway and shouts, "All hail to Queen Cleopatra Selene!"

Lifting my chin with a regal air, I force myself to stride to the raised dais. My gossamer cape billows behind me as if caught by the wind, and the crowd makes way. Behind me, Tala carries the baby in her sturdy Berber arms.

I walk purposefully, pausing only once to keep my balance. Watching me, the king's brow creases with worry. In my white silks, I must appear very pale and frail indeed. But when my son lets out a cry, my frailty is forgotten. My husband launches to his feet, and his eyes fasten eagerly on the newborn. A smile breaks over the king's face. He holds out his arms for the child but I catch Tala's elbow before she can give the swaddled bundle over. "No," I murmur. "Do as we discussed."

Scowling, she lays the babe down on the floor at the king's feet. I've no fondness for this custom either, but I know the Romans. My father was one of them and my husband may as well be. Even so, the king startles when I so publicly offer him the opportunity to reject my child. Perhaps he is remembering that I was no maiden when I came to his bed. His gaze darts to meet mine, a question in his eyes that I do not answer. My expression remains placid, inscrutable, even when the assembled courtiers lapse into silence, anticipating scandal and humiliation.

Many here have seen the emperor's eyes gleam with lust for me. I wouldn't be surprised if they were, even now, counting the months since I left the court of Augustus to take my place as the Queen of Mauretania, and wondering about the paternity of my child. My husband isn't beyond such speculation. He knows already my daughter was not of his get. Perhaps he will reject my son for fear that he has been betrayed again.

Juba hesitates before lifting his robes above his sandals, descending the stairs, and stooping to examine the babe. I resent that he folds back the blankets to reveal my child's sex, but it takes all my strength to remain standing; I've none to spare for irritation.

At the sight of the little phallus, the king smiles and holds the child aloft, naked, exposed. "My son!" Juba cries with joy. A cheer goes up from the crowd and a little bleating lamb's cry goes up from my baby.

Just a few moments more, little one.

I have created a dramatic moment—one that will cause talk in Rome. It was the emperor, my mentor, who taught me such stage-craft, so I know how to ensure that this news reaches him. *Just a few minutes more. Just long enough to give my son his name and I can return to my rooms and collapse in bed.*

"Your son," I agree, taking my place at Juba's side.

It is the king's privilege to name the child. It would not surprise me if he meant to name his son in honor of his own family. Another Juba, perhaps, or Masinissa. But the divine ichor in our son's veins is the blood of the Ptolemies; my legacy is far more prestigious than my husband's. Though it would help to erase any doubt that Juba was the father of this child, *I* am the one who labored hard to bring the child into the world so I say, "His name is Ptolemy."

The joy on Juba's face fractures. "Ptolemy? Why not Gaius, after our patron, the emperor?"

Is that sarcasm I hear? Does he seek to shame me after all? Surely he knows that naming my son after the emperor would invite scandal. Not to mention the fact that I would never name my son after the man who destroyed my family, stole Egypt, and violated me. I shake my head so violently that my dark hair lashes at my face. Somehow, I manage to swallow down my bile long enough to whisper, "Flattery will not sweeten this news for Augustus. Let the baby be named Ptolemy; it will stand him in good stead."

My husband can be an agreeable man—a mild-mannered

king—but I am asking a rather grand concession from him. Looking down fondly at the newborn in his arms, he finally nods. "I'm told the birth was a struggle. You've given me a precious gift: a son to secure our reign. If you wish to call him Ptolemy, I won't refuse you . . . but we'll have to write Augustus. There can be no more delay."

I exhale, relieved and grateful. Motioning to the crowd, I say softly, "Augustus may hear it from them before he hears it from us. Now that the seas have opened, rumor will reach Rome in a week. No more than two." Fear tightens my stomach, but I lift my chin with resolution. "Then we'll reap what we've sown."

Three

DURING the month named for the Roman goddess Juno, our subjects take to the fields to cut down the ripe grain before it is burnt by the high heat of summer. The largest plantations, worked by gangs of slaves, are the first to get their grain to market. Even now, caravans of colorfully saddled mules clog the city streets, bound for our harbor. Camels, horse-driven wagons, and even carts pushed by laborers descend upon us from the hills, all laden down with sacks of oats, barley, and wheat.

If I close my eyes, I can already smell the bread that will be baked with all this grain. It's a sacred scent that calls me to my duty. So why am I listless? I'm healed now from the birth of my son. The illness made my milk run dry, but my infant son thrives at the breast of his wet nurse.

There is no accounting for my overwhelming sadness.

Yet I have no appetite. I'm short-tempered with servants. I hide in my chambers, shunning our court. Though summer bathes my kingdom in golden light, I lurk in gloom. Perhaps it's because I await word from Rome. When Augustus hears of the birth of my son, how will he answer? Will he rage like a possessive lover and mete out revenge? Or will he care at all? Maybe what I do is beneath the emperor's notice now and he will greet the news with indifference. That is the best I can hope for . . .

Alas, I suspect my gloomy mood has less to do with the emperor than with what I saw when consumed by fever. They say I called his name. *Helios.* My other half. Twin. Brother. Lover. King. There was a time I would've gone anywhere with him—disappeared into the desert, sailed away into the farthest reaches of the sea. I'd have abandoned my husband, my crown, my kingdom, and the prophecies too. For Helios and I are of one spirit, one *akh.* We have been together in all the worlds that have ever been or will ever be. That is how I know he lives. We are bound. If he were dead, I would know it. I would be torn asunder. My world could not stand on its foundations without Helios in it. I know this.

What does it matter if I called his name in the shadow of Anubis? I was not in my right mind, quaking with chills and parched by sweats. Perhaps a temporary madness made me see him in the afterworld. I saw Caesarion there too, and did the Romans not tell me he was burned? Would that not have destroyed his soul? No, I cannot have seen Caesarion there and I cannot have seen Helios either, for he lives. I know that he lives.

And yet I cannot be at peace.

I have made of my body a vessel for my goddess, so that the rains might come and the crops might grow. I've swallowed a storm and called it back to my fingertips. I've taken the *heka* in my body and used it to open my womb to new life. There is a birthmark on my arm, the sign of a sail, and the winds are drawn to it, but I know too little of the ancient magical arts of Egypt.

And of the world beyond this one, I know even less.

Only my mage can teach me what I need to know. And so I finally emerge from my chambers with my hair fastened by a white ribbon and a collar of turquoise stones over my robes. I seek out my mage in his apartments. In the guise of Euphorbus Musa, he has become a great favorite of the king because both men share a natural inquisitiveness.

Since leaving the emperor, I've spent many hours in the mage's suite of rooms studying lesser magics of herbs and oil lamp divination. My wizard has taught me to write the words of a spell upon papyrus, then wash the ink into a cup with brown beer and drink it. He has taught me the sacred numbers that carry a chant to the ears of the gods. And he has taught me something of curses, though not nearly enough.

Today he is bent over papyrus, sketching the leaves of some plant while a cacophony of squawking birds in cages on the far wall announce me and my daughter. My Isidora is, as always, enchanted by creatures, standing on tiptoe to peek into the cages, so I let her play with the birds.

Meanwhile, exile has made my mage eccentric and distracted; even with the squawking it takes him a moment to realize we're here. Hobbling along with the assistance of a divination staff, he herds me into a chair that is dusty with pollen. "Majesty, you had only to summon me. You ought not risk your health coming here. After birthing your baby, it will take time to regain your strength."

"I should like to know why the birth of a child has laid such waste to me," I say, wondering how such a tiny baby could've been so very difficult to bring into the world. "You will say that childbed fever saps the strength of queens and peasants alike, but I wear an amulet that says *I am the Resurrection*. Isis is a mother goddess and has made me her vessel. Why should giving birth have been so dreadful for *me*, of all women?"

I expect him to knit his brow in curiosity, or to rub at his chin the way Juba does when worrying over a problem, or even to scratch at his head as when confronted by my inability to work a spell. Instead, he stares with sad, watery eyes that fill me with foreboding. "What is it, Euphronius? Have I displeased the goddess? You cannot think that she's left me . . ."

The mage's fingers squeeze tight on his staff. "Isis will be with you unto death . . . even if you were to abandon her."

It is a rebuke, and I might have expected one, given that he believes I have forsaken my birthright. I will never be Pharaoh, and while the rest of my courtiers dream of the day I will reclaim my lost inheritance, my mage can read my heart. He doesn't need to look into the Rivers of Time to see that all other possibilities flow away from us now. So I admit it. "I will not chase my mother's throne again. I've never forgotten Isis and I've never forgotten Egypt, but they're not the same. Land can be taken from me by force, a crown and scepter wrestled from my grasp, but Isis lives in me and no one can take her from me. You told me—*you* told me—that I carry her wherever I go. I've used her magic here to make Mauretanian fields fertile. I've fed the people on her bounty. That is salvation. That is the true immortality. That will be my legacy."

"If so, it comes at great sacrifice," the mage tells me flatly.

His impertinence stokes my anger. "I am not my mother. I am done fighting Rome. I am done scheming. I am done longing for a lost kingdom. For a lost world. I intend to build a new one, and if you won't help me—"

"Majesty!" he protests. "There is nothing I would deny you."

"Then teach me to see in the Rivers of Time."

The request plainly surprises him. "Majesty, the *heka* we draw, the power and prayer that fuels our magic, is precious and rare. To be used sparingly. You're no temple wizard, pulling magic from the sacred pools. You've awakened powers that are yours alone, but you were not gifted with sight—not every sorceress has it."

He means that *I* do not have it, and he is right. That gift belonged to my mother and my littlest brother, Philadelphus, nearly five years now in his tomb. But I'm desperate. My choices have led me to a path my ancestors have not charted before. How will I navigate the way ahead so that my dynasty might survive? More urgently, how can I go on without knowing the truth about Helios?

It has been a year since I saw him last, but the pain of our separation is still a fresh wound. A pain made more excruciating by what I saw when I was fevered. "Teach me to read the Rivers of Time," I insist. "How is it done?"

My mage calls for his servants to fill an alabaster divination bowl with water. Upon the small altar in his chambers, we light a candle made of sweet-smelling beeswax. We burn incense too that we may be purified enough to invoke the goddess. I sit barefoot before the bowl and press the soles of my feet into the woven carpet. The mage tells me to close my eyes and imagine that it is the warm sand of the desert between my toes. To chant all the names of Isis. To envision a temple to her. To see the silver moon rise over it, glowing on the water of the Nile, shimmering upon the petals of each lotus flower.

"Now draw upon your *heka*," the old man says. "Open your eyes and see into the bowl of water. See the glistening ripples of the Nile and how they turn the shining round moon into the crown of the goddess. See her glorious face shimmer. See what she would show you . . ."

I stare and stare, trying to see the beautiful face of my goddess, hear her words, feel her touch . . . yet all I see is water. I try again and it seems as if the room grows hotter, brighter, and I hear the blaze of torches and feel embers of glowing incense burn beneath my eyelids. I try to draw upon that, but eventually I admit defeat. "It is no good."

The mage bows his head. "The goddess does not bestow all her gifts upon any one person."

"But I see *nothing*."

"Not even the temple and its gold dome?" Isidora asks.

We startle, turning to see that my little daughter has abandoned the birds to stare into the divination bowl. How careless of us to have forgotten her. But Isidora can be quiet when she wants to be overlooked, when she wants to be present for what the adults would exclude her from.

"Do you see something in the bowl, princess?" the mage asks.

"No, she does not," I say, getting to my feet.

I remember being a child both blessed and burdened by magic. I don't want that for Isidora. Moreover, I don't want her to realize that my mage *is* a mage. It's a secret we keep from the king, and I remember what it was like to be a child who carried secrets that could send men to their deaths. I'll have to be more careful with Isidora. We've just celebrated her sixth birthday and I won't steal her childhood from her as mine was stolen from me.

"Come, Isidora," I say. "We've harried the king's physician enough today."

As we make ready to leave, the old man lowers his head in

deference to my wishes, but he stops me before I go through the doorway. "Majesty . . . your birth went hard. You mustn't risk another child now."

A puff of indignant air escapes my lips. "My son is still an infant. I believe the king can be satisfied for the time being."

"Even if the king is not, you must be. As I said, the goddess does not bestow all her gifts upon one person. Not even you."

KING Juba calls for a celebration to mark the birth of our prince, and Isis willing, it will be a good day. Little Ptolemy is still so small, so frail. I want to bundle him up and keep him in a close cocoon, away from the noise and demands of the world, but he is a prince. He must be seen. Neither of us can hide inside the palace forever.

Our processional assembles just outside the courtyard beyond the gates where Isidora makes a game of stepping on Memnon's feet to see if she can make the commander of my Macedonian guard scowl from beneath his fierce helmet. Thankfully, Memnon is made of stern stuff and maintains his Spartan demeanor until Tala rescues him from the torments of my daughter.

Then my niece Pythodorida gently chides her. "Dora, behave like a fine princess today. You don't want to disappoint the king, do you?"

Though my niece is older than my daughter by five years, they're playmates. Together with the other children at our court, they've made up infectious names for one another. Isidora is called Dora. Pythodorida is called Pythia, like the oracle. They are two girls as innocent and carefree as I can make them and both overly solicitous of the king's attention.

When Juba comes into view mounted atop a magnificent stallion, my daughter quivers with excitement. "Papa!"

"There's my girl," Juba says from the height of his horse, and her cheeks glow rosy. "And isn't the queen very pretty today?"

Smiling as if such compliments were merely my due, I refasten my cloak. But if I am honest with myself, I am warmed by his praise, even if it is only flattery. My ladies have brushed oil through my hair to hide its dull brittleness. The drape of purple silk, tied tight at my waist with a silvered girdle, helps disguise the fact that I've become thin. But I fear childbed fever has robbed me of any vestige of beauty. "Let's not be late," I say. "The people are waiting."

The king's merriment is not dimmed by my reserve. "My queen, it's quite unlike you to forget your exalted status. I believe the people are *obliged* to wait for us."

Nevertheless, he wheels his horse round, and I climb into the large gilded *carpentum* with my children and my niece. The trumpets sound and we're off, borne by a fine team of plumed horses in royal purple livery, glittering gold breastplates emblazoned with my family sigil, the eagle and thunderbolt.

The crowd showers us with rose petals. The king's horse tramples them and a fragrant perfume rises up to surround us. The people cheer and it sends a jolt of excitement through me. I adore that sound: the music of my people's love. And I resolve to banish my gloom.

My infant son drowses in the crook of my arm, too regal—or still too raw from the realm of the gods from whence he came—to care about all this mortal fanfare. When I press my lips to his tiny forehead, scenting lavender and milk, my daughter draws closer, tugging at the silvered circlet in her hair. "When you were ill, Mama, they wouldn't let me climb into your bed with you. I feared I might never see you again."

I flinch at her words, pained to think of her trying to climb into my bed and being turned away. Never should she face the terrors of being a motherless child. Terrors I know all too well. Clutching her to my side, I promise, "Don't fear. I will never leave you."

Our noisy arrival in the forum drowns out the bleating camels, the clacking wagons filled with ripened fruit, and the wool merchants shouting their prices. And when I step out of the litter, a prince in my arms and a princess at my side, the crowd cheers again for me, their fertile queen. I am Cleopatra of the royal House Ptolemy, the eighth of my name, but they call me *mother of the realm* and other, more divine titles. I blink against the bright sun, straining to find familiar faces in a sea of people who want me to be the vessel of a great goddess.

"Come this way, Majesty," Chryssa says, guiding me to the dais that has been made ready for us. I take my seat beside Juba upon a throne of ivory, inlaid with mother-of-pearl. Just beneath us, places of honor have been afforded to our children. Though my niece is not royalty, Pythia sits with us as if she were. Augustus took orphans into his family when I was a child; I now do the same, reminding myself that not everything I learned from the emperor was dark and twisted.

Juba announces that this day of celebration is made possible by the grace of our patron, Augustus Caesar. Everyone chants, "Caesar! Divine Caesar!"

The emperor is no god, but the people want him to be—just as they want me to deliver them salvation. So I must mouth his name with everyone else.

Caesar, Caesar, Caesar.

Our ministers make speeches to praise the gods for our new prince. A Greek choir sings a sweet tune. We're treated to a poem by Crinagoras, commemorating the occasion. And then, mercifully, we're free to make our way to the new royal library, an annex to our palace with stairs flanked by gilded marble lions that stand guard over our literary treasures.

Portraits of Alexander the Great grace both sides of the entryway in vivid scarlet and gold, and the cavernous hall is made more inviting by numerous marble benches for scholars to sit upon and tables in niches at which they may read. Modeled after the Great Library of Alexandria, our library boasts three floors and three tiers of galleries overlooking a sunny central court. But the true wealth of this place may be counted in our scroll racks, where copies, and some precious originals, of the most important manuscripts can be found. As we marvel over mosaic floors and climb the stairs to the second-floor balcony, I wonder if it would be beneath my royal dignity to reach out and let my fingers play over my name engraved on the dedication plaque. I'm tempted, for I have a fondness for things that endure . . .

The herald's voice booms, shouting out the coming attractions. Beer and feasting. Dancers and poets. More exotic entertainment too. For the opening act, the crowd parts to reveal a man sitting on the lower level, surrounded by baskets and figs. He plays his pipe, and from the railing, I watch with a growing sense of dread as sinuous serpents rise up from the baskets at the sound of the music.

Below me, six black Egyptian cobras dance on their tails, swaying.

And all the joy of this day flees in an instant.

I watch their scaled hoods spread wide like the *uraeus* on the crown of Egypt. Even from this height, I'm paralyzed by the sight of the asps, their forked tongues flickering out between deadly fangs. I don't notice that I'm gripping the balustrade until my knuckles have gone white, all my effort concentrated upon not swooning and falling to my death.

And I *would* swoon if I were not so filled with rage. Someone has arranged for this. Someone who knows what haunts me. Someone who wants to send me a message and make this occasion a moment of dread. The king must know it, for he calls down, "That's enough. We've seen enough of the snake charmer!"

There is commotion below, some upset at having displeased us. Then Chryssa snaps, "Who could think it a good idea to honor the daughter of Cleopatra by coaxing asps from baskets of figs?"

The story the world tells of my mother's suicide is that she cheated the emperor of his conquest by plunging her hand into a basket where a venomous serpent lay in wait. A legend only, some say, for the serpent was never found. But I was there. I brought her that basket. She was the one bitten, but the poison lingers in my blood to this day. I can still remember the scent of figs in my nostrils, lush and sweet. The dark god Anubis was embroidered into the woven reeds of the basket, the weight of death heavy in my arms. I can still see my mother reach her hand into that basket, surrendering her life so that her children might go on without her. And I *have* gone on without her. I have survived too much to be terrorized by the emperor's agents or whomever else is responsible for this.

If it is a message, a warning from my enemies, I have already allowed them too much of a victory by showing any reaction at all. So I adopt as serene a mask as possible. Juba, however, goes red. "I'll have someone flogged for this."

My daughter blinks her big blue eyes, seeing past my facade. "Are you frightened, Mama? They can't bite us from there. The snakes are very far away."

I get my legs under me, bitterness on my tongue. "Oh, but they're never far enough away."

Four

MY ancestors built the Lighthouse of Alexandria, a wonder of the world. Our lighthouse here in Mauretania is not as wondrous, but it's where I go to find my courage. Leaving my guards behind, I make the long climb up the spiral staircase to the watch room, which does much to invigorate me. There, at the top of the world, I step out onto the gallery, where the stiff ocean breeze reminds me that I am a sorceress who can command winds with her upraised hands. I can defend myself and those I love, if need be . . .

The howl of the wind keeps me from hearing footsteps on the stairs below. It is only the sound of a door crashing open that pulls me from my thoughts. I think it will be the harbormaster or the keeper of the lighthouse, come to attend me.

I am surprised to see the king, instead, purple cape flapping behind him.

He is without a retinue; we are quite alone. And it startles me when the king stands at my side near the rail and takes the unusual liberty of putting his hand over mine. It is an intimacy I've not invited since the drunken night we conceived our son. After all, I didn't take my husband into my bed for pleasure; I took him to bed because I wanted a child, and now we have one.

Nevertheless, I don't pull my hand away. Juba isn't my beloved, but what I remember of our night together is a pleasant memory and I have no urge to spurn him. Below us, big sweating oxen haul wood to the lighthouse to keep the fire fueled so that sailors don't lose their way. Above us, in the tower, the fire burns so hot it warms our backs, and we are silent together, bathed in that fire's light.

When the king finally speaks, he raises his voice to be heard over the crash of ocean waves, which churn into white foam on the dark stones beneath. "Your hands are so cold, Selene."

"I only fear—"

"I know what you fear, but the snake charmer was no threat from the emperor. It was only a tribesman from the Atlas Mountains, come to entertain his king and queen. No one thought better of it." My hesitation must tell him that I'm not convinced. "It was no warning. If the emperor is displeased that we have a son together, he's shown no sign of it in his dispatches to me."

"But has he sent felicitations? No. If Augustus were pleased, he'd have said something by now. I know him. We both know him. The emperor is often silent when he is most enraged."

Then again, Augustus is a new man since returning from Greece, having recovered battle standards from the Parthians without even taking the battlefield. He believes himself a peacemaker now; perhaps he's too exalted to feel jealousy over a discarded lover. Perhaps he's finally tired of me. Perhaps I'm no more to him now than before I was born. That is what I wanted, isn't it? I should be glad of it . . .

The king strokes his thumb over mine as if to ease my anxiety. "Rome is far away, Selene. We have a daughter and a son—a son! We rule over this kingdom and have nothing to fear here."

That is nonsense and he knows it; or at least, he should know it, so I don't dignify it with an argument. "Would you have really flogged someone for my sake?"

His brow furrows beneath his gold crown. "You make the mistake of thinking that because I dislike violence, I'm not capable of it. I can and will protect our kingdom and you."

Against everything and everyone but the emperor, he means.

I have forgiven Juba for the part he played in driving my parents to suicide. But it is difficult to know that he would do it all again. He would do anything for the emperor and give anything to the emperor—even me. And yet, the only way we can live together as man and wife is if we never discuss all the ways we have wronged each other. So I press my lips together and say nothing to contradict him.

Instead, my eyes drift to my city below, and the wall we're building to defend it. Green palm trees and flat-roofed clay houses can be seen in miniature, tiny people swarming through the grid of streets, some of them hurrying in and out of our public baths. From this height, our fine royal capital looks fragile, as if it could be smashed beneath a soldier's boot. But we've built Iol-Caesaria strong, stone by stone. It is my fortress against the emperor. Augustus has sworn never to set foot here and I pray it is one vow he will keep.

IN the morning an imperial flagship bears down on our harbor. Its red and gold banners lead our spotters to believe the vessel belongs to Rome's most formidable military leader, the emperor's son-in-law, Agrippa. My nerves are still raw from yesterday's encounter with the snakes. Now Admiral Agrippa's ship is on our coast and I can think of no good reason for it.

Perhaps the snakes were a warning after all.

I hurry to find the king. He is already at the gate, ready to mount his horse, and I call after him, "Did you know Agrippa was coming? Did he send a herald ahead of him?"

Juba doesn't share my distress; or at least, if he does, he hides it well. "No. Perhaps he means his visit to be a pleasant surprise."

I doubt this very much. The admiral, whose warships sent my mother's fleet and all her dreams to the bottom of the sea, often surprises, but never pleasantly. He loathed my mother as a wicked seductress and he loathes me too because he believes the same of me. Agrippa is not a man to take respite on my balmy shores; he would never come here except on official business.

Perhaps the emperor has sent him to punish us. Then a worse thought occurs to me. Once, when the emperor fell ill, he gave Agrippa his signet ring and named him successor. What if the emperor has finally been bested by one of his many ailments? What if the emperor is dead and Agrippa is now master of Rome?

If so, he has come either to secure our fealty or to invade our shores. He would need no army to conquer us. More than half our soldiers are Roman and would heed his commands before ours. We may rule here, Juba and I, but we're still subjects of the empire. So if Agrippa has come to strip us of our thrones—or even our lives— there's little to be done about it now. There are precious few places in the world that anyone can run for safety from Marcus Vipsanius Agrippa.

Seeking calm, I remind myself yet again that I am my own safe harbor. I've learned to harness the *heka* that swirls in my blood—the ancient Egyptian magic that is my birthright. I've used the winds that answer my fingertips to defend myself before; I can do it now. "How shall we greet Agrippa?"

"I've ordered ready a feast of welcome," my husband says. "There's no time to assemble a royal procession. We'll eschew formality and greet him as a friend."

In this, I follow Juba's lead. He knows Agrippa well; he's served with him both in military campaigns and in the administration of Spain. With shaky fingers, I remove my royal diadem, the emblem of my status as queen, and I leave my purple cloak behind. I would do this for no other Roman save the emperor himself, and oh, how I resent it.

"Be of good cheer, Selene," the king says. "Perhaps his wife will be with him."

That *would* cheer me, and when we go down to the docks, I'm encouraged by the sight of a lady's embroidered palanquin on the deck of the imperial ship. It must belong to Julia, because I doubt Agrippa has ever traveled by litter a day in his life. He's a man who strides, marches, gallops, or sails. He's not a man to be carried any- where. I'm ready to meet him, whatever his intent, but when the plank comes down, only feminine figures swathed in expensive cloth and extravagant jewels emerge from the ship.

And then I see my dear friend.

Julia forgoes the palanquin and walks down the plank in the center of her women. I must hold myself back from crying out her name in gladness. Chryssa, however, shows none of my reserve. From her place behind me at my right shoulder, I hear my freedwoman gasp. "Phoebe! My sister Phoebe is with Lady Julia."

Chryssa has not seen her sister since the days they were slaves together in Rome, so I release my freedwoman from any duty of decorum. "Go," I tell her, and Chryssa hurries down the length of the docks, her sandals clopping as she runs to embrace her sister with wild enthusiasm and tears.

While they embrace, the emperor's daughter approaches me, flanked by her ladies and an escort of guards. "Lady Julia." I smile, my arms outstretched. "We welcome you to Mauretania."

From beneath the veil of a bright saffron palla, Julia's mischievous little mouth breaks into a wide grin. "Always a proud Ptolemy, aren't you? So free to use the royal *we*, even with me."

I had only intended to include Juba in my welcome, but before I can defend myself, Julia squeezes me tight, pushing the air from my lungs. My Macedonian guards grunt in dismay and, in the aftermath of the hug, I strive for a dignified posture, which makes Julia laugh. "Do you feel the swell of my belly?" she asks, smoothing her gown tight over her abdomen so we can see the small bump. "I think I'm with child again, but it isn't contagious." Then she hugs me again. "Oh, I've missed you, Selene. More than I can say."

I've missed her too. She was my first friend, our bond forged in childhood, when we were both at the mercy of her father's temper. We have always been a mismatched pair, her wit and high-spiritedness pulling against my more serious, cautious nature. Our reunion makes my heart fill close to bursting. "I'm overjoyed to see you, Julia. Truly, I am!"

My husband adds his greeting. "We're honored by your visit and offer felicitations if, indeed, you are to give your husband a second child."

"A third," Julia corrects him, pointedly. "Don't forget my little Julilla because she's a girl."

The king smiles. "I beg your pardon. I too have a daughter and take great joy in her."

Isidora is not his daughter, but he's claimed her as such, so I do not so much as glance at him when he says this. Instead, I snap my fingers at a servant. "Princess Isidora will be pleased to have new playmates. We'll have the nursery made ready for your children, Julia."

"Oh, Selene, there's no need," she says. "My children are with Agrippa. Why, I practically need Agrippa's permission even to *hold* them. Now, are we going to stand on the docks all day or are you going to show me this magnificent palace of yours?"

Bewildered, my wary eyes drift to the ship. "Shouldn't we wait for your husband?"

Julia laughs in a way that makes me extremely nervous. "It would be a long wait since I left him across the narrow strait."

I blink. "You *left* Agrippa?"

"Oh, yes, though I doubt he knows it yet. He's returning to Rome by way of Gaul to meet with officials along the way. He sent me by ship, but I decided upon a change in travel plans. And why not? I wanted to pay a visit to my dearest friend."

Instantly, a sweat breaks out on Juba's brow. "Are you saying your husband has no idea as to your whereabouts, Lady Julia?"

She smiles brightly. "That's exactly what I'm saying. Isn't it marvelous? This way, he won't even have to worry. Well, then. Are you going to refuse to receive the emperor's daughter, King Juba, or will you turn me away?"

Stunned, my husband snaps his mouth shut. I'm similarly unsettled. I admire Julia's nerve, but resent that she's trapped us. We cannot refuse to receive her, yet to welcome her is to shelter her in this rebellion against her husband, and can only invite his wrath.

The king speaks gruffly. "Lady Julia, in loyalty to your father we offer you our hospitality. However, this is not how a Roman matron should behave." Julia's women gasp at the king's rebuke and even our courtiers go wide-eyed. But my husband has good reason to be angry. Julia's visit will draw the emperor's attention; she's endangered our peaceful existence here. "It is no true friendship that you show my wife in coming here without your husband's leave. And once you're delivered of his baby, I hope Agrippa beats you like the spoiled child you are."

Without further warning, the king turns on his heel. No one can stop him. Given that Julia has fled here like a fugitive, he's not obligated to show her courtesy. Still, Julia's ladies titter and our courtiers murmur to one another, unsure how to behave. That the king turned his back on the emperor's daughter will cause gossip; perhaps he means it to. This way he can say that he didn't encourage her.

But as the king retreats, his guards trailing after him, Julia snorts with laughter. "Oh, look. I've created a scene."

JULIA is suitably impressed with my marble porticoes, vast mosaics, and sparkling fountains that shoot so high they cool the air with mist. She wades knee-deep through the sea of lavender bushes in my gardens. The shrubs are a greenish grey now, but will bloom purple come springtime. When I tell her this, Julia closes her eyes a moment as if imagining. "Oh, Selene, this is as beautiful as my father's palace in Capri and lovelier than Livia's manor house, with all her white hens."

"Let's not spoil our visit with talk of your horrid stepmother," I say, for we've both been victims of the wicked machinations behind Livia's deceptively placid smile.

If there is any person in the world who loathes the emperor's wife as much as I do, it's Julia, so she shrugs. "As you wish." Then she motions for me to walk with her, far ahead of our ladies. "Isn't it strange to be followed by attendants all the time? We should dismiss them and run wild together, as we did when we were girls in Rome."

Perhaps she remembers a different childhood than I do. "We never ran wild. We only dreamed of doing so."

"Well, we can do as we like now. I'm the wife of Agrippa and the daughter of the emperor. People bend themselves in half trying to please me, for they know that when I return home, I'll be First Woman in Rome."

"Then why didn't you? Return to Rome, I mean?"

"I wanted to see you," she replies, affectionately leaning her shoulder against mine as we walk. "I didn't think I'd have another chance. And now you're stuck with me. Even if my husband is enraged by my visit, he won't want me risking the baby with a trip over the winter's sea just to return to him. So you and I have our freedom. We can have our dream. At least until springtime."

I should scold her. I should convince her to cross the narrow strait at once and return to Spain, where her husband's soldiers can escort her overland back to Rome. But all I can think is that I'll have her until springtime. She'll be here for the rains. She'll see the rich earth of my kingdom turned under the plow during the sowing season. She'll celebrate the Saturnalia with us. I'll have her until springtime, and I mean to enjoy every moment before we're brought to account by the men who rule our lives.

THE next day, we celebrate a wedding.

Though Chryssa is as haughty a Greek as any freed slave might be, she's consented to marry Maysar of the Gaetulian tribes, a Berber chieftain who has advised us since the earliest days of our reign. To anyone who objects to the match, I point out that it was the practice of Alexander the Great to have his generals intermarry with his Persian subjects, and my freedwoman is the closest thing I have to a general.

This makes my courtiers laugh but also serves to remind them of the Hellenistic precept of *harmonia* under which I intend to bring together our diverse and quarreling peoples with all their various languages and peculiar customs. In that respect, Chryssa and Maysar serve as a fine example. In Greek tradition, my freedwoman has cut a lock of her hair and burnt it in offering. But as a bride of a Berber, she's allowed her hands to be tattooed with henna. And when she speaks her vows beneath the canopied tent, she pledges not her heart, but her liver, where the tribesmen believe true love resides.

Julia giggles at this, whispering in my ear, "I pledge in friendship to you, my bladder . . . or would you prefer a knucklebone?"

I jab the sharp point of my elbow into Julia's ribs so hard she yelps. It shocks me to realize how badly I want her to approve of my Berbers; if she discounts them as barbarians, I know that our friendship will suffer. But perhaps I need not have worried. When a chorus of Berber women sing, undulating to wild drumbeats, Julia's eyes sparkle with enchantment. The tribal rhythms are exotic, unique to Mauretania, but the emperor's daughter claps her hands and dances as if she has known them all her life.

As girls, we weren't allowed to dance. Octavia and Livia were of the opinion that dancing was for drunkards and whores. But here, no one stops Julia from doing anything she wants to do, and so she dances until she's dizzied.

Collapsing onto a couch beside me, she holds her belly with one hand, reaching with the other to sample a chickpea salad with barley, mint, and olive oil. Folding the mixture into a piece of flatbread, she motions with her chin to the bride. "I hope you won't regret giving Chryssa her freedom. I'm afraid you'll lose her now."

With these words, she sends a twinge of anxiety through me. As my agent here in Mauretania, Chryssa has become a great lady of commerce, accustomed to bartering and bickering with shippers and bankers and tradesmen. She presides over royal monopolies. Citrus-wood furniture, amber, copper, and purple dye. Were she not a woman, she'd have command of the kingdom's treasury too. But more importantly, Chryssa has been with me since I was a child. Alone amongst my intimates, my freedwoman knows the truth of what the emperor did to me.

Now Chryssa sits beside her new husband, playfully stroking his beard, and I'm irritated that Julia should make me feel anything but happy for her. "Why should I lose Chryssa? As my freedwoman, she still serves me well . . ."

Julia takes a gulp of unwatered wine. "You'll lose her because she's besotted with her groom. There's no room in a heart for two."

Can that be true? Already I love my infant son and my daughter more than my own life. My heart has room for more . . . but Chryssa isn't bound to me by blood, and the thought of losing her nearly spoils my celebratory mood.

It also makes me petty. "Save room for the lungfish, Julia," I say, knowing they have a disagreeably strong taste. "They burrow into the soil and can live for quite a long time breathing air instead of water. The Berbers capture and store them, mud and all, so that we can eat fresh fish even when the streambeds dry out."

Julia eagerly takes some from a passing silver tray. I think she'll gag on it, but she chews with relish, her lips shining with oil. "I predict that I'm to become very fat during my stay and not only because I'm eating for two!" Just then, her eyes dart to where my eleven-year-old niece sits near the king, and asks, "That can't be your daughter, so grown up already?"

"No. My Isidora is abed this hour. That girl is Pythodorida of Tralles, my half sister's daughter."

Curiosity sparks in Julia's eyes. "Another half sister?"

"My father's daughter," I explain, remembering when I first met my half sister on the Isle of Samos, where, in endless captivity, I awaited the emperor's pleasure. "Lady Antonia, or Hybrida, as we called her, after her mother."

Julia sighs dramatically. "How is it that I am an only child whereas you need both hands to count all your siblings?"

"I suppose it's because my father was notoriously fond of women, whereas yours . . ." I trail off, looking away and hoping it's true that Julia is an only child. I have always hoped that my daughter was conceived in love during the storm that once brought Helios and I together and not when the emperor forced himself upon me. I don't want to believe, or give Julia any reason to suspect, that my daughter could be her sister. And I'm relieved when she doesn't press me to finish the statement.

"I'd like to meet this Hybrida," Julia decides.

"Sadly, you cannot. She came with me from Greece but fell ill and died last winter. We found her in bed, curled round my old cat, Bast. They were both gone. I like to think that Bast helped her at the end, like a protectress in the night."

"Oh," Julia says with a sympathetic shake of her head. "I am sorry. It was a bad year. We lost Virgil too so suddenly . . ."

The emperor's poet died of fever, but his death didn't seem sudden to me. Even though Virgil penned vile propaganda against my dead parents, he was my friend, and when last I saw him, he seemed a broken man. He swore to me that his *Aeneid* would be burned when he died, but when he fell ill in Brundisium, Augustus acted swiftly to seize Virgil's work before it could be destroyed. In the end, the emperor lost his poet, but not his poem. Already, the wretched *Aeneid* is the most famous story since Homer's epics. In spite of this, I raise a cup in honor of Virgil and we drink.

"To Virgil," Julia agrees. "And to your sister . . . you must have been very fond of her to let her daughter wear royal purple."

"Quite fond. When she fell ill, I swore to her that I'd bring up Pythia as my own."

About to take another gulp of her wine, Julia stops and gives me a long, hard look. "Are you establishing a little embassy of royal orphans, like Octavia did when we were young?"

"I could do worse than to emulate her. Your aunt was kind to me—even if I didn't recognize it for kindness at the time. There was no reason she needed to gather up all my father's orphaned children . . ."

"Except for all the usual political reasons," Julia says drily. "My virtuous, venerated aunt has a warm heart, but never forget that she arranged my first marriage to ensure that her son would be the next emperor—"

"You loved Marcellus," I counter, unwilling to hear a new version of a sad story.

Julia admits it with a shrug. "I did. We were good companions. We let each other love freely. But don't pretend I have no cause to resent Octavia. When Marcellus left me a widow, she sold me to Admiral Agrippa."

"Octavia did not *sell* you."

"Not for money. For the wages of *spite*."

It's a simplification of a very complicated dynastic game and Julia blames the wrong person for her woes. Or perhaps she understands my role in it, and I stand accused. I argue, "Would you have rather been married to one of the Claudian brothers? Because that's what would have happened if Octavia hadn't given her blessing to your match with Agrippa. Your father would've married you off to one of Livia's sons and then your malignant stepmother would have had us all entirely in her power."

"I would rather not have married at all," Julia says, leaning back with a sly smile. "Here in Mauretania I have a taste of what that's like. You must show me everything. I want to swim in the sea and picnic in the hills. I want to trade for silver jewelry in your market and buy some of these magnificent woven carpets. I want to make an offering in a temple to strange gods and tour your purple-dye factory. I want to see a lion and ride a camel. No, an elephant!"

I wince at the way, in her wild, childlike enthusiasm, she reminds me of my daughter. "You won't like the dye factory or the camels, Julia. They both stink."

"I don't care. You must show me everything before Agrippa comes to fetch me and make us all miserable!"

Five

"THIS is morbid, Selene. Even for you."

As Julia and I settle ourselves under the shady entryway of my mausoleum, I say, "I cannot imagine what you have to complain about. Look at the lovely yellow flowers in these urns and the skillful stonework."

"It's a *tomb*. Hardly the place for an idyllic picnic in the hills . . ."

Though Julia is my favorite Roman, times like these remind me that she *is* Roman. "It's a *royal* tomb and it's the *best* place for an idyllic picnic in the hills. From here we can see the sea and the beauty of Mauretania. Why should I wait for the afterlife to enjoy it?"

"Because there's a sarcophagus inside!"

Truly, she is ridiculous. "What of it? It's Hybrida's sarcophagus and Bast is beside her."

The emperor's daughter makes a strange noise in her throat. "You mummified your cat?"

"She was a good cat. Why shouldn't she enjoy salvation?"

"So we dine with the *lemures*."

When Julia says *lemures*, she means ghosts, spirits of the dead, restless and malevolent, so I'm determined to set the matter straight. "There is no reason to fear the shades, Julia. I've drawn my family's *kas* to this very spot by erecting statues in their likenesses."

"All the more reason for me to fear. Your parents hated my father; I don't suspect their shades will be fond of me. And what is a *ka*?"

"It's one of the nine bodies of the Egyptian soul. It's the part of you that makes you live. A spark. It eats and drinks, which is why I bring meals for my dead. My family is lost to me in this River of Time, so if they can join me here in any way at all, I'm gladdened by it."

Julia sighs as if she must grant me that. "Still, I cannot approve dragging little girls to romp in the tombs of their dead mothers. Visiting one's ancestors should be a somber endeavor. A thing done with all the solemnity of old men who lecture about *gravitas* and *dignitas*."

"Since when have you wanted anything to do with *gravitas* and *dignitas*?"

Julia laughs, conceding the point, while under the supervision of my Berber woman, the children happily play hide-and-seek behind the pillars. As fair as she is, I should worry that my daughter will freckle in the sun, but I don't want to see her covered up before her time . . .

"One day this tomb may be the only place Isidora can be with me," I say, as servants lay a bountiful feast upon our picnic table. "I want her to be happy here. I want to fill this place with warm memories, so that when she comes with offerings for me, the remembrance will be a comfort. She won't fear it. It will already be a home to her."

"Your blood may be Macedonian Greek," Julia murmurs, mirth in her eyes, "but you're more *Egyptian* than anything else."

"I am Mauretanian," I say, as much to convince myself as her. Then, as if to prove it, I lay aside my fears of the hot sun and remove the shawl of my embroidered blue *himation* to leave my shoulders bare.

"You're Mauretanian, then," Julia agrees. "All the better, as far as I'm concerned. Your kingdom is just a few days' sailing from Rome—"

"Depending upon the weather and the direction," I interrupt, which leads me to ask, "Just how did you convince the captain of Agrippa's ship to carry you here against your husband's wishes?"

"Blackmail, of course."

It's the last answer I expect. "The captain of that ship must have a dark and terrible secret for him to fear it more than he fears your husband."

"Perhaps he does," Julia says, plucking a cluster of grapes from a silver platter. "Imagine that the captain became very drunk one night and put his hands on me. Imagine that I gave myself over to him. Now imagine that I threatened to tell my husband about it."

Her words are a cool cup of water thrown in my face. I am the last person to judge anyone for adultery, but I cannot imagine that even Julia would do such a thing. She loves to shock people, and I see that she's enjoyed shocking me, but I cannot affect an air of sophisticated indifference. Remembering her father's new law, the *Lex Julia*, which makes adultery punishable by banishment or even death, I shudder. "You take lovers so freely now?"

She laughs, patting the gentle swell of her belly. "It can be done carefully, Selene. Agrippa's children all look like him. After all, I never take on new passengers until the cargo is full."

With a gasp, I say, "I don't believe you. You wouldn't risk it!"

"Believe it. I do it to punish Agrippa. Even if he never knows about it, I do."

"You don't want to punish Agrippa. You want to punish the man you love."

Julia had been ready to pop a grape into her mouth, but this stops her. "I don't love *any* man."

Her vehement denial reveals the true depths of her heartbreak and I find myself saying, "Iullus Antonius did not betray you, Julia. It was your father who forced him to marry Marcella. Like you—like all of us—Iullus is at the mercy of the emperor."

Julia frowns. "Selene, we shall get on a great deal better during my visit if you don't mention your half brother to me. He's forgotten me, so I do my best to forget him."

I never thought to hear myself defend him, but I say, "Iullus has not forgotten you. When I saw him last, he was bereft."

"Not so bereft that he couldn't perform his marital duty with Marcella," Julia counters. "Iulla and Lucius Antonius, their children are called."

"You have children the same age."

"Iullus has a choice in such matters; I do not."

I know what it is to feel helpless. To feel seething hatred for the men who have lorded over me. So my heart fills with pity for her. "I feared it would be hard for you, married to Agrippa. Do you hate him, then?"

"Of course I hate him," she says, stuffing another grape into her mouth and swallowing it whole. "Big, bellowing Agrippa. I take satisfaction in irritating him to the point of rage. I must be wicked to enjoy his distress as much as I do. But doesn't he deserve it? On the battlefield, they say he's the incarnation of Mars. He's wiped out entire tribes; these past years in Spain he's had his legions hunt the Cantabri to the last man."

Yes, that sounds like Agrippa. "And now he has won . . ."

"He's Rome's best general and has earned a Triumph, but my father will block it—"

"I thought it was at your father's command that the Senate voted Agrippa the honor."

Julia rolls her eyes at me. "You know very well that everything my father does in the Senate is for show! My father will insist that my husband refuse the honor. Perhaps he should. I'm told that Agrippa can't count even a single ancestor amongst the first families of Rome. Not that I've bothered to confirm it, because that would only remind everyone that the emperor saw fit to marry his only daughter to a New Man. And even if I could forgive Agrippa all that, there remains the fact that he's forced me to bear two—now three—children for him."

I wince, remembering a time when I was held down and forced. Remembering it as if it were yesterday. In the remembering, I restrain myself from glancing at my daughter. It was an ugly thing, that night, but I wouldn't trade my beautiful girl, even if it meant I could swim in some other River of Time where that night never happened.

Oblivious to my distress, Julia goes on to ask, "Do you want to know the thing I despise most about Agrippa? It's that I cannot hate him as much as I should."

I too have reason to hate Admiral Agrippa, and yet I've never been able to do it. As much as I fear him, as much as he is my enemy, I've always known that what drives him is not malice—and yet, what solace would that be for all the men he's killed? "Hatred is a heavy burden to bear. Especially hatred for your own husband."

Julia lifts her face to the sun and closes her eyes. "I tell myself that I hate him. Then he comes to my bed with a diligence born of pure patriotism. I swear to myself that I won't be roused by his touch, but I am."

I blink more than once. "Truly?"

"There is something about Agrippa's body," Julia explains, quite unconcerned that she might be overheard by servants. "It's scarred and weathered. It awakens hideously respectable urges in me to bear children and sit all day weaving at the loom."

None of this is what I expect to hear. "You can't mean it . . ."

"Well, not the part about the loom. But the rest of it, I mean every word. He undresses with military precision, lays me flat on the bed, then climbs atop me with a *gravitas* that would be laughable if he weren't so appallingly good at it!"

I'm scandalized and a bit disturbed. "I might have gone my whole life quite happily not knowing this about Agrippa. Have a care—"

"Oh, our Marcella fooled us with her tears on her wedding day. Crying about Agrippa's fumbling hands. She's a liar. Agrippa masters everything he puts his hands to. Even me." Julia sighs, then shivers. "It's such an earnest business, the way he grinds me down into the bed. He tells me to close my eyes and think of the honor of my family and the good of Rome, and I do. I can see myself, a mother of the empire. He excites me. I don't bother to hide it. I don't care if Agrippa thinks I moan too loudly when I find my own pleasure. I don't care at all. It's freeing, not to care."

I speak slowly. "So, then . . . you're not entirely unhappy with Agrippa?"

"What purpose would it serve to be *entirely* unhappy? I'm the daughter of the emperor and the wife of the only man who can challenge him. There are worse fates that can befall a woman."

Perhaps she is thinking of her mother. Poor, ostracized Scribonia, who not only hailed from a family that advocated for the return of the Republic, but had the temerity to give the emperor a daughter instead of a son; he divorced her the very day that Julia was born. Or perhaps she is thinking of *my* mother, who challenged this world of men and came away from it with deadly venom in her blood. "You're right, of course."

Julia likes to be told she's right, so her dark mood vanishes in an instant. "Delightfully, there's more to the world than bedmates and babies. There are advantages to being Agrippa's wife. He took me to Spain and he'll take me to Greece!" Her eyes cut at me, shrewdly. "Ah, but you've already been . . ."

I don't wish to speak of Greece, both because it shames me and because I still carry secrets from my time there with the emperor that are not safe to share. Not even with Julia. "Hurry and finish your lunch," I say to distract her. "We still have an adventure ahead of us . . ."

"IT carries water all the way from those mountains," I boast, sweeping a hand over the path our monstrous aqueduct cuts into the wide sun-drenched vista of Africa. "It stretches farther than your eye can see! We bridged rivers in five places and looped around the landscape where shale or other soft stones are prone to landslides."

Julia feigns a little yawn. "Wake me when you've finished marveling at standard engineering, will you? Honestly, you're worse than Agrippa. We have aqueducts in Rome, you know. Soldiers too."

She's speaking of the Legio III Augusta, which is overseeing the construction. Ordinarily, the officers show me only the barest modicum of respect, but now that I'm in the company of the emperor's daughter, the highest-ranking officer makes haste to welcome us into their camp and boast of their aqueduct.

It's a rough place, here on the river. Alongside the surveyors and engineers, there are men at hard work with picks and shovels. Laborers run pipes, sweating under the sun, while stiff-necked soldiers guard the dusty camp from the raiders on the frontier.

While we survey the marvel from the vantage point of a watch post, I hear Tala sharply scold the children in a Berber dialect I've learned. I turn to see Pythia and Tala's son Ziri standing close together, innocent of any wrongdoing. But my daughter is kneeling in the dirt beside a cage of camp dogs, trying to give them a drink from a water skin.

"What is she doing?" Julia asks.

Groaning, I give a shake of my head. "My daughter can resist no creature under the sky . . ."

My big Berber woman tries to haul my daughter away from the dogs, but Isidora is so intent on the animals in the cage that she actually struggles. "Can't you see he's hurt?" my daughter shouts, slapping at Tala's tattooed hands.

Never before has she treated her nursemaid in such a way and it shocks me. "Isidora! Shame on you. Tala is trying to protect you. You don't know those dogs. Do you want them to bite you?"

"But he's not a dog," Dora cries, sniffling. "He's a boy!"

I march to her side, frustrated by the increasing frequency with which my daughter says strange things to vex me. Peering into the cage, I'm brought up short. There, curled up on the straw amidst the caged hounds, is a little boy with cinnamon-kissed skin. A gash across his dirtied cheek is caked with dried blood and his filthy fingers splay over a festering wound in his side.

I think the boy is dead, so I startle when his agonized eyes pop open and fasten on mine. "Sweet Isis!"

Julia comes up behind me, demanding of the centurion, "Why is this boy in a cage?"

The centurion, who has, thus far, forced himself to politeness for our inspection, clears phlegm from his throat. "He's a raider."

A *raider*, he says! The boy can be no more than eight or nine years old. He's a scrawny, pathetic thing, mangier than the dogs that sniff around him. He is a bag of bones I could rattle to death with one hand, so my lips curl with contempt when I say, "A fearsome warrior, I'm sure. No doubt it took the whole legion to subdue him."

"Just about," the centurion replies. "Little bastard bit half the ear off the soldier who captured him. He was riding with Berber raiders from Numidia. Garamantes, maybe."

The condition of the boy gives rise to my anger. Straightening to my full height, I look the centurion in the eye. "I was told Lucius Cornelius Balbus rid us of the Garamantes. Isn't that why he was granted a Triumph in Rome?"

The centurion shrugs. "We caught the raiders trying to steal the livestock from a farm after they'd set fire to the granary. We spared this one on account of his age. If he lives, maybe he'll fetch a price."

They're going to make a slave of the boy. It's not the worst thing they could do to him, by far. So near to the frontier, it would be risky to try to find the boy's tribe, not to mention more trouble than any legionary soldier would bother with. No Roman magistrate would have any interest in the matter either. What are the soldiers to do? They can't let the boy wander off into the wilderness on his own; given the harsh terrain, he'd be dead in a day. Slavery is the kindest fate for this boy, should he live . . .

"He's hurt, Mama," my daughter sobs. "He's thirsty and hungry too."

"Let Tala give him water. You stay away," I command before turning to the boy in the cage and addressing him in the Berber dialect I've learned. "What is your name? What tribe do you hail from?"

The boy jerks upright, as if not having expected to hear his own language from my lips, but he doesn't answer.

Keeping hold of my weeping princess, Tala says, "He's dull. He has no wits."

Something in the brooding stare of the boy behind the wooden slats of the cage makes me think otherwise. As a child hostage in Rome, I practiced making a mask of my face. When I was older, I learned to slow the beat of my own heart, so that I wouldn't betray myself to the emperor's touch. Having mastered the art of deception, I'm not fooled by the boy's bravado. The spark in his eyes is one that I recognize; it's the enraged and contempt-filled stare of a child who has been taken prisoner.

His defiance is such a sharp reminder of my proud twin brother that I'm nearly undone. "He is one of my subjects," I say to the centurion, though it is almost certainly a lie. "He needs care if he's to survive; does your camp physician believe the best medicine is to lock a wounded boy in a cage?"

The centurion looks not even slightly abashed. "There's a physician back at the fort, not here."

I opt for a conciliatory tone. "Of course. I imagine conditions are very difficult for your men here. Perhaps it would be best to release the boy to us."

Julia raises an eyebrow. "Just what are we going to do with him?"

It's a very good question. I cannot venture into the hills looking for his people. Nor can I find him a competent healer unless I take him all the way back to the city with us. While I consider my options, Dora wrenches free of her nursemaid to offer the boy her water skin. He goes for it with such savagery that I think he'll snatch it from my daughter's hands. But, like a wounded creature brought low by the mercy of a goddess, he only presses his mouth to the skin and lets her hold it for him while he drinks.

She's disobeyed me and behaved very poorly, but the sight of my daughter tending to this poor Berber boy moves me. "Please release him, Centurion. Or must I pay you to do so?"

The veteran soldier kicks a stone in the dusty earth. "He's not worth a bronze coin to you, Majesty. What will you do when he lunges for your face and tries to tear at you with his teeth?"

"My guards can handle a boy."

At my side, Memnon nods, one leathery hand upon the pommel of his sword.

The centurion lifts a hand in surrender, then barks out an order to one of his underlings who returns with the keys to the cage. After a bit of rattling, the boy is dragged out amidst barking dogs. Smeared in blood and dirt, the boy tries to make himself tall. Tries to hide that he's in pain. Again, I ask his name. This time he answers, but puts such animus behind the word it sounds like an obscenity.

"Tacfarinas," the boy snarls.

"Do you know it?" I ask my Berber woman.

She shrugs. "I doubt he's of high status. There is not even a speck of blue dye on his skin."

Yet the little wretch stands before me with the bearing of a prince, glowering at his Roman captors and the rest of us too. We're the enemy. That is what he thinks.

Then he spits at me.

Julia gasps. All my courtiers gasp.

And the Roman centurion snarls, "I warned you he was a little bastard."

Memnon has his big hand wrapped round the boy's throat before I can stop him. This is an insult not to be endured, but the sight of my brawny guard half choking the injured boy fills me with horror. "Memnon, stop."

"Don't hurt him!" my daughter shrieks.

"He *spat* at my queen," Memnon seethes. "I've killed men for less."

I don't ask what men he's killed before and for what reason. I only seek to bring calm. "You're very much mistaken, Memnon. I'm the Queen of Mauretania. My subjects dare not spit at me." Catching Julia's eye, I lift my chin and ignore the wet saliva on my gown. "I didn't see anyone spit at me. Did you, Julia?"

The emperor's daughter shrugs one shoulder. "I saw nothing of the sort."

"There you have it, Memnon. The desert makes a man's eyes play tricks on him. Find the boy some clothing. We're taking him with us."

"YOU speak their language?" Julia asks, reclining in the curtained litter beside me. "Yet you keep interpreters in your employ . . ."

"There are many Berber dialects. I don't speak all of them. Interpreters are still helpful. Besides, subjects will say things to an interpreter they won't say to a ruler. Sometimes it's better not to let someone know that you understand. It's a lesson I learned at your father's knee."

Julia bunches up a quilted cushion beneath her head. "Your daughter is kind."

Still annoyed by the entire episode, I complain, "She's prone to every kind of mischief and—"

"She is *kind*," Julia insists. "She helped that boy even at your displeasure. She defied you and you let her . . ." That I'm too lenient with Isidora has long been a complaint of those closest to me, but this is not Julia's concern. "I fear my children will never be so kind."

"Why wouldn't they be? You'll teach them to be."

"What would I know of kindness?" Julia asks with a shake of her head. "I was never kind. Moreover, if I'd behaved as your daughter did, my father would've killed that little savage boy on the spot."

"You *were* kind," I argue, for when I was her father's prisoner, she offered me friendship when no one else dared.

"No," she says, closing her eyes. "I was a selfish, self-absorbed child. When my children are as old as Isidora, what will Agrippa teach them? My husband isn't a cruel man for the enjoyment of it, Selene. But he is *hard*. If cruelty serves a purpose, he doesn't shrink from it. He's killed many savage boys—just like the one you rescued today. What will my children become with such a father if I'm not there to listen to them and soothe their tears and . . ."

She trails off, and I sense there is some secret she is hiding. "Why wouldn't you be there to soothe your children?"

Catching herself, she gives a false little laugh. "I'm hardly there now. What would I know about mothering anyway? I never had one. Besides, children are sticky little creatures who babble and cling and rumple clothing. It's for the best that Agrippa rips my babies from my arms and gives them into the hands of their nursemaids as soon as they're born."

IN the palace kitchen, the half-starved Berber boy gnaws the roasted lamb off a skewer, then stuffs bits of bread into his mouth as if he'll never see another meal again. He's been bathed and his wounds tended. Euphronius smeared the cut on the boy's face with aloe. As for the wound under the boy's ribs—it looks to have been a laceration from a spear tip—my wizard cleaned it, treated it with a poultice of honey, and dosed the boy's cup with herbs to dull the pain.

Hopefully it will make the boy sleepy and less apt to run away. He's already tried to run, twice. Both times, Memnon boxed him into submission with unnecessary brutality. Both times it was my daughter who got the boy to settle. She soothes the boy like she does her little animals, coaxing him as if he were a cat, letting him approach her, never crowding him. But I think his own tribesmen may be able to make him more comfortable, so I called for Maysar, my Berber chieftain, who stands scowling in the archway. "And what do you expect me to do with him?"

"I expect you to find his people."

Maysar bares his teeth. "Majesty, do you imagine that I know every Berber family in the kingdom?"

"No, but Tala thinks this boy is of the Musulamii tribe. Are they not part of your federation?"

"They're nomadic herdsmen. They travel on the frontier between our kingdom and Numidia. You don't expect me to roam the steppes of Africa looking for this boy's family, do you?"

"The Romans killed his family," my daughter interrupts, having come to my side by stealth.

Surprised, I ask, "Is that what the boy told you?"

Isidora bobs her head, golden curls falling haphazardly in her eyes. "His family returned to their summer grazing lands to find them fenced and farmed by Roman settlers."

"Damned thieving Romans," Maysar murmurs, and the boy's head jerks up from where he's huddled over his meal. Tacfarinas speaks to Maysar in a Berber dialect that doesn't unravel easily inside my ears, but I understand the fear and anger in every gesture. The boy tells a tale of confrontation; of watching his family die. He tells a tale of being the one who ran away. Of being the only survivor . . .

And my heart breaks.

It wasn't *our* Roman settlers who murdered his family, but they could've been. Every year more of the traditional grazing lands are taken for productive use, marked off, fenced in, plowed, and planted. We need those farms if we're to send Rome our tribute of grain, but at what cost?

"We can find some place for the boy, can we not?" I ask.

Maysar replies in Greek so that the boy cannot understand us. "He'd rather run off to join the Garamantes who took him in. I'm not sure I disapprove."

Glancing back at the boy, I say, "Berber warriors begin young, but not as young as this. He was riding with raiders. If he runs with hard men like that, we'd only end up having to bring him to justice someday. Do you want to see him on a cross?"

Maysar sighs and I know why. His romantic notions of the noble warrior ejecting the Roman menace fades more and more each year. "We'll put him to work hauling firewood for the lighthouse. If we find he can be trusted not to run away, perhaps he can tend to the king's horses in the stable."

The slightest flicker of interest lights in the boy's eyes at the word *horses*. Ah, yes. So he is Berber to the bone. And he knows at least one word of Greek. Perhaps he knows *more* than one word. Though he's louse-ridden and hostile, I think he's a clever boy. I have a kingdom full of boys just like him. I cannot save them all, but perhaps I can save just this one . . .

Six

IT'S my husband's habit to visit my chambers on the Ides of each month. Such visits reassure our courtiers that all is well between their sovereigns, and our subjects are comforted to think that their king is a virile man with a fertile wife. They need not know that Juba's visits aren't conjugal in nature.

Other women at court are altogether too eager to share the king's bed. There are young men too who would gladly please him, though I've never heard so much as a whisper that my husband's preferences run that way. In any case, since the night our son was conceived the king hasn't attempted to seduce me and I'm glad of it, for we're estranged by the things we cannot say to each other . . . or be for each other. I cannot give myself to Juba without counting it a disloyalty to my beloved, and I would wager Juba cannot touch me without counting it a disloyalty to the emperor. Oh, we mustered the nerve for it once, but there's no need to repeat it. And so we content ourselves with our cordial alliance.

On the night he comes to dine, I invite the king into my chambers, where we recline on cushions in the native fashion. Slaves wash our hands in rose water, then deliver an array of dishes to our table, several of which are artfully presented in fired-clay bowls decorated beautifully in bold geometric patterns representing partridge eyes and lion paws. The king studies a dish before sampling it, as if he can puzzle out the spices just by looking, then dips his flatbread into a bowl of slow-roasted fowl and olive *tajine*. "I'm told that you and the emperor's daughter made a nuisance of yourselves with the legion. Is it true that you liberated a bandit?"

"He's just a boy, not a bandit—"

"I might've known Julia would lure you into mischief," he growls.

His foul mood tells me that he still worries that when the seas open and we receive word from Rome, we'll be blamed for aiding Julia's rebellion. Perhaps we'll be blamed for much more.

But this has nothing to do with the boy. "Juba, no harm came of it."

"You cannot flit about near the frontier, Selene. It isn't safe."

"Where am I safer than with Roman legions?" I ask, trying not to take umbrage at his implication that he makes *inspections* at the frontier but I only *flit about*.

"Look what the sun has done to you," he complains. "Your skin is burnt, and I gather that if I come close enough to sniff, you'll smell of camels."

"I do not smell of camels! The moment I returned, I soaked in a bath of honey and donkey's milk."

To prove it, I hold out my perfumed wrist. With surprising intimacy, he leans forward and inhales the scent. "So you have. I suppose that accounts for the sour faces of your attendants. They must have spent hours drawing such an extravagant bath for you."

Taking me unawares, he kisses the soft underside of my arm. It's at this moment I realize he may have come to my rooms tonight with a desire for more than dinner. "How solicitous of you to notice the faces of my serving girls. Are you considering taking one as a concubine?"

I ask this only half in jest. I'm a woman and a wife but I'm first a queen; I must know the dynamics of my own court, even if the knowledge pains me, and I suspect it might.

Juba replies with an airy tone. "I'd only take one of your servants as a concubine if I thought it would vex you."

"Perhaps it would."

He raises an eyebrow. "I doubt that, but, as it happens, your serving girls fear you more than they desire me."

Slicing herbed goat cheese for my bread, I counter, "Perhaps they're motivated by love for me and not fear."

"Perhaps." My husband smiles as if our banter is soothing his bad temper. "You did steal my favorite *hetaera* from me, after all."

He speaks of the Lady Circe, who has transformed herself into a grammarian and teacher of Greek. I call upon her from time to time because, even though her beauty is fading, she's wise in the way of men and of kings. Once my husband's lover, she belongs to me now, and it occurs to me that all our court can be divided in such a way. There are those who would kill for Juba and those who would die for me. Only my daughter's loyalty seems evenly divided between us.

"Will you employ another *hetaera*?" I ask.

"Would it vex you if I did?"

To admit jealousy would be beneath my royal dignity and also concede my powerlessness in such matters. If it's true that a king is free to take lovers where he might, then it's equally true that a queen must never grant her husband's whores the status of a rival. To deflect the question, I say, "Such matters are improper to discuss . . ."

"Now you concern yourself with propriety?" he asks, chuckling as we eat together, sharing bits of bread and cheese and almonds. "And this on the same day you let Julia persuade you to take in an urchin boy."

"It was my idea. If you'd seen him there, in that cage, so broken and pathetic. If you'd heard Isidora crying, begging for me to help him . . ."

My husband lifts a hand to wave away the subject. "Say no more. You're right. I couldn't bear Isidora's tears. She's a special little girl."

To hear him praise my daughter moves me. "She is, isn't she? Nevertheless, please know that I'm grateful for the way you've forced yourself to take my daughter into your heart."

"There was no force involved," he protests. "How could I not take her into my heart when your daughter is the only person who has ever loved me?"

The moment the words fall from his lips, his eyes slant away with apparent embarrassment. He sips at the mint tisane our Berbers serve at every occasion, as if I ought to take no notice of the astonishing statement. My stare must tell him that he will have to explain himself, for he finally adds, quietly, "Isidora is the first person to ever open her arms to me without reservation or consideration of my birth or station."

I remain astonished. He's a king, a scholar, a soldier, and a man whose looks turn the heads of even young girls at court. It pains me to think that he's never been loved—or at least, never loved in the way he wanted to be. In fact, it pains me so much that I thrust the thought away. "That can't be true."

"It is. You know I have no memory of my parents or my siblings. Only the *Julii* . . ."

I know exactly what it's like to live as an orphan in the emperor's household, beholden to Romans who can be kind and cruel in turn. "But, Juba, there must've been some friend, some . . . some courtesan . . ."

The king laughs. "I'm not fool enough to believe words of love that fall from the lips of a courtesan. No, Selene. Whereas everyone either loves you or hates you, I'm a man for whom people might feel perfect indifference, as you well know."

"I have never been indifferent to you."

Ambivalent, perhaps, but never indifferent . . .

I don't say it, because I can never find the words to explain precisely what it is that I feel for Juba, and in any case, he is already groaning at my attempt to comfort him. "Enough, Selene. It wasn't my intention to press you for some declaration of emotion. Or press you at all. You've done your duty by me. You've given me a son and heir. It cost you dearly. Euphorbus tells me that if we have another child, it may kill you. So you must never fear that I'll ask more."

I am troubled beyond measure that my mage should speak to the king about such a thing. Has he grown so old and addled that he's lost all political sense? To portray me as frail! "Euphorbus said only that we must not risk another child *now*."

"Ah," Juba says and I cannot tell if he is pleased to hear it. "Nevertheless, we can wait for another prince. There's no hurry."

Stung, I continue, "The old man worries overmuch; he exaggerates my illness. I'm healthy enough. I'm no unworldly girl. I am a child of Isis. The magic of Egypt is in me. I've learned to work *heka* on my own body so I am never with child unless I want to be."

"I find this hard to believe . . ."

How can he doubt me? He's seen my goddess speak to me through symbols engraved upon my palms. He's seen blood drip from my fingertips to be transformed into red flowers when they splattered upon the marble tiles. Has my childbed illness somehow reminded him of my mortality and lessened me in his eyes? The matter must be put right.

My spine stiffens. "Juba, did I not swear to you, the night we came together, that I would conceive a child? Did I not vow it would be a son? Everything I promised has come to pass. I am no ordinary woman. There is no risk in bedding me unless I will it."

In the face of my furious proclamation, the room is silent, and then . . . Juba laughs. I think he mocks me, but his eyes are filled with good-natured mirth. "Madam, if I didn't know you better, I might think you were arguing for me to take you to bed for the sake of pleasure."

Heat pricks at my cheeks and I start to stammer a denial, which only makes my husband laugh harder, and I don't like being laughed at. "Trust that if I were luring you to my bed you would know it."

He is now wheezing in his merriment. He laughs so hard he must dab at the corners of his eyes with a napkin. "I suppose I would. As Cleopatra's daughter, you aren't shy when you want something."

"If this is going to turn into another discussion about how I'm the daughter of an Egyptian whore and well versed in the art of seduction, I—"

"Oh, Selene, don't take offense. I'm not accusing you of immodesty. I remember well that you're the girl who once said that kissing me was the most shameful thing she'd ever done."

I wince that he should remember, much less remind me of it. "That was years ago."

"Have things changed so much since then?"

I have no easy answer for him. My heart belongs to another. But I recall what Julia said about her marriage to Agrippa. He is not the man she wanted, but she's found ways to content herself. Perhaps I can do the same. I feel myself open to possibility. My husband must sense it, for he shifts on his cushions so that he's seated beside me. He doesn't touch me, but lets me accustom myself to his proximity as I've seen him do with wild horses. His voice is gentle but intent. "*Have* things changed, Selene?"

"Perhaps . . ."

"Another *perhaps* . . . but I begin to like that word. It's a word that leaves room for hope." My husband is, at heart, a scholar. It's his nature to test and now he wants to test me. "Shall we experiment with a kiss?"

I stare at his mouth, the curves of which seem deceptively soft. I am afraid to trust them. "This is a silly conversation."

"It would please me to kiss you. As I am the king, should you not strive to please me in all things?"

He says the last playfully, without any true royal hauteur, and I find myself tempted, but wary. "We have kissed for better reasons, Juba. And I cannot think I'd enjoy being kissed *experimentally*. You'll study such a kiss and categorize it like the plants you collect. You'll question the meaning of such a kiss. You'll want to explore my motives and prevail upon me to name my emotions. Then, when I don't answer to your satisfaction, you'll take it into your heart and let it fester."

"You misjudge me, my lady. Those are the mistakes of a younger man who has not yet accepted that his wife, like the moon that is her namesake, is essentially unknowable. Once, I was determined to solve the riddle of you, but I'm now content to be enchanted by your mystery. For example, there was a time I would've peppered you with questions about your magic. I would've made a study of it to include in my treatise on cult worship. But I suspect that would offend you, and I very much wish to avoid offending you. So if the cost of a kiss is that I must not question you—"

"Or speak of it," I caution. "You must never speak of it."

With victory in sight, he grins. "I won't question or speak of it unless you do. Though I intend to kiss you so well that you'll want to boast of it to your ladies."

How little he knows me, even after all these years. "If it were a kiss well done, I should want to keep it secret, so no one could ever tarnish or take it from me."

"Well, then," he says, taking my face in his warm hands. "Here is to silence."

He tilts my head and gently closes his mouth over mine . . .

. . . and I do not want to tell a soul.

IN the days that follow, Juba complains bitterly of the trouble that may come of Julia's visit, and, in spite of the winter sea, he sends a special military dispatch to Rome requesting advice from the emperor on what we are to do with his wayward daughter.

Nevertheless, our court is gayer for Julia's presence and my heart is lighter than it has been in years. When the time comes for winter sowing, I take Julia to my nearest plantation, on a gentle slope in the shadow of Mount Chenoua, where rows of bountiful fruit trees blanket the hills. The villa overlooks the blue sea on one side and rolling orchards on the other, its terrace overgrown with vines of ivy and late-blooming hibiscus flowers. I call it the House of Olives, for the fat olives we harvest in these hills make a fragrant oil when pressed. It's a farm exactly as Cato the Elder described a perfect farm should be, near a well-traveled road, with a vineyard, an irrigated garden, a meadow, and vast grain lands.

When I say as much to Julia, she makes a face. "Why would you spend your time reading Cato? He was such a cranky old man!"

"He was wise in the matter of agriculture," I argue, though I don't follow all of Cato's dictums. Especially not his advice to starve the slaves that work the fields or sell off the old and sickly. Whereas the vast majority of farms in Mauretania are worked by slaves who toil for absent Roman masters, my plantation is worked mostly by sharecroppers. Of course, I'm foolish to take pride in this, because I don't earn as much as I could . . .

Still, I defend myself by saying, "I read Cato as I read everything on agriculture, because your father has set me the task of feeding the Roman Empire."

"Is that all?" Julia laughs, climbing the summit of the hill and shielding her eyes from the sun with one hand. "All he needs from me are grandsons. I'd chide you for exaggerating your importance but apparently you keep a goddess at your beck and call, whereas none of the gods have ever taken any interest in my desires . . . Your plowman's team of oxen seems to be mired in a patch of mud. We ought to call for your overseer."

"The overseer here is an old man; he won't be of much help, but I know that plowman. Let's go down and help him."

Julia is aghast. "You and I?"

"And our guards," I say, smiling at the cohort of Macedonian soldiers who accompany me always. "I keep trying to convince Memnon that when he's ready to retire his sword, he ought to serve as overseer here. Now is your chance to prove you can do a good job, Memnon."

Only because I've addressed him directly does he speak. "Majesty, a Macedonian guard is never without his sword." But because I've pricked his pride with the hint that he may be nearing the age at which he cannot hold a shield, Memnon goes first down the hill into the field to help the plowman.

The rest of us follow. On our way, I stoop down and gather a handful of dirt. "It isn't as black as the river-brought soil in Egypt," I tell Julia. "But it's good earth that surrenders to the plow after the rains. I grow wheat on it, and in the less choice fields, I grow barley."

Julia backs up for higher ground. "You're dirtying the embroidered hem of your *chiton*. It will never come clean."

"I have others." Lifting my skirts to the knee, I walk out into the field, where my guards help guide the team of oxen out of a shallow depression where the rain water has turned the soil to mud.

Huffing with indignation, Julia follows me, and we circle round the powerful haunches of the oxen that toil here in my fields. Both great beasts turn their horned heads. As we pass closely near the sweating animals, I whisper to her, "This always sets Memnon's nerves on edge."

As if on cue, poor Memnon barks at me to get back from the animals for my safety, but we ignore him and I give a little wave to the plowman, who bows deeply. "Your Majesty . . ."

"Last season he taught me to drive the plow," I say.

Julia's eyes go round with delight. "You've driven these animals? With your own hands?"

"Not by myself, of course," I say. "But I have done it."

"I want to learn!"

"Julia, you can't. You ought not exert yourself when pregnant."

It's the wrong thing to say, for she takes it as a dare. "I am not *very* pregnant. Not even five months gone, I would guess, though I seem to be showing earlier and earlier with each child. At any rate, it's your doing that I've come down into this field to dirty my gown and fill my nostrils with the scent of manure. I might as well learn something."

She reaches for the handles of the plow while I try to warn her off. "Julia, you'd be surprised how much strength and steadiness it takes to keep the furrows straight."

In spite of my warning, Julia's hands both wrap round the wood, her knuckles tight as she marvels at the whole contraption. Then the oxen lurch forward. When the plow begins to move, Julia's sandals wobble on the broken ground of the furrow. I reach to steady her, but my interference throws her off balance.

I stagger to catch her before she falls, but lose my own footing in a long slide that takes us both down with a dramatic splash in the mud. Julia wails and I am horrified. "Julia! Are you hurt?"

She looks up, her face a mask of dirt, her hair in filthy strands, one hand on her pregnant belly. "I think—I think I'm unharmed . . . just *filthy*."

She begins to laugh, relieved, but when I join her she shrieks at me, "Why are *you* laughing? This is your fault, you cow!" With that, she launches a fistful of sticky earth that spatters my cheek and clings to my face. Howling, I crawl to her for vengeance, intending to shove her back down in the dirt, but I'm doubled over with laughter as she kicks at me, shouting, "You horrid Egyptian cow!"

I laugh harder, trying to grasp her legs so she can't peg me with the hard sole of her sandal. Julia hoots, tears of laughter streaking her dirty face as we wrestle. Our poor guards think we've gone mad.

But we cannot seem to stop. My sides hurt from laughing, but every time I relent and try to help her up from the ground, Julia drags me back down and I am helpless to do anything but lie on the earth with her and laugh.

"THE emperor's daughter is a menace," Juba announces. He has caught me out in my rooms after my bath and now scolds me like a misbehaving child. "When the seas open again, we will have trouble as you have not imagined. We can only hope Agrippa hauls her away over his shoulder kicking and screaming . . ."

"The plowing was my fault, I assure you."

"You've too much pride to lower yourself in such a way," he insists. "Or you've changed very much, indeed."

"I told you that I've changed."

He comes closer and I see that he's not as angry as he pretends. "I will say of the mud, however, that if you're an example of its merits as a beauty treatment, I very much approve."

His unexpected flirtation makes me smile. "Ouch! My face hurts from laughing too much today."

"I never thought to hear you say such a thing, Selene," he says, cradling my cheek in his palm, taking advantage of the new liberties I've granted him. In truth, I never thought to hear myself say such a thing. In my life, I've rarely laughed with abandon. Never kissed without consequence. Tragedy, sadness, and bitter rage have had the care of my soul.

I'm not sure I would recognize happiness.

But when my husband kisses me, I wonder if perhaps this is it. Here, so far from Rome, we may have found some happiness. It is not love, but it may be happiness. It may only be a happiness born of the things we do not ask of each other and the faults we overlook. It may be a happiness born of concessions, silence, and secrets. But if we *are* happy, it is such a precious and fragile thing that I must cherish and defend it against whatever may come with the arrival of spring.

Seven

WE welcome our son's first Saturnalia with much merriment. At six months old, our little prince's skin is as pale and translucent as alabaster. He now sits up on his own and makes a game of peeking between his fingers. He knows his name too. When I call him *Ptolemy*, he turns to look, and his eyes, like Juba's, are an earthy amber brown.

To celebrate the season, Juba orders fresh pine cut from the forest to be made into fragrant wreaths for every door in the palace. We also use the resin to flavor our wine. Our halls are festooned with garlands and the trees on the grounds have been ornamented with little stars made of hammered silver. I take Dora and Pythia to my private altar to Isis. There I teach the girls to burn frankincense in her honor and we burn so much that fragrant blue clouds of it drift throughout the palace.

It's all very costly, but one cannot be stingy with the gods . . .

This year we'll celebrate more than just the Roman Saturn, whom the Berbers call Ba'al Hammon. My Alexandrians will also celebrate the birth of Isis's son, Horus, who himself is a sun god. Some will honor the Haloea in honor of Demeter or the Brumalia for Dionysus. It's hard to know which tradition they'll embrace, for some Alexandrians consider themselves first Greek. Others Egyptian. Perhaps it is a vain hope, but I want them to consider themselves Mauretanians, now.

One rainy afternoon I find Julia in the receiving hall surrounded by baskets of candles and ribbons and pastries. With the children of my palace, she kneels on the floor, the center of attention. Dora is with her, leaning against Julia's pregnant belly as the emperor's daughter teaches her to tie a bow onto a sprig of evergreen. Dora smiles, and with her lovely little face so near to Julia's, in profile, they look like sisters. The thought wounds me. My daughter. My dearest friend. I cannot bear to think that the emperor is a common thread between them, so I tell myself they're bound by no one and nothing but me. "What are you up to, Julia?"

All the children bow to me as they are accustomed, given that I'm their queen, and this delights Julia. "Why, I'm telling your little subjects all about our days together in Rome. Do you remember how we used to make gifts for the street children on the Saturnalia? How we tied candles and bundles of spices or pastries onto evergreen boughs until our fingers were numb from the cold?"

I do remember, though all such remembrances of Rome are tainted for me. "Did you tell them how you used to steal stewed plums from the pot of spiced wine?"

"Oh!" Julia says, rocking back on her knees. "You've given me a craving. Can we have spiced plums for the Saturnalia? Or don't you think the plums will taste so sweet if we don't have to steal them from Livia's pot?"

"My plums will always be sweeter than hers," I declare.

Julia wants plums, so I give them to her. Wearing a freedman's conical red *pileus* cap, as is the tradition during the Saturnalia, I serve plums at *all* our holiday banquets, and they taste sweeter than ever before. The Romans shout, "Io Saturnalia," and I gather the children in my chambers, where I shower them with gifts, including masks of revelry. I give gifts to my courtiers too. A new set of alabaster lamps for my mage. A thick silver bracelet for Tala. A length of precious cloth for Chryssa. Gem-encrusted inkpots for my poet, Crinagoras, and a vial of perfume for Circe.

Such gifts as these would be too humble for Julia, so I

commission a play in her honor. It is a new version of *The Trojan Women* that makes us all weep. It's one of our playwright's best; everyone agrees that Leonteus of Argos has outdone himself.

Later, still dabbing our eyes and weary with emotion, Julia and I huddle together on a couch by a burning brazier in my chambers, sipping warmed wine. Elsewhere in the palace, we hear revelry that will last late into the evening. I should be there with them in the banquet hall, celebrating with the king, but my quiet intimacy with Julia is a sweet respite. I give her a set of combs and ribbons in commemoration of the first gifts she ever gave to me, and she likes them very much.

"You think me vain!" she cries, but she sets about putting them in her hair straightaway. "And here all I have to give you is the rights to quarry stone in Numidia . . . They fell to me somehow as a gift from Marcellus. I suspect that given all the construction here in Iol-Caesaria, you can make better use of stone than I can!"

It is an astonishingly generous gift. "I'm so grateful. Truly, I cannot tell you how glad I am to have you here for the Saturnalia. I only wish it didn't mean we'll have to face your father's wrath come springtime."

"Oh, Selene, you need not worry about my father's wrath. Did you really believe that I let a sailor of low birth bed me just so that I might blackmail him into sailing across the narrow strait?"

I know the look in her eye when she means to tell me something vital and the hairs rise on my nape. "How should I know what to believe when you play such games with me?"

Julia gives a rueful smile that fades into sadness. "I'm sorry I deceived you. It's just that I wanted time with you that belonged only to me. Time I didn't have to share with my father."

Disentangling myself from her, I begin to sit up. "I need you to explain yourself . . ."

She sighs with regret. "I half convinced myself that I was acting upon my own desires instead of being pushed like a piece upon a game board between men vying for power. I hope you'll forgive me . . ."

"How can I forgive what I don't understand?"

"Fine. I'll make it plain. I left Agrippa at my father's command."

"At your father's command?" But that makes no sense at all, unless . . . "So the emperor means to break from his alliance with Agrippa. Has he grown so powerful in Rome that he no longer needs his best general?"

Julia gives a delicate shrug. "I wouldn't know. I haven't been in Rome since my marriage, and my husband censors my letters. But my father has ways of getting word to me through the soldiers. It was my father who gave me the means to leave Agrippa and come here."

The grinding gears of imperial intrigue have grown rusty in my mind, but now they start to turn again. "*Sweet Isis.* Your father must be planning some move against Agrippa. Is there to be another civil war?"

Julia stares down, twisting her betrothal ring around and around the fourth finger of her hand. "I don't know. I only know this is the only mission my father has ever set for me other than to marry the men he chooses and bear children for them. I couldn't refuse him."

It doesn't surprise me that the emperor would use Julia's desperate need for approval against her. But it *does* surprise me that she remains so stubbornly loyal to such a father. Perhaps it shouldn't surprise me. It is, I begin to think, the Roman way. "Meanwhile, your husband returns to Rome, unaware of the trap . . ."

She has too long been the daughter of Augustus for my implication to startle her. "I cannot believe that Agrippa is in any danger. My father cannot mean to make a widow of me a second time. He simply intends for a new ordering of their partnership. A new understanding. A negotiation . . ."

The emperor once described Julia as a kind of hostage that his powerful and increasingly independent general held against him; now, with Agrippa returning to Rome with his legions, the emperor has sent Julia to me for safekeeping, and I wonder at the significance of that. "Why here? Why did he make you flee to Mauretania?"

"It was the nearest client kingdom, though I'm sure there are other, more personal reasons." She doesn't say what those reasons are and I don't ask. We're both too shrewd for that.

"But, Julia, Agrippa has your children . . ."

"They're his children, or so he insists. My loyalties aren't torn, Selene. I am of the *Julii*. I must do as my father commands. As must we all." Her eyes are strangely intent on me now, all the gaiety gone from them. Then she says quietly, very quietly, "I have never understood what passes between you and my father."

If I have my way, she never will, for it is something too wicked to name. Something I have banished to the past, buried in my dark shadow self, my *khaibit*, which, Isis willing, will not rise again. "There is nothing to understand, Julia. Your father has done me great honor by making me queen and entrusting unto me some part of the grain supply for the empire. He's commanded from me shipments of grain, and I have obeyed."

"That is not all he commands of you now, Selene."

What can she mean by that? I scarcely breathe, so anxious am I. Will the emperor admonish me for having borne the son of another man? In his rage, would he dare to entrust such a missive with his own daughter? Julia meets my eyes and speaks carefully. "My father and my husband need a man to mediate between them."

"Maecenas?" I suggest, for that has long been the role of the emperor's old friend.

But Julia shakes her head. "Agrippa doesn't trust him. He's heard that Maecenas once advised the emperor either to offer me to Agrippa as a bride or to kill him."

That's true. I was there. But I do not confirm it.

Julia continues, "So there is only one man upon which both Augustus and Agrippa agree might make peace between them. That is Juba."

My mouth goes dry as it all falls into place. "Yet you said nothing, all this time?"

"The seas don't open until the month sacred to Mars, so what would be the point of upsetting you when there is nothing to be done about it until springtime?"

I want to shake her. Not only for keeping this news from Juba, but for the news I am afraid she is still keeping from me. In my mind's eye, I see the cobras rise from a basket of figs, but I force myself to ask, "What aren't you saying? What is to be done, Julia?"

"I carry a summons, Selene. My father commands you and Juba to return to Rome."

I won't go, I tell myself. When the sea opens and the ships make ready to sail for Rome, I'll delay. I'll plead illness. I'll plead madness if I must. But I won't return to Rome. I won't return to the emperor's side. I will not be his mistress. I will not play that game again. Never again.

So I say nothing. I don't tell my husband of the message that Julia carries from the emperor. Not when the nights are cold and the sea is rough and we are cut off from the rest of the world. Not when I can lose myself in the daily rhythm of our lives and believe the world we're building here for ourselves can remain untouched.

There will be time enough to tell my husband before the sailing season, so we go on with the Saturnalia. In token of the holiday, I give Juba a bust in the likeness of his father, the Numidian king— something rare that I acquired at great expense. I take pride in this gift, because I don't think my husband has ever even seen a portrait of his father before.

But I worry when Juba unveils it and stares so long at the marbled face. My husband swallows, as if searching the stone replica of his father's image for some reflection of himself. "Now I see why, when I was a child in Rome, I was mocked as the son of a hirsute barbarian. Quite a beard . . ."

"I think he was handsome. Don't you like it?"

Juba clears his throat. "Thank you for such a thoughtful gift, Selene. It's only that I don't know where I can keep it."

I think I understand. We're both the children of Rome's enemies. Like my mother, his father battled Rome and lost. All our lives, we've been forced to renounce our parents. To dishonor their memories with silence, if not denunciation. If my husband should give a place of distinction in our palace to this bust of his father, the infamous Berber rebel, it might be taken amiss by his master in Rome. It might be taken as a symbol that we sympathize with our subjects who would drive the Romans out. But I didn't make this gift with any political purpose in mind . . . or so I told myself at the time. "Keep it in your bedchamber, where only you can see it. No one can fault you for a private sentimentality."

Juba strokes his chin. "If that's true, it strikes me as odd, for it's our private sentimentalities that pose the most danger, don't you think?" I have the strangest sense that this is a veiled barb aimed at me. And when I meet his gaze, I realize that he already knows what I've been keeping from him. He points to a roll of vellum lying half-opened on his writing table. "Julia delivered the official summons this morning. Sealed with the emperor's signet ring."

At a loss for what else I might say or do, I drift to the table, examining the sphinx, the emperor's personal symbol, pressed deeply into the red wax. Written in the most formal language, the summons gives no hint of the emperor's state of mind. Whether he is furious or indifferent to us, we might never know from reading this. It says only that the *Ludi Seculares* will be held in July. It's to be a grand ceremony to announce a new age. And we're required to return to Rome to reaffirm our loyalty along with the other client kings and queens.

"Go without me," I say, my voice hoarse with distress.

"You know that is not possible, Selene."

"There's no reason for me to be there except that he commands it."

"That is reason enough." He rummages on his writing table for a coin that he holds out on his palm. In the world of sovereigns, coins are the surest messengers, and there, engraved on the metal, is the true reason the emperor wants me in Rome. The front of the coin reflects the face of Augustus in profile, but it's the back that is of most interest to me. A star. A comet. Just like the one that was said to mark Julius Caesar's ascension to godhood and the one that was said to herald my birth.

Juba holds it up in the light. "He has minted this coin to commemorate the forthcoming *Ludi Seculares*, in which he will proclaim himself the promised savior. And he cannot be believed by the people unless his claim is acknowledged by Cleopatra's daughter."

The inelegant sound I make is a ghastly mixture of shock, disgust, and outrage. Why, this revelation is only further reason for me to stay away. "Let them believe what they will!"

"Selene—"

"Do you remember that once, the emperor summoned me, and you pleaded with me not to go? You told me to delay. You told me to lie and say the message didn't reach me, or that it reached me too late to brave the journey over the winter sea. You said I should defy him. That I, alone, could defy him."

"Did I?" he asks, careful not to meet my gaze. "I must have been quite drunk."

"It was not wine that made you say it. You offered to help me then, so why not now?"

"Because there is no point." My husband's eyes settle again upon the bust of his father, still half in its wrappings, and he whispers, "Do you see this man, Selene? King Juba, the First of his name. I never knew him. He's only stone to me. Only dust. He's dead. He died while I was still an infant. He wasn't the man who hired my tutors and made certain of my education. He wasn't the man who defended me in my youth. He didn't teach me political strategy or take me with him on military campaigns. The man who did all that was Augustus Caesar. Always Caesar. The only thing I have from the man in this bust is my name. If this is the man you want me to be . . . I fear I will always disappoint you."

I flinch, for I know well what it is to be held up to the example of a parent and be found wanting. "Never would I put such a burden on you—"

"Then don't hold him out as an example to me! Don't ask me to put a statue of him in my bedchambers, where I must see his face every morning upon waking. Put out of your mind that I'm a notorious rebel, ready to throw off the yoke of Roman power."

Heat comes to my cheeks as I realize he suspects me of trying to undermine his Roman sensibilities and I cannot say he's wrong.

"I will not defy Caesar," Juba continues. "The idea that I should prove disloyal to him in any way is a horror to me. I will not send him a refusal or seek to humiliate him or assert our independence. We must go to Rome and you know this."

What I know is that my husband will always choose the emperor over me. The reminder of it stings like a lash across my cheek, and I begin to regret all those kisses that tasted like hope and happiness. My voice trembles with anger when I say, "Go to Augustus in Rome, then. Run to your master when he whistles. But I won't go with you, and you know better than to think you can drag me there."

Some husbands would bend a disobedient wife to their will. Some wives would submit. But I won't be bent and my will is stronger than his. Storming out of his study, I slam every door on my way to my chambers. There I stay, in spite of all my husband's entreaties.

It isn't Juba who persuades me. It's Julia. Coming to my sitting room, and pretending to admire some of the Berber green and red pottery on display, she says, "Oh, be reasonable, Selene. Don't you want to see Octavia? I'm told she doesn't leave the house often these days, but she'll cross the Tiber for you. Do you still own that house overlooking the river?"

"Yes, though it's been empty some years now," I say, annoyed by her transparent attempts to manipulate me with the mention of my stepmother.

"Marvelous. We'll throw our banquets there. I'll invite the youngest and most brilliant people in Rome. Everyone who is anyone important will want to come to pay a call upon the Queen of Mauretania."

"I care nothing about banquets or brilliant people in Rome."

"What of your sisters, then? Why, you and me and the Antonias haven't been together since . . ." She breaks off for we both remember when we were last together. It was just before the fever that took Marcellus and killed my little brother. "Antonia Major is finally with child," Julia continues. "It will ease her fears about childbirth to have her sister near."

"She has other sisters."

"Marcella, you mean." Julia's expression sours as if she's bitten a wormy apple. "That's another reason you must come back with me to Rome. I'll need you to stand between us, so that I don't claw her face."

I sigh. If there were ever a puppet to circumstance, it is Marcella. I'd wager all I own that she played no part in the scandalous marriage arrangements that led to Julia's unhappiness. "You can't blame Marcella for your troubles."

"Remind me of that when we see her," Julia says, taking my hand in hers. "It's one thing to hear of her marriage to Iullus . . . another to lay eyes on them together as man and wife. I won't be able to bear it without you."

"Enough, Julia. That's your world, not mine."

I don't expect to see the hurt in her eyes. "You would truly let me go to Rome without you, given what I face?"

Guilt twists in my belly, but she doesn't know the risk I'd be taking to be at her side. "None of us know what you face."

She stares at me, the giddy light in her eyes winking into blackness. "In Rome, my husband and my father will be locked in whatever confrontation they've dreamed up for each other. It may come to civil war. War, again, and every Roman and every kingdom in the empire will be forced to choose a side. That's why Juba must make peace between them. And you must be there to help him because you're a symbol of the *last* war. I know it. My father knows it. And you know it."

With clear eyes, I return to my husband's study that night. Surrounded by scrolls, he wistfully dips a pen into ink but doesn't set it to paper. We're quiet as my fingers trail over all the comforts he's gathered here. Paintings of old friends he hasn't spoken to in years. A collection of letters from faraway companions he may never see again. A water clock that keeps breaking, but which he will not replace. The silence between us stretches out uncomfortably.

At last he breaks it. "Well?"

"I will go with you to Rome."

He nods once, then returns to his writing.

The next morning, Juba appoints minor officials to look after his interests while we're in Rome and I choose Chryssa to look after mine. Already the disgruntled men in my kingdom say about Chryssa what they cannot safely say about me. That she is an unnatural woman who meddles in matters of state when she should be bearing children and tending to her home. But, like me, she has made this kingdom a calling, and I think Julia was mistaken . . . a heart can make room for many loves.

Still, the appointment does not please her. "What can the emperor want from you now?" she asks. "Why won't he leave you alone?"

"This visit to Rome has little to do with me," I lie, because I cannot bear for even Chryssa to know the truth; that I am still the emperor's possession to toy with. "All the client kings and queens must go to Rome. The city will be filled with royalty. I'll be only one more queen in a sea of them."

But she is not fooled. "And I am a blue-painted Pict from Britannia."

Eight

❀

THE PORT OF OSTIA
SPRING 17 B.C.

WE sail to Italy in ships laden with a cargo of ivory, wooden furniture, pungent fish sauce, and exotic animal hides—all of which are sold by our agents before they're even unloaded from the holds. Other royal embassies have arrived from the East, and we quickly fall into the company of the Cappadocians, King Archelaus and his daughter, Princess Glaphyra.

We must all bear the indignity of being summoned to the emperor to account for ourselves like wayward legates. We all owe our positions to Augustus, and if he wishes to parade royalty before the humblest citizens in Rome, we will all march to his tune. Climbing into wood-paneled carriages with gilded wheels and cushioned benches, we start our painfully slow progress from Ostia to Rome.

Normally, it is an easy day's travel, but with the crowds on the road, I fear that we won't arrive by nightfall. And not an hour into our journey, we come upon King Iamblichus of Emesa, who hails us. Then our followers swell in number so that our combined royal caravan goes even slower, now taking up a long stretch of the road with our supply carts and guards and retainers.

It's a veritable reunion of my closest royal allies—all of whom once tried to persuade Augustus that I should take my mother's place as the Queen of Egypt—and I'm glad to see my friends again. But whereas I was the darling of Greece, Julia is the darling of Rome. The common people wave and cheer her. Maybe they love her because she'll soon be a mother three times over. Maybe they love her because she's young and beautiful and vivacious. Whatever the reason, they *do* love her and I'm glad to see her glow under their adoration, acutely aware that my own status is increasingly entwined with hers. I'm accustomed to being loved or hated for the sake of my parents; it's an entirely new thing to be looked upon with favor because Julia keeps me as her closest companion.

As our journey progresses, my baby boy fusses in my arms. Fortunately, my daughter and my niece keep each other busy with little games, the rules of which only they know. And on the road, the gossip is all good. We hear that there's been a grand reunion between the emperor and Agrippa, their friendship renewed after such a long separation. Everyone we encounter, from fishmongers to mule drivers, tells us the upcoming celebrations shall commemorate the close partnership between the emperor and his son-in-law.

But mine is an ear trained to hear falsehood; I notice the tension in the voices of soldiers newly returned from Gaul. The stories of harmony between Augustus and Agrippa are too bright, too optimistic. We even hear rumor that Agrippa's self-imposed exile six years before was not any true break in his alliance with the emperor, but only a ruse by which the Parthians were lured into peace.

I know this is a lie. And because it is a lie, we cannot trust the rest.

Julia must know it too. With each new cheerful rumor, her rosebud lips draw tighter together.

When we stop to water the horses, we're nearly mobbed by curious travelers. An elderly woman thrusts forward a basket of herbs, crying, "To help with the pains of childbirth!"

Julia's slave girl, Phoebe, takes the basket, and the emperor's daughter says, "I'm no stranger to such pains but I welcome a respite from them. Have you any other advice to offer a good daughter of Rome?"

The woman goes pink with pleasure at being asked and dispenses wisdom about how to steep the herbs in boiling water and the best way to discipline a wayward child. "May the gods bless you, Lady Julia. You're no dried-up old stick living high on the Palatine."

The implied resentment for the emperor's wife is music to my ears. It probably pleases Julia as well, but she's wise enough to take no notice of it. "What welcome will I find in Rome, good matron? Is it true that my father and my husband are fast friends?"

At last we've come upon someone who is unwilling to lie. "You poor thing," the woman says. "Torn between a father and a husband. You've some mending work to do if you will keep them at peace. Marcus Vipsanius Agrippa keeps the company of his own soldiers, and I fear that soon every man in Rome will again be forced to choose a side."

Julia nods gravely, sending the woman on her way with a few coins. None of us speak about what we've heard; we all know the decisions we may have to make if Agrippa and Augustus end their partnership and battle each other for power. Instead, we speak of the upcoming ceremonies, advertised by heralds at milestones here and wide as a spectacle that comes every 110 years, a thing no living man has seen before and will never see again.

Princess Glaphyra asks, "Wouldn't it be fascinating if we could find someone who attended the last *Ludi Seculares*?"

"Impossible," I say. "To remember the spectacle, the man would need to have lived longer than one hundred and ten years, and the gods will not allow any mortal so many years."

"Unless you worship the Hebrew god," Glaphyra argues. "In their book, men live to be hundreds of years old. Perhaps King Herod will outlive us all."

Her father, the Cappadocian king, scowls at her. "I shouldn't have let my daughter learn to read."

"Oh, Papa!" Glaphyra titters. "Don't you want me to learn the beliefs of the Jews? You can hardly marry me to one of Herod's sons and not expect me to wonder if there is more to Judaism than avoiding pork and shellfish."

I'm aghast, and not only because I'm sensitive to the mockery of religion. It is Glaphyra's marriage plans that set my nerves on edge. My mother's old rival Herod has always shadowed my life. Once he tried to convince Augustus to kill my brothers and me. And though

I've never met the man, I count him as an enemy and am alarmed by the way he is growing in power and influence. "I'm afraid news reaches us slowly in Mauretania," I say. "Who arranged this portentous marriage?"

"Herod approached us," the Cappadocian king replies, taking no notice of the edge in my question. "As he received permission from Augustus, I could not refuse the honor."

This tells me nothing and everything.

King Archelaus goes on, "Besides, it's a good match. Herod's son has a better claim to the throne than his father."

This much is true. Herod is king only because he married the princess of the Hasmonean dynasty. Herod's sons have royal blood through their mother, not their father. Aware that Princess Glaphyra is awaiting my congratulations, I say, "I'm sure Princess Glaphyra will bring the light of Hellenism to the Judean court. May she shine like a burning lamp in the dark."

Glaphyra grins at my flattery. "Don't worry. I won't let the Herods dampen my flame!"

The Herods. She has transformed what may become a dynastic name in the careless and amusing way that normally appeals to Julia, but the emperor's daughter is remarkably subdued. Instead of laughing at Glaphyra's cleverness, Julia turns without a word, returning to the *carpentum* to wait. I go with her because I know the impending confrontation in Rome weighs heavily on her mind. The burden of her pregnancy only makes things worse.

In the carriage, Julia leans her head upon my shoulder and asks, "What if I'm not married?"

"What?" I ask, wondering if Julia is overheated, and where that slave girl got to with the fan.

"Agrippa may have decided upon divorce. What if I am the last to know?"

"He'd never divorce you, Julia. It would invite war."

"Maybe he *wants* war. I've always assumed that Agrippa was a faithful hunting hound who would return chastened to my father's side. But what if I'm mistaken? Maybe Agrippa is a wolf."

I cannot say she *is* mistaken. Once, Agrippa was the emperor's loyal champion. But over the years, the warrior learned his own strength and his master's weaknesses. To comfort Julia, I can only say, "Divorce may be the answer to your troubles." After all, in Rome, marriage is a political alliance more easily shaken off than in other places. Nearly every woman in the imperial family has been divorced before. It should not unduly tarnish Julia's reputation. "If Agrippa has divorced you, then you won't be torn between them anymore."

"If Agrippa divorces me, he'll take my children. By Roman law, he can do it. He'll take this baby in my womb too the moment it's born. Just as my father stole me from my mother's arms. I was almost never allowed to see her. I grew up without her, wondering, always *wondering*, if she loved me. If *anyone* loved me. I can't bear for my children to wonder such a thing. I can't bear it!"

A lump rises in my throat. "Oh, Julia . . ."

"In trying to please my father, I may have lost my little ones and caused a war besides! Who would win? *Tell me*, who would win?"

Her husband would win an armed conflict, but Agrippa isn't at the helm of a ship preparing to meet an enemy fleet. He's in Rome, a political arena where Augustus is the prizewinning gladiator. Still, I reassure her by saying, "You're working yourself into a terror over shadows. We face only two strong-minded men in togas on the Palatine Hill."

She calms, either because of my words, or because the caravan is ready to move again and there is no choice for any of us but to go forward.

WE don't reach Rome until evening. Because of the late hour, our Mauretanian retinue goes straightaway to my house on the Tiber River, two bridge spans apart from the city.

It's the house I chose myself when last I lived here; Juba has never seen it. He says our ride from Ostia has left him too tired for a tour; however, I suspect it's Julia's company that has exhausted him. As for the emperor's daughter, I see her swiftly to a guest room, saying, "Whatever we will find in Rome will wait until morning. We'll face it better with a good night's sleep."

I convince myself of that too and retreat to my chambers. Sleep comes swiftly but I awaken when the moon is high, shrouded in gray clouds. I shift beneath the bedsheets, disoriented and confused in the stillness of the night. It is some instinct for danger that has awakened me and now it lifts my every hair on end.

I've long kept the unusual habit of sleeping alone, my attendants banished to a nearby chamber. I'm used to quiet nights. But it is *too* quiet, I think. I should be able to hear my guards posted at my door. Sometimes they lay their spears against the wall and I hear the scrape against the plaster. Sometimes they speak in hushed whispers. Even when they don't speak, I can sometimes hear their heavy breathing if I listen for it.

But tonight I hear nothing.

Rising from bed and wrapping a shawl over nightclothes, I crack the door and find the corridor outside my chamber terrifyingly empty. My Macedonian guards have never deserted their posts. Their absence makes me instantly alert.

Something is terribly amiss. I've a keen sense for danger, nurtured from living so long at the mercy of those who would see me dead. One might think this would prevent me from rushing straight into peril. But my children are in this house, so I take an oil lamp from a nearby table and hurry down the shadowy hall, my steps soft but swift upon the tile.

As soon as I turn into the columned corridor and see men clustered outside the nursery, I know that I've been drawn here by something darker than mere danger.

The emperor is here.

I can't imagine how he came to be in my house, with all the torches dim or guttered out, in the dead of night. Yet I sense him. I know his presence deep down in my bones. I know that he's stolen into my home even before I see two of the emperor's praetorians facing my grim-faced Macedonian guards, swords drawn. I float into their midst, as if untouched by terror. "Is there to be bloodshed, gentlemen?"

"Not if your guards have any sense, Majesty," Strabo says.

He is the commander of the emperor's praetorian guard. If he's here, so is Augustus. The nursery door is ajar and inside I see my son's wet nurse all atremble, her hands winding one over the other as she frets. The fear on her face drives me to push past her into the room, my heart hammering.

I find Augustus hovering over my infant son, his face half-hidden by the dark. We have been too intimate together for me not to recognize him. In military sandals, embroidered tunic, and thick woolen cloak over his bunched shoulders, Augustus doesn't look much like his majestic statues. Strangers are always surprised that he's pale and slight of build. They take it for weakness until he captures them with his piercing gray eyes. Now he turns those eyes on me, the eyes of a predator in the dark, the glowing eyes of a wolf.

And I stop where I stand.

"Caesar," I say, my voice carefully modulated as I lower in deference to him.

"Cleopatra," he whispers, helping me to conjure the shades that haunt us both.

Then with a jerk of his hand, he snaps at the wet nurse, "Leave us!" She looks first to me for permission, but when I nod, she flees, closing the door behind her. Then the emperor and I are alone, and a heavy silence descends. I cannot think why he's come unless it is to punish me . . . or my son. The thought makes me draw closer, wedging my body between the emperor and my sleeping baby. "Why are you here at this hour, Caesar?"

His hand tightens on the edge of the cradle as if he might overturn it with a sharp jerk and spill my baby onto the floor. "I used to love being hailed," he says. "Coming into a city and having every man, woman, and child stream into the streets to greet me. But now I hate such a display. All the petitioners and hangers-on who push and shove to greet me so that I might look favorably upon their cause. Always with their hands out like beggars. Always asking things of me. It's become tiresome. Loathsome. And so what I once desired most has been turned into a poison for me; are not the gods cruel?"

I don't answer; I know that he doesn't want me to.

"Now I must travel in the stillness of night," he continues. "When all the city is sleeping, I steal into Rome like a thief. That's why I'm here at this hour."

"What I meant to ask . . . is why are you here, now, *in my home*?"

"Where else could I see you without the whole world looking on?" He stares with such intensity that I become aware of my loose hair and flimsy nightclothes. It is a stark reminder of the night he took me, when I was still a naive girl. I'm chilled by the memory but not conquered by it. He will never touch me again without my leave. "Why should you want to see me without the world looking on?"

His voice cracks in reply. "Because you've been unjustly torn from me . . ."

So it's to be maudlin self-pity, then. That's better than fury. So I speak to soothe. "It was the will of the gods that you sent me away, Caesar. Remember? I was there in Eleusis when the gods warned you that to become the father of Rome, you must abandon me."

He leans close, his breath a strangely cool caress on my cheek. "I've defied gods before. I would keep every promise I made to you, to make you queen, wife, empress, were it not for the good of Rome."

It's an old dance between us and I know all the steps, but I remain unmoved. I won't allow him to taunt me by dangling the world over my head as he did before. "I don't begrudge you your grand destiny, Caesar. You're a new Aeneas come to found Rome again. Am I not called to stand witness as you herald a Golden Age?"

"You cannot even say the words without seething, Selene."

With a mirthless chuckle, he reaches around me, scooping up my son for closer inspection. I want to lunge at him and snatch my baby away, but I dare not do so while the emperor holds him aloft, staring at my little boy, whose face is wan in the moonlight.

My son. The Prince of Mauretania. A child I named *Ptolemy*. It must have been a fit of madness that drove me to give my son a name that would remind the world that he holds a claim to Egypt. A male child who is kin to Alexander the Great. A boy who can be thought of as a rival to Augustus in a way that I never was . . .

Yet my son looks so fragile, his little head a tender melon that might crack open if dashed against the stone. I'm struck by a sudden rage that the emperor should hold him; that my children should be threatened. The scent of hot metal in the forge rises in my nostrils along with the iron tang of dark magic in my blood. My fingers tighten round the handle of my lamp, which seems to flare with my rage. And I imagine swinging it with all my strength so that the clay pot will shatter against the emperor's skull.

If he moves to harm my baby, I'll do it. I'll beat him down. I'll batter him bloody before the powers of my winds even reach my fingertips. If he tries to harm my son, I'll kill him before his guards even throw open the door to stop me . . .

To my surprise, the emperor merely presses a gentle kiss to Ptolemy's forehead. "Does he know?"

I exhale, still hammering down the molten iron anger inside me. "*What?* Who?"

"Juba," the emperor says. "Does he know about the boy?"

"What should Juba know?"

The emperor speaks the next words slowly and through his teeth. "Does he know that Ptolemy is my son?"

Nine

IN all the years since Augustus took me prisoner, I cannot count the times that he has shocked me. Stunned me. Rendered me speechless with his cunning, his ruthlessness, his unexpected generosity, his boundless ambition, and his madness. Always, his madness. Yet I am utterly unprepared for this.

In my surprise, I must tip the oil lamp, for the wick pops and sparks in bright flame. Still reeling, I murmur, "*Your* son?"

"*Our* son, if you insist upon precision," the emperor says. "You must know how it pains me. To see that you kept your promise to me, though I broke mine. You promised me a son and I promised you so much more, Cleopatra Selene. Now I'm here to confront you in the night, like Aeneas confronted Dido in the underworld after she killed herself of a broken heart. Do not take her example and rebuff me. In sending you away, I only did my duty, but that's cold comfort when I must visit in secret my only son . . ."

Though I am astonished, my voice comes firm. "He is *not* your son."

"Don't deny it, Selene. You played the same game with Isidora when she was born. You've given me a daughter and a son. It's a proud thing. Admit it."

I shake my head, refusing to toy with him, as I would have done before, when I was younger and desperate. "No. I'm sorry . . . Ptolemy is not your son."

The emperor's bony fingers stroke the soft skin beneath my baby's chin. "I counted the months since you left me in Greece, Selene. Surely Juba has too."

This makes me gasp with offense. "My son was born early. He almost died of it. Can't you see how tiny he is for his age, even now?"

"That's because he's of the *Julii*. We're not birthed easily. There is a famous story that one of the Caesars needed to be cut from the womb."

I cannot bear any more of this. I reach for my son, prying the warm little bundle out of the emperor's arms. "Don't even think it. He *cannot* be your son, Caesar. We didn't come together in Greece as a man and woman must to make a child."

"You deny that which was witnessed by the gods themselves?" he asks with an indignant huff. "I took you during the Mysteries at Eleusis. I laid you down on a bed covered in silk to break the curse your goddess laid upon me and to defy the soothsayers who told me I'd never have a son of my own. But your goddess is cruel; she gives me the son I want and denies me a way to make him my heir. Men plan and gods laugh, they say. How Isis must be laughing now."

It's true that I went to his bed in Eleusis, the place where the goddess Demeter searched for her lost child. It's true that together we drank of the sacred *kykeon* and were taken by visions of the world beyond this one. I was prepared to bind myself to him, to give myself to him in exchange for the throne of Egypt. It is *not* true, however, that we made a child. "The deed was never done. You spilled your seed before you could plant it."

"Never in my life have I been unmanned." All at once, he turns on me in such fury I think he might strike me. "Do you expect me to believe that you'd bear the child of any other man? You, my proud Ptolemaic queen? No. You would not. You *could* not. The gods may not let me have you, but that doesn't mean you aren't mine."

I bite back the poisoned words on my tongue at the implication that I should be always waiting for him, like a special couch sent to a faraway palace, reserved only for him when he visits. "You are not my husband."

Augustus seems to take what I've said for a shrewish

reproach—the kind of thing a scorned woman says to the lover who abandoned her. He must think he sees in me a broken heart that I'm desperate to hide, and he reaches for my cheek. "Your denials only prove that Ptolemy is my son. Another woman would try to pass off a child on me to see what advantage it held. Another woman, with such a royal lineage, might beg and plead a kingdom as reward. Another princess of Egypt might even use this child to win back her mother's throne. But you're too proud, too filled with venom. You're a reflection of me so I know you better than you know yourself. The only thing stronger in you than your relentless ambition is your cruel spite!"

I shake my head. He doesn't know me. He only knows my shadow self. My *khaibit*. The part of me that is dangerous and destructive. The part of me I've fought down. I've lied before. I've kept secrets, betrayed vows, and broken faith even with the goddess whose words sometimes carve themselves in my flesh. I've driven men to acts of madness and murder to reclaim what should have been mine. And in the confines of the emperor's household, where my heritage was reviled and my faith suspect, I learned that to survive was to deceive. Indeed, my enemies say that by sparing my life, Augustus allowed a viper into the very heart of Rome. What they don't know is that it was the emperor himself who molded me into the kind of venomous creature that strikes when provoked.

He created my dark soul as a reflection of his own, so I shouldn't be surprised that when he looks at me, it's all he sees. "I don't know what I can say to convince you, Caesar."

"Nothing, Selene. Even Agrippa knows the truth."

I miss a breath. "Agrippa?"

"He can count months too." The emperor strokes the warm bundle in my arms with affection, and in his voice, I hear longing. "Agrippa demands that I deny this little boy his birthright. That I deny my own flesh and blood. That I treat my long-awaited heir as if he were only the petty prince of a faraway land. And little Ptolemy is an innocent in all this, just as Caesarion was."

I'm startled to hear him speak my brother's name—the brother he murdered because two men with the name *Caesar* was one too many. I've always wielded against the emperor his need to repeat history; I've played upon his desire for glory and used the past to torment him. It has never before occurred to me that I've worked into him a poison that also sickens me . . .

"Ptolemy is not Caesarion," I say quietly.

"He's *just* like Caesarion."

I stare into those gray eyes and see myself as he sees me. I'm another Cleopatra, another foreign queen summoned to Rome with a child rumored to be Caesar's. I come with a cuckolded husband, a great entourage, to bear witness to a sort of Triumph. This scenario was the undoing of Julius Caesar; does Augustus not fear it will be his undoing too? "Stop this. We were finished with all this the moment I sailed away from Greece."

His eyes widen, a plea in their depths. "I did not let you go of my own free will. Don't you know how much I want to crown you Queen of Egypt and make our son the ruler of the world? I'll find a way. I'll make our dreams come true."

"Those aren't our dreams. Those were the dreams of your father and my mother, dreams long since dead. I'm content to let them rest. I've buried those dreams. I've come to Rome only at your command, to offer fealty as your client queen. This is the Prince of Mauretania, Juba's son. I bore *Juba's* son."

Augustus forces my chin up so that I must look at him. "You would never allow such a thing to happen unless your husband has become so inconvenient that you desire to be made a widow."

It's the calm, cold threat in his voice that stops my heart. There in his chilly gray eyes is the glinting dagger-tip of his pride. And I realize, for the first time, how I have gambled with Juba's life. It does not matter if the emperor is truly convinced that my son is the fruit of his loins. What has driven him to my son's nursery in the middle of the night is that he cannot bear the idea of another man touching me.

I've been told the emperor has the soul of a poet, but I've always known him to be an actor and playwright, and we're all left to guess at which way he'll turn the plot. If he wants to believe that he has a son, is it more dangerous to play along or to take from him the one object of his desire that fate has denied him?

I'm silent, half-horrified, half-fascinated, clutching my baby to my breast as the emperor asks, "Do you know what I face here in Rome without you, Selene? If I want to keep my alliance with Agrippa, he says I must adopt his son. I'll be father in name, but Agrippa will be the father of the next ruler of Rome *in truth*. That's how he steals my glory. How he seeks to cheat me. Perhaps I'm better off to be rid of Agrippa once and for all. Certainly my wife thinks so."

Of course she would. Such a bargain between the emperor and his greatest general will threaten Livia's position as First Woman in Rome. If the emperor does as Agrippa wishes him to do, Livia would be obliged to give way to Julia, the stepdaughter she tormented.

I find myself unexpectedly delighted by that prospect . . .

My mother was once the most powerful woman in the world, and if I cannot walk in her footsteps, Julia should. So I defend the admiral without whom my family might still be alive. "It's no easy thing to kill Marcus Vipsanius Agrippa, or you'd have done it by now."

The emperor almost smiles at my cool assessment. "Agrippa is as wary of me as I am of him. We've kept the pretense of harmony, but for how long?"

"Julia would have you reconciled with her husband."

"Such a reconciliation will make rivals of you," the emperor says, his gaze still fixed on the babe in my arms. "Julia pitted against you. Her son pitted against yours."

My blood begins to rise to this bait. He's whistling like a master to a well-trained hunting cat, calling to the dynastic ambitions that have been bred deep into my Ptolemaic bones. But he has done it before and I turned it away. The price was too steep. The world for my soul. It's still not a trade I'm willing to make. "You must do what's best for the empire."

AUGUSTUS is already gone when Juba enters the nursery. "What did he want? What did he say?"

"Nothing," I reply as my innocent baby nuzzles against my breasts.

Juba slants a dubious gaze at me, his eyes taking in the loose hair that flows over my shoulders. Here I am, having greeted the emperor in the middle of the night, dressed in little more than what I wore to bed. It would be enough to make any other man suspicious and Juba knows he has better reason than any other man. "Do you mean Caesar was silent? Utterly silent?"

Knowing the emperor as he does, this prospect probably alarms him more than if the emperor shouted and raged. And I am so shaken by the visit that I tell him the truth. "The emperor has convinced himself that Ptolemy is his son."

I watch my husband wrestle with his emotions until his mouth thins into a straight line. "I see."

Laying the baby back down in his cradle, gently untangling a fist from my hair, I ask, "Aren't you going to ask me if it's true?"

"No," Juba says.

Remembering a long-ago day on the deck of a ship when my husband wouldn't hear the truth about how Augustus violated me, I turn to glare. "Go on. Ask me if I've deceived you."

Juba sits in an alcove by the window, folding his hands in his lap. "I didn't ask you the day you laid this baby at my feet and I'm not going to ask you now."

"Doesn't it matter?" I ask, lashing out at him though it is the emperor who has me furious. "You're already playing the father to another man's daughter, so why not a son? Or don't you want to know? I think you're so beholden to the emperor that you cannot bear to know all the insults he's done you."

In the face of my tirade, Juba's tone is calm and even. "I'm not going to ask because if the torn trust between us is ever to be mended, one of us must give way. I've thrown down my weapons on the chance that you'll do the same."

My cheeks sting with embarrassment even as the heat of my temper drains away. "I thought—"

"You thought I'd accuse you, as I've done before. You thought I'd treat you coldly."

Coming to his side, I say, "I'm sorry."

He looks weary. "As am I. I know that I've taught you to guard yourself against me but I'm a man of learning. I'm trying not to repeat my mistakes."

And I'm trying not to repeat mine. I want to reassure him that he is Ptolemy's father—to give him the gift of honesty, freely given. But when I start to speak he presses his lips to mine. Not softly. Not experimentally. Not playfully. He kisses me with a desire and perhaps an expectation of more. But more I cannot give him, not here in the shadow of the Palatine Hill . . .

"MY father was here," Julia says by way of morning greeting. She usually sleeps late; I hadn't expected to see her so early. "Don't bother to deny it." Julia sniffs. "The slaves know everything. Phoebe says you rose from your bed and that you went to the emperor half-dressed!"

I'd expected recriminations from my husband—not from the emperor's daughter. As we sit down together in my *triclinium* for the morning meal old-fashioned Romans insist is a gateway to Oriental corruption, I say, "I only went to see that my children were sleeping safely and was taken by surprise by the way your father stole into my house."

Julia's beautiful face twists in bitterness. "I thought he might have come for me. Isn't that foolish? I hoped that my father might have come to take me home. That he came to say, 'Well done, Julia. I know what you risked to obey my command and I'm grateful.' But he didn't even ask for me!"

"Of course he did," I say, sipping at wine vinegar and water, a mixture Romans swear by to awaken the senses. "I told him you were quite big with child and shouldn't be awakened. I told your father he must let you have your rest."

She knows I'm lying and her nostrils flare, but before she can accuse me, Tala rounds the corner to announce that we have a visitor. "There's a Roman at the gate most eager to see Lady Julia. King Juba has gone out to greet him."

Julia's head snaps up. "Who?"

"Admiral Agrippa," Tala replies.

The emperor's daughter goes pale with fright, lifting both hands to her face. To calm her, I say, "Go back to your rooms, Julia. I'll see what I can do to make your husband leave."

Julia laughs bitterly. "No, Selene. Not even you can make Agrippa do anything. I wondered which of them would come for me . . . would it be my father? I admit it; I even wondered if it would be Iullus. I just didn't think it would be *Agrippa*."

Steeling her spine, she snaps her fingers at her slave girl and Phoebe helps her rise up out of her chair; for Julia is so pregnant now it takes both of them to get her upright. Then we all go out to the front of my house to greet the admiral where he is mounted upon a warhorse accompanied by *lictors*, the ax-wielding guards that denote his office and power.

Agrippa is a big man with a thick brow over his fierce eyes. He has the bearing of a commander, and even though he's aged since I saw him last, the graying temples and weathered face only make him look more dangerous.

Fortunately, he and Juba appear to be in amiable conversation. My husband has maintained good relations with the two most powerful men in the world. Juba has no mind for intrigue—he is ever willing to swallow Roman lies and propaganda—but he has always said that he wished to bring about a more peaceful world, and in spite of my reservations, I find myself earnestly hoping that he may accomplish it.

Agrippa dismounts and falls into stride with the king, entering our courtyard. "Welcome, Admiral Agrippa," I say, forgoing almost all the formalities of address. It isn't as if my whole royal court is looking on, after all. "It seems that our little home on the Tiber has become a veritable embassy, which the most important men of the Republic feel compelled to visit."

He takes my meaning at once. "Caesar was here?"

"Indeed, he was," I reply, hoping the invocation of the emperor is enough to still Agrippa's hand if he means to do violence. But Julia fearlessly pushes past me to face her husband.

The two of them stare at each other and the courtyard falls into silence.

Agrippa is the first to break it. "Pack your things, Julia."

"I'm delighted to see you too, my darling husband."

Agrippa grinds that massive jaw. "Don't call me *husband* when you ran away from me like a rebellious slave. I should thrash you within an inch of your life."

Moving to her side, I'm ready to defend her, but Julia lifts both her hands in invitation. "So do it, Marcus. Right here in front of the royalty of Mauretania. Better still, take me to the forum and beat me. Humiliate the daughter of Augustus and the granddaughter of Julius Caesar the god. I'll wear the bruises proudly before your legions. Before your children. Do you think that will endear you to them? Or do you think the bruises will serve as evidence of the lowbred *New Man* that you are?"

I'm surprised to see him flinch, surprised that she knows how to cut him. "I thought you'd been lost at sea, you wicked woman. When I heard nothing from you, I thought you'd been lost or taken by pirates. Do you understand? I feared you were *dead*."

Julia lowers her chin, perhaps a bit chagrinned. "Wickedness wasn't my aim. In this, I was an obedient and dutiful daughter."

Agrippa grunts, as if this were the only excuse that might appease him. "Then rejoice, because your father and I hope to soon be in accord."

"That doesn't mean I have to go with you."

He glowers at her. "Get your women and your things and follow me meekly or I'll haul you over the saddle of my horse and carry you off like a Gallic slave girl."

Julia sighs. "For such a brilliant strategist, you're terribly simpleminded at times. There *are* other options . . ."

Agrippa raises a brow. "Such as?"

"You could extend a hand to me. I might take it. I might walk *with* you away from this house, where all the people can see us warmly reunited. Why, you might be vulgar enough to press a kiss to my cheek. And if the stars align, I might forget that you're just a coarse soldier, not fit to put hands on me . . ."

I'm slack-jawed at her nerve and even more astonished that Agrippa seems prepared to bargain. He crosses his meaty arms over his chest and asks, "What would such a performance cost me?"

"Not much, for I confess I'm more pleased to see you again than I thought I'd be."

I swear I see a blush creep under his stubble. "Don't trifle with me, Julia. We're neither of us very fond of each other."

"Oh, yes," Julia says cheerfully. "You despise me and I think you're a perfectly contemptible old goat, which makes my sentimentality all the more confusing. Perhaps it can be explained by way of the fact that we're having another baby. Perhaps it will even be another son, which is all you care about, isn't it?"

Agrippa barks, "What do you want, Julia? A gown of Coan cloth? A strand of pearls? Tell me now, because I'm not going to stand here all day while you heap insults on my head. What do you want this time?"

"I want my mother," she says, the thread of hope in her voice pulled tight. "I've been scarcely permitted to see her since the day my father took me from her arms. I want to see my mother."

It's such a pure, simple request that one would have to be a monster to deny her. In this one thing, Agrippa is the only man in the world who can give Julia what she wants. She's gauged him; she's chosen the precise moment when he wants to irritate the emperor without damaging the relationship beyond repair. She's made a careful calculation, and I'm reminded that she is, after all, the daughter of the world's foremost manipulator.

I am not the only one who learned at the emperor's knee . . .

Agrippa rubs at the back of his neck. "Your mother has a reputation as a respectable woman. I can't see the harm in it. I would permit you to see Scribonia today. Will that suffice?"

Julia's breath catches in scarcely contained joy. Then Agrippa thrusts his big hand out to her. Julia stares at it, this beckoning hand with its scars and calluses ruddy in the morning sunlight. She's making a choice, I realize, and there have been few enough of those in her lifetime. Perhaps she savors it. Julia gives me a brave smile. Then she steps forward and slips her delicate hand into his. Moments later, the two of them go out my front gate, the distance between them closing with each step.

NOT long after, Iullus Antonius arrives at my door fitted out like a military staff officer, in a cuirass and military skirt, the flaps of which slap against his thighs as he marches into my house. My Roman half brother is some manner of tribune but I don't know which kind. It doesn't matter, really. He has whatever authority Augustus gives him, and since he married the emperor's niece, he's benefited greatly.

"You're too late," I say, leading him into my *triclinium*, where the morning meal has gone cold. "Julia already left this morning."

Iullus scowls at me with as much resentment as the day he met me. "I only *just* heard she was in the city. You might have sent word to me."

"If Julia had asked me to, I would have."

His hands flex on the back of my couch—a blue one from Mauretania, with a carved citrus-wood edge. "To whom did she go? Augustus or Agrippa?"

When I tell him, he looks stricken. It takes him more than a few moments to compose himself. "As it happens, I didn't come here for Julia."

Lies do not come as easily to him as to me, but it is a brave attempt, so I pretend to believe him. "Oh?"

"I came to speak to your husband about what the emperor expects from him in the coming days." Iullus is puffed up with importance as one of the emperor's closest companions—as if the emperor had not already been here, in the night, desperate to rekindle *our* old intimacy. But if it pleases Iullus to think that he's now the favorite, I'll let him think it. After all, the emperor threatened to make me a widow, a fear made all the more potent when Iullus says, "The emperor will meet with Juba tonight on the Palatine Hill, and he wants to see him alone."

Ten

I don't know how it will go between my husband and the emperor. I'm afraid. If after ten years of separation, the two men meet in violence, I'll be to blame. If they embrace as brothers, I might also be to blame, for we're all bound together by a singular crime.

In any case, I don't want to bear witness to their reunion, but when my husband leaves, I find myself uttering prayers to Isis for his safety. And when Juba returns home that night quite unharmed, I'm relieved beyond measure.

I press him for details in the privacy of our *triclinium*, where we take our ease upon dining couches strewn with pillows dyed in saffron and blue. The king sends his cupbearer from the room, then pours himself some wine, but he cannot hide his conflicted emotions behind the rim of a cup. "I gave the emperor an ivory fibula pin for his cloak, carved like the sphinx on his signet ring." *An odd token*, I think. A reminder that the emperor is every bit as unknowable as the desert riddler and just as deadly. Juba adds, "He received it gladly and threw his arm around my shoulder as if I were his long-lost son."

But the way Juba's fist suddenly clenches at his side, I worry there has been some confrontation. "And then?"

Juba takes a gulp of his wine. "He said nothing of his late-night visit to our nursery. Instead, he spoke of old times, when we would drink wine together by a warm fire, talking about the tragedy of Ajax. He said that he'd suffered without me at his side all these years, but that it was a sacrifice he needed to make for Rome. He said I was a good king and better than my father before me . . ." The throaty emotion in Juba's voice tells me that he still falls easy prey to the emperor's praise. "He greeted me very warmly, Selene."

Personal warmth has never been one of the weapons in the emperor's arsenal. Indeed, I doubt Augustus can even feel love. At least not the way other people do. He does form attachments, however, so perhaps his regard for my husband is genuine. Unfortunately, those the emperor keeps closest to what passes for his heart are often those to whom he is most cruel.

One glance at Juba as he averts his gaze tells me that he has, indeed, endured some manner of torture. "What did he say to you, Juba?"

Twice Juba starts to speak before he finally swallows whatever is choking him. "He said that every man is, alone, barbarous and pathetic, capable of any dishonor, and that he is no different. The emperor told me that he has committed great wrongs for which he seeks redemption. That it is only the fellowship of a man's friends that keeps him from wandering off civilized roads. He says that he needs me now, as he has never needed me. That I've been called to keep men from drawing their swords; to keep friends marching together on a road to glory."

I am rendered quite speechless by this secondhand account of the emperor's expert manipulation; apologizing for his crimes without admitting fault, blaming Juba's absence for his poor decisions, all while begging for help. The brazenness of it stuns me almost as much as the way it has affected my husband. As I stare at him, Juba drains his cup, swallowing the wine down in several gulps. When he is finished, he leans back against the pillows and I see what wars inside him.

He is a father who wants to protect his child. A son who wants acceptance from the only father he's ever known. Perhaps even a husband who would defend his wife. Certainly a newly made king who wants to be of some consequence . . .

"You think me quite a self-important fool, don't you, Selene? To think I may play some instrumental role in the age to come."

"No, I don't." My husband wasn't born under a prophecy; no one expected anything from Juba except that he would eventually betray barbarian leanings—an expectation he has frustrated his entire life by becoming the most learned and civilized of kings. And yet, from the first day I met him, empire building was on his mind. When I was still too much of a child to understand the ways in which the world had changed, my husband explained them to me with a determination to help Augustus make the world a better place.

However misguided my husband's loyalties have been, whatever his role in my family's downfall, Juba has never wavered in that ambition. And now, even I must bow to it. "I think you neither self-important, nor a fool. You've steered a difficult course between Augustus and Agrippa so that they both might rely upon you. It positions our kingdom very well. It's excellent statesmanship."

Hope shines in his eyes. "I don't think it will be so very difficult to reconcile them, do you?"

I'm not so certain. Six years ago, Agrippa broke with the emperor and left Rome. The falsehood that he was driven away by a jealousy for the emperor's nephew has become accepted as truth. But now Marcellus is dead and Agrippa is not the same man who fled Rome in a pique of temper. Agrippa has been tested. He's more confident. He's more ambitious. And I tell Juba as much.

"But I suspect Agrippa does not desire more power for himself," Juba muses. "All Agrippa wants is for the emperor to adopt his son."

I make an indelicate snort. "What Agrippa wants is to stop the emperor from claiming *Ptolemy*."

Juba stiffens, his eyes meeting mine. "Then it is in my interest to help him, is it not?"

There is a part of me—a dark shadowy part—that rises up unbidden, with ugly ambition. I surprise myself with thoughts that our son's future could be greater than Juba and I have ever dreamed. If Juba could set aside his paternal pride, we could have more power over the emperor than ever before. The night Augustus hovered in our nursery he all but *begged* me to reach for the world. I could take it. I could rule it or destroy it . . . and if Juba were to conspire *with* me . . .

But he will not and I would never ask him to. I will not abuse his loyalty as the emperor does. And though I was born to intrigue, I will not exploit my innocent child. Not for Egypt, not for the world. I *will not* trade the world for my soul, I remind myself. I have not come to Rome to campaign for power. So, should I feel threatened or flattered that Agrippa finds himself struggling against me in a war I'm not even fighting?

ACCORDING to my husband, the emperor and his son-in-law are taking pains to avoid each other, relying upon Juba as their intermediary. It is, perhaps, the wisest course of action. Once, they hammered out a peace treaty with my father in the full view of their legions—whose unwillingness to bear arms against Mark Antony forced the bargain. They both learned from that mistake. They are now clever enough to keep their quarrel as shrouded in secrecy as their reconciliation must be. Only a few of us are aware that while the whole city prepares to celebrate, this fragile truce might fall apart at any moment.

Meanwhile, the children make nuisances of themselves on our terrace balcony, where they throw little pebbles toward the river. "Are you trying to hit the Tiber?" I demand, smoothing back my daughter's golden curls into the ribbons meant to remind her that she's a princess.

"We're trying for the island," Dora says.

"You'll need a much stronger arm for that. Aren't they clever, the Romans? To shape Tiber Island to look like a boat. Do you see the obelisk that makes the mast? That came from Egypt."

My niece bobs her head with interest, but my daughter's somberness makes me fear she remembers her time here as a child. Isidora was only a babe in my arms during the famine, when the sick and starving thronged the island, seeking help from the Temple of

Asclepius. If I close my eyes, I can still hear the cries of the dying floating up to me from the river, and I fear my daughter remembers it too.

"Mama, will you take us to visit the island?" she asks.

"We'll pass over it every time we go into Rome, where there are far more important things to see. I'll take you myself to the Temple of Venus Genetrix, where you can visit a golden sculpture of your grandmother."

Pythia's eyes light up, but Dora only gives me an indulgent smile. "There's a snake on that island and he calls to me."

She's always been a peculiar child. Helios once said that looking into her eyes was like seeing into the Rivers of Time, and it is true. Is it so wrong of me to wish that she could be just a normal girl, at least for a little while longer?

"Don't be foolish," I say, dismissing what she's said as the fancy of a child's imagination. But her words linger. It was a snake that took my mother to the afterworld. Snakes are guides for the dead and if one calls to Isidora, I will keep her from it. And so I do not bring the girls to visit Tiber Island.

Instead, we cross swiftly into the city, then take a litter up the Palatine Hill. Fierce-looking praetorians greet us before the laurel-decked entrance of the emperor's residence. The modest front of the household in which I was once kept prisoner does not fool me. I know that the gates will open upon a collection of buildings and sprawling gardens, ornamented with priceless artwork, all joined together with the majestic Temple of Apollo.

I find it no small irony that once inside the sacred walls of Rome, I'm obliged to leave off my symbols of royalty, removing my crown and setting aside my purple cloak lest I offend the Romans who claim to tolerate no monarchs. And yet here upon this hill, in the heart of their city, is the seat of the true king who rules over them all.

The emperor calls himself only the *Princeps*, the First Citizen amongst equals. But here stands the evidence to the contrary: an imperial compound that has steadily grown into a palace, garden by garden, monument by monument, year by year. Like a slow and steady bricklayer, he's accomplished this, like everything else, one plodding step at a time, so that it is now too late for anyone to complain.

Anyone, of course, except Agrippa.

I find Octavia in the sewing room amidst looms, spindles, and baskets of shining white sheep's wool. To the fascination of my girls, I explain that in my youth, all the women of the emperor's household toiled here, so that the emperor could claim he kept his women to the old Republican traditions.

Today, only Octavia and her daughters work at the tasks. My stepmother wears a drab *tunica*, a dark *stola* overtop to symbolize that she still mourns for her son. Her head is covered with a black shawl too, making her face look heavier and more severe beneath it. It worries me to see that the corners of Lady Octavia's mouth turn down and little lines have etched themselves there as if she's forgotten how to smile.

But the moment she sees me, she does smile. So do her daughters. There's a great outburst of chatter as we all exchange glad embraces. In my mind's eye, my half sisters, the Antonias, will always be little girls, quick to mimic their mother and me. But now Antonia Major is married and swollen with child. And at nineteen years old, Minora is betrothed. Together with Octavia's oldest daughter, Marcella, my half sisters have become the solid foundation of the imperial family.

These are the women of the *Julii*. They are family of the emperor in a way that his wife and her Claudian sons can never be. It's the emperor's sister who has provided him with prim women of good reputation, beholden to no other political alliance, which is why they still reside with him on the Palatine and likely always will.

Kissing Marcella's cheeks, I say, "I'm glad to see you haven't forced little Marcellina to take up the loom yet."

"Marcellina isn't so little anymore," she says. "Besides, Agrippa has taken her from me. Now she must call Julia mother, and we both know Julia would never deign to dirty her hands with useful work."

It's unfair. All of it. That Agrippa should take Marcella's daughter simply because they've divorced is a cruelty. That Marcella should resent his new wife for it, doubly so. Julia had no part in the arrangements; indeed, she's struggling with her own resentments, and it pains me to think of my two childhood friends so at odds. "Surely Agrippa lets you visit with your daughter . . ."

"Of *course* he does," Octavia snaps. "The girl is coming today, in fact. Agrippa is no brute. He treated Marcella with respect."

Octavia's quick defense of the admiral reminds me that the twisted affections of the imperial family reach far beyond the perverse quadrangle at its center, made up of Agrippa, Marcella, Julia, and Iullus. The political marriages have hurt nearly everyone, including Octavia, though some of her wounds are self-inflicted.

This isn't the tone I wished to set for our reunion, so I force a smile and wave a hand as if to disperse smoke from a kitchen fire. "This room is just as stuffy as I remember it! Are you going to make my royal entourage stand in the corridor, or shall we all go out into the gardens and have a proper visit where the children can play?"

Octavia's hands halt over the shuttle of her loom. "You brought the children?"

"Yes, and I want them to enjoy themselves . . ."

The corners of Octavia's mouth threaten to lift into another smile. "You have very unorthodox ideas about children, Selene. No doubt you'll spoil them rotten and turn them into little tyrants."

"No doubt," I reply. "That is why I need your guidance."

"Well, then," she says, pushing her stool back from the loom. "I'll go out by the fishpond for a spell, but I can't spend all day dallying—I have to attend to my work at the theater. It will never be done in time for the games at this rate."

The Antonias exchange a look that tells me their mother has been fretting about this for some time, and that my visit is a welcome distraction. So we all go out into the verdant springtime.

There in the gardens, I present my children to Octavia one at a time. My daughter is a prettier little girl than I ever was and Octavia praises her golden hair, calling her a veritable Venus. Then I present the dark-haired, sloe-eyed Pythia, and Octavia gives a wistful sigh.

"Antony's first granddaughter . . . a shame what happened to her mother. To be married off to a Greek merchant!"

Pythia lifts her chin ever so slightly, rancor burning in her eyes, so I send both girls off to play at the edge of the pool. "This is my son," I say, giving my baby over into Octavia's outspread arms.

She takes him eagerly. "Ah, a healthy little prince for Mauretania. He has Juba's eyes, doesn't he?" I'm grateful that she notices. "You'll make a proper little barbarian, won't you?" Octavia coos at my little Ptolemy, who takes no offense, blinking up at her with a sweet gurgling smile.

Just then, a fish splashes in the pond and I can't help but taunt her. "Fishponds, Octavia? When did you become so grand a lady as to demand only the freshest fish for your dinner table? And are these saltwater fish? Do you have slaves haul ocean water all the way from Ostia for your convenience?"

Octavia huffs. "The *piscinae* weren't my idea! It's all the fashion these days to have lampreys and mullets. These were a gift from Agrippa."

"Who knew the admiral could be so extravagant?"

"So says the queen of a grand palace by the sea," Augustus interrupts, emerging from a nearby archway in a broad-brimmed hat and short tunic that exposes his spindly legs. "I'm glad to find you here, Selene," the emperor says, motioning to me with two fingers. "Come. Walk with me."

WHEN I was a girl I took pride in the way the emperor singled me out for his attention, but it now distresses me. Nevertheless, one does not refuse a request to walk beside the emperor . . .

We stroll in the gardens where he shows me a fruit tree I've never seen before. A gift from the kingdom of Pontus. *Cherry*, the emperor calls it. "It isn't new to Rome, but it is rare. Like you, Selene."

I turn from him, resisting his flattery. "Is it also poisonous?"

He snorts. "No. Cherries are sweet and fleshy . . ."

I don't want him thinking of my taste or flesh, so I say, "Perhaps

I will acquire some of these fruit trees for my palace in Mauretania, to which I should like to return as soon as possible."

At this, the emperor abandons his wooing in favor of the business he has in mind. "The Senate meets today to authorize persons who would not normally be allowed to participate in the Secular Games . . ." The Romans can be very insular when it comes to their rites and rituals. "I want all of the city to take part. Slaves, mourning women, and even foreign queens."

"That is why you summoned me, is it not?" I cannot resist plucking the ripening berries, so round and shining in the sun with possibility. Tasting one, I find that cherries are all sweetness. Juicy pleasure on my tongue. Such untainted sweetness is so strange to me, I cannot decide if I love this fruit or detest it.

"I mean for you to have a special role in the festivities," he says, and the sweetness in my mouth turns sour. "During the day, I must share the glory with Agrippa. But in the evenings, I will invoke the gods of Rome to herald a new age."

"Isn't that the duty of the Pontifex Maximus?"

"I cannot very well call Lepidus back from exile to perform his priestly duties, can I?"

"Why not?" Marcus Aemilius Lepidus was the third man in the alliance my father once made with the emperor. The triumvirate. An agreement to divide up the Roman world between the three of them. But during the civil war, Lepidus was so inept as to make enemies on all sides. "I have always assumed that you let Lepidus live because he is harmless . . ."

The emperor scowls. "I do not let traitors live because they are harmless. He lives because he is the High Priest of Rome."

"Julius Caesar was the High Priest of Rome and it did not stop the assassins from plunging knives into him," I say, my voice trailing off as I realize my error. If there is anyone he truly reveres, it is his adopted father. He would do nothing to invite comparison between himself and the men who assassinated the dictator.

"Precisely the point, Selene! I cannot execute Lepidus unless I wish to be blamed for every calamity that befalls Rome—for the people will see in it the wrath of the gods. When Lepidus is dead, I will take the pontificate for myself. The ceremonies I will perform in the coming weeks will help to establish my place as the highest religious authority in Rome. That is why I'll have you at my side."

He says this to me as if it has already been decided, but I will not allow myself to play the role of the emperor's mistress, fueling the sort of gossip that destroyed my mother. My mother was foolish to allow Julius Caesar to commemorate her with a golden statue for all Rome to gawk at, but she was the Queen of Egypt and she was in love with her Caesar.

I am neither.

"I'm not your wife and I have no place at your side."

"Has your time in balmy Mauretania dulled your wits? I'm not asking you to take part as a notorious woman or an exotic curiosity. I want you at my side as the priestess of Isis that you are."

He's the first to call me a priestess. Though I've given voice to my goddess through my own flesh and blood and ministered to others in her name, never have I donned the robes of a priestess. Never have I submitted myself to the initiation of her holy order, nor suffered the privations they endure to find communion with her. Isis has called me her child, never her priestess, but hope creeps into my breast. "Do you mean, then, to restore Isis worship to Rome?"

"I cannot do that," he says, and I think I hear a genuine hint of regret. "Imagine what mischief Agrippa and his champions could make for me if I'm seen to welcome back the foreign goddess of Cleopatra with her daughter standing beside me. No, Selene. In these rites, I must call upon Roman gods and show that I mean to restore the old ways. It's an honor I offer you, to be here at the start of a Golden Age."

I'm not honored but offended, for I understand the nefarious political reason behind this strange request. He remembers the last time I was in Rome—when conspiracy threatened his power and Isis worshippers rose up in insurrection. In this city alone, thousands of Isis worshippers believe that the goddess speaks through me. Augustus knows it all too well. He knows too of the prophecy at my birth, that I would help to usher in a Golden Age. My presence at his side would give a silent nod to those who believe in that prophecy . . . those who believe in me. My presence would tell them that if I have a place at the emperor's side, then they too have a place in his empire.

It is one lie too many. "No. I'm sorry. I must refuse."

He stares at me with those intent gray eyes. "You rebuff me now at the merest provocation, clinging to your wounded pride. Selene, don't you see what I mean to give to you in the years to come? Once it's mine and only mine, I mean to give you the whole world."

"Well, I don't want it," I tell him flatly.

"Yes, you do, Selene. *Yes, you do.*"

Eleven

THE next day, I receive an intriguing invitation to the Temple of Vesta. Draped in pure white, the chief Vestal Virgin is waiting for me inside the well-tended gates. She's a woman of such height and stature that we meet each other with a level gaze. "Welcome to the House of the Vestals, Your Majesty."

"I thank you for the invitation, Virgo Vestalis Maxima. To what do I owe this rare honor?"

"You may call me Occia," she says with a musical voice, leading me into the shade of the courtyard, where the statues of her predecessors watch over us. "I've asked you here because Augustus wishes for you to take part in our sacred rites. He tells me that you have refused . . ."

"And he's asked you to change my mind?"

"Yes. Though I would have tried whether he asked or not."

"I cannot imagine why."

"Your Majesty, I've been tending the hearth at the heart of this city since I was a girl. I was unusually young when I rose to be the chief Vestal. Twenty-two. The same age that you are now. That was the year your father broke with your mother to marry Lady Octavia and all Rome believed that the civil wars were over. We were wrong."

I thought Vestals beyond such worldly concerns. Whenever I have seen them before, floating in a cloud of white wool, trailing the end of sacred processions, they've seemed like captive birds set out to please the eyes. I begin to think I have misunderstood something vital. "No one is sorrier than I am that no lasting peace for the world could be made."

"Perhaps a lasting peace can be forged now, Your Majesty. That is what we mean to ask of the gods in our sacred rites." Though her unhurried steps give the impression of a tranquil stroll, I begin to think she is leading me somewhere. "When I became the chief Vestal, I thought myself every bit as pure as I'm meant to be. Pure in body, pure in heart, pure in deed. I was proud. I dutifully kept the fire burning in the Temple of Vesta. I fetched water from the sacred spring. I made the salted flour that sanctifies Roman rites. I was a very proud young woman."

And I am a proud queen, so I cannot fault her.

Other homes display ancestral masks or graven images of Roman warriors on horseback or the conscript fathers in the Senate, but here, in this college of priestesses, they surround themselves with the memories of women who have served before them with duty and distinction. I've seen marble carvings of goddesses and nymphs and queens, but never before have I seen statues honoring mortal women for their spiritual dedication. And I am captivated. "Pride motivates us to do our jobs well."

"Pride is a mirage," she says. "You see, I thought I could secure the blessing of my goddess for Rome, but there have been many dark days since the year I became the chief Vestal. War and famine. Proscriptions, men murdered, and blood in the streets of Rome. I believe the dark days were a punishment from the gods, that they started here . . . and that they started with you."

"With me?" We stop before a carved wooden door with a large bronze handle. It's reinforced with bands of iron. I stare at it without comprehension. "I'm afraid I don't understand; I have never been here before."

She opens the door to reveal two pretty Vestals inside, one holding a lamp and the other filing some document away in an iron box. They both dip in reverence to the chief Vestal Virgin, who waves them away. From the doorway, I catch only glimpses inside, of chambers filled with metal plates, scroll-cases, and various strange artifacts.

Occia does not invite me to step inside. "Vestal Virgins are thought to be incorruptible, Your Majesty. That is why we can give testimony at a court of law without even swearing an oath. We are entrusted with treaties and contracts . . . and the wills of important men."

Gooseflesh rises on my arms and I'm quite suddenly chilled. Her expression tells me I have every reason to be. Her gaze is faraway. She is remembering, lost in another time.

"You are the Vestal Virgin who surrendered my father's Last Will to the emperor, aren't you?"

She nods. "Octavian—that is what he was called then—came for it in the dead of night with torches and soldiers, demanding to inspect Antony's papers. I stood here, my back against this very door, using my body to bar the way."

"Do you mean for me to believe he did violence to force you?" I whisper, for I won't believe her. Like a Roman magistrate, her very person is sacrosanct. No man would dare lay hands on her. Not even Augustus, I think.

Occia squints. "No one should blame us, he said. Was he not an imperator? We tried to reason with him. We made plain to him that this would violate our oldest trusts and traditions. But he said Rome's protection should never extend to her enemies and that your father's Last Will would prove him to be an enemy. In the end, we told him that if he held the gods and goddesses of Rome in so little esteem, he could take it and suffer their wrath. So he took it . . . and then we all suffered."

There can be few things more sacred than the arrangements one makes to preserve one's memory after death. My father entrusted his words—the last words he might ever say to his family and countrymen—to the Vestal Virgins. And the emperor took those words and used them to start a war. *Antony is no Roman now, but an Egyptian who wishes to be buried in his beloved Alexandria.*

"I had always assumed it was a forgery," I say.

"It may have been. I never read Antony's will, but if the document the emperor revealed to the Senate was an expression of your father's true desires, then his love for your mother was such that he couldn't bear to be parted from her, even in death. The family Antony wished to honor was *yours*. So I am right to say that the suffering started here and with you, at least in part. That is why I hope you will take part in the rites, Your Majesty. Your father cannot absolve me, but perhaps you can stand in his stead."

I hold tightly to my resentments. My hatreds must be pried from me before I will cast them away. I have struggled these years to master the dark, vengeful side of my nature lest it rule me. Forgiveness does not come easily. It has been difficult enough to reconcile myself to an alliance with the man who destroyed my family and to a marriage with the flawed man who helped him do it.

Now they want more than my forgiveness. They want me to ask even the gods to forgive them.

Such a galling request churns in my belly. It is too much. I can offer only a shake of my head and an upraised hand as if to forestall anything else she might say. Then I turn and walk away, trying to find the path that will lead me out.

The chief Vestal follows, calling my name. It is only when she matches my stride that I hiss, "If you think that Augustus is sincere, you are mistaken, Virgo Maxima. The emperor wants me at his side while he performs rites that he knows should be performed by the Pontifex Maximus. He wants me with him to lend religious authority to his performance, nothing more."

I come to a halt at the foot of the steps that lead up into the Temple of Vesta, my body arrested by a familiar sensation that makes my fingertips tingle. Is it *heka*? Here? Watching me carefully, Occia pinches dead blossoms from a nearby vine. "Have you the gift to see into a man's soul, Your Majesty?"

Not all men, I think, but I have seen all that I need to see of the emperor's soul. I've glimpsed the greatness of which he is capable, but I've also seen the writhing snake pit of madness and ambition. "I'm no stranger to the bargains that must be made for political gain," I say. "Land, money, ships, slaves, marriage, alliances, taxes, and tributes . . . these are the currency of statecraft. I understand too that rulers must make bargains with the gods. But my faith is not a commodity; it's something as pure white as the gowns you wear. To wield it falsely would be to stain it."

"Majesty, I pluck these dead blossoms so that the other flowers may bloom bigger and brighter. It is for my own pleasure that I tend to the task. But does the plant know why or care? What matter does it make to great gods why we do our duty to them, so long as we do it?"

She speaks perfect sense in the Roman way of thinking; we worshippers of Isis bewilder them with talk of faith and mystery and communion. "It matters to me."

"Then perhaps your prayers for a Golden Age will be more powerful than mine," she says, starting up the stairs into the round Temple of Vesta and beckoning me to follow. It is not a large temple. The whole of it centers on a single flame, an eternal fire, tended by these women since the dawn of Rome. The fire represents light, and life itself. Life for the city. Life for civiliation.

Yet, it is an austere hearth, a tiny sanctuary beneath a domed roof.

And I am moved by the simplicity of it. Not only by the sight of these guardians performing their hallowed duties, giving their lives to this flame, but because the magic in this place rushes at me like water. I might drown in it if I do not let some of it flow into my body and the amulet at my throat. Perhaps I am entitled to take it, for has not Isis told me that she is all goddesses? Does this place, this Roman place, belong to her too?

I find Isis now even where her name is never spoken. And yet, I hesitate because the echoes of ancient prayers I hear are not the same kinds of prayers that women make in a Temple of Isis. These are not prayers to turn a lover's gaze or make a womb fertile. Not prayers to save a dying child or bring home a lost sailor. The prayers I hear are for *Rome*. They are prayers for the well-being of the people as a whole. They are prayers for the preservation of the state.

How have I missed this crucial piece in understanding the people I have so long considered my enemies? Rome is male in every part, I have argued. Certainly everything the emperor has ever done before now has led me to that conclusion. But here in the heart of the city, at the center of everything Romans have believed about themselves, is the idea that only women can defend their way of life.

Chaste women, to be sure. Women who cannot be mothers or wives or lovers. But women, still.

"Your Majesty," Occia says to me, her voice lilting low. "They say you are one of those persons for whom the veil is very thin between our world and the divine. Given the rapture on your face, I think they speak truly. I'm told that you have used your gifts to feed your people and give comfort to those in your faith. Perhaps our rites will have no meaning to you and will do no good for the world. But if we do mark a new age—is it not right that you should be there?"

IT still irritates me to lay aside my royal purple garments for the festivities, but I settle upon a green *chiton* with a large Greek key embroidered on the hem. My shawl is so white it looks as if it's been chalked for a Roman election. But for jewels, I wear showy amethyst earrings to match my mother's carved ring. I cannot bear to forgo purple entirely, after all.

I take so long to dress that Juba is forced to set out ahead of me and I must pass over the bridge to Tiber Island in a covered litter with my own entourage following behind on foot. While the heralds shout invitations to the people, I cross the crowded island, then take the second bridge to the newly constructed Theater of Marcellus.

I confess, I did not much care for Roman architecture when I first came to this city as a girl, but since then, I have marveled at the grand domed Pantheon Agrippa built on the Campus Martius. And now I am impressed by the new theater, for this three-story semicircular structure is one of the finest I've seen. A honeycomb of archways and pillars, it's covered in travertine. Ramps rise up to flower-bedecked platforms leading to airy corridors in which theatergoers may gather and converse. My only complaint is that the columns are a mix of Doric, Ionic, and Corinthian, which ought to please the Hellenistic queen in me, but I think it may be too much altogether.

Of course, I will not say so with Lady Octavia fretting near an entryway. Flanked by the Antonias, she's cornered some hapless official. "It's not finished," she's saying. "All of the paintings haven't been hung. The statues haven't been put into place. You've covered part of the structure with canvas but I can see the exposed bricks at the foundation in the back."

"There's nothing to be done about it now," says Minora.

Then Antonia hurries to add, "People will be watching the play, not worrying about the brickwork, Mother. Trust in the emperor's judgment."

"Well, I've done that for a lifetime and where has it gotten me?" Octavia snaps. Then she sees me. "Selene! What honor does it do my Marcellus to let the people see a shabby unfinished theater?"

"Surely it's better than to keep the people out," I reply, nodding to the crowd that is assembling while the orchestra readies inside. "It can't be right to celebrate the Secular Games without remembering Marcellus. The games come only once in a century; there won't be a second chance for you to see them celebrated here."

Octavia purses her lips in consideration. "That's true . . ."

I know how to move her because we share a singular trait. Like me, Octavia has survived those she loves. Like me, she struggles to carve some legacy from the ruins for her beloved dead. So I say, "A hundred years from now, the people won't remember the diamond-patterned bricks or even the plays they see this afternoon. They'll remember your son's name. They'll remember that Marcellus shared in this glory."

"Yes," she breathes, releasing the fists she's made of her hands. "Yes, they will. That's all I can give him now."

Minora leans to whisper in my ear. "She's like this all the time. We couldn't even get her to dress prettily for the celebration; not even jewelry." Unfortunately, she doesn't whisper quietly enough.

Octavia stiffens. "My ears haven't failed me yet. Jewelry isn't for women like me. It's for you girls to make yourselves beautiful for your husbands."

"Nonsense," Minora argues. "Jewelry is to impress other women. Most men wouldn't know the difference between an emerald or a pea."

While I gape at my little sister's surprisingly tart observation, Antonia holds up a pair of golden leaf dangled earrings. "This is a special occasion," she insists. "Livia is wearing jewelry. Let me put these on you."

Octavia snorts. "I most certainly will not."

"If you don't want to shine, I may take it as license to do something scandalous," I say, to tweak her. "It's not too late for me to don an old Egyptian-style wig and have myself carried in by oiled slaves dressed in loincloths. I'm Cleopatra's daughter, but I was brought up in your household. How will that reflect on you?"

"You're a wicked girl," Octavia scolds, but she lets Antonia fasten the earrings on her.

Hearing that the emperor's wife is soon to arrive, I make a swift retreat up the stairs to a small antechamber. Seated upon a luxurious couch draped in fleece, I wait for Juba. Unexpectedly, I am joined by an older man whose hair has been dyed black, in contrast to his graying eyebrows. Given this strange vanity and charismatic smile, I am left to assume he's a stage actor.

"Your Majesty," the actor says in strangely accented Greek, bowing with a dramatic flourish. "We have a few moments before you will be ushered to your seat."

"Have you seen my husband?" I ask. "King Juba of Mauretania?"

"No, but I don't suppose that he's run away, my dear. Unless he's been told about tonight's play, in which case any sane man would find the nearest exit."

My guards stiffen that he should address me with such familiarity, but I find myself stifling a laugh at the old man's wit. "What is tonight's play? I didn't even think to ask."

"It isn't worth asking. You know these Romans. For them, it's all comedy and pantomimes. I myself prefer a good Greek tragedy."

The man's geniality puts me at ease. "Do you have a favorite?"

"*Medea*," he says at once.

"Ah. That's very good, but such a fiendish tale of revenge has always disturbed me."

He looks surprised, as if a queen may not be as horrified by the murder of children as any other woman. "Indeed, Majesty? Do your sympathies go to Jason who led the Argonauts or to the sorceress who triumphs over him?"

Wading into an argument that's raged for hundreds of years, I insist, "No one triumphs in that play. Jason's ambitions bring calamity down on his house and Medea cannot ruin him without ruining herself." It's the same iron-jawed trap I've been caught in all my life. "Besides, there's no triumph to be had when you must sacrifice your own children to it."

My charming companion smirks. "We'll see if you still agree when you're my age and your children show you so little respect that you wish you'd left them on a hillside."

"Your children can't be so bad as that . . ."

"Oh, they are. My sons take after their mother. They're high-handed and proud. I look forward to fetching them home and teaching them a lesson."

Fiddling with the embroidered edge of my *chiton*, impatiently watching the doorway for Juba, I ask, "And where is home if not Rome, sir?"

The genial gleam in his eye slowly changes into something sharper. "Somewhere we appreciate tragedies. Somewhere we notice that Medea escaped with *Helios*, who tried to drive his father's chariot but set the world on fire."

My eyes snap to his, for no one speaks the name *Helios* to me by accident. "Do I know you?"

His smile is like the edge of a silvered knife. "I'm Herod. King Herod of Judea."

Twelve

MY blood runs cold. It isn't done that one sovereign meets another without introduction or warning. He must have arranged to come upon me this way, or had someone arrange it for him. He would only do such a thing if he wanted to shock me or frighten me or both. Since I cannot let him have the satisfaction, I smile as if I admire his nerve and answer him in his own language. "I think I've heard of you. You were one of my father's allies, weren't you?"

My performance gives him pause. Perhaps he did not know that, like my mother, I speak his tongue. Or perhaps he didn't expect to be put on the defensive over the matter of alliances abandoned more than a decade ago. "I was the best friend your father ever had, but now I'm an even better friend to Caesar."

"So he's told me," I say, to remind him that I have the emperor's ear. "Yet, in all our conversations together, Augustus never intimated that you were such a humble king. Why, to greet me without an introduction or even a retinue . . . is this part of the pageantry? I know the emperor likes to present himself as simply the First Citizen of Rome, but do you mean to outdo him by masquerading as an usher? Should I rub a little dirt on my cheeks to get into the spirit of the thing?"

His grin widens. "I come to you this way in the spirit of friendship. I didn't think you'd receive me warmly if you knew my name."

My other enemies are familiar to me; I've grown accustomed to Agrippa's stoic enmity, Livia's petty resentment, and the emperor's ruthlessness. They have always been perfectly obvious. Herod, by contrast, is a cipher, so I cannot let my mask slip for even an instant. "Why wouldn't I receive you warmly, King Herod? I still owe you thanks for a coin you commissioned in honor of Kore . . . a gift you sent to me when the emperor and I were in Greece together."

"Much has changed since then. I fear that you've been poisoned against me. You must know how it is to practice a faith that is suspected here in Rome. There are always people willing to slander those who are called to serve only one god . . . or goddess."

This I cannot argue.

Perhaps sensing that he has me in his thrall, he continues, "No doubt you've been told that I'm a monster who mutilates the genitals of young boys and eats babies after midnight."

It's a step too far and now I'm done with the charade. "What I've been told is that you have a penchant for killing queens."

He grimaces. Good. I've found a sore spot. I'm tempted to twist the knife by mentioning the wife he murdered by name, but I hold that in reserve. "Didn't you try to persuade my father to kill my mother?"

Regaining possession of himself, the older man admits, "I did. Had Antony taken my advice, he'd be emperor now. Indeed, you might be the Queen of Egypt in your mother's stead. Yes, I tried to persuade Antony to kill Cleopatra but there was no malice involved; I gave him my best political advice. In the end, he followed his heart and now we all live in the world he left behind. My actions were that of a friend."

Some friend! I go from cold to hot. His rational accounting of his actions offends me. I can think of no reason not to be frank. "Does a friend argue for the slaughter of Antony's children? I'm told you pleaded with Augustus to kill me and my brothers when we first came to Rome. Do you deny it?"

Herod affects a wounded expression, hand to his heart. "You've been woefully misinformed, Cleopatra Selene. It was only the boys I thought Augustus must be rid of. Only your brothers; not *you*. Why, I even made an offer to marry you when you came of age."

"Oh, well, then. How can I hold it against you?" I try to dislodge the thought of Caesarion strangled, Antyllus cut down at the foot of Caesar's statue, Philadelphus writhing in a fever that may well have been poison. And Helios? No, I best not think of him . . . "Did you mean to make a wedding present to me of my brothers' heads?"

Herod lifts both eyebrows as if surprised by my sarcasm. "I didn't know you were so fond of your siblings. Your mother certainly didn't care for hers . . ."

"I'm not my mother." And it's true. I loved my mother, I admired her, and I grieve for her. But I walk my own path. "I'm no one that you've ever met before, King Herod."

His eyes narrow with a hint of approval. "It's fortunate, then, that we have this time in Rome to get better acquainted . . ."

A gruff voice interrupts us. "Herod?" I look up to see Juba in the doorway and my husband's glance tells me that he had no idea to expect the King of Judea. "To what do we owe the surprise of your company?"

Herod's mature and practiced geniality never falters. "Ah, Juba, how good to see you again, my old friend. I came to pay tribute to your queen. When I hear about one of the world's wonders, I like to see it with my own eyes. She is as has been reported to me . . ."

"By whom?" I ask.

Herod ignores me. "We'll be sitting together tonight, your royal family and mine. The greatest king in the West and the greatest king in the East, come together as friends for the glory of Augustus."

Herod flatters himself. Juba is certainly the greatest king in the West, but Herod is only one of many in the East. Herod's is a troublesome kingdom, providing Rome with neither a great abundance of grain nor mineral wealth. Judea is notable only for the strategic importance of its location and the unusual religious traditions of its people. And Herod is notable only for his bloodthirsty reputation.

My husband does not point any of this out. "Perhaps we can

take the opportunity to discuss how to better share the talent of the empire. With our competing building projects, the engineers, architects, and artists have learned to play us against one another and extort outrageous fees."

This is a bit of diplomacy on Juba's part, for he knows, as well as I do, that Herod boasted of building two cities to frustrate our own efforts. For now, though, Herod is happy to let the engineers and architects and artists take the blame. "Indeed! Perhaps these profiteers would be less bold in their demands if they knew we shared a friendship. An alliance between our two families might be taken by Augustus as a sign of harmony in his empire."

Before I can make an indignant reply, we hear music from the orchestra indicating that we will soon be called to our seats. "Alas," Juba says. "It's a discussion that must wait."

Herod makes an elaborate gesture of farewell and then withdraws. The moment he is gone, I launch up from my couch, but before I can utter a word, Juba takes hold of my arm, "Calm. Be calm."

"Herod is not to be trusted!"

Juba dips his head to look me in the eye. "I know this, wife."

Why am I always ready for an argument with Juba, always leaping into combat even when there is no enemy on the field? It's a habit I must break myself of, so I moderate my tone. "He's not what I expected, not what I expected at all. I assumed he'd be a nasty brute . . ."

"He is, but he's also a chameleon. He's a Jew when he wants to be a Jew, but does not keep their traditions. He's a Hellenized king when he travels, but his interest in philosophy is not genuine. He's a fawning friend to Augustus while sneering at Roman ways when he can get away with it."

Juba's evaluation dispirits me. Herod is an actor after all, good enough to charm even the emperor. But that does not explain why he came here tonight. "Why should he come to us looking for friendship?"

"He needs allies," Juba explains. "Herod isn't popular in Judea—or anywhere else."

"Herod *has* allies. Augustus allows him great latitude. He has the friendship of Livia and Agrippa too. Why, he's even strong-armed Archelaus of Cappadocia into giving over his daughter in marriage. Who could make Herod feel so vulnerable that these aren't friends enough?"

"That I cannot guess, Selene, but if he wants our friendship, we should give it to him. It serves us no purpose to grant him the status of a rival."

I cannot disagree. I don't trust Herod—all the more so because I found it difficult to dislike him—but he can be no threat to me now. It's the quailing little girl inside me that fears him; I shouldn't let her rule the queen I have become. If forcing myself to smile at Herod means more engineers and architects for Mauretania, then I must find a way to make common cause.

The musicians hail us with a royal march as we're led into the crowded theater. The first row is reserved for Roman senators, in their best purple-bordered togas. Behind the senators sit the money-eyed equites, knights of the Republic . . . or what is left of it. Finally, in the upper rows, the plebs, the common citizens of Rome, find their seats. A special area is roped off, reserved for royalty and foreign visitors, and we find our places there.

Juba and I are well received by the crowd. The people remember our tributes of grain. They remember Juba as a scholar, soldier, and tamed barbarian. They remember that while I am Cleopatra's daughter, I'm also a daughter of Rome. They cheer us and we wave to them. The crowd also cheers for the two sons of Herod, who have lived in Rome now for years.

But no one cheers for Herod.

The King of Judea pretends at distraction as his sons find their seats. Alexander and Aristobulus are men now, both handsome, sitting close together, straight-spined like fellow soldiers who have been through some manner of battle. My heart goes out to these

Judean princes, for they've been kept here in Rome far from their homeland. Perhaps they've considered themselves hostages, and I know what that's like. But I catch the glance they exchange when their father leans over to whisper something to them.

And then I know.

I know exactly who makes Herod feel so vulnerable that he would seek even *me* out for a friend. He fears the popularity of his sons. Those young men both sit as stiffly near their father as if they had a scorpion at their back, and perhaps they do. These are the sons of Queen Mariamne, the Hasmonean princess whose bloodline put Herod in reach of the throne. He murdered their mother and now he's come to fetch them home . . .

I cannot imagine having such a father. My own father refused to harm my mother, though it cost him his life. Not even Augustus could bring himself to do away with Julia's mother. Which tells me that though I boasted of being no one Herod had ever met before, he is something I have never encountered before either. No matter how advantageous an alliance might be, no matter how witty or charming Herod is, I decide he must *always* be my enemy, or I will have betrayed everything good still left inside me.

The trumpets sound and we all look up to the imperial box. There Augustus and Agrippa stand. There they are, the two men upon whom the fate of the empire rests. One broad-shouldered and brawny. The other frail and shrewd. Neither man spares the other a glance. Like a courageous Sabine woman, willing to throw her body between her warring husband and father, Julia stands with these men, one hand upon her pregnant belly. With glittering eyes and a dazzling smile, Julia wins the hearts of the crowd in an instant. They are on their feet for her. I stand too, for it is Julia's moment. Glowing in our admiration, she is the strand that connects everything. This is her dead husband's theater. She is widow, wife, mother, daughter. She is First Woman in Rome.

We rely upon her to hold these men together, to be the conduit between them that keeps their ambitions and hostilities at bay. She need not share this rare moment of recognition with anyone else, but as the crowd adores her, Julia sweeps one arm back, turning to acknowledge the older woman behind her: Lady Octavia.

Octavia gives a quick shake of her head, her face frozen in an expression of Roman *gravitas*, as if she thinks herself unworthy of recognition. But brash, lovable Julia grabs Octavia by the arm and pulls her to her feet. And in spite of everything, my own eyes glisten with pride for them both.

The crowd applauds the matriarchs of the *Julii*. They cheer for Octavia because she has shared with all these Romans, their darkest times. Wife of Mark Antony. Sister of Octavian. Mother of Marcellus. She's suffered torn loyalties, lost loved ones, and sacrificed in the hope of a better future.

They honor her. I honor her too and not only because of the kindnesses she's done me over the years, but also because I know what she has sacrificed to keep Livia from power. Julia is Rome's darling only because Octavia made it so . . .

By instinct, my eyes seek out the emperor's wife, seated to the side in shadow. Livia wears a soft smile of serenity that scarcely disguises her smoldering resentment. This might have been *her* moment, but Octavia has stolen it from her and delivered it into Julia's hands. When Octavia came to suspect that Livia was responsible for her son's death, she retaliated with an unbending resolution to box the emperor's wife into irrelevance. And for that, we might all be grateful.

THE play is exactly as Herod predicted: utterly forgettable. Rome's artistry resides chiefly in her ability to organize, build, or destroy on a massive scale; her playwrights, when not stealing from the Greeks, are middling at best.

Fortunately, just when I think I cannot sit through one more moment, the show is over. As soon as the performers take their bows, Agrippa makes a hasty exit. He has always been an active man who can never sit still for very long, but I think it is the pretense of accord with the emperor that his general cannot maintain—not even with his pregnant wife as a buffer between them. He considers himself a man on the verge of war, and because Agrippa is who he is, he cannot bear to be sitting beside his enemy.

As we watch him shoulder his way out of the crowd, something strange happens. My husband and I glance at each other, and reach wordless agreement on what must be done. Juba must follow Agrippa. He must seek out the brooding general and playact the part of the aggrieved husband.

At least, I *hope* it will only be playacting.

Meanwhile, I must join the emperor in his religious rites. Juba's trust in me is a new and fragile thing, and I don't know how much weight can be safely stacked upon it. And yet, I'm emboldened by our silent conspiracy. To be, for once, in such perfect harmony with my husband is as welcome as it is unexpected.

We both rise, splitting our retinue neatly in half as we go our separate ways. Falling in with the emperor's entourage, I pull my *palla* over my head and I go out into the torchlit night where the priests of Rome burn a cloud of bitumen and sulfur to rid us of lice and mites. We purify ourselves by walking through the strong-smelling smoke. On the Aventine, acolytes at the Temple of Diana give out baskets of wheat and sacks of barley and beans to be offered to the gods. The emperor and the college of priests lead a grand processional to the river, where three different altars are illuminated against the black sky.

The bleat of the sacrificial lambs can be heard as they're lured to the places they will find their end, but my ears are filled with the sound of the Tiber River as it flows by.

The emperor raises his hands and invokes the gods of the West. Jupiter and his wife, Juno. Apollo, and his ruthless twin sister, Diana the Huntress. He invokes Neptune, the god of the sea, and Minerva, the virgin goddess of wisdom. He invokes Venus, the goddess of love, and Mercury, the fleet-footed messenger. He calls Ceres, who brings the grain, and Vulcan, who pounds in his forge. Then Mars, who brings war, and Vesta, whose hearth the Vestal Virgins tend.

He even calls upon Hercules, that demigod of so many labors from whom both Juba and I claim descent. Then he calls upon the Fates, and when he does, the emperor's eyes seek me out and beckon me to his side.

The Fates. I feel their shadow over us. How have our destinies become so closely entwined? Part of it is the emperor's doing. Part of it is my doing. My quest for Egypt, my desperate desire to save what remained of my family and our legacy drove me to cleave to this complicated man, in whom so much wickedness and potential reside. But perhaps there are forces greater than either of us who have drawn our lives together in a single thread. And I am afraid to know what will happen if it unravels.

So I go to his side, where I see the sacrificial knives laid out on a cloth of gold, glinting in the torchlight. The emperor means for me to hand him the knives with which he will sacrifice the lambs.

The emperor shouts, "Now we call upon Pluto and the forces of the underworld. We call too upon his bride, Proserpina, whom the Greeks call Persephone or Kore, goddess of springtime!"

In Greece, they called me the *New Kore*. She is the wife of the dead. She is also Isis. And in the crowds, I can see Isis worshippers nodding beneath their conical *pileus* hats of liberty—the same ones we wear for the Saturnalia—as if they believe he is acknowledging *her* by acknowledging *me*.

But one should never play such tricks with the gods.

I want no part of this. My throat swells closed. No. I will not do it. I am not shy of animal sacrifice. It is not the blood but the lie at the heart of this sacrifice that gives me pause. I cannot do it. I tell Augustus this with a barely perceptible shake of my head. He waits, but I make no move to help him. I will not hand him the knife. Finally, one of the priests of Rome does what I will not. The emperor makes short work of the first lamb, whose warm blood mists in the air before it collapses.

A priest is near to collect the blood, which he drips on the altar to the gods of Rome. But there are still two more lambs. "We call upon the Fates to receive our sacrifice," Augustus says, plunging another knife into a struggling lamb, forcing its head to crash to the stone, air puffing from its nostrils before it breathes its last.

Hearing the death rattle of its comrades, the last lamb panics and pisses itself. The creature has soft, innocent eyes that remind me of my little brother, now in his tomb. This last lamb's wool has magnificent curls like those my father wore in his hair. This last lamb will bleed on my feet like the Prince of Emesa did when he died.

I think to call an end to this; to plead mercy for this last lamb, but I cannot. Instead, I step back. I step back from this. I step away before the emperor cuts the lamb's throat. And I do not stay to see the lambs burnt. I flee to the Sellisternia, the sacred banquet in honor of the Great Mother Goddess, hosted by the matrons of Rome. Entering the hall, I am still shaken, though I try to disguise it. Blessings are said over the cheese and herbs. Small portions are set out for the great mother, but I eat little. The taste of parsley and coriander in the cheese is not strong enough to overcome the bile at the back of my throat. Underneath the drums and flutes that play for the revelers, I hear Roman women whispering with distaste about the wives and daughters of Asiatic kings who have dressed with insufficient humility.

Their barbed remarks make me glad I chose my garments carefully. Fortunately, Princess Glaphyra of Cappadocia is so lovely that she's spared their contempt even though she wears a headdress made of thinly pounded gold leaves that tinkle whenever she moves. She sits beside me, and urgently whispers, "I've met my bridegroom and he doesn't want me!"

"I'm sure you're mistaken," I say.

"I'm not," Glaphyra cries, wringing her hands. "Prince Alexander said his people won't accept me. That I'll taint his claim to the Judean throne. That any children we have won't be seen to properly belong because they won't have a Jewish mother."

"That can't be true. King Herod cannot secure his shaky dynasty by making bad marriages for his sons. Especially not for the son who will follow him onto his throne."

Glaphyra worries at her bottom lip. "Alexander promises that he'll treat me gently—that I'll never have want for jewels or baubles—but says I'll never be his queen. When it comes time to take his throne, he says he'll set me aside for a more suitable woman."

Tears pool in the corners of her eyes and I can think of nothing to say to ease her mind. "Have you told your father this?"

"Of course!" she whispers so vehemently that her entire golden head tinkles. "But Papa says that these are just the words of a resentful young man. That when I bear sons for Prince Alexander, he'll feel differently."

If he doesn't, he'll have to contend with the wrath of the Cappadocian kingdom. Given that Judea cannot afford to make enemies, the objections of the young Herodian prince to his new bride will have to be overcome, but such calculations aren't likely to soothe poor Glaphyra. "I'm sure your father is right. Feelings do change in time," I say, reflecting hopefully on the fledgling understanding I have reached with my own husband. "*Everything* changes in time . . ."

THAT day, all manner of games and entertainment are held, to the joy of the populace. Chariots run special circuits in the circus. Plays are performed in wooden theaters, and pantomimes erupt in the streets. I learn this from Tala, who takes the children to see all these marvels and brings them home excited, babbling about puppet shows. Then Juba returns early with an unwelcome guest.

We receive King Herod with all due honors, of course. Nothing else can be done.

I have refreshments served and make Crinagoras recite some verses for us as we sit down together with a few of our most entertaining courtiers. Still, to have the King of Judea here, in my home, discomforts me in every way and I'm relieved to hear him say that he cannot stay long.

"Perhaps I ought to have sent an emissary," Herod says, reaching for his wine with an aged hand. "But when in Rome, they say it is best to do as the Romans do. I thought we might get straightaway to our business without the usual formalities."

"By all means," Juba says.

Herod swirls the vintage in his cup, sniffing at it before he swallows. "My son Alexander will marry Glaphyra of Cappadocia, but I have other sons in need of brides. I'm told there is a Princess of Mauretania."

A sudden chill sweeps through the room as nearly every one of my Alexandrians turns hostile glances in the direction of our guest. No Eastern king can have designs on a Ptolemaic princess without turning greedy eyes to Egypt, and they all know it. Most of my retinue once graced my mother's court; some of their families have served mine for hundreds of years. They are nearly as haughty and proud as I am—maybe more so. And they seem plainly horrified by the idea that the Ptolemaic dynasty has fallen so low that I might entertain a marriage proposal for my daughter from a foreign prince, much less the King of Judea.

But where the direction of this conversation receives a cold reception from my courtiers, it sparks a flame of maternal protectiveness in me. "My daughter is only six years old."

Herod smiles, tipping his cup to recognize me, as if amused I should enter the conversation without invitation. "I was told she was nearly seven, but that is of no matter. Send her to Judea and the wedding could be postponed until she turns twelve."

"Twelve!" I cry indignantly.

Juba puts a hand on my knee to still me.

Herod tilts his head, as if bewildered by my reaction. "Is twelve not the legal age at which girls may marry by Roman law?" Indeed, he seems so puzzled that he may not even realize how distasteful his proposal truly is. Even the emperor insisted upon the age of *fourteen* for the girls in his household.

"Twelve is the legal age," Juba replies. "But my queen is very attached to our daughter. We would not part with Cleopatra Isidora so soon."

It is the politic answer, so I do not interrupt.

Herod lifts his hands in a gesture meant to be conciliatory. "Normally, I'd want the girl to live in Judea until she's of age, but we're men of the world, Juba, and kings besides. We can indulge the sentimental urges of our women. Cleopatra Selene, content yourself to keep the girl until she's twelve and then we can celebrate a wedding."

I am about to say something undiplomatic when Juba breaks in with, "I need time to consider this offer, and, in any case, we could not let her go until she was fourteen."

My husband says this as if he will be the one to make this decision. As if he is actually entertaining this preposterous idea, a thing that plainly discomfits our courtiers as much as it outrages me. From his dining couch, my poet's eyes narrow to a squint. Even Memnon, standing at his post by the door, clears his throat.

Still, Juba's insistence that Isidora be fourteen before she marries should dissuade Herod. The King of Judea's sons are grown. He would waste almost a decade before Dora comes of age, during which time his sons will weary of waiting.

Strangely, Juba's demand does *not* deter Herod. "Fourteen, then."

I can no longer keep my silence. "We have not agreed to this." With Princess Glaphyra's words still ringing in my ears from the night before, I say, "Surely there are more suitable brides for your son. Perhaps a Jewish girl?"

King Herod gives a look that seems to indicate he expects my husband to keep me in better order, but Juba merely dips a bit of flatbread in spiced olive oil, which forces Herod to deal with me directly. "I am a Jew, Queen Selene, but my subjects dispute this. The more closely I keep Judaic tradition, the more they hold me in contempt. There is no pleasing them and it holds no benefit for Judea to please them anyway. Better that my people adopt Hellenistic culture and learn to comingle. It is for this reason I prefer to marry my sons to gentile princesses."

It is a perfectly reasonable explanation. Perhaps his sons only *imagine* that he seeks to eliminate them as legitimate rivals for his throne by marrying them to princesses who do not worship the god of the Jews. I too would find it hard to trust his motives were he my father, but Herod's words have such a pragmatic ring of truth that they cannot be entirely discounted.

"Nevertheless, my daughter cannot be part of your plans," I say. There is no advantage in mingling my Ptolemaic blood with Herod's; if anything, it is a distinct disadvantage, as can be read in the hostile expressions of my courtiers.

Juba attempts to soften the blow of my refusal by saying, "Our daughter is so young that we're forced to be cautious. I have only two children, after all."

King Herod's response is a tapping foot upon my tile and a scowl that makes plain we have offended him. Then he forces a leering grin onto his face. "Come now, Juba. Surely not just the two children. You're a young man, but not *very* young. Have you no natural children of concubines or harem girls?"

My cupbearer actually gasps at this effrontery but I do not betray the slightest emotion. Such an impolitic question, put to my husband in the presence of his wife, is either meant to shame me or to insult Juba's manhood. Nevertheless, I keep my chin high and my posture regal, coolly regarding Herod down the length of my half-Roman nose.

"If there are any such children, I am unaware of them," Juba says mildly, as if he had not noticed that everyone in the room has stopped talking, intent upon his answer. Fortunately, my husband's infuriating mildness seems to be an asset in discussions such as these. It is a manner that I cannot adopt as my own, but I cannot deny its merits. Especially as it seems he has effectively ended the conversation.

"Well, then," Herod says before taking his leave. "We can address the subject again at a later date."

The moment Herod is gone, I dismiss my courtiers. Then I am on my feet, pacing back and forth upon the black and white tile. The vulgar mention of illegitimate children makes me wonder exactly what Herod knows or suspects about me or my daughter. Does he suspect that Augustus might be her father? Surely not. If he did, he would never allow one of his sons to marry her.

He would want Dora for himself . . .

No, Herod must be an arrow shot at me from someone else's bow. Livia's perhaps. She would delight in taking my daughter from me. Or perhaps it is Agrippa, knowing all that he does. Yes, it must be Agrippa, who wishes to diminish me and my line at all costs.

And what shield do I have against him?

Thirteen

"I apologize," Juba says, watching me pace. "I shouldn't have invited Herod here. He is an obscene man . . . but you can expect more proposals like that one. Dora is a prize. Herod can't resist the lure of that Ptolemaic prestige."

He is trying to ease my humiliation, but I fear it is more than prestige that Herod is after. Insofar as I still hold a claim to my mother's Egypt, so does my daughter. She would help to legitimize any ambitions Herod might have for his dynasty to swallow up Egypt. Perhaps Herod thinks to become Pharaoh . . .

Herod is as vindictive as he is hungry for power; the chance to seize even parts of my mother's kingdom as she once seized parts of his must tempt him greatly. He has already risen far higher than anyone might have predicted, and such men do not perceive limits on their ambitions.

And yet, Egypt now belongs to Rome and such an ambition is too great even for Herod to dream.

Another reason to suspect he is merely Agrippa's puppet.

Later, while my servants dress me for the evening's festivities, my niece hovers in the doorway. Then Pythia shuffles in, biting her lower lip. "Your Majesty . . . would you offer *me* in marriage to one of Herod's sons?"

Aghast, I wave away the servant who is trying to fasten my garment with a pin ornamented with pearls and emerald beads. "Pythia! Why would you even suggest such a thing?"

My niece's cheeks pinken. "I overheard King Herod's offer. I didn't mean to eavesdrop but the doors were open and I heard what he said. And I—I need a husband." She speaks very quietly, but very earnestly. "My mother told me that I would need a good husband to better my station. She hoped that you might find a husband for me. Girls can marry when they turn twelve and I am almost thirteen now."

I'm determined that the children in my household will be children as I never was and it vexes me that a girl of Pythia's age should worry to better her station. "You do not need a husband. Not yet. You're the granddaughter of one of Rome's finest generals, the niece of a queen, and the heiress to a great fortune in Tralles. You want for nothing."

"I do need a husband. I need a husband if I mean to write my name in the scrolls of history. If I mean to avenge all the wrongs done to our family."

Tilting my head, I stare down into her unreadable dark eyes and ask, "What wrongs do you imagine you must avenge?"

"They call my grandfather a traitor to Rome. They call my father a filthy foreign merchant, though the Romans funded their wars on his treasury. They all but banished my mother for the sin of having married him. I must become *something* to show that everything they said about our family is a lie."

That is when I realize that I have shielded her from nothing. She has only let me see what I wanted to see. Little Pythia. Always well behaved. Agreeable to her tutors and obedient to all who have authority over her. She is an orphaned girl who seems at ease in my court, living amongst strangers, but mourns for her dead mother and perhaps secretly pines for her lost home.

Sweet Isis, am I looking down into the face of the little girl I used to be?

She is not like Dora. My daughter has no shadow self. No *khaibit*. No dark soul. But I see now that Pythia is like me. Even at her young age, she burns with a dark ambition. And I am rocked by the strange sensation that I am staring at my very self. Taking her hands in mine, I make a solemn vow. "I am not going to give a twelve-year-old girl to any man. But I promise you, as I promised your mother, that I will make a fine future for you whether it be in Mauretania or Rome or somewhere else altogether."

But it is a promise too easily given, for we learn before the night is through that the show of unity between the emperor and Agrippa is only pretense and that we are, indeed, on the verge of war.

TWO of Agrippa's most trusted men have been found dead, apparently drowned in the Tiber River. Before the evening's religious rites, there is apparent retaliation. Two senators—lackeys of the emperor—are found dead in their homes. One of them had his head bashed in by tiles and debris from a suspicious roof collapse. The other seems to have slit his wrists open in a bath, but there is no explanation for the curious stab wound betwixt his ribs.

It is happening again, the people whisper. The purges. The civil war. It is coming. If Augustus and Agrippa can pretend to be at peace while killing each other's men, they will surely lay waste to all of Rome before it is over.

Augustus has pretended friendship with Agrippa in daylight, but excluded him from the evening sacrifices. In reply, Agrippa's soldiers have been spreading word that these rites will not carry the religious authority of the Pontifex Maximus.

Agrippa knows Lepidus is a thorn in the emperor's side. He reminds the emperor that there is still some power in the Roman world that he does not possess. And Augustus always wants most what he cannot have . . .

That is why the Secular Games and all the attendant festivities are to continue and almost certainly why the emperor sends his praetorians to fetch me. Juba stops me in the hall as I am leaving the house. "You will keep your own guards near you, yes?"

My eyes narrow. "Am I in danger?"

It is a foolish question. I have always been in danger. But with the power of Isis that is mine to command, I do not fear the ordinary. If a man should come at me with a weapon, my winds would take him down. It is only the threats I do not see coming that I fear.

"Agrippa believes that you are an obstacle," Juba says quietly. "He believes you are the reason the emperor will not agree to his terms for peace."

"The emperor does not like terms being dictated to him by an underling—that is why he will not agree," I say, though we both know it is only a small part of the truth. Another small part is that I *am* to blame. At least, the emperor's obsession with making me his very own Cleopatra is to blame. And have I not always used it to my own ends?

"Nevertheless, Selene, be mindful tonight of how vulnerable you are."

Vulnerable. I am that. Everything in this city is a reminder to me of my past and the future I could have had. *Could* still have, if I walk another path. I am again tangled in the web I worked so hard to escape from and I do not know which move to make to keep from being devoured.

"I will be mindful," I say, turning to go.

Juba stops me again. "Selene? Your father's soldiers. The ones who still serve in the legions. If Augustus and Agrippa go to war . . . whom will they choose?"

My breath catches. "Why do you ask?"

"Because I want to know if they will protect you. And if I am to force these men to bargain with one another, I need to know to whom your father's men will pledge their swords."

"I try never to rely upon Roman soldiers to protect me," I say. For what good were my father's men in Egypt? They abandoned my father and they abandoned us too. "As for the rest of it, they will choose Agrippa. Unless I pleaded with them, and maybe even if I do, my father's men will choose Agrippa."

"You sound so certain . . . but it was Agrippa who sent their comrades to a watery grave at the Battle of Actium. The emperor did not fight them himself . . ."

"That's why they will choose Agrippa. There will be less shame in it for them."

But there will be nothing but shame for me, because I must side with the emperor. If Agrippa sees my children as a threat now, he will always see them as a threat. The admiral is a danger to my children and me. The emperor is a danger too but he would defend my children because he believes that they are his. So I will side with the emperor as I have always done. There is no escaping it. There is no escape from him, after all.

THAT night the emperor invokes the primordial goddess of child-birth and the Vestal Virgins bring forth the sacred cakes. Augustus wishes for me to be seen with him during these rites, but I stand stiffly, aloof, resisting the emotions that had so shaken me the night before.

I hate every moment of these rituals. I hate this farce. I hate more that I am any part of it. And at the late-night banquet that follows, I am, again, dispirited.

Julia, by contrast, is infused with energy. In spite of the advanced state of her pregnancy and the tensions swirling in Rome, she is somehow radiant and wide-awake, dragging me from couch to couch to meet her friends and the artists she patronizes. One of them is Ovid, who shows a dangerous contempt for the proceedings, one that goes well beyond even mine. When Horace taunts him with reports that Ovid doesn't even believe in the gods, the younger poet merely replies, "It is convenient that there be gods, and, as it is convenient, let us believe there are."

"Why associate with such an irreverent poet?" I whisper to Julia.

"Oh, spare me, Selene," she says with a roll of her eyes. "Your poet is more irreverent than any other . . . Besides, if you read Ovid's love poetry, you'll know perfectly well why I prefer him. But mainly I advance Ovid to frustrate Horace, who wants to take Virgil's place as Rome's foremost poet."

Julia is a stubbornly loyal creature, in her way. As a young wife, she was as unfaithful to Marcellus as he was to her. But as his widow, she has defended everything and everyone he ever loved. Even Virgil. "Stay close to me," Julia whispers, yanking on my wrist. "Marcella is here and if I see her, I cannot think what I will do or say."

"Adopt a pleasant tone. You have a stepdaughter in common—"

"Marcella and I have entirely too many people in common. That is the problem. How many different ways are we related? She is my cousin, my sister-in-law, my husband's former wife, and now she has married . . ."

She trails off, but she doesn't need to say it. Marcella has married Iullus Antonius—the man Julia loves. With all his machinations, the emperor has managed to turn his family into one of those vulgar comedies in which every woman pines for the wrong man, every man ends up in bed with the wrong woman, and every child is without a father.

"What a miserable state of affairs . . ."

"With one entirely unexpected exception," Julia replies. "I don't know if you've seen him yet, but our sour, dour Tiberius positively dotes on Vipsania. He's still boring and brittle as a stick, but he's sweet to his wife, Selene. Truly. Without any regard for his own interests. It's as if he's forgotten he's Livia's son long enough to actually love someone."

I wonder if, finally free from his mother's absurd quest that he should marry Julia and become the emperor's heir, Tiberius may have finally found a measure of contentment. One glance at Vipsania across the banquet tells me that she is happy too. Dipping her head to whisper to my giggling half sister, Vipsania is the picture of a joyful wife.

"Minora doesn't seem displeased with her betrothal either," I say.

Julia pops a little ball of cheese into her mouth. "Minora and Drusus will find themselves well matched when they wed. She always knew it would be Drusus for her. Who else was left in the nursery once you went off to Mauretania?"

I'm struck by a sudden and vivid memory of our childhood. The day Philadelphus knocked us into the pool and Julia and I flung white ribbons of water at him. Minora and Drusus squealed and splashed and climbed all over us. Closing my eyes, I remember the laughter. We all laughed that day. Even Helios, who so seldom laughed. The remembrance is a sharp arrow of pain.

I ought to push the memory away, but I let it linger because I cannot have the sweetness of Helios without the bitterness of having lost him. Indeed, I savor the memory, drinking deeply of my wine.

Not in at least a hundred years have the women of Rome participated so fully in the business of the state. Regardless of the lateness of the hour, the rumors of impending bloodshed, and the supposed solemnity of this banquet sponsored by the most prestigious women in Rome, they chatter with excitement.

Only Livia sits quietly at the far end of the hall, watching with detachment. And I am surprised when she motions to me with her finger.

"Goodness, you've drawn the eye of the harpy," Julia says with a laugh. "Well, you can't keep avoiding her. Go on. Don't worry. Livia's claws have been clipped."

Though Julia's popularity has brought Livia low, I cannot be seen to snub the emperor's wife, so I stiffen my spine and make my way through the crowds to take the empty edge of the couch upon which Livia reclines. When I do, the emperor's wife sucks in a big breath as if it takes courage to face me. Perhaps it does, since the last time we were alone, I threatened her life, vowing that if she should ever put my daughter in fear that I would make her disappear. Though I've yet to master my magic to the extent that I can do such a thing, the earnestness of my promise was not lost on her.

But I am just as wary of her. Cautious as a cat, I ask, "What do you want, Livia?"

"I want to know where you went wrong, of course," she says, tapping one of her bony fingers against her lips. "Since you've returned to Rome, you've put on a masterful performance, as if you were content to be merely the Queen of Mauretania and the wife of a Berber. Yet we both know you aimed much higher when you made yourself the emperor's whore on the Isle of Samos."

I shrug because I know better than to allow Livia to see what truly matters to me. "We must all content ourselves with the roles the emperor chooses for us, mustn't we?"

Livia plucks a flower from the wreath around her neck and crushes it between her fingers in contemplation. "Oh, I wouldn't have admitted it then, but you did worry me. You bewitched my husband. I'm told he considered divorcing me and putting you in my place. But somehow you aimed too high. You overshot. I want to know how you failed."

Pride makes me ask, "Are you so sure that I failed?"

"He cast you off," she insists. Then her contemptuous eyes flick away to another woman entirely. The plump matron who has drawn Livia's ire must be Scribonia. Long banished from social gatherings in Rome, the emperor's former wife is now openly received thanks to Julia. Scribonia has emerged from veritable exile to take an honored place in her daughter's retinue, a circumstance so abhorrent to Livia that she says, "This city is filled with the emperor's cast-off women. He has cast off all of them but me."

That's all she has left to cling to. Her social position in Rome is superfluous. She has only a few loyalists left amongst the women of the city, but none of them are seated with her now. Her influence is gone. Her ambitions for her sons to rule the empire after Augustus are all shattered. The horrible things she's done have all been for naught. I take some measure of satisfaction in that, enough to make me say, "No one deserves him more than you do. In the darkest chamber of my soul where hatred resides, you have etched your name again and again, Livia. Even were I to forgive all that you've done to me, you've hurt those I love, so I am glad you have the emperor and that he has you."

"And I'm glad you hate me, Selene. So very glad. Because one day you will realize that we're just alike. Then the self-reverence with which you carry yourself will melt away and leave you to hate yourself just as much."

It is an accusation that makes me boil over with rage. "We are *nothing* alike."

"Aren't we? When I was fourteen years old, I was given over to an older man to be his bride, just as you were. My first husband was considered to be worldly and intelligent, like yours. A civilized man of middling ambition."

She is trying to insult my husband, I think, so I do not dignify it with a reply.

"It was my duty to my family to be a good wife," she continues. "To give him sons and learn to love him no matter what weakness I saw in him." Her lips curl with scorn. "He got me with child right away. My son Tiberius can make nothing easy on anyone, so the birth was hard. While I was screaming, my husband told the midwife to cut the baby out of me. She protested, telling him that it was too soon for such a drastic course. That it would kill me. But my husband said, 'Better a dead wife than a dead child. I cannot make sons easily, but I can find another woman to bed.'"

I'm too fascinated to stop her now. With a coldness that makes me believe it, she explains, "They tied me down so that I couldn't struggle against my death. The midwife told me how great my child would be if it was a boy. How he would honor my name and bring it glory. Would not any good Roman woman wish to die to ensure such a thing? She wanted my assent to kill me. She even offered to cut my throat first to make it quicker and less painful."

I stare at Livia to see if she feels anything about this at all, but she goes on without emotion, as if describing something that happened to someone else. "That is when the child finally slithered out from between my legs. It didn't matter that I was tired and frightened and so very injured. They put the babe on my breast. They could have sent for a slave—some slut from the kitchens with milk in her breasts—but if they would take my blood for the baby, why not my milk? For that squalling brat they would drain me of everything."

I say nothing to Livia, because I *can* say nothing to her. The birth of my own son was not easy. But no one threatened to cut him free of my body and leave me to die. Livia is the same vile creature she has always been, but she is telling me how she was made. And I find that I want to know.

"My first husband was one of your father's men," she says, and when my eyes widen, she adds, "Oh, yes, I was in Antony's camp then."

The mention of my father's name alarms me, for it's rarely mentioned in public. As he was declared a traitor and his birthday named an unlucky day, I look over my shoulder to see if anyone has heard, but Livia and I are alone together in this alcove, both of us trapped by the past.

She draws closer and I can smell the herbs on her breath. "Your father came to congratulate my husband on his new son. I heard them laugh about the beardless boy who meant to fill Julius Caesar's shoes. That was the first time I heard the emperor's name spoken. In laughter. They refused to honor him with his adopted name, Gaius Julius Caesar Octavianus, *Divi Filius*—the son of the god. Instead, they laughed, calling him by the name he was born with. *Gaius Octavius Thurinus*. Or, when they were drunk, they called him just *Octavian* or *the boy*. The boy had no army, they said. No breeding. He was the descendant of slaves. All the boy had was his adopted name and hubris. And he would be easily defeated."

Would that he had been, I think.

"That was the last time I ever heard anyone say Octavian's name in laughter. The next time I heard it, it was spoken in panic by our slaves as they fled in terror, abandoning us to *the boy's* marauding soldiers."

She is talking now about the dark days of civil war. Days when blood ran in the streets of Rome. Days when my father and the emperor struggled for power . . . the days that shaped us both. "He captured you?" I guess, fascinated.

"Just listen and let me tell it!" she snarls. "I was an ailing girl with an infant at my breast and thugs at my gate. My husband snatched our son out of my arms and commanded me to stay behind to delay the soldiers. He meant that I should let them dishonor me and my family name. Give myself to rutting soldiers . . ."

To protect my children, I can think of nothing that I would not do. But to be a girl—just a child myself—and given such a command by my husband, by the man who was bound by honor to defend me . . . if it were anyone but Livia telling me this story, it would break my heart.

She must see something akin to pity in my eyes, because she laughs. "Oh, do you think I would let men violate me and live on, shamelessly, as you do? No, the soldiers were too intent upon looting our valuables to concern themselves with me. So I slipped out the back into the garden, climbed over the low wall, and fled to my husband. When I caught up with him he simply put little Tiberius into my arms and told me that the boy was hungry."

The dark tale is starkly at odds with the revelry around us and I am eager for it to end. I have changed my mind. I do not want to hear more about Livia's sufferings because the fiendish woman has dared to remind me of how she brought me to the emperor's bed, then gave me poison to drink the morning after. "May no other girl ever know such suffering."

"Why not?" Livia asks. "Suffering is what makes us. You've certainly worn your suffering like a mantle. It is always in your eyes, in your every breath. You never let any of us forget it. You wallow in it. But all anyone thinks when they look at *Livia* is how high she's risen."

"Oh, I assure you, that is not all I think when I look at you."

She doesn't hear me; in a sense, I don't even think she's speaking to me anymore. "Have you ever smelled your own hair burning? It is a horrible stench. My husband never gave a thought to my safety. I was nearly burned alive when Octavian set fire to the town where we fled. Like a wolf, Octavian was always on our heels. I knew that if ever the wolf got too close, I would be the bait."

I will not let this story soften me, I think, for she has ever been my enemy, a threat to everyone I love, and I do not forget. But this story haunts me and will linger in my mind.

Livia must know it because her smile is chilling. "I decided that when the wolf got close enough I would let him snap me up in his jaws. I was already the wife of a ruthless man, so why not be the wife of the *most* ruthless man? A man who would never be sent fleeing into the night. A man who would stop at *nothing* to win. Octavian was that man."

"So you let the wolf catch you," I say.

Livia smiles mysteriously, examining a simple golden ring upon her bony finger—the one that must have been her betrothal ring to the emperor. "I caught him. When your father married Lady Octavia to make peace, we were able to return to Rome. I suggested a dinner party—how could it be unseemly to host Mark Antony's new brother-in-law? My husband agreed, and a day later, Octavian reclined upon our dinner couch. I let him know, with whispered words and a glance, that I was his for the taking, if he should dare such a thing in my husband's house. So he dared . . . that very night. He took me in the gardens, then brought me back to my husband's couch still red-cheeked and flushed, utterly shameless. He loved that shamelessness—and I knew then, it was the wrongness of it that fed his appetite."

That is how she seduced the emperor away from Julia's mother. And she has been clinging to him for survival ever since. Livia thinks we are alike because we have both played the emperor's strumpet in the name of survival. She sold her very soul for her ambitions; I nearly did the same. But I turned away before it was too late.

Haven't I turned away? "You sicken me, Livia."

"Only because you tried to play my game and failed. I want to know what you did that drove Augustus to cast you off and run back into my arms."

She assumes it was the emperor who stepped back from the abyss. That he took his fill of me and sent me away when he was done. Even my courtiers think this and I'm not at liberty to contradict them, because the emperor must think it as well. And yet, I have finally come upon the one person to whom I can speak the truth, because Livia will not believe it, and even if she did, she cannot repeat it.

"He did not cast me off, Livia. I cast him off." The shock on her face gives me such satisfaction that I go on boldly. "I didn't want him. I *never* wanted him. Not when you helped force me into his bed. Not when I was at his side on the Isle of Samos, striving for my mother's crown. He gave it to me, you know. He put the crown of Egypt upon my brow and he pressed the scepter into my hands. He promised me a greater place at his side than you have ever enjoyed. But I would not live as *that* man's wife, even for the whole world. I drove the emperor back into your arms because it's what you both deserve."

She draws back as if I've slapped her, gulping in air. Let her think on that. Let her suffer knowing the truth. I don't care. And I feel a moment of triumph as darkly thrilling as it is dangerous.

Fourteen

JULIA is the glittering center of the party. It is difficult to convince her that she must go home and to bed because until she does, none of the other matrons of Rome dare leave. I nearly have to haul her outside into the dark.

The moment the humid night air touches my cheeks, however, I regret having done so. An escort of minor officials have gathered to see guests home, led by none other than Iullus Antonius. Julia sees him and her fingers clamp down so hard on mine as to cause me pain.

Iullus cannot take his eyes from her, but he greets me first, with unusual gallantry. "My sister, the Queen of Mauretania . . . Lady Julia . . ."

The unspoken longing between them after their heartbreaking separation is so suffocating that I feel certain everyone else must be holding their breath. But no one else seems to notice the anxiety on my Roman half brother's face and the mask that descends over Julia's.

Their love is a secret. And the way Julia's fingernails dig into my palm makes me wish it was a secret I didn't know. "How good to see you again, Iullus Antonius," Julia says. "How long has it been?"

"More than three years," he replies stiffly. "Almost four."

Her grip tightens on my hand. "I trust the years have been good to you. Certainly your loyalty has been well rewarded. I'm told that my father relies upon you and Tiberius for everything. Much has changed since I've been gone."

In the moonlight, he drinks her in, head to toe, his eyes burning with emotion that he dare not express openly, but still, he comes close. "Some things never change, Lady Julia. Some things are as eternal as the flame in the heart of Rome . . ."

I feel the tremor that goes through her hand. "Horace told me you'd taken up poetry, Iullus Antonius; now I believe it."

"Any man may be a poet if he is graced by a Muse," he replies. "And you have always been mine. May I escort you home?"

It is a plea to walk alone with her as they used to do in the gardens. He wants to take her aside from her attendants so that they might speak privately. Once, Julia would have readily agreed. I know she is tempted. She stares at him, weighing his proposition for long moments, her heart beating so loudly that I can hear it. She wants to go with him, but she is married to a man who will never forgive such impropriety. It will be disaster if she goes. I will not *let* her go, I decide.

Thankfully, Marcella emerges from an archway and the spell is broken. One glance at her rival seems to bring Julia to her senses. She gives a polite nod to Iullus's wife. "Thank you for the offer, Iullus Antonius, but no." The effort seems to makes her cruel, and she turns to show off her swollen belly. "I'm sure that Admiral Agrippa has sent a litter to fetch me now that I am great with child again . . ."

Then she walks away with me, her eyes straight ahead, never looking back. But I look over my shoulder and see the knob in my half brother's throat rising as if he cannot swallow it all down.

IN the morning, I have slaves bear me away from the city in a covered litter to visit the tomb of my little brother Philadelphus. I find his crypt well tended, the stonework in good repair, new paint upon the carved garlands and fresh flowers strewn upon the entryway. The Antonias vowed to me that they would tend his tomb and perform the rites due a child of Isis . . . and I am grateful when I see a little brazier with the fresh ashes of costly incense.

Then my steps come to an abrupt stop at the sight of a Roman soldier wearing a red-plumed helmet inside. I gasp, astonished. "Drusus?"

Turning from the wall behind which my brother's sarcophagus is safely bricked in, the dashing military commander removes his helmet and tucks it under his arm. "Ah, Selene. I didn't mean to give you a fright."

Clutching my basket of offerings, I ask, "What are you doing here?"

"I stop here when I can," Drusus replies sheepishly. "Today I was nearby on an errand, and Minora asked me to make an offering for Philadelphus."

"That's very kind of you," I say, reminded that my youngest brother spent as much time in Rome as he ever did in Egypt. He was as much *theirs* as he was mine, but even though I'm touched at the sentimentality of Livia's youngest son, I want to make my offerings alone.

Fortunately, Drusus does not stay long. He's always busy with somewhere to be. And so he leaves me to make my offerings to the statue of Philadelphus—where I think my little brother's *ka* may reside. I give him milk and barley cakes covered with honey, figs and dates and little pastries with beans in them. They were his favorite at the Saturnalia . . .

Then I tell him of all that has happened since I came to Rome. As I speak, I know that Augustus and Agrippa are making another sacrifice on the Capitol, this time a cow to Juno. But it's always what Augustus does in darkness that most concerns me. Since I'm named after the moon, perhaps that's only right. They tell a story of my goddess that she knew the secret name of Ra. Perhaps, like her, I was born to glimpse the souls of men at their darkest hours and know them for who they really are.

These gloomy thoughts are a reflection of Livia's words. I told her that we're different because I didn't want Augustus; but perhaps she never wanted him either. I told her that I cast him off, and even though it is true, I did so only for my own survival. How many times on the Isle of Samos did I wish to throw myself into the water and drown?

Once, I nearly did.

I let the emperor send me away because I would never have been able to live with myself otherwise. Livia's sense of self-preservation isn't stronger than mine, nor are her ambitions greater. The only difference between us—the only true difference—is that I have tied myself to the emperor in the hope that he might one day be a better man.

I know the emperor's dark side. I know the chained monster inside him that he unleashes to ravish young girls. I know the cold ruthlessness that slows his blood and makes him murderous. But I also know a side of him so pathetic and vulnerable that I have always been able to exploit it. He longs to be a great man. He longs to *be* the hero that the world needs.

Caesar. Aeneas. Apollo. These are the names he wants as his own and I have given them to him. I have used him to have my own way. He's given me riches. He's saved men on my word and killed others because I wanted them dead. If I have such power over the emperor, if, like the goddess I serve, I know his *true* name and can wield him as a weapon—can I not also make him lay those weapons down?

I have done it before. I have convinced him to spare men's lives. I have persuaded him against war. I have changed him in ways large and small. And that is why I return to my house on the Tiber to don the garb of an Isiac priestess.

Tonight I will go to the emperor wearing a clean linen tunic, the threads of which come from a plant so that no harm is done to a living thing. Dyed in bright colors to represent the various facets of my goddess, it shows how she can be found in every beautiful thing given to us in nature. Tied between my breasts in the sacred knot of the *tiet* is a black-fringed cloak weighed down in silver stars.

In my hand, I hold the *ankh*. The symbol of eternal life.

For those who believe me to be an incarnation of Isis—or my mother reborn—the sight of me dressed this way has a powerful impact when I make my way to the emperor's side that night. Whispers swirl around me asking whether the ban on Isis worship has been lifted. The crowd parts for me not only because I am a queen, but because they sense the *heka* that tingles at my fingertips.

Augustus might well object to an apparition of my forbidden goddess here, in Rome, where she may not be worshipped by name. But whatever he tells himself, he *is* worshipping her on this night. He *is* sacrificing to Isis.

And I will help him do it.

The emperor's gaze sweeps my way and I stop where I stand, lifting my eyes in challenge. This is my price. If he would have me call upon my goddess on Rome's behalf, then I must be allowed this latitude to appear as her priestess. I have chosen this moment so that he cannot forbid it. I've chosen to ask forgiveness rather than permission.

We are seasoned bargainers this way; we no longer need words to negotiate. He gives one curt nod, and I find a place in the shadows beside him. The cow he will sacrifice tonight is heavy with an unborn calf. She's a pretty heifer, snowy white and without blemish, adorned with garlands of flowers. Standing over her, beside the rushing birth waters of the Tiber, the emperor asks the great mother of all things to give birth to a new Rome.

When he has said all the sacred words, he looks to me to hand him the knife. I'm standing close enough to him that I might plunge this blade into his heart and rid the world of Augustus forever. But his body has always been at my mercy in some way or another, no more now than ever before. I have nursed him to health and shielded him from harm so that he might finally bring about some good in the world. And tonight, he is trying to. He is begging the gods to give Rome a new start—to clean the sin from this world and from his heart.

"It is not blood that she wants," I whisper.

My voice is quiet but he hears me over the gurgling river beyond. He draws nearer until our torchlit shadows mingle on the ground and the rest of the world, all the priests, all the worshippers, all the citizens who watch and wait, seem to freeze in place.

The emperor asks, "What does Isis want?"

Once, I looked for the words of my goddess to reveal themselves upon my arms in blood. Now that I'm older, I think she carves them inside me where only I can see. They are no less painful for it. I'm saddened by the certainty of what she would have of me now. For Isis does not cling as hard to her hatreds and resentments as I do.

I may have been born to usher in a Golden Age, but the people don't care if it's mine or *his*. Their lives turn on small things like food in their bellies, the security of good laws, the prosperity of peace. What dynasty should rise or fall is nothing to them if it costs them everything else they love. They've known too many dark days to fight for a Republic anymore. It has all become empty talk for them.

I would gladly blame the emperor for this. I *have* blamed him. But this is what ninety years of civil war and instability has wrought. Now all they want is peace and *order*. They are hungrier for it than they are for bread.

And he wants to give it to them.

When I speak, my voice is still a whisper, only for him. "She wants a true sacrifice. You must make peace with Agrippa. You must forgive him for his defiance. You *must* forgive him and give people peace and security at long last. You must adopt Agrippa's son as your heir, Caesar."

The emperor's eyes narrow as he whispers, "You know what I sacrifice should I do that."

His fantasy that little Ptolemy is his son is potent. Having me close to his side during these proceedings lets him dream he might claim us in the future. This is a fantasy that must be cut out of him just as my hatred must be cut from me. "Caesar, Romans sacrifice the best horse, the winning horse, the October Horse to the gods. They do not sacrifice the losing stallion. It must *hurt* to surrender it . . . or it is no sacrifice at all."

As the wind begins to pick up, the emperor looks thoughtful, as if he is hearing a truth he already knows. "And what do you sacrifice?"

What have I not sacrificed? Yet, still, I must surrender to my goddess the bitter bile in my spleen toward these people. These

Romans. For their sake, my mother, my father, my brothers, and all their dreams of a different world have been sacrificed and burned like the lambs.

This is all that remains. These people. This empire—a thing I can only shape if I recognize my kinship with it. I must forgive those soldiers who abandoned my father at Actium; I must forgive men like Plancus and Juba whom I once called traitors. I must forgive even the emperor . . .

I must bury my *khaibit*, that shadowy, vengeful part of myself that fights the Romans, plots against them, pretends that their fate is not my fate too. That this empire is not the same one my parents fought and died for. Always I've been taught that forgiveness is a tender, uplifting force, but forgiveness can be sharp as a knife. Forgiveness will cut me this night and I will bleed. "What do I sacrifice tonight?" Taking the knife, I see that my hand is strangely steady. "Why, tonight I become Roman."

I press the hilt into his palm. Our fingers touch and I let the spark of my *heka* flow into his hand, into the knife, and into the night. He's seen words called forth upon my body, engraved in blood. He's seen me call the wind with my upraised hands. But he's never felt the force of my power as he feels it now. I yield it to him, using my hopes and dreams for a new world in the hopes I will make him blossom the way I once made a hillside in Mauretania bloom with flowers.

His eyes widen with the sensation, then widen again as we connect. The tendrils of magic wrap around him and bind us more tightly than anything else ever has. More closely than carnal knowledge. If I have never before truly bewitched him, this time I do, and the ruler of the world nods to me his surrender. He will do what is right. He will make peace.

My winds scour the night and make it clean, sweeping away the pains of the past to make room for a new world. I pray that Isis lifts any curses she has laid upon these people . . . even upon the emperor himself . . . and that she fill our hearts with forgiveness.

As the people cover their heads and huddle together, Augustus holds the sacred knife above the cow. Isis does not want blood, but the gods of Rome do, so Augustus slashes the poor animal with swift mercy. The cow falls before Occia, and the rest of the Vestal Virgins crowd close to pull the unborn calf from its dying mother just as I was ripped away from mine.

The cow and the calf are burned by the Vestals, their ashes to be used in remembrance of this night at all holy occasions in the coming year. And I stand in the wind, trails of salt on my cheeks where my tears have burned away.

IN the days following, Juba brokers a private agreement between the emperor and Agrippa. The emperor's wayward general agrees never to celebrate a Triumphal parade. In so doing, Agrippa vows to decline the honor that would make him a veritable king for a day, even if his soldiers should hail him as imperator after a victory on the field of battle, even if the Senate should vote one for him. With this vow, the general agrees to support the idea that *all* Roman generals are, in some sense, merely legates of the *Princeps*, the First Citizen.

In exchange, the admiral is given large swaths of property in the East including the Thracian Chersonese. Agrippa is also given *proconsular imperium*, so that he may never be outranked wherever he travels. Moreover, he is granted the unusual *tribunician* powers that make him a colleague of the emperor for the next five years. And while Agrippa is extorting these favors from the emperor, his wife gives birth to a little boy named Lucius Vipsanius Agrippa.

It is a name the baby does not keep long because the emperor adopts *both* of Julia's sons under the laws of Rome.

Six years ago, the whole city was in a near state of insurrection at the idea that the emperor intended his nephew Marcellus to take the part of political heir. I remember the riots. I remember how I feared the whole mob would turn against the emperor's family, then come for me and mine. Those dissenting voices are strangely silent now. The adoption of little Gaius and Lucius is a far more obvious danger, an unsubtle dynastic move, and yet there is nary a protest.

Perhaps we are all willing to pay any price for the peace we begged of the gods.

As reward for his service, my husband is given a small fleet of warships with which to guard against piracy. He is also named *patronus coloniae* over the Roman settlements in our kingdom. There will be no question now of any disgruntled Roman appealing our rulings to the emperor. With Agrippa ready to start off for the East and the emperor's legions in Germanic Gaul, my husband is now the foremost authority in the West.

That is all very well for Juba, but I have my own ambitions. I have my own calling. On the night the emperor's astronomers present to him a bronze device used to predict the movement of the stars, I find Augustus in the room dedicated to his ancestors.

"I did my part," I tell him, with the masks of the *Julii* there to witness it. "Now I want permission to celebrate my goddess in my kingdom."

Watching the gears turn in the device, Augustus asks, "You give nothing freely, do you?"

"You allow Isis worship in Egypt," I argue. "There is no reason to forbid it in Mauretania."

"*You* are the reason. In Egypt, there is no more queen. There is no pharaoh. The priesthood is beholden to me. But in *your* kingdom, they will look to *you* for a savior."

"Have I not delivered those who worship me into your hands? You have allowed Herod to rebuild a temple and his people do not recognize you as *their* messiah. Let me build a temple for Isis in Mauretania, where my Berbers will honor Rome too."

"I won't pay for an Iseum. Not a copper coin."

"I'm not asking you to pay. I am asking you to make peace with Isis as you wish her to make peace throughout the empire. Give me your blessing and I'll return to Mauretania and trouble you no more."

"There is nowhere I am untroubled by you, Cleopatra Selene," he says, lifting his head so that our eyes meet. "There is no hour in any day that I do not resent the way you have been torn from me."

I swallow in the face of what seems to be earnest emotion. "It cannot be otherwise, Caesar. We begged the gods for peace and paid their price. We have shaped a new world and must be content."

"I am not content," Augustus says, pinning me with an intent stare. "I will never be content and neither will you."

"I *am* content, Caesar."

"You are lying. You are lying either to me or to yourself, Selene. But I will allow you to return to Mauretania with Juba. I will allow you to build your temple. So long as you are mindful always, in both matters—in all matters—that you are mine."

PART TWO

THE GROWING

Fifteen

WE make harbor just before the autumn rains begin to fall. The rains are welcome in our kingdom, but late, and I cannot help but think it is my fault for staying away so long in Rome. This land needs me. If I had performed the proper rituals for the god of the river, I could have made the rain come sooner. But I did not and now the farmers are in a frenzy to get their seeds into the earth for the winter sowing.

The sharecroppers hurriedly sow barley. The shepherds make ready to slaughter their fatted calves. The vintners rush to make their wine and turn the remaining grapes into raisins. And I have an overripe matter of my own to attend to; I dare not wait another moment to begin my temple lest the emperor change his mind about allowing it.

Calling my advisers to the tiered benches in our council chamber, where they may lounge beneath linen draperies and potted cherry trees that I have brought with me from Rome, I say, "I intend to build a great Iseum in honor of my goddess. Can we afford it?"

This question should go to my husband's master of the treasury, but it's my freedwoman who manages our monopolies, and my own riches. And so I do not like Chryssa's hesitation when she rises from her seat to address me. "That depends, Majesty. Will we take donations from the wealthy Isiacs who have come to your city to be free of persecution or will the temple be dedicated in your name alone? How big will the Iseum be? Will the walls be made of brick or stone?"

"Questions for an architect," I say.

"That will cost us too depending on the architect's skill and reputation."

"I will have only the best for Isis," I insist.

With a severity matched only by the tight braids that make up her elegant coiffure, my freedwoman says, "You will not have the best. The best architects in the empire are in the employ of Augustus or they work for Agrippa."

Tugging at my pearl earring in irritation, I say, "Surely not *all* of them."

She spreads her hands in helplessness, so that her gauzy blue shawl billows from her arms like the wings of my goddess. "We've sent agents to recruit the talented ones in the East. But they are easily wooed away by King Herod, who pays them a ransom."

It is not the money, I think. Talented architects and craftsmen would flock to a true Ptolemaic queen. But they have begun to think of me simply as the wife of a Berber. It is difficult to face the diminishing reputation of my dynasty . . .

From the corner where he has been idly plucking at the strings on my *kithara* harp, Crinagoras says, "Have you considered a Roman architect, Majesty?"

I scowl, because every Roman architect in Mauretania is otherwise occupied with roads, markets, warehouses, public baths, city walls, and the king's gladiatorial arena. I want to say that there is no Roman who could build a worthy temple to my goddess because although they are genius builders, they lack for artistry in their souls. But have I not just declared myself Roman? "Who do you recommend?"

My poet replies, "I rather like Publius Antius Amphio. He is shamelessly ambitious. Arrogant too."

Chryssa winces at the suggestion. "The amphitheater builder? Majesty, he is a greedy whoremonger. He is more prideful than most of his kind. Resentful too. On more than one occasion, I've heard him speak disparagingly of your Berber subjects."

"I've heard you do the same, Chryssa," Crinagoras taunts my

freedwoman, plucking at another string. "But you married one, didn't you?"

To prevent them from bickering, I ask, "Well, what do we know of this Publius Antius Amphio?"

"He *is* a greedy whoremonger," Crinagoras confirms. "But he believes baths and walls and useful buildings are too humble for his talents . . . he won't be difficult to manipulate into accepting the project for a fee that will not bankrupt the crown."

"Why must we manipulate him into it?"

Crinagoras snorts. "Because you want an artist, Majesty. And as the greatest artist in your employ, trust me when I say that you must appeal to vanity."

To that end, I give my court poet permission to put out two rumors. The first, that I am seeking a Greek architect to oversee the construction of a grand Iseum, not believing any of the Romans up to the task. And the second, that I have specifically rejected Publius Antius Amphio because I do not approve of the work he has done on the amphitheater.

Two weeks later, Amphio seeks an audience with me and haughtily submits a sketch for my perusal. The design isn't what I envisioned— not exactly anyway—but it *is* ambitious. I approve of the Egyptian influences. I'm pleased by the central lotus altar and *ankh* panel above the door, but my experience forces me to ask, "How would a building of this size, with this footprint, support a heavy dome?"

The Roman architect approaches me without permission, positioning himself at my elbow and rudely pointing over my shoulder. He stinks of stale perfume, as if he has just come from a brothel. "It will not be that heavy, Majesty. Look at the next sketch. See this honeycomb of recessed panels? It is a coffered concrete dome with a central window to the sky. Like the Pantheon."

I've seen the majesty of the Pantheon. It is a grand structure and my goddess deserves something as grand. Perhaps Amphio is the man to give it to her. "Do you worship Isis?"

The Roman looks down at me over a crooked, hawkish nose. "You take me for an Isiac? I am no woman or slave or prostitute."

Fighting back irritation, I ask, "What god do you worship, then?"

"I worship the forms of nature. Mathematical ratios. The sacred cohesion of sand and lime and stone."

I begin to see why he must pay women to spend time in his company—and it is not because of his nose. "So are you a Pythagorean or a Cynic?"

"Neither. I am not a philosopher. I am not a priest. I am a builder. I will build you a temple that brings mortals to their knees, but do not ask me to hold with mummery and witchery and superstition."

I dismiss him without further consideration.

This temple is to be my greatest work. It is to save the belief in Isis that has sustained wretched people in their darkest hours. I cannot entrust something so sacred into the hands of a man so profane.

There must be someone else. I will find someone else.

MY husband is indifferent in the matter of my temple, but the proposed Iseum is greeted with mixed reaction by our courtiers. On the one hand it pleases the Isiacs amongst us who seek a familiar goddess in this strange land. On the other hand, it displeases many of my Alexandrians who take it as evidence that I will never lead them home as the Queen of Egypt.

None take it harder than my mage. He absents himself from court, withdrawing to his chambers, where I find him sitting on his balcony alone, feeding seeds to little birds who peck around his feet. "Don't you want to see Isis honored with a temple?"

His eyes flutter closed. "Your mother was going to build an Iseum in Dendera, alongside the temple for Hathor. When she pledged the funds, your mother was carved there. Caesarion too. And I saw myself, in the Rivers of Time, as the chief priest. What a fool I was."

Sliding onto the bench beside him, I put my hand beneath his, catching some of the seeds in my palm. "You were never a fool. Not everything we envision for ourselves can come true. The world changes. Or, as you would say, the river flows in a new direction. We must swim in it and see where it leads."

"That has always been your gift, Majesty. Even without the small magics I have taught you, you swim the treacherous currents, no matter where they lead. Your parents . . . your brothers . . . the rest of us sink. We drown."

Letting the seeds fall for the birds, I take his hand in mine, stroking the knuckles and veins that bulge beneath his aged and liver-spotted skin. "I will not let you drown, old friend."

"I thought I would return to Egypt. There, where the gods know my name. Here, not even men know my true name. And when I die, they will forget me."

I do not like to hear him speak of dying. "The gods will know your name, Euphronius. Because I know it and what I build here will be remembered."

"Will your mother be remembered? Or will all anyone knows of her be that which the emperor tells them? The paintings of her, the stories they tell, that is not the Cleopatra I knew. Not the queen I served. Not the Egypt I remember."

He wants to go home. He dragged himself across the world to be with me, leaving everything he knew behind, and I can give him no solace. "If you want to return to Egypt, if you want to leave me, I would release you. I would thank you gladly for your service and send you with my tears and all the gold you could carry."

He stiffens, affronted. "I return to Egypt with my queen or not at all."

That even Euphronius cannot see the importance of what I do here in Mauretania reminds me just how acutely my royal prestige relies on the idea that mine is a court in exile. My power resides chiefly in people remembering that I am the heir to the world's greatest dynasty. That I am Cleopatra's daughter.

And so I commission a coin that stuns poor Master Gnaios, our gem cutter and sculptor. "In your mother's image, Majesty? You want me to make a coin honoring Queen Cleopatra?"

"You do remember what she looked like, don't you?"

"I remember that she was—she was . . ."

He reddens.

"An enemy of Rome? The emperor's nemesis?"

Now he begins to sweat. "Do we have the emperor's permission?"

"We don't need it. The emperor has vested in us autonomous powers of coinage." This does nothing to calm the poor artist. He frets, stammering that we will give offense to the emperor until I am forced to demand, "Do you think you know Augustus better than I do? My mother is long dead now, no danger to him. He is not frightened by her image. He delights in it. Has he removed my mother's golden statue from his family temple? He has not. I have even heard that he took one of the pearls he stole from Alexandria and split it in two halves for earrings, to adorn that statue. He will not take offense."

I believe every word I say. But I also know Augustus will see the coin differently than others do. He will not see it as a challenge to Rome—as the glorification of his enemy—but he *will* see it as a message from me, a reminder of all that has passed between us, and my promise that I would be his Cleopatra. That much will incite him. But not to fury. So long as I do not cling to vain hopes to be made queen over all the lands that belong to me by right, I can only stand to benefit from the emperor's preoccupation with the past. And so I issue a coin that reminds the world that mine is still House Ptolemy.

MY son's first word is *horse*, a thing that delights the Berbers because they are all mad for horses. Indeed, horses are so important to the Berbers that, under the old kings, horses were counted in the census. Unfortunately, our first attempt at a census proves to be a disaster.

When our city-dwelling subjects learn they must register for taxes and military recruitment, the proclamation is greeted with grudging cooperation here in Iol-Caesaria, but in the faraway city of Volubilis, it provokes the Mauri tribesmen to violence. One of our magistrates is killed in the fighting.

"There must be a response," Juba vows, apoplectic before our council. "Those responsible for killing the magistrate must be brought to painful justice."

I regret that I have chosen this day to allow the girls to sit in the council chambers. My daughter swishes her feet back and forth, alarmed when the men call for vengeance. And Pythia's eyes widen, but she leans forward, interested and intent.

"What kind of justice shall it be, Majesties?" Maysar asks, coming before our throne in the long burnoose of a desert nomad. Always protective of his Berber brethren, he argues, "Your largest tribe is the Mauri, and yet the people near Volubilis have never seen the royal family that rules over them. They do not know the king and queen who tax their lands and ask their sons to be soldiers. I do not argue that men who murder should be left free to do it again, but if you send Roman soldiers to hunt them down while counting Berber tax money safely behind these walls, they will not see it as justice."

"What do you suggest?" I ask, annoyed. "Should the king wrap himself in the blue cloth of your people, mount his horse, and ride after these brigands himself with a sword at his side?"

Maysar shows a glint of teeth. "I wouldn't serve King Juba if I didn't think he could do just that."

My husband does not seem to hate the idea, but I find it absurd. "That is *not* what you are suggesting, is it?"

The Berber chieftain shrugs. "I do not think it the worst plan, but perhaps you will like better the one where you move the seat of government to Volubilis. You have won the loyalty of Berbers here. Why should you not do the same in all your cities?"

Maysar has never seemed to understand that the farther we are from Rome, the fewer resources at our disposal, and I snap, "Volubilis is more than twenty days' travel from Rome in the *best* conditions and at least two weeks from Iol-Caesaria. That city is an indefensible, landlocked outpost at the foot of the Atlas Mountains, totally unsuitable to serve as a capital."

"I do not mean that you should settle there, Majesty, but a

presence is required. Why not move your court there for a short time?"

Because I don't want to. Because Iol-Caesaria is *my* city—the city I saw in my mind's eye and helped to build from almost nothing. It's Alexandria in miniature, a mirror of all I lost in Egypt. Moreover, if there is an uprising in Volubilis, are my children not safer here? I could not leave them, after all.

To my surprise, Juba says, "I'll go, Selene. You'll look after the children and rule here in Iol-Caesaria while I'm gone."

We have only just returned to our kingdom and now he thinks to leave again? His ready willingness to part from me is a jolt I do not expect. But it is, perhaps, only the most sensible solution. I can make no argument against it. We cannot ask Romans to put down an uprising in our own city; Juba must go. Except that . . . I do not want him to.

When my husband braves the cold and drizzly afternoon for his daily ride, I insist upon joining him, though the rain soaks through my cloak and puts a shiver into my bones. Our breed of Barbary steeds, sleek and fleet-footed, often take top prizes in the chariot games in Rome. Nevertheless, I always feel unsteady upon these fierce horses, as if they might bolt out from beneath me.

Juba, however, is a fearless rider who does not stop for rest until we are miles from the palace, at the edge of a coastal lake. Leaving the horses to our guards, I follow him in no good humor. But before I can complain, Juba catches me unawares, asking, "Have you been to this lake before? I would like to give it to you. The rights for it came with the many honors Augustus paid me before we left Rome. I think you and your freedwoman will make good use of it."

Shielding my eyes from the gray drizzle, I allow my gaze to skim the surface of the water, where I see nothing special at all. Not even a fishing boat. "I don't understand."

"Look by your feet, Selene. Amber washes up here."

I'm suddenly a little warmer beneath my damp cloak. "Truly?" Stooping down, I'm amazed to find a raw chunk of the yellow stone and clasp it in my hand. I know it is very valuable when polished. I know it has strange qualities. It burns, and when it does, it yields a scented oil. Sometimes, when it is polished to a sheen like glass, one finds insects inside it. Rising up again, I say, "It's beautiful. Do you believe amber is, as they say, the tears of the sun, fallen to earth?"

Juba gives a curt shake of his head. "No. I would say it is a gum stone, maybe honey hardened to a rock. But since the Greeks believe amber belongs to the sun god Helios, I thought you should have the rights to this lake and mine the amber from it as you will."

It is a gesture both practical and sentimental, the kind that appeals to me best. It calls to mind my beloved twin, but I need my husband to believe the emotion he might see in my eyes is the longing of a grieving sister. For Juba, like the Romans, has long believed my twin is dead. Still holding the amber in one hand, I touch his arm with the other. "Thank you. What an extraordinary gift. I am more grateful than you know."

"I will be gone in Volubilis for some time," Juba says. "It might take a year or more to establish peace. We will have to each keep our own courts . . ."

"When would you go?" I ask somberly.

"A week from now," he says, his eyes on the horizon. "Tomorrow, if it pleases you."

"Well, it does not please me," I say, puffing my displeasure into the air.

"No?"

"No! You will miss the Saturnalia . . . the children would be so disappointed."

Most children know their nursemaids better than their parents, but my husband is such a large presence in my children's lives that I know they will take it hard.

"I will send the children little gifts and letters," is his mild reply.

I stand there, my chest rising and falling with some emotion I don't understand. He is a king; he has duties. I know this better than anyone. Mauretania cannot prosper if we do not bring our tribesmen to heel. But I don't want to him to go. Not now when we have only just come home. Not now when we are finally learning to be good to each other.

As I struggle for the words to explain myself, he lifts an eyebrow. "Would it not be easier for us to be apart, Selene?"

I frown, more confused than before. "Easier? Why would you think it easier—" Then I know. And I go hot, my fist curling round the amber as I consider hurling it in anger. "What did Augustus say to you? Or did he threaten you?"

Juba catches my wrist. "He said nothing to me about you, Selene. Nor did he threaten me. Why would he?"

I want to shout at him for being so naive. I want to tell him how the emperor all but vowed to make me a widow if I should ever give Juba a child. But I bite back the words, caging them behind my teeth, because there is no way for my husband to respond that will not do more harm than good.

If I tell Juba of the emperor's threat and he refuses to believe me, then whatever trust there is between us will be smashed. Then again, it is no better if my husband *does* believe me. If I say that Augustus still claims me as his own, Juba may well decide that I am still the emperor's property. My husband has, after all, given me up before. Or perhaps he will, like a coward, decide to come to my bed only in secret, resigned to a profaned and infertile marriage bed. How will I ever look at him without despising him if he does?

There is a chance Juba would fight for me—a thing I had not realized, until this moment, that I desperately want. But what a wretched woman I would be to encourage rebellion when no one but Agrippa can fight the emperor and live to tell the tale. No. There is nothing I can say. Nothing that will not destroy my husband or destroy me.

So I stand there, silently seething in the damp mist of the lake.

"This isn't about the emperor, Selene. It's about you."

"Oh, I think you are wrong. It is always about him."

"Was it the emperor who issued a coin celebrating the infamous Cleopatra?"

I meant to tell him of the coin myself once Master Gnaios was done with the design. I did not think someone would show it to the king before I did! "It is only to remind people that our children are heirs to the House of Ptolemy. The coin will—"

"Did you think to ask me, first?"

I cough, damp and cold and cross. "I am empowered to mint my own coins without your approval."

He rubs at his face, as if to master his emotions. "Give me a son, you said, and we will forget Augustus. But now you know, now you have seen, that the emperor has not forgotten you. That he still desires you. Perhaps you thought to stay with him in Rome, even if it set every tongue wagging."

The emperor said I can never be content, but I have smothered my dark ambitions and my hunger for revenge. On the last day of the Secular Games, I bested my *khaibit* to make room for the better parts of me. How can Juba doubt me now just because of a coin? I see now that I was unwise to commission it without informing the king, but I am too angry to admit it. "Yes. I could have stayed with the emperor in Rome and set every tongue wagging. But did I? No, I set sail for Mauretania with *you*."

This seems to soften Juba. "You did nothing to encourage him in Rome? This coin is not meant to provoke him now?"

"I did not mint the coin to provoke Augustus," I say, my throat pained under the emotion swelling there because I suspected it *would* provoke him, but took the risk anyway for a greater purpose. "It was not my *aim* to provoke him. Nor did I encourage him in Rome. And if you dare . . . if you dare to accuse me again after all these years—"

"I'm sorry," he says harshly.

"I did not encourage him!"

"I *am* sorry," he says again, trying to soothe me. I will not be soothed. I am shaking my head, a distraught girl again, caught in the memory of how I told him I'd been forced, how he would not believe me when I needed him most. "Selene, it was not my intention to accuse you."

I do not know if he is speaking of now, or then. It is still a wound more raw than perhaps either of us realized. And I am guilty too because part of me believes he has no right to be angry that I honored my mother this way and another part of me believes he has every right. "Then what did you intend, Juba?"

"It is only that I must know what you want, Selene. You say you chose Mauretania. Well, if you have now thought better of it, I must know. I cannot bear to do this again . . ." He looks away. "I cannot bear to always be the one to hold you back from what you want. There are two cities in this kingdom that need rulers; there is no reason we must live together, always in each other's way, trying to make a solid thing out of something hollow."

I flinch at the word *hollow*, then swallow my anger and my pride. He is making a sincere offer to step aside in deference to my ambitions. For my sake—or perhaps for the sake of our children. But I *did* choose Mauretania. "I have not changed my mind."

He does not look as if he believes me. Instead, he stares off at the southern horizon, as if he were eager to pack up and go off into the wilderness without another word as he did when we were first married. Will he make me say it? Must he hear me speak the words aloud? "I don't want you to go to Volubilis, Juba. I don't want to be apart."

"You know I must go," he replies. "And if there is to be fighting, I cannot have you or the children there with me. There is no choice to be had. I must go and we must be apart."

"Yes, you must go," I admit. "But you do not have to stay away. And I don't want you to."

"You don't?" he asks, reaching for me as if afraid to believe it.

I meet his gaze. "No. I don't."

Rubbing my arms against the damp chill, he asks, "For the sake of the children?"

By the gods, must he humble me so? I have already said enough. I have already said too much. "Not *only* for the sake of the children."

With a sudden jerk, he pulls me closer, wiping the mist from my cheeks, staring at me all the while. "Selene, someday, we will be called to Rome again and you will be tempted. You must know that."

I do not want to know it. I do not want to admit it. I do not want to think about it. So I say, "I only know that this is your home . . . and that I will be here waiting for you when you return."

THAT night, the king comes to dine in my chambers but we leave our meal untouched. In the light of the moon, he draws me into his arms and kisses me. I return his kisses with eagerness, dizzied by the scent of cinnamon on his skin. When he touches me, I touch him too.

There is a moment that he hesitates. A moment in which I am afraid he will ask a question I cannot answer or say something to pull me from this blissful, mindless pleasure. But I think he must know that the price for this pleasure is silence, because he stops only long enough to blow out the lamp so that what we do we may do in darkness.

Sixteen

IT is easier this time. When I last ruled Iol-Caesaria in the king's absence, I was only seventeen years old. Then, I arrogantly assumed I knew best until I came up against my own ignorance of the day-to-day administration of a kingdom. Since then, I have learned a great deal about governing, and, perhaps more importantly, I am no longer easily questioned or dismissed.

There are, to be sure, a few men on our council who bristle at a woman's authority. Some who attempt to bully me. But it is the ninth year of my reign. The king's explicit command that I am to be obeyed, paired with my own independent stature, renders such men a mere inconvenience.

Truthfully, I am also more patient. Once, keen to prove my worth as Cleopatra's daughter and a queen in my own right, I took umbrage at every offense. Now, placidly seated on my pearled throne wearing my gold crown and purple cloak, I happily indulge the long haranguing lectures of our most bombastic Roman advisers.

Then I do as I like.

When I am not tending to the business of the realm, I am worrying.

I worry always for Helios, never knowing where he is or whom he is fighting or what danger he faces. But my beloved twin is a child of Isis with powers beyond those of ordinary mortals. With a back as broad as a bull, Helios is stronger than ten men put together, a demon with a sword in one hand and fire in the other. He has made himself into the legend *Horus the Avenger*.

My husband is no legend, but a mortal man, so my worry for Juba is more acute. Juba is neither a hardened fugitive nor accustomed to fighting. Yes, he has experience as a cavalry officer, having fought beside Augustus in Spain, but I am fretful every day that we do not hear word of the king's expedition. And Juba is gone *two months* before we receive our first report from Volubilis.

The king writes that his soldiers captured the men responsible for murdering our magistrate, and that he presided over the trial, condemned the guilty men, then had them stripped naked and crucified alongside the road. I shudder to read this. Crucifixion is a lingering public death meant to humiliate and intimidate. It is not a death for warriors. It is a death for slaves and lowly criminals . . . which is why the king chose it. These men must not be lionized by other tribesmen; their rebellion must not spread. Of course, any pity I may have had for these crucified men swiftly diminishes upon reading a second message telling how armed rebels descended from the mountains one night to attack my husband where he made camp. Juba and his men were able to repel the attack without serious injury, but it is an act of untold brazenness to attack the king!

How can this be happening all because of a census? Everywhere in the civilized world people know they must be counted and pay taxes or make tribute. Berbers say they do not want Roman soldiers ruling over them. Well, if that is so, then they must allow their sons to enroll in Mauretanian legions. Berbers say they want to remain an independent kingdom. Well, if that is so, then they must contribute to our enterprise. I would say as much to Maysar, but my Berber chieftain is with the king, serving as his emissary at my behest. And with sullen sighs, Chryssa makes plain that she is not at all pleased about it, given that she is now expecting their first child.

THE emperor's answer to my coin comes in equal parts seductive, grandiose, and appalling.

Augustus has had himself named Pharaoh of Egypt.

I despair to hear such news from Lady Lasthenia, but do not

doubt her. Her society of Pythagoreans comprises a formidable network throughout the world and my disheveled scholar is usually the first to know everything. Here, it is to my advantage, even if what I am hearing horrifies me.

Pharaoh. A title passed down from antiquity to Alexander himself, then conveyed upon my ancestors. It was my mother's title. Perhaps I never deserved for it to pass to me, but it should have gone to Helios, who fought for Egypt when I could not. And for all I know, he is still fighting . . .

Putting my face in my hands, I take a moment to compose myself. Then Lady Lasthenia and I walk together amongst my withered cherry trees, none of which have acclimated well to our hot climate.

It should not surprise me that Augustus should want this title. Hasn't he wanted all the others? Perhaps he thinks he needs it if he is to be the savior all the world wants him to be. The savior who is prophesied to come out of Egypt. But why now? I fear he has done it now because of me. With my coin I honored my mother, Cleopatra VII, the last Pharaoh of Egypt, forcing him to conquer her all over again. When I find my voice, I ask, "The emperor will go to Memphis to be anointed?"

"No," Lady Lasthenia replies. "But he had his likeness carved at Dendera."

"Not Dendera!" This will break my mage's heart. It is already breaking mine. "Did he tear down the temple walls or merely erase my mother's name there? Tell me."

Always cool-tempered, Lady Lasthenia lowers her voice in response to my outburst. "Neither, Majesty. He had himself carved near to her."

My hand presses flat to my chest in surprise. "Do you mean to say that Augustus had his image carved there *with* my mother's?"

"Yes, Majesty. According to my sources."

Moments pass in which I try to order my words into coherence. Augustus is a genius and a madman, and in this I think he is both. He has ensured that his name will be entwined with my mother's long after the papyrus scrolls of history turn to dust. Perhaps this is his way of making things right. His way of honoring Isis as he promised to do on that night when we sacrificed together in asking the great mother of the world to cleanse us of our sins and to give birth to a new age.

Were it not for my Ptolemaic pride, perhaps I would see this as a gesture of his true greatness. His willingness to preserve my mother's legacy along with his own. His willingness to honor the ways of Egypt and give her the pharaoh that she needs. I sacrificed my hatreds to help make him a better ruler, and perhaps he is becoming one . . .

So why does this dig at me like a nettle beneath my skin? Why do I suspect there is, still, some game behind this and that he is waiting for my next move?

Pharaoh.

He's taken my mother's kingdom, her children, her crown, and her title. Now he has proclaimed himself her heir. Just as I am her heir. Just as my children are her heirs . . . and I am more aware than ever that he can make them his heirs too, these children of mine that he believes are his own . . .

To My Friend, the Most Royal Queen of Mauretania,

Rome is so very dull without you. Thank heavens I will be leaving it soon! Though it is against custom for a wife to accompany a governor on his travels, I've persuaded Agrippa that petty little rules like that apply only to ordinary people.

Meanwhile, Livia's sons have been sent to subdue rebels in the Alps. It seems like dreary enough work for a competent soldier like Tiberius, but I fear young Drusus is not likely to distinguish himself in battle. Though his mother has the temperament of a gorgon, he was always good-natured. I can scarcely believe how quickly time has passed that the boy we grew up with is now old enough to fight.

Oh, well. I suppose that's what all boys do.

Anyway, since Drusus and Minora are soon to marry, for the sake of your half sister, I will make a little offering at a shrine for his protection. I would hate to think of Drusus stuck with some barbarian's spear atop a frozen mountain.

Especially since I shall soon be enjoying the balmy weather of Greece!

Speaking of Greece, have you heard that this Olympic Games may be the last? Somehow, they have run out of money, and are too proud to ask my father for more than he has already given. They prefer to think of the games as the province of Hellenes, I suppose, and since you are the most prominent Hellene I know, you can probably expect a request for an outrageous sum.

Julia's warning still leaves me utterly unprepared for the plea that comes from Greece. Were my husband here to see it, he would sneer at the sum. I too am overwhelmed by the expense, but where can Hellenism find a champion if not in Cleopatra's daughter? My ancestors would never allow the Olympic Games to perish and neither can I. I am Mauretanian now, not a barbarian, after all.

I pledge nearly all the profits of my new amber lake to the games, though it pains me to do so because I fear it leaves me with too little in my treasury to woo a renowned architect when he arrives with letters of recommendation and an ambitious plan for my temple. "Do you know him?" I ask my mage. "This Necho of Alexandria?"

"I know *of* him and I know the names of the men who vouch for him in his letters." My mage says all this stiffly, for he still sees for me a different destiny, and even now, he will not surrender to defeat. "But it is not too late to turn your attention to a worthier project, Majesty. You have learned small magics from me in Mauretania, but think of what I could teach you in Egypt and how great your powers might be there. With your hands alone you might summon such winds to bury legions in the sand!"

I remember a time when Augustus wanted me to do just that. It was then, and is still, beyond my imagination, not to mention outside my reach. "You still dream of me battling the Romans,

Euphronius? As my twin summoned such fires that he burned
Roman legions into dust? Or did he lose that battle?" I do not ask
it to be cruel; I have forgiven the wizard his part in luring my twin
into a battle that lost him everything. Even, as the world believes,
his very life. I ask only because the old man needs to be reminded
that I have no desire to bury armies in the sand. More war is not
what I want. "This is my kingdom now and you must accept it."

"But there is another path to Egypt now, Majesty. Augustus calls
himself Pharaoh, but he does not name Livia the Queen of Egypt
nor does he have children by her to put onto the throne after
him . . ."

I have not told my wizard that the emperor believes himself to
be the father of my children because I feared his mind would turn
in this direction. Still, I think he knows. Perhaps he saw it in the
Rivers of Time before his magic slipped away from him. "You have
seen my children on the throne of Egypt?"

"Once," he answers. "Long ago."

I should not have asked. Curse him for putting this new hope
in my breast! It is now more difficult to beat down my ambitions,
to deny the legacy of my Ptolemaic blood. I told Juba that I choose
Mauretania and I have. For me. For myself. But can I deny my
children what is theirs by right?

Simple practicality hardens me. "My son is not even two years
old and my daughter only a girl of seven. There will be time enough
to think of their future."

"Easier said by a queen of your years than a wrinkled mage nearing the end of his."

I will not hear talk of that. My mage has been with me in one
way or another since the day I was born and I cannot imagine a time
without him. And he will have to make common cause with me on
this Iseum. I tell him as much, and set him the task of persuading
Necho of Alexandria to work for a lower fee than he might normally
command.

In this, my mage is successful. But there are still other details to
work out. Necho chooses a site in the Greek quarter of the city, high

on a hill. My freedwoman tugs at her silver earring when she hears the plan. "Brick walls?"

"They will be faced with marble," Necho explains in the council chambers, spreading his sketches upon a table, the legs of which have been carved into gilded sheaves of grain. "It will save the kingdom a great expense."

A healthy consideration for the cost is certainly the way to please Chryssa, but I have other concerns. "Will brick walls be strong enough to hold up a magnificent dome?"

"Majesty, not even the emperor's architect objects to brick walls," my new architect says. "Vitruvius himself points out that brick is used in temples throughout Greece. We need not waste time quarrying and cutting stone. Brick will allow us to begin without delay. I am told that your amphitheater is nearly completed and we will have an army of slaves to put to work."

At this, my freedwoman scowls. My mage does not look pleased either. I am equally unsettled.

Though slavery is a way of life everywhere in the empire, it is a complicated matter in Mauretania where my Berbers call themselves the *Amazigh*. Free people. They resent the idea of captive men toiling in the blazing sun. We came here at the command of the emperor with shiploads of slaves. More arrive every day to work the giant plantations owned by Roman senators who administer their lands from far away. I cannot rid my kingdom of slavery. I cannot even rid the palace of it, should I desire to do so. Juba owns thousands of slaves and many of them serve at my pleasure. But I have heard priests and priestesses of Isis speak against slavery. "Can we afford to hire tribesmen and freedmen?" I ask.

"Your amber would have gone a long ways toward funding that," Chryssa says, though, as a Greek, she knows full well why I pledged it to the Olympic Games. When I make no reply, she takes a deep breath through flared nostrils. "I will find the money," she says, and I do not ask how.

Then my new architect goes down to one knee before me in

submission, praising my intention to give my goddess a throne. "Together we will honor Isis as is befitting, Daughter of the Moon."

And so I sign the order in Greek as my mother once signed hers. *Ginesthoi.*

Make it so.

"WHY are there crickets in my hall?"

I ask this standing in the threshold of the schoolroom where a horde of insects chirp and hop across my feet. Our lady grammarian has a Berber boy by the hair. Tala's boy, Ziri, is too red-faced with laughter to even notice that his tutor is reaching for a leather strap. And meanwhile, his partner in crime, the boy we saved from the cage, is emptying another clay pot of crickets onto the floor, to the shrieks and laughter of the other children—even my Dora and Pythia too.

No learning can take place in this chaos, so I clap my hands together at the children. "Go capture those crickets before they get all over the palace. Go now!"

At my command, the children jump up from their benches and Ziri uses the distraction of my presence to wriggle out of Lady Circe's arms. She cries after the boys with uncharacteristic shrillness, "Run, then, you little brats! When I catch you, I'll strip the hide off your backs."

"You don't actually whip them, do you?"

Her answer is laced with indignity. "Of course I do. It is the only thing the little savages understand."

By this, she means the Berber children. Lady Circe is a well-educated Hellene whose salon has become a popular place for our most arrogant Greek philosophers to gather and sneer at those beneath them. Lady Circe has never approved of the king's insistence that all the children of our court take their education alongside our own children, whether they be Roman, Greek, Egyptian, or Berber.

But in this, Juba and I are in complete agreement. Even the emperor, for all that I loathe him, provided the boys and girls in his household with an excellent education. We can do no less. These children are more than just children. They are all that I have to rebuild my family's fallen dynasty so that I may not be the last of the Ptolemies . . .

"How well is my daughter taking to her studies?"

"Princess Isidora has a natural talent for language. Her other tutors say she has a mind for philosophy, mathematics, and science."

This pleases me. It pleases me *too* much. "Are you saying this because she is my daughter or because it's true?"

Lady Circe smiles, her voice smooth silk. "Who would dare lie to you, Majesty? But do not think it is all good news. Your niece is not quite as gifted. Answers do not come easily to Pythodorida . . . she struggles at her studies. But Pythodorida works hard for the answers, Majesty. In this, she is a good example for your daughter, who must learn that not everything will come easily to her."

I do not treat my children as little adults, as queens and kings from the cradle. I coddle them as I was never coddled. This is not the way of the Ptolemies or the Greeks or the Romans. But I know how adversity can shape a child for the worse. I shield my children from everything, because I was shielded from nothing. And I do not need to justify myself to Lady Circe. "What of the other children? Are the Berber boys always so disruptive?"

"Tala's boy shows promise, but Tacfarinas . . ." She sighs. "Let him go back to hauling firewood for the lighthouse. He is no good for anything else. He will never appreciate what you have done for him, Majesty. He steals wax tablets from the other children. He breaks inkpots. He looks for ways to create mayhem. The only way to make that boy behave is to bloody him."

I have seen him bloodied before, and so I say, "No, I will not have it. I don't want the children beaten."

"You risk a reputation for softheartedness, Majesty. Strapping the children will do them no real harm. Trust me when I say that I've met grown men who would pay for such treatment."

Though she amuses me with such talk, I raise an imperious eyebrow. "Which reminds me that you ought take a new name as yours calls to mind a profession you've left behind."

The retired *hetaera* who was once both my husband's lover and Herod's spy smiles indulgently. "It is a profession I may need to take up again if you don't allow me to discipline my students. I propose a bargain. If you allow me to thrash those boys, I'll change my name to anything you think appropriate."

One glance at her leather strap and I'm reminded of a beautiful golden-haired boy who was beaten for his insolence in the emperor's home. My beloved twin, whose flesh was rent for protecting our family honor. A youth who promised that he would always, always defend me and that I would be his queen. She cannot know the things that haunt me, so I only say, "Keep your name, then, Circe, and I will bear up under my reputation for softheartedness somehow."

Seventeen

❧

CHRYSSA gives birth to a healthy boy, dark like his father. "Your Berber chieftain will burst with pride when he returns with the king," I promise her, but I do not know when that will be.

Juba has settled his court in Volubilis, where he says the buildings are holdovers from the Carthaginians, so old that they boast the Punic style. The people of Volubilis are not hungry or lacking for useful employment, but their city is in need of defensible walls and public baths, new marketplaces and a basilica too.

The expense for these projects makes me dizzy to comprehend, but I think we were wrong to pour all our wealth into Iol-Caesaria. It has created resentments elsewhere in the kingdom that now need a remedy. As a gesture of goodwill, the king gifts the city of Volubilis with his prized bronze bust of Cato the Younger. I match his gift by sending overland a statue of the goddess Kore that was given to me during my sojourn with the emperor on the Isle of Samos.

I have just made the arrangements for the statue's transport when my niece comes rushing into my chambers, her black hair damp with sweat, her cheeks scarlet, as if she has run the whole way.

"We were nearly eaten by a lion!" Pythia cries, breathlessly telling the tale. "Tala took us to the market to choose new sandals. We were only halfway there when we heard shrieks. Then people ran in every direction at the sight of an escaped lion from the amphitheater."

That accursed amphitheater! It has only just been finished and already the gladiatorial arena is a danger. "Well, what happened then?"

"Everyone ran from the wounded lion but Dora rushed to it and began to speak to it!"

I gasp, covering my cheeks with both hands. "Where is she now?"

"With the physician, but she isn't hurt. Tacfarinas pulled Dora out of the way while Tala distracted the lion, but Tala was slashed and Euphorbus is tending her wounds now. Tala would have been eaten too if Dora hadn't told her to plead with the lion in your name."

"*What?*" I ask, still weak with fear.

"Dora told her to talk to the lion and he might let her go. So Tala shouted that she served a great Ptolemaic queen. And when the lion cornered Tala against a market stall, she begged him to spare her in your name, for she was the caretaker of royal children. You should have seen the lion stare, listening to each word as he limped back and forth, pacing in front of her. Tala told the lion that the Queen of Mauretania would be very displeased with him if he should make a meal of her and pleaded with him to leave her in peace. So he did."

"*What?*" I say again, unable to comprehend it.

"Like a king, he listened to her petition, then set her free. He limped off into the street and left us alone, though I don't know where the lion is now."

"Sweet Isis!" Standing on wobbly knees, I rush to the chambers of my mage, where I find my daughter helping to bandage three claw marks on my Berber woman's big thigh. "Is it true, Tala? You were slashed by a lion?"

My Berber woman tells the story just as Pythia told it, and I turn to my daughter, not knowing whether to clutch her against my breast or thrash her or both. "Why did you run toward the lion? What could you have been thinking?"

"He had a spear in his flank," my daughter says. "He was badly wounded from the gladiator arena and needed help."

Yes, I will thrash her, I think. For the first time in her little life,

I will thrash her until she is howling. It is only that I am still so weak with fear that I cannot make myself do it. "You could have been killed. You could have all been mauled to death in my market, far from me where I could do nothing to stop it." The thought that I could have lost her—that I could have lost any of them—has me shaking all over. My emotions are so volcanic, I do not trust myself to touch her. "You are not a physician, Dora! You cannot heal every creature that crosses your path. Surely you understand danger. You will have no dinner tonight and you are *never* to be out of my sight again, do you hear me?"

Fear has made me a shrieking harpy and my daughter begins to cry, turning to Pythia to hold her and wipe away her tears. How galling that she is not afraid of a lion, but now she is afraid of me.

My mage rests his comforting palm upon my shoulder. "Majesty, it all ended well. Tala's wounds are shallow. No lasting harm has come to any of them."

Even Tala—who should be angrier than I am—seeks to pacify me. "If it scars, I'll be glad of a keepsake. I'll be the woman who spoke to a lion in your name. Maybe your poet will even write of me."

There are not enough thanks in the world for my Berber woman. She saved my children at the risk of her own life and I will never be able to repay her. I will gift her with a poem or with whatever else she likes. She may behave in any way she pleases in my court, I decide. I do not care how insolent she is.

And the Berber boy, Tacfarinas. He must be rewarded too for pulling Dora from the lion. Only I cannot think on it now, for I am too shaken.

Later that night, Dora crawls into my bed and I curl around her, cuddling her close. I cannot get enough of her. "If you had been there, Mama, you would have helped the lion. That is why I wanted to help him. And it is why he didn't eat us. He knew it too."

She is wrong about me, but I do not correct her, because I am too touched by her innocence. She is nothing like me. I was never so pure of heart. Never so filled with empathy. She cannot have learned this from pragmatic Juba. Nor can she have inherited it from the emperor, for he has a heart of stone. This quality in her can only have come from Helios, the boy who gave every last coin he owned to beggars. In this, she *must* be his daughter. And for that, I am grateful.

To My Friend, the Most Royal Queen of Mauretania,

How I love the East! On our progress, we've been to Taenarum, Gythium, Sparta, Corinth, and Athens. Never—not even when you've described it—have I imagined to be honored and feted this way. The moment we set foot in a place, they call for the stonemasons to dedicate an inscription to us. We give them money and they erect buildings to us. Why, Agrippa even has a college named after him in Sparta now, which, given that he is as grouchy as a Spartan, seems entirely appropriate!

We attended the Festival of the Muses at Thespiae and I persuaded my husband to stop at a shrine to Asclepius for treatment of his feet. Agrippa apparently thinks he is still a young man who can march with his legions without consequence, but I know better. The physicians at the shrine insist that he must soak his feet at night in hot baths of vinegar. This helped ease his pain, so I intend to make a large donation to the next temple of Asclepius that I come across.

Who knows? Perhaps they will carve my name in the stone if I do.

One of my favorite cities so far is Mytilene. Isn't your poet from there? It has a beautiful harbor and all the people are clever and hospitable. They call me the new Aphrodite, for she is my ancestress, but I'm not sure I like seeing myself carved as the goddess herself. Unlike you, I am content to be a mortal woman.

A very rich, pampered, well-traveled mortal woman.

At any rate, as part of his bargain with my father, Agrippa owns mansions wherever we go, each more exotic than the one before. My husband insists on buying priceless artwork rather than seizing it, but the citizens have little choice but to sell us whatever we want at whatever price we say. Because of this, I am now the guilt-ridden owner of a lion sculpture and a painting of Ajax and Venus.

If you want them, let me know and I will send them to you.

It will sweeten your disposition for what I have not yet told you. Namely, that King Herod has traveled to meet us. He is still no admirer of yours. He bristles at the mention of your name and complains that you think your blood too good to give your daughter over in marriage to his sons.

He went on this way so tiresomely that I felt the need to tweak him. I asked if he would erect a statue of me as a naked nymph in the middle of Jerusalem, and he was so terrified of Agrippa's reaction, he could not look at me for the rest of the day.

It is not all fawners and festivals and flowers, though. People come to me to appeal to Agrippa on their behalf. Sometimes I even do it! I have no explanation for this. Perhaps when I visited you in Mauretania, I was too much taken by your example. I've begun to write letters to my husband about political matters, practicing clever turns of phrase. More distressing, the other day, when I should have been shopping for jeweled lamps, I caught myself spying a good place for an aqueduct!

I fear you have ruined me.

You may have heard about Queen Dynamis of the Bosporus, who has now had three husbands in one year, leaving me little room to complain about the frequency with which my father weds me to men I don't love. I begin to suspect, however, that Agrippa loves me.

I went without him to see Ilium, where the Greeks conquered the Trojans, because it thrilled me to think that I might walk in the footsteps of my ancestor, Aeneas. (Certainly it will make my father green with envy.) I sent word ahead of my impending arrival, hoping for an escort in light of the winter rains. Alas, when my entourage reached the banks of the

Scamander River, only a few villagers greeted me and I was obliged to set forth in a fishing boat, which overturned halfway.

I don't know if you've ever plunged headfirst into swollen floodwaters, but I cannot recommend it. The shock of the frigid water was like needles into my spine and when I gasped for air, I breathed water instead. The praetorians were so terrified to see me disappear in the black water that they splashed in after me, but my mind went black before they reached me. I thought—for just a moment—that this might be the way the gods wished to reunite me with Marcellus, for I still remember that dark night in Lake Avernus before he died . . .

Next I knew, I was vomiting water onto the muddy bank. The shivering did not stop even after they wrapped me in furs and put me before a fire. I must have looked like a bedraggled *lemur*, because when Agrippa and I were reunited, he exploded with thunderous rage, threatening to burn down the whole city of Ilium and throw children from the towers as Greeks did so long ago.

In terror, the citizens of Ilium claimed that I sent no word ahead of my arrival or they would have sent a proper escort or guided me to a bridge that would afford me safe passage.

But Agrippa would hear none of their excuses. He accused them of having tried to kill me, and fined the city so heavily I can't imagine how they will ever repay it. I think for men such as him, this is love. And I think for women such as you and me, it must be enough.

I am still thinking about her letter, days later, when Pythia asks me if I have given any more thought to a marriage for her. "I am thirteen now. Crinagoras says that when you were my age, you married King Juba and became a queen and a mother too. I am not too young."

I was nearly *fifteen* when I married, and even then I did not want to be a wife or mother, as my poet has good reason to know. The politician-poet is meddling again, and it vexes me, but I do not say this to Pythia because I know what it is to be an orphan, desperate for a family to carry on a lost legacy. "Do you have a husband in mind?"

"I will be content in your choice for me," my niece replies. "But I should like for him to be an important man. A senator. Or a prince. Perhaps a king, if one can be found."

She aims high, but shouldn't she? Pythia is a wealthy heiress and I have given her the finest education possible. She has studied in my throne room too. There is no man in Mauretania worthy of her and because I do not know the first thing about matchmaking, I reply to Julia's letter and ask her advice.

I must grudgingly admit that my girls are not little children anymore. There are things I must teach them. Things my mother taught me. It is time to take them to the source of the Nile.

HOW excited the girls are to learn we will go by camel, wrapped in Berber shawls against the heat of the sun with turbans upon our heads like desert nomads. They run to the library to peek at maps purporting to prove that Egypt's Nile finds its source here in Mauretania. They bicker over what to take in their satchels. And they pester my poor mage with questions when they learn that he is coming too.

They know the old man as the king's physician, wise in the ways of potions and rituals. They know he is a worshipper of Isis, yes, and that he may know a magic spell or two. But they do not know that he was once Cleopatra's most trusted wizard and I worry for his true identity to be revealed. I worry more that he is not healthy enough to make the trip, for the journey nearly killed him last time.

Alas, he will not hear of being left behind. "Where Isis is summoned," he tells me solemnly, "that is where I belong. If we want autumn rains, we must go now to meet the god of the river."

Chryssa will stay behind to look after the city in my place. With Tala, I leave something more precious to me than the city or the whole kingdom—my baby boy. Ptolemy is two years old now. Old enough to climb stairs and jump into my arms with boisterous enthusiasm, but I cannot take him on a journey into the wilderness. This is a duty for queens.

So I kiss my son's pale cheeks and surrender him into Tala's arms before mounting the camel that will take me into the desert once again. Atop *their* camels, the girls delight in this grand adventure and their excitement becomes my own.

We leave in the heat of summer, the cracked earth an oven beneath us, baking what once was grass into straw. The tribesmen hail us when they see our caravan leave the city. Women hauling bundles of twigs to burn in the hearths of their mud-brick houses stop to wave. Children drop their buckets of water and run to us for little trinkets and coins. Indigo-clad shepherds driving their flocks of woolly sheep stop to salute us with their crooks.

When we reach the wilds, the girls are delighted by the macaque monkeys who call to us from the forested hills, where pine and cedar and oak offer us cool shade beneath their green finery. We are charmed by the colorful bee-eater birds with their bright plumage in green and blue and yellow. By the ripening pears on the fruit trees. By the scent of wood smoke when we make our fires at night and sleep in tents beneath the brilliant stars. And by the far-off roar of a lion, warning that there is more than one king in these lands . . .

For the sake of my mage, we travel slowly and stop often. Thirsty, sweaty, and stinking of camels, I worry that the girls will tire and want to go home. But they seem to treasure my undivided attention now that they have me to themselves, away from court. When at last the marshy scent of the river reaches our noses, I know we are near to the place Juba discovered. The place he says is the source of the Nile. The place I first became Isis and learned the true nature of my power.

The girls sense it too. I have taught them Egyptian gods and they see Hapi in the hippos, glistening pink and gray in the water. They see Sobek in the yellow-eyed crocodiles sunning on the far shore. I tell them that we are soon to meet Osiris. I tell them how, when I was a young girl, my mother took me on her barge to Aswan so that I could see her become a vessel for Isis.

We stop where the green river is widest. With the blistering sun this high, I wear the thin white linen that Romans find so scandalous. Even so, perspiration pools between my shoulder blades. The girls sit together under a cypress tree, fanning each other with ostrich feathers, watching me prepare on the riverbank.

"If we were in Egypt, white-robed priests would gather here on the banks of the Nile," I say. "Musicians would play double-reeded clarinets, serving girls would throw pink flower petals into the water, and worshippers would kneel in homage to me, their queen, the New Isis. If we were in Egypt, I would give them the blessings of our goddess. Then I would visit the Nilometer to see how high the river has risen, which would tell me if this will be a fat year or a lean one. Here in Mauretania, though, it is not the flooding river that brings the grain. Here, we need rain. To get it, I must go into the river as a bride. A queen must be divine wife to divine husband."

Pythia narrows her eyes. I think she may have some notion of what I am saying. But Dora, my exuberant seven-year-old, pulls the ribbons from her hair, asking, "Can we swim now? We should have brought Ptolemy with us. He loves to splash in shallow water!"

"We did not bring your brother because there are some things only queens can do . . . and I mean for you both to be queens one day."

This awakens Pythia's ambition, and her curiosity too. "There are things kings can't do?"

"Can a man suckle an infant?" I ask, unbinding my hair. "He cannot. Neither can a king nourish his kingdom. He can protect and defend it. He can rule his people justly. But a king cannot feed his people except through Isis. This is why, in Egypt, no man comes to be Pharaoh without wedding Pharaoh's daughter."

My daughter nods absently, distracted by a lazy bee and I hope I was right to take her on this journey at so young an age. "I need you to listen, Dora. Every year in Egypt the river rises to wash away all the dead vegetation from the dry, cracked land. Then it leaves black fertile soil in its place. Every year in Mauretania, the rains must soak the earth to make it easier to plow. Then the farmers grow their wheat, and the laborers cut the wheat with their scythes, and the bakers make it into bread."

"I know *that*," Dora says.

"Then tell me why the Nile rises. Tell me why the rains fall," I command.

"Is it part of the Mysteries?" Pythia asks, glancing at the mage.

Euphronius sits quietly by the river, soaking his feet, a little smile of reverie upon his face. This is as close to home as he can be—and as close to home as I will ever be again. But one day, my daughter may rule all these lands. Egypt, Mauretania, all of Africa. Isidora has the claim. I must now teach her the power inside herself. "It is love that makes the river rise and the rain fall. No man can rise to create life without a lover, and neither can the god in the river."

Both girls look puzzled, so I explain, "Before the dark god Set cut Osiris into pieces, he first drowned the good god of grain in the Nile. It was on the banks of this river where Isis first wept for her murdered husband. This is where she brought him back to life with her magic. The spirit of Osiris lives here now, in the depths of the water. Here, he waits for his love, for Isis, and each year he swells to make love to her."

Pythia's eyes light with sudden insight. "And she comes to him in the person of a queen . . ."

"Just so," I say, removing the amethyst ring that once belonged to my mother but became my betrothal ring to Juba, a king, but a mortal man. "You must always love your kingdom like a faithful wife or it cannot prosper. Today I will meet the Nile like a bride to a bridegroom."

"I'm too little to be a bride," Dora points out.

I sigh at her innocence, even as I am determined to guard it. "Not for long, my sweet. One day, you'll be a beautiful maiden, then a loving mother, and then, hopefully, a wise old crone. But of these three, it's your life as a mother that will serve your people best."

"And please the king," Pythia adds.

I stiffen, my grip tightening on the betrothal ring I have just removed. "Have a child for Isis, for your kingdom, and for yourself before you do it to please any man. Your children will be rulers, and their divine ichor will come to them through their mother's milk— no matter who their father might be."

With that, I set the ring aside and wade into the shallows, my thin linen shift soaking tight against my body before I remove it, for the god. My breasts are not as firm and high as they once were, but since I have had two children of my own, perhaps the god will find me more womanly, more comely.

"What of the crocodiles?" Pythia asks, eyeing them nervously.

"Queen Selene is a vessel of Isis," my mage whispers, forgetting himself. "And when she is Isis, crocodiles will never harm her, for she is sacred to all the beasts of Egypt."

The river is as warm as a lotus-scented bath, and the frogs sing to me a song that makes my fingers tingle with *heka*. Magic is already flowing through me and not much longer will I be myself. While I am still mortal, I hold out my arms to the girls. "Come. Meet Osiris."

Eighteen

PYTHIA cautiously moves into the water, using rocks to steady her. But Dora leaps in with a splash. Her little feet don't reach the bottom, and she flails in the water until I catch her under the arms. "You carry Isis with you wherever you go, but remember that the god waits here, pining for love. For surrender and rapturous embrace. One day, you will be Isis, but now I must be."

Already, the Nile's green waves lap at my consciousness, drawing me into the marshy reeds of a waking dream where life teems. I have seen this before. I saw it the day my mother put a frog amulet around my neck and called me the Resurrection. Now my wizard does the same.

"*She is the Resurrection,*" he prays. "*She brings life from death. She gives to her kingdom an heir, she gives to her people their daily sustenance, and she gives Isis an embodiment on earth for Osiris to love.*"

I cannot make room for Isis inside myself until I loose my hold on my daughter, trusting her into Pythia's hands. Like Demeter, I must let my daughter go if I am to have her back again.

My skin tightens as the goddess comes to me, for she is so much bigger than my frail body can easily hold. I feel the stretch of her in my bones, her happiness and eager joy swelling my heart until it aches in my chest. She longs for the man she loved and lost—and I know how that feels. I may never see Helios again in this life, but perhaps I will find him again just as Isis finds Osiris through me. She smiles with my face, lifting it to the sun. She lays me back in the water and swims, arm over pale arm, fingertips brushing the lilies that float on the water. She calls to him with my tremulous voice.

And he comes to me. He caresses me with the silky stroke of silt. He kisses me with the brush of a heron's feathers on my cheeks. The hot sun is a lover's breath on my face, my neck, my breasts. He wants her. He loves her. He waits for her always. And he has her, through me.

I take my hopes, my fears, and my dreams and release them into the water with my *heka*. I let them go. I give them to him. In return, he promises me a year of plenty.

The air grows damp, heavy with dew. The birds flock. The fish leap. The reeds grow thick and green. And when I rise from the river this time, shaking the water from my hair, I am struck by the sight of the girls waist-deep in the river, praying with my mage. I am struck by it because Dora has her hands in his, *heka* dancing in her eyes as if she were drawing it from the river.

"You are going to be a very great wizard," she says to him.

The old man is so mesmerized that he admits, "No, Princess. I was once, but no more . . ."

"You will be again," Dora insists. "I see it."

At these words, my poor mage staggers, and my girls help him down to the mud, both of them tending him. They have him well in hand, stroking his cheeks with water, bringing a hat for his head.

In my life, I have so often lamented all I have lost, but I am truly blessed. The bounty promised me in that river is not merely grain. It is in my girls too. I came to teach them, and they have taught me. For I realize, in this moment, as they care for my mage, that I am not alone. My joys, my burdens, my legacy . . . they carry them too. Everything that has been prophesied of me is also in their power.

For they too are daughters of the Nile.

THE mage needs a soft bed, water aplenty, and an escape from the infernal heat of the sun. As soon as we return to the palace, I call for servants to carry him to his rooms, to bathe him and rub his chapped skin with aloe. He is determined to fast in prayer and study, but I make him eat a hearty meal of eggs and stewed lentils followed by cakes made with finely ground nut flour, still warm from the oven. And when I realize that his teeth and gums hurt him, I cut up his eggs and cakes into tiny pieces.

This infuriates him. "Majesty, leave it for servants to do!"

"Are we not all servants of Isis? Even queens? Now finish your lentils."

He sulks at my bullying, but he eats. When he is fed and settled into his bed and I have taken my own bath in lavender water, I reflect on what I have seen and what I have done and what I have still left to do. I have again gone to the river and made of myself a vessel of Isis. But still, there is no temple for her in my kingdom.

The next morning, I summon Necho of Alexandria before my throne.

He does not answer my summons.

Instead, Publius Antius Amphio appears before me, and for once, he does not stink like a brothel. He is freshly bathed and bows a little more deeply than he ever has before, expressing his gratitude at my return, a thing which, in and of itself, makes me suspicious. "Why so solicitous, Amphio?"

"Oh, I am in a very good mood today," he says. "I thought I would escort you to the site of your Iseum, where, no doubt, Necho of Alexandria is hard at work."

It does not surprise me to hear the professional jealousy in his voice. In the past few years, he has been tasked with designing baths and marketplaces and warehouses; nothing so grand as a temple. But when we are almost to the work site, I sense more than petty resentment from Amphio. Indeed, he can barely disguise a sneer.

Soon I realize why. The carriage stops at the foot of the hill where a foundation has been cut into the soil and bricklayers toil. I am disarmed by how little progress has been made. Why, it barely looks as if any work has been done at all. And Necho is nowhere to be found . . .

The foreman sees me and my guards and comes swiftly, wiping mortar on his tunic. "Majesty! We were not warned of your visit or we would have taken some trouble to welcome you."

"Tell her what you're doing," Amphio barks at the foreman.

"We are laying bricks, of course," the foreman replies.

But glancing up at the workmen, I see that they are not laying bricks. They are pulling them down. "What, exactly, is going on here?" I demand to know.

Amphio is only too happy to show me, offering his arm to help me climb up to what *ought to be* the base of a magnificent temple. Over the foreman's objection, the Roman architect takes hold of a brick and taps it on the ground, then crumbles it in his palm. My eyes widen. Either this Roman has strength beyond normal men or . . .

"These bricks were cured only this summer in a too-hot sun," Amphio explains. "They were not fired in a kiln. Nor were they given time to dry all the way through. It is the kind of mistake not even an apprentice would make."

The bricklayers fall silent in agreement and I am forced to ask, "Are you saying this is the doing of Necho of Alexandria? That he ordered inferior bricks be used on my Iseum?"

Amphio grunts. "That and more. See here. Look at the foundation. This is not good ground to build on. That is why—"

"I've seen enough—"

Insolently, he raises his voice so that his words run over mine. "*That is why* you see this tiny crack here. One day it will become a very large crack. Then your precious goddess—I assume you will make a statue to her—will come tumbling down with the rest of it."

"You are saying that my architect is incompetent? Necho is known by name and reputation as a great talent."

Amphio bleats with triumph. "I am saying he's a fraud! Any letters recommending him were undoubtedly forged. I doubt very much that the man who has presented himself at your court is Necho of Alexandria or any sort of architect at all. What I am saying, Majesty, is that you have been duped."

*   *   *

THUMBING the hilt of his sword, Memnon growls. "Necho must be ridden down, captured, and beheaded."

Chryssa is even thirstier for vengeance. "A beheading is too good for the thief. To think how we sponsored countless smelly *garum* factories to pay for nothing!"

Time wasted. A fortune squandered. How is it that I continue to fail at everything I was supposedly born to do? Brooding, I decide, "We're not going to behead him. We're going to let him disappear into the desert."

Chryssa's eyes bulge. "*Why* would we do that?"

"Because I cannot let it be known what a fool I am. Yes, I was a credulous *fool*. Now I'm going to pay a heavy price for that foolishness without even the satisfaction of seeing justice done to a man who would steal from a goddess!"

Publius Antius Amphio leans idly back on his seat, braced upon both elbows in supreme satisfaction. "It isn't a total disaster, Majesty."

By the gods, I want to cut the insolent smirk off his face. "Say what you mean, Amphio."

His smirk widens to a grin. "Now you have the chance to start again. A hill in the Greek quarter amidst all the clacking wagons and crowded streets was never a good place for your Iseum."

"You think you know a better place?"

"Aye and so do you, madam. Wouldn't you like to open your linen drapes and be able to see your great vain tribute to your imaginary goddess? Wouldn't you like your temple to be, like the Parthenon in Athens, the first thing *anyone* sees?"

He has my rapt attention now.

"Build it on the island with your lighthouse," he suggests, with a sweep of his hand. "Build it there and it will be the first thing anyone sees coming to this city and the last thing they see before they leave."

I close my eyes, imagining it beneath the flutter of my lashes. The blazing fires of the lighthouse reflected off a golden roof like a glow of salvation. A temple that will dazzle in daylight and shine like a beacon in the night. A temple here, near my throne. A proclamation to all who come to our shores that Isis has come again to her throne through me. And it is an arrogant, godless Roman who gives me this vision.

"Will you build it?" I ask, opening my eyes again.

Amphio sits up. "If I am given a free hand I can start in the springtime. We'll use concrete where convenient, but we'll also need travertine—quarried and cut into blocks. We'll need bronze struts and iron bands. We'll need marble for the facing. We'll need gold, Majesty. Lots of gold."

Chryssa pales, nearly paralyzed by this litany of expenses. I think she will say it cannot be done.

But her eyes meet mine and she says only, "I will find the money."

"I want to learn curses," I tell the mage. "And don't pretend you haven't mastered such spells, because I have scented dark magic on your clothes since I was a child."

"As your mother's wizard, it was my place to master them. But dark magic is not an art you want to learn."

"I cannot send soldiers after Necho of Alexandria, but he should not escape justice completely. You must show me."

He teaches me the incantations and rituals to call forth my *heka* and turn it to vengeance, but I realize that he is only humoring me when he adds, "Of course, you would need some essence of him—his urine, his semen, his saliva. Something of his body."

This I do not have. "Should I send servants to search his empty apartments for a stray hair or nail clipping?"

"Majesty, I have told you before that all magic cuts its way out of you. Curses have especially jagged edges and hooks that take chunks of you with them. Even with careful wording, dark magic may come back upon you. It is a thing to be feared and used sparingly, which is why the laying of curses is work for mages, not for monarchs . . ."

But he cannot do it for me. He drew his magic from the Temples of Isis in Egypt and has too little to spare. I draw my magic from wherever I feel her presence. That is why my blood is infused with *heka* and he, having forsaken Egypt to follow me, has withered in his powers. If a curse is to be laid upon this villain, I must be the one to do it. But before I can send for servants to scour the architect's room for some trace of his person, my mage asks, "Majesty, do you not think Isis can avenge herself without your prompting?"

This question strips me of my high-minded reasons and makes me suspect that the honor I seek to avenge is my own. In the matter of the architect, I allowed myself to be guided by too much prejudice and too much pride. Can I justly curse Necho of Alexandria—or whatever his true name is—without also cursing myself?

"He is beneath you, Majesty," the old man advises. "Save your wrath for worthier opponents."

Grudgingly, I accept his counsel. I do not want to be like the emperor used to be, punishing most severely the faults in others that found a source in himself. Augustus was a man who seldom forgave and never forgot, and I am desperate to believe that he is my apprentice now, and that I am no longer his . . .

THE king returns at the head of a legion.

A year and a half my husband has been gone, and in that time, he has raised troops enough for a light infantry and a fearsome cavalry. I know better than to ask too closely as to how this was accomplished. Juba has equipped them with the finest mounts and says our Berbers are the best horsemen in Africa. Some are archers, others carry javelins, and some fight with swords, but they are all trained for quick strikes, and even the Romans praise them for agility on their fleet-footed mounts.

After their parade into the city, the king dismounts, greeting me formally. I greet him just as formally, though it is a struggle not to smile. At fourteen, Pythia bows with poise. I have taught Dora to bow to the king too, but she is so excited that she runs to him, crashing into his legs. Juba stoops to kiss her hair, then scoops our son out of my arms. I fear that little Ptolemy will not know his father, but he laughs as if he only saw him yesterday.

I throw a fine banquet to celebrate the king's return, during which Crinagoras recites his new poem about the lion that would have eaten my Berber woman did she not command him in my name. Juba is amazed by this story, asking for details I had not thought to, such as whether anyone else was harmed by the lion before it was captured or killed. He wants the lion's pelt to present as a gift to me, but I remind him that it was Tala, and even the half-wild boy, Tacfarinas, who were heroic and deserving of reward.

"Yes, what will you have of us, Tala?" the king asks.

She shrewdly turns away his largesse, insisting that she would rather hold a favor in reserve one day when she might need it more. Such is the practicality of Berbers.

"Surely you want something, Tacfarinas," the king says, motioning to the boy. "Maysar tells me that you will grow up to be a true horseman."

The Berber boy seems startled by the praise and pushes out his chest. "I can ride without saddle cloth or reins. Give me two javelins and a round shield of hide and I can harry my enemies."

This makes our soldiers laugh, for it is a proud boast for a boy so sleight of build. Give him two javelins and a round shield of hide and he would stagger under the weight. Still, Juba rubs his chin and pretends to consider it. "Perhaps, when you are of age, you would like to serve in my cavalry and harry *my* enemies?"

Delight shines in the boy's eyes. "I would gladly serve a true Berber king."

My husband raises his goblet in a toast. "What am I if not a true Berber king? I am Juba the son of Juba. I am a descendant of Masinissa. Kin of Jugurtha too."

Of those names, only Masinissa was loved by the Romans. The rest were rebels and the boy must know it too. "Will you join with our Berber brothers in fighting the Romans near Egypt?"

I shoot a potent glare at Lady Lasthenia, who is to bring me such news before I hear it anywhere else. "What fighting near Egypt?"

It is the king who answers me, reminding me that when he moved his court to Volubilis, most dispatches from Rome were sent there too. "There is a rebellion on the border of Egypt, near Cyrenaica. The Garamantes who survived the campaign fought by Lucius Cornelius Balbus have made alliance with other tribes. Publius Sulpicius Quirinius is leading legions into the interior of Africa."

"We should fight Quirinius," Tacfarinas insists, heedless of the many Romans in our court who would count this akin to treasonous rebellion. "We should come to the aid of our Berber brothers."

Seeking to tamp down the fire in the boy's words, Juba says, "I did not raise a legion to go to war, but to see that we don't have to. Have our brothers not had enough fighting, Tacfarinas?"

"But this time, they will *win*. The Garamantes worship Egyptian gods. They have with them a warrior forged of fire. *Horus the Avenger* they call him, and he will burn all our enemies to dust."

With my hand, I cover a gasp. *Horus the Avenger.* Still fighting Rome on the borders of Egypt. If it's true—if it is not just a rumor, not just legend—then it is proof that Helios still lives. It has been years since I saw my twin with my own eyes, kissed him with my fevered lips, caressed his cheeks with my fingers. And this news awakens me as if from a long sleep. It puts a terror in me that my twin may yet be caught, captured, dragged before the emperor, and revealed by name. No, not Helios. He would die before giving Augustus that satisfaction. But oh, he is not dead. If it is true what the Berber boy has said, then Helios must be somewhere in this world, and the relief I feel is such that I am suddenly dizzied . . .

When I sway, Juba stares at me, and I am forced to look away. Heedless of how his words have affected me—indeed, how they have shocked the whole court—the boy goes on. "We should ally with the Garamantes, Majesty. Do that, and we will fight for you to the end."

Juba should grab Tacfarinas by the tunic and shake him, threaten him, and make a great show of displeasure, but the king surprises me by laughing. "Well, if the Garamantes have a god such as Horus on their side, they hardly need our help, do they?"

The king's jest cuts the tension. Laughter rings throughout our hall. Even the Romans laugh. Only Tacfarinas stands before his king red-faced, for he has been made to look like an inconsequential little boy. Sensing the boy's shame, Juba says, "Come work in my stables, Tacfarinas. I will have you as my groom and give you a horse of your own."

It is too generous a gift for even a resentful boy to turn aside, and Tacfarinas bobs his head in submission. I think Juba will regret this offer, for Tacfarinas will most likely take his horse and ride off into the hills where we found him, never to be seen again. But perhaps it would be better for us if he did.

That night, as the banquet draws to a close, leaving us to finish up the dregs of our wine with only a few intimates, talk turns to our new settlers. Some are Isis worshippers. Some are merchants and moneylenders. But most are discharged soldiers, fresh from the legions, who are to be settled in our lands in keeping with the promise that Augustus made to them. It is their payment for many years of service, but they come at the expense of our Berber tribes, who must make way for these settlers.

Berber grazing lands are being turned into farmland, and the arrival of settlers brings a flood of court proceedings surrounding property. The need for magistrates is so patently obvious that not even the Romans object to my presiding over disputes. "You are, perhaps, a better judge than I am," Juba confesses.

"To the contrary," I protest, glad of his return and hoping he can sense it. "You've memorized every point of Roman law and understand how to make them work with our own. It is only that I find out the liars more easily than you do."

"You have help in that, do you not?" the king asks, gaze falling upon Chryssa. "Your freedwoman has made a terror of herself to every farmer, merchant, and shipowner who does business with the crown. I am told she makes them account for every copper."

"Is that true?" I ask her.

Chryssa is unrepentant. "If the king and queen wish to forgive the thievery of their subjects, it is within their powers. Your Majesties, it is for *you* to be benevolent, but your council should be merciless with those who try to steal from you."

Whatever happened to the sweet slave girl who first knelt to me in homage, so timid even in speaking the name of Isis? Her freedom in Mauretania has made her bold, but then, has it not done the same for me? I glance at the king to see what he thinks of Chryssa's exacting standards.

"I cannot find it within myself to argue with your freedwoman," he says. "So long as such officiousness does not end in her murder at the hands of an aggrieved banker."

Maysar idly strokes the weapon at his hip. "Hopefully fear of her fierce Berber husband and his big shining sword should serve to protect her."

We all laugh. Then, with eagerness in his eyes, Juba reaches across the couch to lace his fingers with mine. "Come, wife. We should leave our companions to their reunion and indulge in a happy reunion of our own."

Nineteen

MAKE the arrangements swiftly, Julia writes. *And your niece can be a queen before the year's end.*

Apparently, King Polemon of Pontus is in dire need of a wife. Julia has secured Agrippa's permission for him to marry Pythia, so we will not need to ask the emperor. Unfortunately, King Polemon has a different bride in mind. Throwing open a chest of exotic gifts, fragrant herbs and spices, shining silks, and golden leaves pounded thin as papyri, the king's emissary says, "My king offers this and more for your daughter, Cleopatra Isidora, heir of the Ptolemies."

Juba gives the answer we've been giving since Herod's proposal. "Isidora is too young and my wife will not part with her yet."

Wearing a cone-shaped hat and a robe of silver mesh, the emissary glances to where Pythia sits with the rest of my women. "Your princess looks ready for marriage. If a girl so beautiful has not already caught the attention of men twice her age, she soon will. Especially when you leave her free to be seen by all those who come to court."

If he thinks to argue his way into a marriage agreement, he has miscalculated. I do not like his manner and my husband likes it even less. Juba snaps, "That is my wife's niece you look upon so boldly and without my leave."

Another girl might blush and let her pretty dark eyes fall to the mosaic floor, but fifteen-year-old Pythia lifts her chin. I've not raised her to hide in the women's quarters or veil her face from the gaze of men and I feel strangely proud of her for this decided lack of modesty. So I say, "If your king is content to have my niece—as the emperor's daughter assures me he is—we might consider it. But a marriage between the King of Pontus and my daughter is quite impossible."

We should not have to say it. He should have known better than to ask, but Herod set the shameless example . . .

The emissary withdraws to consider. And that night, we bring out the maps. Pythia runs her fingers over the vellum, murmuring, "With the combined kingdoms of Pontus and the Bosporus, we would have dominion almost over the entirety of the Black Sea . . ."

It would be a marriage of great advantage to us, but I don't think Pythia understands what it will entail. "King Polemon is not a young man. You would not be his first woman, nor his first bride."

Fortunately, she is not naive, this girl that I have helped to raise. "I hope he is old. I hope he is *very* old, so that he will need my companionship, comfort, and care. I can give those things. They are a small price to pay for a throne."

They are, to be sure, less than the price I paid for mine.

She understands the way of the world. She has no romantic notions. What a magnificent queen she will make! But it hurts my heart to think of parting with her. "You would be amongst strangers, Pythia. Do you understand how far away those kingdoms are?"

"I've been to Pontus. My father owned an estate there. I remember because when we went, my mother bought me a hat of pure snowy white rabbit fur to guard against the cold."

The pining in her voice echoes deep within me. I have tried to make Mauretania her home, but always some part of her heart is in the East. "Pythia, you've no need to leave this court. There is always a place for you here. You are as a daughter to me."

Her dark eyes soften. "But I do not have the blood of the Ptolemies. I cannot be a daughter to you."

Taking her face in my hands, I say, "Isis brought us together and your mother gave you to me. Don't you know that I love you?"

My heart breaks at the sudden tears that spill over her cheeks. Have I never said this to her before? Surely I have. But somehow

I have never made her believe it. What a wretched woman I am. Wiping the tears from her cheeks, I say, "Pythia, know that I love you and that you don't have to go."

"But shouldn't I? If I *did* have the blood of the Ptolemies, what would I do?"

I smile, bittersweet. "What would a princess do when a golden crown and glorious future is in her reach? She would snatch it up with the unrelenting grasp of a Ptolemy Eagle."

She will have him, I decide. No Eastern king will refuse my niece, the granddaughter of Mark Antony. Pythia is a kinswoman to the imperial family through the Antonias. She is their niece as well as mine. And if she wants King Polemon for a groom, she will have him.

EVERYONE wants Isidora. Julia's inquiries on behalf of my niece have touched off a flurry of betrothal offers for my daughter that I suspect would never have taken place if we had sent Herod away in utter disgrace. The offers become a topic of discussion in the council chambers with our advisers. Resting comfortably on his ivory throne, my husband observes, "The Emesans do not even ask a dowry."

"Princess Isidora's bloodline is a dowry richer than the Emesans deserve," Lady Lasthenia says crossly. "What foreign prince is worthy of a Ptolemaic princess?"

"None of us are," my husband says, sighing with amusement.

He seems not to realize that a good number of our advisers are not at all amused. Many of them are status-conscious Alexandrians who are indignant at these proposals of marriage from lesser kings. "We are not entertaining the offers," I say, hoping to forestall criticism.

"Not now anyway," Juba adds. "But one day Isidora must leave us for some foreign prince."

This gives me a start. "Why must she?"

Juba tilts his head to slant me a glance. "Who else is she going to marry? Her brother?"

The king asks this with a contemptuous laugh and several Romans laugh with him as if none of them realize the insult. For nearly three hundred years my family practiced brother-sister marriage, a tradition all-but-abandoned by my mother with the gravest consequences. When Juba and his men laugh, they are laughing at my family. Humiliation scorches my cheeks, and our Alexandrians stiffen in their seats, a schism in our court widening before my very eyes. Lady Lasthenia reddens, arguing, "King Juba, this is the way of royal dynasties in the East."

"Not all of them, surely," Juba says with a tight smile. "Or we wouldn't be receiving all these offers."

My poet takes up the argument, going on to list all the kingdoms that follow the practice of brother-sister marriage, finishing with, "Why, at present, there is only one sister left for the King of Commagene to marry off because he married the other."

At last, Juba seems to sense that our courtiers do not see the world with Roman eyes, but he is not chastened. "Well, they may do as they like in the East, but it will not happen here."

My nostrils flare at the autocracy of his words, but I keep my silence.

Crinagoras rises to his feet to address the king again. "Having served in many royal courts I would remind you that there are good reasons—good political reasons—not to give hope to foreign kings that they may lay claim to your throne or to the bloodline of the Ptolemies."

At this, Juba turns to face me. "Is that what you want, Selene? Our nine-year-old daughter and our four-year-old son to cease being innocent siblings, everything corrupted between them by a betrothal?"

The pain this question causes me is acute—a band of agony squeezing tightly at my throat, suffocating any reply I might make. He asks this of me as if the notion were absurd. A disgrace. So distasteful an idea that I should be ashamed. And I am ashamed, for his words are not only a slap to the traditions of Egypt, but a condemnation of the love I found with my twin—a love I have hidden and denied, a love I have sacrificed at an inestimable price to my soul.

Of course I don't want our children to marry. I cannot even imagine it. Ptolemy runs after Isidora when she is at play and she is patient with his boyish ways. She holds his hand when he goes up and down the stairs and coddles him when he falls and cries. Everything they do, they do in innocence. They are a sister and a brother, nothing more. They are not like Helios and me.

No. I absolutely do not want them to marry. And yet, the king has called me out in front of our entire court. "What I want is to make a wise and considered choice for Princess Isidora. One that is in keeping with my duty to our kingdom and the distinguished lineage of my ancestors . . ."

It is as tempered a reply as anyone could possibly expect from me under the circumstances, but it seems to anger the king. Or perhaps Juba is smarting from having been lectured to by the Easterners in our court who will always see me as my mother's heir and him as the husband who was forced upon me by the emperor.

In a rare fit of temper, my husband dismisses our council, retreating with his Roman companions, leaving me behind with only a few of my intimates.

"That was a most unfortunate dispute," my poet says.

"Do not make much of it," I warn. "Do not make record of it in your poems. It was only a disagreement and it is years before a decision must be made about Isidora's future."

"Nevertheless, the king seems unprepared for it. He is too much Roman . . ."

In spite of the fact that Juba has wounded me, I argue in his defense. "Maybe we are too much Greek or Egyptian. Our Berbers have their own royal traditions. Why, they even divide their kingdoms between all their sons."

"Which has proved a disaster for them!" Crinagoras has had an unusually long career, serving as an ambassador for his home of Mytilene long before I was born. He politicked with my mother, my father, Julius Caesar, and Pompey the Great, and has made the acquaintance of nearly every king in the empire. I am fortunate to have him at my side, even if he is vain, boastful, and dismissive of my Berbers. "King Juba has no standing upon which to show you such disrespect."

"Juba didn't grow up in a royal court. He doesn't understand."

"That much is plain. If King Juba gives the impression that he will happily accept a foreign prince for his daughter, what will happen to your reputation? Your bloodline is your claim to Egypt. Your claim to the legacy of Alexander the Great. It is bad enough, they say, that your mother let two Romans sire her children, but at least those Romans were the most powerful men in the world. Now *your* children's blood has been diluted with that of a jumped-up barbarian—"

"You speak of your king!" I hiss, whirling upon him.

"He is not my king," Crinagoras reminds me, unrepentant. "I am a free citizen of Mytilene. I serve Cleopatra's daughter . . ."

"You do not serve me when you speak of my husband with scorn. There are limits to my tolerance and I will send you back to Mytilene within the hour on the leakiest ship I can find if you do not recant."

"Your Majesty," he begins, only a touch more conciliatory, "I am merely repeating what is said of your husband. These are not my words. I know that King Juba is a civilized king. Perhaps the most civilized king. But he does not behave in keeping with the expectations for a *Hellenistic* king. He has not paid visit to Greece. He's sponsored no monuments in Athens. He shows no interest in sponsoring the Olympic Games and allowed your contributions to be dwarfed by King Herod. Already you find it difficult to lure artists and engineers and scholars to Mauretania—and those that *do* come, come because of the prestige of being able to say they served in a Ptolemaic court. Without that, what do you have?"

LATE that night, Juba comes to me, stumbling, drunk, and angry. We are, neither of us, in any good temper. But I do not want to quarrel. I missed him too much when he was gone, so when he puts his hands on me, I let them roam and pretend that wine has not made him clumsy. As the servants melt away, snuffing out candles and lamps as they go, I let the king pull me down onto a bed piled high with embroidered pillows. Encircled by a canopy of gauzy linen that sways in the sea-scented breeze, I let him strip me of my clothes. I remember how it was when I went to meet the god in the river, where my womb opened like the blossoming of a lily. When my body became an instrument of life. I want another child, so, like the goddess opened herself to the god, I try to open myself for my husband.

But I cannot do it.

You would never allow such a thing to happen unless your husband has become so inconvenient that you desire to be made a widow.

The emperor's threat echoes in my mind. I do not want to be a widow and now I can think of nothing but how I gamble with my husband's life. When it is finished, I know that I am not with child. I think Juba knows it too. Years now, he has kept to the terms of our bargain. When we come together, he doesn't speak of it. He doesn't ask me questions or force me to examine my desires. He doesn't press me to name my feelings or even to acknowledge what we do together when we are alone. He doesn't try to unmask me or to delve beneath the surface of what I am willing to show him. And because he has not demanded that I give him my whole self, I have been able to give him a small part. If he sees that the seeds of my fondness for him might blossom into something more—he has been wise enough not to say so.

At least until now.

In the dark, his words are whispers against the pillow. "Do you love another man, Selene?"

The question catches me by the throat. *Do I love another man?* I am only half of one soul—I came into this world with another—and to be without him is a wound that never heals. It is a wound I bandage over with the fabric of my life in Mauretania. It is a wound so deep and hidden that it is not safe to touch. *Helios.* Horus the

Avenger. Whatever name they call him now, he is my twin, my other half, and the strength of everything I do.

Yet the purity of our bond would be something Juba considers *corrupted*.

It does not matter, I tell myself. It was Juba that I married, but Helios was always the husband of my heart and now I am a guilty adulteress, no matter what I do. I cannot let myself love Juba without betraying my very soul, and I cannot love Helios and give myself wholly to the man in my arms . . . even though I want to.

I want to. I *want* to. But why should it matter? Where in all the royal marriages of the world would it matter?

My husband waits on my answer, but no good can come of telling him the truth. It will only wound him or enrage him or both. I resolve to lie to him as I have lied to him for years. But Juba's hands are now so gentle as he strokes me, that in this moment of intimacy, skin to skin, I cannot force myself to speak words of deceit.

The king takes my silence for an answer. "Will he take you from me?"

"No," I say, and it is true. My twin will fight for Egypt. He will fight the Romans to the end of his days. But he has left me to this life. He has left me to this man. He will not take me from Juba.

Juba has always believed that it is Augustus who stands between him and my heart. It is the farthest thing from the truth, but it is a lie that protects us all. If Juba knew my brother was alive, he would betray him to the emperor. And if he knew that Helios had been my lover, he would hold me in contempt for more than a betrayal of our marriage bed.

Once, I would not have cared whether Juba held me in contempt. He would not have been able to pierce my Ptolemaic armor with his disdain. But that is all changed now. And so I squeeze my eyes shut, praying that he does not ask me to explain myself. By the gods, let this be the end of it!

The king should close his eyes, sink into the cushions, and let

Dionysus carry him off in drunken dreams, but he asks one last question. "Will you dishonor me with him?"

He does not ask if I *have* dishonored him, for he has always assumed as much. In this, he simply asks a promise. I don't know if I can keep it but I make it anyway. "No. I won't."

My husband exhales and I know we will not speak of it again. We will both pretend he has never asked these questions and that I never answered them. We will forget these words like the nonsensical things uttered in the madness of ecstasy when a man and a woman come together in the night—words that cannot be examined in the light of day. Words that *must* not be examined in the light of day.

Twenty

"*HORUS the Avenger*," Euphronius mutters.

He is almost always to be found in his rooms now. His eyes have become so cloudy that it is hard for him to see, making it too difficult for him to walk the grounds of the palace on his own. So isolated is he, here amidst his old magic wands, dried herbs, and caged birds, that I cannot imagine how he has come to hear the gossip.

"You have heard about the fighting near Egypt," I say, irritated that his servants have not swept up the birdseeds from the tile. What if he should slip and fall? "Who told you?"

"The stable boy. Tacfarinas. He comes with Dora to read for me sometimes. I cannot read the recipes for my own potions anymore. I cannot sketch plants for the king's books anymore either, but the boy can do it."

Setting aside my surprise, I try to cheer him. "The king intends to name a plant after you. Euphorbian, it will be called."

I think this will make him smile, but he glowers. "That is not my name."

I had hoped that our trip to the Nile the previous year would have lifted his spirits, but he seems older, frailer, and more defeated than I have ever known him to be before. Pressing my lips together, I ask, "Do you want to go to Helios? To *Horus the Avenger*? I told you again and again that he lives and now I can even tell you where he will be found. Near Cyrenaica, on the border of Egypt, fighting with the Garamantes."

The mage's lips turn down at the corners, his whole face droop-
ing, jowls and all. "Majesty, he will not be found there. He will not
be found in this world."

I groan in frustration, throwing myself down upon a dusty couch
amidst dusty scrolls and stray feathers. "Even now you will persist
in telling me that my twin is dead?"

"Do you know what made me a powerful seer, Majesty? It was
not that I saw into the Rivers of Time. Many magicians can do that.
Some of them—including your mother—could see all the possibilities. All the potential in the world. But I always saw things differently. When I scried, I saw only the directions *my* River of Time
could still flow. I tell you now, when I left your twin brother in
Thebes, I knew I would never see him alive again. All other possibilities flowed away. Helios disappeared from the Rivers of Time.
He simply disappeared."

It is a crushing thing to hear, a thing I refuse to hear. "For you,
perhaps. Perhaps *you* will never see him alive again. But I have seen
him with my own eyes."

"Maybe you are the only one who can."

"What do you mean by that?" I ask shrilly. "What can you
mean?"

Pressing his cheek against his staff, he says, "You were born sacred
twins, two halves of one soul. Perhaps you can see him because you
are now joined together."

The word *joined* makes me blush. I have never spoken to my
mage of how I took Helios for a lover, though it is unlikely to shock
him. Perhaps I have not spoken of it because the Romans have taught
me to be ashamed. Or perhaps it is because what passed between
Helios and me was never tradition, or legacy, or politics. Our stolen
nights on the Isle of Samos are the only memories of true love that
I will ever have. Our lovemaking was *lovemaking*, secret and sacred.
Ours alone.

I will not share those nights with anyone else, even by speaking
of them.

"Majesty, if Helios lives in this world, he does so inside of you."

"Then where is he?" I demand. "I do not see him now. And I long for him. You have no idea how I long for him." He must think me a madwoman, and maybe I am. I have lost too many people not to be a little mad, I think. But I will go *completely* mad if I allow this talk to continue. "Helios fought the Romans with the Kandake of Meroë in Egypt. Now he is fighting with the Garamantes. You heard the boy say it. Tacfarinas said the people whispered of a mage called *Horus the Avenger*. That is where you can find him, Euphronius. With the Garamantes. Not here. Not in me."

"There are always rumors in Africa of *Horus the Avenger*. It is a story as old as the world, and people tell it because they want to believe in it. They want to hope when hope is lost."

"I have not lost hope," I say. "And you are wrong to let yourself lose faith in it."

The old man's head bows at my chastisement. He is silent for many moments. When he speaks, it is with grave resignation. "I have been wrong about a good many things, Majesty. So let me help you in the one way I might still be useful. Let us take no chances with your new Iseum. Let me help you consecrate the spot for Isis before Amphio's workers break ground."

Can this mean that he has given himself over to my vision of how our goddess must be saved, not in Egypt, but here in Mauretania? This does lift my spirits. And because I do not wish to argue with him anymore, I am swift to agree.

The mage insists on being shaved bald for the ritual, and dresses in linen as a priest of Isis must. We go alone when the sun has set, because my goddess is the mistress over the moon that is my namesake. It is slow going, every part of it difficult for him, even though he leans upon his staff on one side and my arm on the other. My poor mage is so much older now than when we started this journey. He is brittle only in bone and near-broken in spirit. I hope this rite will inspire and rejuvenate him.

Beneath the silver glow of the moon, he encourages me to go barefoot onto the soil, walking patterns the mage taught me long ago, searching with my feet for any evil spells. My toes curl into the earth, searching for the *heka* of pain or suffering, the lingering laments of the dying. Sensing no tales of woe, I go to my knees. Pressing my hands to the ground I push a tiny bit of my magic into the soil and draw it back in again, communing with the island, letting it speak to me, delighted when it tells me only the stories of sailors and fishes.

"It is a good place for an Iseum," I declare, holding a lantern high.

"Are you certain, Majesty?"

For a moment, I think I have missed some trace of dark magic. Then I realize he is not asking me if this site is fit for a temple. He is asking me if I am certain of the course I have chosen. There was a time when I was uncertain—a time, even, when I doubted my faith. A time when I turned from Isis, her worshippers, and all their hopes for me. But I am on the right path now. Even if Helios is alive, fighting a world away, I was born for a different battle. "Before she died, my mother said that rulers choose what ink to write in. Blood, sweat, or tears. Well, I have written in all three."

"You have had little choice in the matter, Majesty . . ."

"Perhaps the gods will remember it that way. But in my hour of judgment, when my heart is weighed for sin, I would have Isis know that I used the hands she wrote upon to do work that glorified her and lifted up others in her name. People have looked to me and called me savior. They ask me for salvation and they will find it in this temple. It does not matter that it is here and not in Egypt. Even if my name is never whispered after I am gone, even if this temple crumbles to dust, they will still speak of Isis. And I will have saved her . . ."

Tears glisten in his rheumy eyes. "But I will still have failed. I was to see you restored to Egypt. But I have failed in everything. I failed your mother. I failed Isis. I failed you."

I put down the lamp, take his wrinkled face in my hands, and make him look at me. "You never failed my mother. You never failed Isis. And no matter what I have said in the past, you never failed me. You have given your whole life to us. Your queens do not forget. Not Isis, not my mother, and not me. Tonight we begin something new. Something pure. Something that will live on long before we pass into the Rivers of Time."

There is no question in my voice. No sadness or doubt. Only faith. He hears it too. He withdraws from my touch, taking up a censer of burning incense. "Then I will help you. In this and in everything."

Lighting candles in a circle on the soon-to-be sacred spot, I pour Nile water into a lotus cup. Facing Egypt, I lift the bowl and let moonlight touch its surface with silver before calling upon the blood, the power, and the purifying winds. My gown billows into the sky as the forces of Isis cleanse us of all that has come before. And in a cloud of fragrant smoke, my mage calls upon the eternal flame of our goddess to make this place her own.

Bathed in pale moonlight, he walks in the circle we've made and hums a song I have never before heard. Like a murmur of butterfly wings, like the music of flowers when they spray pollen into the sky, like the first ripple on a calm pool of water. I do as he has taught me, making the bones of my feet hollow things through which my *heka* may flow, and I feel my lightest magic mix beneath me with the tinier but more potent tendrils that belong to the mage.

The world spins beneath me as he makes himself a part of this place, boldly venturing forth like a lion, noble as an elephant who never forgets. He gives all his magic to this ground, like marrow squeezed from bone. He gives himself to my land of salty ocean spray, hot winds, and desert grasses. He gives himself to my kingdom, to Isis, to me. He plants himself here, in this soil, like the seeds of what will become an endless sea of grain.

And then I know he is dying.

He taught me once that it costs nothing to take magic into your body, but it will carve its way out of you. It is carving its way out of the mage now, leaching from his bones, ravaging his body. I try to stop him. I reach for him, trying to push the life force into him. But what I give of myself he will not take. How desperately I cling to him, trying to keep him here in this world with me. But always I have been his student, and even now he has more to teach me.

He is no longer a man of failing sight, sagging skin, and bent back. He is a child of Isis and made of more than these bits of flesh and bone. He is, on this night, a breathtaking mirror of the gods. He is not weary and old. He is a young man again, towering in determination and joy. How happily he shows me the essence of him. How lightly he lets go of all that has ever held him here as he consecrates this sacred ground. He makes himself as peaceful as a silver thread, glimmering in moonlight, as light as a feather, as free as a floating drape of silk.

And then he falls.

I cradle him in my lap, my tears falling upon his cheeks. Why, *why* did he insist we come here this night, keeping from me his true purpose? He knew. He *knew* what he would do. But never would I have let him do this, if *I* had known. "That is why," he says, with a peaceful smile. "Do not mourn. Princess Isidora saw it truly. I have become a great wizard again. I have lived long and I am not gone."

The curve of his smile becomes the waves in my ocean. His breath becomes the night mist. His open palms become the petals of lilies floating on the Nile. The spark in his eyes becomes the fire in my lighthouse. And I know now that I must never, ever let it burn out . . .

I pack his magic wands carefully in fine-spun silk cloth and set them into a chest with the divination cups and alabaster lamps and magic amulets. His books and sketches I will give to the king, but I do not know what to do with the bundles of herbs and incense.

The birds I set free.

I am still standing there by the window with an empty cage when I hear someone knock at my mage's door. Let them knock. I will not answer. I made plain to the servants that I do not want to be disturbed. But whoever it is braves my wrath by coming into the room without my leave.

"Selene?" It is the king. I know his voice. But it seems so far away. "What are you doing here?"

"I am mourning."

Juba comes to my side, taking the cage from my hands, his eyebrows furrowed. "I know it took you some time to warm to my physician and I am glad he won you over, but I'm sorry to see you so very sad at his passing . . ."

He does not know what Euphronius was to me.

He has never known.

And that is my fault.

"He was a priest of Isis," I say, tilting my head back to swallow my emotions down. "A great wise man of Egypt. He was my mother's wizard—a man feared by even the Romans, in his time."

Juba shakes his head in confusion. "Are we speaking of Euphorbus Musa? Brother of the emperor's physician?"

I turn to face him, wondering what difference it makes now. This is one lie amongst so many. Why is it that now, after so many years, I feel the need to tell him so many painful truths? "We misled you. He called himself Euphorbus at my command. His name was Euphronius and he was my mother's wizard. He was the mage who helped Helios escape from the emperor all those years ago."

My husband's eyes fly wide as if he cannot decide to be furious or appalled. "Do you mean to say that for *years* now, you have let me shelter one of the emperor's enemies, here in my court?"

Nodding, I say, "I was afraid that if you knew who he really was, you would tell the emperor. I was afraid you would have given the old man over to the Romans to be tortured or killed."

Juba's jaw snaps shut and he stares hard, clenching a fist. But he docs not say that I was wrong to fear it. That *is* what he would have done and we both know it. I was right to keep it from him. I was *right* to do it.

Suddenly, the king throws down the cage with a clatter. "Who else knew? Half our court hails from Cleopatra's Alexandria. They knew him, did they not? Memnon, Lasthenia, Crinagoras, and the others . . . all this time, they said nothing!"

"Many of my mother's intimates took new names after the war," I explain, quick to defend my favorites. "They keep one another's secrets as a matter of survival."

Juba stares at me as if he cannot quite fathom that I could have deceived him about such a thing and for so very long. "What of Musa? Did you never worry the emperor's physician might deny having a brother?" His eyes go wider at my silence. "By the gods, Selene! Just how intricate a conspiracy did you weave?"

"Musa knows. And I think Dora knows. When I took the girls to the river, I think she saw him true. She has the gift of sight—a gift he had too."

It is too much for the king to hear. He shoves his fingers through his hair, squeezing his eyes shut. "This is madness."

"It doesn't matter now," I say, blinking back tears. "Euphronius is dead. The emperor cannot hurt him now. Augustus need never know the truth unless you tell him."

"Tell him?" The king laughs with bitter indignation. "What purpose would it serve to tell the emperor what a gullible fool I have been? Better for him to question my loyalty than to know I have been a blind half-wit. A mockery in my own palace!"

"You are not a mockery."

"Oh, no? Then why tell me this now . . . unless it is to laugh at me? I would never have known the truth. Why tell me now, after all these years?"

I meet his eyes in plaintive desperation. "Because there is no one else I can tell but you. Because I am filled with sorrow and there is nowhere else I can turn but to you."

Why do I give him power over me? I have made myself so vulnerable! He can betray me to the emperor. He can punish my loved ones. He can purge our court of my favorites. He can walk away from me in my grief. Then who would be the mockery? All our marriage, I have shielded myself from him, guarded my heart, determined never to allow the mask to slip. Now I stand before my husband more naked than I have ever been. And he is so angry, I am afraid of what he will do.

What he does is open his arms.

"Then turn to me," Juba says hoarsely. "If there is nowhere else you can turn but to me, then turn to me."

With a small sob of surprise, I step into his embrace. He tugs me close and I bury my face in the folds of his tunic. He strokes my hair and urges me to lean on his chest, to let him cradle me in my sadness. I am afraid to lean upon him, but when I finally do, I am surprised by his strength. He does not have the wide shoulders of a sailor or the bulging sword arm of a soldier, and yet maybe there is some manner of iron inside him after all.

WE cannot honor my mage with the funeral he deserves and I won't bury him under a false name in Mauretania. I send him to Egypt. He said he wouldn't go home without his queen, so I have his sarcophagus filled with my coins—the ones honoring my mother. He was hers before he was mine. Before that, he belonged to Isis and Egypt. So that's where I send him.

It costs a small fortune to have him embalmed and carried to Alexandria and ferried up the Nile to the temples of Philae and buried with the other priests of his line. To have his true name carved in such a way as not to attract the notice of mortal men, but to catch the eyes of the gods.

I worry I have done the wrong thing in telling Juba. The king is colder to our Alexandrian courtiers—especially my favorites, the ones he knows helped me to deceive him—but he does not send them from court or strip them of their positions. He may never trust them again, I think. He may never trust *me*, but in matters such as these, he should not, because I will never turn over my loved ones to the emperor. Juba will. He has not denied it. He cannot deny it. We will forever be at odds in this. There is no room for compromise. If he'd known about my mage, he would have given him up, and if he even suspected that Helios was still alive, he would betray me to the emperor. I would never forgive Juba for it and I would never forget. It would be the end of this fragile solace we have found in each other.

And this fragile solace has become so vital to me that I dare not risk it.

So I content myself to accept my husband's compassion and mourn my wizard. Though I have sent him to Egypt, some part of him is still here with me on the spot where Amphio has broken ground for the Iseum. I *feel* my mage and his magic. And it makes me more determined that this temple be worthy of his sacrifice.

Before the rains come, I go to inspect the work site myself. Watching Amphio order the workmen about their tasks with a testiness I have not seen in him before, I ask, "Has something gone wrong?"

Amphio holds up his hands. "Nothing I cannot fix, Majesty."

"I'm told you're confiscating tree trunks in bewildering quantities. What's that siege engine there? A catapult? And why are you ferrying mountains of ash? Explain yourself."

In reply, Amphio leans against his measuring stick and scowls. "Do you want me to build your temple or teach you construction?"

Sweet Isis, if I did not need this man's talents I would send him packing. I have faced down more impressive Romans in my time. But I cannot banish Amphio. At least, not yet. "Inattention cost me greatly with my last architect. I will not repeat that mistake."

"Your last architect was a huckster who told you whatever you wanted to hear. I'm going to tell you something you don't want to hear. The ground on the island is not as stable as it should be on the far end." I groan because this must be the site for my temple. My wizard died to consecrate this spot. It must be here. It *must* be.

Amphio condescends to explain to me, "To make it stronger, we use that machine to drive piles of fired olive wood into the ground. It is no catapult, but rather, you may think of it as an enormous hammer . . ." He loves to make me look foolish and I have given him the opportunity, so I have no one to blame but myself. Chastened, I merely listen. "We drive the piles as close together as we possibly can, then fill the spaces between them with ash. When finished, it will be like solid bedrock."

"I see."

"I doubt that you do."

"I don't like you, Amphio."

"I will try not to lose sleep over it, Majesty."

Indignation makes me huff but before I can cut him down to size, he adds, "You don't need to like me. You merely need to have faith in me. Since you believe in an invisible deity, believing in a mortal architect should be easy . . . and soon the magic of my craft will rise up before your very eyes."

THE letter from the King of Pontus arrives before winter; he agrees to accept my niece as his bride. Pythodorida of Tralles, the daughter of an Anatolian Greek financier, will become Queen of Pontus and the Bosporus. She will be the most powerful woman on the Black Sea.

Juba reads the letter over in his study, pinching the bridge of his nose.

"It's only a headache," he says when I press him. "Euphorbus used to give me a tincture . . ."

He trails off, grimacing at the mention of my dead mage.

"Let me call for another physician."

He gives a shake of his head. "It is nothing."

I worry he will shrug away my attempt to soothe him, but I dare to put my fingers into his hair anyway, gently stroking his scalp. He reaches up for my hands and holds them. "You wrote to the emperor, Selene. Is that how you arranged the marriage for Pythia?"

Having taxed my husband's patience to the limit over the matter of the mage, I dare not dissemble now. "Yes. I knew if the emperor took an interest, the King of Pontus would not refuse her."

"The emperor has never cared about your niece before. Never gave her a thought. A letter from you and all is changed . . ."

"He wants the wedding to be celebrated in Rome."

"Ah, the price!" Juba says, bitterly.

Taking a deep breath, I say, "I'm sorry. I sent the letter before the mage died . . . before you and I . . . The point is, I'll never again do such a thing without consulting you."

"Of course you will. You always do what you think is best." I hear frustration in his voice, but maybe a tiny bit of admiration too. "And I suppose I cannot condemn you for it without being held to account for all the things I do without consulting you . . ."

It's no easy thing to share a kingdom. My mother didn't like sharing hers. For most of her life, she was glad to rule alone. But my husband has taken large steps to close the distance between us; it would be dishonorable not to meet him partway. "Juba, I am *truly* sorry. I will try to do better. I'm sure you doubt it now, but I hate to be the cause of your anger. And I don't want to go to Rome. Help me think of some way—"

"I'm not angry, Selene," he says, surprising me by kissing my palm. "We must return to Rome anyway, wedding or no."

That's when he shows me another letter, this one from my Roman half brother, who has been elected praetor for this year. In September, Iullus will host a celebration for the emperor's fiftieth birthday. Other client kings and queens will go and if we are not amongst them, it will not only offend the emperor, but cast a pall on what ought to be my half brother's moment. Iullus is older, more experienced—and I think smarter—than either of Livia's sons, but he has been passed over for duties that would win him prestige and power in Rome. Augustus has transformed him into a glorified errand-boy. But what I see written in a torrent of invisible ink is that he hopes to prove his love and loyalty to the emperor. Two gifts Augustus will never accept from him.

Iullus has always done everything the emperor has ever asked of him, but he is Antony's son; nothing he does will ever be enough. Nevertheless, the emperor expects a triumphant homecoming from Gaul, and we have been—quite effectively—called back to Rome.

Twenty-one

AT sixteen, my niece is a dark beauty, eager for marriage. Meanwhile, my fair-haired daughter is nearly eleven now, the same age I was when I first came to Rome. And my son is an exuberant five-year-old who hates when the servants use irons to curl his hair in the Greek style.

I am glad to show my children Rome, this time. It isn't Alexandria, but neither is it a city of brick and mud. I cannot help but admire the way Augustus has transformed the center of the world into a showcase of marble. Of course, my enjoyment of the city is made possible by the fact that the emperor is absent from it.

The emperor is still in Gaul with his wife and her sons, which means that the only real enemy I have in the city is Admiral Agrippa, just arriving from the East with a grand contingent. Traveling with him is my niece's bridegroom, King Polemon of Pontus, and I cringe at the sight of the man. He is as old as I expected. I did not, however, expect to find his face scarred by a sword slash. The scar does not make him grotesque, but it gives him a hard, mean look, and the thought of his hands on Pythia makes me want to bundle her up and flee back to Mauretania.

Fortunately, Pythia does not seem frightened by the appearance of her betrothed. While watching his processional into Rome, she only touches her cheek in the place where the old king is scarred. "Do you think it hurts him? Should I gift him some of Dora's willow powder for the pain?"

"What powder?" I ask, glancing at my daughter in the crowd assembled to welcome Agrippa back to the city.

"I found it in the physician's room before you emptied it," Dora says matter-of-factly. "Euphorbus taught me how I could use it for my animals when they get sick. He taught me about all his plants, so I did not think he would mind if I took some after he died."

Should I scold her when the gift of his knowledge is her birthright? No, I cannot. Now that he is dead, she will never know how much more the mage would have done for her than teach her about his plants, and this thought makes me sad.

My sadness is banished, however, when I am reunited with Julia. The emperor's daughter doesn't wait for me to call on her. She comes straightaway to my house and throws her arms around my neck, nearly dragging me down under the weight of her enthusiasm. "We will have your niece's wedding at my newly refurbished villa. We're neighbors now, here on this side of the Tiber!"

In spite of the treaty between them, Agrippa will not sleep under the emperor's roof as he once did. I cannot be sorry for it, because it means that Julia and I can visit away from the Palatine Hill, where we have always been subject to the utmost scrutiny and censure. And surely she *will* meet with censure for her wild appearance. "Julia, is that a wig or . . . is your hair blue?"

The emperor's daughter laughs. "I dyed it with woad to hide that my hair is going gray. I am only twenty-five. I refuse to look like a crone before my time."

"Well, the color is very . . . dramatic!"

"You should approve. I took the idea from your blue Berbers. Consider it a tribute."

"I will, then," I say, clasping her hands as we sit together in my gardens on a bench by a little fountain. How glad I am to see her! "I cannot thank you enough for your efforts on Pythia's behalf."

"Oh, it was nothing," she says with a wave of her bejeweled hand. "Agrippa is keen to please me these days. I gave him another daughter when all he needs is sons, but he seems quite taken with little

Agrippina. She has his stern bearing already—a little Athena in the making—and Agrippa no longer considers me the *worst* mother in the world. Wait until you see how he indulged me with the villa. It is a sprawling stucco monstrosity on the outside, but I've painted the interior walls with exotic scenes from Egypt!"

"Why?" I ask, in amazement.

"To needle him, of course. He insisted we must have a sweaty gymnasium in the house where he can apply his fitness regimen in private. So, in retaliation, I made a guest room for you and turned it into a veritable shrine to Isis. You're painted there as her priestess, wearing a high crown and feeding two majestic lions from a libation bowl to represent each of your children."

"Julia!"

"Well, I meant them to be lions, but the artist made them look rather more like panthers . . ."

"You painted me?" I ask, breathless at her nerve. "You painted *me* as a priestess of Isis, in *Agrippa's* house? You've lost your wits!"

"Oh, there are so many rooms for him to ramble about in, he hasn't even discovered it. He noticed all the scantily clad women on my bedroom walls, though, in every sort of nude pose and carnal embrace. Nymphs, dancing girls, and seductive sirens . . ." Here, she trails off with glittering eyes, trying to hold back laughter. "He says that they make him feel so unvirtuous that after he climbs off me he has to punish himself with a cold bath!"

Julia howls at Agrippa's expense and I clap my hands over my mouth, unsuccessfully stifling a laugh. We are still laughing about it, weeks later, when preparing for the wedding. While I brush Pythia's thick hair, Julia strokes the saffron bridal veil and asks, "Do you know how children are made, dear?"

"Julia!" I cry.

"*What?* Surely she ought to know more than we did at her age. I can assure you, Livia told me nothing useful whatsoever on the morning of my first wedding. You don't want your niece to be ignorant, do you?"

"I'm not ignorant of how children are made," Pythia says stoutly.

"She's seen horses bred," I explain. "She's been raised in a court filled with debauched Alexandrians. I have not stifled her and kept her chained to a loom."

Julia tilts her head, with a mock-gesture of dismissal. "Oh, well, then. If she has seen horses, she must know everything, though I daresay her expectations may be disappointed in terms of girth and vigor . . ."

This time I glare. "Julia!"

"Oh, fine! I'm going," she says, leaving us to ourselves at the dressing table. I stand there, overwhelmed with the need to brush Pythia's thick dark hair, which is even blacker than mine. The feel of it in my fingers calls up some memory from long ago and I realize that I'm thinking of Octavia on my own wedding day. "Julia can be vulgar, but . . . if there is anything you would know, Pythia, I would tell you . . ."

Pythia blushes, either shy or mortified. "There is nothing."

"Don't think your new husband is permitted to hurt you simply because he's king," I say, stroking the brush through her hair. "Remind him that you are the granddaughter of Mark Antony. Make clear from the start what you'll tolerate and what you won't. Bargain if you must, but remember that you're not chattel and don't be ashamed, because what happens between a husband and wife is sacred to Isis."

"Of course," she says, squeezing her eyes shut as if *willing* me to stop talking.

Once her hair is brushed smooth and glossy, I use the traditional spear-shaped comb to divide it into the fashion of a Roman bride. "You know that I would go with you to Pontus if I could."

This finally gets her to smile. "But then everyone would bow to you and not to me."

I smile too because I see that I have no cause to worry she might let anyone bully her. Then she surprises me by asking, "Will you give me your blessing to style myself in the Ptolemaic fashion as Queen Pythodorida *Philometor*, the mother-loving? For Isis, for my mother . . . and for you."

My heart swells so that it's hard to speak. "I would be honored, Pythia. So honored."

THE wedding is accomplished under a full moon and the breakfast banquet the next morning is extravagant. The King of Pontus has us dine on sweetmeats, sausages stewed with plums and pomegranate seeds, delicate cheeses and honeycombs, saffron cakes, and stuffed capons. Every course is served upon trays of silver and gold. I am especially impressed with an array of grilled fish glistening upon a special serving platter in which peppery *garum* sauce flows over them from the spurting mouths of sea dragons.

I steal glances at Pythia, who sits beside her groom, smiling shyly at him. That gladdens my heart. Then the conversation turns to the Olympic Games, which are again imperiled. There is an expectation, of course, that I will be the one to save them. An expectation I must frustrate, given that my coffers are strained by the construction of my Iseum. But when pressed on the matter, I cannot admit that our wealth is finite, so I am left to argue that the responsibility ought to be shared.

They agree, of course. The kings of Pontus, Cappadocia, Emesa, Cilicia, Commagene, and so on. They all nod their heads and make vague promises about the gold they will contribute, but they do so with sidelong glances at my husband as if they blame him for my reluctance.

Only a barbarian king would allow the oldest traditions of the Hellenes to perish. That is what their courtiers whisper snidely behind their napkins. But Juba either does not notice or does not care, for we are in favor with the emperor and perhaps that is all the prestige that either of us needs.

Alas, my niece's wedding is destined to be overshadowed by the impending return of the emperor. As the day of his return approaches, everyone in the city seems to become more and more agitated. Poor Iullus makes elaborate preparations for all the Senate to greet the emperor before he reaches the city gates. He stockpiles flower petals in urns to be rained down on his hero upon entering Rome and positions runners at mileposts.

He would have done better to position a trumpeter in my atrium . . .

I know to expect him this time, in the dead of night. And on the day his heralds announce his imminent arrival, I dress for the occasion, garbed in a modest white *chiton* bordered with a blue wave pattern at the ankle and with my hair held tightly in place with sharp hairpins. I intend to wait in the *tabulinum*, passing the time reading Sallust's history of the Jugurthine War—the war Rome fought against my husband's Berber kinsman. But when I pull aside the curtain in the entryway, I find the king already sitting there. "Why are you awake at this hour, Juba?"

"The same reason you are."

My hands go to my cheeks. "You shouldn't wait with me."

"You shouldn't wait at all. If Caesar comes tonight, I'll greet him."

"What good do you think that will do?"

Juba looks me straight in the eye. "It will shame him."

"No," I say with a shake of my head, hating to be the one who must speak hard truths to him. "He will shame you. He will command you to fetch your wife for him. He will stand here and command you, a king in his own hall, to leave us. And you will obey."

My husband flinches. "You think me such a damnable coward . . ."

"No more of a coward than I am. Juba, you will obey because pride—your pride and mine—is not worth the price to be paid if we defy him. Pride is very costly. It would cost us both much less if you simply went back to bed."

He knows this. He has always known it. That is why he has always let the emperor have his way. It is why *I* have so often let the emperor have his way. That weakness in Juba is a mirror of mine. But tonight, he argues. "You ask me to pretend not to know Caesar is beneath my roof, carrying on with my wife as he once did with the wife of Maecenas."

I burn to be compared to my predecessor, the emperor's

shameless mistress, Terentilla, but try hard to remember that this is no easier for my husband than it is for me. "Augustus will not put hands on me. I'll receive him with refreshments and good cheer. I'll listen to him complain about how the gods taunt him, how Fate denies him what he most desires, how he has sacrificed all for Rome. Then I'll say whatever words are necessary."

"*Whatever words are necessary*," the king repeats slowly.

"If he comes tonight, it's because he sees in me and the children a fantasy. He is nearing his fiftieth birthday and he wants to believe what every man wants to believe at the end of his life: that he leaves behind a son to carry on after him. But it is *only* a fantasy. No harm can come of it now. You have nothing to fear."

My husband's fingers go to his temples, rubbing there as he contemplates what I've said. At last, he surrenders and rises to go. Before he does, he turns. "I am not afraid of the emperor's fantasies, Selene. I am afraid of yours."

I do not tell him what I am afraid of. I am afraid the emperor will take one look at my son, who looks more like Juba now than he did as a babe, and know the truth. I am afraid the emperor will fly into such a rage that he tries to murder my family in their beds. Never will I let him do it—I would kill him first—but either way, I am afraid blood will be spilled.

Memnon hears the rattle of the chain at the gate before I do and pokes his head round the corner to warn me. I put down my scroll and go out into the atrium, where the emperor is unfastening a decorative cuirass that weighs heavily on his shoulders. He lets it fall to my tile floor with a clatter, dropping a parade helmet there too. Almost four years have passed since I saw him last, and the years have not been kind to him. His hair is whiter. His skin is pallid and looser, his arms thinner than before. But those accursed eyes of his are just as penetrating as they have ever been.

"Caesar," I say, dipping low and humble in greeting.

To my surprise, my humility does not seem to please him. "Is that how you greet your Pharaoh?"

Pharaoh. How he needles me! My mother was Pharaoh. My

brothers ought to have been. I do not care what the terrified priests of Egypt say, this man will never be the true Pharaoh of Egypt. Nevertheless, I bow. "All hail, God-King."

Augustus arches a brow. "If I did not know better, I would say you were mocking me. What new divine powers do I have now as Pharaoh, do you suppose?"

"I could not guess, Caesar."

"*Pharaoh.*"

He wants to make me say it. "I could not guess, *Pharaoh.*"

"Can't you?" he asks, coming closer. "I have power over the wind. I have power to commune with other gods. I have power over all the magic and spells you know, because I have power over you, my Cleopatra. Is it not said by the Egyptians that a man cannot become Pharaoh until he has wed Pharaoh's daughter? I made you my bride during the Mysteries at Eleusis. And here you are, still mine."

He wants to set a tone for our reunion, I see. "You have come a long way. Won't you join me for some refreshment?"

Alas, the emperor has not returned from the provinces in the middle of the night for wine and olives and cheese. "Take me to see the boy," he says, shivering against the night air.

"My son is abed, asleep."

"All the better," he replies. "Take me to him."

What if I don't? If I refuse, maybe it will put an end to this farce. But maybe it will prolong it . . .

My son does not even stir when we creep into his room. Ptolemy has decided he is too old to sleep with his Berber nursemaid but we keep a lamp by his bedside because he is still afraid of the dark. He sleeps with both little hands curled up beneath his dimpled chin and I gently stroke the dark curtain of infuriatingly straight hair from his brow.

Augustus sighs, leaning over my son's bed, staring at his face as he once stared at mine. Then all at once, he draws his fist against his lips. "By the gods! What have you done, woman?"

My blood goes to water. When my son was still a babe in his cradle, the emperor was sure of his patrimony. But now? What does he see, looking at my precious boy? I see Juba in his features, but there, by his mouth and eyes, I see my older brother Caesarion too. I do not know which resemblance the emperor will latch onto, and I cannot speak.

I am too afraid to speak.

"My Cleopatra." The emperor exhales, eyes bright and manic. "Look what you have wrought. Look at this fine little prince you have given me . . ."

I say nothing, grinding my teeth against delusions that would be pathetically comedic were they not the key to our survival. Augustus cannot live forever, I tell myself. He will leave this empire behind for a younger man, or perhaps one in better health. Agrippa or his sons will rule Rome. When that happens, I will be left with only the protection of my magic. But for now, we are all at the emperor's mercy.

So I say nothing.

The emperor's eyes soften as they rest upon my son. "He has the blood of Alexander, the blood of Aeneas, and the name of a dynasty that goes back hundreds of years. No one will ever dismiss him as unworthy . . . and that will make him a better ruler, Selene. The things I have done that haunt me still are things I would never have done if I did not have to fight for my name . . ."

I do not know if this is true or not, and there is an argument to be made that men who must fight for power learn better how to use it. But the emperor is lost in his own thoughts and he says, "You've made me want to do better, Selene. I want to rule more justly, so that when our boy grows to manhood, he may take pride in me as a father."

An unexpected tenderness at the sincerity of his words tries to steal into me. "What child of yours would not take pride in you?"

It is too flip an answer. It wounds him. The emperor was vulnerable for a moment, but now he hardens again, demanding of me, "Should our son not have a *bulla* like a true Roman boy?"

He speaks of the protective amulets worn round children's necks. But if I were to give Ptolemy such an amulet, it would be an

Egyptian one, such as my mother gave to me and my brothers before she died. I still wear mine, the jade frog at my throat. But I have another. The collar of gold worn by my little brother, Ptolemy Philadelphus. I should give it to my son, who is named in his honor. I can, even at this moment, imagine it glittering on his neck, a tribute to his true heritage.

But then I remember one of the last things my little brother ever said to me. *Give this to your daughter. You may be tempted to give it to the son you'll bear, but it's meant for her.* "He does not need a *bulla*," I say. "He is a child of Isis and she watches over him as do I."

"Good. Watch over this precious little prince you have given me, Selene. Or perhaps I gave him to you. It is gods who grant life. Goddesses and women are only the fertile earth in which seeds grow. They are the soft bed upon which men and gods find comfort. Goddesses and women nurture what gods and men allow to prosper. Is that not so?"

My nostrils flare as I consider an answer. "I always nurture that which is given to me."

"Thank me, then, for the life of this boy."

Chilled to the bone by the implied threat, I swiftly say, "I am grateful."

"And your niece. Was the wedding to your liking?"

I inhale sharply. "It was. Thank you. Again. We are so grateful."

"Now thank me for the girl," he says. "Thank me for Isidora."

I stare at him, dumbly, fear and anger swirling together in a familiar storm.

"I remember the night we made her, Selene. I think of it often and with pleasure. I remember how you fought me. How I had to hold you down. How you sobbed and cried out in pain when I breached your maidenhead. You made me conquer you. But in the taking, I gave you something very precious that night, did I not? Thank me."

I would sooner stab him. This sickness is what no one else understands about Augustus. He cannot hold regrets as other men do for very long. He cannot allow himself to have been the villain. He wants so badly to be a giant that he makes himself into a small, *small* man. A line draws itself inside me and I cannot cross it. "I will never thank you for what you did to me that night."

"You wanted me to do it, Selene. You looked my way as you spoke your wedding vows. You seduced me with a painted face and loose hair and bare shoulders. You knew you were mine, and dared me to take you with every flutter of your eyelashes. You wanted me to do it. You wanted it to happen just the way it did. And have I not always given you everything you wanted eventually?"

There is suddenly a swarm of hornets in my mouth eager to be unleashed. I can scarcely swallow over the sting. I didn't want him to do it. I won't take the blame for his crime. But the accusation humiliates me. He has taken nearly everything from me, but he would argue that he gave it all back. In some twisted way, it might even be true. What would he give me now? Egypt is no longer in his power to give. Not while Agrippa breathes. And at this moment I am so filled with revulsion, I do not think I would take the crown of Egypt from his hand even if it were freely offered. "Your generosity is a thing of legend, Caesar."

He smiles as if he finds my anger amusing. "Do your children not thrive on it?"

"They do. So do Gaius and Lucius. I've seen your sons and know you must take great pride in them."

Now he scowls. "You are the one who said I must make peace with Agrippa and adopt those boys. I would never have done it—I would never have given away the inheritance of our little prince—if you did not goad me to it during the rites. Don't you know how difficult it would be now to undo it all?"

So that is what he wants. He wants to undo it. He wants to disinherit Julia's boys, break with Agrippa, and abandon all those pledges he made to the gods at the *Ludi Seculares*. And he wants me to beg him to do it. That is why he came here this time, to provoke me. He has already written my part.

"I am sorry," I say, because I want no part in this.

"You *should* be sorry. You convinced me I must surrender to

Agrippa's demands. In the moment your courage was tested, you faltered. But our son will not falter. What a hero, what a king, what a pharaoh and emperor he will be. He has the sweet face of a choirboy, but look at those tightly squeezed fists. When the time comes, *he* will grasp hold of his destiny and never let it go."

WAR has broken out and no one seems to know it but me. Indeed, the Senate votes to dedicate an altar to *peace* and to sponsor a thanksgiving for the reunion of Augustus and Agrippa. After four years, they are again together in Rome. In public, they clasp hands as friends. They are seen to walk together in the company of the sons they share, Gaius, a little older than my boy, and Lucius, a little younger.

Unlike the last time we were together in Rome, soldiers are not tight with tension, trying to guess how their loyalties will be tested. The people do not invent bright and cheery gossip to disguise their terror of civil war. They do not notice the artifice with which the emperor loudly proclaims Agrippa to be his dearest friend, closest colleague, trusted ally, and son-in-law.

Even Agrippa does not seem to notice it.

The admiral does not like my presence in the city, much less in his house. He scowls when he comes home to find me in his villa, visiting with his wife. Yet when we meet in passing, he forces himself to civility. He mentions favorably the quality of our Mauretanian grain tribute. He even compliments me on the poise of my niece, the new Queen of Pontus, who has been charming the social set in Rome.

In spite of his age, Agrippa is still healthy and built like a bull, but I remember Julia's letter about the pain in his feet and notice that he limps a little now. Dora sees it too, and as we are making our way out after a visit with Julia, she dares to address him directly. "Admiral Agrippa, you should drink an infusion of ground chicory root each morning and eat berries with your dinner."

He is caught unawares by her, staring at me with suspicion as if I have a raised up a little witch. "Some hemlock too while I am at it?"

"Dora, go," I say, pointing a finger. "Tala is waiting outside."

My daughter leaves, and Marcus Vipsanius Agrippa and I are left in his giant atrium with all the garish Egyptian artwork on its walls. "Be wary, admiral."

"When you are near, I'm always wary, Cleopatra Selene."

"Not of me."

He quirks a brow. "Who, then?"

I cannot tell him outright that the emperor is considering breaking their alliance. It is too dangerous to tell him, but I say, "There are very few people in this world who can harm you, Marcus Vipsanius Agrippa. I am only warning you to be wary of the ones who can . . ."

We stand there staring at each other until he rubs at the back of his neck. He knows what I mean—what I am warning him of. But I fear he does not believe me. "By union small things become great, by division the greatest fall to pieces. If you are here to sow trouble—"

"I am not here to sow trouble. I am here because I am Julia's friend."

His eyes soften at the mention of her, though he complains, "I suppose I have you to blame for her profligacy. She spends treasure faster than I can seize it."

"Even if she continued this way the rest of her life, she could not spend all your treasure. You have become a very great man. You have done exceedingly well for your family and honored your ancestors. I do not begrudge you."

He nods stiffly. "Then leave me to my own affairs and go on home with you and be the good matron Octavia taught you to be."

When I do go home, I find Iullus there, complaining to my husband about his rivalry with Tiberius. Livia's eldest son has already served as Consul of Rome, but Iullus, as a praetor, is on his heels, always a step behind. Their political ambitions have pitted them against each other again and again. But my half brother has been denied the coveted military command that would make all the difference.

"Tiberius has me worried that the birthday games will not be grand enough," Iullus complains. "He intends to outdo me with a lavish affair to celebrate the emperor's homecoming and success in Gaul."

"There will be honors enough for Augustus this summer," Juba says.

But I worry there can never be enough.

Twenty-two

WERE I to list the dizzying variety of parades, ceremonies, and official celebrations that we are obligated to attend in honor of the emperor, I would exhaust myself all over again. In their attempt to outdo each other, Iullus and Tiberius treat us to such an endless barrage of feasts, games, and entertainments that even the children begin to find them tedious.

Then there is Drusus and all his pomp. Still as genial as he was when we grew up together on the Palatine Hill, Livia's youngest son has, nonetheless, surprised us all by maturing into a military commander of the first order. Bold and energetic, with a keen mind for strategy, he's earned honors for routing bandits from the Alps. He dresses the part of a hero from the short cut of his leather military skirt to the laces of his sandals, which have been dipped in gold. Given the way girls swoon when Drusus passes through the forum, I worry for my poor half sister, Minora, who must burn with jealousy as his wife.

But it is said that Drusus does not stray from her bed. It seems that there is no fault that can be laid at his door, except for the persistent rumor that he would like to return Rome to her old Republican traditions when elected officials held true power.

If it is true, I think he must be alone in wishing to revisit that sort of chaos.

One morning on the way to yet another parade, Pythia frets, "Am I doing everything right? There are so many rules to follow as queen!"

She seems content in her new marriage, and says nothing against her new husband whatsoever. Dora reassures me that Pythia is happy, so I resolve to be happy too. After all, there is nothing unusual about their marriage; it is only that the emperor has made me leery of what older men might do to a girl . . .

On the emperor's birthday, on my way into the circus, I am unexpectedly approached by an old rival: Lucius Cornelius Balbus. Given the enthusiasm with which the Roman greets me, bowing with a flourish in a way he never did when he served on our council in Mauretania, one might think we were long-lost friends. And after a few moments chatting with the bombastic soldier, I forget that we were anything but.

It is strange how I can hold a perfect memory of every crime Livia or the emperor ever committed against me and mine, but time has worn away at lesser resentments. I cannot even recall now the cause of my quarrel with Balbus—something about gladiators, I think. Is it age or maturity that makes us forget such things?

In any case, Balbus has come to Rome to dedicate a theater in his own name. Unwisely, I think. Years ago, Balbus made the near-fatal mistake of celebrating a Triumph to mark his victory over the Garamantes—something I doubt the emperor has forgiven. But Balbus longs to leave a legacy, and he surprises me by asking after the son of one of his freedwomen. "Iacentus, I named him, as I always suspected he was mine. He's a good Roman-trained soldier. I hope he'll have a fine future."

I know just the young man he's speaking of—an ambitious soldier with piggy eyes that should have made me suspect the relation. Since I too am here to assure the future of my children, I am pleased to inform him, "King Juba speaks highly of his competence. I see no reason that Iacentus will not advance at our court."

Balbus is so puffed up with pleasure at my answer, and his own self-importance, that he invites me to join him in his procession to the imperial box, where he intends to approach the emperor. Of course I cannot accept, because Augustus has made it clear that women and men should not be seated together at occasions such as this one.

Instead, I climb up to the rows reserved for the women of the imperial family and take my seat beside the emperor's daughter.

Julia makes quite a sight, blue hair boldly styled, elegant jewels dripping from her ears, and an Egyptian-style gown that is so scandalously transparent, even I am shocked by it. "Have you ever seen such a fine weave, Selene? Certainly much better than anything we ever did at the loom."

Octavia gasps, removing her own shawl to cover Julia up. "You will be mistaken for a *hetaera* in such a garment!"

"Don't be silly." Julia laughs carelessly. "Not even the wealthiest *hetaera* could afford a *kalasiris* gown like this one."

It is strange that Livia does not join in the argument, since the emperor's wife normally torments Julia at any opportunity, but she merely smiles a strange little smile. I soon understand why. From across the arena, the emperor has seen Julia's attire and glares at her with such cold disapproval that we both feel the chill.

Julia has grown used to doing as she pleases; she will have to remember now that we are again in her father's sphere.

She is shrewd enough to dress modestly the following day, greeting her father warmly before we enter the stadium. The frost in his eyes abates as he takes in the layers of garments that cover her nearly head to toe. "Now, this is a more becoming dress for the daughter of Caesar."

Julia smiles her brilliant smile. "That is because yesterday I dressed to please my husband, but today I dress for my father's eyes." It is a perfectly calculated defense; he cannot fault her. And yet he will fault her, I think.

For whatever pleases Agrippa now seems to displease him.

Later, when we are seated together on an uncomfortable bench in the arena, Julia confides, "I wish I'd not said that in front of Octavia. I am a horrible, wicked, selfish woman to flaunt Agrippa's desire in front of her."

Fanning myself to disguise that I am bored half to death by the chariots racing below, I say, "You have four children with the man, Julia. His desire for you is no secret."

She flutters her lashes and smiles. "He wants another baby."

"You sound pleased by the idea . . ."

"I am. Agrippa is, at heart, a simple man. It isn't difficult to make him happy. Do you know what a relief that is for me? I know exactly what he wants and when I give it to him, he forgives me all else. Besides, I think I'm starting to like children. My own anyway. Fortunately, it gets easier to birth them each time . . ." She glances at me and pales. "Oh, I'm sorry, Selene. I really *am* a horrible, wicked, selfish woman."

I'm puzzled by her mortification until I realize, with dismay, that she thinks I'm barren. She thinks that because I have not had more children that I *cannot* have them. She thinks I—the vessel of Isis—am *barren*! Do the rest of them think it too?

My cheeks burn with humiliation. I am still burning with it that night when I return home to find my husband pacing the length of the *impluvium*, the shallow pool that catches rainwater in our atrium. When he sees me, he crouches down to wash his hands. "I had to save Lucius Cornelius Balbus today when he made an impolitic remark to the emperor."

It is a sweltering summer in Rome and my sandals are too tight, so I slip them off, sit beside my husband, and dip my feet into the pool. "Balbus doesn't seem to understand that his career is at an end."

"Well, he understands now," Juba says soberly. "Augustus accused him of plotting against the state."

"Balbus can scarcely plot a course on a map."

My husband doesn't laugh. "Augustus was ready to bring Balbus up on charges. He must have been ready to do it for quite some time. I had to persuade him to allow Balbus to retire to his estate in Spain . . ."

I realize, with a start, how I have come to take for granted the emperor's milder temperament. Gone are the days when he murdered men with indifference and told me to have a stronger stomach when viewing their entrails strewn upon the road. In spite of all he said in my son's nursery, in spite of his resentment of Agrippa, he *has* changed and I have helped change him. But that doesn't mean he isn't still deadly. "Lucky for Balbus that you were there . . ."

Juba turns and captures my gaze. "More than lucky. Augustus needs me, Selene, and I do not want to fail him. He *needs* me. He does not rely so much upon Maecenas anymore. Tiberius and Iullus are too busy arguing with each other to give the emperor good counsel. Octavia keeps her own counsel, as she should, and Livia . . ."

He does not say it. I know. Livia seethes with impotence, her path to power blocked by two little boys named Gaius and Lucius. She can never hope to be First Woman in Rome now. Her sons will never rule this empire. Agrippa's machinations have always stood in my way, but they stand in her way too—and I am glad of it.

TO my surprise, there is one celebration in Rome that I quite enjoy. It is the thanksgiving in the month named for Julius Caesar, a processional intended to consecrate the ground for an altar to peace.

The *Ara Pacis*, they will call it when it is built.

To dedicate the ground, every member of the imperial family is to take part in a parade. Julia and Agrippa walk with their little ones. The Antonias, with their husbands and children. Tiberius and Vipsania and their infant son. Marcella and Iullus and their children. Livia and Octavia too.

Only a few of the visiting royalty in Rome are invited to take part and my family is foremost amongst them. We are the only royals to march with the emperor's household. I admit, it gives me some pleasure to see Herod excluded while Juba and I, children in hand, walk together with the imperial family.

And what a glorious day it is, under a clear blue sky.

The emperor leads the ceremony as if he were the Pontifex Maximus—which he is not, a thing I know still vexes him, and he makes no secret of it. He still mutters darkly about Lepidus having the temerity to live on, when Augustus would rather he were dead. But it does not stop him from usurping the high priest's place, directing the *flamens* of Rome, the priests wearing strange spiked leather caps, to perform sacred rituals to consecrate the ground.

I would describe these rituals if they moved me, but they are nothing compared to what my mage did to consecrate ground for my temple in Mauretania. What does move me about this ceremony is what happens when the solemn duties are at an end.

The dignified march I have come to expect somehow transforms itself into a stroll of all Rome's most important citizens, talking and laughing as artists sketch us on scrolls. What was a procession becomes more of a summer picnic. A reunion with all of us feasting and reminiscing while the children play jumping games with sticks and lines of chalk on the pavement.

With a grandchild in each arm, Octavia meets my eyes and smiles, for it is exactly as she hoped and neither of us wants the emperor to undo it. In the dark, the emperor talked to me of my son's destiny, but now in the light of day, even Augustus cannot help but enjoy himself just as things are. He is surrounded by family, all of them finding a way, on this one warm afternoon, to be happy.

All except for his wife, of course, who sits slightly apart from the rest of us beneath a shade tree watching the idyllic scene unfold with wistful regret. This is not as she would have it, but it is exactly as it should be. If the emperor could take my husband's example and love his family without regard for who sired them, Augustus would see himself as the patriarch of this enormous brood.

Little Gaius and Lucius admire him. They want his attention and approval as a grandfather and a father. He could give them a different life than the one he gave Julia. He could keep Marcus Vipsania Agrippa as his good and loyal friend. He could reach inside himself and find the part that inspires such loyalty from men like my half brother, Iullus, and my husband, Juba. And so I pray the emperor abandons the man he is with me in the dark and embraces the man he is now, lit up by the summer sun.

"SAY that you'll stay in Rome through winter," Julia pleads with me. "I want to spend the Saturnalia with you before I must trudge through the mountains."

"What mountains?" I ask.

Julia waves a dismissive hand. "There is some uprising in the new province of Pannonia, south of the Danube River. I think the duty should fall to one of the Claudian brothers, since Livia's sons are now so popular and eager to impress. But my husband itches for battle. Only the gods know why he insists I go with him. After all, he's just going to leave me behind at Aquileia, but I think he wants me nearby. Say you'll stay until I must go!"

Julia is persuasive, but we stay because this may be the last Saturnalia we celebrate with Pythia. And it is a merry one. Like all children, mine love the Saturnalia. Freed from studies, Dora spends every last moment with Pythia and my son sets aside his *toga praetexta* in favor of a simple tunic and freedman's cap to play all day with the children of the imperial family.

They spend the holiday playing ball, jumping ropes, running about in masks, and eating so many pastries that they spoil their suppers. Julia and I allow it. Neither of us wish to inflict our own strict upbringing on our children. So we let them run wild through the emperor's halls on the Palatine, a thing that puts us at odds with Octavia's daughters, all of whom try to enforce some manner of discipline.

On the day the boys learn how to make slingshots, Marcella forbids them from the garden, saying, "Put those rocks down. No stones! I'll strap you if you shoot even one pebble."

They promise, then use their slingshots to shoot coins instead, smashing a row of expensive Greek vases in the emperor's dining hall. "This is your fault," Marcella hisses at Julia. "You let them do anything. Now the emperor will punish them when he should punish you as an unfit mother."

But when Augustus learns that it was my son who taught the other boys to shoot coins instead of pebbles, he laughs. "They are only vases. There are a thousand more vases in Greece for the taking. But I have only one Prince of Mauretania!"

Marcella drags her son away by the ear, Julia makes a token effort to scold her boys, and I try to decide what to do with my son. Still clutching the slingshot, Ptolemy is sheepish, but a little proud too because he senses the emperor approved of his antics.

Ptolemy's father, however, does not approve. Furrowing his brow in a way that makes my son gulp, Juba says, "You're going to be punished. Not for playing. Not for using coins in the slingshot—that was rather clever—but because you broke things that have a history. Things that people made with their own hands. Things that told a story. So we're going to fetch the shards back from the slaves, get some *gluten taurinum*, and use it to put all these pieces back together again. That is how you're going to spend the rest of the Saturnalia until it is done."

That night in my chambers, I watch the two of them work together with the pieces, big and small, until poor little Ptolemy is bleary-eyed. Juba makes him stay awake, makes him good and tired, before sending the chastened boy off to bed. My husband is still kneeling on the lion-skin rug, hovering over the puzzle of the broken vases, when I close the door and bar it behind me. Juba looks up at me and raises an eyebrow. And when I kneel beside him, he warns, "Careful. Some of the edges are sharp."

I put a finger over his lips to silence him. When he is quiet, I kiss him. He seems startled by it, frozen with surprise, for I rarely initiate such intimacy. So I kiss him again, until I make him understand that my lips have not fallen upon him by mistake. He pulls back, a question in his eyes. I answer it by unfastening my girdle. Then he lifts me up onto the couch and we are quick about it.

What we do here in Rome seems more illicit. I think that makes it more heated. Furtive and fumbling. Panting and primal. Though my husband is older now, I take more pleasure in him than before. Maybe the spirit of revelry that is the Saturnalia has gotten into me. Maybe it is the spiced wine. Or maybe it is because I can imagine no other king in the empire kneeling upon a rug to take a boy in hand.

I want another child. I *desperately* want another child. If we are to secure our dynasty, we must risk it. We must again risk the emperor's wrath. Perhaps this frenetic act will give me the courage to prove that I'm not barren. But when I try to open my womb for Juba, when I try to use the powers gifted to me by my great goddess to bring new life into this world, I cannot.

You would never allow such a thing to happen unless your husband has become so inconvenient that you desire to be made a widow.

WE cannot leave Rome until the sailing season. Thus, everyone leaving overland departs before we do. Julia is the first to go because her husband refuses to let the snow keep him from his campaign. Eager to crush the rebellion in Pannonia, Agrippa sets out on a winter march with his legions, and his wife follows. I am there on the road waving to her as she goes, but I am not alone. Mounted on a bay stallion, Iullus is there too, breathing puffs of silent longing into the cold morning air.

Julia waves back at us with a wistful smile, letting a flower fall from her hands as her carriage rolls away. When I start for my house to escape the chill, I look back over my shoulder to see Iullus get down from his horse, take the flower from the cobblestones, and press it to his lips.

In February, the Eastern kings begin their journey and my niece must go too. "My friend Strabo will join Pythodorida's court," my husband says. He means Strabo the historian and geographer, not the emperor's praetorian of the same name. "We will exchange letters often, so you can be reassured of her safety."

I am grateful, both for my husband's consideration and that Pythia has found her place in the world. It's only the rest of us who will be miserable for her absence. On the day of her departure, my son clings hard to Pythia's knees. "Will we never see you again?"

"We'll meet again here in Rome," Isidora says, as if she has seen it come to pass. I think she is only being brave, though, because my daughter cries inconsolably when Pythia is gone. Dora was fond of my mage, but this is a harder loss. It is the first time she learns that not all friendships can go on unchanged even if the love remains the same.

"LEPIDUS is dead," the emperor says, smiling with such predatory satisfaction that the lamplight gleams off one tooth. Juba and I are taking a meal with the imperial family and they seem as surprised by this news as we are. Our hands filled with goblets, napkins, lettuce leaves, and eggs, we all fall silent.

"Lepidus is dead," the emperor repeats, saying it in the way one might announce that there will be gold-dusted honey cakes for dessert. He holds a scroll aloft over the remains of our meal in case we doubt him. "The Pontifex Maximus is dead."

Iullus makes a toast. "Good riddance to the worthless Lepidus, then."

Grudgingly, we lift our cups. All but Drusus, who pointedly pushes away his wine.

Livia's youngest son pulls himself upright from his couch, his flashy military sandals settling on the floor. "I do not celebrate the death of *any* Roman. We should *mourn* the Pontifex Maximus and honor his public service."

Drusus gets away with it, as he gets away with everything, because he is charming and because his sentiments are always proper Roman sentiments, which no man who wishes to remain in public esteem can contradict. "Of course," the emperor says, hiding a sneer behind a gulp of wine. "This is how I mourn."

In truth, none of us here have any reason to mourn Marcus Aemilius Lepidus. A party to the Second Triumvirate, he was the least of the three. His relative ineptitude—and his priestly title— kept him alive as an example of the emperor's supposed mercy. And yet I wonder, "How did he die?"

The emperor spears a chunk of smoked lamprey on the end of his knife and brings it to his lips with relish. "Who knows? Why should you care?"

It does not matter, I suppose. The long exile of Lepidus is at an end. Whether it ended with murder or illness or accident, that chapter is closed. Augustus is already the highest governing authority in the empire; now he will have complete dominion over religious matters as well. "I will stand for the vacated office of Pontifex Maximus," the emperor declares, as if anyone would oppose him. And on the sixth day of the month dedicated to Mars, the emperor is elected by popular acclaim.

With this power, the emperor will now select all priests and give them their offices as a sign of imperial favor. But no priest of Isis is a member of the priestly college and he will not appoint one. So it is all meaningless pageantry to me.

Amongst the emperor's first act as Pontifex Maximus is to seize the Sibylline Books, those ancient prophecies that have guided Rome since before it was a Republic, and which gave the people belief in holy twins who would bring them a Golden Age. He says that it is to safeguard them, and he moves them to a vault in the Temple of Apollo that he has built atop the Palatine Hill.

Then he purges them of everything he deems suspect or inconvenient. All the verses that speak of a savior who will come out of Egypt, all the visions of a fiery sun god who will burn Rome, all the prophecies that made my twin brother such a danger to the emperor's regime, all gone.

He will make it as if Alexander Helios never existed . . . and that I was never anything more than a captive treated generously by the true savior. Augustus is the chosen one, the messiah, and now, as Pontifex Maximus, imbued with the solemnity of a holy father who must guide the Roman state. It's the role of his lifetime, and I cannot think how the play might have ended any other way.

But as in all the best plays, tragedy is always the partner of triumph, so I am eager for my family to exit the stage. We've been away from Mauretania for nearly a year and the longer we remain within the emperor's circle, the more it poisons my heart.

Twenty-three

ON the Ides of March, we leave for the port of Ostia. The children ride with me in a four-wheeled *carpentum* with gilded sides and thick purple drapes to keep the cool mist of morning at bay. But no sooner do we set out upon the road than hard-riding imperial troops force us to give way, sending us into a ditch.

The wheel cracks with a thunderous sound and the entire *carpentum* lists to one side. Inside, we all fall against one another. Bracing my children with my arms, I hear them both howl, with fright or excitement or both. As it happens, we are only jostled, not harmed. Once reassured of this fact, I climb out, prepared to hurl abuse at the ranking Roman officer, but see only a cloud of dust in his wake.

My husband's furious stallion paws at the ground, anxious to ride after the rude cavalrymen, and my husband seems much of the same temperament. When his eyes fall upon our mud-spattered children and the wreck of my carriage, he shouts, "I will have that officer's name and the skin off his back!"

I don't have the slightest urge to dissuade him from his wrath when the sour-faced coachman explains that the carriage cannot be fixed without a new wheel and axle. As he and the other men in our retinue try to haul it out of the ditch, another cadre of grim-faced soldiers ride past us the other way. They do not even stop when Juba hails them, as if a royal banner gave them not the slightest pause.

It's curious, because my husband has long served in the military; he has some semblance of rank and status. Whatever the business of these men, it is more urgent than their fear of reprimand.

Anything that causes soldiers to fly down the road arouses my instinct to flee. But Juba says, "Something is amiss, Selene. Let's turn back."

"Our place is in Mauretania," I say, trying to remind Juba that our business in Rome is done. He has grown too accustomed to being at the emperor's right hand. I must break him of this. He must remember that he is a king. "Our kingdom awaits us . . ."

My husband stares back over his shoulder at Rome. "I am going up the Palatine for answers."

"Our ship is waiting for us in Ostia. Whatever the news, it will reach us eventually!"

Juba's voice takes on a firm tone of command. "Selene, you can't really mean to leave without knowing what we might face . . . What happens in Rome matters everywhere."

It is a winning argument. He is right. Mauretania is our kingdom, but part of the Roman Empire too. So I let Tala see the children back to our house on the Tiber and I go with the king.

We find a great throng of people at the gates to the imperial compound, all of whom are being denied admission by the praetorians, but we are allowed to pass inside, where we find the imperial slaves fearful, some of them crying.

"What is happening?" Juba asks. "Where is the emperor?"

"Gone," someone replies. "He went to Agrippa in Campagna."

Confused, I say, "But Agrippa is in Pannonia with Julia . . ."

Juba sets off up the stairs, two at a time, in search of Tiberius or Iullus. Meanwhile, I search out Octavia and find her standing in the middle of her corridor staring at nothing, as if she does not hear the wailing slaves. She is holding a scrap of paper in one hand, crumpling it in her fist. Like the statues that adorn each alcove, she is perfectly still. Her expression is beyond bleak—all light in her eyes extinguished.

"Octavia, what has happened?" She does not answer me. She doesn't move at all, as if she'd turned into one of the pillars that must bear up under the weight of the roof. And I want to shake her. "Tell me!"

Finally, she says, "Marcus Vipsanius Agrippa is dead."

With those words, the whole world shifts beneath my feet. I'm sure I've misheard. After all, what could fell such a colossus? "Do you mean that he's been wounded in battle?"

"He never made it to battle," she replies, her voice stony and remote. "Agrippa started for Pannonia but immediately fell ill. Julia convinced him to withdraw to Campagna to get well, but there he died."

Octavia is looking at me but I don't think she sees me. She's seeing beyond me into a world without Agrippa. Into a world where all our planning, all our sacrifices might be for naught. My hands go to my face. "No, not Agrippa. Except for his sore feet, he's never been ill a day in his life . . ."

"It must have been the plague," she hisses, the first sign of any emotion. "We should've known when we learned about the death of Lepidus, but we celebrated. Now the gods have their justice for our hubris. Plague is racing up the coast and it's taken Agrippa."

The suddenness of it leaves me confused. That and the fact that Agrippa was not on the coast when he took ill. He and Julia were on their way to Pannonia, in the other direction. I saw them go! "How can you be sure?"

"The emperor received word that Agrippa was ill—so ill that he might not survive. So he hurried to Agrippa's deathbed to be by his old friend's side, to inhale his last breath, as the *paterfamilias*. But he was too late. Too late. He writes to say that Agrippa is dead."

Agrippa was the ruin of my family and my nemesis, but he was also a bulwark against utter political calamity. Now I know why military dispatches were sent with such haste that we were forced from the road. The emperor may have resented him, but Agrippa was the empire's most able general. Without him, the legions are likely in chaos.

"Agrippa is dead," Octavia says again, her lips trembling on his name. I hurt for her. She loved Agrippa so much that she gave him up. She gave him her own daughter Marcella in marriage and when that was not enough, she saw to it that he married Julia. Then she did everything in her power to ensure that Agrippa's children would rule the empire.

My hand goes to my throat, thinking of Julia now. That my dear friend should be widowed again is a travesty; I cannot even imagine the horror of her position, holding vigil over a dead husband in the midst of a plague. Perhaps Julia has her little daughters with her, but what of her sons? "Gaius and Lucius . . . where are they?"

Octavia closes her eyes. "They must be with Livia."

Cold seeps into my body from the floor. I've always had a preternatural ability to sense the likely political ramifications of an event. It is what has allowed me to survive and to spar on the political stage with the emperor himself. Even in my state of shock it takes me just a moment to work out that with Agrippa dead, only two small boys stand between Livia and everything she's ever wanted.

I run. I don't stop for my ladies; they are forced to chase after me. Breathless, I burst into Livia's house and search for her. With a sense of dread, I find her in the kitchen hovering over four-year-old Lucius with a silver spoon in hand. Instinctively, I lunge forward, knocking the spoon away and sending it to the floor with a clatter.

Livia barks in outrage. "What do you think you're doing?"

"What are *you* doing?" I demand, grasping Lucius by the shoulders with one arm and catching Gaius with my other. In my protective embrace, Gaius squirms and Lucius begins to wail.

The emperor's wife glowers at me. "Let them go. Look how you've upset my sons!"

"They're not your sons. They're Julia's."

Now seven-year-old Gaius begins to cry too, struggling to get away from me. And I realize that though these two boys have been at the center of my hopes, I'm frightening them. They aren't frightened of Livia; they're frightened of *me*. Fortunately, Livia is also frightened of me and keeps her distance. "They haven't been Julia's sons since the day the emperor adopted them. They are my husband's sons, which makes them mine."

"Am I to believe that you're such a loving mother that you regularly take time from your day to feed them from your own hand?" I remember two other boys who were once in her care. Marcellus and Philadelphus, who both died of a mysterious fever. Did she feed them too? "Why don't you take a taste from that bowl?"

Livia sniffs. "I don't care for porridge. Why don't you?"

Wrestling Gaius into submission, I grind out, "Eat the porridge, you poisonous bitch."

Livia gives a tight smile, but she isn't one of my subjects. Unless I assault her here and now, she can defy me with relative impunity. So she toys with the bowl, lifting it halfway to her lips. "I cannot decide if it would satisfy me more to prove you wrong or to leave you always wondering . . . the latter, I suppose." She dumps the porridge into the slop pot, where rotting remains of previous meals make a noxious stew. "I'm afraid I'm not very hungry."

I should force her down onto her hands and knees and make her gulp from that bucket. Failing that, I should take it to test on some creature . . . but what proof would it be from a slop pot? Not knowing whether or not Julia's sons have been told about Agrippa's death—I give her a warning look, holding the boys tight. "I'm taking them with me."

"Do you think the praetorians would allow you to take a step out of the gate?"

"I'm not afraid of the praetorians."

This is not entirely true, but it convinces her, which is the important thing. "Maybe not, but you fear Augustus, and he will not thank you for kidnapping his sons. Some might even see it as a move to eliminate your own bastard's rivals."

These words are cold water flung into my face. That she would accuse me of doing harm to Julia's children and call my son a bastard—that she should dare to even mention it in the presence of servants and my breathless ladies who hover in the doorway—is a testament to her own guilt. Still, she is not wrong that there are rumors about me and mine . . .

"Selene?" Juba pushes past the servants, making his way into the kitchen. His bewildered glance darts to the howling boys, their faces streaked with tears. "You've told them?"

"No," I say. "Not yet. Where is the emperor?"

"He is on his way back to Rome," my husband replies. "We'll wait for him."

I do not argue. We cannot possibly leave Rome now. Especially not now, not with Livia poised to murder Julia's sons. My voice *trembles* with fury. "As it happens, Lady Livia is most concerned after the health of these children. Should they catch a fever in the next few days, for example, or take a tumble down the stairs . . . should they so much as sniffle . . . she knows it would grieve the emperor and how great a risk such a circumstance might pose to her own health."

Livia sneers, half-amused at my threat.

Juba is not amused. Through clenched teeth, he asks, "Selene, *what* are you going on about?" Each word of his question is edged with a bite that tells me he does not see Livia as a danger. That he thinks I am mad to suspect her of anything.

Meanwhile, I can hardly accuse her more plainly in front of crying children who want nothing more than to escape my clutches. Yet as I relinquish my hold on Julia's sons, I lean to whisper in Livia's ear. "I swear by Isis, so long as there is breath in me, you will not benefit from harming these boys."

AGRIPPA'S funeral train rolls into the city with the greatest solemnity and it seems as if all the citizens in Rome come out to see him. Beyond the professional mourners, there are Agrippa's clients and the soldiers who served him, whose grief seems so genuine that it is difficult not to join them in wailing lamentations. The admiral makes a shocking sight where they prop him on the rostrum, a wreath on his head, two coins over his sunken eyes and one in his mouth. I suspect that Agrippa—a strong, proud bull of a man— wouldn't have wanted people to look upon his wasted body. He is finally spared the indignity when the emperor has a curtain drawn in front of the body before giving the funeral oration.

The emperor is generous with his praise, which now he can well afford to be. He promises that his son-in-law's ashes will be buried in the tomb of Augustus, so that he might never be parted from his good friend in death.

At this, Julia flinches. It is her first reaction visible to the rest of us, since her pregnant belly is swathed in mourning clothes and her face is concealed behind the mask of one of Agrippa's ancestresses. After the funeral pyre has been assembled, she pours perfumed oils onto the wood and lays fragrant spices beneath her husband's body so we will not choke on the fumes of the dead. Agrippa is burned in a fire so high that no one can stand close to the flames without being seared.

That night and into the next morning, Julia performs every duty expected of her with grace and composure; she stumbles only once when pouring wine onto the embers to turn them to ash so that she may collect the remains. And when she stumbles, it is Iullus Antonius who steadies her.

AFTER the funeral, Julia returns to her father's home on the Palatine Hill and says to her slave girl, "Phoebe, find my mother. Bring my mother to me. Until then, I will see no one but the Queen of Mauretania."

Then Julia slams the door, pressing her forehead against the wooden frame, taking deep gulps of air. I watch her battle to stave off sobs, but it is a battle she loses. Everything I know of friendship I've learned from Julia's example, so I wrap my arms around her shaking shoulders. "Oh, Julia. I'm so sorry. To lose your husband, so suddenly . . ."

At this, her head jerks up, her sobs hiccuping to a halt. "It wasn't sudden. Do you think Agrippa would meet anything without a fight? It was a horrible struggle. It went on and on for weeks."

"*Weeks?* But—"

"My husband took ill before we even got to the mountains! I sent word to my father at the start of the month that I was taking Agrippa to Campagna and that he must meet us at once, for I feared my husband would not live long."

I can make no sense of this. "The messenger must have been delayed. Such things are common. Messengers are waylaid. Ships are sunk. Horses go lame. News reaches us in Mauretania sometimes swiftly, sometimes not at all."

"Oh, no, Selene," she says, fury glinting in her tear-filled eyes. "My father received the message. He sent word back that I must be exaggerating Agrippa's illness. He said that I must not spread panic in the legions, for it would embolden our enemies in the Senate and endanger my children. So my dying husband and I were silent while we waited. We were silent while my father dallied in Rome to be made Pontifex Maximus."

Every hair lifts on my nape as I remember the night the emperor told us that Lepidus was dead. Did he know, even then, that his greater rival was so very ill? I can scarcely believe it. Were we all there, standing in the forum, cheering while Agrippa lay on his deathbed? I don't *want* to believe it. "There must be some mistake."

"There is no mistake," she hisses. "Agrippa knew he was dying. All that remained was to pass on his last breath to his *paterfamilias*, an honor he wanted to bestow upon my father. He kept his heart beating in his chest long after the battle was lost. I sent message after message, but my father did not start out to meet us until he *knew* he would arrive too late to help Agrippa die. He made sure of it."

That is not the impression here in Rome. All anyone will remember is the emperor's mad scramble to reach Agrippa's bedside. All anyone will remember is the great tragedy that he did not get there in time. But that is not what Julia remembers.

Smearing her tears with the backs of her hands, she says, "My father must have been afraid to come because of the plague. Musa tells him that plague leaps from person to person, like a mad *lemur*. What a coward. More fearful of his health than of betraying the man who was once his truest and most loyal friend."

Maybe that is the explanation. Augustus has always hidden from danger even at the expense of his honor; and he has seldom passed up an opportunity to spite a rival, which is what Agrippa had become, in the end. But can it be only chance that Lepidus and Agrippa should die at once? "You are sure it was plague, Julia?"

"I am sure of nothing but that I have never seen any man fight so hard against his death. Agrippa strained and gritted his teeth. He endured the humiliation of being washed and fed by me until he was too weak to protest. Those strong hands withered in mine. One night, I saw he could bear it no more. I told him that there was no shame in this defeat; that there is one war every commander must lose. He couldn't speak, but put his hand on my swollen belly. Then he sighed and I knew it would be the last sound he ever made. So I kissed him. I put my mouth on his dry, cracked lips and I breathed him in. I took Agrippa's last breath. *I* took it."

She is not crying anymore. That is done. She squares her shoulders with something of the strength of her dead husband. "He's inside me now. Not just in my child, but in our breath and bones. We have him, Selene. We have Agrippa. Me and his unborn child. I've never been so happy to be pregnant before. I've never been so glad of anything in my life."

I stay with Julia well into the night.

I am filled with sorrow for her and her poor children. But it is more than sorrow. Her suspicions have unleashed the dark and angry shadow in my soul. I thought I had defeated my *khaibit*, but some part of me still hates this city and would see it all turned to ash. Here atop this hill, the emperor has built a palace virtually on top of the fabled house of Romulus, a thatch-roofed hut that has been carefully preserved to honor Rome's founder. Like me, Romulus was a twin. He killed his brother for Rome, and I have been left to wonder if I somehow did the same.

Two crows land at my feet, their raven wings flapping as they fight over a charred piece of meat that is still smoking from the flames. It is from the funeral, I realize, from the sacrifice made at the funeral of Agrippa. Now the birds are squawking and squabbling over the scraps like two Roman generals . . .

Juba nudges me gently. "The litter is waiting."

Still, my eyes are on the crows as they take to the sky. The events of the past few days have filled me with white-hot anger. A vengeful *heka* rises in my blood, setting it to boil, and I release it into the wind lest it consume me. I want to punish Livia and the emperor and everyone who has helped bring about such heartache, but there is nothing I can do but smolder. Or is there more magic inside me than even I know?

I wonder because the next morning we learn that the hut of Romulus has burned to the ground. Two crows, they say it was. Two fighting crows, they say, dropped charred meat onto the roof and it somehow caught fire . . .

. . . and now Rome's oldest monument is ash.

It is an omen the emperor takes seriously. He commands the entire imperial family to make ready to travel to the outpost of Aquileia. The official reason is that suppressing the insurrection in Pannonia now falls to Augustus with the greatest urgency. In truth, I think it is the emperor's intention to flee the plague. Or perhaps he fears that his legacy—like the hut of Romulus—will go up in smoke.

I might almost take satisfaction in his fear if it weren't for the fact that Augustus insists that he must have us at his side. He says he must have Juba's help fighting in Pannonia, which is utter nonsense. My husband is no great Roman general, and has not nearly enough battle experience to make himself a worthy successor to Marcus Vipsanius Agrippa even if he *were* a Roman.

Juba will not hear of my objections, however, for the emperor has preyed upon his great weakness. My husband needs to be needed. It has always been thus. Perhaps I have made it worse by so seldom admitting that *I* need my husband. I fear it is true that I do need Juba—more every day. Perhaps if I confessed it, I could turn him from the emperor, but need is a vulnerable thing . . . and I am not brave enough to be that vulnerable.

Instead, I find the courage to confront the emperor, climbing up the stairs to his private study where I once cowered as a girl. "Let Juba go," I say the moment the doors are closed at my back. "If you will have grain for Rome, food for your soldiers, we must return to Mauretania."

The emperor is thrusting scrolls into a pouch, making such haste to depart the city he doesn't even wait for slaves and secretaries to do it for him. He does not look up when he says, "You can set sail from Aquileia."

"But our ship is waiting for us in the port of Ostia."

"Then send a messenger to your ship's captain to meet you in Aquileia, because I will not let you go to Ostia."

"Why not?"

"Because I will not let you expose my children to plague!" he hisses with an angry fling of his arm that nearly topples the golden dolphins he stole from my mother's baths in Egypt. "I am taking you as far away as we can get from the illness without actually crossing over into the provinces."

I cannot decide if he is truly trying to protect us or if this is another performance. "Is the plague really so dangerous?"

He shoves another scroll into the leather pouch. "Dangerous enough to kill Agrippa. Damn him and the mess he left me."

"Are you certain it was plague that killed him?"

His eyes snap to mine. "What makes you ask?"

More than once the emperor spoke to me of killing Agrippa. Now I search his expression for the pretense of grief or the satisfaction of murder. All I see is *rage*. I think he is angry at Agrippa for having had the temerity to die at an inconvenient moment. The emperor used the death of Lepidus to his advantage, but there has been chaos in the wake of Agrippa's funeral. With some legions on the cusp of mutiny, the emperor has been forced to send dispatches to his military commanders beseeching them to be stricter with their soldiers.

I stare and stare, as if I can see through his skin and bones to get to the truth. The emperor's shoulders are knotted in tension. His lips curl in a slight snarl the way they do when his aching teeth are bothering him. And I think he is innocent of Agrippa's death.

If he had sent someone to poison his wayward general, he wouldn't be able to hide his smugness from me. He would want me to know. If he did away with Agrippa, he would want me to appreciate his work. He would *need* someone to appreciate it.

"*What* do you mean by that question, Selene?"

I clear my throat. "It is only that Julia was with Agrippa when he died and she is not ill of plague. None of her children are."

"A good thing too, because Ptolemy is not old enough to be named as my heir. Think! If I should be without Gaius and Lucius to conceal our true ambitions . . . think how my enemies would be emboldened."

Which enemies does he mean? Having worked all his life to be a man without peer, the emperor now imagines himself abandoned and assailed on all sides. He once despaired to me that we now live in a world with only little men, but he has made that world. He is an old man without young ones to succeed him. He is the king of kings without any prince old enough to inherit his kingdom—not even my prince.

That's what decides it for me. Yes, he considered killing Agrippa, but did not want him dead *yet*. He would have waited for a time and place of his choosing—not when one of the provinces is in rebellion and all the children are still so young. He delayed going to Agrippa's side because he was cowardly and petty and because he needed the extra time to cement his power in Rome as Pontifex Maximus.

He may have killed Lepidus, but he did not kill Agrippa.

The only person for whom Agrippa's death is convenient is Livia.

She might have given Agrippa a tonic before he started his journey. She might have sent a slave to do it in her place. In any case, she is now mother to the only good generals Rome has left. Between Tiberius and Drusus, the Claudian brothers now have the legions. And Augustus has finally begun to appreciate the threat posed by his own wife . . .

Twenty-four

AQUILEIA is a frontier town, a veritable fortress against the tribes to the north. Just south of the Alps, the air is colder here and scented with the brackish water of lagoons. My children think this is a rugged springtime adventure and wonder if we will continue up into the mountains and camp in the wild where they've been told they might see wooly bears.

But all the niceties of civilization follow wherever the emperor goes. We are swiftly ensconced as guests into the villa of the wealthiest man in the vicinity. Aquileia is equipped with baths and a marketplace and a basilica for public business, and until the plague passes, this will be the new seat of government.

Something King Herod uses to his immediate advantage.

One night, returning from a foray in the hills with Roman soldiers, Juba says, "The entire royal family of Judea is coming here."

This has me up and out of my chair. "All the more reason to pack our bags now and be on the swiftest ship home . . ."

Still wearing armor, my husband rubs the back of his neck where his helmet has left a red mark. "You go, Selene. Take the children. But I cannot leave Caesar. At least not until autumn. Perhaps the uprising will be over by then."

I want to tell my husband how foolish he is being. I want to tell him that the emperor doesn't need him. That the emperor doesn't even *want* him here. That he is no Roman officer, but a king of a faraway kingdom and is not meant to fight like a lowborn soldier.

I want to tell him that he is only being kept at the side of Augustus so that *I* will be kept here too. But these are the things that would break him, so I grind my teeth. "I hope you have at least spoken to the emperor about the settlement of veterans. There must be a better way to reward these soldiers at the end of their careers than with the grazing lands of our Berbers. Why not a lump sum of gold?"

"Because every soldier dreams he will one day pound his sword into a plowshare and retire to his farm like the old Roman hero Cincinnatus."

"Oh, yes, the idyllic agrarian soldier . . . The dream might be a credit to them if so many soldiers did not immediately sell their land holdings in Mauretania to the richest noblemen in Rome."

On this subject, Juba and I have enjoyed many spirited discussions, but there is no point prattling on about it because we are largely in agreement. He nods. "I'll speak to the emperor after Herod's visit."

And that will have to mollify me. "Why is Herod coming anyway?"

"There is to be a trial."

"A *trial*?" At this news, my eyes widen and I imagine the King of Judea being dragged before the emperor in chains. "What has Herod done?"

A cool mist has descended from the Alps, and in the dampness, Juba slicks his hair back and stops to warm his hands over a brazier in our rooms. "Herod isn't on trial. He's bringing his sons to be tried in a Roman court of law. Herod is bringing them as prisoners. He accuses them of treason."

At this, I nearly choke. "Treason?"

"It's a contemptible business, isn't it? He doesn't dare try his sons in Judea. The boys are both well loved there. For that matter, they're well loved in Rome too. Herod cannot act against them without a Roman decree or he'll be torn by the mob, either in Judea or in Rome."

"Isis forgive me, but seeing Herod at the mercy of the mob *would* be worth staying to see . . ."

Juba smirks at my thirst for Herod's blood. "You won't see it. Herod has chosen his moment well. He drags his sons here to Aquileia where no one knows them. Where no one can defend them."

"Still, he takes a horrible risk just for spite."

"Indeed. Romans will say that a king who cannot keep peace within his own family cannot govern a client kingdom. Herod risks being stripped of his throne. If he cannot establish good governance, all Judea may be turned into a province as a lesson to the rest of us."

Juba does not have to explain it to me. We should be present, whatever comes, if only to serve as a dignified counterexample to the sordid spectacle, lest every kingdom in the empire become another province for greedy Roman generals to loot. We cannot leave for home if we want to have a home to return to . . .

THE emperor sends Juba back up into the mountains to brave the arrows and javelins of the Pannonian tribes. Meanwhile, we celebrate my son's sixth birthday in Aquileia with a party for the little army of imperial and royal children who fill the rustic villa courtyard with shrieks and laughter. Under the supervision of their nurses, they chop at one another with wooden swords, then chase one another on wooden horses with gilded wheels and gemstone eyes. Meanwhile, Dora supervises a makeshift hospital for little clay dollies, much to the delight of the younger girls.

I'm glad the children can take delight in the world, even as the rest of us feel it reshaping under our feet. Livia does not attend the celebration. Octavia, who has scarcely spoken a word since Agrippa's death, excuses herself to take an afternoon nap. Never have I known Octavia to be idle a day in her life, and I glance to Julia in surprise, but her gaze is far away. Too far away to care.

We'd all worried what would happen if the emperor should die but none of us gave a thought to losing Agrippa. It hadn't ever seemed possible. It still does not. "It's your turn," I say to Julia, prompting her attention back to the dice that lie inert in her hand. I've taken it upon myself to cheer her when I can, teaching her games from ancient Egypt that can be played upon a lovely carved wooden board. "Julia—"

"I thought I already won," she says.

"That was only the first round." I run a thumb over the polished ebony of my game piece until it hits a rough edge. "It isn't the whole game. There is an element of chance to it, but there's strategy too. You race your ivory pieces—"

"My father likes to roll dice, not me," she says, pushing away from the table. Then she blinks, staring at the sun. "Selene, you've no gift for false cheer. If I wanted to be amused I'd call for musicians or mimes or . . . monkeys. I seek out your company because you're good at mourning."

She may not intend her words to sting me, but they do. "I never forget my dead, but today I celebrate the birth of my son. My children are the blessed salve for my wounds, and you'll soon have *five* children to comfort you in your darkest days."

Julia snorts indelicately. "Oh, *spare* me. Have you taken to heart my father's lectures about motherhood?"

"Of course not," I say, laying my hand over hers. "But you told me you were glad for this child. Surely not all your happiness died with your husband. You were *Julia* before you were the wife of Marcellus. You were *Julia* before you were the wife of Agrippa—"

"And I was Caesar's daughter before any of that," she says bitterly. "I can never outgrow his authority . . ."

Just then, Augustus enters the courtyard and we jump to our feet—except for Julia, who is too heavily pregnant to jump. The slaves and children all bow to the emperor until he waves them back with one hand, saying, "I'm told there is a young prince who celebrates a birthday today!"

The emperor motions for my son to come near. The children all quiet and gather round, eager to see what great honor the emperor wishes to bestow. How strange it is to witness Augustus go down to one knee before the little Berber prince he wishes so desperately to believe is his own son.

Ptolemy shows no fear. To the contrary, my son smiles his dimpled smile and gives the formal military salute of a Roman soldier. It's a precocious gesture that charms the emperor. "Are you ready to fight the barbarian hordes for me, young Prince Ptolemy?"

My son brandishes his wooden sword in eagerness. "At Caesar's command!"

The emperor smiles more indulgently than I've ever seen him smile at anyone. "Then I think you'll need this." Augustus snaps his fingers and slaves bring forth a miniature set of parade armor, complete with a tiny carved breastplate in gleaming gold and a leather military skirt, studded with gems. My son gasps in delight as the slaves fasten it over his tunic.

I don't think I've ever seen my son so overjoyed.

"But what's missing?" the emperor asks playfully. "What could it be?"

"A scarlet cloak?" little Gaius asks, wrestling with envy.

"Not quite," the emperor says, and another slave comes forward to unfurl a purple cape fringed with gold. "Scarlet cloaks are for everyday soldiers, but Ptolemy is kin to Alexander the Great. He shall wear royal purple like the king he will become."

At this I cringe, for the moment the purple cape is fastened over Ptolemy's shoulders he reminds me of Juba. With long arms and legs, and skin kissed by the desert, he looks more like his true father every day. Whatever I see, however, the emperor does not. "And now, then, young Ptolemy, what's missing still?"

"A helmet," Ptolemy guesses.

"Not a helmet for Ptolemy, but a crown," the emperor replies and rises to receive into his hands two toy reproductions of sacred emblems. When a client king is vested by Rome as a friend and ally, he receives an ivory scepter. Now, with mock solemnity, the emperor places an exact reproduction into my son's hands. Then, whilst Ptolemy is still marveling over the scepter, the emperor places a golden crown upon his head. "There now, you are king for a day."

My children have been taught proper manners, but such is my son's excitement at his gifts that he launches himself against the knees of the emperor, hugging them in gratitude. I give a sharp intake of breath—and all the court titters—but the emperor indulgently pats my son's head. "Off you go now, my little king."

With the lavish gifts dispensed, Augustus meanders to where Julia and I sit astonished. "You'll spoil him," I say, wishing he hadn't called such special attention to my son.

"Oh, I think he'll make a just king," Augustus replies, pointing to where Ptolemy has set up a mock court from which to preside. Peering down at our game board, the emperor takes up one of the ivory pieces, examining it carefully. "What's this?"

"Selene's teaching me a game," Julia says, frostily.

"When it comes to games, you can have no better teacher."

The emperor smiles at me, meaning in his hooded gaze.

And Julia's shrewd eyes miss nothing. "Unfortunately, the games that interest both of you hold no appeal for me. Once my child is born, I wish to return to Rome and retire into private life."

I'm not sure which of us is more surprised by this announcement, but the emperor speaks before I can. "You wouldn't last two days in private life. You crave the attention of the crowds too much."

Because I agree with him, I say nothing. Julia lives to be adored. Even in her grief, she is sure to never, ever be alone. The very idea of such a vibrant woman shutting herself up in a house and wearing mourning clothes every day is absurd. But Julia argues, "I don't see why you should object, father. Your laws say that Roman women have some right to independence once they have borne three children. Well, this child will be my fifth. Surely I qualify to live my life as I please. I've done all that you've asked of me. All that you ask of *any* Roman woman."

"You're not *any* Roman woman," Augustus snaps. "You're my daughter."

She cannot bury her resentment over the emperor's delay in reaching Agrippa's bedside; she cannot even hide her contempt. "Yes, I am your daughter. When you remember it and only then."

"See that *you* remember it when you remarry, which you must now do."

This comes as a cold shock, for Agrippa is not even three months dead. Julia blinks, but recovers swiftly. "Who would you have me marry this time?"

"Someone suitable. You're too dangerous to leave unmarried. You know that, Julia. You must remarry."

She raises her chin. "No. I won't."

For a moment, Augustus stares at his daughter in confusion, unaccustomed to being refused. While he stares, Julia pushes her pregnant girth up from her chair so that she can meet him with a level gaze. "I will not remarry, father. I've given you my children, my youth, my heart . . . you've no right to steal the years remaining. I will not do it. I will not do it simply because you say I must."

Whatever drives her to defy him is a dangerous impulse. He sometimes accepts rebellion from me, but never from her. His arm draws back and his fist closes. It is only because he is slow that I am able to throw myself between them before he strikes her. "Wait!"

Scarlet with rage, the emperor trembles, his arm still upraised. "Hear how she speaks to me!"

"We shouldn't argue in front of the children," I say quickly.

"Let them see how a father disciplines a rebellious daughter!"

Julia ought to shrink from him; she ought to apologize. Instead, she stands behind me, her black garments rustling in the wind like leaves. She is an imperious oak tree of grief. Her stoic silence, her absolute *composure* enrages the emperor even more.

Again, his arm comes up and this time I know he really *will* strike her if I don't stop him. Desperate, I grasp the emperor's cloak, pleading. "Let me speak to you before you do anything rash. Please, I beg of you."

My intimate touch has the desired effect; Augustus allows me to lead him into the house, where I hurriedly whisper, "She doesn't know what she's saying. She's a wounded animal, lashing out blindly. She's broken by grief."

He gnashes his teeth. "Why should she grieve so bitterly for a husband she never wanted in the first place?"

"Does she not owe some loyalty to Agrippa's memory, especially when she is wracked with guilt for having always put her father before her husband?" In this, I mean to remind him of how Julia left Agrippa in Spain, at her father's command. "She's always honored you above everyone else—"

"Where is her filial piety now?" he growls, though his high color is fading. "The contemptuous look she gave me just now would be cause to end a life were she a man."

Fearing a time might come when my children displease him, I say, "You jest that you have two wayward daughters you must indulge. Julia and Rome. Well, it is no jest. Your daughter is near her time of birth, mantled in sadness. This time, this *one* time, you must indulge Julia."

"She must remarry. I cannot indulge her or forgive her!"

"You *can* forgive her. Surely that much is in your power."

He narrows his eyes. "One day soon, I will show you what is in my power."

"GREAT Caesar, what offense have I done these sons of mine that they should plot against me?" King Herod's question, made without any apparent irony, booms theatrically through the crowded basilica.

It is greeted with a murmur of disapproval in the audience. Even Augustus, seated upon his curule chair, wearing his oak-leaf crown, is forced to raise an eyebrow at Herod's nerve. Undeterred, the King of Judea plays the aggrieved father. "Have I not bestowed upon these two young men the finest opportunities, entrusting their education into the hands of Rome? I've given them royal princesses to wed. Whether they asked for servants or spending money for fine clothes, I've never refused either of them if I was able to provide it. And yet their minds are bent on hatred for me."

Herod's sons make a pitiable sight, red shackle marks upon their wrists. The younger brother swallows, the apple of his throat bobbing. The older brother glares daggers at Herod, but is wise enough not to interrupt.

"Even though I'm their sovereign king," Herod continues, "even though I have the power of life and death over them, I bring them before *you,* great Caesar, for justice. Though I have uncovered their parricidal plots—schemes so vile that any other king would put them to death—my love for them is such that I forbear the rightful vengeance of a king or a father. I *risk* my own life to bring them here and submit the matter for Caesar's judgment as if they were my equals and not my subjects."

Someone in the audience snorts. Someone else laughs. By this scorn, Herod ought to measure his words, but he's too caught up in his tirade. "They've written letters to stir up revolt. They've con-cocted poisons to slip into my food. They've hired assassins. I've borne this misery in silence for years now, but no more! Punishment must be done, lest I live the rest of my days in fear."

Though Herod claims close friendship with Augustus, he seems not to sense the emperor's distinct displeasure. Knowing the mood behind the emperor's every gesture, if I were in Herod's place I would silence myself. For though Augustus loves a spectacle, he loves best those spectacles that he creates himself. *This* matter, made so public, is an embarrassment. The accusations Herod has laid at his sons' feet may result in their execution. Herod wants them dead. He wants his own sons dead so much that he will risk infuriating the emperor. Everyone in the audience seems to recoil in collective realization of it.

Glancing from face to face, I search for Herod's allies. Not one Roman displays sympathy. Nor can I find a gesture of support from the mingled royalty or foreign officials. Nicholas of Damascus, one of my old tutors, now in the service of Herod, looks green. It is only amongst the Judean royal family that I finally find Herod's ally. His son Antipater anxiously perches on the edge of his seat. He stands to benefit from his brothers' deaths and I think his anxiety is eagerness.

Herod roars, "Great Caesar, I wouldn't sully your ears with tales of vile treachery if it were not for the pollution of my sons' minds. Both are blinded by low ambition to seize my throne and mur-der me."

"What proof do you offer?" Augustus asks quietly.

This ought to terrify Herod, for the emperor is never so

dangerous as when he withdraws in quiet fury. Nonetheless, the King of Judea continues boldly, "Courtiers tell tales of snide remarks my sons make when my back is turned. They have somehow convinced Jews in my country to call them the *true* heirs. And when I admonish my sons, they answer with biting words, scarcely disguising a roll of their eyes. Disrespect is where treachery starts, Caesar. You cringe to hear it, but you're a father too. What would you think if your own daughter showed such disrespect?"

A collective gasp sucks the air from the room and all eyes turn to where I sit next to Julia in the gallery. Herod must be a madman to compare his sons to Agrippa's mourning widow. He must be *absolutely mad* to impugn the character of the emperor's daughter, even by implication, for at this moment, Julia is more popular than the emperor himself.

Julia's response is to turn her head and whisper to her slave, as if she had not been listening, but I narrow my eyes at Herod to show my derision. He has gone too far. Surely he will pay for it.

Alas, Herod made his career not in stepping back from a breach but by compounding his error with such audacity that he must be forgiven. "If your daughter were to disobey you, Caesar, would it not lead you to the inescapable conclusion that she plotted your murder?" It is an absurd premise, but Herod knows exactly to whom he speaks. "Augustus, I submit to you, the only child who does not fear a father is the child who intends to ensure the father will not live long enough to take vengeance."

Herod hits a nerve. A pulsing raw nerve—one that I doubt he reached for on his own. He cannot have learned of Julia's quarrel with the emperor from his own spies. He learned it from someone else. Someone taught him how to play upon the emperor's paranoia. Someone has positioned his bow and pointed his arrow.

Someone is aiming for Julia . . .

Twenty-five

FROM her seat in the gallery, Livia's tiny twitch of a smile tells me I was a fool to ever think that Herod was Agrippa's creature. Now I realize that he must have belonged to Livia all along. She has rid herself of Julia's husband as an obstacle. Now she must be rid of Julia and her boys. Livia may not be able to poison them, but she can poison the emperor's heart against his own daughter.

It is, I admit, the best play, because in her widowed and pregnant beauty, Julia is loved in a way that Livia has never been loved nor ever will be. And if the emperor makes common cause with his daughter—if he takes Julia as his political helpmate, a role that she has always longed to fill—the Claudians will remain powerless. The only way that Livia's family can rise to power is by cutting Julia down and getting her out of the way.

Livia must see just such an opportunity in Julia's refusal to remarry, which infuriated Augustus.

The quarrel must be fresh on the emperor's mind because Herod's comments about disobedient children make Augustus lower his head, rubbing his temples as if to quiet a roaring pain. If anyone provokes him now, an execution will follow. One snap of his fingers and someone will die. So I am breathless with fear when my husband, seated at the emperor's side, leans over and whispers to him.

A moment later, Augustus calls a break in the proceedings. Then the emperor retires with my husband and the small retinue of men who now make up his shrinking inner circle. At my side, Julia smiles as if untroubled, but whispers, "If Agrippa were still alive, he would tear King Herod's head from his neck . . ." Then she rises from her seat, giving an affectionate wave to the crowd. "I'm going to rest."

I go with her, escorting her down the shadowed corridor of the basilica, where we are set upon by Princess Glaphyra, whose beautiful face is swollen with tears. "Lady Julia," Glaphyra whispers by way of greeting, a sob in her throat. "Your Majesty."

Julia knows that nothing good can come of meeting with the wife of the accused prince, so she abandons me. "I would invite you to dine, Princess Glaphyra, but I'm afraid I don't feel well. Selene, stay and be reunited with your friend."

When Julia goes, Glaphyra grasps my hands beseechingly. "I beg your help. King Juba is a great favorite of Caesar, as are you. Can you persuade your husband to speak on our behalf?"

"I'm quite certain that my husband is doing so even now."

"Tell him King Herod has vowed to kill us, whether Augustus grants him permission or no."

I find this hard to believe. "Not even Herod would defy the emperor . . . but in case I am wrong, you should flee Judea at the soonest opportunity and return to your father's kingdom."

The unhappy princess grips my hands harder in desperation. "Herod has the power to call back any person who flees from him from anywhere in the empire. He says that Caesar has favored him with this authority, granted to no other king."

With an indignant laugh, I disabuse her of this notion. "Herod claims a great many things are granted to him and him alone. Think the way Romans do. In their eyes, you'll always belong to your father before you belong to Herod or even to your husband."

Glaphyra inhales, taking in my words, then squeezes her eyes shut. "I can't flee. Even if I could leave my husband, Herod has my sons. My two little boys . . ."

At this, my throat swells with sympathy for her plight.

She gathers her composure, opens her eyes, and meets mine. "My husband and his brother and my sons are all that's left of the Hasmonean dynasty. Herod wants them dead. He is a man with a rotting heart who suspects intrigue behind every pillar; he's not fit to rule Judea. Truly, he is not fit. Tell me how to make the emperor see it."

There is no one alive who has danced on the edge of the emperor's blade as often as I have, so perhaps she has asked the right person. Herod appealed to the father in Augustus. The emperor will be thinking of Julia and her recent rebellion. So I tell her, "Your husband and his brother must be humble."

"My husband and his brother are both proud men . . ."

"Their mother was also proud. That is why Herod executed her, is it not? They must be *humble*."

Glaphyra nods as if she understands, but the way she dissolves into tears makes me doubt that my words will do any good. Glaphyra leaves me, returning to the chamber in which the trial will soon resume. "There goes a pitiable princess," I say, when my husband comes upon me. "Do you believe in the innocence of Herod's sons?"

Juba shrugs. "Herod offers no proof of guilt."

"But do you think they are innocent?"

"I think . . ." My husband hesitates, his amber gaze dropping to the floor. "I think that I'd rather die than see my children dead, no matter what crime they might ever commit."

It is a sentiment that prompts me to put my hand in his, though the Romans think it is vulgar for a husband and a wife to show such public affection. "Say we will never become like the Herods."

A sound of light amusement rumbles up from my husband's chest. "Do you fear that beneath my scholar's robes I disguise a bloody tyrant?"

I fear that I will never know Juba as I know my own soul. I fear I will never sense his presence when I walk into a room nor feel the tug of *heka* pull between us, two halves of a soul straining to reunite. Juba is not my twin. He is not my other half. He is always a foreign creature to me, one with strange habits and customs. He is neither fire nor ice. He is a man I think I will never wholly understand. But of *this* I am absolutely certain: Juba is no tyrant.

In all the empire there may be no other king like him.

And, perhaps for the first time, I realize how fortunate I am to call him my husband. It is only the circumstances under which we came together that put us at odds. If we had met in another place, another time, I would never have resisted him. By the gods, if I were a different woman and came before this king, I would have held nothing back . . .

Pressing his lips very briefly to my forehead, Juba says, "The trial is starting again. We must go."

We return to the hall, where Prince Aristobulus sobs as if bewildered by the danger in which he finds himself. I advised that they be humble, but truly, they are wretched. The eldest prince reaches for his brother's hand in comfort, and this spontaneous display of fraternal love moves the crowd to groan. These two princes have said not a word and yet women weep for them in the audience. Grown men rub their eyes and the current of emotion that flows through the crowd seizes even the emperor's cold, withered heart. "Fear not to speak before Caesar," the emperor tells the princes.

Dramatically, Glaphyra's husband turns to face Herod, his accuser. "Father, that you have brought us before the emperor, the savior himself, is proof that you mean to save us. Still, how can we live knowing you believe us guilty? If you truly believe we're such fiendish conspirators, it's better that we die."

I hold my breath at this bold and dangerous gambit. As every eye turns to look at him, Herod seems to suddenly notice the crowd. He sees hostile faces, women weeping, men ready to shout in favor of the princes, and his expression changes to one of affected sorrow as he considers a reply.

Prince Alexander speaks again before Herod can. "It's an easy thing for your advisers to say that my brother and I want to take your throne in revenge for our unhappy mother. But could not such an accusation be made against any young men in our circumstance? Suspicion is not proof. Let any man come forward and testify that we have procured poisons. We beseech any man who has witnessed conspiracy to speak of it now."

Not one person steps forward. The floor remains empty. The emptiness stretches on and on, which fuels the prince's righteousness. "Our mother is dead, this is true. But isn't it possible her death has served as a warning to us? We cannot confess to evil deeds never done, but we are sorry for any conduct on our part that has let you believe the worst. Before Caesar, we put this to you. It is a terrible thing to be falsely accused. Yet we cannot bear for our father to live in fear of us, so if you are not convinced of our innocence, then we desire to die."

Pandemonium breaks out with shouts in favor of the princes. Whereas Herod is late to appreciate the sympathies of the crowd, the emperor can plainly see that any order of execution will cause a riot. Herod has made himself hated. There is not a slave or senator in the room who does not count the King of Judea a deranged fiend. Should the emperor sanction Herod's butchery, Augustus *too* will be seen as monstrous . . . and for no political gain.

So when Augustus turns to Herod, a chasm has opened between them. One wrong word and Herod will fall into it. I'm eager for it. *Do it*, I think, *and you will be destroyed.*

Unfortunately, Herod sees the danger. At this last crucial moment, he wisely takes a step back. "Like the rest of you, I am moved by the words of my sons and apologize to you, Caesar . . ."

Augustus waits, his fingers steepled beneath his chin.

Herod begins to speak, then stops. Begins again. Stops.

"Oh, why apologize, King Herod?" Augustus finally breaks in. "Though your sons are surely innocent of the crimes of which you have accused them, they are not *entirely* blameless. After all, it is the duty of a child to behave with such subservience to a father that such suspicions would not be believed by anyone."

Here the emperor's gaze lifts to the gallery as if seeking out his daughter, and I am glad Julia made a hasty retreat. The emperor clears his throat. "I admonish you to be reconciled with your sons. Dismiss gossip and rumor in the future. Harbor not suspicion for your sons, but affection."

It's both a command and a reprieve. The emperor's evenhanded justice allows the king to save face. But the truth is seen in gestures, not words. Augustus does not embrace Herod. Instead, he summons the two princes forward. Knowing they've been spared, they both drop to their knees in supplication, but the emperor lifts them up, one after the other. The gesture is understood by all. Augustus has given his personal endorsement to the two princes.

None of this is lost on Herod. "I shall send an amended will to you, Caesar, for your approval. I shall restore these sons to the succession."

"Make whatever provisions you like," Augustus snaps, as if envisioning an endless stream of paperwork every time Herod wishes to punish someone. "Divide your kingdom evenly between your sons for all I care; I don't need to approve every change."

Herod forces himself to smile at this chilly response and bows graciously. "This is a great honor, Caesar, that you grant me the authority to dispose of my kingdom as I see fit. How many other client kings may say the same? I will do it now, if you so desire. In the spirit of harmony we have found here, I will make such arrangements before all assembled."

It's another blunder, and Augustus narrows his eyes. "You would do better to keep your final arrangements to yourself. I would not want, after all, to deprive you of the power over your kingdom, or your sons, while you live."

With that, the emperor turns on his heel. In a swirl of red cloaks, his praetorians snap to attention and assemble at his back, and then they are gone.

MY poet writes an amusing verse mocking Herod, but he is wise enough to show it only to me in the privacy of my apartments. "I thought to pass it off as the work of an anonymous epigrammist, Majesty, but my style is too distinctive, my talent unmatched."

The poem amuses me but I blot it out with ink from my reed pen. "Let the moment pass unheralded, Crinagoras."

"Don't you want to immortalize Herod fleeing with his tail between his legs like a broken dog?"

"Herod is not broken," I say, bitterly.

"Bruised, then." Crinagoras takes a seat without being bidden, draping one leg casually over the other while admiring the length of his own thigh. "So bruised that he is trying to buy his reputation back in the East. Nicholas of Damascus shared with me a bit of gossip that the King of Judea has promised to fund the Olympic Games in perpetuity and they've appointed him to preside over the coming games . . ."

"Yes, I know." For hundreds of years my family funded the Olympic Games. There is even a gymnasium there named after my illustrious ancestor. Of all the reasons for my enmity with the King of Judea, this is surely the most petty, but it irritates me like a rash I cannot scratch. "Herod will get away with it. All of it. Augustus has done nothing to punish him. He allowed Herod his show trial, he allowed Herod to make veiled accusations against Julia, he allowed Herod to go about boasting that he is King Herod *Philokaiser* . . . the friend of Caesar. And what's more, Herod has now convinced the emperor to give him the profits from the copper mines in Cyprus."

This sobers my poet, who understands the importance of that last bit. Cyprus was part of the Ptolemaic empire—part of the kingdom that should have been mine. Part of the kingdom that could still belong to my children. That Augustus took my ancestral lands for himself is painful enough; that he should cede any part of it to the King of Judea is beyond endurance.

Crinagoras is plainly shaken. "So Herod *does* want Egypt. He dares to think . . . he will try again to arrange a marriage with your daughter."

"Yes. He will keep trying. He is that brazen. The rest of the world thinks King Herod is the emperor's exotic pet lion—a creature to let loose in the arena for amusement or to set upon enemies when convenient—but one that needs periodic beating with a whip to keep tame. But I know better than to trust Herod can be tamed or that it is the emperor who holds the whip."

"Then Herod is your rival," my poet says, slowly.

"Yes. Herod is my rival," I agree. Herod is my rival in the way none of the emperor's friends or mistresses have ever been. Herod is my rival because he has intuited the emperor's need to be appreciated by those who *understand* the full measure of what he has accomplished.

Herod is part of the old guard. He has been playing the game longer than any of us. He knows how to woo the emperor, to seduce him on an equal footing, withholding from him the empty adulation of the masses. I have seen him do it before; he did it even during the trial when he spoke to the emperor as one father to another.

It has taken me far too long to realize that the emperor indulges Herod much as he has always indulged me. Herod is a threat. If not to me, then to my dynasty. But I will never let Herod have Egypt. I will never let him have my daughter. And I will never again think of him as a petty irritant. I must crush Herod under the heel of my silvered sandal by whatever means necessary.

I am a Ptolemy. Our motto is *Win or Die.*

I must find a way to engineer his fall. "You know that Herod once sent Lady Circe to my husband as a gift, as a spy."

"You should do the same to him, but he has so many wives I do not see how he could find the room in his bed for a *hetaera* too."

My poet has finally drawn me to the point of our visit. "I intend to put a spy in his court, but it cannot be a whore. Herod does not trust women. Yet, he is vain enough to trust flatterers . . ."

"Your Majesty," Crinagoras says carefully, "I believe you are about to do something *enormously* foolish."

Knowing that he has guessed at my intentions, I glance up over my cup of warmed wine. "Am I?"

"Yes," he drawls, drawing out the word. Then, just when I think he will refuse me, he smiles. "You are about to quarrel with the world's greatest living poet. Without regard for his unsurpassed talent and the damage it will do to the beleaguered state of the arts in your kingdom, you are about to dismiss me from your service. In a fit of royal pique, you are going to take offense to a wonderfully witty remark that amuses everyone but pricks at your Ptolemaic pride."

"You are not as witty as you think you are, Crinagoras."

"Exactly what you will say before dismissing me from your service, seizing what pittance you pay me, and leaving me resentful and without passage home to Mytilene. Why, I will be forced to beg the indulgence of the Judeans to set sail with them . . ."

He looks satisfied and amused with this plan.

"Do you think Herod will be fooled? I worry that he will never offer you employment knowing that you're an intimate of mine."

"Did he not steal Nicholas of Damascus from your mother? Herod attracts malcontents. He'd like nothing better than to stick it in your eye."

"But can you do it? You're a poet, not a spy."

"Entertainers make the best spies. We're easily overlooked."

It occurs to me that Crinagoras may very well have been spying upon *me* all these years. He's been within my most intimate circle, privy to many of my secrets. And he's right. It is very easy to overlook a poet—even one as ostentatious as mine . . .

But my goddess can see into the heart of a man and know his true name, and I think this too may be in my gift. My poet has seen me through very dark days and I trust him. "It would be a very great risk, Crinagoras."

"I need the excitement," he replies, eyes dancing with delight at the opportunity to make mischief. "When I first came to serve you, it was all storms and sorcery and royal pathos worthy of Homer. Now you've become so dreadfully domesticated . . ."

"Domesticated!"

"Oh, that's very good. See how easy it is to offend you with a witty remark?"

My jaw snaps shut. "How would you get information to me?"

"Infrequently. I might send it with someone I trust or put it in a poem as a coded message you could read with a cipher. Lady Lasthenia is better suited to this kind of scheming . . . but she is in Mauretania and here I am, bored and willing. How long would you have me stay in Herod's court?"

"Until you found a way to destroy him."

"Splendid," he says. "Then I offer my services without hesitation."

Ah, what a shiny prize he offers me. "If we really mean to do this, we must tell King Juba."

"Very well," Crinagoras says, daring to roll his eyes at me. "But on the matter of your domestication, I rest my case . . ."

JUBA does not like the idea. "If your poet wants to leave, let him leave. If he wants to serve Herod, let him serve Herod. If he is caught sending you letters or receiving Mauretanian gold, we will be implicated."

Perched on the edge of my husband's writing table, where I seek to win his approval—or at least distract him with peeks at my breasts and the scent of my lavender perfume—I say, "Then let us be implicated. How many letters did your *hetaera* send before you realized she was Herod's spy?"

Juba pretends to write upon a scroll but leaves only a scribble. "I knew what she was all along."

I do not believe him. "Still you took her for a lover?"

He lifts his eyes from the page to stare at me in challenge, knowing that he has been caught in a prideful lie. "I took Lady Circe to bed to arouse your jealousy."

"That was poorly planned, since I did not learn of your love affair for nearly a year."

"It was not a love affair," he snaps, trying to ride it out. Then color floods his cheeks. "I was lonely."

I smother a smile, for I am charmed beyond measure. "Why,

husband, I did not know that loneliness could lead to such bad political judgment. I shall endeavor not to leave you lonely again . . ."

His hard stare melts and he murmurs, "That might be best. For the good of the kingdom."

"Ah, *for the good of the kingdom*, what would I not do?" I ask, pressing an affectionate hand to his cheek to soothe his embarrassment. "Will you consent to send Crinagoras to Herod's court?"

"Will you obey me if I refuse?"

I consider my answer. "Yes . . ."

He considers my hesitation. "But then you will find another way to spy on Herod without telling me . . ."

"Possibly."

"And you will resent me as an unworldly king . . ."

"Probably."

"And either way, we will quarrel late into the evening?"

"Certainly."

He leans back, stretching his neck. "And just so I understand all the pertinent facts . . . even if I emerge victorious from this quarrel, I will lose a great deal of sleep tonight."

"You will lose several nights' sleep and not for any pleasant reason."

He smirks. "Then you have my consent, Selene, because I must be up before dawn to ride out with Roman soldiers into the hills . . ."

I would like to quarrel about that as well, for I am fearful every time he rides out with the emperor's soldiers to face a hailstorm of arrows, but that is an argument I cannot win. Furthermore, I'm sure to make a fool of myself in such an argument when I'm running hot with desire for him. I do not understand this desire and how it can flourish in the grief and danger and drama of Aquileia. This is not a desire born of love or duty or sacrament. I fear that my husband has taught me to desire for desire's own sake.

The realization of it embarrasses me, but not so much that I pull away when he leans in for a kiss. Perhaps he only means it to be a tender kiss good night, but it swiftly turns hungry and breathless and in its aftermath, I am shy. "Juba, I thought you wanted a restful evening . . ."

"Suddenly, I am not so very tired . . ."

Good thing too, because we do not sleep.

THE dismissal of my poet is easily managed the next morning. Then Crinagoras sails away with the Herods and I do not know when, or if, I will ever see him again. My mouth goes sour with the taste of sending someone I care about into mortal danger. It is what rulers do, but if it all goes wrong, how will I forgive myself?

Soon after the departure of the Herods, at the end of the month sacred to Juno, Julia gives birth. She asks me to play the part of the handmaiden and deliver the news to the emperor. I find him on the terrace overlooking a makeshift arena in which his soldiers have arranged an early-morning cockfight for his amusement. The emperor has been shown all the wonders of Greece, but in Aquileia, this cacophony of birds and men consumed with mindless bloodlust in the shadow of darkly forested hills is apparently the best sport to be found.

"It is a boy," I whisper in the emperor's ear. "Big and healthy. Julia would like for him to be named Marcus Vipsanius Agrippa Postumus."

It is the emperor's prerogative to choose the boy's name, but he says, "I suppose it is only right. He's Agrippa's only son by law, as I've taken all the others."

I hear the note of satisfaction. Was it all for show, how hard he fought against adopting Gaius and Lucius? Or is it only now that Agrippa is dead that the emperor imagines the adoptions as a private victory over his ambitious general? "Shall I tell Julia you're pleased by the birth of your grandson?"

Staring down at the cockfight, he replies, "You shall tell Julia that she must marry Tiberius."

Neither the screeching of the birds nor the nip in the morning air chills me so much as the emperor's words. "Tiberius? You cannot mean it. You cannot possibly mean to let Livia have her way."

The emperor clenches his teeth. "It's a necessary measure."

"You are handing your empire over to the Claudians!"

"I am handing nothing but Julia to Tiberius."

"That will be enough. Tiberius already has your legions. Now he will have your daughter too. What can Livia have possibly said to convince you to wedge her family into power at the expense of yours?"

As the birds battling below us scratch and peck and claw, Augustus says nothing. Normally, he would challenge me to work out for myself the reasoning of his political decisions, but whatever is behind this one, he would rather I did not know. That is what shocks me, and my mouth drops open. "You *suspect* her. You suspect her of doing away with Agrippa. And you fear—"

"I fear nothing."

I give a bitter laugh to stave off sudden bitter tears. "You fear *Livia*. You are afraid of your wife, and you should be because you can't touch her now. You can't do anything to her without risking that her sons will turn the legions against you in vengeance. You can't even divorce her or get rid of her now. She has you *trapped*."

"Tread carefully, Selene," the emperor warns.

I go on, heedlessly laughing, near hysteria. "She has outsmarted you. She has outsmarted us all. Now the Claudians will have their way . . ."

"They will *think* they do," Augustus snaps, punctuating his words with a slap of his thigh. "With Tiberius as my son-in-law, there will be no need for them to scheme."

Tiberius is now the empire's most notable general. He's achieved more than any of his ancestors in more than two hundred years. All that, with a bloodline far more prestigious than the emperor's. "Don't do it," I plead with him. "For the love of the gods, give Julia to someone else. Find someone strong enough to stand against Livia. Someone who needs Julia and her sons to cement a claim. Do not clear a path for the Claudians. Create a *rival* for them."

The emperor glares at me. "Who? You tell me who, Selene."

"Iullus Antonius! He's a soldier. He has my father's legacy behind him. He might hold it all together. My half brother would defend Julia and her children and you."

When the emperor leans forward, I think he's considering it until I see the malice shining in his eyes. "I would sooner see Rome *burned to ashes.*"

"Then you just might see it burn."

"Listen well, Selene. I will never give Mark Antony that victory over me. I *took* his daughter to my bed; his son won't take mine."

This pronouncement is a slap to the face—a stinging reminder of how he took me by force. He told me I wanted it and he is not the only one to have accused me. My own husband blamed me for the emperor's lust. Even I tried to convince myself that the emperor would never have done it without Livia's encouragement. Now I know better. Now I know what was in his mind from the first moment he came to Alexandria. He wanted to *take* everything my father had, and when my mother escaped him in death, he turned his eyes to me. He was *always* going to rape me; always intended it. Nothing I did or didn't do would have changed that. It was never my fault or Juba's fault or even Livia's fault. The crime was all his.

Below us, a rooster falls bloody and defeated into the dirt.

While the men cheer the victor, the emperor insists, "Tiberius must marry Julia. If my health should fail me while my heirs are still little boys—"

"Then they'll all be at Tiberius's mercy. Julia and Gaius and Lucius . . ."

"Not only them, Selene. You and your children too. Everyone who belongs to me. The only way to hinder the aspirations of Tiberius is to bind him to my legacy. My daughter must be his. My sons must be his. This will tie his hands."

The Tiberius I remember was a sour boy and a brooding young man who kept his own company but was never cruel without provocation. The trouble with Tiberius has always been his willingness to cater to his mother's overweening ambitions. With the emperor gone, Livia will be free to take her revenge on all those she despises. We will be at *her* mercy, and perhaps that is what the emperor intends to protect us against.

"It will be Tiberius," he insists. "It *must* be Tiberius. Not Drusus, not Iullus, nor any other man I have not observed since his boyhood. We both know Tiberius's nature. He never takes a risk if there is no promise of reward. He will be grateful to me for this marriage and it will buy us time, for he will never act against me if he believes that he must only wait for me to die . . ."

"It's a gamble. You'd rely upon Tiberius's character and gratitude?"

"And his love for my daughter. I'm told she can be very charming."

"Tiberius is besotted with his own wife. He doesn't want Julia."

"She can change that. And you must persuade her to do it."

Twenty-six

❧

"SO now I am to seduce my own stepbrother for the good of Rome?" Julia bares her breast for her infant son, who is her child in a way none of the others have been. Sitting beside her on a couch in the inner courtyard, I sense in her a new mother's fierceness. "My father doesn't even have the courage to ask it of me. Instead, he sends the daughter of the woman he called the world's greatest harlot to give me lessons. You don't mind being used in such a way?"

She's entitled to her bitterness, so I take no offense at her words. Her position is altogether too familiar and it pains me to argue on her father's behalf; I would not do so if I saw any other way. "The emperor intends to ask Tiberius to marry you. If you appear . . . unwilling . . . Julia, you do not want to be blamed for providing an excuse for Tiberius to refuse."

Julia's nose wrinkles as if she has smelled something foul. "Either way, I will have the blame."

I take a breath before telling the truth as I see it. "I believe that your father is trying to secure your welfare. Yes, he is thinking of his own legacy and selfish desires, but he is also thinking of you and your children. What would happen if your father died tomorrow?"

Julia's eyes drift to the window with an expression that is either worry or wishfulness. "I would be a prize for the highest bidder, no different than now."

She's being stubborn. She doesn't know what it is to grow up at the mercy of a man who considers your every breath a danger to his ambitions. I've lost four brothers to the emperor's fear and it would be naive to believe he's the only man capable of such monstrous acts. A man who wished to rule Rome would smother Julia's little children in their beds if given the chance.

And that is to say nothing of what Livia might do.

I must make Julia understand. "Until your sons come of age, they are in danger. We know Tiberius isn't ambitious for his own sake. If you win his heart, he may defend your sons against his mother. Against all. He may come to love your children as his own."

"Now you're thinking of *your* husband, Selene. Not Tiberius."

I dare not ask what she means by that or what she knows.

The baby in her arms hiccups round her nipple, then screws up his face to cry. "There, there," Julia murmurs. "You cannot cry, Postumus . . . not when you look so much like your father, who never cried at all . . ." The baby screams instead, and she says, "Yes, screams are better than tears. Better that you bellow like your father . . ."

Truthfully, little Agrippa Postumus wails louder than any babe I've ever heard, and I remember the way the Admiral's booming voice could shake a room. I wonder if it is this reminder of her dead husband, of taking his last breath, that stiffens Julia's spine. Because when Julia looks at me, I don't see the girl who gave herself over to one wild impulse after the next. I see a woman who knows the world and her own place in it. "My answer is no. I will not woo Tiberius. You may tell my father that I am no whore."

IN the end, the matter is decided by Iullus Antonius.

He waits until the celebration of the Neptunalia, when the citizens camp beside the River Aquilis and splash in the water when the afternoon sun gets too hot. Of the Roman festivals, this one requires the fewest formal prayers and was Admiral Agrippa's favorite—for he believed that Neptune had granted him his naval victories. Perhaps it is for this reason that Julia arranges for the sacrifice of white bulls, enough to honor the god and feed the people of Aquileia too. The mouthwatering scent of meat roasted over campfires fills the air and we are all on hand to celebrate.

The imperial family has settled in to dine in a lavish tabernacle, complete with garlands wound round every tent pole and flower petals strewn upon the tables. It is in this idyllic setting, where luminescent glowworms light the darkening sky, that Iullus announces, suddenly and without warning, "Caesar, I would marry your daughter."

It is such an outrageous statement, so bold and out of place, that everyone ignores it. As if our ears had all played tricks on us. As if his words were just a low murmur on the evening breeze, a sound only imagined. Inside the tabernacle, children shriek protests against nursemaids who usher them to bed, guests continue to eat heartily, and slaves still scurry between couches fetching platters, filling wine cups, and wafting giant fans made of ostrich feathers.

In truth, I would wonder if *I* heard wrong were it not for the narrowing of the emperor's eyes.

Before I can prevent it, Iullus lumbers to his feet, struggling to pull the end of his toga into proper position over one arm. His low baritone is not unlike my father's. And this time it carries. "Caesar, give Julia to me and I will seek no other honor as long as I live."

The crowd's laughter dies away. But the uncomfortable silence does not stop Iullus. Nor does he see the urgent warning in my expression. He does not even flinch from the gorgon's glare Livia shoots him from her couch. There is only one woman he sees. And that is Julia.

Still garbed in mourning, the emperor's daughter is sprawled on a low couch beneath garlands of flowers and fruit, blinking at Iullus with tears in her eyes. It is plain that he has taken her utterly unawares and she is not the only one . . .

The emperor folds his arms and gazes upon the son of his conquered enemy. Surely Iullus must see that is all he has ever been to Augustus. He must see the malice in the emperor's eyes, the pure contempt. Any fool would see it, and Iullus is not a fool.

But he is worse than a fool; he is a man in love. "Caesar, all my life, I have defended what is yours. Your name, your family, your legions, your empire. Allow me to defend your daughter and her children with my sword and I swear by Jupiter, it will be my honor and only ambition."

The emperor's reply is pure venom from a seething maw. "You are nothing *but* ambition, Iullus Antonius. I gave my niece to you thinking it might satisfy your appetite, and this is how you repay me?"

It is a small mercy that Marcella retired early for the evening. Perhaps Iullus told her what he intended, or perhaps her absence was the permission he needed to blunder forth. And blunder forth he does with a heartbreaking, wine-soaked passion. "Your niece is a woman of the greatest value, second only in virtue to your daughter. Marcella has been a good wife to me. But it is Julia I love—Julia I have always loved—and I would take her as my wife for all my life long."

Love. Like a buffoon, he has said the word aloud. It forces Julia's hands to her face but elicits nervous laughter from the rest of the onlookers, all of whom scoff at love. They are hypocrites, every one of them, for I have learned that Romans *feel* romantic love like any other people . . . it is only that they fear it more.

At Iullus's declaration, Livia laughs, giving a casual toss of her head that belies the stiffness of her posture. But I do not laugh and neither does the emperor. His eyes are a winter storm, his lips drawn tight and mean. I know this icy expression, for I have seen it countless times before. This is the face of a killer. It is the cold face of death.

My hapless half brother is staring at mortal danger and every part of me wants to scream a warning. I want to rush at Iullus. I want to shield his body with my own and threaten to call down magic in his defense. But I'm frozen in terror that the emperor will blame me for his folly.

Instead, he blames Julia, turning to his daughter, ominous thunder rolling below his words. "I wonder . . . would such an arrangement be agreeable to you, Julia?"

One glance at her father and she knows, as I know, that he has murder on his mind. If she confesses her love for Iullus, it will mean his death, so Julia steadies herself, rises to her feet, and says, "No virtuous Roman daughter would opine on such a matter. Any arrangement my father finds agreeable is one that I welcome . . ."

This is too timid to stop what Iullus has put in motion. The emperor's fury has been unleashed and he will not be humored. "Nevertheless, I am an indulgent father and wish to know my daughter's preferences in the matter."

Julia glances at Iullus, who laps up the eye contact with canine hope. All his life he has endeavored to live down the reputation of our ancestors, the *Antonii*, whose wild love for life has always been our undoing. But now raw emotions play across his face, and it is Julia who retreats behind a cool mask.

Sweeping her lashes low, she says, "If I do have a preference, a hidden softness for a man, it is not for *Iullus Antonius . . .*"

She says his name with disdain and Iullus stumbles back as if a blow has caught him square in the chest. As if he did not understand that she is battling for his life. His mouth opens to drag in a pained breath. He is lovelorn. He is suffering. And I hope—I pray—that this deep wound will appease the emperor's bloodlust.

But that is a vain hope, for the emperor now finds his feet, and we all watch the horrid drama acted out before us. "If not Iullus Antonius, then whom would you wed?"

Julia's complexion goes to ash but she mimics shyness. "I've whispered his name in confession to your wife . . . but even I am not immodest enough to say it aloud."

Livia's smile is slow, triumphant, and chilling. "Tiberius."

Julia averts her gaze, one hand to her face as if she were blushing, but there is no flush on her cheeks. It's Tiberius whose cheeks redden. Never at ease in his own skin, he looks as if he'd like to crawl out of it now. He holds his wife's hand, actually gripping Vipsania's fingers. Vipsania turns her head to shield her eyes from onlookers and we're all frozen in an awkward tableau.

A married man in love with a widowed beauty who claims she would rather bed down with her own stepbrother. Not even the most vulgar playwright could write such a farce. Such a hideous farce.

And yet Julia's theatrics save the day. The emperor plainly enjoys the humiliation of Iullus. If his humiliation were water, the emperor would bathe in it. He is spitting in my father's face through Iullus, and it is the happiest I have seen him since he told us that Lepidus was dead. "Well, then, Tiberius Claudius Nero, can you refuse an alliance with me and my beautiful daughter, her heart so tender for you?"

Tiberius goes to stone, but we all know what his answer will be.

I want to go home. I want to board the first ship and sail for Mauretania. I would *swim* if I could. But Julia begs me to stay until the wedding and I cannot leave her. Not even when we learn that she's to marry Tiberius in November. It means I must stay on until after the sea closes even though the dispatches we receive from home are increasingly distressed at our absence. I will miss another sowing season, another growing season, another quiet winter in my beloved kingdom.

My only consolation is that I see my half sister Minora joyfully reunited with her husband. Drusus has been campaigning in Germania, where he took a fleet of ships into the North Sea and ran aground during the low tide, suffering untold casualties. It is a near catastrophe for his campaign, and in retreat, he'll winter with us in Rome. Augustus wants him with us—his punishment for failure in Germania, I suppose.

As a married couple, Drusus and Minora are famously well suited. Young and handsome, gay and charming, they're beloved of the people in the way Julia and Marcellus once were. But this time, it is a real romance. Drusus is as much known for fidelity to his marriage bed as he is for his fierceness against the Germanic tribes. And with little children in her arms, Minora is the picture of a happy

Roman wife. Perhaps the emperor hopes their marital accord will distract from the colder, more calculating arrangements being made for his daughter.

Or perhaps he hopes they will cheer his sister.

Our poor Octavia.

All Rome remembers when she swooned at the mere mention of her son's name in Virgil's poem. We saw her grieve for Marcellus, deeply and bitterly. Her sadness was an exposed wound, the scar visible to everyone. But her lingering grief for *Agrippa* is hidden . . . and festering. She was not Agrippa's mother, his sister, his daughter, or his widow. She was nothing to him in the eyes of the world. She gave him up to win a dynastic game. Now she is defeated, and I can say nothing to comfort her. I know, as she knows, that in spite of our efforts, we've failed.

Unless Julia's children survive to be men, the Claudians will rule.

News of the betrothal between Julia and Tiberius has reached every corner of the empire and Livia is now ascendant. When we make our processional into Rome, Livia rides in a gilded carriage beside Augustus, clutching Julia's little boys in her talons. Her message is simple: The man who rules Rome today and all the men who might rule Rome tomorrow . . . they all belong to her.

Livia has usurped Julia's place as the mother of the empire.

And Lady Octavia is forgotten. She stops weaving. She says the wool is inferior. The dye is no good. The loom is broken. But I see the way she rubs at her hands, the joints of which are swollen. I think she is in pain, though she does not complain of it. And in the weeks before Julia's wedding, Octavia takes to her bed.

The Antonias and I worry over her, fretting when she turns food away. When her daughters abandon their husbands and move into Octavia's house to care for her, I can do no less. I take my childhood bed in the room with the loose brick in the wall, where Octavia imprisoned me . . . and sheltered me.

Octavia's daughters and I make ourselves a nuisance to the household slaves. We see her shiver and demand a bigger fire in her room, more blankets for her bed, hot cider for her to drink. We see her flush and we demand she be carried out into the courtyard to breathe in the fresh air. Antonia takes on the management of the household, ordering supplies, seeing to repairs, supervising the servants. Marcella rules the kitchen to see that her mother is fed the most healthful foods and ones she can chew easily. Meanwhile, Minora takes on all Octavia's public responsibilities, giving to charities, making the final decisions on the Theater of Marcellus . . .

I'm left to discuss Octavia's health with the physician when she's asleep and to read to her when she is awake. She asks to hear the sixth book of the *Aeneid*, when the hero goes down into the underworld and sees the shades of the dead by the River Lethe. And when I finish the verse, Octavia says, "Should we hope it's true that the dead drink of this river to forget their lives? It would be a mercy to forget the pains of this world, but what of the pleasures? Would I surrender the shame and pain and loss if it meant I must also give up the memory of my children? Of my loves?"

I don't want her thinking of this; reaching into the realm of the dead before her time. "That isn't what Isis holds forth for us in death, Octavia. We do not forget ourselves. We do not forget the faces of our children or our loved ones. We are joined with them in the afterlife and walk beside the gods."

Octavia smiles indulgently, closing her eyes. "Perhaps I should like an Egyptian afterlife . . ."

That smile stops my heart, for it's altogether too peaceful and grows more so as she drifts to sleep. It alarms me so much that I hold my hand over her mouth to feel the warm puffs of air, to assure myself that she is still breathing. When I am finally reassured, I leave her to sleep, and find Iullus in the courtyard, sitting on the edge of the cistern, rubbing his hands together against the autumn chill. "How does Octavia fare?"

"Resting now," I answer. "But stay for supper. She'll be happy to see you."

"I doubt that, Selene. I doubt that anyone is happy to see me after the Neptunalia. Certainly not my wife and just as certainly not my mother-in-law."

He doesn't have to explain himself. Anyone who wasn't present when he asked for Julia in marriage has heard about it now. And though Marcella holds her emotions close, her husband's declaration of love for another woman has embittered her. Marcella has been snappish, and it isn't only her mother's illness that's to blame.

I sigh. "They know you meant no harm to anyone."

Iullus tilts his head. "Are you defending me?"

It seems to shock him as much as it shocks me. "I suppose I am, and not for the first time either. It was an ill-considered thing you did, but your intentions were good."

He swallows, reaching for a leather pouch on his belt. Unlacing it, he says, "I have something for you."

He withdraws two matching cameos and presses them into my palm. One is a carving of my father, his curly hair wild. The other is my mother, her features rendered on onyx. I recognize the style, for the artist, Master Gnaios, now serves in my court. "Where on earth did you come upon these?"

"In one of our father's villas. A small one in Ostia that I was allowed to inherit. I found these in a niche by the bed. They must have been overlooked . . . at any rate, I've no use for the cameos or for the villa. I'll happily sign it over to you if you like."

He says it with the pretense of contempt, and once I would have believed it. Iullus forged his whole identity around being anything, anyone, but Antony's son, but even contempt would not cause him to give away what wealth he has left, nor would he give any thought to the sentimental value of these cameos if he weren't suffering a winter of the soul. "Why are you in such a generous mood, Iullus? Don't you want to leave anything for your wife and your children?"

"For it to be taken by my neighbors when I am officially proscribed?"

It has been a long time since the bloody purges in which men were condemned, stripped of citizenship, and hunted down for the reward money. Still, the idea of proscription strikes the heart with terror and I am not immune. My fist closes tight around the cameos.

"I'm glad you're finally wise enough to fear the emperor, Iullus, but if Augustus wanted to be rid of you, he'd do it with less fanfare."

He shrugs, lips turned down, drawn tight. "He won't have to do anything."

It isn't the flatness of his eyes but the catch in his voice that fills me with foreboding. He's ready to take his leave, but I catch him by the wrist and hold tight. "Don't you dare!"

He looks down at me, his expression as bleak as my father's after the Battle of Actium. "It's the only way, Selene. It's the only thing I can do for honor."

"Honor be damned," I say, my nails digging into the very wrists he intends to slit. Or will he take his sword and position the tip beneath his ribs, falling with his weight upon it? It won't be poison. It won't be a venomous snake. He's a Roman. It will be bloody . . .

"Let go, Selene. The emperor wants me dead and if I wait to be proscribed, Marcella cannot marry again and my children will inherit nothing. Our family . . . the *Antonii*—"

He doesn't finish. Perhaps he *cannot* finish. He has never wanted to carry our father's name or family legacy. For all his resentments and pettiness, Iullus has never wanted anything but to please the emperor and to love Julia. My heart breaks for him. Truly, it does.

"Our father was a drunken general," Iullus rasps. "A besotted fool in love. A weak-willed man who had the whole world in his hand and lost it. But I? I am even less than that. I am nothing."

I shake my head violently. "It isn't true."

"Give me a sword and I can outfight Tiberius and Drusus. I could outgeneral them too, if Caesar would give me a command. But he will never do it, Selene. He will never let me lead men. He will never let me become anything. Now I've lost Julia. She won't even see me. I have nothing. I am *nothing*."

"You're my brother," I say fervently, as the meaning and weight of our connection finally settles upon me. He *is* my brother. He is the only one of them left to me, the others dead or . . . gone. "I won't let you give your life for honor. I'll work the vilest magic I know to keep you in this world, I swear it. If not for my sake, then for Julia's.

For Marcella. For the Antonias. For your beautiful little children. You're not *nothing*, Iullus. You're a father."

"That has to be enough?" he asks, eyes red and wet.

Taking a deep breath, I say, "Our father *was* a drunk. He *was* a besotted fool in love. You didn't know him, but he was everything you said and more. A womanizer. A spendthrift. An overgrown boy. But I would give anything to have him back."

"Because he was honorable and brave. Yes, I've heard—"

"Because he was my father and he made me feel cherished. You have a tender heart for your children too. I know you do. Think of them before you do this."

Iullus does not want to hear me. "A child needs an inheritance more than he needs love."

"Oh? How have you enjoyed your inheritance, Iullus Antonius?"

He doesn't answer but I can't hold him any longer.

Twenty-seven

ON the evening of Julia's wedding, she sits like a queen amidst a hive of slaves. Phoebe plaits her hair, another slave anoints her feet, and a third paints her lips red. All the while, the emperor's daughter stares into a polished mirror with dead eyes.

Julia has asked me to serve as the *pronuba*, the matron of honor. I don't know if she asks it of me because she needs me at her side or because I am the only friend she has who has not yet been divorced or widowed. Either way, I sit by a basket of flowers and try to choose some for her wreath. "Octavia sends her regrets," I say, separating out the yellow blossoms from the red. "She is too ill to attend your wedding."

Julia shrugs. "It's a good excuse. Perhaps I should have thought of it."

"Her illness is no excuse. She isn't well. Neither is Iullus Antonius."

At this, Julia sighs, waving the slaves away until we are alone with her flowers, her flame-colored veil, and the gown we will fasten with a belt of gold and rubies, shaped into a symbolic knot of Hercules. But if I think she means to address what I have said, I am wrong. Instead, she says, "I have decided to give Phoebe her freedom while she is still young enough to enjoy it. I hope she does something utterly irresponsible with it like spend all her fortune on a chariot race or take up as a scandalous stage actress like Cytheris."

"Julia—"

"Do you think I should sell the villa? I want there to be at least one thing that Agrippa touched that Tiberius will not be able to take."

I don't answer, but thread together the flowers for her bridal wreath. By custom, she should do it, but she has no interest and there are more important matters to discuss than her slave and her villa. "Iullus says you won't see him."

Now Julia's temper flares. "Of course I won't see him! You know why. Of all people, you know."

It would endanger him, certainly, but given what I think he means to do, I'd rather she take the risk. I know her life will be made more difficult if she must look into the eyes of the man she loves on the very day she must marry another, but I'm frightened for Iullus. "Don't you worry what he will do for honor, Julia? If you have some message, I'll carry it to him."

She shakes her head, tears sparkling in the corners of her eyes. "There is nothing I can say. Do I ask him to absolve me? For that matter, should I kneel in front of Agrippa's death mask and beg his forgiveness too?"

"There is nothing for either of them to forgive," I insist. "You're doing what you must for your children. It isn't forever. Soon your sons will be grown and—"

"Tell Iullus that whatever we shared was long ago. It was a girlish caprice on my part and he must forget it. He must forget, because I feel nothing for him."

I give a sad shake of my head. "I'm not going to tell him such a cruel lie."

She fingers her garnet ear bobs, which hang down like two fat drops of blood, and when she speaks again, she nearly spits the words. "Why not? He ought to know the truth, which is that my father is right about me. I've always been an unfaithful whore."

The vehemence with which she accuses herself startles me and I set the bridal wreath aside. "That's another lie."

"Oh, it's true. I was unfaithful to my first husband more times than I can count. When I ought to have been coaxing Marcellus to make a child, to continue the line of the *Julii*, I bedded Iullus like a common strumpet. We did it everywhere, you know. Even in your house, in that dark corner behind your statue of Hercules!"

It does not shock me. "Marcellus gave you leave."

Julia fists her gown as if she might tear it. "Yes and I justified it because I was in love. I told myself that Iullus was my *true* husband, so there was no betrayal . . . until I married Agrippa. Almost ten years I was the wife of that hulking, lowborn, grouchy old general, and I learned to love him too, in my way. Iullus and Agrippa. I loved them both and therefore betrayed them both."

It is too near a thing to my own private guilt for me to offer any sensible reply. Then Julia bursts into sudden laughter. "My father has put me on a silver denarius. He is on one side of it. I am on the other, as a goddess. Which one does he choose for me? The virgin huntress, Diana with a quiver of arrows. It's perfectly *hilarious*, isn't it?"

I don't laugh, but Julia cannot seem to stop. "It looks nothing like me, but I suppose it is the wage I've earned. Tonight, my step-brother is going to make me his wife. Though I *gag* at the thought of him on top of me, I'm sure I'll learn to love him too. Because, as I said, my father has just the right idea about me after all. I will prostitute myself cheaply!"

Perhaps it's what she must tell herself, the story she must believe in order to do this. If this is the armor she needs to marry Tiberius, I ought not strip it from her. But I know Julia is every bit as virtuous as anyone could wish her to be, for there is no one in all the empire with a more steadfast or stout heart.

LET no one say that Julia does not try to be a wife to Tiberius. She makes herself pretty, charming, and amiable. It is Tiberius who broods with weepy eyes when the wedding vows are exchanged in torchlight. Several times I catch him searching the crowd as if to find the wife he divorced and discarded, but Vipsania is gone.

In the weeks that follow, Julia is kind to Tiberius. She tries to amuse him with talk of philosophy and recitations of poetry. She takes his little son, for whom Tiberius has the utmost affection, to her hearth and her heart. In short, Julia throws herself into the role her father has chosen for her and utters not one word against the sour-faced husband she's been saddled with this time.

Anything Tiberius asks of her, she does. Anything that interests him, she takes notice of. Anything that pleases him, she pretends is a pleasure to her as well. I worry that Julia was not built for duty; surely this pretense will break her. Yet she shows no signs of distress when she pays a call to us at the house where Octavia remains confined to her sickbed.

To celebrate the Saturnalia, Julia comes with a train of slaves bearing candles, fruits, pastries, and sweet-smelling incense. She sits with us, cheerfully sharing gossip until poor Octavia cannot keep her eyes open. I tuck the blankets under Octavia's chin, then see Julia out. We are nearly to the door when we cross paths with Iullus Antonius in the atrium, his arm draped in a purple-bordered toga, the mark of his senatorial rank. His formal clothing is a choice out of step with the holiday, during which the men of Rome customarily wear colorful dinner clothes in the style of the Greeks. But then again, I suppose Iullus feels as if he has not much to celebrate . . .

Julia and Iullus stop and stare, drawing closer, close enough to touch, forgetting my presence entirely. She is bundled against the cold in a fur-lined cloak pulled up around her head like a veil. Her lower lip trembling, she whispers, "Io Saturnalia, Iullus."

He reaches for her, as if to cup her cold cheek with his hand, but she stops him in one deft motion, laying her palm on his forearm with the utmost politeness. She gives him a smile filled with apology, forgiveness, and infinite loving grace. Then she kisses his cheek in farewell, moves around him, and takes her leave. As she goes, his big shoulders sag; he deflates before my eyes like an emptied wine-skin. I hurt so badly for him that my own knees threaten to buckle.

And that is the first time I truly know that Julia is stronger than any of us.

Turning to my half brother, I ask, "Did you mean it when you told the emperor that if allowed to defend Julia and her children, it would be your honor and only ambition?"

"You know I did."

"Well, you cannot defend her if you are dead."

He shuts his eyes tight. "Will you *never* mind your own affairs?"

"Julia needs you now more than ever. If you love her, you will protect her even without the reward of having her for a bride."

"Just how am I to do that when I have been left so powerless?"

I tell him, very seriously, "You must become powerful, Iullus. You must reconcile with the emperor; it should not be difficult because he enjoys having you close at hand to abuse. He is an old man in ill health. He cannot live forever. And when he dies, Julia and her sons will be at Livia's mercy, so you must be ready."

Iullus holds up a hand to silence me but I will not be silenced. I have given it much thought, and I have made a plan. "You must make yourself a lion in the Senate, Iullus. You must reach out to our father's old allies and woo them. You must make common cause with the richest men in Rome and everywhere else. You must seek office. Even if it means virtually nothing to be a Consul of Rome anymore, it will raise your stature and be followed by a proconsular command in the provinces, where you can raise legions for any war to come . . ."

Years ago, he would not have hesitated to go to Augustus and reveal everything that I said, casting me in the worst possible light. The fire in his eyes tonight, though, tells me that he will not. And so I stoke the flame. "Many men die for honor, Iullus. Be one of the few who live for it."

WE try to hush the children when they run riot through the snow-dusted courtyard so that Octavia can get her rest, but she says that she likes to hear her grandchildren at play.

"You're too hard on the children, Minora!" Octavia scolds, coughing into her kerchief.

At this rebuke, my exasperated half sister turns to me. "Strange how she would have shouted at us to stop dallying and make ourselves useful when we were their age."

I laugh both because it is true and because Octavia is regaining her health. Though it is a frigid January day, she asks to be carried into the dining room to share our meal, and though she cannot hold a cup without spilling it, she does eat. We will see her through this winter, I think, and then she will recover. She will champion her grandchildren. It is all decided for my generation, but *these* children are the future of the empire. Livia be damned!

My son and the boys of the imperial family are a merry band of mischief-makers who love nothing so much as rough-play, but Dora is no longer content to rule over a fiefdom of infants and toddlers. At twelve, she is caught between a child and a woman and when I see her staring pensively into the rose water with which the slaves bathe our feet, I tilt her chin up. "Perhaps it's time you had some special gowns made for you with pretty embroidery."

"I will only get them dirty and you will scold me for it." Dora sniffs, for she has never found a plant she did not want to dig up nor a filthy wounded animal she did not want to clasp to her breast.

"Yes, I will scold you and embarrass you and demand of you things that you cannot give, but that is the way of it between mothers and daughters. It will give you something to talk about with your brother when I am in my dotage and the two of you have no one else but each other to complain to about all of my faults."

Dora smiles at my teasing. "We won't complain."

"You will, but before then, we'll go to the market and shop for cloth together, shall we?"

Her pink smile falters. "Shouldn't you stay with Lady Octavia?"

"Musa says she is getting better."

Dora shakes her head, just once, a golden curl falling over her eyes. "No, Mama. The snake on Tiber Island has whispered to me that she will get no better."

THE snake on Tiber Island is wound round the staff of Asclepius in his temple of healing. It is not a real snake but a sculpture, and I bring my daughter there to prove it. As we make our way through the throngs of sick who have come for cures, Dora shows no fear of the old broken slaves, dressed in rags, huddled on pallets, coughing blood into their hands.

She wishes for me to give them coins and I send my guards to do so, along with a generous donation to the temple itself, but Isidora is not to be so easily convinced that her whispering snake is not on this island.

"Do you keep serpents here?" she asks one of the priests.

He surprises me by saying, "Many, Princess Isidora. Would you like to see them?"

She insists, and because I took her here in my ignorance, I am now bound to follow the priest as he leads us into an antechamber. At the sight of the courtyard where the slithering creatures bask in the light, coiled upon rocks and under brush that has been arranged for their comfort, I break into a cold and clammy sweat.

I know that serpents are a symbol of eternal life. They have appeared in my visions. Miraculously come to life on the riverbanks when I have worked the magic of my goddess. I ought not fear them, but it seems that my dread of snakes gets worse with age, not better. And in this room there are so many of them that I can scarcely breathe. There are at least twenty serpents slithering over one another on the floor. Maybe thirty. I lose count in my terror. I tighten my grip around my daughter's hand, fearing she will rush to these creatures as she once rushed to a lion.

"He's not here," she whispers. "My snake isn't here."

Thank Isis for that! "Why do you keep them?" I ask of the priest.

"These are the sacred red-eyed snakes," he explains. "They have no venom and their skin, sloughed off, helps with regeneration. Do you seek a remedy, Majesty?"

"Something for the Lady Octavia, perhaps."

I buy a tincture. Then I take my disappointed daughter out of the temple and hurry to the bridge that will lead us home. But as we are leaving the sacred aisle, Dora suddenly reaches into the foliage. Before I even know what she is doing, she has drawn a live serpent from the brush. One glimpse at that forked tongue and

I shriek. Memnon must think we are being murdered, for he draws his sword, but Dora lets the serpent coil around her wrist. "Mama, it's not dangerous. It has no fangs."

She is wrong. It does have fangs. Tiny ones, but the snake makes no move to strike her. Memnon seems prepared to lop off the snake's head at my command, but while I clutch at my pearls he says, "Majesty, it is just the same as the snakes in the temple. See the red eyes?"

I do. The priests said this kind of serpent held no venom. It must be a very young snake, because it is so small that Dora can hold it in one hand as it loops around her fingers. "This is the snake that whispers to me," she insists.

My teeth grind together as my stubborn desire for her to be a normal girl must give way to the truth of her gifts. "What does it say to you?"

She tilts her head thoughtfully. "I think it says it will help me become what I must be."

She wants to keep it. Of course she does. Because it is not enough that at home, in Mauretania, she has a menagerie of animals including a Barbary macaque that Juba brought home for her from one of his expeditions. Now she must have the serpent too, and I cannot deny her because she too is a child of Isis, and though her magic is nothing I understand, it is real.

ALAS, my daughter was right about Octavia. Her hair begins to come out in great clumps. When she sleeps, it becomes more difficult to wake her. For the first time, she complains of the pain. To relieve it, Musa gives her a tonic, explaining to my curious daughter that it is a brew of henbane and poppy syrup. The Antonias do not like the way this concoction makes their mother murmur strange things, but if she must leave us for the afterworld, I am grateful for anything that will ease her way there.

In February, the day of the Lupercalia, Octavia nags her daughters to leave her bedside and go down to the forum and put themselves in the way of the young men who lash at the crowds with thongs of goat hide. It is a fertility ritual and Octavia insists that we must all have more children—especially me. Can she know how much I want another child? Does she know that I have tried and failed? To make light of it, I ask, "Will you never stop trying to make me into a respectable Roman matron?"

"Will you never forgive me for it?"

She wants my forgiveness when she has forgiven me everything, even that I am Cleopatra's daughter? Emotion swells painfully in my chest and I wish I had never spoken a harsh word to her my whole life long. "Octavia, there is no room between us for resentments."

She softly caresses my cheek with her gnarled fingers, which still have about them the earthy scent of bread. I remember when her hands were sturdy and strong. I remember when she towered over me and it pains me to see her so delicate and frail. I press my lips to her shaky hand, trying to say with a kiss what I cannot say with words, and her eyes go misty.

"Your father once ran in the Lupercalia," she rasps. "In the year your mother came to Rome. How young and magnificent he was . . . bare-chested, clad only in goatskin. Along the route every girl crowded close, hoping he would single her out and strike her with his strip of hide. He passed me by, but then, catching my eye, he circled back again to strike me. Right here," she says, taking her trembling hand from my cheek to lay it over her chest, her breast, her heart. "It worked too. Because he gave me three daughters. The Antonias . . . and you, Selene."

Her love for him has become love for me, and I am humbled in the face of it. Overcome.

But it is not my father's name Octavia says when she is restless in her sleep. It is her son Marcellus she calls for. Sometimes Agrippa too. And, at the end . . . Isis. "Tell me of your winged goddess," she whispers, dosed so heavily on Musa's potion that her pupils are wide. The first time I spoke of my goddess in her presence, she flew into a rage. But that was long ago. Long before she saw me bleed, the words of the goddess carved into my palms. Long before she took Philadelphus to her bosom, and witnessed his gift of sight. Long before she asked me to pray to my goddess to spare her son's life.

My goddess does not guard against death, though; she conquers it. Isis ensures that death is not the end of all things. And so, here under the emperor's roof, I tell Octavia all I know of my goddess. Mother. Magician. Goddess of Women. Queen of the Dead.

My half sisters too, in hushed whispers, invoke my forbidden goddess, for I taught them how, years ago. We gather round Octavia's bed with our sacred amulets. Antonia with a tiny *ankh*, the symbol of eternal life. Minora with a bead carved like a scarab beetle, the symbol of transformation. And me with the jade frog round my neck that reads *I am the Resurrection*.

We are with Lady Octavia until her final moments. Then she asks for her brother, the emperor, and he comes to her bedside. He shuts the door on us, so I do not know what passes between them. I do not hear Octavia's last words. I only hear the world as it is without her, more hollow and silent by far.

Never again will anyone mother me. I won't be scolded for dallying, I won't be lectured on the proper way to raise my children, I won't be tut-tutted for my clothes or for my foreign ways. I will not be worried after in the way Octavia worried after me. I will not be loved the way she loved me.

She loved me even though I was a sullen and resentful child. Even though I reminded her so very much of my mother and gave her every reason to despise me. So if ever the emperor's sister won a victory over my mother, it was this: I loved Octavia too, and I loved her longer.

Octavia mothered me for almost twenty years. For almost twenty years, I basked in her praise and shrank from her disapproval. Almost twenty years, she has been the touchstone of my life. Now she is dead and *Isis* is the only mother I will ever know again.

Twenty-eight

❦

SOMEONE has been here before me. Behind the bent bars of the locked temple gates, I find that someone has swept up the crumbled stone, the desiccated plants, and the crocodile bones. Inside the inner sanctuary of the Temple to Isis where once my blood blossomed into flowers, I find an array of melted candles upon the cracked altar. Though the statue of Isis is weather-beaten and unadorned—no priests have dressed her or fastened jewels upon her ears—the marble has been scrubbed clean of paint and the moss that once grew in the neglected folds of the white stone.

As always, the smile of my goddess, compassionate and mysterious, warms me against the cold. The hum of *heka* in the stonework tells me a secret—that she has been worshipped against the emperor's command. She is still worshipped here in Rome. Now she is more beloved here than ever before and no chained gates can stop it.

"Wait outside," I tell Memnon. "I want to be alone."

He leaves me, but I am not alone. I have been drawn by an instinct in my sadness over the loss of Octavia. I need the comfort of my goddess. I need some sign that Isis will champion Octavia in the afterworld. I need to find the strength not to cry every time someone mentions Octavia's name.

But not only that. I feel that I have been drawn here by a prayer. That I have been called here . . . and in my weeping, I hear an echo that makes my heart begin to thud in my chest.

I do not need my eyes to see him in the shadow at the farthest reach of the temple. The scent of him is too familiar. The rush of his breath, the slight thump of *heka* in his blood that pulls me to him. I sense him with every part of me. With every fiber of my being. I know my twin as I know myself.

And that is my undoing.

Can it be possible that, at long last, my beloved twin has come for me? When Helios emerges from the shadows, I drink him in, drowning in equal parts elation and despair. The weathered lines of his face are deeper with age. The size of him is still impressive. Helios is as big a man as our father ever was. His hair, darker now than it was in his youth, is still a lion's mane of thick tawny curls.

He holds out to me a warrior's hand, then squints as I shrink back. "Don't you know me, Selene?"

"Of course I know you," I whisper through lips gone dry and cold. "But you cannot be here. You cannot have found me here, in the middle of Rome."

"Where else would I find you on the day of Octavia's funeral? Will you not take my hand?"

"No," I say in anguished disbelief, steadying myself against a pillar for fear my knees will buckle. "Because it will not be real. You are in Africa. You are fighting with the Garamantes. *Horus the Avenger*, they call you. When I heard it, I knew that you were alive. I knew you were still alive in this world with me. Still *real*. But if you are here. If you are here now . . ."

He steps forward and captures my hand. His is as warm and alive as any hand I have ever known. His fingers are leathery as they tangle with my own and my hand seems tiny in his calloused palm. It is the calloused palm I have always sought during my darkest hours. "We are one *akh*, Selene. We'll always find each other."

That is true. He is part of me and I am part of him. But have I dreamed him up, summoned his spirit to comfort me? For the first time, I wonder—truly wonder. "You cannot be here . . ."

"But I am."

I shake my head so hard it dizzies me. "No. On the Isle of Samos, I was the only one to see you. No one *else* sees you."

Helios frowns at my ravings, adjusting his sword belt and stiffening his spine. "Shall we go out together into the street and be seen together?"

It is no serious question. We could never be seen together without risking our lives. Trembling at the nearness of him, at the unbearable nearness of him, I whisper, "Seven years we have been apart. I never thought to see you again. Why now?"

He brings my fingers to his lips, kissing them softly. "News of Octavia's death brings me here. When I learned of it, I knew you would suffer. My ship was not far, so I came for you."

"You never cared for Octavia."

"But you spoke well of her . . . in spite of all."

My beloved speaks in sympathy but I hear only reproach. "Yes, in spite of all, I cared for Octavia. I still do. I cannot hate the whole world and prosper in it!"

He allows me this outburst of grief, nuzzling my fingers against his stubbled cheek. By the gods, the feel of it makes me a girl again. I am lost in the sensation . . .

"But you *are* prospering, aren't you, Selene?"

"Yes," I say, as if it were a guilty confession. "Again, in spite of all."

Helios stares at me hard. "I wanted you to prosper. I wanted you to succeed where I failed. There is no world for me if you are not in it, carrying our name, caring for her . . ."

Does he speak of Isis or my daughter? I cannot think clearly. And looking into the verdant depths of his eyes, I can barely stand. Perhaps he senses the shaking of my knees, because Helios ducks away, spreading his scarlet cloak at the base of the statue, giving me a place to sit before I fall. Then, with his hand upraised, he uses his *heka* to make fire leap into the brazier and set all the candles ablaze.

In the firelight, we stare at each other anew. With my fingers, I trace the lines of his face, looking for new scars. And he—he stares at me with a longing that echoes deep in my soul.

"*Sweet Isis*, how I have missed you," I cry.

I still remember the taste of his kiss. The feel of his body as it moved with mine. And now, the scent of him, the warmth of his caress, brings the memory back to me so vividly that I am moved to tears. I cry for myself, for him, for our family, for Octavia . . . all my griefs mingle together. While I cry, he holds me, stroking my hair, my cheek, pulling me tight against his broad chest. "Hush. I am here, now."

We speak of days long past, when we lived together as children in Octavia's house, in fear of her wrath. We remember the wall that separated us then. How we were forced to whisper to each other at night through a hole left by a loose brick. Then I must tell him about our wizard and how he died. I tell him about Bast too. I can see these things hurt him to hear, but combat has hardened him. Helios does not sob like I do. And he is reluctant to tell me of his travels, his ships, and his wars. I fear it is because he must be fighting Romans, stealing from them when he can. "Helios, I cannot bear for you to have become a pirate."

"Don't you know what I am?" he asks.

But when I shake my head, he only reassures me with irritating vagueness. "I am no pirate."

Perhaps he lies to me. I do not mind. I do not mind if all of this is a lie. Every precious moment is a reprieve from the world outside. "How long will you stay with me?"

"I am always with you, Selene. I am always where you need me . . ."

Now, that *is* a lie. It is the kind of lie we tell when people are torn from us, never to be reunited. The kind of lie that is meant to lessen the blow. But nothing will ever blunt the pain of our separation for me. "How long will you stay in Rome?"

"How long will *you* stay?" he asks with a note of frustration. "You swore that you would break free of the emperor, but here you are."

"I have broken free of him. I've made myself as free as I can while protecting my family. I swore it to Isis and I swore it to you and I swore it to myself. I'm doing all that I can to keep that vow. Do not take me to task. Only tell me how long we have together . . ."

He sighs, shaking his head with resignation. "Until moonrise.

Should I stay much longer, I will be too tempted to burn Rome to the ground, and I imagine you are still against that plan."

My smile is bittersweet. "Yes, I am against it. It was our father's city and Octavia's too. It is a city that receives my children warmly now."

My smile fades at his anguished expression and the defeated slope of his shoulders. "When last I saw you, there was only the girl."

Nodding, I look away. "Now I have a son too. Juba's son."

Helios exhales sharply. As if he knew already, but hearing it again from me opens a new wound. Then he braces himself for another. "You are content, then, with Juba?"

I do not know how to answer. What I feel for Juba is not contentment. Neither is it what I feel now for Helios. This reckless passion that causes my heart to beat so wildly. This desperate longing. This pure love that has endured between us from the womb to this very moment. This love between two children of prophecy who came together on an altar as a young god and goddess. This perfect divine harmony between me and my twin.

And so I wish I could tell Helios that it is only friendship that Juba and I share. But that too would be a lie, and Helios would know it. He would see it. He would feel it. Swallowing hard over the lump in my throat, I can only say, "Juba has given me a family. He has given me a son and my daughter a future. Together, we are rebuilding the House of Ptolemy."

Helios bows his head, and I see that even this gentle answer has cut him to the quick, but he says, "Good. That is good. That is what I wanted for you and for Cleopatra Isidora."

He speaks her name with such reverence that it breaks my heart. "She is nearly grown now, a girl of twelve. If you could see her—" Here I break off, because he is not her father and he cannot see her. Even if Helios was the one who gave life to her, and not the emperor. Even if Helios was the only thing that kept me from swallowing poisons to rid myself of her when she was still in my womb. Still, he is not her father. It is Juba who claimed my daughter. Juba who taught her about elephants and monkeys and the bounty of our kingdom. Juba who carried her upon his shoulders. Juba who protects her. No other man ever has. "Helios, has there been no woman, no children, no home for you?"

"Only you," he says hoarsely. "There will never be another. Your happiness is my happiness. The life you live, I live too. The rest is denied me, so you must live well for us both."

I do not like these haunting words, for I cannot imagine loving a man as unselfishly as this man has loved me. "I think you are telling me that you are not real."

"I am as real as you are . . ."

In some fit of madness, I cry, "If you are real, then come away with me! We are leaving soon for Mauretania. I can make a place for you. You can serve in the guard or—" I break off, knowing that I'm a desperate fool to even suggest it; it isn't workable. What if my husband were to catch a glimpse of Helios? He would know him. What would he do? My twin is an outlaw, an enemy of the emperor. Juba's loyalty to Augustus has always been stronger than anything else. It would be a terrible risk and, perhaps, a cruelty to make Juba choose between loyalty and love.

As I am now being forced to choose between them.

I want to trace the beautiful outlines of Helios's lips. I want to thread my fingers through his curls and pull him to me in a kiss. I want to lose myself in the warm circle of his arms. I want to recapture the love that was ours on the Isle of Samos. It is still a temptation. It is a temptation so strong that I feel my chest pried apart by the swelling ache of my heart. I want another stolen night with Helios. A lifetime of them.

But perhaps that was a different lifetime . . .

If I were free to run away, I would follow Helios into snowy mountains, into the sands of the desert, into the foam of the sea. For I love Helios. I love him still and always. But there is no place for us save this one; a secret sanctuary where no one must ever find us together. And when he reaches his hands for my body, to embrace

me as a lover, to take me here in a temple, as he has done before . . .
I remember that I am not free.

Other bonds now hold my heart. I remember too the questions
Juba whispered to me in the dark.

Will he take you from me?

I answered honestly then, for I will never leave my kingdom or
my children. And I will never leave Juba. Helios does not ask it of
me, but when he tilts my chin to him, hunger in his eyes, I must
answer a different question.

Will you dishonor me with him?

My twin has lost everything. I cannot bear for him to think that
he has lost me too. But I don't know how to do this again. How can
I make love to him again and let him go? How will I remember it
if I do? My lovemaking with Helios has always before been untainted,
a thing of beauty and secret sustenance. I never felt shame for it
because he is my brother nor for any other reason.

But this time I would feel shame.

I would despair of betraying Juba this way, even as I despair now
of betraying Helios. Taking my twin's hands in mine, I stop them
from undressing me, though it pains me more than I ever thought
it could. I sob with the effort to deny my own desire and his, and
because my heart is torn in two, every explanation I try to give tastes
false on my tongue.

Anguish howls through the hollows of my soul when Helios nods
his head in surrender. "It's all right. I don't need to make love to you
to be inside you. I don't need to lay a hand on you to touch you.
But I will never so much as brush my lips against yours without
your leave."

There is something about what he says, about everything he has
said, that makes me question what River of Time I am swimming
in. He is here with me now, but I do not know if he is here in the
mortal world or in the divine. We are in a temple, and I might have
summoned him with my grief. I fear it is a thing I must never do
again, whether he is real or imagined. "I don't know how to do this.

I don't know how to love you and say good-bye to you, over and over, never knowing if I will see you again."

At this, he presses a kiss into my palm. "We will always see each other again. I taught you once that under your skin, between your bones, there's space for other, more fluid things. Like blood. Like *heka*. Like fire and wind . . . and *love*. So long as you live, I live. We were born together. We will die together. And I will always seek you out . . ."

I have lost Helios. Again. And this time, forever, I think. In spite of his promises, I think I will never see his face again. Never hear the comforting rumble of his voice. Never hold his hands in mine. He is gone. All gone. And I let him go without giving him every part of myself that I could.

I hate myself for it, even if I would have hated myself if I had done otherwise.

Once, I could return to Juba from another man's bed and feel no remorse. No longer. But I am so wrecked by the loss of Helios that I shy away from my husband's touch in an inconsolable fog, unable to concentrate on anything.

Unable to endure public scrutiny after the loss of *his* sibling, the emperor has withdrawn to our house across the Tiber, where citizens are not free to approach him. In the days following Octavia's funeral, the emperor spends his evenings by a warm fire in our study, cloistered with Juba, reminiscing or making battle plans or whatever else it is the two of them discuss when I am not in the room.

We indulge the emperor as our guest—what other choice do we have?—but he notices our servants packing our trunks and readying for our springtime journey. And when I come upon him in the dining room, he insists, "You and Juba cannot leave me now, when I am utterly abandoned."

He means Octavia, of course. If he can grieve—if he is human enough for that—he is grieving for his sister. She was the moral center of his family. Like a Vestal Virgin, she tended the fire at the heart and hearth of the *Julii*. Now the fire has gone out and his inner circle has narrowed again. Octavia was always his true dynastic partner. The only person who knew him since childhood and still loved him. And I cannot help but think that if he were Egyptian, he might have married Octavia. Perhaps he would have been a better man if he had married his sister, who encouraged his good qualities, instead of Livia, who has helped goad him to every evil. Had he married Octavia, the whole twisted mess he's made of his family might never have come to pass. But of course, he is Roman and would think taking his sister to wed more depraved than all his other wicked deeds . . .

Now he is isolated, unsure of whom to trust, and aware that Livia holds unspeakable sway. He cannot harm her without unleashing her sons, both of whom are woven so tightly into his family and his structure of power that he cannot shake them.

And so, bereft, the emperor leans upon me and my husband. He asks me to play my *kithara* harp for him as I once did to nurse him back to health. He makes himself at home on my terraces, indulging in the little game my children have made of throwing stones at the Tiber River. He plays ball with Ptolemy in my courtyard and he gifts Isidora with a golden bangle studded with amethysts and emeralds that he looted from Greece.

When we're alone, taking a meal of peeled grapes and olive paste on warmed bread, I warn him that the bangle is too expensive a gift, for my daughter is prone to mislay jewelry and only recently lost a ring while planting seedlings in a pot garden outside her rooms. But the emperor waves this away. "Let her be careless with such riches, for they are a fraction of what I want to give her. If you would only give me a little more time, you will see how I intend to honor you and our children."

That he clings to this dangerous fantasy that my children are his, that *I* am his and there is some future for us together, hardens me against his attempts to play upon my sympathies. That he dares speak it aloud here, in my home, where servants might hear, hardens me even more. "My kingdom needs me, Caesar. You do not. You're wealthy and powerful beyond anyone's wildest imagination. You're worshipped throughout the empire as a living god. Everything is as you would have it."

"Nothing is as I would have it, and you know that."

Remembering all that Octavia sacrificed, and all that I have sacrificed, and all that Helios has sacrificed, I say, "We chose our path."

He must hear my bitterness, because he turns on me and bellows, "If you leave me, you leave without my son!"

The room goes cold, or perhaps it is only that my blood drains away from my limbs to pool inside a heart swollen with rage. I've always known that I would kill to protect my children. A metallic tang coats my tongue as dark magic bubbles up inside. I taste iron. I taste blood. I swallow them back long enough to say, "Ptolemy is only six years old. He needs his mother. He needs to learn the kingdom he'll inherit. He's been too long from Mauretania."

"I'd give him more than a frontier kingdom. I'd give him *much* more."

Juba warned me I would be tempted. I've given up my own ambitions for Egypt, but I cannot help but hope my children will return one day. That they will rule all North Africa as their ancestors did. Yet seeing Helios again has reminded me that I know better than to make bargains. "When my son comes of age, give him what you will, Caesar. Until then, he must stay with me."

I am appalled when my husband does not agree. Later that night, amidst piles of scrolls and trinkets he has collected for the journey home, he says, "Let Ptolemy stay in Rome to befriend Gaius and Lucius; let him become their indispensable companion. This way, when those boys are old enough to wield true power, they'll look upon our son with favor."

From a couch near a cage filled with songbirds, I shoot to my feet to confront him. "Foster our son under Livia's care? Never even think it!"

Juba tries to persuade me with cool reason. "Do you want the Romans to think of our son as a barbarian? They need to think of him as a kinsman. You're quick to point out he's the grandson of Cleopatra and Mark Antony. Should we give him less of an advantage than Herod has given his own sons?"

But in this matter, I cannot be reasoned with. "Herod's sons were nearly killed for their father's jealousy."

"They were saved because Augustus knew them. Because the Romans knew them. That's what saved their lives. That is *all* that saved their lives, Selene. It's an important lesson for us."

Grinding my teeth, I stubbornly argue, "We are *not* the Herods and I will *not* give up my son."

Juba becomes just as stubborn. "Ptolemy needs a Roman education. I thought it could wait, but now I have changed my mind."

If my husband thinks this will settle the argument, he is much mistaken. Just the thought of leaving my baby boy tears my heart to shreds; I cannot bear it, and I will make my husband's life a torture until he changes his mind back again. "You would abandon Ptolemy?"

"Of course not. Your sisters would watch over him. Julia too. Ptolemy would never be without friends and allies here in Rome . . ."

Seeing that his words are of no comfort, Juba reaches to embrace me, but I shrink away from him. "No. Don't you dare. Don't even think to touch me if you mean to leave our son here as a hostage. For that's what he'd be. I could not live a day in peace knowing Livia had her claws to my son's throat."

"You fear Livia overmuch."

"Do I? I think you are naive. She meant to poison Julia's boys when Agrippa died. I know she did."

"Oh, for the love of the gods!" Juba shouts, raising a fist into the air. "It has been nearly a year since Agrippa died and no harm has come to those boys."

"Because Livia's moment of opportunity passed, but there will be another and she's waiting for it."

"Stop making up stories like a terrified child. Think like a grown woman. Think like the queen you are. This is an opportunity that other kings vie for, Selene. The chance to have their children grow up at the emperor's knee. We both know how fond Caesar is of the boy—"

"He is more than fond. I've told you that he believes Ptolemy is his son. He wants Ptolemy for himself. And he will ruin him. He will blacken his soul. He will leave a stain on our son just as he left one on you and me. Would that Augustus had never heard our son's name! That our son could live in a world untouched by the emperor."

Juba's hand comes crashing down on the table. "Then call your magic winds and scour the world of Caesar. Do it if it's in your power. Go on." When I stand there blinded by impotent rage, he continues, "No? Then we deal with the world as it is. We live in an empire. If our children are to rule after us, they must know Rome. They must know the imperial court. They must understand politics and intrigue."

His certainty batters against my resolve and fear makes my voice shaky. "Ptolemy is still a baby, Juba. He plays with wooden boats in the fishpond and kicks a ball in the courtyard. He's still sometimes afraid of the dark, especially when there is thunder. And you would plunge him into a sea of danger?"

"The other royal boys his age have already begun preparing for kingship. Other princes already jockey for position in Rome, sharpening their swords for whatever may come. They will all know one another when they come of age. They will know one another's strengths and weaknesses. Would you leave our son unprepared and unarmed?"

"I would arm him with *our* beliefs, with our hopes for him—"

"Stop." Juba pinches at the bridge of his nose, his head bowed. "There's no point to this argument. In the end, we *both* know that Ptolemy must stay in Rome."

"I only know that the emperor commands it, and as always, you're eager to obey. Is there nothing you will ever deny him?"

Juba's head snaps up. "And how often have you refused him?"

My nostrils flare at this reproach, but I am silent. It is beneath me to list all the ways in which I have frustrated the emperor, and

I refuse to be brought to account on the matter of fidelity to our marriage bed. Especially after turning Helios away.

At my silence, Juba storms over to his scroll rack, flinging rolls of papyri as he searches for something. "You think I can't say no to him? You think I would bleed our child like a sacrifice so long as it did not displease the emperor? Is that what you think?"

He is shouting now, but I am just as angry. "What else can I think when you ask me to leave my son at his mercy?"

In answer Juba hurls a scroll at me, the wooden rollers at each end giving it a dangerous momentum. Before it hits me, I catch it. Then I realize that it isn't a weapon; he means for me to read it.

Snapping it open without a care, I begin to puzzle its contents. What I see sends me fumbling for a chair. It is a marriage contract that names my daughter, Isidora. In this contract, Herod agrees to pass his kingdom into the hands of any prince my daughter should bear for him, and in exchange, Augustus cedes parts of Egypt and Cyrene, over which Isidora would be queen.

I clamp one hand over my mouth. *No.* I cannot believe it. She would be queen in name only; Herod would rule in her name. Augustus means to give portions of my ancestral kingdoms over to the girl he believes is his daughter, but at the same time deliver her into the hands of that monster. "She would never survive as Herod's bride!"

Juba gives a shake of his head. "Herod wouldn't dare harm her, but every wife in the harem and every prince who stands to inherit would resent her as a rival and an outsider. Which is why I refused. Augustus believes he can mend a rift by marrying Dora to Herod or one of his sons. But I have *refused*. Three offers now I have refused, though Augustus grows ever more impatient."

From the scrawled note on the far margin of the paper, I can see that for myself. In the note—which I recognize as Augustus's own writing—he takes my husband to task for sentimentality, insisting that my daughter is of marriageable age and must be wed where it will serve the most advantage. "Why didn't you tell me of this?"

"Because I knew you would be frenzied with worry. You've

already been brought low by Octavia's death. Ever since the day of her funeral, you have been in a daze, as if you would be somewhere else, anywhere else, but here. Moreover, if Augustus should become enraged, I wish for the blame to fall on me."

I am astounded to realize that Juba thinks he is protecting me. That he is willing to risk the emperor's wrath not only for me, but for the daughter he knows is not his own. It is a humbling realization. "This is the emperor's command and you refused?"

Still fuming, Juba shouts, "I refused him absolutely! Would Caesar take my kingdom and nail me to a cross like a common criminal, still I would not consent to give Isidora over to Herod. Never would I leave *either* of our children defenseless, Selene, but you cannot hold them forever. There comes a time when you must cut the cord that ties them to your womb."

These are the last words he says before slamming out of the room. It is our first violent quarrel in so many years that it leaves me gasping and raw. I nearly sob in its aftermath. I *would* hold my children forever. Both of them. I would hold them and never let them go until the last breath left me. But this is not the way of the world. I cannot pretend that difficult decisions will not need to be made. Moreover, our quarrel convinces me that if I do not make plans for the inevitable, someone else will make the plans for me . . .

Once I have composed myself, I look for the king. I find Juba alone on the terrace, wondering over the little piles of pebbles he finds there. It is past the dinner hour and the moon hangs over a city both dark and cold. Wordlessly, Juba picks up a pebble and flings it. Neither of us looks to see where it lands.

"Two years," I whisper, my breath puffing steam into the night air. "Please give me two more years."

Two years will be enough, I tell myself. Time enough to teach Ptolemy to be less trusting of the world. Time enough for Dora to become a woman. At fourteen, maybe she will want a husband as much as Pythia did. By all accounts my niece is happy, and a mother should want happiness for her children, even if she cannot be a part of it. "I beg of you, Juba, just two years more . . ."

He agrees and together we go to the emperor. We promise Augustus that in two years' time, we'll arrange an appropriate marriage for Dora and send Ptolemy to be fostered in Rome. Augustus doesn't like our answer, but when he sees that we are united, he relents.

Or at least, that is what he wants Juba to believe.

Before we leave for Mauretania, the emperor makes me understand the price for this indulgence. "In two years, you will bring my son to me, Selene. He will take his rightful place at my side and so will you. In two years, you will both come to Rome to stay."

PART THREE

THE HARVEST

Twenty-nine

✦

THE KINGDOM OF MAURETANIA
SPRING 11 B.C.

TWO years can pass in the blink of an eye. In the flutter of a bird's wing. In the space between two breaths. Two summers, two autumns, two winters, and two springs. Not long. Not nearly long enough. Yet, for me, these two years must last a lifetime. All the memories I wish to make with my family, I must make now. Everything I mean to accomplish, I must do now. Everything I want for my kingdom, I must have now.

Perhaps that is why I am so mortified when our advisers report just how much has gone wrong in our absence. More squabbles between our settlers and natives. More discontent in Volubilis. The harvest is not as bountiful as it has been in past years. Our treasury is not nearly as full as when we left. And our subjects resent that we have been gone so long in Rome.

Chryssa is distraught to deliver this bad news. She's grown plump, having recently given birth to another little boy. Her hair is neither curled nor oiled, as if she has not given servants time to attend it. The fact that she is not even wearing jewelry tells me that my absence has driven her near to the breaking point. "You said you'd be gone a few months in Rome! I am only a Greek freedwoman and the wife of a barbarian. I am not the Queen of Mauretania."

I should have been here, ruling my kingdom. I should have gone to the river, offering myself as Isis. I should have done all the things a queen ought to do. But I would have had to abandon Julia when she most needed me. I would have had to abandon Octavia as she lay dying, and I will never regret being with her in the end. It was as important as anything else I have ever done, and it is what Isis wanted me to do. This I am sure of.

I am less sure of my other decisions. Was I right to let Helios go? Was he even there at all? And what of sending Crinagoras into danger? No, that was prescient, because in two years, the emperor may press Herod's case as a marriage prospect for my daughter again. And he may not care if we approve of the marriage or not.

That must never happen. Herod must be brought down.

Unfortunately, the first report I receive from Crinagoras is from a dancing girl who travels with a troupe of performers. It is during a banquet that she drapes herself scandalously over my husband's knees and passes to him a note from my poet that he, in turn, passes to me. Crinagoras reports in salacious detail that Princess Glaphyra has made enemies in the Judean court. They dislike her for her royal bloodline and for her beauty, and there are rumors that Herod would like to bed her himself. But none of this tells me how I might destroy the King of Judea.

And so I am irritated with everything, my plans frustrated at every turn. Why, it doesn't even look as if any progress has been made on the Iseum, so I call Amphio to account, forcing him to come before my throne in his formal toga. "I hoped to see more done," I complain. "I was gone in Rome nearly two years. Perhaps if you spent less time with women of questionable virtue—"

"Patience, Majesty," Amphio says, with an infuriating smirk. "The amphitheater took twelve years to complete and that was done with an army of slaves. Since you've been gone your tribesmen have not once, but twice stopped work, demanding higher wages. Even still, in that time, we have built the base, fashioned the drainage for your pools, and framed—"

"You must work faster."

"I cannot, Majesty. We have only a thousand workers. I would like it better if we had three thousand. That is to say nothing of the stonecutters, carpenters, masons, and artists—we will need more money to lure the best. If I'm to build faster, I'll need more men, more wagons, more everything. With the resources you have given me, no temple builder in the world could do better. It may be ten years more before it is done."

A decade more! I've already reigned as queen over Mauretania for thirteen years. In ten more years, my daughter will be twenty-two years old; she will be married with children of her own by then. And my son? Why, he will be old enough to ride with the legions. Where will I be in ten years? Where will I be in two . . . ?

THE king calls me to join him in the royal library adjacent to the palace. Once I have gone up the stairs between the watchful gold lions, he meets me in the central court, then leads me into one of the storage rooms where thousands of scrolls crowd the little cubbies on the wall. On a wide table of fragrant citrus wood, he spreads open a manuscript, his hands weighing down the ends. "I need you to verify the authenticity of this scroll, Selene. We can't have our librarians filling this place with forgeries."

He is right. To pass off a forgery as an original manuscript is a serious crime and we cannot have our reputation tarnished with a library full of ignorance and fakery. Still, there are librarians better equipped than me to detect such fraud . . .

Nevertheless, I glance down and the familiar writing makes me gasp. "Oh, Juba. These are my mother's words, written in her own hand."

He smiles with great satisfaction, edging from the table so I may take a closer look. "You recognize this manuscript?"

Here my mother turned her scholarship to medicine. Cures for fox mange. Treatments for scalp and skin diseases. A complicated list of weights and measurements. How Isidora will love this book, written by her own grandmother . . .

"This is the original, Juba. How did you get it?"

My husband looks abashed, clearing his throat nervously. "At rather great expense and with devious skullduggery engineered by your Lady Lasthenia. I suppose you will not approve of my raiding the Great Library of Alexandria, but who has a better right to the works of Cleopatra than you? I meant it as a gift, and I hoped it would please you."

The blush upon his cheek banishes all my reservations about raiding the Great Library. "You can hardly have pleased me more . . ."

I want to tell Juba the truth. *Sweet Isis*, I want to tell him everything. I want to tell him that the emperor intends to steal us away from him. I want to tell him that if Ptolemy goes to Rome, I must go too. I even want to tell him about Helios, though I know he will never understand . . .

No, I cannot. If I tell him these things, it will ruin what time we have left together. There is nothing my husband can do to change any of it. Telling him may ease my burdens, but it will only add to his. Perhaps I will tell him later, when I have a plan. When I have thought of a way out. Until then, I have two years. Two years to be the best mother, the best queen, and even the best wife I can be. And so I kiss my husband and keep my secrets.

"HOW can he afford it?" I demand of my advisers. "Tell me how Herod can sponsor the Olympic Games, give spectacles for his people, fund cities and expeditions, and still afford to build his temple in Jerusalem?"

I would put these questions to Crinagoras if I had any way of contacting him. Instead, I must wait for the next dancing girl he sends my way. I am forced to rely upon Lady Lasthenia. "Augustus gives him money," she says, absently tugging on a strand of her hair that looks to have been chewed on the end. Her fingertips are stained with ink, but we do not keep the Pythagorean scholar at court for her noble appearance. "Herod also taxes his citizens heavily."

"That can't be it," I say with a shake of my head, remembering how our Berbers resented the tax. "Not all of it anyway. If his subjects are poor, they cannot pay. What do they grow? What do they make? What do they sell? Dates and wine. They have no metals to speak of. They are a small kingdom; their farms produce far less grain than ours. Yet Herod can afford these great building projects and completes them with great speed and finesse. How is he doing it?"

Chryssa offers her theory. "Spice traders cannot reach imperial markets without going through Judea. He profiteers on access to Rome."

"Then of course, there is the tomb raiding," Lady Lasthenia adds, almost absently.

We all stare at her, for it is an outrageous accusation, even against Herod. Truthfully, the way she keeps her gaze low tells me that she is hesitant to level the charge. "It's rumored that he raided the tombs of his predecessors. King David and King Solomon. Jews in our city say that it was such an abomination against their god that the bodyguards who helped haul the loot away perished in a burst of spontaneous flame."

"Or Herod killed them to keep them quiet," I say, though I can never hear about spontaneous flame without remembering my twin's gift with fire. *Sweet Isis*, the thought of Helios still wounds me. How I sent him away as if he were only a brother now and not my lover, my love. But this temple will be for him as much as it is for me and for Isis. It will be the way I honor him and what he has given up.

"I might ask what kind of king desecrates the tombs of other kings," I say, "But then, we are speaking of Herod, a villain such as I have never before imagined." I will not emulate him. To honor my goddess, I cannot ask the emperor's help. I will not tax my subjects into impoverishment, I will not extort and bully our traders, and I will not raid the treasure of dead kings. But I will raid the ocean. "We will need more factories to turn the sea snails into purple dye. We'll make ten times the amount of dye."

Chryssa considers. "Majesty, if we make ten times the dye, you'll flood the market and send the price so low that every beggar on the street will be wearing royal colors."

"Then let it be said that Cleopatra Selene clothed the whole world in purple majesty. I won't mind as long as we have the money for the Iseum."

*   *   *

I have come to rely upon Juba to poke apart my arguments and reveal their weaknesses, so when I tell him about my intentions for the dye works, I am ready for him to find some flaw in my plan.

Seated amongst inkpots and maps and the pieces of that damned broken water clock that litter his writing table, Juba only waves away my idea and thumbs through sketches of plants that I recognize as having belonged to my mage. "Do you remember the plant I named after my physician?"

"Euphorbian. It can be used as some manner of purgative, as I recall."

He taps at the sketch of a cactuslike specimen. "It might be a topical cure for snakebite."

Can he know how such a revelation fills me with bittersweet pain? It was my mage who made me carry a basket of figs to my mother—the basket in which an asp waited to strike her dead. Though I was just a girl, the wizard made a killer of me, and for many years, I resented him. I forgave him long ago. Still, he spent his final days searching out a cure for snakebite . . .

"Does it work?" I ask.

"We should test it on a condemned prisoner. I might have one in mind." Then, without warning, Juba roars, "And in the future, you would do well to discourage Isidora from keeping company with the Berber boy!"

I take two steps back, without the faintest idea why he is shouting at me. "What has Ziri done?"

"Not Tala's boy. The stable boy. *Tacfarinas.*" Juba growls, snapping the scroll noisily in his lap, urging me to examine the sketch more closely. "Isidora told me that he drew many of these plant sketches. He still draws them for her in your garden where she has a little plot of dirt. I came upon them together and they were holding hands."

A thousand times have I seen the children together in the gardens, grabbing each other round the waist, clasping hands as they run, for Isidora is much younger, in her way, than I was at the same age. "They are happy to be reunited after our trip to Rome. I am sure it was done in innocence."

The king does not look at me. "No boy his age takes any girl's hand in innocence. He is no fit companion for a princess. He is a Numidian barbarian."

"As are you by blood."

That finally provokes him to look at me. "And you have made clear for the entirety of our marriage that I am not worthy to touch the hand of a Ptolemaic princess. Consider me convinced. Isidora needs more supervision. She should be accompanied everywhere, and if Tala cannot do it, then you must see it done by . . . by *eunuchs*."

"Shall we import some from the East? I'm sure our stiff-necked Romans would take delight in the sight of perfumed eunuchs whispering in the ear of their princess." When I see that he is not amused, I sigh. "Dora takes pity on Tacfarinas, nothing more. Whatever you imagine you saw in the garden was kindness to a boy with a wretched past."

The king's frown deepens. "Selene, I *imagined* nothing. Isidora is thirteen years old; it is long past time you speak to her about what will be expected of her."

This sobers me. Two years I bought for her. Time is racing by and I am no closer to a solution. Always I have imagined that I would have my daughter with me; that when I am gone, she will wear my crown and carry on my legacy as another Ptolemaic queen in a long, proud line of them. I have taught her to love Mauretania as I love it. But the emperor seems intent on marrying her to a foreign king.

In his way, I think Augustus is trying to do well by her, but he has given us precious few names of potential suitors, and I will not accept Herod or his sons. Taking a deep breath, I say, "If I plead with him, Augustus would approve Ptolemy for her."

Juba tilts his head back with an air of frustration. "Not this again."

"I don't like the idea either, but between us we are both orphans without relation. They call me the last of the Ptolemies and we have only two children by blood; we cannot afford to send either of them away."

The king stands abruptly. "My son will never marry his sister, Selene. Such an abomination will never happen, here."

Abomination. Again, he wounds me. "My ancestors are not the only royals to marry brother to sister. The Seleucids—"

"Stop," Juba says, one finger pointed at me.

"In Pontus and Commagene and—"

"I have heard it all before in our council chamber. Our advisers say no man becomes Pharaoh but through Pharaoh's daughter. They say royalty must imitate the gods. They say it is done for the sake of stability. They say that a pure bloodline frustrates the ambitions of rapacious men. I don't care. I know that our Easterners expect us to marry our son and daughter to each other, but this is not Egypt, and our courtiers will have to learn to live with disappointment just as I have learned to live with their resentment."

"Have you considered what it means to marry a Ptolemaic princess to a foreign king? Any man my daughter marries can lay claim to Egypt and Cyrenaica and Numidia and Mauretania. All North Africa. You do not realize it, because you do not aspire to be a ruthless conqueror, but Augustus realizes it and that is why he has approved so few names. He knows, as I know, that any child Isidora bears may serve as an excuse for war—as an excuse to take or destroy everything we have built."

"That is not the way of the world anymore, Selene," my husband says, with wide-eyed optimism. "No kingdom dares to move against another in violation of Rome's will. That is why we serve Augustus, is it not? He forces the peace."

"It is better to guard against disaster instead of hoping it never comes to pass."

Juba rubs at his face. "Selene. Enough. Not long after our wedding night, you held me at knifepoint and vowed that you would see me dead if I forced you to bed. I believed you as you must believe me now. You will need to see me dead before I allow our son and daughter to marry. It will not happen while I draw breath. So make your choice. Pick up a knife or surrender this perverse idea."

It is, I suppose, a testament to how things have improved between us that taking up a knife is never a serious consideration. "Must you be *quite* so dramatic? I only want my daughter to wear my crown here in Mauretania, where she is beloved. I am grasping for something that will allow me to keep my daughter and prevent her from being ripped from her home, the way I was ripped from mine."

"Now we come to the truth," he says, softening a bit, reaching to stroke my arm. "Isidora will never be taken from our home as a prisoner, Selene. She will never walk in chains. She will merely marry beneath her, and it has not turned out so badly for you, has it?"

He's trying to charm me and it is working. "That's not the point."

"I know. You want to maintain your dynasty in the way it was— so that your children can return to *Egypt*. But Isidora cannot marry Ptolemy and there is no one else of suitable rank. Isidora will wear a crown, Selene, but it cannot be yours. The sooner you prepare her for it, the better."

I tell her in the early summer, on the day of her first moon's blood. My daughter is not shocked or frightened by her menstrual bleeding. She understands the breeding of animals and knows she can now bear a child. Nevertheless, we take Isidora to my chambers and my ladies make much of the occasion. Tala and I teach her to use rags to soak the blood. We tell her to give no credence to the superstitions that in a bleeding woman's presence, bees will die, dogs will go rabid, seeds become sterile, plants will dry up, and fruit will rot on any tree she sits under.

"Really, *men*! Where do they get these ideas?" my daughter asks. And when we have her laughing at this silliness, I take her aside and tell her what it means to be a woman. What it means to be a royal princess. And all that the emperor would have of her.

"He is thinking grandly of your future," I say, forcing a smile.

"Must I leave Mauretania?" she asks, her voice swelling.

The question nearly breaks my resolve, but if I do not make myself serene, I will frighten her. If I am not strong, how can she be? So I swallow a gulp of air and smile even wider. "Yes, but you will come to love a new kingdom just as you love this one. You will marry a prince or perhaps even a king."

Her soft hands tremble in mine like captured birds. "I don't want to marry a prince or even a king. I don't want to marry a stranger. If I must marry . . . if I must marry, I would marry . . ."

She is on the edge of confiding something, but draws back.

How astonishing.

My daughter has had little cause in her life to hide things from me. She has never been one to lie about her misdeeds. Always, I have tried to be the person in whom she might confide. But I realize, for the first time, that she *has* become a woman. It is not the blood that made her so. It is a secret. A secret she is keeping, even from me. How is it that Juba stumbled upon it first? "Isidora, you are a royal princess. Your Berber boy can be nothing to you."

The sudden stain of red on her cheeks pains me. Oh, my poor girl. I have warned her, more than once, about overfamiliarity with our subjects, but her heart is too big. Taking her into my arms, I hold her close and stroke her hair. "We are Ptolemies. I think we are not meant for private passions . . . we are meant for *more*, and it is very hard. I know. But you will become a great queen like Pythia."

Isidora's eyes slide from mine. "I've never seen it that way. When the waters shimmer for me and flow into the future, always I see myself here in Mauretania."

What she says ought to comfort me—for if she sees truly, it means Mauretania will not lose her. But I remember when my little brother Philadelphus told me that he would always stay in Rome, he meant that he would be buried there. "You don't know what you see, Isidora. You're too young to try to see into the future."

"I have always done it and I am not so young," she says, tilting her chin at me in sudden defiance. "Sometimes, I see a wide river with currents that churn up mud. In the water, in the brown and green and white rapids, I see things that haven't happened yet. If I'm a woman now, I should learn how to understand these visions. You should teach me."

"I cannot teach you to read the Rivers of Time. It was never within my gift. Moreover, I have only ever seen it as a burden to those who *do* have that gift. It might be better that you did not learn any magic at all."

"*Heka* flows into me whenever we go to a place of worship," she says, trying to show me how much she already knows. "It flows into me and makes me see more clearly, though it makes me feel so very ill. Do you know why?"

So she has been keeping more than one secret.

"That is the *heka* sickness you speak of," I explain. More than once, I have fallen victim to it. Never have I forgotten the day I nearly lost myself in the magic of the sirocco. There are mortal dangers too. Already Augustus has made plain his intention to use my daughter by marrying her off. How else might he exploit her if he knew that I'm not the only sorceress in his power? "It's dangerous to work magic, Dora. But more dangerous by far to look into the Rivers of Time. That magic cost our family everything. Do you understand me?"

She straightens, a perfect imitation of my most regal posture. "If it's dangerous, then isn't it better that I learn from you how not to fall ill from *heka* sickness? Isn't it better to learn from you than from a stranger in some foreign court where I must rule as queen?"

I recognize that stubborn set of her jaw. Whatever else she may be, my daughter is a Ptolemy. She has always known what she wanted and I cannot say she is wrong to want it. Two years, I remind myself. Less than two years now. There is no time to wait for anything.

In surrender, I rise from my couch. I take her to my iron-banded strongbox, unlocking it to show her my precious treasures. I show her silvered stars that were gifted to me by a Syrian magi. I show her the pearls that once belonged to my mother, but now belong to me—a long-ago gift from the emperor himself. And then I show her the golden serpent bracelet that my mother wanted me to have.

Sliding it up my arm until it coils tightly against my bare skin, I explain, "My mother had the gift of sight, as you do. She saw that one possible future was one in which she would have a daughter. One in which her daughter would bring her a snake with which to end her life. Because she saw it, she entrusted this bracelet to a friend and told him to tell her daughter it was not her fault. Because she saw into the Rivers of Time, she was able to reach back for me and offer me this comfort. But it is the only good thing to come of her sight."

I don't think Dora is old enough to possibly understand the significance of what I am telling her, but I was just her age when this serpent was given to me. My daughter tucks errant strands of golden hair behind her ears, and says, "How strange that my grandmother gave you a snake and you gave me one too."

I tilt my head, then I remember. "What happened to your Asclepian snake?"

"It hunts in your gardens and sleeps in the tree by my room. When I am troubled, I listen for anything it might whisper to me. It was born in the temple and it knows things that physicians know."

This would be useful, but I still do not like the thought of my daughter keeping company with serpents. Alexander the Great's mother slept with snakes and used them to work her own magic, but it is not a magic I understand. And what I do not understand, I have good reason to fear.

Nevertheless, I move aside a length of cloth and draw from my strongbox a precious amulet. A collar of gold. "Before my mother died, she gave me the jade frog amulet that I wear. I am never without it. She gave my brother, Philadelphus, this collar of gold. He wore it until . . ." Here I pause, remembering my little brother on his deathbed, and I do not think I can continue.

Dora lays her hand atop mine. "Until?"

"He wore it until the night he died. He said that you should have it. He *saw* that you should have it." Her eyes light up with wonder at this revelation, but I caution her. "I will give you this amulet to wear and I will teach you how to use it to channel your *heka* so it does not overwhelm you. Every day, after you've completed your other studies, you and I will practice magic together. But only if you vow to me that you will never try to look into the Rivers of Time unless I am with you. Do you agree?"

She pretends to agree and I pretend to believe her. Then I fasten the chain around her neck and hold her tightly, knowing, just as my mother knew, we are nearly out of time.

Thirty

"TEN denarii," says the merchant.

"Three," insists Tala, using her height and stature to intimidate all those who crowd round us in the marketplace. She never leaves her room without donning every piece of jewelry she owns, and her tinkling silver makes her more impressive.

"But the queen agreed to *ten*," the merchant says, holding up the painted pot that I mean to send Julia as a gift.

"Because the queen doesn't know you're a cheat," Tala accuses, pointing out flaws in the workmanship I do not see. I would rather pay more than the pot is worth, but then I remember the expense of my temple and I let Tala haggle.

In the crowd, my subjects press close, grabbing for my hands, trying to touch my gown, my hair, anything within reach. Memnon hates that I allow this, and he uses a brawny arm to shove back anyone who lingers too long. When my Berber woman returns to my side, triumphantly holding the colorfully painted pot aloft, we walk ahead of the other ladies, Memnon opening a path for us ahead. "Tala, did you know about my daughter's fondness for Tacfarinas?"

She grunts in the affirmative. "You gave him to her like a puppy from a cage. How can you complain now that she wants him on her leash?"

"She must go to a marriage bed far from here."

"And you're going to ask me to go with her," my Berber woman says, stopping to put a hand on her broad hip as if challenging me to deny it. I cannot deny it. If Dora is to be queen of some foreign land, she must take with her a royal retinue and the preparations for it must be made as soon as possible . . .

"I was born a chieftain's daughter, not a serving woman," Tala says. "In the hills, I had a house for winter and another house for summer and a tent for when the tribes journeyed into the steppes. I slept in my own bed and set my own table, one carved from wood and polished with wax until it gleamed. I had goats and sheep and a donkey to carry firewood and buckets of water from the wells. I was commanded by no one under my roof—not even my husband. But when he died, my people put me in your household to see what kind of queen we would have. I stayed because you were a spoiled know-nothing who needed me. I took your daughter to my breast because I had milk. For you, I left the ways of my people behind. Now you ask me to leave behind the lands of my ancestors too?"

I put my hand to my brow both to shield me from the too-bright sun and to hide my shame. "It is too much to ask of you."

"Yes, it's too much to ask," Tala says gravely. "I wouldn't go with her because you *asked* it of me. Or even if you commanded me. But I'll go with her because deep in my liver where it cannot be cut out of me without killing me, I love your daughter as my own. I won't let your child go alone somewhere that frightens her any more than I have ever let you do it."

Moved, I put my hands to my cheeks and shake my head. "But you have a son too. And a . . . a man."

"Captain Kabyle is a sailor. Surely there will be a harbor in whatever kingdom your daughter marries. And as for my son, I call upon you now for a favor once promised me. Make my son a great man in Mauretania," she says. "So if ever I return home, I can boast to all the tribeswomen who have mocked my choices. I'll watch over yours if you watch over mine."

I release a violent breath, dizzy with relief and gratitude. This is an easy promise for me to make for it is also a promise I feel in my heart—or in my liver, as the Berbers say.

* * *

WHEN servants try to curl my son's hair in the fashion appropriate
for a Hellenistic prince, he squirms and risks being burned by the
iron, so I take it upon myself. As it happens, I have him perched in
my lap, a lock of his hair wrapped round the hot tong, when the
king pokes his head into the room.

Usually when the king wishes to tell me something, he sends a
messenger or waits for a meal together, so I am immediately wary
of whatever it is that might trouble him enough to seek me out.

"We were away in Rome too long," Juba says, leaning against
the door. "I have just received a letter from the magistrate in Volubilis and I fear the people of that city will not remain pacified
without a royal presence there. I must go back. We will have to
divide our court again, as we did before."

The last time Juba went to govern Volubilis, he was gone for more
than a year; we no longer have time to spend so freely. "Must you go?"

The king shrugs. "I like it no more than you, Selene."

"We can go together," I say. "We can move the whole court to
Volubilis."

Juba scowls at the idea, for moving a seat of government will be
an immensely inconvenient undertaking. But I am suddenly desperate to convince him. "We'll all go, and it will be a grand adventure.
We can show the children the wilds of Mauretania. Ptolemy needs
to know the lands over which he will rule . . ."

Especially if he is to spend the rest of his youth in Rome.

Before Juba can protest, I kiss the top of my son's head and ask,
"You'd like to see more of Mauretania, wouldn't you, Ptolemy? We'll
go west and see all the places Hercules slept. We'll dig out lungfish
from the riverbed for our supper."

He is a seven-year-old boy; it is the lungfish that gets his attention. "I can get my own supper? Can we hunt for antelope too?"

I promise, "If you catch one, you can put the horns over
your bed."

Ptolemy is almost convinced. "Would I have to go in the carriage or could I ride a horse?"

"A horse," Juba vows, smiling down at the boy he put in a saddle almost as soon as he could walk. "You can ride beside me. If you make it all the way to Volubilis without complaining, I'll give you your very own stallion."

This is too exciting for Ptolemy to endure in the cage of my arms. He springs up to embrace his father, forcing me to fling the iron away before we are both burned. "Ptolemy!"

But I cannot be angry.

The king ruffles Ptolemy's hair, ruining my handiwork. "Run, boy, before she catches you and makes you into a pretty Greek." Once my son has scampered off, my husband asks, "Are you satisfied? We'll never hear the end of it now if we don't find antelope."

"You're the one who promised him a stallion," I say, fetching the hot iron, where I see it has dented the wooden chest at the foot of Ptolemy's bed and scorched the floor. "I will never understand why everyone in this kingdom is so smitten with horses. I've always preferred cats."

Threading an arm about my waist, my husband says, "You are part cat, Selene. Aloof, mercurial . . . You really mean to go with me to Volubilis?"

To hear him so hopeful makes me ache inside. Chryssa will be outraged to be left behind again, to look after my interests here. But I can endure her censure in exchange for Juba's smile. "Yes. I want us all to be together . . . until we can't be."

IT will be a journey of two weeks, half at sea and half overland, into the fertile plains of Mauretania. We go first to Tingis, our Roman colony near the Pillars of Hercules, where the strait is so narrow that on the sunny day we make landfall, we can see Spain across the waters. The Romans receive us with unexpected enthusiasm now that Juba is the patron of the colony, and we are tourists for a day in Tingis, walking the beaches and learning of its history from our guide.

Dora shrugs off her brother's attempts to play with her in the surf, too grown-up now, she says, to walk barefoot in the sand. But when I remove my sandals and run with Ptolemy, letting the sea foam tickle my toes and leaving footprints in my wake, Isidora relents. The king joins in and we spend an hour heaping up piles of sand to build a little city in miniature, with walls, a lighthouse, and a temple too. Hopefully Amphio's version of my temple will be stronger than the one I make, as my sand temple collapses under the weight of the dome I try to shape.

"This is as far west as Hercules ever traveled," the king explains to my children, both of whom are descended from the great hero. "In penance for a great crime, he was ordered to do labors. His tenth was to capture the cattle of Geryon, a monster who once lived here."

With our entourage, all of whom are now happy sightseers, we climb into the cave of Hercules, the very spot where the hero is said to have slept. I marvel at the hissing sea spray beneath. Ptolemy, Ziri, Tacfarinas, and the other boys climb on the wet rocks where the sea rushes in, and I fear they're going to be swept away. I call down to Ptolemy to be careful, and he calls back up to me, "What *was* the great crime of Hercules?"

"He committed murder in a fit of rage," I answer.

Later, back on the beach, Isidora asks, "Why didn't you tell him Hercules murdered his children?"

"I would rather little Ptolemy did not know such horrible things. Truthfully, I wish you did not know either."

Dora leans forward over the frothing water, thoughtful. "What could drive a man to such derangement?"

Fixing her hairnet—for she has let it slip—I blame it away on the gods. "Hera cursed Hercules so that when he looked at his children, he thought they were the children of his enemy. He didn't believe his children were his own."

"Does it matter so very much?" Dora asks.

I glance at Juba where he walks with his son on the beach, hand in hand. "To some men more than others."

I can imagine the sad solitude of Hercules brooding here alone in his cave. But I cannot imagine how he might have ever found redemption. If I lost my children, I would wander the world like a destructive madwoman, like Demeter did when she lost Persephone. And in truth, if I lose my children to the emperor's plans, I may end up doing just that . . .

WE go next to Lixus, a city nestled in a forest of cork oak trees so old that they saw the Carthaginians rise and fall. It is here they say that Hercules found the Garden of the Hesperides, where a bite of a golden apple conveys everlasting life. I cannot blame my husband for sending search parties into the hills to find this mythical orchard, because I too want every moment we have together to last forever. Every laugh of my children. Every sun-soaked step they take at my side. Every story my husband tells them, each word precious to me.

After two days of leisure, we are ready to make our way inland to Volubilis. "War elephants?" I ask, disarmed by the intent gaze of the great creatures who are to accompany us. Clothed in wrinkled gray skin, with big rounded ears and fearsome tusks that extend to a sharp point, the elephants do not look at all tame. We stand on the road, our baggage train assembling under the hot sun, accompanied by soldiers and every manner of official we might find useful.

In the chaos of travelers, pack animals, and the flies that plague us, only Maysar seems to hear my distress. "We do not plan to use them for battle," the Berber chieftain says. "But if we want people to remember that our king is a Berber king, we must remind them that he is Juba son of Juba, who rode in battle against Romans with elephants carrying turrets on their backs."

This was not a winning war strategy for Juba's father, but it would be churlish of me to point it out. Elephants have been a symbol of royalty and power since Alexander's time. Even before Hannibal so famously took elephants across the Alps to attack Rome, my Ptolemaic ancestors tamed them for war making too. So I attempt to get into the spirit of the thing. "Well, then, how do I mount one?"

From horseback, wearing the flowing burnoose in the tradition of our tribesmen, Juba turns to us. "The queen is not going to ride an elephant into the city. When we get there, I will ride an elephant and lead the others through the gates, and she will follow in a *carpentum*."

I do not think he intends to offend me, but he does. "I am not a woman in your baggage train, King Juba. I am as royal a queen as you are king. There is no reason I should not ride at your side atop an elephant."

Juba snorts. "Only the best reason: You're a dreadful rider. You can barely stay astride a horse. What will become of your royal dignity—not to mention your royal bones—should you fall from an elephant and snap your neck?"

"Oh . . . I had not considered that possibility." Still, I am a *little* aggrieved. "But if you are riding into Volubilis on an elephant, so am I."

"You are an audacious woman," the king says with an exasperated shake of his head. "Set a better example for your daughter, Queen Selene."

"I intend to," I call after him.

As he rides off, I grin because I know he is not angry. In fact, I do not think I have ever seen the king so happy. He is a man who loves to learn and it does not matter if learning comes to him in the form of a scroll or an expedition into wild lands. Having us here with him for each new discovery seems to bring him great joy.

I feel it too.

Our baggage train stretches at least a mile as we snake our way through the tall grasses with our slaves and servants, our sack-laden camels, the wagonloads of provisions pulled by donkeys, our horse-mounted soldiers, and our war elephants. By day we travel like the nomads, crossing the steppes alongside herds of goats and sheep. At night, we burn fragrant sagebrush and juniper to keep warm. I love the shimmering grasses of our fertile coastal plain. And we *do* see antelope. However, when Ptolemy breaks away from our group to ride one down, I begin to regret encouraging him to such adventure.

"Ptolemy is fearless!" Juba exclaims that night in my tent, taking a simple meal of dried fruit and nuts, served with thick slices of cheese.

Because we are alone, I reply, "Yes, he is fearless. Which makes me all the more afraid for him."

Propped up on embroidered pillows, the king takes a handful of raisins, then says, "It's a mother's way. I know how afraid you are to send him to Rome, but you must make peace with it."

"I can't. If there is *any way* we can keep him, we must."

He dismisses my plea out of hand. "It will do him good to live apart from us. To live in a place where his mother and father are not the highest authority in the land. He will learn to see things differently."

I will never leave my son alone in the viper's nest that is Rome. I will never abandon Ptolemy to the emperor as my mother was forced to abandon me. I will never leave my son undefended against Livia. If Ptolemy must live in Rome, then I must live there with him. This would be my decision whether it was the emperor's desire or not. Perhaps it would comfort the father in Juba to know that I will be there to keep his son safe, but it will not comfort the husband in him.

If I cannot think of another way, we will be parted. And when that happens, Juba will have his memories of me and little else. So I resolve to give him the best of me now. "You said once to Herod that if you had natural children by other women you did not know of them."

The king's fist closes around the raisins and he glances up at me. "Has this been troubling you?"

I hesitate, weighing my words, wondering how I once thought myself so clever with them. "I have not been able to give you another child and . . . I know there have been women. If there are children, you should have them with you. If you brought them to court, I would receive them warmly."

He raises an eyebrow. "And their mothers?"

"I would pretend not to hate them."

At that, the king laughs, which is not the reaction I was hoping for.

Taking a deep breath, I cling to my dignity. "Have I not treated Lady Circe well?"

The king throws his head back on the pillows. "Too well, I think. Don't fret. There are no such children, Selene."

He thinks this will reassure me, but it saddens me, for his sake. "Are you quite certain?"

"Reasonably certain. But, if there were such children, I would not want you to receive their mothers warmly."

Confused, I slant him a glance. "You would prefer jealousy and backstabbing harem politics?"

"Unquestionably. It would please me to see you fly into a jealous rage."

I fold my arms over myself because I believe he is mocking me. "That is not how a queen behaves." It would also be the height of hypocrisy on my part.

"But if you were not a queen—"

"I have *always* been a queen."

"But if you were *not* a queen, and simply a woman in my baggage train, then how would you behave?"

"Any way you wished me to, for you are still king in that scenario."

I do not mean it as flirtation, but it comes out that way. Heat flashes in his eyes, and he tugs me down onto the pillows with him. "You would not have me unless I was still a king with a baggage train. Even if you were a louse-ridden peasant, you would be hard to impress." As he teases me, he caresses the length of my arm, pleasure humming in his throat. "But if I should take a woman when we get to Volubilis . . ."

"I would unleash a crocodile in your bed to eat you both."

The sentiment delights him. He laughs, bends his head to me, and crushes me with a kiss that lasts until morning.

In the end, Juba teaches me to ride an elephant. The trainers pick the most docile one, a cow who kneels on command. As it happens, there is no ladylike way in which to mount an elephant, but the king pulls me up into a saddle made of soft woolen blankets so that I may become accustomed to the creature.

In the saddle with Juba, holding tight to the rope, I am more afraid of falling than I am of this gray giant whose bulk could crush us in an instant, so I am grateful when the king's arms come around me to keep me steady.

Having spent years exploring our kingdom, Juba tells me, "Elephants touch to greet one another. They wrap their trunks together and stroke one another's faces. And when they die, they bury one another."

"How extraordinary."

"Even more extraordinary is that their families are led by the females."

"What clever creatures."

I feel him smirk against my hair, but the king holds me fast. Hour by hour, plodding step by step, I become more sure of him and slowly let go of the ropes . . .

HOW many times have I made a grand procession into a city? The first time, it was as the emperor's chained prisoner, dragged behind his chariot into Rome. The second time was in Athens, where I rode beside the emperor in his chariot, amidst rumors that he had taken me as his mistress. This time I am no one's prisoner and no man's mistress. This time, in the fifteenth year of my reign, wearing a pearled crown and a gown made of cloth of gold, I ride a monstrous creature into a city over which I am queen.

Our elephants have been painted in pigments of turquoise, ochre, and carnelian. Their massive heads have been draped in decorative enameled shields that extend partway down their long trunks. They trumpet for us when our heralds blow their horns, and I ride at the king's side into the gates of Volubilis.

It has the desired effect. Startled citizens throng into the streets, some shrieking with excitement, others silent in awe. But oh, the noise we make. The trumpeting of elephants and the stamping of their feet, the clash of cymbals, the rumble of our carriages and wagons, and the thunder of horse hooves on the pavement. When the crowd roars—in approval or dismay, I cannot quite tell—I fear our elephants will startle or stampede. It also occurs to me that the king and I are quite vulnerable to arrows here, so high and conspicuous. But I am a Ptolemy. I have never feared my people and I never will. Our goal here, as everywhere in the kingdom, is *harmonia*.

We must all learn to turn our differences into united strength.

When our brave processional is over, the king cries out to me in approval. "What a sight you made!"

Domesticated, indeed . . .

I am sorry that Crinagoras is not with us. My poet would have written verses comparing me to some many-armed Indian elephant goddess. Or perhaps Dido as she rode into Carthage. I know he will regret having missed the elephants, but I take comfort in the latest missive from Judea, in which Crinagoras sends word that he believes Herod to have been taken by some sort of illness of the genitals. How he knows this, I do not ask, but it makes me more determined than ever that Herod will never marry my daughter.

The rest of our entourage sets immediately to the task of making Volubilis our seat of government. It is not a big city, but it has its advantages. It is a paradise in the wilderness, surrounded by a quilt of green and gold fields that blanket the hills. Still, as a grim-faced magistrate shows us the way to the palace, I wonder aloud if it was wise to build a remote city so far inland.

"Berbers are not afraid to be far from water, Majesty," Maysar replies.

No, they are not. They are hardy men who can strike and disappear into the desert, scattering like sand on the wind. It is why they have never been truly conquered, these people. I am not the only one to think it. "This city will need a better wall," one of our Romans says.

The palace is very old; it was built when Carthage still ruled, and the Punic architecture is a marvel to me. Everything I touch is a historical wonder. I am heartened that the simple red and white mosaic floors greet me with only one symbol—the one for Tanit, so similar to the *ankh* of Isis. This grand, flat-roofed house with sandstone columns and staircases that lead to rooftop terraces is not so impressive as the palace we built by the sea. Still, I am enamored by an inner courtyard filled with rows of fruit trees intersected by hedges of shrubs and little gutters of running water.

Is that cherry? It is! Here in the cooler weather of the steppes, it grows well. And looking up, past the fruit trees, I discover a tower capped with a pyramid. Ah, it comforts me to know there is Egyptian influence here too.

The next day, the king insists that we inspect the stable yard, which stinks of straw and manure and liniment. From behind a stall door ornamented with golden lions with emerald eyes, a groom coaxes forth a cream-colored stallion fitted with a plume upon its head. My son is slack-jawed at the sight of the awesome creature, its glossy coat stretched over powerful muscles.

"He is yours," Juba says as the horse snorts, pulling against his golden bit. "In keeping of my promise, Ptolemy."

When the horse stamps and gives a roll of its eyes, I cannot think the king means to give such a fierce creature to my son as a mount, but my boy is fearless, after all. Approaching the horse's side, Ptolemy strokes its nose, then uses the roots of the stallion's mane to vault himself up onto the saddlecloth while all the Berbers cheer.

The stallion is a racer, Juba says. Faster than any other in our stables. And my son names him Sirocco after the windstorms that sometimes beset my land. The fierceness of this horse has me beside myself with worry, but the king himself vows to help Ptolemy train his new mount to perfect obedience.

Meanwhile, I must keep a vow of my own. Every day, when Dora has finished her studies in mathematics, geography, philosophy, and music, I teach her to use magic without letting the *heka* ravage her. I teach her to use her collar of gold amulet to channel the power inside her, but she finds it difficult to do as I instruct.

She cannot call the winds; we try it, but she fails. She cannot throw fire from her hands either. There is a moment when I think that she can—a moment that I think I hear flames roaring in my ears, when I think I glimpse the torches spark with our efforts—but then the moment is gone, and Dora says she felt nothing.

This should not surprise me. She has no strange birthmarks in the shape of hieroglyphs. Nor was she born under a prophetic star. But her way with animals is not simple affinity. I think her understanding of their wounds and how to heal them is not something she learned from my mage. Though it still makes me shudder to see, it does amaze me that she listens for wisdom in the whisper of her brown snake's scaled skin as it coils around her wrist. And what she can see in a simple pool inspires in me both awe and terror.

"There are so many currents," she says one day, staring at the surface of the water in a divination bowl. "So many different paths for the future. How do I know which way *our* river is flowing?"

"If you knew that, my sweet, you would rule the world, and perhaps you shall."

Thirty-one

❧

GRASS, wood smoke, and fresh apples perfume the air on the day we join the residents of Volubilis for their orchard festival. Children are sent with baskets to see who can gather the most fruit while women gather near the presses to squeeze cider out of the misshapen ones.

With lazy bees buzzing about and the mountains mantled in the colors of an African autumn, Juba and I hold court beneath a canopy. Nearby, Tacfarinas keeps watch over the horses because even though all our royal horses are of a fine breed, my son's impressive pearl stallion has become an attraction.

Meanwhile, I keep a wary eye on my children, afraid they are going to fall out of the apple trees and break their bones. I am thus distracted when our subjects come before us to offer gifts of welcome.

One mountaineer sets down a small chest before us, a gift of silver for the king, he says.

"My queen is more likely to make use of it," Juba jests, offering the chest to me. Silver is an extravagant gift from hill people and I make ready to find some way of rewarding them for their generosity, but when I open the box, I do not see any silver.

I see only a bundle of beautifully woven cloths.

"How exquisite," I exclaim, eager to praise the mountaineer, who is suddenly shy, withdrawing from our dais. Reaching into the bundle to find the treasure inside . . . I am suddenly attacked.

"No!" Tacfarinas cries. The boy hits me hard, wrenching my

shoulder and knocking me to the ground with the weight of his whole body. The chest of silver flies from my hands, crashing to the ground a few feet away while chaos erupts around us.

With my face pressed into the dirt, I see only the feet of the retreating mountaineer, who shouts in Berber, "Remember the cruci-fied heroes of our rebellion!"

Shouts and screams erupt all around us. Several of Juba's guards run after the mountaineer, but Memnon draws his sword, shouting at Tacfarinas. "Get off the queen, you little bastard, and I'll kill you quickly instead of drawing it out as you so richly deserve!"

But Juba yells, "Everyone out of the tent!"

Gasping under the bulk of the boy, I can make no sense of what is happening until I see the black scorpions swarming Memnon's feet. "Don't move," I whisper to my guard, but it is too late. I see that he has already been stung, and when he realizes it, he begins to crunch the scorpions beneath his sandals.

Tacfarinas rolls me away, and moments later, Juba's guards have me by the arms, the rest of them dispatching the venomous crea-tures. "What is happening?" I shriek, though it is not difficult to understand. Someone is trying to frighten or kill us.

And poor Memnon is the unlucky victim. One scorpion sting will cause discomfort; it need not be fatal for a grown man. But Memnon's been stung in at least a dozen places. His heart thumps so loudly in his chest that even I can hear it as we drag him from the tent and try to lay him down. "No, keep him upright," Dora says with great authority, rushing to Memnon's side. "Hold him standing to keep the poison from spreading and tie off his legs."

Everyone listens to her because none of the rest of us have the first idea of what to do. I am too stunned to stop her when she kneels at Memnon's feet, her new embroidered gown crushed beneath her knees in the dirt.

Her examination is too much for Memnon, who insists that the pain does not vex him, even though we can plainly see the redness and swelling where he has been stung. He is shamed to be tended to by the royal princess, who once, as a small child, stepped on his feet to see if she could make him lose his composure while he stood stiffly for parade.

But my daughter is no longer a small child. She pulls a dagger from Memnon's belt and uses it to cut the ribbon from her hair in half. She uses each half to tie off his legs just above the knee. Then, without hesitation, she slashes open one of the welts. Her golden hair spills over her shoulders as she bends to suck the poison, and we are all stupefied when she stops to spit it out, blood running down her chin.

"By Jupiter!" Juba cries. "What is she doing?"

"I have no idea what she is doing," I confess, holding him back. "But she seems to know . . ."

My daughter has become, quite suddenly, a commanding presence, snapping orders to the servants to hurry Memnon back to the palace. And no one dares disobey her. Not even me.

Memnon's breathing shortens and becomes labored. By the time we reach the palace, he is soaked with sweat, too weak to protest Isidora's ministrations. She insists that he drink a tonic of thistle and calendula, and he does, but I leave the room because my presence is one more indignity than he can bear.

In the courtyard, I find the boy skulking nearby, arms folded over each other, head bowed. "You may have saved my life," I say.

Impertinently, Tacfarinas only tightens his jaw with pride, as if he now considered his debt to me repaid. But he will not get away so easily. Rubbing my shoulder, for it still pains me from his attack, I ask, "How did you know there were scorpions in the box?"

His pallor turns to ash. "When you opened the lid, I saw a black scorpion, from the corner of my eye, Majesty."

I find it difficult to believe he could have glimpsed into the box before I did, but perhaps I am making too much of it. Or perhaps he has already made friends with the bandits and rebels of this place.

In my experience, men and boys of nefarious intent tend to seek one another out. I do not press him on the matter because of one important thing. Whatever he knew about that box and the men who delivered it to us, he threw himself in harm's way to defend me. He may sympathize with his Berber brethren who resent us.

Indeed, he may resent us just as much. But he risked his own life to save mine, and what more can one ask of a boy like him?

THAT night, my husband is in a black mood. "I should never have agreed to bring you all to Volubilis. I thought it was safe here. How many more men must I crucify to avoid a rebellion . . . or have I already caused one?"

My hands go to Juba's shoulders, kneading the flesh there, trying to push the tiniest bit of *heka* into his sinews and bones in order that he might find some relief. "There are always men such as these, Juba. We can never win all of them. But we must win *most* of them and I think we have. We weren't set upon by a cavalry from the mountains or pelted with arrows from on high. Assassins are usually men who cannot find compatriots to fight with them, so they resort to scorpions in a box. It is a desperate thing."

"A thing that may have killed Memnon. Even if he recovers, we cannot go on as we have been. You have your guards. I have mine. It is all haphazard. That must change now. We will organize a royal guard of praetorians, modeled after the emperor's own *corporis custodes*."

"Don't you worry to anger Augustus with our presumption?"

"I spoke to him about it when we were last in Rome. He said he would not allow it in other kingdoms, but he would sanction it for us if we thought it was necessary. I am now convinced it is necessary."

I have no more arguments even though I do not like this idea. I have known no other security in my life but for my Macedonian guards. Moreover, it feels disloyal to even discuss such a thing while my poor Memnon might not live to see the morning . . .

WE are all amazed when, by sunrise, my daughter seems to have cured my trusted guardsman. Dora asks, "Can you feel your tongue, Memnon?"

"Yes, Princess," he says, gruffly, unable to meet her eyes.

"Then the worst of it has passed," she says, inspecting his hands. "Have your fingers always curved that way?"

"No," he answers, suddenly snatching them away. "I mean, they were this way before the scorpions."

"Your little toe on the right foot is bent strangely too," she says. "And when I saw you reach to pick an apple in the orchard, you grimaced when you lifted your arm over your head. How long have you had such pains?"

Memnon wants nothing more than to flee, but I command him to answer her. "The past year or so, Princess Isidora. It does not hurt. A little soreness. Nothing more."

"It is a special pain of the joints, Memnon. It will get worse if untreated. You must season your food with turmeric. It is a spice from Parthia. It is costly, but we can provide it for him, can't we, Mother?"

"Of course," I say, saddened by the realization that my poor Memnon is getting old. Always I remember him as the fearsome soldier who stood outside my door. But like the rest of us, he cannot be forever young. "Perhaps it is time you retired your shield, Memnon, and took your ease on my plantation as overseer. Your shoulders might pain you less if you did not have to carry a sword."

He stiffens as if I have commanded him to suicide. "A Macedonian guard is never without his sword, Majesty. *Never.*"

So Juba's new scheme will not go easy, I think. Memnon's honor will never endure his being set aside. I will have to divine a new duty for him, special and urgent, that I can entrust only to him.

SOMETHING about Volubilis changes me.

I am not the darling of the Hellenes here, always required to serve as the example of fine Greek culture. Neither am I an exotic magician. To the contrary, the Berber natives are accustomed to wisewomen and tell stories of Juba's grandfather, King Masinissa, whose mother was a sorceress.

There are fewer Romans here, and because I am not challenged, there is no need to fight for my place as queen. Indeed, my worries about our safety here are put at ease when the native Berbers capture and turn over the rebel who delivered the box of scorpions.

Normally, I am keen to see terrible justice done to anyone who tries to harm me and mine, but I leave this to Juba because he asks it of me and because I wish to do as he asks. Somehow, I find myself able to be a different kind of woman here. A softer kind of woman. The kind of woman who obeys the king and does not resent giving him his way.

And every day Juba does not abuse my deference to him, I find myself more eager to oblige. I resolve never to refuse him when he desires me. Two years, I remind myself. Much less than that now. That is all the time we have together. And I want another child.

More importantly, I want to give Juba another child. One the emperor can never claim as his own.

If the emperor has me and Ptolemy at his side, he will forgive Juba for touching me. I will *make* him forgive it. So whenever the king comes to my bedchambers, I set aside my fears and call upon the magic that makes me fertile. But every time, my goddess denies me. And it is with the greatest bitterness I begin to fear that my womb is barren after all.

We do not let the people forget our entrance into the city. Juba has a coin struck with elephants to remind them. The coins are put into wide circulation by means of gifts and grants to the tribes who come down from the mountains to treat with the city elders. We keep busy repairing crumbling buildings, cleaning out faulty drainage, commissioning new roads and marketplaces and artwork for the public buildings.

And Juba wants to build a wall. "Strabo writes from your niece's court that the King of the Bosporus constructed a wall nearly three hundred and sixty stadia in length to protect against attacks from nomads . . ."

"Sometimes a wall keeps attackers out," I say, "but it can also be used to trap people inside. Is that not how Julius Caesar defeated Vercingetorix?"

My words give Juba pause, as I mean them to. He has been in a quiet fury since the day Memnon was stung by scorpions, and even after dispensing with the culprit, he has behaved more like a general plotting a campaign against barbarians than a king seeking to civilize them. I don't blame him. I know it's the Roman way to respond to every setback with a fortress or catapult. It's what he's been taught. But my husband is as responsible as anyone for teaching me that when there is no defense left, you must resort to diplomacy.

During the winter solstice, we recognize the Berber sun god Ba'al Hammon and their moon goddess Tanit. I host a banquet for every prominent Berber family in the city. It may be too much to ask the proud, horse-mounted tribesmen to forget that we are foreigners, but I think their women can be won over. My daughter and I approach these women during the celebration with our hands tattooed in henna, Berber designs bold on our skin. We speak to them in their own tongue, and when they do their tribal dance with drums, a line of chiseled men facing a line of colorfully dressed women, we join them.

We start the dance veiled as a symbol of our isolation and need for enlightenment, but the veils are abandoned when the dancer feels the spirit of the movements has captured her. We throw our hands to the north, south, east, west. Then we reach for the heavens and for the earth. A gesture to the past behind us and to the future before us. It is a dance of abandon and blessing—and I feel the *heka* rise in me as I flick it from my fingertips, always from the liver, where true emotions reside.

Then begin the gyrations and the tosses of head that make a music of tinkling silver jewelry worn by every Berber woman of status. I dance, though I do not know all the steps. I dance until my feet hurt. I dance until the sweat wets my hair and soaks my gown to the small of my back. I dance in firelight until I cannot dance anymore.

I collapse on a couch with the king, who makes eyes at me as if he wants me alone. But everyone else's eyes are on my daughter, whose very fair coloring is a curiosity here in the hills. She is not Berber by blood, but she knows their dances, their stories, their crafts, and the meaning of their symbols. Tala has made her a Berber in a way I can never be.

They watch my daughter because she is the granddaughter of Cleopatra. They watch her because she is the princess and because she is beautiful. But they also watch her because they seem to know that she is theirs. One Berber boy in particular has reason to think she belongs to him, for while the rest of the people watch Isidora, *she* is watching Tacfarinas, flashing her eyes at the stable boy every time she claps her hands or tosses her golden hair. And I worry at the kind of magic she is working now and if it will be her downfall.

THE children grow so swiftly.

My daughter has become a young beauty. The sullen Tacfarinas has sprouted up in height such that he towers over the others. He will be a big man, I think. One with powerful arms. And already, the hint of a beard makes itself known like the soft fuzz of a peach on his upper lip.

Tala's son is now a boy of fourteen, and while he eschews the Roman custom of wearing the *toga virilis* as a mark of manhood, he insists on a new name. When he was born, his mother called him Ziri, the Berber word for moonlight. Now the charming little name has become an embarrassment to him and he insists on being called Mazippa, after his father, a Berber of the Mauri tribe, who died before he was born.

In the way of young men his age, Tala's son bristles when anyone but Dora calls him by his given name, but I am glad of his bourgeoning pridefulness because I have plans for him. Grazing lands must become plantations. We must have grain. But there is no reason whatsoever that the greatest landholders in Mauretania should all be Roman. And so I encourage Ziri—or rather, Mazippa—to learn the skills needed to manage a great estate. *Make my son a great man in Mauretania*, Tala said to me, but the boy will have to do some of his own making . . .

My little Ptolemy is growing big too. In the spring, he celebrates his eighth birthday with a hunting trip and returns with the head of an antelope, which he proudly presents to me. Trying not to retch at the sight of the bloody thing, I praise him lavishly and announce that we will have roasted antelope for our feast. Alas, I do too good a job at disguising my distaste because Ptolemy says, "I know you said I could mount the horns over my bed, but if you want them, Mother, I would give them to you."

"I would not dream of stealing your prize, my generous little prince!"

"You would not be the first to try," he says, boasting about how raiders from the hills tried to chase the boys from their prey. "They fled when they saw our royal banner, though."

The story makes me wilt with fear. Only a stern lecture from Juba about how boys must become men keeps me from forbidding such hunting trips in the future. Instead, I use my terror for an opportunity, confessing to Memnon that I can trust no one but him to watch over my little prince in this wilderness city, where raiders and assassins appear from the mists.

I work myself into such a state that Memnon promises to take up his post outside my son's door, and I feel I have done well. Though Ptolemy is no easy child to manage, the burden on Memnon will be less. He will not be required to stand at attention for hours at official events or march in my processions. He can bark at my son and make him obey rather than chase after me and suffer my imperious ways.

So I resign myself into the custody of my husband's new commander of the palace guard, the young praetorian Iacentus, whose ambition and keen sense of authority has him establish a rotation of professional soldiers around the royal family in the model of the emperor's elite guard.

To My Friend, the Most Royal Queen of Mauretania,

How I hate Aquileia! It is as cursed as everything else that Tiberius and I share. My new husband and I made a son here in the shadow of the Alps. (Do not be shocked; there is nothing else to do here where the nights are so dreary, the wine hardly passable, and no decent poet can be found.)

Alas, our poor little baby did not live to see winter.

Livia says we must not grieve in an excessive or unseemly way. Our son was only a few days old when we lost him and, according to her, hardly a real person at all. But I tell you, Selene, I have never been so sad. I am so sad over the death of my babe that I think I am ill. I have no other explanation for what's wrong with me. I take pleasure in nothing. Wine tastes sour. Jewels do not sparkle. Fires do not warm me.

Phoebe tells me shared grief should draw a husband and wife together. Nevertheless, I am certain that I am done with this farce and that Tiberius is done with me. There are some rifts between husband and wife that can never be mended. I think the loss of a child will smash even the strongest of foundations, and our foundations were made of clay.

Do you know that when last we were in Rome, my husband saw his former wife? Tiberius was so overcome with regrets for having divorced her that he followed Vipsania through the streets calling after her with apologies and tears in his eyes. You would think such a thing would be a humiliation to me, but it only makes me sadder.

Unfortunately, the story so enraged my father that he sent Vipsania away, where Tiberius cannot see her again. No matter what I say, my husband is convinced it was my doing. Now we cannot stand the sight of each other, so I am returning to Rome where I am loved by the people, where I can watch over my children and my interests.

Especially now that Livia's youngest son has become a Republican.

Can you believe it? Fair Drusus, who owes nearly all his success to the fact that he is the stepson of the emperor, now argues that my father should renounce his authority and give power back to the Senate. Drusus makes no secret of his sentiments. Everyone knows it. Even my father knows. Tiberius showed my father one of his brother's letters to warn that the emperor must pay respect to the more democratic institutions of Rome or there may be rebellion.

Yes, those Claudian brothers, such champions of the people!

I might admire it if I didn't know it would be at the expense of my sons and of the plebs, who have been lifted out of poverty by my father's governance. No one believes that these Republican sentiments are anything other than an excuse for Rome's nobles to dominate and impoverish the people while warlords make war again . . . Why, not even Iullus Antonius believes it, and he has the most to gain, for he has surprised us all by standing for consul this year and being elected to the post.

Reading what I have written here, I realize this is a wretched letter. I should burn it at once if only I did not think you would take some pleasure in learning that Herod is ruined . . .

Thirty-two

✤

HEROD is ruined. I learn it not just from Julia's letter but from all the other messages that trickle in, reminding us that there is still a world outside our idyll here in Volubilis.

Herod has made so many enemies that everyone seems eager to tell us about his fall, but the most vivid account comes from Crinagoras, who arrives to tell us in person. Puffed up with self-importance and pride, my poet-turned-spy appears before us sunburned and complaining of the journey, spouting verses about how he would rather have been born a shepherd than to ever have dipped his oars in the bitter brine of the Aegean.

We receive him gladly in a private room overlooking the olive orchards, and I am nearly as grateful to be reunited with my poet as I am to hear the news. Luckily, he is eager to tell us everything. "The Judean court is not a happy one. Everyone is always suspected . . ."

"But not you?" I ask.

Crinagoras, who had been admiring his reflection in a silver tray, huffs with indignation. "Not me, of course. I promise you, Herod was entirely taken in. I was the milking goat from which he eagerly sucked every milky drop of gossip. Herod was all too pleased to offer patronage. *He* never doubted that my greatness would reflect well on him."

Impatient, Juba says, "Go on . . ."

Crinagoras sprawls insolently upon the couch, accepting wine and honey cakes from our servants. "You must know, of course, that Herod is still determined to kill his sons, so he arrested and tortured the court eunuchs until he obtained incriminating evidence. I took it upon myself to send word to King Archelaus that his daughter's life was in danger, and he came straightaway to Judea. The King of Cappadocia was forced to pretend he was so angry on Herod's behalf that he wanted to kill his own daughter and son-in-law with his bare hands. Through careful questions—which I helped him practice beforehand—he let Herod eventually convince him of their innocence."

"Clever," I say. "But strange."

Juba is appalled. "Then Herod is *truly* mad."

"He was always mad," I reply. "We are all simply so accustomed to madness that we no longer recognize it. Now, Crinagoras, tell us the rest. How did Herod fall from favor in Rome?"

My poet smirks. "I'm getting there . . . I urged King Archelaus to stay in Judea and pretend at friendship with Herod, who was keen to start a war with the Nabateans. We convinced Herod that he should attack without securing permission from Rome. Was he not a sovereign king? Would Caesar make King Juba and Queen Selene ask permission if Mauretania fell under attack? Nay, we said. Was Herod any lesser king?"

I lean forward, disturbed. "Did people die for this?"

"Herod would have attacked anyway, Majesty, and he would have received the permission he sought. But in this, he fell victim to his own vanity. Now Augustus is furious with Herod for taking unauthorized military action."

When my mother plotted our escape after Actium, it was the Nabateans who burned her ships, and in so doing, condemned us to our fate. I decide that my poet's strategy is fair vengeance. "You're sure Augustus is angry with Herod?"

"Caesar refuses to receive any of Herod's ambassadors and has sent a letter revoking Herod's permission to call himself *philokaiser*. There is some question of whether Herod even remains a friend and ally of Rome."

My eyes widen with great satisfaction. Herod will not be trusted with even a portion of my ancestral kingdoms now, and we need not fear that Isidora will be sent to Judea. The only way the news could be better is if Herod had been stripped of his throne. "He *is* ruined!"

"So it seems, thanks to a little help from your poet."

"Oh, Crinagoras, you will be rewarded handsomely!"

"Not handsomely enough, I'm sure—especially since it is not a service I can perform twice. When King Herod learns that I've returned to your court, he'll realize he was deceived."

"I hope he does," I say smugly. Because Herod is *finished*. The thought that I had anything to do with his downfall is a cause for celebration and I say so. Then I send my poet off to be pampered by slaves, as he complains of aches and pains and trials and tribulations endured to reach this backwater city in the wilderness.

My mood is buoyant and when I rise from my couch, I nearly dance in a circle.

"You're fetching when you gloat," Juba remarks idly, his stare traveling up my legs.

"I can't help gloating. That Herod has finally made such a spectacular mistake is sweet news . . . better than a mouthful of ripe *cherries*."

It is all sweetness here and I thank Isis for it every day.

UPON our leave-taking, the elders of the city present me with a glorious gift. It is a giant platter carved in intricate detail by the finest silversmith in Mauretania. It is an extraordinary portrait of me draped in an elephant headdress, like a fearsome Carthaginian queen. In my arm, I hold a cornucopia filled with the bounty of Mauretania topped with the crescent moon that is my namesake. There is a sistrum rattle, to represent Isis. A *kithara* harp like the one I sometimes play. And a lion and a lioness to represent my children. I am moved by the beauty of the piece, but startled beyond words to find a representation of *Helios* too.

Who could know me so well, as to put all these things of meaning upon one portrait? "Don't you like the gift?" the king asks, as I stare. "You are beginning to worry them." Trying to speak over emotions that swell in my throat, I find that I cannot and the king frowns. "Now you are beginning to worry *me*."

It must have been Juba who told them what to carve. He chose things that brought me joy. Symbols of what means the most to me. Of what I am. Of what I want to be. Only someone who loved me could choose a gift like this for me.

Sweet Isis, my husband loves me.

When we married, he only wanted me as he imagined a wife must be. No man could have loved me and refused to believe that the emperor raped me. No man who loved me would have accused me of inviting it. But the man Juba has become . . . that man loves me. And what if I love him too?

Overwhelmed with emotion, I reach for his hand, asking myself that very question. What if I love him? And yet, it is a question I must not answer, because it will all come to nothing if I am forced to stay in Rome at the emperor's side . . . and I have found no plan, no scheme, to avoid it.

EVERYTHING begins to go wrong the day we return to our royal harbor city on the sea. We pass through the gates of Iol-Caesaria in time for the summer wheat harvest, when every road in the city is clogged with people and donkeys and wagons bearing sacks of grain.

When we enter our grand palace, Ptolemy shows off his antelope horns and lets out a whoop at the soldiers who hail him as a returning prince. But my daughter seems dispirited. She complains of the summer heat, even though the ocean breeze sweeps across my wide walkways. She refuses to take our homecoming supper with our courtiers, and hides away in her room.

Worried that she has fallen ill, I call her name at the door. She does not answer. When I knock, she does not open it. When I try to push the door open, I find it barred. I cannot imagine any good circumstance in which my daughter might bar the door against me. For a brief moment, I wonder if she has locked herself in with the stable boy. So I pound on the door, vowing that I will bash it in if she will not admit me. What I fear, of course, is that she *can't* admit me. That something terrible has happened.

"Guards!" I cry.

That is when Isidora finally opens the door, her eyes bloodshot, her hand trembling. By the gods, she *is* ill. She is so ill she can barely stand. She sways on her feet, and I see the whites of her eyes before she collapses into my arms. Iacentus helps me carry her to the bed. It is only then that I smell the magic, sweet and smoky, floating in the hazy air of her bedchambers. Her divination bowl is tipped upon the floor, Nile water wetting the tiles, and I watch in dread as her snake slithers through the puddle and disappears under her bed.

So my daughter has been felled by *heka* sickness. I do not know whether to be furious or relieved. "Fetch some cold water and a cloth," I command one of the slaves gawping at us from the doorway.

Dora moans again but doesn't open her eyes until the candle has almost burned away. She wakes to find me wiping the sweat from her brow, and she lowers her eyes, abashed. "I just wanted to know what lay ahead for me in Rome. What sort of husband I might have . . ."

I do not shout, though I want to. "Nevertheless, we agreed you would not try to read the Rivers of Time without me. I knew you were too young to understand the dangers of that particular magic and now you have proven it."

"If I'm old enough to be a wife, I'm old enough to be a sorceress," she insists. "You can't control everyone and everything, Mother."

Well, that much is true, I conclude. But I have learned to master everything over which I have authority, and as long as my daughter remains with me, that includes her. "I *will* have your obedience."

Her eyes do not drop in surrender the way they should. "You should be encouraging me to read the Rivers of Time. I could use my gifts to warn you and Papa of dangers or foretell opportunities . . ."

I am too hot with temper now for this to persuade me. "My mother, my brother, and my mage could read the future and it did no good for any of them. It did harm. No, Isidora. I am done with this now and so are you."

She narrows her gaze. "You just don't want me to know the truth. When I see into the Rivers of Time, don't you think I see what you could do?"

She has never spoken to me with such disrespect, but I keep my voice even. "You have no idea what I can do."

"I know you can break Papa's heart!"

It is too much. I have let her have her way too many times. "You don't understand your visions and you are forbidden from this magic. If you disobey me, I will keep you from the stables. Oh, yes, I know you like to go to the stables. I know *whom* it is you go to see. So do not test me."

"I won't do it," Isidora announces flatly, several days later.

"Wear the white one, then," I say, exasperated with her. I am accustomed to being obeyed by my subjects in the smallest thing. How is it that my daughter becomes more willful by the day? "Wear what you want to the council chambers. Only stop dawdling."

Taking a big breath, she turns to face me. "I'm not talking about the *chiton* I will wear."

Are we to argue about magic again? I give her such a withering look that it should cow her. I am her queen and more importantly, I am her mother. At the moment, however, she seems not to care about either of those things.

"I won't be packed off and sent away like some chest of jewels, delivered to a foreign king as a bride. I don't want to leave Mauretania. It isn't right to force me. It isn't."

There she stands, flushed with righteous anger, her arms folded tight against her chest, and what am I to say? I was fortunate in the match the emperor made for me. Will she be as fortunate? "This is the way it is for women. Wherever would you get the idea you should have any choice in the matter?"

Her eyes blaze. "From the example of my grandmother."

So she *has* been listening to me when I speak of our heritage—when I speak of the women in our line . . . I might say to myself that my mother chose her husbands. She chose Caesar. She chose Antony. But were they choices? Both men were a means to keep Egypt. "Your grandmother always chose the good of her kingdom, Isidora. As you must. You're a princess and you have a duty."

"I never asked for this duty."

I should have her on her knees begging forgiveness for such ingratitude, but because she's my daughter, I calm myself. "Nonetheless, the emperor commands that you be married. There is nothing we can do to change that."

"Then curse the emperor!"

Catching her by the elbow, I hiss. "You must never let anyone hear you say such a thing."

"Why? Will he take your crown? That's all you care about. Only your kingdom and your crown. Not me or my happiness. I know what my duty is, and I'll do it, but you don't even care how much it hurts me!"

To hear such words from her. If she had slapped me, it would not sting as much. I want to grab her and shake her, but I have never laid hands on her in anger before. "How wrong you are."

"I love Tacfarinas and it doesn't matter to you at all."

"Of course it doesn't. You are a Ptolemaic princess and he is a common tribesman. But for my interference, he would be a slave. Don't make me regret saving him from dying in a cage like the dogs he bedded with."

"So now he's a *dog*," she says, skewering me with contempt-filled eyes.

"That's not what I said."

"It's what you meant and I hate you for it!"

The word *hate* knifes into me. I am smote to the heart. Still, even in my agony, some small part of me is gratified by her show of temper. Never did I want her to be a vicious and vengeful girl, but I take some small pride in the fact that she should stand up for herself . . . even against me. "You may hate me," I say, a tremor in my voice, "but I love you more than any crown. More than any private passion or ambition. I have sacrificed for you more than you will ever know."

"I don't want to know. I don't care. The emperor may send me away, but I'll never . . . I'll never . . ." Whatever she was going to say is drowned by tearful sobs. And when I try to wrap my arms around her, she wrenches away.

FEELING miserably sorry for myself, I sulk in my gardens, hiding in a sea of lavender. Unfortunately, my freedwoman knows exactly where to find me. "Good news, Majesty. Captain Kabyle has found islands off the west coast that were used by the Carthaginians to make dye. They're still equipped with vats. They're even called the Purple Isles. We'll reopen them immediately."

This *is* good news, for we have already opened five new dye factories and we are already in need of more. Still, I cannot even smile.

"It's what we hoped for, Majesty. We can now afford to double the workforce on your Iseum. The walls of the inner sanctum are up. Amphio has recruited some of the finest sculptors . . . Why aren't you pleased?"

Because I was a fool for thinking the Iseum would be complete before I left Mauretania. Amphio warned me he'd need ten years—did I think he could complete it in two? I would have liked to see it finished before the emperor took me captive again, but perhaps that is only a vanity on my part. In the end, it is Isis who must look upon this temple with pleasure . . . not me.

Chryssa stoops in front of my bench to look me in the eye. "Has someone died?"

Thinking to explain my devastation, I tell her about Isidora.

She doesn't seem to understand. "Oh, I'm certain the princess means nothing by it. It's what children say to their mothers. Surely you remember what it was to be a girl her age."

"When I was a girl her age, I didn't have a mother to hate." Then I blush with shame. That is not true, is it? I did have a mother and I did hate her, for a time. For too long a time, I blamed my mother for dying. For leaving us. For risking our lives for what murky visions she saw in the Rivers of Time. Then there was Octavia. How I resented her. How I fought against her every kindness. I blamed Isis too. For her remote mystery. For not saving us from the emperor . . .

Blinking my eyes against the sun, I whisper, "I never wanted Dora to know a moment's suffering. I didn't want her to grow up carrying the burdens I carried."

"Then why are you shocked that your daughter behaves as she does? She wasn't a queen before the age of nine. She was no one's prisoner. She's never been dragged in chains behind a conqueror's chariot. She's never feared for her life. Frankly, she's never stumbled over an obstacle that couldn't be removed by her parents. You've never before denied her anything she wanted."

My freedwoman must mean to comfort me, but her words plunge me into despair. She is saying we have spoiled Dora. Maybe she is right. Perhaps I have failed my daughter—and now, because of it, I will lose her. She will hate me forever. She will think I betrayed her . . .

What if I have? It's true that I've never before denied her anything that she wanted. Why should I have, when she has never wanted anything that revealed an inner cruelty? I *taught* her not to accept the world as it is, but to endeavor to make it better, so is there really anything so very odd about her objection to being sent away to be the bride of a stranger just because that's how it's done?

I should fight harder for her. Demeter fought for *her* daughter when she was taken away. Surely there is some plot, some scheme I can fashion for my daughter's sake.

When one comes to me, I go searching for Juba. I find him

reviewing new scrolls he has acquired for our library. Shooing away the scribes, I say, "You helped Lucius Cornelius Balbus retire to an estate just across the strait, in Spain. He's not royal, but he is wealthy and in need of a wife. Balbus could return to Mauretania to marry Dora. They could both live here. As a wedding gift, we could return all the lands I bought from him. Even the House of Olives."

Juba rolls the scroll up and slides it into the appropriate hole in the rack. "A Roman for Isidora? Now I know you are desperate. But it cannot work. Augustus has never forgiven Balbus for celebrating a Triumph, and I would not agree to the match because that is too much temptation for a man like Balbus. Do you want your son to be the next King of Mauretania, or do you want to trust that Balbus isn't ambitious enough to use his marriage to wrest the throne away from us?"

He makes a good point. "I cannot believe I'm suggesting it . . . but can we consider Tacfarinas? Perhaps we can cast the match as part of the policy of *harmonia*, a marriage to bring our peoples together."

Juba is only momentarily stunned. "Such a marriage would fly in the face of the emperor's policy against marriage between persons of different social ranks. That is to say nothing of how we'd be laughed at in every corner of the civilized world."

A long, frustrated sigh escapes me. "I do not disagree. I just needed to hear you say it . . ."

Juba gives a rueful shake of his head. "The boy is not landed nor the son of a tribal chieftain. He is not even *Mauretanian*. Our subjects might go into bloody revolt out of jealousy that we should raise up one Berber tribe over the other. And if our legions could not crush that rebellion, our kingdom could very well become a Roman province. It could be the end of everything, and you know it. Perhaps it's time Isidora knew it too . . ."

Thirty-three

JUBA takes my daughter on a small sailing ship to view the harbor that day. I do not know what argument he makes. I only know that when they return, Isidora is subdued. She is no longer openly insolent, only cool and distant. She withdraws into her books, into her sketches and her pouches of powders.

Seeking out the king in the confines of his study, where he is testing his broken water clock against a candle that has been marked off by the hours, I ask, "What did you say to her? Did you threaten her?"

The king's eye twitches in annoyance. "Do you take me for Herod?"

No, he is not Herod, I remind myself. He is not Augustus either, but he has never before faced the challenge of a rebellious daughter. "She took what you had to say to heart?"

"I explained to her that as a father, there is nothing I would not do to indulge her. But that as a king I must do what is best for all the people who live in our kingdom. All the Romans, the Greeks, the Egyptians, and the Berbers too. Boys just like Tacfarinas. I reminded her that both her parents were orphaned by rash decisions that led to war. Then I asked if she would be the cause of other people's suffering . . ."

Even explained so reasonably, it is still a momentous responsibility. "Poor Isidora."

The king snuffs out the candlewick and smears the soot between his thumb and forefinger. "Save your pity for me. I had to demand her obedience as if she were a subject at the foot of my throne. Then I promised that if she would take up this duty, we would abide by her choice amongst the men the emperor will approve for her."

"How did she answer?" I ask, coming to his side.

"She said she will consider her answer."

My eyes narrow in suspicion, wishing that I had been the one to reason with her. "As quietly as that? She does not say that she hates you?"

My husband smiles softly, cupping my chin with compassion, no doubt smearing me with soot from the candle he snuffed out. "I am not her mother, Selene. She doesn't have to cleave from me to understand herself. You must not take it so hard."

IN the autumn, Captain Kabyle returns to Iol-Caesaria with new maps and big hunting dogs from islands he discovered off the coast. The muscular hounds have massive square heads and short, coarse coats. Juba is so impressed with these canines that he decides to name the islands after them.

The Canary Islands, they will be called.

Strangely, my daughter shows no interest in the dogs. With a distant stare she has perfected in recent months, she announces that she prefers her snake. So the finest specimen of the island breed, a bitch of silver fawn coloring, is given to my son. Ptolemy throws his arms around the neck of the hound and names her Luna. "It's because she's silver and beautiful, like the moon and my mother."

I am neither silver nor especially beautiful, but such courtly manners in my son charm me. The dog, however, does not. She guards my son aggressively, growling even at his friends. One afternoon, the boys dress for a hunting trip in tunics with striped sleeves. They carry with them traps for birds and Ptolemy whistles for the hound to join him. They are gone only a few hours before they return, half carrying Tala's son, whose leg has been bitten.

"Luna caught a hare!" Ptolemy cries. "But when Mazippa reached for it, she attacked him."

The other boys taunt Tala's son for the dog bite, saying he cannot be a fierce Berber warrior if he cannot defend himself against a hound. The matter is only made worse when Dora calls him by his childhood name. "It's not Ziri," he snarls, in obvious pain. "It's *Mazippa*, Princess."

I'm less concerned by his wounded pride than by the scandalized gasps that fill our hall when our princess apologizes to him, then kneels to wash out his wound. When she was a girl, her behavior was tolerated, but now she is on the cusp of marriage and the court has expectations of her. Expectations, of course, that she cares nothing about. If she did, she would not be wearing such a plain gown with her hair styled as carelessly as a scholar's.

I would scold her, but I do not relish another quarrel with my willful daughter. Juba is less hesitant. "Get up off your knees and send for Tacfarinas to take the dog to the stables! The bitch is covered in nettles and needs to be better trained to life at court."

My daughter stands up, her nostrils flaring. "Tacfarinas is gone. This morning I told him that the emperor desires that I should marry. That my father the king and my mother the queen command it. And that I intend to do my duty." Her chin bobs in pride on the last word, even though her lower lip trembles.

I reach for her hand but she stands on her own, tall and strong.

"Tacfarinas is gone?" Juba asks, with obvious surprise. "Without leave?"

My daughter swallows hard. "He didn't think he'd be missed."

That is the end of it. Or so I hope. But my daughter comes to me that night in her nightclothes and slips under the covers. She clutches me round the waist, breaking into sobs. "I'm sorry. I don't know why I said such things. I love you. I don't hate you. I don't hate anyone. I don't know what to say to make it better."

I stroke her silky hair. "Oh, sweet girl. Words do not matter now." All that we need to say can be said in the brush of my lips against her tear-soaked lashes and in the clutch of her arms. She clings to me, crying through the night, sniffling quietly, trying to stifle her sobs when she thinks I have fallen asleep. But by morning, she is dry-eyed.

"You did well to give him up," I tell her. "Rulers know great wealth and power. We build cities. We shape kingdoms. We change the lives of our subjects and their children. We write history with our own blood, sweat, and tears. Sacrifices must be made for such a privilege. We must give up certain things to achieve the rest."

"Like you gave up the man with the golden hair?"

In dull shock at her words, I smooth the bed linens over my knees, noticing every wrinkle. How long has my daughter been holding this question in the secret chambers of her heart? She cannot have remembered Helios there, on the Isle of Samos, where he said she looked into his eyes. She was too young. How could she know him? But then, my daughter does not see with her eyes the way normal people do . . .

In the end, it doesn't matter whether she saw Helios alive as I have comforted myself to think I have seen him. Or if she has only seen another River of Time where we lived together as husband and wife. It only matters that my daughter is asking me, one woman to another, the most important question she might ever ask. She may hate me for my answer. It might be kinder, wiser, to lie to her. I could deceive her—yes, even her, with that penetrating otherworldly gaze. But I must trust her. I must trust that, like Pythia, I have shaped her into a woman who can hear the truth. "Yes," I say, with a simple lift of my chin. "Just like I gave up the man with the golden hair."

It wounds me to say that. There is such finality to it that I shudder.

"Did you love him?" she asks.

The question cuts me even deeper. "With all my heart. With all my heart and soul."

Fingering the collar of gold amulet at her throat, she gives a mournful sigh, then glances up at me again. "Still, you gave him up so you could marry Papa and be queen?"

"No. I gave him up so that *you* could be queen."

She blanches and asks no more questions.

I allow the servants to dress me, then I go with my daughter to the library, where she asks to see maps she has never shown any interest in before. She wants to know her choices—where she might marry according to the emperor's wishes and to what benefit for our family. Listening to her pose questions to the king, I am so filled with pride that I must brush tears from the corners of my eyes; for I have lost my child, but I have my daughter still.

"LET us delay our trip to Rome a few more weeks," I plead with Juba, refastening his ivory fibula pin so that his royal cloak will fall better. "We need more time to settle our affairs."

He catches my hands and holds them against his chest. "It's almost November, Selene. If we don't leave now, we risk sailing in winter storms."

"I swallow storms. The last thing I'm afraid of is a *storm*."

"You are only afraid of Rome, I know," he says, bringing my fingers to his lips. "But the rest of us are afraid of storms and shipwreck, so you must indulge us. Besides, we gave the emperor our promise. The *Ara Pacis* is complete and if we are not there in time for the dedication this winter . . ."

It's a bitter reminder. The emperor finished his grand altar to peace in two years, but Amphio hasn't finished my Iseum. I'm afraid of what I might say or do to my temple builder should we cross paths, so I do not go to the site to inspect it. Instead, I take Isidora to my lighthouse and we climb all the way to the top so that we may look down upon the kingdom we may never see again.

Here, with the wind howling and sky bright overhead, I wonder if I have ever done anything worthy. The emperor says he found Rome a city of brick and turned it into marble. Well, I have done the same in Iol-Caesaria. I have made this city a reflection of everything that has made me. Will I be remembered for it? Will I be remembered at all?

There is not a schoolchild in the empire who has not heard tales of my mother and my father. They made war. I have tried to make peace. They made wild gambles. I have taken plodding steps. They clothed themselves in legend. I have played my part in someone else's glory.

They told the world that they were gods.

I have merely tried to honor mine.

And now I must return to Rome, to the emperor, with everything unfinished. I am so very miserable at the thought I could sob. Why haven't I thought of a way to keep the emperor from destroying our life here? Wasn't I smarter than this, once? Has motherhood made me irrational and featherbrained, or am I just tired of fighting?

Glancing at my daughter, I know she struggles with her own disappointments. But she has gotten ahold of herself and I must do the same. Fine, then. Maybe it is all unfinished. Isn't it for everyone, in the end? Not even Alexander accomplished everything he set out to do before he died, and I am not dead yet, though being at the emperor's side will make me wish I were.

I must bear up under this and find a way to turn it all to my advantage as I have always done. Just as my daughter is now learning to do. With a stiffened spine, I take Isidora's hand and we return for what I hope will be a peaceful evening.

Instead, we find my palace in chaos. It seems as if every courtier in the city is crowded in the throne room, where there is also a horse standing on my marble floors. Yes, a horse. A hobbled mare, burrs in her coat, ribs protruding at each side.

Chryssa is there too, and my freedwoman tries to warn me away from the unusual scene with a frantic motion of her hand. Soon I see why. With the mangy horse is the boy. That *wretched* boy, wilder than when we first found him, teeth bared in a snarl at his Roman captors.

I suppose Tacfarinas is no longer a boy. A hint of a beard gives a rough quality to his square jaw as it juts out over a thick neck and well-muscled shoulders. He is filthy beneath the ropes in which he is bound, as if his accusers dragged him in the dirt to bring him to trial, but there is a potent masculinity about him now that he has become a young man.

At the sight of Tacfarinas, my daughter stifles a cry with her palm. I wish she had not seen him. Would that Isidora had never laid eyes upon him in that cage all those years ago!

Chryssa whispers to us that Tacfarinas has been captured in the hills by Roman settlers and stands accused of banditry. Of horse theft. Dora shakes her head in disbelief and tries to go to him. Catching her by the back of the gown, I give her a firm tug to remind her where we are and who is watching.

She squeezes my hand as the Romans make their case before the king. Seated on his throne, Juba hears the complaints with an air of placid attention, but his fingers flex in agitation at his side. I doubt the Romans would have bothered to bring Tacfarinas to trial if they didn't know he had been in the service of the king.

Indeed, Juba makes no pretense of not knowing him. "Tacfarinas of the Musulamii, you stand accused of stealing this mare from a veteran farmer, under the cover of night. What will you say to these charges?"

Tacfarinas swallows, his dark eyes flashing with resentment. "I would say that there is nothing here in Africa that has not been stolen first by Romans."

It startles me that several Berbers in the audience shout their agreement. While waiting for the cheers to die down, Tacfarinas turns and his eyes fall upon Dora. They soften when he sees her; I will give him that. But when she mouths his name, trying to warn him against further rebellion, he looks away.

The king sits taller. "Did you steal this mare?"

Tacfarinas jerks his head up as if he would deny it. Then, as he takes in the array of powerful men in togas situated around him, his shoulders droop and the spirit seems to go out of him. "Yes, I took the mare."

"Guilty! Guilty!" These cries go up from the Romans.

Dora gives a slight, desperate shake of her head and I tug her hand to keep her still. The king's expression is grim, for we all know the penalty for such a crime. The boy does not have Roman citizenship, which means the punishment will be worse. He will be flogged—there is no question about that—but his freedom and his very survival are in question too.

The Romans call for Tacfarinas to be cast from a cliff or made into a slave while some of our Berbers shout for mercy. At the calls for death, my poor daughter's breathing begins to stutter. Her wild little pants make me fear she will swoon. I decide to spirit her away, but she will not be moved. Terror has turned her into deadweight. The king sees Dora's distress but he has no choice in what he must do. I know it. He knows it too.

"Nothing else to say?" the king asks Tacfarinas.

The Berber boy remains mute.

The king tries to goad him into speech. "I would have you answer this. You were not watched closely in the royal stables, where the finest steeds are bred. Any horse was yours for the taking if you wanted to steal. Why steal this broken horse and not one of mine?"

Tacfarinas's insolent stare cuts up to Juba. "You're not starving your horses, Majesty. You didn't tie them to a fence and leave them in the sun with no water. That's how I found this mare. When I tried to give her a drink from my water skin, this farmer hurled abuse at me and drove me off. So I came back for her at night."

The settler doesn't deny the accusation, but makes a threatening gesture with his fist. "What cause did you have to be on my land in the first place, you young pirate?"

The boy answers, "I need no cause to sleep on the lands of my ancestors."

None of this will help him. It is no crime to starve a horse. We have little authority to tell our settlers how to treat their slaves; we cannot tell them how to care for animals. That Tacfarinas tried to free the sickly mare can be no defense and I suspect he is guilty of far greater crimes. I do not think it an accident that the Roman veteran called him a pirate . . .

Juba asks, "How old are you now, Tacfarinas of the Musulamii?"

Tacfarinas falls silent again. Perhaps he does not know how old he is; the Berbers do not count their years in the way we do, so the king answers for him. "You are sixteen. Maybe seventeen. Old enough to serve in my legions. Our kingdom needs soldiers and I know you have fight. I sentence you to be flogged . . . and then conscripted into service for a minimum of twenty-five years. Let it be done as I command."

Chryssa blanches at the sentence and I remember her screams when the emperor had her flogged. My daughter has never seen such a thing, but she is unable to restrain herself for even another moment. "No!" Dora cries, trying to break away from me; she tries to run to her Berber boy, but I have too strong a hold on her. My guards hurry to surround us, helping me to usher the princess away.

As we go, I hear the tearing of the boy's tunic as he is stripped for his flogging, and I shudder to think of what a bloody mess the scourge will leave him . . . if he lives through it.

Hiccuping and near hysterical, my daughter cannot be calmed. "It's my fault," she wails in the privacy of her chambers. "When I told him I was to marry, it hurt him so badly."

Arranging the coverlet on her bed, I insist, "We all face disappointments—we don't all behave so recklessly as that boy always behaves. You're not to blame."

"I *am* to blame. If I didn't tell him I was to marry, he wouldn't have run away. He tried to save the mare because he saw another creature in as much pain as he was. And if I wasn't so fond of Tacfarinas, Papa would have never sentenced him so harshly."

I stroke her cheek. "How wrong you are. Were you not so fond of that Berber boy, he'd be dead now. Or a slave."

"He'll think conscription worse than slavery. He'd rather die than fight for Rome."

"He'll serve in *our* legions, not Rome's. It may do him good, Isidora. One cannot commit a crime and escape without consequence. It was for *your* sake that the king gave him a place in the army where he may yet bring honor to his people."

She groans in misery. "Twenty-five years he must serve, and I'll never see him again. The last memory he'll have of me is that I stood by my father's throne and did nothing to help him."

I know well the guilt in staying silent. Of walking away from the one you love. "There is nothing you could have done to help him. If you had said anything, it would have gone worse. The king would have been forced to punish him more severely so as not to appear as if he were disregarding the law just to please his daughter."

But Isidora will not hear me. She does not shout or fling hateful words. She does not have to. It is all in her eyes. Her eyes see a world filled with injustice and that I am part of that world. She does not want my comfort. I am forced to leave her curled upon her bed, tears falling on her pillow.

Leaving her, I go straightaway to the king but he has gone to supervise the conscription himself.

I do not see him again until the next afternoon.

I catch him at his meal and ask, "Is it done?"

The king takes a roasted quail egg from the platter and stabs it open with his knife. "Tacfarinas is bloody but alive. He is now in the custody of the *decurio* for our cavalry. The boy is a skilled rider; he may have a career ahead of him when he heals." Then Juba heaves a sigh. "I went to see Isidora late last night . . . She will not speak to me."

"Well, she cannot bear the sight of me either."

"You aren't the one who sent her Berber boy away," my husband says with a rueful shake of his head. "I did that and I fear she will never forgive me."

"She'll forgive you and she'll forget Tacfarinas."

At this, my husband gives a bitter laugh. "Not if any harm should come to him. Boys who die young live forever in the tender hearts of the girls who loved them."

TO cheer my daughter, we host a farewell banquet, and during the festivities, our courtiers all speculate on what fine royal groom will win her hand. Several young girls volunteer to serve her, wherever her new home might be, so that she will have her own ladies at court.

Before the banquet is over, Tala points to two young

handmaidens, one from the kitchens and the other the daughter of my washerwoman. "Not those two," Tala says, bracelets jingling on her blue-tinted arm. "They're fawners and flatterers and frivolous girls. They'll tell Princess Isidora whatever she wishes to hear, but they won't keep her secrets or help her to guard herself or her reputation at court."

When my niece married the King of Pontus, I did not worry about court intrigues, for there has seldom been a girl as guarded as Pythia. But my daughter guards herself against nothing. Isidora will be very fortunate to have Tala with her to speak hard truths and bolster her strength, just as I have been fortunate to have my Berber woman with me all these years.

"You choose her attendants," I say, comforted to realize that in this, and in so many other things, Tala knows best. What kind of queen would I have become without her Berber wisdom? I will miss her frankness. I will even miss hearing her bicker with Chryssa, the two of them exchanging barbs that are no less sharp for their mutual respect and affection.

I will lose both of them now. The two women who have served as my closest companions since I first became queen. For Tala will go with Isidora, and I will leave Chryssa here in Mauretania, where she has her own children to look after . . .

I cannot count the number of times I have said good-bye to Chryssa. I have given her up a little bit at a time. First to her freedom. Then to her happy marriage. Then to her beloved children and the house she bought in the hills—the one she thinks I do not know about. She has feared my reaction to the idea that she has a life of her own that has nothing to do with me or my treasury. Truthfully, she has been right to fear it.

I do not let go easily of the things I love.

But she doesn't need me anymore, I think, and so our farewell is especially bittersweet. All the more, because I think she knows, I think she senses, that I will not return from Rome this time.

In the privacy of my chambers, she says, "Don't go."

Sitting at my dressing table, I nearly upend a number of little green glass perfume bottles and amber kohl pots. "When the emperor summons me, I always go." I must go. It is too late for schemes or plots or plans, since Juba and the emperor both insist my son must be educated in Rome.

"This time feels different," she says, eyeing me carefully as she unfastens my pearl earrings, falling back into our old intimacy.

I stop her, catching her hands and forcing them against the folds of my royal purple cloak. "You're not in servitude any longer, but I am. I haven't freed myself from Augustus; but I've freed *you* from him. And I am glad."

These are not mere words. It is the truth. Striding confidently through the palace, giving orders to servants and subordinates, calling officials to account and harrying them until they will agree to nearly anything to escape her, Chryssa is no longer a beaten slave. She is an impressive woman and part of the legacy I leave behind. I will not leave behind a finished temple to my goddess, but there are people I have helped, people I have loved, people who love me. Can there be better work than that?

Thirty-four

WE set sail for Rome in late October. We are not delayed by storms, though I briefly consider calling one in the hopes it will buy us time. Or at least drown my son's dog, which barks incessantly every time a gull flies too close to the ship. When we make landfall, I try to persuade Ptolemy to leave the dog with the sailors, to guard over the ship's hold, but my son is as in love with his dog as he is with the pearl stallion Juba gave him. So we are stuck with the slobbering hound and the fierce but beautiful horse.

Our trip from Ostia to Rome is unimpeded. Nothing delays us. Not the weather. Not plague. Not a broken wheel on a carriage. The servants at our house on the Tiber know to expect us, and everything is ready when we arrive. A thing that, for once, annoys me.

Again, we reach Rome before the emperor does. He is coming from Gaul in the company of Livia's sons, both of whom are returning with more military glory. Drusus has been elected as one of the two consuls this year, and though Tiberius has earned a Triumph, Augustus will not allow him to celebrate one. He is to have a lesser parade, an *ovation*, which tells me how jealously the emperor guards his privileges, and just how much the emperor has to fear from Livia's sons.

Julia complains bitterly of it when we are reunited. "Do you know that I must arrange the festivities for Tiberius? Not too lavishly, lest I offend my father, and not too humbly less I offend my husband. Men!"

Still clasped in Julia's embrace, I tell her, "I'm sure you will manage precisely the right balance."

"Who says I want to?" But I know she will do her duty as she has always done. And she will do it with her very own stamp and style.

When Juba and I settle into our home on the Tiber, we find gifts waiting from one of my daughter's new suitors, the new King of Emesa. He is the son of my old friend Iamblichus, and he sends Dora a gown embroidered with gold and silver threads and a tapestry depicting the Emesan cult's sacred stone being carried in a golden chariot by four horses.

Of course, Dora is more interested in the stone than the dress. Running her short, ragged fingernails over the tapestry, she asks, "It is a black stone they worship in Emesa? Not a god or a goddess?"

"The stone is a meteorite," I explain. "They say it was cast down from the heavens by their god, whom they call *Elagabal*, the invisible sun god." I say this with respect, for the Emesani people are a people of great faith . . . and I too have a place in my heart dedicated to an invisible sun god. "The King of Emesa is the chief priest of the cult."

I am careful to say no more than that, for I want her to choose freely of the men the emperor has approved for her hand in marriage. This must be my daughter's choice, as much as it can be. That is why we break with custom and allow her to meet her suitors before the emperor returns to Rome.

We host a small dinner for her suitors under the guise of welcoming the visiting royalty to the city, including my niece, the young Queen of Pontus, who bursts through the doors of my house with glad tidings and warm embraces. Pythia and Dora hug each other until they cry and my eyes are damp too. At this happy reunion, Pythia has her servants present me with a cloak made of the fur of silver foxes from the cold mountains near the Black Sea. She has a cloak for each of us: white rabbit for Dora, reddish-brown sable for Juba, and spotted lynx fur for Ptolemy.

Pythia is eager to tell us about her children, two boys and a girl, all of them under the age of three. And Julia cannot resist quipping to me behind her hand, "It would seem that watching horses breed was very good preparation for your niece after all."

Indeed, Pythia already has three children and I only have two, though I have lived twenty-nine years now, going on thirty. And my husband is younger than hers. But anyone who might think the Queen of Pontus is a mere broodmare is quickly disabused of this notion when she impresses our guests with her knowledge of business and governance.

She is exactly as I taught her to be and has given her children proud names. Zenon after the famous orator. Marcus Antonius Pythodoros after my father, and Antonia Tryphaena after both my father and my mother's line. That her husband, the elderly King of Pontus, is both attentive and indulgent enough to allow her to name her children this way makes me feel badly for ever doubting him, and I give him a place of great honor at our feast. Is it too much to hope that Dora will look upon this example as proof that such marriages may turn out happily?

We've invited some of the more popular members of Roman society, including Julia's favorite poet, Ovid—whose style Crinagoras dismisses as puerile and salacious. Of course, that's exactly why we invited him. We want the event to be so informal that every gesture my daughter makes won't be scrutinized for political import. We don't want the banquet to be an official matter of state. The more frivolity the better because we want Dora to meet the men who vie for her hand in such a way that she might decline their attention and not cause public embarrassment.

Though I know Dora would rather greet her suitors in a simple white *chiton* with her hair thrown up carelessly in a comb, I make sure to dress her carefully. "A queen can use her appearance to make an impression," I tell her. "You can have as many appearances as a goddess. You can dazzle a man in a pleated gown with high slits that show peeks of your thighs. Wear purple if you wish to emphasize your royal bloodline. Wear a modest veil and pretty little flower patterns on your hem if you wish to seem vulnerable or make people underestimate you . . ."

My daughter nods politely at my advice, but I am not convinced she is listening.

When I'm finished, her golden hair is swept up, knotted at the back, held in place with an exquisite golden hairpiece carved in the likeness of a rising goddess and studded with amethysts. Her peplum gown, dyed a most royal shade of purple, brings out the beauty of her eyes. Oh, but she is a fair princess, delicate and perfect, with plump rose-pink lips.

Such is her beauty that Juba stares at her when we take our places in our dining room, which has been festooned with pine for the coming Saturnalia. Then, she beams at him and Juba mutters darkly, "Good gods, none of them deserve her."

When the servants bring silver trays of baked eggs, asparagus, and oysters, we introduce Isidora to the guests, including her suitor, the young Emesani king, who is quite handsome under his dark ringlets and closely trimmed beard. The moment this king sees my daughter, he plainly wants her in the way a man wants a woman, and his eyes smolder like black coals. I search Dora's eyes for any hint that the young king's hot gaze can make her forget her Berber boy, but Dora is politely remote. She thanks her suitor for his gift, engages in light conversation as etiquette dictates, but otherwise gives the royal stranger no encouragement.

"I don't like how he looks at her," Juba whispers to me.

"How else should he look at her?"

"I don't know," Juba confesses. "But I don't *like* it."

When the second course is served, the recently widowed King Archelaus of Cappadocia arrives. It pains me to see how our old friend has aged since last we saw him. Not even his ornate crown can disguise that he's balding and has lost a few teeth. He is, I should think, the suitor a girl should least wish for. And yet Dora smiles brilliantly when he presents her with an oak chest carved with the symbol of a serpent wound tight round a branch.

It's the symbol of Asclepius. A reminder of her serpent. Not a poisonous cobra intent on murder, but a snake meant to teach us how to shed our old skin and learn to live in a new one. My daughter's eyes light up and she cries with delight, "A medicine chest!"

Then she throws open the lid and marvels over the contents of each little pouch of herbs she finds inside. King Archelaus listens patiently as she natters on about this rare plant from the East or that new poultice from India.

From across the room, Crinagoras smirks, obviously guilty of having meddled in the matter. Having once told King Archelaus how to trick Herod, Crinagoras obviously advised him how to win the affection of my daughter too. By the gods, my poet is a wily old thing. I'm not entirely sure I approve.

At any rate, Isidora spends the rest of the dinner with the old Cappadocian king. I want to urge her to pay more attention to the King of Emesa, who is at least still young enough to give her children. But we have already asked much of Dora. If she prefers a man old enough to be her grandfather, then that is whom she will have. Better Archelaus than Herod. That is what I keep repeating to myself.

At the end of the evening, when we make our farewells, the King of Emesa's words are tinged with sadness. "It was my father's wish that our families be bound by blood and kinship, but I fear your daughter would rather be the Queen of Cappadocia."

I try to soften the blow. "Oh, don't be hasty to draw conclusions. It is only that she has known Archelaus since she was a little girl . . . He is a familiar face and knows what sort of things capture her imagination."

"I should have thought to give her a box of dried weeds . . ." He laughs at himself, good-natured for a man who has been snubbed, and I decide that I like him even if Dora does not.

Clasping his hands, I say, "I too would have our families bound by blood and kinship, for I have not forgotten your father's friendship on the Isle of Samos, nor have I forgotten that a Prince of Emesa once gave his life for me. I have a son who will need a wife. Perhaps there is an Emesani princess who longs to see the beautiful mountains of Mauretania . . ."

He grins and I see that he likes the idea. And I am grateful that we part friends. Meanwhile, all Rome waits for the emperor's triumphant return, and Augustus sends word that my son is to command a troop of boys in the Trojan Games.

I know these games to be quite dangerous, involving horse-mounted drills and mock-fighting. Boys have been known to break bones and I do not want my son to take part. I remind my husband that once, years ago, my twin was forced to rescue Livia's son, Drusus, from being trampled in the melee. But my husband reassures me that Ptolemy is a better rider than even my twin brother was at that age and I know this to be true.

Moreover, Ptolemy is overjoyed at the news.

When it comes to horses, my son's Berber blood serves him well. He doesn't even use a saddlecloth atop Sirocco. He is accustomed to galloping in the plains of Africa and riding down antelope. But to command troops in the Trojan Games will require much discipline, and so Ptolemy goes to the stables every morning to practice while we await the emperor's entrance into Rome.

One evening, the king presents my daughter with a necklace—a sardonyx cameo with a perfect little portrait of our family. Juba carved on one side and me on the other with Ptolemy upon my lap. My daughter is plainly touched by this gift, clasping it to her breast and promising to wear it always so that she may think of us in faraway Cappadocia.

"It's to be Archelaus, then?" Juba asks.

Dora nods. "I think he will be kind to me, Papa. He reminds me a bit of you."

Yes. I can see it now. No king in the empire can match Juba's scholarly mind, but Archelaus of Cappadocia is intellectually curious and has a fatherly manner about him. I doubt that Dora will ever know love or passion with him, but he will allow her to be whatever she wishes to be . . . and there are worse fates for a princess.

"If that is your choice, I'll make the arrangements," Juba says.

"Yes," Dora says bravely. "That is my choice."

I dread the moment we must let her become a bride, but Juba is in good humor, lifting himself onto one elbow and glancing about the dining room as if he cannot see our boy. "And where is Prince Ptolemy?"

"Right here!" Ptolemy calls from where he is sitting on cushions.

"Did you get taller since this morning?" Juba asks, feigning at surprise. "Why I scarcely recognize you. Oh, well, never mind, then, I suppose you are grown enough for these."

In a flash, Juba presents a quiver of golden arrows to Ptolemy.

I protest immediately. "Those arrows aren't blunted. They're sharp at the points."

"Mother, these arrows aren't for *shooting*," my son tartly informs me with a roll of his eyes as if I have never before seen the Trojan Games. "They're just to be slung over my shoulder while I take my troops through the maneuvers."

Tala cuffs him for impertinence, but he's so proud, so tall, so earnest about the Games that I can only ruffle his hair before he goes off to bed. Ptolemy gets almost to the archway before rushing back to hug his father in thanks. He hugs me too, dimpling me a smile before pressing a quick kiss to my cheek.

Then he runs off like a ruffian.

Together, Juba and I laugh. We cannot help it. And when we are alone, the king reaches into a pouch at his hip. "Don't think I forgot you, Selene. Where is it? Ah, yes, here is another cameo for your collection."

This cameo is also sardonyx, cleverly carved where a layer of whiter stone meets the bloodred color. On one side is a likeness of my daughter and on the other, a likeness of my son. Two portraits of my children. Like my jade frog, this is another kind of sacred amulet—one that I will wear with the first.

I thank Juba over and over again, then let him fasten it upon my neck, saying, "Master Gnaios has become even better at these. I recognize his handiwork. You must have had this made long before we came to Rome."

Our fingertips brush as we straighten the chain, and the king murmurs, "Yes, and it wasn't easy to keep it secret from you all these months."

Oh, how my heart hurts for the secret I keep from him. The time we have now is so precious, for when he realizes I will not return to Mauretania with him, he will think himself abandoned. He will never forgive me. Not even if, in his heart, he knows that I have no choice in the matter. But I hold a hope—surely a vain one—that he might still remember me a little fondly. That is all that I can ask for.

"I have something for you too," I say.

His hands drift down the front of my gown and his lips whisper against my neck. "Oh?"

"It is a silly thing," I say, suddenly embarrassed. "Nothing as lovely as this cameo. Nothing grand or expensive . . . except for the box."

"With such an introduction, how can I resist? Show me."

I lead him to the study, where I pull back a curtain to present a strongbox with my Ptolemy Eagle laid in gold over a silver thunder-bolt, much like the one that held my mother's crown and scepter. This one holds nothing so grand, and when I open it, I explain its humble contents. "A veil, to remind you of our dancing in Volubilis. Whorled snail shells we collected on the beach near the cave of Hercules. A golden apple, for our time together in Lixus . . ."

These and other trinkets I have collected in remembrance, but now I worry he will find them to be strangely sentimental. Given the tilt of his head, I think he does. "What is this?" he asks, reaching inside. "A braid of hair?"

"Yes. I cut mine and Isidora's and Ptolemy's and braided the hair together so that you might have it if you should ever need reminding of us . . ."

He brings the braid of black and brown and golden hair to his nose, inhaling deeply of its scent before lifting his eyes to mine. "Selene, I shall keep this box of treasures and value it more than a chest of gold, but know that I never need reminding of you or the children. We're here in Rome because Isidora is to marry and Ptolemy is to have his education. It is only a change for us, not a good-bye."

I kiss him so that he cannot see how much it pains me to know he is wrong . . .

IT is night when Augustus summons me.

"I'll go with you," Tala says, hastily wrapping an indigo blue shawl over her dark hair. But I know she dreads to go out into the cold night, and her teeth already chatter with anticipation. "Nothing good happens at this hour, Majesty. Especially not here, in this city of schemers and cutthroats."

Nevertheless, I must go. And I must go alone. I tell myself that it is better that Augustus has summoned me upon his return to the city. It means that I do not have to wake the king. It means less of an affront to my husband's royal dignity and mine. And it means that whatever happens will not happen in the house where my children sleep.

So I fasten my new fur cloak on my shoulders, the weight of it giving more gravity to my steps. I look in on Isidora before I go, comforted to find her bundled beneath a woven blanket, her flaxen hair fanned out on her pillow. Ptolemy too is tucked safely into his bed, faithful Memnon outside his door.

I do not visit the king's chambers, however. If Juba were awake, I could not face him.

Instead, I follow the emperor's praetorians.

I think they will escort me up the Palatine Hill to the emperor's residence. Instead, they take me to the Campus Martius, the site of the new altar, lit by torches and the full moon. Passing into the enclosure, I encounter the square, squat *Ara Pacis*. The emperor's monument is more modest than I would have guessed. The steps are not very many, nor very steep. It isn't until I'm halfway up that I see the detail, the Greek key pattern that separates each panel, and above it, a story of Rome and a story of the emperor's ambitions.

To my right, a colorful frieze of pious Aeneas, the emperor's hero, his head partially covered with his toga, pouring out a libation, always ready to sacrifice to the gods. With him, his son Julus, from whom the *Julii* claim to descend. To my left, a depiction of Romulus and Remus, twin princes, sons of Mars, thrown into the Tiber River to drown, then rescued by a she-wolf.

To enter the *Ara Pacis*, one must pass between both these foundation stories, these reminders with which Augustus irrevocably ties himself to Rome's greatest heroes.

These are legends, but a man of flesh and blood waits inside. Augustus stands upon the raised podium before the altar table. He is alone. Solemn. Pensive. "Just the queen," he says to his guards and they withdraw.

Anxiously, I dip low in deference to him. "I bid you glad homecoming, Caesar."

He takes my hand as I alight the last few steps, and in spite of the chill, his skin is warm, his palm sweaty beneath mine. That is curious, for I have ever known the emperor to be a man who runs cold. "Ah, Cleopatra. I have been waiting a long time for this reunion."

"Only two years. Not long at all."

Augustus swallows, as if overcome. "Much longer than that, as I am about to show you."

He leads me into his monument, the thing of himself he expects to endure. The interior is open to the night sky and the moon glows down on a riot of color. Blue Corinthian capitals bend to fit inside each corner. The carved walls boast of green palmettes, yellow festoons, and red garlands. There are also ritual cups and platters, fruits and ribbons and bovine skulls. As I catalog the various patterns and symbols, the emperor watches every flick of my eyes, desperate for my reaction.

I consider carefully before I give it. There is no *heka* here. Not yet. But I can well imagine that there will be. This will be a sacred place of gladness. Of thanksgiving. Of goodwill and gratitude for the Golden Age.

All my life I've watched the emperor tear things down, and finally, he is proudest of what he is building. I am stung with jealousy . . . but also deeply moved. "It is lovely," I admit. "It is beautiful beyond what I might have imagined . . ."

He preens, running a reverent hand over the altar stone. "This is where the Vestals will make a yearly sacrifice for peace."

"To do it, they must turn their backs on the field of Mars," I notice. "To make peace, they must turn their backs on war. Very clever."

He smiles like a man who knows a secret. "But the artistry, the true artistry, is on the outside. Come. Walk with me, Selene."

Back down the stairs we go, hand in hand, into the moonlit night. He leads me past Romulus and Remus to the north wall where a grand procession is carved in high relief. It features senators and other important personages carrying laurel branches. In the carving, two senators stop to talk to each other, so lifelike that I might almost stop and lean in to overhear. It's a strange piece, as if the artist had frozen a real moment in time and reproduced it with all its flaws.

Then I see Julia carved on that wall, and realize that the artist *has* captured a moment; this is the processional from years before, the happy thanksgiving celebration we shared to consecrate this ground. Oh, how I remember that day. Agrippa and Octavia were still with us then, and Julia was smiling, as she is in the carving, trailed by her children. Gaius, Lucius, and little Julilla, and baby Agrippina too. My heart warms at the portrait of Julia's brood, then my throat tightens as I see my beloved Octavia, illuminated by moonlight.

The emperor's sister is brought to life here, where all the gods and all the generations might see her holding two laurel branches in her hand. *Sweet Isis*, how I have missed her. Would that I could reach out and touch Octavia's cheek and find it warm. But if I were to reach out, the illusion would break apart like a reflection on the water. That's what this monument is—a glimpse into the past, as if it were a River of Time flowing the other way.

"Come," Augustus says when I linger too long in loving memory. "There is more."

We turn the corner, where I see Roma wearing a battle helmet, sitting atop a pile of captured war trophies in victory. We have come to the street entrance where the people will see the monument in its splendor, and the emperor's hand clutches mine so hard that I'm forced to look up into his eyes, which are smoky gray. He has always been ice, but tonight I see the spark of something in him. "Look, Selene. Up and to your left."

I do as he says.

To my surprise, green eyes, just like mine, capture my gaze. I am looking at a face like my own, more feminine, more idealized, her hair wavy instead of curled in the Greek style. But the nose, straight and long like mine. Her expression intense, like mine. The breasts, round and full like mine. Perhaps my eyes play tricks on me, perhaps I'm a vain woman to see my own features, but then I see the winds . . .

. . . and my heart begins to pound.

This is no simple portrait of me, the Queen of Mauretania, on his monument. This is something else. Something grander. Something *unimaginable*. It is an earth mother, two babes in her arms, one of them offering a pomegranate. A goddess flanked by the *aurae*, nymphs of the breezes, one atop a swan and the other on the back of some manner of serpent. The *aurae* attend her. They are in her power. Just as my winds obey me.

He has made me into a goddess in the heart of Rome.

My hand trembles in his; the other covers my mouth to hold back a sob of awe. Staring, dumbfounded, I soak in every detail. With only stones as her throne, this goddess dwarfs a bull and a lamb at her feet. Fruit spills from her lap. Grapes and acorns. Tall grasses and reeds recall Egypt to mind. And there, by an overturned urn, is a heron. A *heron*. Sacred in Heliopolis, a city named for the sun, like my twin . . .

I cannot move. I cannot breathe. I cannot tear my eyes away. The trembling moves up my hand into my arm until it overcomes me and I shiver from head to toe. Cold bites at my nose, at my cheeks, at the tips of my ears, but it all fades to numbness.

"Who is this goddess?" I murmur.

"Does it matter? She is *Tellus*, the very earth itself. She is *Venus*, my ancestress. She is *Pax*, the peace we have wrought. She is *Isis*. She is *you*."

I shake my head, unwilling to believe that he's done something so reverent and momentous and marvelous for me. I am shocked. I am wonderstruck. I am overcome with sentimentality. With this monument, he has finally touched me where his hands could never reach . . .

Myriad emotions wrestle free of my heart, causing tears to spill over my lashes. Tears of joy. Tears of awe. Tears of fear. "Why have you done this?"

"It's no golden statue in my family temple," the emperor replies, his throat bobbing, evidence that he too feels deeply. "But it is no less a statement of who you are to me. The fertile earth, the mother of my children, the goddess who has guided me to this Golden Age."

This monument has been years in the making. Longer than just the two it took to build it. *Years* he has planned this gesture. It is part of his grand delusion, so it ought not pull at my heart like it does. I don't want to be touched by it, but I am, oh, *I am*. Stupefied, I let him tilt my chin and in an instant we're back on the Isle of Samos, and he's offering me the world. "I do honor you, Selene. Can you see that now?"

"Yes," I whisper, enthralled by its beauty. "Yes, I do see it, Caesar."

"And we are bound, do you see that too? We have always been bound."

First by tragedy and treachery and violation. But now this monument, this *Ara Pacis*, will bind us together in a new way as long as it stands.

He has bound us together with peace, forever.

This thought is both dark and light, like this night, glinting silver beneath the moon. Never before has my mind been so clouded, so murky and confused. I am a queen. I am Cleopatra's daughter. I am the chosen child of Isis. I am worthy of this monument. I have *earned* this man's reverence, time and time again. It is only right that I should have some part on this altar to peace. It is only right that I be remembered for the thing I was born to bring about . . .

And yet, it sends shivers down my spine. I am a Ptolemy and I am proud. But I am also a survivor, and some ominous voice, deep within, cries out to be wary. Perhaps Romans will look upon this frieze and not recognize me in it; it isn't a Roman likeness, warts and all. It's a perfected vision of me. Perhaps people will pass it by and think only of whatever goddess pleases them best. Venus. Ceres. Tellus. Isis. It may be that the name *Cleopatra Selene* will not enter their minds. But when they see the winds . . .

"Caesar, what will they think you mean by this?"

"Ah, my Cleopatra. Let me show you what I mean by it."

Thirty-five

I stumble along beside him in a daze. Now we come to the wall of the monument where the carved processional continues and I see a likeness of Augustus. He is carved surrounded by the priests, wearing their distinctive leather caps with the strange pikes, and his *lictors* with their bundled rods and axes. In the carving, he holds up a wand of augury, as if he can foretell the future of Rome.

My eyes stop at the portrait of Agrippa. The admiral is a ghost on this panel, like Octavia. I'm gladdened to see him as he was. Big and strong, decidedly awkward in ceremony, his head covered. As he was in life, he stands at a position of most prominence near the emperor. And just behind him, holding the hem of his toga, is a little face that steals my breath.

Ptolemy.

There is my son in the princely garb he will wear for the Trojan Games. There he stands, on this wall, looking over his shoulder at Livia. The air whooshes out of my lungs and I falter. For a moment I don't think I can stand. The emperor catches me with a hand at the small of my back while I struggle to finish a sentence. "You put . . . you put my son . . . you carved my son . . ."

"Our son," the emperor insists. "That is why I put him here at my side, as Agrippa was once at my side. I gave Agrippa my signet ring when I thought I might die, but you nursed me to health and now I shall give it to our son."

"Oh, gods," I gasp, then repeat it, again and again. "Oh, *gods*!"

"Calm yourself, Selene. I am laying the foundation to claim Ptolemy as my heir. When he is Emperor of Rome, he will point to this monument as proof of his worthiness. I'm a descendant of the Trojan Aeneas, and here is my son, dressed as a Trojan, at my side, do you see?"

I do see. As I fear everyone will see. My senses rush back to me, and I fear the keenest danger. Julius Caesar honored my mother with a statue, and was murdered for his trouble. What might the Romans do now were they to know that the emperor meant to name my child, a foreign prince, his heir? "Augustus, what have you done?"

"I have claimed my son in the only way I can."

My breath stutters; my knees weaken. "Do you think you're fooling someone? To put Gaius and Lucius on the other side of the monument, on the other wall, far away from you, and here my son—"

"He is not the only foreign prince on the monument."

"But the others are *hostages*!"

When I was a girl, the games I played with the emperor were mine to play. That my own children should be part of the emperor's madness was never my intention. This monument is a web of his creation and mine, but now my children are caught in it too. Though it is a midwinter's night, I begin to sweat. "*Sweet Isis . . .*"

The emperor thinks the Romans will not see what he intends until he wants them to see it. And it is true that everything on this monument can be denied. Each symbol carries more than one meaning. The placement of my son can be argued away. But there are some for whom no arguments will be persuasive. Livia will know, in one glance. She will *know*, and she will take it as a threat most dire. "Your wife will strike back. And when she does, she will have two sons at the heads of your legions, both willing to defend her."

"Why should she strike? I have honored her too. This monument will be unveiled and celebrated on her birthday. Can she complain? No. Have I slighted her sons on this monument? I have not. Look there and see Tiberius. Look a little farther and you see Drusus and Minora talking to each other, grouped together with their children.

I've given them a place of great prominence. Have I slighted Gaius and Lucius on this monument? I have not. They are my adopted sons—"

"They are not Livia's sons and she will never forget it."

He raises a hand to cover half his face. "Selene, enough. *Enough.* Can't it be enough for you to know that you will prevail over her in the end?"

I don't want to prevail over Livia; I want to survive her. But she is not the only deadly scorpion in my life. I am loved in Rome, but I have enemies here too. Roman senators may not be powerful enough to throw off the yoke of Augustus, but my family is an easier target for their ire. If they have ever feared my influence over the emperor before, this will scare them witless.

"For the love of Jupiter, Selene, are you really so timid? Haven't I taken us safely this far?"

I round on him fiercely. "I don't want you to take me anywhere. I've told you before that this is behind us. I am so tired of this lunacy. So *exhausted* by it. I don't want what you think I want!"

"I don't believe you," he says, giving me a little shake. "You want your mother's Egypt and you want the world. You and I want the same dream . . ."

"You're wrong. I have grown and changed and now everything I want in Rome is something I brought here with me." If his angry expression is any indication, he thinks I mean Juba. Because I don't know that he's wrong, I hasten to add, "I'm building a kingdom. I'm building a sanctuary. I'm feeding the empire. *Mauretania* is where I want to be. I am only here because you command it and because I will not abandon my children."

"What of our son? The grandson of Cleopatra and Antony. A Ptolemaic prince, kin of Alexander. I will not let you deny him his rightful place at the center of the world."

He has found in me a weakness, a terrible weakness. I can accept for myself a destiny my mother never wanted for me, but for my children, the last of the Ptolemies? I want the world. *Isis forgive me,* I want them to have the world. Every cunning instinct in my bones, every ambition that has driven me in my life, every dark desire for vengeance and victory screams inside my blood to embrace this moment and even this man, if need be.

This scream, this desperate scream echoes inside me until it is answered with perfect, tranquil silence. For though some part of me is shadow, another part of me is light. I want the world for my children, yes, but I would not gamble their lives for it. I have made this decision already once before on the Isle of Samos. I have made this decision *more* than once. I made it here in Rome the third night of the *Ludi Seculares* when I offered up my hatreds and ambitions for peace.

I have made this decision every hour of every day since then.

And at long last, it is no longer a struggle.

I am at peace with it. I am. And now I know what I must do.

JUBA is sitting up awake in his chambers, staring into the fire. I am chilled from the winter night, but I hesitate to come nearer for warmth when his words float to me in the shadowy darkness. "When I heard you leave with the praetorians tonight, it occurred to me that you might not come back . . ."

Taking a deep breath, I say, "But I *have* come back."

My husband bows his head, his voice quiet, distant, and contemplative. "I started to remember all the little things you've done in recent days that felt like you were saying good-bye . . . or have I imagined it?"

There was a time I could have deceived him. There was a time that he could not see past my masks and could not breach my walls. He once asked me if he was married to a stranger and I glibly answered, *Aren't we all?* But he knows me better now. "I'm not here to say good-bye."

I decide to start from the beginning, or at least as near to the beginning as I can bear. I tell him that Augustus once demanded a son from me. I tell him how I manipulated the emperor on the Isle of Samos, promising to give him a son if he would give me Egypt.

I tell Juba how I stoked the emperor's lust to such a white-hot flame that he wished to set Livia aside and put me in her place. I tell him that I, Cleopatra Selene, had in my grasp everything my mother ever wanted. And that I turned it away.

My husband knows, or has guessed, most of this story, though there are moments in the hearing of it that he shows genuine surprise. Still, it is only when I come to the part where the emperor threatened Juba's life if I should ever bear his child that his surprise turns to furious denial. "Caesar would *never* harm me," he says.

"He would. I remember his words plainly, for I have wrestled with them for years. He said, '*You would never allow such a thing to happen unless your husband has become so inconvenient that you desire to be made a widow.*'"

The look Juba shoots me is withering. "You would say anything, wouldn't you? *Whatever words are necessary.* Don't lie to me. He needn't put the threat to you. Augustus has had ample opportunity to threaten *me* over this matter, so why hasn't he?"

Because it might unite us, I think. Better to keep us forever in discord. However, I am already asking my husband to hear hard truths about a man he admires, a man he loves. Oh, yes, even now, I can see how my husband still loves the emperor. How he defends him as a son would defend his father to the very last breath. "Maybe he only said it to frighten me, but it *did* frighten me, Juba. Can you not understand that? Augustus has kept me in terror since I was a girl and when I was no longer frightened for myself he made me frightened for everyone else."

The king doesn't answer. Nor does he invite me to sit, so I stand there on stiff legs, trying to find the right words to make him understand. "Juba, Augustus told you he would foster Ptolemy under his roof. What he did not tell you is that he intends to keep him. And me. He does not want me to return to Mauretania. He wants both of us by his side here in Rome."

The king rises from his couch, folds his arms, and stares at me coldly. "That's what he had to say to you tonight?"

Miserably, I shake my head.

"Then when is he supposed to have made such a demand?"

This is already so much more difficult than I ever dreamed it would be. "Two years ago."

In wide-eyed shock, my husband cries, "Two *years*!"

Though I hate every moment of this confession, I do not spare myself. "I wasn't going to tell you until I had to. Not until the last possible moment. Not until I'd exhausted every option or excuse. Because I didn't know how I could bear the way you are looking at me now."

My words do not thaw him at all. "Oh, ho! I think you underestimate yourself, Selene. Surely you are not exhausted yet. Surely you had it in you to spin a few more lies. You may have kept me in ignorance at least until it was time for me to return to Mauretania. Perhaps even longer than that."

This is going very badly, but still, I must try. "I never wanted to deceive you. It is only that I hoped you might never need to know. I hoped that I would find some way, as I have so often found a way, to turn it all around. But what the emperor has done now . . . I cannot undo."

Taking another deep breath, I tell him about the altar to peace. About the long-ago procession of thanksgiving depicted. I tell him about the Tellus panel where I am carved as a goddess with two children upon my knee. I tell him everything I can remember. Every inane detail. It all comes out in a rush, my words tumbling over themselves until I am nearly panting for breath.

Juba paces as he listens, but he doesn't interrupt or ask questions. He doesn't speak at all, which makes it that much more difficult to go on. Yet I must go on. I tell him how Ptolemy is carved upon the monument and where he is placed and why. I finish by saying, "I am so afraid for our son, I don't know what to do."

Never have I doubted myself more than now. What has happened to the schemer inside me? I can think of nothing! That is why I have come to Juba. I need his help more than I have ever needed it.

The king stops his pacing and comes toward me, still staring. Every moment that goes by in silence, I shrink a little more. I am not frightened in the way so many wives would have good cause to be frightened. Juba isn't the kind of man to rage violently. Instead, he lets his pain ferment into bitterness. "So, as always, you wait until there is nowhere else to turn before you turn to me . . ."

That isn't true. He is the *first* person I turned to this time. The *only* one. Still, I do not dare defend myself. It is only Ptolemy I must defend. "We cannot go to the dedication of the *Ara Pacis*. We cannot stand there while the crowds look at our son carved on those walls. We must find some excuse to leave the city. Some excuse to spirit Ptolemy away."

The king snorts. "We must go to the dedication, Selene. Everyone must go."

"Not everyone is carved in living color on the altar's walls."

"That is why we must go," Juba says, grinding his teeth. "We must stand there together and behave as if it was nothing out of the ordinary. We must stand there, side by side, as if our mockery of a marriage were not impugned there in marble for all to see." I wince at the word *mockery*, but it does not stop his tirade. "Yes, Selene, we must stand there shamelessly smiling at one another as if it were of no consequence. Because it is of no consequence. It is only stone."

Few things last longer than stone, and I feel certain that if he had seen the monument for himself, he would understand. "Augustus is using the *Ara Pacis* to soften the ground for what he means to do. He means to claim Ptolemy as his own son. He thinks to make Ptolemy the next Emperor of Rome."

My husband gives a bark of dark laughter. "You must enjoy this game. Playing the emperor's whore. You must take as much pleasure from it as he does. Most adulterers do their filthy fornications in a bed, but not the two of you. You need never touch in the dance you do. You have shamelessly teased and tormented each other to a fever pitch and now you are both hungry for release."

Here he goes too far. "Do I look flushed with pleasure? Look at me and, for once, truly see me."

But he turns away. He storms away. With his cloak trailing behind him, he slams past furniture, overturning a small table in his anger and haste to flee from the truth. When he gets to the door, he flings it open.

"Juba!" I cry.

And he stops. He *stops*. His hand hovers there, gripping the door until his knuckles go white, his shoulders rising and falling with each heaving breath.

To his turned back, I speak urgently. "When I was a bruised and battered bride I tried to show you the marks Augustus left on me, but you wouldn't look. You wouldn't believe me. I was fourteen years old. I was the same age Dora is now. I was a frightened girl, all alone in this world. I asked you to believe me, but you wouldn't. This time, I am *begging* you to believe me."

Juba does not move. Neither of us does. He stands there and stands there. I gasp when he closes the door again, then strides to where I stand. He comes close enough that I feel his breath on my face, but we do not touch. With a stony expression, as if steeled for ferocious battle, he lifts his gaze to my face. I do not shield myself from it; I let all my masks fall away. Let him see me. The truth in me, the falsity of me, my virtue and my vice. All of it. Trembling, I say, "This is the truth: Ptolemy is your son and mine. I do not want the emperor to claim him. I do not want to be at the side of Augustus. Not now. Not ever."

Staring, Juba breathes in. He breathes out. His voice is hoarse when he speaks. "If that is true, then lay aside your trembling, because it will never happen. Whatever Caesar has been telling you, whatever he has promised you, he will never do it. You think you know him. You think you know him better than anyone else. But I have known him longer, Selene. I've seen him toy with adversaries for years. For decades. He tells them what they want to believe—"

"He is the one who wants to believe Ptolemy is his son, not me."

Juba lifts one hand as if to grant me that. "Perhaps the desire is all his. Still, you must understand that these fantasies are private indulgences. He has many. Things to help him find relief from the realities he cannot escape. In the end, he always does that which will assure his esteem in Rome."

My husband is telling me that I am nothing to the emperor but a very expensive *hetaera* with whom he plays the most intricate bedroom games. Perhaps he is right. It would be better for us all if it were true. Unfortunately, I cannot believe it. "The *Ara Pacis* is not a private indulgence. It will be unveiled days from now before all of Rome."

"Tell me, Selene. Which hero is depicted on that monument?"

"Aeneas."

Juba nods as if I have proven his point. "Not Alexander. Not Julius Caesar. Not Mark Antony. None of the men who took an exotic or forbidden woman for a bride. He chose Aeneas. He chose the hero who abandoned his African queen. He will never jeopardize his legacy. Not for you or even for a son of his own. If you believe otherwise, if you *truly* believe otherwise, it is a vanity."

He puts a terrible doubt in me. Can I have been so foolish? I think of all the promises the emperor has made to me. All the promises he has broken. Has my Ptolemaic pride blinded me to the truth that the only promises he has ever kept were the ones most convenient to him? I am shaken but not convinced. "It is not my vanity that carved me with the winds as a goddess. How will our enemies answer it?"

My husband adopts the tone he uses to lecture. "We do not have enemies, Selene. We have a rival in Herod, that much is true. But here in Rome? We have friends and allies. Julia adores you. Tiberius and Drusus were your childhood playmates, and I would happily serve either of them should they come to power. I understand that you do not care for Livia. She resents you because of the emperor's fascination, and two strong-willed women will undoubtedly come to conflict."

I shake my head violently. "No. You don't understand at all if you think Livia and I loathe each other because we are strong-willed. There is a long trail of dead men and boys in her wake. I cannot prove it. I have never been able to prove it . . . but she is a poisoner more dangerous than the emperor himself."

"That is a *vicious* rumor," Juba says, as if he thought better of me than to spread it. "One that might well be hurled at Isidora one day for her love of plants and potions."

My fists clench because in this one thing, I am utterly certain. "I know Livia works in poisons because she tried to give me one." I remember what she said the morning after the emperor forced me to his bed.

I've provided you with an honorable exit. It won't be as dramatic as your mother's end, but unless you have the power to conjure up Egyptian cobras, a goblet of poisoned wine will suffice.

When I tell him, Juba narrows his eyes. "Did you drink it?"

"Is that what you think I should have done for your honor and mine?" I ask, fury rising inside me. "All this time, you have been wishing that I took my own life . . ."

"No," he snaps, taking me hard by the arm. "No, Selene. I ask because I want to know how you are so certain the wine was poisoned."

Damn him, examining my claim like a tutor before a classroom. Demanding proofs that I cannot give, but which I know in my heart, in the deepest part of my heart, are true. "You think I imagined the danger?"

He gives a long-suffering sigh. "I think you have seen so much death in your time that you are overvigilant against every possible threat. You have lost so much that it has made you paranoid, prone to hover over your children and live in constant terror for them. If everything you've said is true, people will gossip about your surrendered virtue and mock me, but they'll assume Ptolemy is just one more of the many children on that monument and they will put it from their minds."

I want it to be as simple as that. I desperately want it to be. "So we should do nothing. We should pretend as if it is nothing. Will you still see it the same way when Augustus insists on keeping me and Ptolemy here in Rome?"

The king grimaces. "I'll speak to Caesar about this. It is a conversation long overdue."

This answer, given so seriously, makes my stomach churn. "You don't believe anything I've said, do you? Because if you did believe me, you would know to fear for your life in having such a conversation. I have told you everything and still you don't believe me . . ."

"Have you told me *everything*? Tell me there are no more lies. No more secrets between us. No more fugitives hiding in my court. Tell me that I know everything now."

I have told him everything that is mine to tell. I have told him every part of the story . . . except for those having to do with Helios. I cannot tell him that. If I tell him Helios is alive, he will reveal it to the emperor. And if he should try to persuade me that Helios is dead, another thing I have only *imagined*, it will break me.

At my hesitation, Juba takes me by the shoulders. "What else?"

My voice quavers. "You will not thank me for telling you . . ."

"Tell me, damn you!"

We are at the edge and neither of us can back away. If I tell him, we will fall. If I refuse to tell him, we will fall. We will fall and we will not survive it.

"Selene, you tell me or Augustus can keep you for all I care."

This threat makes me want to shout at him that it can be over, then. That if he is willing to abandon me to the emperor, again, then I do not want him. But I would be lying. I do want him. I fear that I have fallen in love with him. I fear that I love him *desperately* and that he is breaking my heart. "Juba, can't you see that for you, I am stripped bare of everything but this one secret? It is not a danger to you. It is not a danger to our children. It is not a danger to our kingdom."

I hear him swallow. Then he asks, "Are you my wife or no?"

I don't understand what he means by this question. I answer it with the truth as I know it. "I have been your wife since the night we conceived our son. Not before then. Not the day you married me. Not the years after. You were no husband to me then either, but I swear to you by Isis and everything I hold sacred that when I returned to you from the Isle of Samos, I became your wife. We made a family and a marriage beyond what was written in the contract."

"Has that marriage no value to you?"

"You know it does. Let me have this one mystery. Don't make me tell you. I ask for nothing else. Because if I tell you, you will betray me and none of it will have any value at all . . ."

He snorts. "So I am to trust in you while you put no trust in me."

I lay my palms flat to his chest, beseechingly. "I am no good at trust. Or honesty. Or laying myself bare. But I am trying, Juba. I am trusting you with my son's life. With my life. With all my secrets save one. I have put myself in your hands. Can it be enough?"

"I don't know," he says harshly.

It is not the answer I hoped for. "You don't *know*?"

"That is what I said. I don't know. You've had two years to consider, Selene; I will need more than just one night."

Thirty-six

IN the wee hours of the morning on the day the *Ara Pacis* is to be unveiled, I dream of mobs swarming my house, intent upon tearing me and my children from our beds and dragging us through the street. I do not want to go. While Tala natters on with the mistress of my wardrobe about what I should wear for such an occasion, I lie back down again in my bed, grateful for the Roman design of the house that keeps away sunlight. My daughter peeks into my chambers to ask, "Aren't you feeling well, Mother? I can make you a tincture before we go . . ."

Though my head is pounding, I say, "I just need a moment to myself."

She squints. "Perhaps your humors are imbalanced."

"Perhaps I like them that way."

She laughs and I am glad, because I regret my sniping tone. My daughter is only trying to tend to me. It may be the last time she ever does. Soon she will be the Queen of Cappadocia. And before that, she will see me carved on the emperor's altar. Others may not see, but my daughter always sees. So I force myself to get up.

My hair is styled in the knotted coiffure made popular by Octavia and I don only small pearl earrings for adornment. For garments, I wear a modest blue *tunica* with yellow fringe, covered by a matching shawl and my fur cloak.

I will need the fur-lined cloak, for it shall be a very cold January day. It is made all the colder by my husband, whose crisp civility belies the storm inside him. The slaves must sense it, because they jump to his commands, preparing him for the day as if he were about to ride into battle. The king has not a spare word for me and I do not press him.

And as we go out into the winter afternoon, I stare out over the other side of the river, where the crowds assemble for the dedication. I know the difference between the normal clamor of the city and voices that are gathered together in anger, echoing off wood and brick and marble. I listen closely, my ears searching out for the slightest sound of jeering or discontent, but I hear none.

When we reach the site of the dedication, the crowds part for our royal entourage, but we do not hurry to take our customary place closest to the imperial family. Juba and I hold back and linger with the other notables in Rome, many of whom blow warm air into their hands and eye the sky for bad bird omens that may send us all home.

We endure speeches, rituals, gift giving, and pomp. Augustus is both solemn and proud to show off his new gift to Rome, and the people murmur and point at this symbol or that while I hold my breath.

They are most interested in the red granite obelisk that he stole from my mother's Egypt and the bronze lines in the travertine pavement that mark the degrees of the solar year. Henceforth, on the emperor's birthday in September, the shadow of the obelisk will fall upon the center of the altar of peace. He has made of it the gnomon of a sundial. With this bit of artistry, he is saying he was born to bring peace. He is saying that he is the savior. Augustus has made himself a sun god at last and obliterated the memory of Alexander Helios . . .

Clutching my son against me, I take great pains not to look in the emperor's direction when he is hailed again and again. It is Livia I watch. I watch for every false smile and every twitch of her predatory eyes. Perhaps she has prepared herself. She is surrounded by her kinsmen. One can't turn a full circle in the crowds today without seeing a Claudian of one stripe or another. Every man, woman, and child with a claim to the Claudian name has crawled up out of their holes to find favor in Augustus's regime.

Livia has accomplished for her family what I could not accomplish for my own—a feat that deserves my grudging admiration. The emperor's wife seems untroubled by my presence and, in fact, utterly unaware of me. It is a pretense, I know, but is it because she is afraid of her husband's plans or because I am now so beneath her?

Who does the emperor lie to, I wonder? Livia or me? Who sees the true face of Augustus?

Maybe none of us do.

My husband and I stand side by side, keeping our children close. Juba performs the role that is required of him, but has no talent for this sort of playacting. His laugh is bitter and his only words to me a sharp rebuke. "Stop holding the boy round the neck or you'll suffocate him."

Ptolemy, who is keen for his independence when other boys are watching, is grateful when I loosen my hold on him at the king's command. And my son's eagerness to squirm away makes me feel even more of a fool. I don't know what it is that I was expecting under the bright sun on this crisp afternoon. Did I think people would gasp at the scandal? Did I think senators would come rushing at us with daggers? From the street in front of the altar, a few women impolitely point at me and whisper behind their hands. Perhaps they have always done it, but today I notice, and it is very hard to pretend that I do not. But I am jumping at shadows, I think. All along I have condemned the emperor and Herod as paranoid and mad, but now I wonder if that is what I have become. What they have turned me into. It is a humiliating thought . . .

We stay only as long as propriety requires.

That night mobs do not swarm my house. From the city across the river, we hear only the sounds of merriment, late into the evening. No furious senators send letters of rebuke. Indeed, we hear no complaint from any quarter. Can I have been too proud to admit that I am of no threat to *anyone*?

I am just a client queen from a kingdom at the far edge of

civilization and my son is only the Prince of Mauretania, not the next Pharaoh, nor the next Emperor of Rome. There is no danger to my son because I am the only one gullible enough to believe a thing Augustus says . . .

In the morning, Ptolemy insists he must visit the stables and work with his prize stallion, practicing his drills for the Trojan Games, and I cannot deny him. I cannot go on fearing every phantom shadow and see danger lurking everywhere. My son must be known to the Romans and respected. If Ptolemy is to rule over *anything*, I cannot hold him back. Juba is right. Perhaps he has always been right about everything.

ON the day Julia distributes salt and olive oil to the poor, she insists I go with her. Most charity in Rome is done with great fanfare and accompanied by a lasting monument, but she prefers spontaneity. Unfortunately, her spontaneity takes us into the Suburra, a run-down neighborhood of questionable safety. "Did you ever suspect Livia's son would turn out to be such a bloody-minded imbecile?"

With a wary eye on the ruffians in the street, I ask, "What has Tiberius done now?"

"Not Tiberius," Julia says with exasperation. "My husband is just a miserable lump. I'm talking about *Drusus*. Don't tell me you haven't heard how our new consul is preparing for his return to Germania, vowing to win the noblest spoils by hunting down a tribal chieftain and bringing back his armor!"

"It's just talk," I say dismissively, for the *spoila optima* is the highest honor a Roman general can achieve, considered greater even than the military Triumphs that the emperor has denied him. "Drusus says it to excite his soldiers."

"Oh, no, Selene." Julia shifts in the litter, jostling it so that I must grip the edge not to be tossed out. "I've heard tales of Drusus rushing onto the battlefield ahead of his armies, chasing great big fur-clad warlords through German forests and thickets. He's going to get himself killed. The only good news is that Livia is beside herself, wondering how she could have possibly raised a man who champions the *Republic*."

I doubt Livia is truly vexed. For it is the same old strategy of putting a brother in each camp. Drusus agitates for a return to the Republic so that the emperor cannot pass his powers down to his heirs. But Tiberius is the stepfather to those heirs, and if Augustus dies before his grandsons reach majority, then Tiberius will take power with or without a Republic.

Either way, the Claudians win.

Julia continues, "If Agrippa never celebrated a Triumphal parade and was never given the honors of a Triumphator, why should Drusus get them? He thinks he can call the emperor's bluff and *force* my father to allow it. That's what an idealistic fool Drusus is."

Either that, or he's more ambitious than I ever gave him credit for. Noble Drusus. Always affable. Always ready with a kind word. He is so unlike every other member of his family that it has never occurred to me he might be the best politician of them all.

Julia peeks out the curtains at the rough crowd that has started to follow us. "It's a dangerous pretension. You ought to speak to your sister about her husband."

"I'm done meddling in Roman affairs."

At this, Julia rolls her eyes. "You're so very sour today! Well, if you aren't going to help me save Rome from the idiotic heroics of her generals, the least you can do is make yourself useful handing out salt and oil to the poor."

"Why can't you have slaves hand it out?"

Julia twists her finger into a lock of hair, dyed purple today to cover the gray . . . speaking of pretension. "Because I'm a woman of the people!"

"Well, I'm a Ptolemaic queen."

"Exactly. And your presence increases my stature," Julia replies, her eyes narrowing a little too shrewdly for my taste. "After all, you're a goddess on my father's monument whereas I am depicted as a mere mortal woman."

Acid burns in my belly, tempting me to deny the accusation. I *would* deny it, if I were speaking to anyone else. "It doesn't look very much like me, does it? I swear to you, the Tellus panel wasn't my idea. I didn't ask it of him."

"Of course you didn't. What could you stand to gain from my father making a fool of himself?" Her voice is light with amusement, but it must be the very question she's been asking herself.

What *do* I stand to gain?

If the emperor's obsession with my son is real and not the pretense Juba thinks it is, then it comes at the expense of Julia's sons. I want Julia to be the First Woman in Rome. I want her sons to fulfill their promise and have all that she would wish for them. But I want a brilliant future for my children too. That is the weakness in me the emperor has preyed upon, and I am frightened that Julia might sense it.

I ask, "What did Livia say about the *Ara Pacis*?"

"Do you think Livia would say anything to me about it?"

"Tiberius, then."

"My husband is even less likely to share. You know he despises me."

"No one could despise you."

She gives a dismissive flick of her fingers. "Tiberius does."

"That's unfair. You've done nothing but reconcile yourself to being his wife."

Her shoulders droop. "Maybe if our son had lived, things would have been different . . ."

"I'm so sorry," I say, reaching for her hand.

She lets me take it, her eyes wistful. "You wouldn't think it, but Tiberius is very sentimental. His grief for that baby was wild and without reason. He wished the child was never born, so he wouldn't have felt the pain. And of course it is my fault the child was born. Livia has him convinced that I've always had designs on him. Even when I was married to Agrippa. So Tiberius fancies me a temptress and dares not even look at me."

I am altogether too well acquainted with the way men will blame their own lustful desires upon the women who aroused them. I am also aware of how difficult it is to have a husband who will not look at you. "Perhaps time will change him."

Julia gives a toss of her dyed hair. "Let him despise me. I don't care. I don't even care what my father thinks of me. I have my *own* partisans now. Soldiers who would fight for me as Agrippa's widow. Men who report to me on the doings of everyone from my father to the lowest senator. I mean for my sons to rule this empire, Selene, even if I never have an easy night's sleep until it comes to pass."

THE emperor's daughter arranges for my husband and me to interview an imperial shipbuilder who used to serve Admiral Agrippa. We need such a man to take a position in our court. Nevertheless, Juba insists that he has urgent business elsewhere. Given my husband's brusqueness, I suspect the urgency is simply to avoid me.

My son is also up and away into the bright February morning, eager to return to the stables. At least Ptolemy lets me kiss his cherub cheeks before he goes, a thing I treasure because I do not know how much longer it will be before he won't accept cuddles and cosseting without embarrassment.

Once he's gone I rummage through the scrolls in the cubbies that line the wall in our study for something that will make me seem less than hopelessly ignorant on the matter of shipbuilding. In the end, I give up. When the shipbuilder comes, I quickly offer the man a position; if he was good enough for Agrippa, he is good enough for me.

Wanting to give my husband no reason to be more displeased with me than he already is, I carefully slide Juba's dusty old scrolls back into their holders. That's when I hear Dora scream.

At the sound, I dart out into the atrium, where I see every slave, servant, and courtier turn to the peristyle garden. Guards rush to defend us against unseen danger and we find Isidora sitting alone beneath the grape arbor, her bags of herbs scattered around her and a divining bowl, filled with water, clutched in her trembling hand.

I sense the *heka*—it tingles up and down my arms—and I know she's been reading the Rivers of Time against my wishes again. Alas, I cannot fly into a rage at my daughter's willful disobedience because I'm too terrified by the tears in her eyes . . . and the way her lips are tinged with blue.

"Dora?" I grasp at her hands. They are ice cold. How long has she been sitting out here without so much as a cloak to shield her from the bite of winter? My daughter trembles, red-rimmed eyes so filled with horror that I cannot imagine what she has seen, or what she is *still* seeing. She screams again, her eyes looking through me. And I am afraid for her. I can see that she is being swept away to some other place and I feel helpless to stop it. I shake her. I shout at her, "Isidora!"

I give her my voice to latch onto, to swim her way back to me, but she is fighting strong currents of magic. It isn't until after I drape my own cloak over her shoulders and try to rub warmth into her arms that she begins to groan. "Oh, Mother, no . . ."

She knows who I am. That much is good. "What is it?"

My daughter dissolves into sobs, and it is difficult to make out her words. She is shouting at someone I cannot see. She is warning them to run away!

Iacentus helps his princess to her feet but she cannot see him either, a thing that plainly disturbs him, even under his professional veneer. I send for Musa, the emperor's very own physician, for if there is something physically wrong with her, I will trust no one else to heal her. Then I take her to her room, swearing that I will search it and confiscate every potion, talisman, or magic item I can find.

And I will kill that snake, wherever it is.

As I get her to bed, she sobs, "Ptolemy run!"

The blood drains from my face. I feel it go, nearly taking my sanity away with it. Where is Ptolemy? I start for his room, then remember he is at the stables. I don't want to leave Dora, not like this, when she is so fragile, drowning in the Rivers of Time. But now I must find my son.

There is a commotion downstairs. Banging at my gate. The sound of boots on tile as people rush into my atrium. It is the shrieks that send me running down the stairs two at a time. That is when the scent of smoke gets into my nostrils and I feel a terrible thunder underfoot. The house seems to shake with it, and someone cries, "There's a fire at the stables!"

Thirty-seven

OUTSIDE, black smoke rises from the stables like a pillar into the sky. Spooked Barbary horses with perfect pedigrees gallop wildly through the street in front of my house, smashing carts with their back hooves and rearing up at anyone who approaches them. Rushing out into the madness, I have a near miss with my son's stallion; the big horse's eyes roll with fear, his mouth foaming with fury, a gash on his shoulder and a smear of blood upon his fair mane.

One trampled man howls in pain, while others try to wrestle the horses into submission. My guards shout warnings, but I am only dimly aware of the danger from the horses; my eyes are on the fire beyond. "Ptolemy!" I cry, sprinting toward the fire, dodging broken gates and smashed carts. Even before I reach the stables I'm nearly overcome by a wall of heat that warps and bends the air. I can hear nothing but the roar of fire as it blazes in brilliant red and orange.

I throw both my arms up, summoning my magic to clear the smoke away with my winds. The sail-shaped birthmark on my arm tingles with power but when I hurl a pillar of air at the flames it only fans them and forces them to jump higher. Somewhere in the stables, I hear my son's dog barking and I know they must both be inside.

Screaming Ptolemy's name, I break away from my guards and sprint into the burning stable, stumbling over something that feels human. It is the body of a man whose head has been split open, his face to the dirt, unrecognizable. Still, I know the dead man's hands—hands that have protected me. It is Memnon, sooty fingers clutched round a dagger.

Where his sword and shield may be, I don't know.

I let out a cry of grief, but I cannot stop for him. Again and again I hear the dog bark. Frantically, my eyes sweep the conflagration for the sight of my son. All I find is the end of a familiar blue cloth. Crawling beneath the flames, I follow the cloth like a ribbon, knowing with each turn of it on my hand that it will lead to bitter tears. For this is Tala's turban. "Tala!" I shout. "Ptolemy!"

Sooty smoke dims the air around me, and the heat scorches my lungs with every breath. But I surge forward until I find the barking dog and find my Berber woman on her back in the dirt, her unseeing eyes wide open, staring at the sky. In the cradle of her tattooed arms . . . I find a broken boy.

Not my boy. *No.* No, this cannot be Ptolemy. I curse my lying eyes, for my little boy, *my* little boy, has always been so perfectly formed. This little boy's arms bend in ways they should never bend. His legs are shattered, splintered bones bloody and exposed. And his little lips, that precious mouth that has kissed me so fondly, are caked with dirt and stretched open in wordless agony like a frozen scream.

But I scream for him. Oh, I scream.

Falling to my knees, throwing myself over his body, I scream his name again and again. My son will not answer. Perhaps he cannot answer. He is trampled and bloody in more places than I can count. Choking on sobs and smoke, I'm afraid to touch him, afraid to hurt him more than he has been hurt. I fear he is far beyond pain now. He doesn't feel the bones piercing through his flesh or the gush of his life's blood as it stains the earth. I put my hands on his wounds. I *will* my own life force into his body. I call on my *heka* to make him live. I wail to my goddess, for Ptolemy cannot die.

I will do anything for her. *Anything.* But she must help my child.

He is my baby, my precious boy, and this cannot be happening. For if he is dying, then I am dying with him. Let him have my blood, my bones, my blistering flesh . . .

A beam creaks overhead, breaking free of its moorings and crashing down in a spray of sparks. Beyond it, I see Iacentus and his men braving the smoke and flames to get to me. We are all going to burn, I think. We are all going to burn alive. Then something happens to me. In the roaring inferno of my grief, I become a thing apart from myself—convinced I am caught up in some otherworldly lake of fire and I must master myself and my magic to escape it.

Whatever else I do, I will not let my son burn to ash.

Ptolemy will not burn.

I think I see a flash of golden hair. A man with broad shoulders who beats his way through the flames to rescue us. *Helios.* I call to him for help. He sees me and holds out his hand. Fire seeks him out, leaping into his palm.

Except he is not here.

It is not his palm.

It is mine.

The flames are not leaping into his hand. The flames are leaping into *my* hand. I catch fire like a torch, but I do not burn. The fire does not consume me; I consume it. I inhale soot and ash until it is part of my blood. I drink in flame until it licks the inside of me and flares in my eyes. I find the magical core of this fire and catch it between my teeth, sucking in its heat, its luminosity, its sparks and suffocating smoke, making room for it inside me just as my twin once taught me.

Under your skin, between your bones, there's space for other, more fluid things. Like blood. Like heka. *Like fire and wind . . . and love.*

I eat the fire. I swallow it whole, down to the last shining ember. And when it's inside me I stand covered in soot in a blackened stables, with quaking guards and a barking dog.

I grab up the broken body of my son, staggering under his weight.

"Take Tala," I command. "Take Memnon too . . ."

That is the last thing I hear, for all the sound and sensation in the world ebb away. The winds come to me, summoned by the hot tears on my cheeks. I do not hear what my guards shout to one another as they find Memnon, their fallen comrade. I no longer hear the incessant barking of the dog. I only know that they all crowd round me in the circle of my winds as the ash swirls high. And with my son in my arms, I leave that burned-out place, a trail of his precious blood in our wake.

Returning to my house, we are met by my daughter, still wild-eyed but in possession of herself. She has fought her way back from the Rivers of Time and now rushes forward to help me.

We gently lower my son's mangled body to our table in the *tabulinum*. "Oh, oh no, please no," Isidora moans, backing up until her back touches the wall. "Poor little Ptolemy!"

Then someone sends for the king and pulls the curtain shut.

I realize that it is Musa, and remember that we summoned him. Good fortune too, for we need him desperately. The physician examines my son where horse hooves have crushed and broken and left him bloody. Then he says softly, very softly, "Majesty, Prince Ptolemy is dead."

My son is dead. The words are more devastating than any I have ever heard before. The possibility is so horrible, the mere contemplation of them makes me push the words away. It isn't *possible*. Ptolemy kissed me only this morning, boasting about the little bruise he'd taken from another boy's wooden sword. He is badly hurt, but he can't be dead. It's unthinkable. Numbness spreads through my arms and fingers like armor, preventing my fear and horror from breaking through my certainty that my son still lives. "No, you are wrong."

"I'm so sorry," Musa says, with the tenderest sympathy. "But he's gone."

He is trying to say Ptolemy is dead? My son is dead of so many wounds we cannot even know the one that killed him. That is what he is trying to say to me. And though I shudder, I must hear it because I am a mother, and Ptolemy needs me in life or death.

"Reset my son's broken bones," I whisper through lips gone cold.

"Majesty, it will not help him . . ."

"Do as I say! Set the bones." Ptolemy's legs may not heal in this life, but he will need them in the next. If he is dead—but no, he can't be—if he is dead, it is even more important that we do this for him.

The physician doesn't want us to stay in the room while he sets the bones. Musa doesn't want us to see him push and pull at my son's limbs like they were slabs of meat on the butcher's table. Wringing her hands with helplessness at what she foresaw but could not prevent, Isidora seems ready to stand at my side whatever horror will come. But I send Isidora away. She will not see this, but I will not abandon Ptolemy now.

If my little boy must suffer this, I will suffer it with him.

I stay. I watch. I see things that no mother should ever see. I see things and hear sounds that I will never describe to a soul. Things that destroy me. Shatter me.

I am going to fall to pieces. I know it. I didn't cry when they told me that my twin was killed. I did not shed a tear at the death of Ptolemy Philadelphus, after whom my son was named. Never did I lose my composure when I saw Octavia pass into the world beyond. I have borne much with a regal, uplifted chin. I have borne it all under cold, hard armor.

But this I cannot bear.

The moment I breathe too deeply, everything that holds me upright will collapse and I will come tumbling down. So I do not breathe deeply—determined to hold the broken pieces of myself together just long enough to care for my son.

Just long enough for that, I tell myself.

When Musa's grisly work is done, I send slaves scurrying for water. I wash Ptolemy myself. His little hands and feet, still soft and small. The little dimple of his chin. His hair, dark and straight and perfect. Why did I ever insist that it must be curled? If only he would open his eyes, I would never make him curl his hair again . . .

How can this be happening? I loved this boy from the moment he was a flutter in my belly. I dreamed for him such grand dreams. Now all the things I taught him, all the things I wanted for him, all for naught. All the scrapes I kissed, all my worries, and all my love did not keep him safe.

I was to protect him; that was my sacred charge, and here he lies dead in my house while I still breathe. The injustice of it cannot be borne. When I have finished bathing him, tremors build inside me.

My hands shake. Then my arms. Then I quake all the way through to my soul. Excruciating pain breaks through whatever is left of my defenses and it hurtles me into the darkness. My chest tightens.

And from far away, I hear my own keening wail.

My legs fail and I sink to the floor, the world falling beneath me. My ladies rush to attend me where I crouch, dizzied. On my hands and knees, I begin retching and sobbing by turns. When they try to lift me from the ground I slap them away because they cannot help me. They cannot wake me from this nightmare. They cannot make my son breathe again. And that is the only thing I want.

I am still on the floor when Juba bursts in with his men, their boots thundering on the black and white tiles. My husband throws open the curtain and jolts to a stop as if he has crashed, headlong, into a wall of torment. Surely someone has told him. Surely they did not let their king come to see this unprepared. And yet my husband's mouth falls open at the sight of me on the ground.

Then he looks upon our son, and a sound explodes from his lungs—a horrible sound.

I watch those lean legs of his as he comes closer, and I see that they are shaking. He reaches for the sheet of cloth that covers our son's most grievous wounds, and I clasp him at the knees. *"Juba, don't look. Don't!"*

He doesn't listen or perhaps he doesn't hear me. He pulls back the cloth and I feel the shudder that goes through him right to the marrow of my bones. For once, my husband is unable to master himself. "Oh, *gods!*" He cries out again, and again, as if he can summon all the powers on high. He hurls his voice toward the sky as if to command their attention. As if to demand an accounting. *"How? How could this happen?"*

I don't know. The fire. The horses. I shake my head helplessly, still clinging to his knees. I know only that it must be my fault.

SOMEONE sees to it that the stables are searched for survivors. Someone else arranges for the escaped horses to be rounded up and stabled with neighbors, though they do not find my son's magnificent stallion. Sirocco is gone. Stolen, most likely. Stolen from us like the boy who sat astride him like a conqueror.

Someone calls for the *libitinarii*, but I do not want Roman undertakers for my son's funeral. I will have him embalmed in the traditions of Egypt. This is the only decision I make.

In the days following my son's death, Juba and I are both so insensible we frighten our servants. Wisely, they closet my husband in his chambers where he may give private vent to his grief. He is a king and must not be seen this way, even by the household staff.

But I am a mother and I care nothing for that. I sit beside my son's body where he rests in the atrium, his feet to the door. I sit still, staring, hollow. I am emptied of tears. Dried of everything but grief. Sorrow has carved me out again until I am nothing more than a shell. I do not notice the daylight when it comes or goes. I do not eat. I do not drink. I do not sleep.

I am not hungry, for I feed on remorse. I am not thirsty, for I drink from a well of suspicion. I am not tired, for my mind is spinning. I am remembering, reckoning, and burning for revenge.

I should never have brought my son to Rome . . . this festering cesspit that has always meant misery for me and mine. My son was in danger the moment he set foot here, and I didn't safeguard him. What kind of queen am I—what kind of mother am I—when I cannot protect my own children? Isis hid her son in the reeds until he was strong enough to fight for himself. I should have done the same. I have failed in many things, but this is more than failure. It is the damnation of my soul. I feel certain that I have killed my own child. Like Medea, like Hercules, I have killed my own child.

And there can be no redemption for me. I will never forgive

myself. Perhaps that is why I do not want the forgiveness of my goddess, even when I feel her reach for me, *heka* tingling in my fingers and hands. I hesitate to lift my palms to see what Isis is writing in my skin with stinging cuts and slashes. It is only a torment of the flesh that will heal, whereas the agony of my son's death cuts deeper than sinew and bone. These hands of mine were only yesterday bathed in my son's innocent blood and that is why my goddess has come to me, I know. But I let my hands dangle at my side, letting blood drip from the tips of my fingernails until it puddles beneath my chair.

"Mother, you're bleeding!" my daughter says, rushing to me as if she would bandage my wounds. Has my poor Isidora been sitting with me all this time? I do not remember her coming or going, but it is her presence, the tears of grief in her eyes mingled with fear, that makes me lift my arms.

"This is how my goddess spoke to me when I was your age," I say, letting her marvel at the hieroglyphic symbols that engrave themselves in my skin, with bright carnelian blood. Feathers and owls and vultures and twisted wicks. The language of ancient Egypt scrolls over my palms and wrists, blood flowing like ink from a reed pen.

"What does it say?" Isidora asks, and so I read it for her.

I am the Mother of the Dead. Your child will suck at my breast and taste my sweetness. Through me, he will be reborn.

My goddess is salvation. Because of her, death is not the end of all things. She is a goddess of mercy and compassion. She offers me the comfort of knowing that my child will be taken into her loving embrace . . . but how can I rejoice when I know that I will never again have him in mine?

It is on the second night of my vigil that I hear what I think must be another stampede, but is the emperor's men as he comes to darken our door. Augustus has returned from some errand in Ostia, disheveled and unshaven. Someone must have sent word to him because his eyes are bloodshot with a grief he has no right to claim.

Rushing to the side of Ptolemy's bier, he clasps my son's feet, weeping.

I have never seen Augustus *weep* before, not even in the depths of his grief for Octavia. Now I watch him sob. I hear his laments. But they do not reach me. He says something to me. I don't know what. I don't care what he says. I don't care at all. I have no pity for him. I do not bow to him. I do not even stand.

Tearing at his tunic, he cries, "After all they have denied me, how can the gods be so cruel as to take my son?"

My mind cannot turn away from the unspeakable pain my son must have suffered before he died, but Augustus only asks how the gods could take something from *him*. As always, he puts himself at the center of the tragedy. Perhaps that is where he belongs. My voice quavers. "You dare to blame the gods?"

"Who else should I blame?"

My whisper becomes an outraged shout. "It was no bolt of lightning that struck him dead! It wasn't the gods that killed my son. It was you."

His bleak eyes meet mine and he staggers back. "What?"

"My son was *murdered*," I cry rashly. "He was taken from me by your enemies and mine. My son was murdered because of you and what you carved on that accursed altar."

In the face of my rage, Augustus actually softens. "No, Selene. I was told there was a fire. A stampede . . ."

I will not believe it. I know better. I've always known better. "Who started that fire? Who opened the stalls? I saw those horses. Something—*someone*—spooked them."

"The flames could have been started by anything. An overturned lamp . . . the fire must have sent the animals into a panic."

"It was not the fire," I insist. "Where is Memnon's sword? He was never without it. My guards searched the ashes for that sword, but I know they'll never find it. Because someone took it from him. That's why Memnon died with a *dagger* in his hand. He didn't die choking on smoke or dodging the deadly hooves of runaway stallions. He died fighting. He died fighting for Ptolemy."

"Selene—"

"My son was a prince. He was always watched, never alone. They all knew it. All your enemies. All of mine. So they murdered my son's faithful guard and they murdered my Berber woman before they murdered my child. Then they let horses trample the bodies to cover their crime."

Augustus takes my arms and shakes me. "Who would dare?"

Livia. Livia would dare. I want to name her. But this act doesn't bear her signature. Poison is her weapon. She doesn't strike in the open. This act, so haphazard, with so much potential to go wrong, would be the crime of someone far less prudent. Someone who deals in brutality and mayhem. But who?

Tiberius commands men to slaughter on his behalf, but he is painfully cautious and unimaginative. Drusus is bold enough, but would my sister's honor-obsessed husband kill my son? Could Drusus have possibly convinced himself that the only way to restore the Republic was to murder my child?

Surely not.

Then there is Herod. By now he must have surmised that Crinagoras was my agent, my instrument in bringing him low. Herod would want vengeance and has agents in the city . . .

As these thoughts consume me, I cannot make my lips name a culprit, for the moment I do, I will bind myself to fatal revenge. No bond of kinship, no debt of honor, no command of any deity above or below will keep me from dealing bloody justice to the person or persons who did this. It is only this knowledge and the swelling of my throat that keeps me silent.

The emperor strokes my arms. "Oh, my poor Selene. You are searching for villainy . . ."

I shake with denial, my heart filled with guilt and bitter bile. Someone is to blame for this. Someone *must* be to blame for this. It is too unnatural that a child should die before his mother. I can make no sense of it. I will not hear reason. I will not believe that my beloved boy could be taken from us in such an indifferent happenstance as an overturned lamp . . .

Augustus tries to calm me, saying, "No one would dare kill my son."

And thus he repeats the lie, here in Juba's house, once again. My head jerks up and I rake him with a vicious glare. I want to fly at him and tear his face open. I want to make him bleed the way I am bleeding inside, and I scream, "He was not your son!"

The emperor's eyes narrow into slits. I see the danger there, but I do not care. For once, I am reckless. Too consumed with pain to do anything but tell the truth. "He was not your son, you madman. You *madman*! He was mine and Juba's. Now he's dead because you're too vain to admit that you cannot sire a son of your own."

No one has insulted the emperor for a very long time. Certainly none who lived to tell the tale. And my words are more than insult. They are deadly missiles launched from a catapult and they crash into the fiction he has built around himself. He literally shakes from the impact. "Never say that again—"

"Or *what*?" I fling his hands away from me, despising his touch. My hair, loosened from its adornments, flies wild in my face and I feel the storm inside me rise hot with fury. If I were in my right mind, I would remember how much I still have to lose, but I am broken free of my moorings. Now I am all avenging shadow. I know how to wound him. I know better than anyone. And I *want* to wound him. "What will you do? Will you rape me again? Will you raze my kingdom to the ground? Or will you kill my daughter too? You fiend! What will you do?"

When he only blinks, I rave on, spittle flying from my lips. "The only thing you won't do is kill me. No. You will shove me down just to see if I can stand up again. You will destroy the world and make me watch. That is what you have always enjoyed. From the day you captured me, you have gloried in tormenting me. You delight in forcing me to tears as you rob me of everything and everyone I have ever loved. That is your monstrous, sadistic thrill. So what will you do to me now? What will you take from me next? Make your threat plain."

My heart thunders in my chest and my fists clench at my sides, ready for anything. Yet I do not anticipate the softness of his hand on my cheek. "How wrong you are, my Cleopatra. What I wanted most was to give you everything . . ."

He believes it. He believes it with all his twisted heart and soul. Everything he knows about himself and the legend he created depends upon this belief. And in this moment, I want nothing so much as to strip him of it. It is the lie of his lifetime . . . and mine. It is the lie that killed my son. And I will not have it.

"I am *not* your Cleopatra," I say, forcing the words out calm and clear. "Listen well, you petty, *pathetic* man. I am not your goddess. I am not your lover. I am not your bride. And I am not your Cleopatra."

His hand slips to my neck in warning, as if he would choke me. Perhaps I have goaded him to end my life and give me a merciful escape from this pain.

Alas, his fingers do not squeeze. "You've lost your wits, my poor girl . . ."

"I am not your poor girl. I have never been your *anything*."

"That's a lie," he says, forcing me to look into his eyes. "You bound yourself to me before I ever touched you. When I was dying, you nursed me back to health. Did you not offer yourself to me during the sacred Mysteries at Eleusis? Did you not call upon the gods to bring about a Golden Age in my name? You and I are two parts of a single story. Deny it."

My lips part to scream my denial. To swear that I have never felt anything but hatred for him. To vow that I am bound to him by nothing. But I catch a glimpse of my daughter in the doorway, pale with fright. By the gods, she looks like *him*. Small ears, a delicate little nose . . .

If he is a part of her, is he not also a part of me? I have never loved him, but I have felt more for him than hatred. I have felt pity, gratitude, and even awe. I remember all the times I used his weakness. I have used him to gain power and wealth. I have used him to kill. And now it has come full circle. First, because of him, I brought death to my mother. Now, through him, I brought death to my son.

All along, I've told myself that my hatred for the emperor was something I hid in my *khaibit*, my shadow. But he *is* my shadow. The emperor is a reflection of everything that is weak and wicked inside me. And this is what we have wrought together. A dead boy, his little bones crushed under the weight of our ambitions. And a trembling girl in the doorway, her eyes wide with fright at our discord.

"Deny it!" Augustus cries, clasping me hard.

I cannot deny it. We *are* bound. We are a curse to each other and the world. Unless someone puts a stop to it we will both live on long after everyone else we love is destroyed. I must stop it. I must make an end to him, even if it means my own end . . .

And in that moment, I decide that I must kill him.

It is as if Isidora has already seen me do it, for she rushes to my side, trying to break us apart. "Please! Please, stop!"

Then her pleas are cut off by another voice, low and menacing. "Get out."

It is Juba in the archway, his swollen eyes dark with fury. For a moment, no one moves. No one can believe that the king should speak to his emperor this way. And yet Juba lifts a hand and points one of those long elegant fingers directly at Augustus. "*Get out!*"

The cold leaches into the emperor's hands. "This is none of your concern, Juba."

Juba advances upon us with clenched fists and murder in his stare. "I swear by Jupiter himself that if you don't take your hands off my wife—"

"You *threaten* me?" Augustus's eyes dart to the door where his praetorians stand, ready to kill at his command.

But Juba is beyond reason. He grabs the emperor by the tunic, tearing him off me, nearly lifting him from the floor. "Must I *throw* you out, damn you? Because I will, Caesar, by all the gods, I will. I will *hurl* you from my doorway into the street."

The praetorians rush in, swords drawn, ready to cut Juba limb from limb and I act by instinct to defend my husband. My hand flies up, fingers extending with *heka* as a torrent of wind races up my arm and blasts out of me. But it isn't wind.

It is a ball of fire . . .

Strabo tries to duck out of the way but it catches the emperor's chief praetorian by the shoulder, sending his cape into flames. Strabo screams as it catches fire to his hair. One of his comrades tries to beat down the flames while the others crouch down in loose battle formation and I send another stream of fire after them, an explosion of blinding flame.

On my arm is a birthmark in the shape of a sail, a sign of the wind. Fire has never been my power. That is my twin's magic, not mine. How has such a magic come to invest itself inside me and how long has it been there? There is little time to wonder. Wild-eyed and terrified of my powers, the men scramble to their feet and flee, abandoning their emperor in my clutches. And I am still determined to kill him. It is Helios's rage that rises up inside me like the flames I have swallowed. My twin's burning, murderous certainty. The same certainty that was in his eyes the night he came to kill the emperor in Greece. I stopped him then, but now I cannot remember why . . .

The emperor doesn't see the danger in my eyes. He does not see that the moment my husband releases him, I am going to wrap my arms around him and incinerate him with every last drop of *heka* in my blood. He does not see it, but Isidora does. She grabs my still flaming hands, shrieking, "Stop! Do you think Ptolemy can't see us? He has yet to enter the afterworld and have his heart weighed against a feather. Would you make his heart heavier with sorrow to see us tear one another apart?"

At her words, Juba releases the emperor—flings him away—but the damage has been done. Augustus eyes me and my husband as if we were hunting dogs gone rabid. We all stand there, heaving breaths, the air so charged that any spark may bring more violence.

Isidora sinks to her knees before the emperor. "Forgive us, Caesar. We are mortals and we suffer as mortals, forgetting ourselves in our grief. We haven't your strength to accept wounds with stoicism. Please come back another day when we can learn from your example how to mourn without causing distress, for we are all your children and we need our father's guidance . . ."

Our *father's* guidance. I am struck dumb by her careful choice of words. She knows. She knows Augustus is the man who put her in my womb. He wants to be bound to me, and Dora now offers herself as the strongest tie. He is moved by her, I can tell. And how could he not be? She is heart-wrenchingly beautiful. He could never look into her tear-filled blue eyes and not want her for his own. My Isidora is not proud or guarded like Julia. She will not hold herself back from him. As always, she offers her whole heart. And I am afraid he will eat it raw.

Thirty-eight

I do not know what Augustus will do now. He leaves my house wide-eyed and shaken. Perhaps he realizes that he came as close to death at my hands as he has ever come. If he is finally afraid of me, it will go better for everyone. But he is not the only one left in fear. Our servants are too afraid to attend us. The world is upended and our place in it uncertain.

Since the day I met Juba, I have goaded him to rebellion against the emperor. Now he has done it. We have all said things that cannot be unspoken and done things that cannot be undone. My husband has seen me use magic, but never has he seen me throw fire. And yet I think he is more shocked at his own behavior than mine. As he slumps against a marble pillar, I see the devastation written all over him.

What have I done to him? I judged Herod a monster for tearing his family apart, but look what I have done to mine. When my husband rises again, he grips his tunic, snapping it straight. Then, with a look of grim purpose, he storms through the scorched archway toward our front gate.

I follow, calling after him, "What do you mean to do?"

"I am going after him," Juba says.

"To what purpose?" I demand to know. "To what possible end?"

Juba grips the iron bars, his biceps tight and trembling, his breath puffing in the cold air under an overcast sky. "I don't know."

"Please don't chase Augustus. If anything, we should lock the gates against him and his men."

"Lock the gates against me, if you like, but I'm leaving."

I hold the shattered remains of myself lest I fly apart. "And where would you go?"

"To hunt down that horse," he says with clenched jaw. "When I find that stallion, I'll sacrifice him and bury him with the boy."

My husband wants vengeance too, and if he cannot have it against Augustus, he'll have it from the stallion. I know what Juba is thinking. He is thinking that this animal threw our son. That the majestic horse trampled our little Ptolemy beneath his hooves. So eager to find blame, I should think the same. But I remember, "Ptolemy loved him, Juba. He loved that horse. Let Sirocco go. I beg of you."

The king turns to me, his eyes bleak as the winter sky. I think he will strike me. I think he will rage as I have never seen him rage. Instead, he shrugs his assent. "As you wish, Selene. Who am I to deny you?"

With that, he storms away into some dark recess of our house.

I cannot go after him. I have no right.

Instead, I go back inside and place my cloak over my son. Ptolemy does not feel the cold anymore, but I tuck it under his chin as if he were merely asleep. Then a whimper and a howl cuts through the winter air. It is Ptolemy's dog keeping vigil by his bier, licking bloodied blistered paws that I realize only now were burned in the fire at the stables. The creature is skittish, shying away. She was faithful to my son. She was there with him at the end. My son loved this dog and everything he loved is now precious to me, so I stroke the animal's neck to soothe it while the hound blows air through its nostrils in distress.

Dora stoops beside me and tears the hem off her garment to make a bandage. I help her wind the cloth round the dog's paws and tie it tight. Then Dora clutches at the collar of gold amulet round her neck and declares, "Augustus will forgive you. I have seen it. He will forgive you anything."

"I don't care if he does," I say.

It is Juba's forgiveness I want and I do not deserve it, so I will have to content myself with vengeance. "You saw it happen in your divination bowl, didn't you? You saw your brother's death."

Dora nods once, sadly. Perhaps if I had allowed her to work her magic, she may have seen it long before it happened. When there might have been time to save him. The thought hammers another nail of guilt into me. "Did you see who started the fire, Isidora?"

Tears spill over her lashes. "No. I only saw the flames and the stampede . . ."

"Fetch your divination bowl. I'll give you my *heka*. I'll hold your hand and pull you back if the currents of the magic carry you too far. I want you to look into the Rivers of Time and tell me who did this to Ptolemy."

She rests her hand atop mine. "The Rivers of Time flow into the future. They have never shown me the past." It is another crushing disappointment. She must see it on my face. "Could the wizard see the past? Could my uncle Philadelphus? If they did, maybe I can too. I'll try."

"No." I remember with bitter certainty. "They did not see the past. Forget I ever asked such a thing. And when we go back home, things will be different between us, that much I vow."

"But I'm not going back," she reminds me gently, as if I'm addled. "Don't you remember that I'm to marry King Archelaus and be Queen of Cappadocia?"

"That's all done now, Isidora. You will never live anywhere but where you wish to live. You will never marry unless you wish to. And if you become a queen, you will be queen in your own right, for you are now the sole heir to Mauretania."

IN the seventy days it takes for my son to be properly embalmed, my Roman sisters flock to me. First the Antonias, then Julia and Marcella too. For my sake, they do not quarrel. They come carrying garlands and elaborate candelabra and vases of oils and ointments for my dead son. They whisper words of sympathy, their faces grave. Minora tells me that I am still young enough to have another child, and I forgive her, because I know she only says such a thing in a spirit of compassion.

The truth is that I am barren and, even if I were not, my husband recoils anytime I come near him, a thing that makes my pain deeper and more desolate by far. My husband loved Ptolemy as much as I did. He is the only one who can possibly know the loss I feel. He is the only person who could possibly understand there is an emptiness in me where Ptolemy used to be and it can never be filled. If there were any comfort to be had, I would find it in Juba's arms. But I know we will never be happy again.

The soul of my dead son is now in my keeping and I can think of little else. I cannot even grieve properly for Tala, my friend who served me so long and so well. Nor can I properly grieve for Memnon, my brave champion. I am too lost, adrift, and broken.

My sisters pray with me, invoking my forbidden goddess, but my prayers to Isis are bitter. My heart is hard. I want the darkest magic to fill my being and I am bewildered that Isis should allow the days to grow warmer when my son is so cold. How can flowers blossom when my world is so gray?

I am resentful on the day Minora comes to my house carrying baskets of pink posies and red roses for my rooms, because she believes their brightness will cheer me. But she cannot know that the scent of roses will always remind me of the birth of my son, and the way I awakened to see him the first time, with that perfume in my nostrils.

She is not alone. Her children are in tow, and her husband, Drusus, is with her too. Ptolemy's dog springs up at the sight of the tall military general, growling with such ferocity that I want to command my guards to throw Drusus out and slam the gates shut. Instead, I tell a servant to take the dog, then rise from my couch to face the newest Consul of Rome.

Filled with suspicion, I am brought up short by what Drusus holds in an outstretched hand.

"I don't think you'll remember," Drusus says, offering a boy's golden torque to me. "But I wore this many years ago when I rode in the Trojan Games. Your twin saved my life that day. I've always kept this torque as a lucky token and a remembrance of Helios. Now I give it to you to bury with your son because he should have lived to earn one of his own."

I'm moved by the sincerity with which Drusus says these words, his voice choked with emotion. For years, no one in the imperial family has dared to mention my twin by name. Now Drusus dares. And with these words, he reminds me that he is not only Livia's son, but my brother in marriage, and a boy I knew well. That doesn't mean he is innocent, but if he is guilty, he is the most audacious fiend ever born . . .

"Take it, Selene," Minora says, her eyes shining with love and admiration for her husband's tender gesture. In the crook of her arm, she cradles little Claudius, their youngest. When I look at them together, a family in the truest sense of the word, I wonder how it is I can suspect Drusus of treachery. He is beloved by everyone. By his wife. By the Romans. By the Gallic tribes he ruled as governor. He is even loved by some of the Germans whose country he has ravaged. He is a hard soldier, battle-tested, and he is a canny politician; there burns in him a bright ambition, paired with exquisite charm. I must ask myself, is he the best of the Claudians or is he their cleverest villain yet?

I don't know. I can't know. So I take the gift and thank him gladly for it. I bid him fond farewell, for he is shortly to leave again on campaign in Germania. I embrace him, kissing both cheeks with all the affection I have conceived for him over the years. Then, when Drusus is gone, I take the token he has given me, and using a silk cloth, I rub the oils of his fingertips from the gold. At the small altar in my home, I offer this cloth to the fire, drawing the *heka* from my blood where it boils blackest.

And I intone a dark curse upon him.

I do not care what the curse claws out of me, for I am already hollow. And so I speak a spell that any evil he has done to me or mine be revisited upon him. If he stands innocent, let Drusus find glory and happiness in this world, but if he has stolen my son from me, *by the power of Isis,* let him meet with painful justice.

ONE gray afternoon Julia finds me sifting through the ashes in the burned-out stables, searching for Memnon's missing sword. I wave her away, telling her that her feet will get dirtied with soot and her fine stola may snag and tear on broken timber.

"This stable should be knocked down," she insists, flinging herself onto the makeshift seat of a broken beam. "Juba should order it."

But Juba is not giving orders. My husband is like a shade in the house. I sense his presence, but he is never there when I look for him. He doesn't leave his chambers unless he is sure not to see me. So I make excuses. "He is occupied with other matters."

"What other matters? He must have told you that my father has commanded him to return to Mauretania . . ."

My husband has not told me, but I am not surprised. "So we are banished?" I ask, seeing a glint of metal and stooping to find only the remains of an ornamented bridle.

Julia's lips tighten. "Not you, certainly. Only Juba. And not officially. It's only that my father commands your husband to set sail before the Lemuria."

This is more bad news, compounded by ominous meaning, since the Lemuria is a springtime festival in remembrance of the dead. "How did you learn this, Julia?"

"I told you before, I have my own partisans. I have spies amongst my father's secretaries and messengers. For the sake of my sons, I make it my business to know what Caesar does . . . That is how I know that my father's chief praetorian is badly burned, though I do not know how it happened. I know King Juba has fallen from favor but I don't know how that came about either. But, as always, you do . . ."

"Juba quarreled with Augustus," I say, using my fingers to wipe clean the heat-warped metal bit with a sharp edge.

Julia's gaze is just as sharp. "I suppose we both know that quarrel has been a long time in coming."

She is never quite what she pretends to be. She is not merely the flighty girl in need of censure and a strong hand. She is not merely a shallow hedonist who basks in the good fortune to have been born the daughter of Caesar. She has always hidden a keen mind and a depth of spirit. She is not blind to her father's madness. Did she guess that his love for my son was at the expense of her sons?

My hand clenches hard on the warped metal as the horrifying realization washes over me. There is no one who would have more cause than Julia to kill my Ptolemy. The idea leaves me gasping for breath, my heart galloping in my chest. Could it be possible that I see treachery when I look into the eyes of my first, and best, friend? My bloodless lips begin to stutter what I do not even want to contemplate. "Did you—have you some involvement—do you know something about Ptolemy's death?"

She tilts her head. "Oh, Selene. You can't think—"

"*Sweet Isis*, swear it was not you!"

If Julia were guilty, I couldn't bear it. I would rather be dead than live with the knowledge of such betrayal. But I would kill her first. I would kill her where she stands. I would kill them all . . .

I feel the pain in my hands and think it is my goddess again carving into my flesh. When I look down, I see that I *am* bleeding, but only because I have cut myself on the warped metal.

Julia sees it too, and her eyes fill with worry.

"Watch and listen," she says softly, taking the metal from me and making a swift slash across her palm, opening a wound. At the sight of her red blood mixing with mine on the metal edge, I start to shout my protest, but she hushes me. "Pay attention now. I am showing you that when you are hurt, I am hurt. I am showing you that I could never wound you without wounding myself. Could you ever bring yourself to harm *my* sons?"

I am, in this moment, a danger to all of Rome. There is in me a fiery avenging spirit that desires nothing more than murder. If need be, I would slaughter Livia and her sons. I would slay the emperor and his minions. I would bring to the world not a Golden Age, but a world of carnelian blood that turns the Tiber red. There is something, *someone*, in me that would destroy anything that remains of the emperor's legacy. Does that include his grandsons?

No. I am not a murderer of children. That is the only virtue I still cling to. I exhale, relieved to speak the truth. "Never, Julia. I would never harm your children."

She nods. "It is the same for me and you must know that. You are the only person in my entire life who has been true to me. I swear to you by my blood, by Isis, Juno, and every other god and goddess I know. I did not hurt your son. Nor would I stand by and let someone hurt him. You know my heart, Selene. You *know* me."

She laces her bloody fingers with mine and I wince in pain at her touch. But she's right. I do know her. I know her heart, for it is constant, no matter what she might say. Julia is no murderer of children. She is no monster. I am the monster. Grief has made me hate the whole world and suspect even those I hold most dear. I begin to tremble. "I'm so sorry. I am going mad. I am going mad!"

Julia pulls me into a forgiving embrace, stroking my back to soothe me. "It only feels that way. Take solace that this is the worst you will ever feel. When my baby died, I told myself that nothing could ever hurt more. That if I could stand this, I could stand anything . . ."

"That is you," I whisper. "Not me. I can't do this. I can't."

"Yes, you can. For your daughter, you will. What other choice do you have?"

No other choice at all . . .

Julia's forgiveness calms me. Her strength keeps me standing. Her hand keeps mine steady. And when the moment has passed and I can stand on my own, she asks, "What will you do about Juba?"

"I will go with him," I say, for in that, there is also no other choice.

Julia nods, knowing this is farewell. There is nothing more we need say, and we clasp our hands even tighter, quietly bleeding into each other as we have done in one way or another from the very start.

* * *

ON the day of the Floralia, prostitutes dance in the streets of Rome, drinking and celebrating. I do not celebrate the rebirth of the world, but I acknowledge it. The world is changed. For me, everything is changed. Rome will always be the place my son died and now that the embalmers have finished their work, I cannot wait to leave. But there is one thing I must do before I go.

I make a visit to the emperor.

My last visit, I vow.

This will be the last time I make my way up the Palatine Hill. The last time I stand at these gates. The last time I inhale this distinct scent of bay as it floats down from the laurel trees on either side of the entryway. The last time I will climb the stairs of the emperor's house and enter his private sanctuary . . .

But at the foot of the staircase, the emperor's wife blocks my way. Beneath her severely conservative hairstyle, her eyes narrow. "Augustus will not grant you an audience. After what you and your husband did, how dare you even show your face here?"

Just the sight of Livia gives rise to a primal hunger for vengeance. I do not know if she stands guilty of my son's death, but my fingertips grow warm with the desire to burn her to ash and then call down my winds and scour the earth of her. I am holding myself back from such violence only by the thinnest of threads.

Perhaps she knows it, because she takes a breath and stiffens her spine. She is afraid of me and she should be. Restraining the surge of fury in my blood, I tilt my head. "You stand before me while my son lies cold and dead, and you ask how *I* dare? You are braver than I ever gave you credit for . . ."

"I did nothing to that boy," she vehemently declares.

She has never been eager to exonerate herself before, no matter what I have accused her of, so perhaps she is telling the truth. I do not trust myself to judge. I do not trust myself, but there are other darker powers that I now put my faith in. All at once, I lunge at her, snagging my fingers in the knot of hair above her brow.

"What are you doing?" she shrieks, trying to pull free of me. But she is an old woman now and I have the strength of a mother lioness. I yank hard on her head, driving her to her knees, tearing her gray hair out by the roots. Then I hold a fistful of it in her face, knowing I will make a curse of it. "What am I doing? I'm making you a vow, you cold, grasping bitch! If my son died for your ambitions, you will suffer. You will suffer what I have suffered. You will lose your sons too, one way or another. And you will die, unloved and alone. You will *rot* like carrion left for vultures, stinking of all your vile deeds."

She gasps, clutching at her scalp, her eyes bulging. "I did nothing to your son . . ."

I tuck her hair into a pouch on my belt, then leave Livia there, stepping over her to march up the stairs.

"I did nothing to him!" she cries after me.

Fortunately, the praetorians do not stop me. They do not even look me in the eye. The emperor should have left orders to refuse me entry, but his vanity prevents him from guarding himself from me. He will not kill me and he will not defend himself from me because to do either of those things is to end it all.

He will not end it. But I will.

Stepping into his private study, his so-called *Syracuse*, I brace myself for the mocking golden eyes of the statue, *Fortuna*. Instead, I find that Augustus has turned that fickle goddess to the wall and draped her in black. The emperor is also draped in dark cloth that hangs on his wiry frame in a way that makes him look old and tired. He hasn't shaved yet today and I see how white his whiskers have become. They emphasize puffy jowls that give away his age. He was never truly the vigorous young soldier he is depicted as in his statues, but he never seemed so old as he does now.

Perhaps he does not hear Livia below us, still shrieking her innocence. Instead, he stares out the window, overlooking the garden where my son once played with the children of his household. I can imagine the laughter of the boys. I can imagine glancing into the yard and seeing my son playing with them. That is why we brought him to Rome, after all.

The emperor must be thinking the same. "Ptolemy will be borne by the greatest men in Rome for his funeral," he murmurs. "I will carry his bier. Tiberius, Drusus, and Iullus have all agreed to take part in the procession."

"Oh, have they?" My son was the Prince of Mauretania. He should have been Pharaoh of Egypt. He might have even been the next Emperor of Rome. He died too soon for us to know how brightly his star could burn. I would give him a grand funeral. I would have him carried in an elaborate coach, so laden down with jewels that it must be pulled by a hundred white mules. I would see mourners by the thousands at the sides of the road. But I will do none of these things because I will not give my enemies anything more of my son.

Certainly I will not have my son carried through the streets of Rome where Livia may silently gloat over his death. "There will be no procession," I declare.

"There *must* be a procession," the emperor insists. "If the people are to accept that a foreign prince will be buried in my mausoleum, they must see the imperial family honor him in the streets."

He wishes to have my son beside him for all eternity? Augustus banishes Juba, but wants my boy in his tomb. I should be angrier at this revelation, for the emperor's love for Ptolemy is narcissism. It is vainglorious folly. What he mourns most is the loss of his own legacy, his own glory. But he *does* mourn. The human part of me that survives my sorrow recognizes his suffering. And insofar as Augustus loved my son, it is no longer in me to be cruel to him.

It is no longer in me to be anything to him.

"Ptolemy is not Roman," I say. "I will do for him what was done for Alexander. I will wrap him in sheets of gold pounded so thin that we will see his face through the covering. I will put amulets in his hands and over his heart and tokens of remembrance in his sarcophagus to take with him into the afterworld. I will fill his tomb with wax *shabti* figures, to go ahead of him and herald him to the gods so they know the spirit of a great prince is to join them. But my son will be buried on a hill in Mauretania where I built a tomb for my family. There I have placed statues of my loved ones so that their spirits may watch over him. And I will visit him and perform the rites that will sustain him in the afterlife."

Augustus turns angry eyes my way. "You mean to take Ptolemy to some remote, inaccessible tomb in a faraway, barbarous frontier where I have vowed never to set foot?"

"Oh, yes. I am going to take my children and leave you to the disaster that you've created, as I should've done all those years ago."

He grinds his teeth. "This is a disaster of your making as well as mine. Did you not curse me to this fate? Did you not speak the words that threatened my heirs would fall before me if I did not appease Isis?"

"Those were the words of a goddess."

"A goddess who let Ptolemy be struck down!"

That is hard to hear. It is a forbidden thought I have not allowed myself. A bitter thought that puts doubt in my heart. Isis did not protect my child. She did not save my child. I don't know why; I will never know why.

He thinks he does. "Your goddess took him because he was my son. It is her curse. After all the ways in which I have sought to appease her, this is how I am repaid? I am done with Isis, that faithless Egyptian whore."

I stand there swallowing my bile, searching my faith. Here I stand, a child of Isis. Still her champion. I should defend her, but I fail her in this, as I have failed her in so many ways.

"Let Ptolemy be buried with me," Augustus says, his voice turning from anger to pleading. "He was my only son."

"You have two sons, Caesar. Their names are Gaius and Lucius—"

"You will not leave me, damn you!" For a moment I think he will strike me, but he knows better than to test my strength. Instead, he reaches for my heartstrings. "You know that I am surrounded by enemies and rivals. You would not leave me to a pack of jackals, with no one to trust."

"Trust Julia. Take her for a partner." He snorts as if the idea is ridiculous fantasy, so I strive to convince him. "Julia's interests align with yours. Cleave to her and her sons as if they are the only family you will ever have—because that is true. You will need them to hold the Claudians at bay. Treat them well and your love will be repaid a thousand times. Help Gaius and Lucius become strong men who will honor a Golden Age."

"You aren't leaving me. This is about Juba, isn't it? You wish to make a grand gesture for his sake. Fine, then. Have your way. The King of Mauretania can stay in Rome as long as he likes so long as you take your place at my side."

"My place is with him, in Mauretania, and I am going home . . ."

He shakes his head with furious denial. "This does not end it, Selene."

"It ended the moment my son took his last breath."

"We have a daughter together too."

"No. We have nothing together. Let there be an end of it between us, you once said to me. I obey that command."

"Now I command you to stay. Obey me or—"

"Do you remember you once wanted to bring me with you to Parthia?" I show him the palm of my hands, which have so often told our future. "You asked me to bury the armies of your enemies in sand. I said I could not do it and you called me a liar. Perhaps you were right. Think what you have seen me do with these hands. Think of the winds I have commanded. Think of the fire. *Think* for one moment of whose armies I might bury if provoked. I am taking my family to Mauretania and you will leave us in peace. If you do not, if you send ships after us, I'll send your navy to the bottom of the sea."

I hear the catch in his breath, see the whites of his eyes as fury overtakes him. But he is considering my words. He is wondering what I would dare and how he might stop me. "You cannot do it, Selene. No more than your mother could. If your mother had that power, she would have won the war. If you had that power, you would be in your mother's place now, the Queen of Kings, the Empress of the World . . ."

"Are you so sure that I'm not?"

His brow furrows in confusion.

I don't wait for him to figure it out on his own. "You have turned to me, again and again, to help you in your quest for power. I have nursed you. I have nurtured you. I have helped guide you and curbed your worst instincts. I have invoked gods on your behalf. You have prospered through me and through everything you have taken from me. Like Isis, *I* am your throne. It has been thus since the moment I discovered I had the power to destroy you . . . and chose not to. I was born to bring about a Golden Age, and through you, I may still do it. So has it never occurred to you that *I* am the ruler and *you* are the vassal?"

He startles visibly, a hand lifting shakily as if to slap me. We are face-to-face, here in this room where I once cowered at his feet. Where he once grabbed me and shook me until I was weak with fear. He doesn't grab me this time. He does not dare. Once, I imagined we were two towering colossi on either side of a road, but we are both cracked and crumbling now. He is old and tired and broken. And I—I am divided against myself. Some part of me is determined to kill him, here and now. But the other side knows it is enough to ensure that he will never harm me or my loved ones again.

"You started a war with my mother," I remind him. "But not only her. You made war on Isis too and called it a just war. *Justum bellum*, you said. She told you the war was not over and so it is not. She will win. Isis always wins. That is why I am leaving and I am never coming back. I will never again answer your summons. Not for any threat. Not for any promises of riches or glory. This is the end."

He stares, but nothing changes behind his gray eyes. He doesn't accept what I'm saying. "You have run from me before, Selene. You'll come back."

"No. You will never see me again."

The flat finality of my words, spoken like an oracle, finally reaches him. He stares, rattled as I have never seen him. He looks as if he is shrinking into himself, falling into a pit of inner blackness, and though I should let him, I offer him one last chance at grace. "Caesar, if you ever cared for me, if there was ever a moment of genuine feeling in your heart, if I have ever pleased you, if you ever pitied me or admired me or wished to give me or my children anything, give me this: *Let me go.*"

When I say it, he nearly crumbles before me. His face screws up and then the words burst out of him like a plea. "I *can't*! You are my Cleopatra and I am your Caesar."

Perhaps I should remind him that Julius Caesar was parted from Cleopatra, that Aeneas was cleaved from Dido, that Cyrene lived apart from Apollo . . . but these are all dangerous pretensions. Bitter loss has taught me that there is peril behind wearing masks.

In the oldest Egyptian stories, Ra was the king of all gods and creation, but Isis held power over him because she learned his secret name. The name the emperor was born with is no secret, but it holds just as much power. He is not wily Julius Caesar. He is not pious Aeneas. He is not sun-drenched Apollo. He is not Set, the evil god of the desert. He is not Jason . . . and I am not Medea.

I lean forward, and speak the truth. "Hear me because I am going to tell you who I am and who you are. You are Gaius Octavius Thurinus and I am Cleopatra Selene of House Ptolemy. You built an empire, and I fed it. This is our story. The whole of our story. And this is how it ends."

PART FOUR

THE BREAD

Thirty-nine

I do not stay to watch Augustus suffer or to see him draw himself back together. I stay only long enough to meet his eyes one final time. Mine, green as the Nile. His, a stormy gray. I will not forget his eyes and he will not forget mine. But we understand each other now as we have never done before.

He sees in me not only the cowering girl who has always made common cause with him, but also her fiery twin—the one who would burn everything he has built to ash. I am dangerous to him, and for the first time, he knows it.

While I draw breath, he will never again threaten Juba's life with impunity. Nor will he take my daughter from me unless she wishes to go. That much we understand. And so I leave him.

I leave him atop the Palatine Hill and cross the bridge to Tiber Island. I cross again to my home with the black and white tiles where my children threw stones from the balcony, and I do not look back.

We hoist black sails in Ostia and carry our son's sarcophagus to Mauretania. We make harbor in the shadow of our lighthouse and my unfinished Iseum. We are met by our royal guard, mounted on horseback. Beneath helmets adorned with smart plumes that bob up and down as they ride, the riders break into two ranks, forming an honor guard for our sad procession.

King Juba is grim-faced, his back stiff, his gaze so faraway that I'm unsure if he even cares that we have at last returned to our own kingdom. But I am comforted. My son died in Rome, but he was born here in Mauretania. He played here on these shores, collecting rounded pebbles from the beach. There, in the market, where Tala took him to taste honey and laugh with merriment at the actors in the streets. This city, Iol-Caesaria, is another child that Juba and I birthed together.

For that alone, I would hold it always close to my heart.

Our court is in mourning. We give Tala's embalmed body over to her son so that he may bury her in the traditions of the Berbers. Ziri—or Mazippa as he is now called—and his people will paint her in red ochre and make a tomb for her in the side of a mountain. I take upon myself the expense for it. In honor of Tala, I also give her son a royal grant to vast plantations, making him the greatest Berber landholder in Mauretania. He will always have a place in our court, I assure him. Always a seat in our council chambers or at our table. Where he has no mother now, I bid Mazippa to consider me in her place, if he should feel I am worthy, but I know I am not.

In memory of Memnon, our Macedonian guards cut their hair in solidarity and sorrow. I commission for Memnon's tomb a new sword, for he should never be without one, in life or death. Then I begin to make arrangements to return him to Egypt, from whence he came.

It is then that Lady Circe tells me that Memnon once asked her to put his last wishes in ink, for he himself could neither read nor write. She shows me the parchment, where he made his mark, a crude blot of ink. And there I see written that Memnon wished to be buried wherever I am buried, in Mauretania or Egypt, for he would never willingly leave his post.

These words would break me if I were not already broken.

On the day of our son's funeral, our people line the streets from dusk to dawn to pay tribute to their lost prince. For Ptolemy, they give coins and silver jewelry, fine woven carpets and polished furniture, little ivory toys and silken clothes to carry with him into the afterlife. They loved their prince. Truly, they loved him.

We carve his name where the gods may see it. We perform all the sacred rites. And we seal him in his tomb with half the wealth of our kingdom. I do not count it much of a sacrifice, for we have already lost our greatest treasure . . .

At every step of the funeral and the feast that follows, Juba is at my side, stoic and silent. When we return to the palace, he takes my dazed daughter to her chambers, brushes her tears away with his thumbs, and tucks her into her bed as if she were still a small girl. He does all that is expected of him as a father. All that could be desired from a king. But there is nothing of a husband in him.

He does not seek comfort in my company. He does not speak to me. He cannot even look at me, and I fear whatever was between us died with our son. When I wake in the morning, Juba is already holding court. When I go to meet him in the stables before his daily rides, he is already gone. When I offer to dine with him, his slaves tell me he has retired to bed. We live in the same palace, but slip past each other like dim spirits in the necropolis.

I think we will live like this the rest of our lives, for it is all smashed.

All ruined.

Everything destroyed.

I must know how I swallowed a fire and why sparks now snap to my fingertips whenever I desire them to. If I can throw fire now, what can that mean? I think it means I imagined Helios always in my darkest moments, always coming to my rescue when no one else would. But perhaps I was always my own rescuer and I have survived everything on my own.

Who, then, is Horus the Avenger? A legend or *lemur*?

I will never know the truth of it. But if I have conjured up Helios in my sorrow, then why isn't he here now? I have never suffered more than with the loss of my son. So if Helios is only a comfort that I give to myself, then why isn't he here?

Perhaps, he *is* here. My mage once said that if he was alive anywhere in the world, Helios was alive in me. I feel him inside me even now. Perhaps when the Romans said he died in Thebes all those years ago, he did. If that is true, Augustus has nearly died more than once at my hands. If it was not Helios who nearly assassinated the emperor during the Eleusinian Mysteries . . . then it was me.

I remember the night of Agrippa's funeral, I watched the crows fight over a scrap of meat and felt anger flare up inside me. The hut of Romulus burned before dawn. I think it was my doing. I think there has been a war inside my soul between an avenging sun god who wants nothing more than destruction and the moon goddess who pines to bathe the world in peaceful splendor.

If my wizard were alive, I would put these questions to him. I would demand that he answer them. I would demand that he tell me the truth, and I would stay with him until I could understand and believe it. But the wizard is long dead. So when the moon has risen, I go to the island upon which my Iseum is being built, and I reach for his essence, for the wisdom he gifted me here.

Thinking I am alone, I light candles in the nearly finished inner chamber and leave my tears where masons will build the altar.

How it enrages me when my search for spiritual guidance is interrupted by Publius Antius Amphio.

"I beg your pardon, Majesty," he says, from the dim recess of an archway. "I was only just told that you had come to inspect the Iseum. I had hoped you would come in the daylight."

He looks as if he had been abed and roused by panicked workmen before rushing here with his toga askew. The end of it trails on the ground when he bows. Since, in all the time I have known him, he has never made any real pretense of respect, I worry what bad news he might have for me.

Gathering up my candles, I take in the work he has completed. The piers of the Iseum look to be tall and strong. The stone walls look to be solid, tightly constructed, perfectly in order. Above us, the impressive dome has been laid over a temporary olive-wood frame. But Amphio's mood is so subdued that I ask, "Won't the dome hold on its own?"

Amphio, who has grown balder since we met last, stiffens. "It will hold, Majesty. Once it is set, we'll remove the frame. The concrete layer, being one piece, will exert pressure downward rather than out. It will hold."

"You're sure?"

He nods gravely. "I swear it to you upon my life. What's more, I won't wait for you to execute me if it fails. I'll stand beneath the dome when the centerings are removed as proof that I'm a genius or a fool."

He is many things, but not a fool. "Tell me, then, why it is that you seem so sad when you should be boasting. What can have gone wrong *now*?"

"There's nothing wrong with the Iseum, Majesty, save that I have not finished it sooner. I don't believe that Isis exists, but you do. It would have pleased me for you to have found comfort here in your grief."

If he is mocking me again, I will have his head. But one glance at his stern face with its hawkish Roman nose and I know he's sincere. "Prince Ptolemy would have made a very great king," he says.

Though he is a stiff-necked Roman, he does understand compassion. He does understand suffering. In spite of the fact that he claims no gods for his own, he somehow understands our need for them. His humanity is evident in the beauty of this temple he is building. And for the first time, I am sure that even Amphio has a soul. He may not know it, but Isis and I do.

IN the first days of summer, there comes for us a letter from King Archelaus. This letter catches us unawares because we thought nothing of the King of Cappadocia when we sailed away from Rome with the girl he meant to wed. In our grief, we broke the betrothal without offering recompense and I cannot imagine that a king of his stature would easily forgive such an insult. Yet he sends heartfelt condolences for our loss.

Perhaps our long-standing friendship accounts for his willingness to overlook this slight to his royal dignity. Or perhaps this letter has less to do with friendship than with the plea of the emissary he has sent with it. "King Archelaus asks your intercession in a matter most dire," the ambassador explains when we receive him in our mostly empty throne room, where potted palms droop wearily in the corners. "The King of the Jews has again taken it in his mind that his sons are plotting against his life and has again put them both in chains. Princess Glaphyra too is being held against her will."

The king and I are so numb with our own loss that I only murmur, "*Again?*"

"Herod sees enemies round every pillar. He's expelled friends and ambassadors from Judea. The country is in disarray. We fear that our Princess Glaphyra may be put to torture or executed."

I glance at Juba for his reaction, to see if he has anything to say. He is silent on his throne, distracted, his eyes on the colorful paintings that line our walls. I force myself to be the queen I still am and clear my throat. "We are grieved to hear this news. How can we be of assistance?"

The emissary steps closer, his sandals sweeping softly on the marble floor. "The emperor hesitates to act against Herod on King Archelaus's word alone. But if the emperor were to hear censure of Herod from voices he trusts and esteems, we believe he will strip Herod of his throne."

Juba's head snaps up as if he finds it surprising that news of our fall from favor has not spread to all corners of the empire. "Caesar is not interested in anything we might have to say about this matter. Your king would have a better chance of success if he were to sail to Judea himself and steal his daughter away in the dead of night. We can offer no help to you whatsoever."

It is a flat and impolitic dismissal; there is nothing I can do to take the sting out of it for the Cappadocian emissary, who stiffly backs out of the room with a frosty farewell. If we had not already made an enemy of Archelaus by breaking the betrothal, we will surely have made one of him when he hears how his emissary was treated in our court. And yet my concern is for Juba. I reach for his hand, but my husband flinches away and I am reminded of how much he hates me.

I make a gift of ivory to the Cappadocian emissary to make amends for my husband's harsh refusal, but I cannot think of what else I might do. That night, turning the problem over in my mind, I cannot sleep. In my aimlessness, I drift to the empty room where my son once slept. I touch the wooden chest at the foot of his bed. I sigh softly as my fingers find the indentation left by the hair-curling iron I once flung away because my son was so excited to run to his father's arms.

The memory rips through me, bittersweet. I light the tiny lamp beside his empty bed. Then I climb in and press my cheek to his pillow, hoping to catch a scent of my boy and remember how preciously he tucked his little fists beneath his chin. By day he was as fierce as a Berber warrior, but at night, what a sweet babe he was . . .

Thinking I am alone, I am startled by something cold and wet against my hand and look down to see the nose of my son's dog. *How soft her ears are*, I think as I stroke her big ugly head. Luna climbs up into the bed next to me and I stroke her, wondering if she too is searching for my son. She was there with him at the end, barking and barking. She might have abandoned him to the fire, running away in fear as the horses did. But she stayed with him, a loyal hound indeed.

Luna's silver paws have healed up nicely, but she is shy of flame now, her eyes wary when I lift the lamp to get a closer look at Isidora's handiwork. "Poor dog. You will never forget and neither will I."

My son did not die in a bed, in the arms of his mother. He died near this dog, and I want to be near him. I whisper my son's name and offer the bewildered animal the comfort that I cannot give to Ptolemy. I stroke her, searching the warmth of her coat, reaching for any tendril of connection to my son's spirit.

All at once, the hound lifts her head in alertness at a noise at the door and I glance up to see Juba there. We have startled the king as much as he has startled us, and he gruffly asks, "What are you doing here with Ptolemy's dog?"

"I don't know," I whisper. "Were we all drawn here by the same impulse?"

My husband has grown a beard—a thing that bewilders me, given his sensitivity to being mocked as the son of a hirsute barbarian king. He is generally fastidious about keeping his cheek clean-shaven as a Roman would, so this beard, like everything else about him tonight, is a sign of his desperate grief.

"I'll go," Juba says, turning to retreat.

"Wait, Juba, please . . ." But when he stops, I don't know what to say. I want to rush to him. I want to grab his hands and fall to my knees and beg his forgiveness. It would not matter, though, for I cannot forgive myself. I think to suggest he divorce me and take a new wife who can give him children of his own, but where would that leave my daughter? So I only ask, "Will you write to Herod? Perhaps you can persuade him—"

"Herod will not rest until his sons are dead."

What horrible irony that we would give anything to have our son back and Herod is still trying to kill his. "Won't you try?"

Juba scowls. "There is enough to be done in Mauretania. There are trade agreements to be reached, letters to dictate, military posts to be built, and justice to dispense."

He wants to retreat to his study into a pile of scrolls. He wants court cases in quick succession. He wants to send advisers scurrying to gather more information on this problem or that. He wants to work with a feverish determination that will hold the grief at bay. I know, because I have done it too. "Not even the greatest king can send sadness into exile . . ."

My husband swallows at the word *exile*, glancing around our son's empty room. "I am mindful that our court is watching us, Selene. They worry what is to become of our kingdom, and I can't let them see that I am not even king enough to care."

"You care, Juba. It's only that you can't feel it now. You are numb—"

"I am everything but numb, Selene! By the gods, I *wish* I were numb. What a relief it would be not to have to hide the truth."

It is the first time in months that he has spoken to me beyond that which was necessary. I take it for a fissure in the wall he has built to keep me out, so I screw up my courage and say, "You needn't hide your grief from me."

"No. To you, I am entirely exposed. But what does it matter? Ptolemy is dead and buried. No prayers or pleading or tears will change that. So what are we to say or do with so many eyes upon us?"

We both live public lives. We have always been watched and studied. But whereas I have embraced the attention, Juba has shied away from it more than once. Maybe he was right to. Perhaps running away is the only thing that helps. "We can go where we're not watched."

"And where would that be? There is no such place."

"I know a place . . . and I will take you there, if you will let me."

Forty

IN silence we ride up into the wheat fields that blanket the hills with their tall golden stalks, each head swollen with seeds. It is not a far ride to my plantation, where the blossoms of the olive trees have begun to give way to the growing fruit. My groundskeeper has already cut chunks from the wheat fields to test the crop for harvest. Some of this scythed wheat has been bundled into tawny sheaves to dry under the bright summer sky, and hope steals into my heart . . .

If there is any place where my little family and I might find respite, it will be here, at the House of Olives. I have happy memories of this place. Of Julia and I rolling around in the muck, flinging dirt at each other. Of teasing Memnon that he ought to retire here. Of my children learning to press oil and hiding behind vats in the fermenting yard. Of my husband asking questions of our sharecroppers, always keen to learn something new . . .

But that was Juba as he was before. Always inquisitive and interested. With the death of his son, the light has gone from his eyes. He has withdrawn so far into himself that he does not even bother to return the greetings of our housekeeper, who welcomes us with a promise of spicy sausages, eggs, fresh-baked bread, and a hot mint tisane.

When my daughter and I settle into our rooms upstairs, Isidora lingers by the window, asking, "Where is Papa going?"

I look out to see my husband walking through the olive orchard. "I'm sure he has gone to speak to one of the plowmen," I say, so as not to alarm her. But *I* am alarmed because Juba is without his guards.

Bidding my daughter to go down for a plate of the housekeeper's rustic fare, I seek out Iacentus in the yard. "Why aren't you with the king?"

"He commanded us to stay behind, Majesty. He wants to be alone."

Yes, Juba wants to be alone. That's why we came here, isn't it? I don't know why I should feel so unsettled. My husband is not likely to meet with danger on a farm . . . unless that danger is from himself. I try to shake away that fear, telling myself it is only because I lost both my mother and father to suicide that such thoughts occur to me. Knowing my husband's temperament, Juba is more likely to simply walk off into the wilderness.

But then I remember Iullus and what he contemplated in the face of the emperor's disfavor . . .

I try to shrug off these worries and follow the scent of sausage roasting in the kitchen, but Luna starts barking. Perhaps she only barks at the cows being led into the barn but the sound makes me remember. I remember how she barked when my son lay trampled in the dirt. How she barked when Drusus came to call upon me at my house. Her bark brings back to me the darkest moment of my life and panic overtakes me.

Gathering my skirts in my hands, I start out after the king. He is at the edge of the olive orchard now, crossing the road into the wheat fields, and if I do not catch up with him, he will disappear in the sea of grain. "Juba!" I call after him, but he does not turn. Walking faster, I hurry past the water well, past the wagon filled with manure, past servants hauling buckets of water. I call again, but the king does not answer.

He only walks faster, as if to escape me.

I pick up my pace, wading into the field after him, calling his name, until I am running after him, the wheat stalks slashing at my face and scraping my limbs. "Juba!"

All at once, he whirls on me. "What do you *want*?"

I hold my ribs, breathless with fear and exertion. The blood is pounding in my ears, and I am too afraid to say what I really want. "I only want to know where you are going."

"*Away,*" he says, taking a sword from his belt to chop his way through the grasses as if it will speed his progress away from me. Stubbornly, I follow him, even though I know I should leave my husband to grieve.

Farther and farther we go into the grain field, until I am as lost in the world as I am in my soul. Julia once wrote that the loss of a child will smash even a marriage of the strongest of foundations. The foundations of my marriage were like Necho's sunbaked bricks, likely to crumble away under any weight at all. If my husband hates me, it is no more than I deserve. All these years, I have taken for granted his affection and now it is gone. Still, I need to reassure myself that my fears are unfounded. "Why do you have a sword, Juba? What are you going to do?"

This stops him. He turns to look at me, sweat dripping from his fine dark brow. "Are you worried I am such an incompetent fool that I might cut myself?" When I press my lips together, he must see what I fear, because he blinks. We stand there, staring at each other as if over an abyss, and his eyes go hard. "No, Selene. Though I want nothing more than to lie down in the earth and die, that is no way out for a king. There is no way out for me."

I exhale, glad that he knows it. Grateful beyond measure that I am the fool. And yet I cannot be glad that he is in such pain he would wish for death. He has never known grief like this before; he has never lost anyone that he loved so deeply. Being well practiced at mourning has not blunted the pain for me, but Juba has not even that pitiful defense. And I have done this to him. I could not have known where my choices would lead when I was only a girl, playing with Augustus for the world. I didn't know that someday I would have a new family to be harmed by the decisions I made. But does that excuse me?

As Juba begins walking again, I cry, "I would do anything to take it back! To make it all different. I am sorry. I am so sorry—"

Juba rounds on me with bloodshot eyes. "You *apologize* to me? You stand there, seeking forgiveness?"

Forgiveness would be far too much to ask, so I say, "I only need you to know of my regrets, but that is a selfish urge too. If you wish to be alone, if you cannot bear to look at me . . . I'll leave you and Isidora here and return to the palace. Just tell me what you want and I'll do it."

"I want you to blame me!" he roars. "Why don't you say it, Selene? I know you must think it. You must think it every moment of every day. Say that it's my fault our son is dead."

I am so stunned that I nearly stumble. The sweat pools in my palms and I stare at him, trying to understand. Can it be that what I have seen when he looks at me with those bleak eyes is not hatred but guilt? *Sweet Isis*, does he believe I would lay our son's death at his feet, as I laid the baby there at his birth? There are so very many people I have condemned, myself most of all, but I have never held my husband responsible. "How could I blame you?"

I reach out for him, but he catches me by both wrists. Then the calm, reasoned shell of the king cracks open to reveal the raw man inside. He shouts in my face, "I was the one who insisted we foster him in Rome! You never wanted him to go. You told me the truth about Caesar's obsession. You warned me again and again that our son would be in danger. You begged me to believe you. You *begged* me, but I wouldn't listen."

I let him scream at me. I let him shake me. I do not care if I fly apart. I only care that now he does believe me. He does. "You suspect someone?"

Juba grinds his teeth together. "I don't know who. I don't know anything. I only know that I was not with our son when he died. I was not with Ptolemy that day. I gave him that stallion—that ferocious stallion. Yet I imagined I had some more important business. I left him alone. So blame me. *Damn it*, blame me."

He stands there, bracing for the mortal blow of my accusation. Welcoming it, I think, like a gladiator who is done with life. But I would not willingly wound him, and the bitterness leaches out of my pores. "Yes, you gave him that stallion, Juba. And so much more. You gave him a father to admire, a father who showered him with love. Juba, you did not leave Ptolemy and he was not *alone*. I will not blame you. I will never blame you . . ."

His hands tighten painfully on my wrists, then he tries to thrust me away. "I will blame myself for all my life . . . so leave me be."

He is a vigorous man, kept fit by horse riding and practice at arms. His body is stronger than mine, but I do not *let* him thrust me away. I grab his arms and cling to him. "For the love of Isis, I don't want to leave you. I want to hold you and be held by you. I know I don't deserve it, but I want to grieve with you and share with you whatever comes of this day."

He shakes his head, as if it were too late. As if the bridge between us is broken and there is no way back. He tries again to push me away, but I won't let him go. I know Juba and what he does with his pain. If history is any guide, he will soon gallop off to the wilderness to make his maps or write his books. Perhaps he will take some pretty Greek *hetaera* with him. It will be as it was when we were first married, still strangers to each other, pried apart by our own disappointments. It will be as if Ptolemy had never been born.

That, I cannot bear, so when he turns from me again, I grasp him round the waist, fighting Juba as I have never fought anyone. I don't use my magic. I use my arms, my legs, my whole body. My fingers clutch at his clothes, my nails dig into his skin. Anything to keep him here with me.

"Selene!" he cries. "Let go."

"I *won't*," I say, my voice breaking. I hold on as if my life depended on it, and his too. "I won't let you go. Not this time."

His attempts to escape me become more violent and I am sure he bruises me in his desperate attempt to get away. But I don't let go. We grapple and he becomes breathless with his efforts to dislodge me. I am tall, like my father, and I make of myself a deadweight. My gown tears in our struggle and we tumble down to the earth. We hit the ground so hard the breath explodes from my lungs, but still, I don't let go of him.

Then, there is surrender.

All at once, I feel him shudder in my arms, for I am drawing the grief out of him. It starts as a moan, then dissolves into a keening wail. He chokes with sobs, his whole body quaking with despair. He is drowning in it. And instead of pushing me away, he clutches at me, his fingers digging into my back. I let him soak my hair with his tears, here in the field where the grasses shield us from the world.

I kiss him. Soft kisses to start, on his head, on his shaking shoulders, on his tear-soaked beard. Then our lips meet in shared anguish, touching off a desperate hunger to feel something, anything but pain. We kiss again, longer, harder, my face in his dirtied hands.

Then, by silent assent, our kisses become something else, more frenzied and hungry. His hands are on my face, in my hair, on my breasts. And my hands are on him too, yanking his tunic up. Grief has stripped us of all grandeur. Here on this field, with my back on the earth, I am humbled. I am no goddess and he is no god. I am no queen and he is no king. He is only a man and I am only a woman.

We make love. And I realize that it *is* love.

How have I denied it so long?

I want him. I need him. This time, I give myself to him completely. And when we are both spent, I whisper the truth against the salty sweat of his neck. "I love you."

Heaving with ragged breaths, he murmurs, "Don't say it, now. I cannot believe it, now."

He rolls off me and we stare up into the glow of the afternoon sun. His hand tangles in my hair. I breathe in the warm desert scent of him.

"All my life I have dreaded for you to see me this way," Juba whispers, as if afraid his voice might carry on the shimmering sea of grass.

How strange that he should dread for me to see this side of him, when it is precisely the unexpected rawness of him that I am drawn to. "Why should you fear such a thing?"

"Because I am exposed. I never wanted you to realize that I am an empty man, a paper king. Without Ptolemy, I am of even less substance. A man without weight. A man without family . . ."

"No, Juba. No." I feel his pain as my pain. That is how I know it is love between us. For all that I have repudiated it, it is there. Juba has not always loved me well or faithfully, but he has loved me with a long and patient constancy that has outlasted even the resentments of my hard heart. And I love him. I love him so much it aches beneath my breastbone. I must find a way to convince him. If only I knew the words . . .

"You are not empty, Juba. You are filled with patience, foresight, and resolve. I would live all the rest of my days with you, and when I am dead, I would be buried with you in the mausoleum on the hill. I would be your family. I *am* your family, if you will let me be."

He gives a sad smile, as if he dares not hope for it. "But it is only the three of us now."

In my life, I have played many grand roles. Isis, Kore, Cleopatra, Dido, Demeter, and more. All of them queens or goddesses. But here, now, with Juba, I am only an ordinary woman. It is this ordinariness that offers us a chance at more than we have ever had before. I decide, then and there, to embrace it. "We will make it enough. We'll find a way to need no one else, Juba. We'll find a way."

I think it's true what I said that day in his arms, smeared with tears and sweat and dirt, my skin sticky and itching from the crushed grasses that made our bed. Together, we are enough. But sometimes the gods see beyond the truth and bless us with gifts we did not think to ask for.

I did not use my magic in the field with Juba. I did not invite my goddess into me. Yet in the hottest days of summer, when farmers bring in the last of the grain harvest, I feel the spark of *heka* in my womb. Barren so long, I tell myself it is nothing. It is a vain hope in all this sadness and I cannot afford another disappointment. But I am craving figs. Fresh figs. Dried figs. Fig sauce. Any kind of fig.

I ask for figs in the morning and before I go to bed, telling myself all the while that I am a half-wit.

I am thirty years old. What barren woman my age suddenly bears fruit?

Then, one day, my daughter asks me if I know that I am with child. "You are swollen at the breasts," Isidora says. "Your hand keeps drifting to rub your lower back and you do not sit as long in council before you excuse yourself to pass water."

Everything she says is true. There are other signs too. I cannot remember the day of my last moon's blood. My nipples have darkened. I feel heavier upon the earth. Perhaps it is possible. My mother was thirty-two when she birthed her last child. Octavia was thirty-three.

Am I not as strong as either of them?

My hands go to my cheeks with excitement.

Sweet Isis, I am going to have a baby!

The sheer force of such unexpected joy brings a smile—a thing itself that makes me feel so ashamed that I cover my mouth. What if someone should see me smile and think I have forgotten poor Ptolemy? How can I smile when I have lost my child? What will I tell Juba?

It is better to wait to tell until I am sure. After all, we are both so fragile. In the daytime, the king and I are gentle with each other. At night, we hold the grief at bay, as if we have both discovered in each other's bodies the only elixir for our pain. Our lovemaking has an urgency to it. It is still, for both of us, a desperate thing. But I have kept enough secrets from my husband for one lifetime. So I decide to tell him when he comes to me in bed that night.

After he is spent, I draw the long fingers of his hand over my belly and whisper, "I am with child."

Still breathing hard from our exertions, Juba shakes sweat-damp hair from his eyes. "What?"

I tell him again. "We're going to have a baby . . ."

This time he blinks, his lashes tickling my cheek. *"What?"*

He nearly makes me laugh. "A baby, Juba. We're having a baby."
Abruptly, he sits up, fingers still splayed over my womb.
Discomforted by his stare, I ask, "Must I say it again?"

"You had better."

"I am with child."

His brows furrow. "But I thought—"

"We were wrong."

Now he shakes his head in denial. "You can't be sure of this . . ."

"I am. I am a vessel of Isis. These things are in my gift."

It is meant only to be a proud boast, but his expression darkens.
"Your last birth went hard, Selene. Euphorbus said you ought not
risk another child."

"I've had years to regain my strength and, in any case, it's done.
It's too late to worry now."

His expression clouds over. "It is not too late. There are herbs
women take to stop a child from growing. I've heard of them from
soldiers, and Isidora would know them too."

Is he suggesting that I rid myself of this child? Does he think I
would be the cause of another death? I am a mother lioness in fury,
ready to tear and shred, but then Juba says, "I couldn't bear to
lose you."

Quieting my anger, I let myself understand the import of his
words. I let myself understand that he would sacrifice a legacy, a
child, and his responsibility as a king. He would sacrifice it all for
me. He is my king. My husband. My love. "We are going to have a
baby, Juba. I am not afraid."

He *is* afraid, but a hint of a smile works its way onto his face.
And now we have a secret that we share together.

"HOW did he die?" I demand of the Roman soldier who delivers
the news.

The soldier is a leathery veteran with a jagged scar from lip to
ear. I've little doubt that he's lost comrades in the field before. Yet
he is fractured, his eyes shining with tears. "It was a fall."

"A *fall*?" I ask, my voice echoing down from my throne. "How should such a great warrior die from a fall?"

"He fell from a horse and was trampled and crushed under the creature's weight," the soldier chokes out, unable to disguise his distress even before our assembled councilors. "His leg was shattered and the wound festered."

The crowd gives a collective gasp at such a painful, ignominious death. Some make sacred signs to ward off evil, but I am calm and clear-eyed with my son's faithful hound at my feet. "*Trampled*, you say? His bones shattered . . ."

These words fall from my lips with bitter satisfaction, though I do my best to disguise it. Is it only tragic coincidence that Drusus, the brightest star of the *Claudii,* should perish by the same means that took my boy? No, I do not believe it is coincidence. It *cannot* be only happenstance that such a fate should befall Livia's son while new life grows inside me.

Then the soldier says, "It was sorcery that did him in."

The hall goes silent, every eye trained upon this messenger, who sucks in his lower lip, then blows it out again, as if summoning his courage to speak of magic in the presence of Cleopatra's daughter. "The night before battle, our poor general was awakened by an apparition. A woman of superhuman size commanded him to depart and foretold that the end of his life was near. We retreated for the Rhine, but ill omens followed us. Children weren't allowed on our march, but two boys were seen in camp. One with straight dark hair, the other with golden curls . . . both riding fine royal mounts. Then we heard a woman keening for her lost child, but when we searched for her, we could not find her."

Two spirit boys on horseback. One dark. One golden.

Ptolemy . . . and Helios.

It was my keening, wailing curse that killed Drusus, and all the soldiers heard it.

It was Drusus, then, who murdered my child. And this vengeance upon him is the work of my goddess. I give silent praise to Isis for it. Always, Isis hears me. Always, she is my fiercest champion.

And I must be hers. That is why I cannot allow myself to take pleasure in her wrathful justice. Instead, I let her soften my heart and remember his wife and all those for whom this news will bring the greatest sorrow. "What of my half sister, Antonia Minor?"

"Safe in Rome, Majesty," the soldier reports, wiping at his eyes with his brawny forearm. "It was his brother who fetched our brave commander home. When Tiberius finally heard of the accident he rode two hundred miles in a single day and night to be at his brother's side."

If true, such an incredible feat would be an unsurpassed speed record. To ride so far in one day he would have to waste horse after horse . . .

"By the time Tiberius reached the fortress," the soldier continues, "Drusus had taken with fever. Tiberius held our poor general's hand on his deathbed."

I try not to begrudge my enemy the love of his brother in his dying moments, but then I remember Ptolemy's broken body in the dirt and my heart hardens again.

The soldier goes on, "So great was the esteem of Drusus even amongst his enemies that the Germans agreed to a truce so that his body might be carried on the shoulders of his men. Then, once they reached the Rhine, his *lictors* broke their ceremonial axes and accompanied his body back to Rome. All the way, Tiberius walked, on foot, in front of his brother's funeral carriage."

Tiberius *walked* all the way back to Rome? Such an ostentatious display of piety might be thought a cynical ploy, but I can well imagine doing such a thing for my dead brothers, had I been allowed to. Of course, I was not . . .

Tiberius is now Livia's only living son. The only hope of the Claudians. For the sake of Livia's ambitions, Tiberius has lost the wife he loved, married a woman he despises, and lost his brother too. He is alone now. I might even find it in my heart to pity him. I *do* pity Minora. My poor widowed sister must now rear up all Drusus's little children, the eldest of whom is officially to be called *Germanicus* as a posthumous honor to his dead father. My nephew is now a six-year-old boy with a very big name.

It is my sadness for these innocents that prevents me from seething when Juba suggests we make tribute to the memory of Drusus here in our kingdom. Let Drusus be honored, I decide, for the sake of all those who loved him. For the part of *me* that loved him. Because it will also be my private memorial to vengeance, my mark of triumph over him, knowing that he died by my hand . . .

Justice was done and more is yet due. Livia said that she did nothing to my boy, but she sent her son after mine, didn't she? It is not enough that Livia has now *lost* her son the way I lost mine. It is not enough. I want to destroy her. I want to crush her into dust.

But when I retreat to the room in the palace where the colorful painting of my winged goddess smiles down upon me, I find myself strangely reluctant to work more dark magic—and not only because I find my daughter there, her head bowed in worship, expensive incense upon the altar.

"What are you praying for?" I ask, my hand atop her head.

"For our soldiers," Isidora replies. "I've made an offering to Isis to protect them, for if a general like Drusus can meet such a fate, what dangers lay in wait for a simple cavalry officer?"

I do not think it is our soldiers she prays for, but rather one particular soldier. "Is Tacfarinas an officer already? We are not at war, my sweet. There is no danger to your Berber boy . . ."

I say it only to comfort her, because there is always danger if we look for it. And perhaps there is danger even in what I have come to do. I remember well the acrid stink of death in my nostrils when I cursed Drusus, and later, when I offered Livia's hair to the flame. I remember too the words of my wizard. *Curses have especially jagged edges and hooks that take chunks of you with them.*

When I worked dark magic, I was empty, carved hollow with grief. I did not care how the magic tore at me, bleeding me with each incantation. But I am not empty now, I remember, laying my hand gently over my pregnant belly.

Dora watches the trail of my hand and asks, "Did you come to pray for the baby?"

I do not want to tell her that I have come for vengeance, but my daughter must be made to understand the way of the world. "When you looked into the Rivers of Time, what have you seen of Livia? I ask because she is my enemy and she is yours. You must never trust her or anything that comes from her. She is a *monster* . . . and we must always keep a wary eye upon her."

"You must not worry yourself about the emperor's wife, Mama. You must not worry yourself about *anything* right now."

What has Juba told her that she thinks I am so frail? "That is advice for village women. I am the queen—"

"Childbirth is a danger to village women and queens alike. If it will ease your mind, I will tell you what I have seen of Livia. I have seen her die. Always, she dies alone. She dies alone and afraid and frustrated. And her son leaves her to rot. That ought to satisfy you. Does it?"

No, it does not. It's what I cursed Livia to and though it is not enough, it will never be enough, I must find a way to let it be. For I carry inside me a great gift. A new baby. More than that, I have my daughter and a new love with my husband—a new marriage, truth be told. Everything is new. Everything is begun again.

I am not like Livia. I will not live in a cold and corrupt marriage. I will not risk everything for the sake of ambition or vengeance. I will leave Livia to her fate . . . and embrace mine.

Forty-one

THE KINGDOM OF MAURETANIA
DECEMBER 9 B.C.

HOW can we celebrate the Saturnalia? Without Ptolemy to squeal over his gifts, without Tala to paint our hands in henna and scold us for being spoiled, without Memnon to watch over us, how can we be merry?

But when I glance out from the balcony at my city, my heart is gladdened at the sight of rain-soaked children playing in puddles. Colorful awnings in the marketplace shelter revelers, and vendors hawking roasted meats and sweet treats peddle their wares in every covered doorway. The spirit of my people is defeated by nothing. They are bowed by neither sorrow nor rain. They thrive in the searing sun of the desert, the hardscrabble life in the mountains, and the fierce struggle for survival in the city streets. They never turn away an opportunity to rejoice, and I take a lesson from them. Life is a bargain between bitter and sweet. Because there is a surfeit of bitter, we must savor the rare sweet.

So the king and I observe the Saturnalia. Together with our court, we give thanks that our cold, dark nights will soon surrender to warmer days. We give thanks too that I am with child. Whatever else has happened, our kingdom still prospers and we still have Isidora with us.

She is a young woman and a scholar besides. There is not a scroll about medicine in our library that she has not read. Nor is there a day that she does not pester the king's new Greek physician. I wish that she showed as much interest in the governing of our kingdom as she does in medicine, but she has lost the boy she loved and her brother too. I will not take one more thing from her.

She performs the rites at the Saturnalia for us. And we allow her to host a banquet of her own for the young people of influential families, Greek, Egyptian, Berber, and Roman. As always, I am concerned by my daughter's inability to maintain a proper distance between herself and the subjects over which I intend her to rule, but she has a rapport with the future leaders of our kingdom and that should stand her in good stead.

In truth, with that disquieting snake so often wrapped around her arm, I think she frightens them a little. And that is a good thing in a future queen.

On the one day of the Saturnalia that it does not rain, the king and I attend a play in our theater. It is Leonteus's lighthearted version of the story of Hypsipyle. And though we are all great admirers of the dramas written by our court tragedian, his *comedy* is dreadful. The story begins when the goddess of love curses all the women on the isle of Lemnos with a disagreeable body odor. The rest is such bawdy farce that our sophisticated Alexandrians actually boo.

Later, bundled in woven blankets by the fire, Juba shows me a critique he's written in mock-tragic language on his wax tablet, panning the play. How I have missed Juba's dry wit!

We laugh together at the expense of our playwright, but then Juba's smile falters, as if he felt it some disloyalty to our son that he should ever laugh again. My own laughter dies away too. How long will we feel this way?. Will every moment of levity be banished by the memory that our little Ptolemy is shut up in his tomb? Probably so. I think we will feel this pain until the moment we die.

But Juba and I are still alive and I make sure to remind him of it.

CAN it have been a year since my son breathed his last?

The violent winter rains are but drizzles now and I count the days. It feels as if my boy was alive only yesterday, and yet it also feels as if I have lived a lifetime since. The king is unsure of how to mark the occasion. He does not know if he should dedicate a memorial for Ptolemy or a feast in honor of our forthcoming child.

I argue that we should do neither. In truth, we are both still too fragile for a public display. I also worry that Juba may have memorials enough to arrange if the birth does not go well. I told him I was not afraid to give birth to another child, but perhaps I should be.

Three times now I have awakened to blood on my sheets and pain in my abdomen. And three times now Chryssa has called our new Greek physician to my rooms. Unfortunately, he is worthless. Overfamiliar too. A young pup who seems to believe childbirth is beneath his expertise.

I would rather have the midwife, though she is not much help either.

Knowing that it is too soon for the baby to come, I will away the pain, pushing it aside. Tala would tell me not to complain of my ailments and I miss her stern advice. Would that she were here to paint her tattoos on my belly and work her Berber magic . . . but she is not here.

We lost her, as we lost Memnon and my precious son.

We will not lose this baby, even if it kills me to bring him into the world.

I do not tell Juba, but I know the baby will be a boy. What I do not know is whether or not the baby will live. What if our baby should perish, wasting away in his cradle as Julia's little boy did? The king and I could not bear it, so I do not worry my husband with my troubles. Nor do I let him plan a celebration, the memory of which might fester if it should all go badly.

Instead, I make a private pilgrimage to our Royal Mausoleum with offerings of wine, olive oil, milk, and honey—libations for my dead. The ones who are buried here and the ones I have drawn to me.

There is my son in his sarcophagus, a crown of antler horns above his head. There is my mother's statue in a queenly pose and my father's bust with eyebrow raised in mischief. There is my cousin, Petubastes, in black basalt. And there are my brothers, Caesarion,

Antyllus, and Philadelphus. They are all here, their names carved in stone.

Even Helios. Perhaps he is still alive somewhere in the world, but I doubt it now. I think he is inside of me. And either way, I have betrayed him. If he is dead, I never properly mourned him. I never found his body. Never bound his wounds. Never performed the Opening of the Mouth that he might breathe again in the after-world. Never did anything for him but build this tomb and carve his name in stone that the gods might see it.

Yet, if he is somehow alive, I have betrayed him in a different way, for I have given him up. I have matured beyond our youthful love and taken another man as a husband. I have taken another man as my king. I have taken another man to my heart.

Love for Juba is not the same as for Helios. It could never be the same because I am not the same. But I love Juba. Oh, I do. I love him in a way I did not understand I could love. It is an impure, tainted love, no less beautiful for its roughened edges and lack of illusion. For all its flaws, my love for Juba runs deep and wide.

So I will think no more on Helios today. For the good of the child in my womb, I must keep my thoughts small. I must take each day as it comes, shrinking the weight of my world so that I can bear up under it.

WHEN the yellow primrose blooms in our gardens, we receive another emissary from King Archelaus in Cappadocia, carrying grim news. "Herod and Augustus have mended their rift, Majesty."

Even with a cushion at my back, I cannot sit comfortably on my throne in my advanced state of pregnancy and this news makes it worse, agitating me beyond reason. "No, you must have this wrong . . ."

Juba clutches the arms of his throne chair as if to keep himself from flying out of it. "Do you mean to say that the emperor has forgiven Herod?"

I can scarcely believe it. Neither can the child in my womb if the kicking is any sign. But the emissary replies, "He has, Majesty. Nicholas of Damascus convinced the emperor that Herod had been misjudged in the Nabatean affair. Augustus has forgiven Herod and given him permission to take his sons to Beirut and try them for treason before a court of Roman officials and other men of importance."

So there is to be *another* trial. While I try to decide who benefits, the emissary continues, "Princess Glaphyra and her husband tried to flee to the safety of Cappadocia, but were found out and arrested. Now Herod believes King Archelaus is part of a conspiracy too."

I wish he *had* conspired with us against Herod. Would that we had all banded together to destroy Herod when he was weakest. We assumed he was finished, but now he has somehow ingratiated himself with the emperor again. The damned King of Judea is like some mythical creature from the depths that cannot be slain by ordinary means. Always he rises again when we least expect it. In this, he's like Augustus . . . and me. "What would you have us do?"

The emissary explains, "We beseech King Juba to travel to Beirut and serve as one of the judges."

My husband's expression is curiously blank. "Herod has not invited me to sit in judgment over his sons. I don't see how I might intervene."

"Your Majesty, with all due respect, you are the King of Mauretania. He cannot easily turn you away."

The emissary shouldn't need to remind Juba of his power and reputation. We rule more territory than all the other client kingdoms put together. We have fostered friendships throughout the empire. My husband is esteemed not only for his marriage to me and his connections to the imperial family, but also for his learned scholarship and diplomacy. The Cappadocian ambassador is right. Herod can't easily turn Juba away.

And yet, I fear that Juba will refuse this plea.

To forestall this, I tell the emissary that I do not feel well, and that we would be honored to speak to him again in the morning.

Then I call for servants to escort him to well-appointed chambers and command that he be treated as a most honored guest. He withdraws from our chambers, his shadow retreating between our marble pillars.

When we are alone, Juba turns to me in concern. "What is the matter? Is it the child? Shall I call for the physician?"

I do not feel at all well, but say, "I only wished to buy time to consider King Archelaus's request."

"There is nothing to consider. It is a fool's errand."

"Even so, there is no reason to give a hasty answer."

Juba broods and I know what has darkened his mood. It has darkened mine too. Herod is now favored in Rome again while my husband is in virtual exile. It is so unjust that it forces me to exclaim, "Let the two of them reconcile, then. Herod and Augustus. The two *madmen*. It is no wonder they are bosom friends. Why, they are just alike, the bloody tyrants."

Juba's lips thin. "Are they truly alike, Selene? Can I have been so wrong, so blind, all my life?"

I feel the weight of my husband's stare. Oh, my poor Juba. He still loves Augustus. Even now. Once, his devotion infuriated me. Now it fills me with the most tender compassion. For my sake, Juba is estranged from the man he has lionized. Now, again, for my sake, he will condemn himself for loving such a man. He looks to me to tell him if his hero is *all* villain and I cannot do it.

"No," I say, cupping Juba's cheek with my hand. "Herod and Augustus are not the same. Augustus has brought some peace to the world—good will come of his legacy. You were not blind. There *is* greatness in him. You were not wrong in that. It is only that we must have no part in it now or he will ruin us."

WE make ready the birthing room. Stacks of linen tower over pots of ointments and bottles of oils. The new birthing chair boasts a fleece covering. Juba even commands that a small dais be fitted into the corner where musicians will play to soothe me during my birth pangs.

This makes me laugh. "I'm more likely to hurl a chamber pot at the head of a hapless musician than to allow one to pluck at a harp while I am on a birthing chair."

Juba laughs too. "I'll tell the musicians to wear battle helms."

Isidora does not share our merriment. In fact, she leaves the room in a sudden fit of melancholy. Later that day, when Juba goes to attend a Berber festival involving camel races, I make my way to the library, where I am told my daughter is attending Lady Lasthenia's lecture on mathematics.

Alas, I do not find her in the lecture hall. Nor do I find her in the pillared gallery surrounding the pool in the courtyard. Instead, I find her tucked away in a reading niche with a letter that she hastily sets aside in favor of a scholarly treatise, the vellum of which she pulls over her lap.

She will have to do better than that if she means to hide something from me, but I pretend not to notice the missive behind her back. "What are you reading?" I ask, sliding onto the bench beside her.

"Herophilos's treatise on midwifery," she replies.

"Ah . . . is that what has you skulking about? You're worried about the birth of the new baby?"

Shamefaced, Isidora gives a miserable nod of her head. "I should have warned you of danger. But you and Papa were barely speaking to each other when we returned. I didn't think the Rivers of Time could possibly be flowing this way . . ."

"Why don't you tell me what you've seen?"

She stares down at the sea of green and blue tiles that make up the mosaic beneath her sandaled feet. "The baby could die. I've seen the birth go very badly."

I hear myself swallow. "Have you seen it any other way?"

"Yes," she admits, but it does not cheer her.

"I suppose you have little reason to rejoice at a new baby. When we left Rome, I told you that you were now sole heir to Mauretania. With this baby, that will change again and no one consulted you . . ."

At this, she takes umbrage, stiffening her spine. "I'd be gladder than you know to have another brother. In truth, it would be a very great relief to me."

She knows it will be a boy, then. "A relief? Even though your future will be put in doubt again?"

"I am not in any doubt. If your baby lives, the Romans will make him king and I will be content to let him rule."

"Oh, Dora, this baby is not yet even born and there is time to arrange for a throne for you yet . . ."

She draws her knees up to her chest. "What if I don't want to be a queen? Must I have a throne for you to love me?"

The question forces me to gasp. "What a question! You need be nothing but yourself for me to love you. I'm your mother; nothing could destroy my love for you. Even when you speak nonsense. Of course you want to be queen."

With a tremor in her voice, she insists, "No. I never wanted to be queen. Not of Mauretania or any other place. I am not like you or Pythia. I cannot sit still in council. My mind wanders when claimants come before your throne for justice. I've studied the laws because it makes you and Papa smile when I do, but I've no gift for picking out the liars or the cheats. I'm made uncomfortable by the false flattery of ambassadors and I would much rather suck the venom from scorpion wounds than sit through a banquet wearing my hair in tight braids and combs, with jewels weighing down my earlobes and pearls choking me about the throat."

Listening to her, I am agape. And when she glances up at my horrified expression, she hurries to add, "I'll always do my duty to my family and my kingdom as you've taught me to do. If I'm to be Queen of Mauretania, I'll try to follow your example. But I would be happiest healing the sick and teaching others to do the same."

It is too much. "Isidora, you are a Ptolemy. You are meant to wear a crown, not serve as a court *physician*." My poor daughter is confused. With the uncertainty about her future, perhaps it is a consolation to tell herself that she does not want to be queen. She deserves a mother's kindness, not reproach, so I moderate my tone. "We need not discuss it now, Isidora, but I hope this baby can be good news for all of us."

She starts to smile, but it is only halfhearted. To tease a *true* smile out of her, I say, "And in the meantime, you have your letters. I am guessing that the one you hide behind your back is from your Berber boy, no?"

Isidora shakes her head quickly. "No, it's not from Tacfarinas."

Still, she crimsons, convincing me of her guilt. "There is fear written all over your face. You say you don't want to be queen, but even as a royal princess you must learn how to hide what you're feeling. You're not a good liar, Dora."

"I'm not *any* kind of liar. It isn't from Tacfarinas!"

"Then why don't you show me?" I ask, since she is now clutching the letter.

When she makes no move to relinquish it, I try to pluck it from her hands and she tries to pluck it back. I laugh at our comic pantomime, but then I see the red seal that I know so well. A symbol of a sphinx, pressed into the wax with a signet ring. My laughter becomes a cry of alarm as I realize that the emperor is writing to my daughter.

Tearing the letter from her hands, I demand, "What does he say?" I am furious to realize that my Isidora has more on her mind than boys and brothers and babies and thrones. Skimming the letter, I see nothing of import. Mindless little anecdotes and a complaint about his slave—a *nomenclator* whose job it is to remind Augustus of the names of important men to help him avoid political embarrassment. Apparently this slave did not do his job well and when he asked the emperor if there was anything he ought to bring to the forum, the emperor replied, *Letters of introduction, I should think, since you know no one there.*

"What does he mean by this?" I ask my daughter.

"I don't know . . . I think it eases his mind to confide in me the things that vex him in his day."

I crumple the letter. "He has written you before?"

"A few times . . ."

"When did this start?"

"After Ptolemy died. He asked if I would write to him about my studies and about what happened here in our kingdom. I knew you wouldn't like it, but I was afraid to say no. I was afraid of what Augustus would do to us after that day when Papa had him by the throat and you used fire against his praetorians."

Oh, why didn't I kill Augustus that day?

I know why. I know exactly why. He is still better for me and my family, better for the world, than those who might follow him were he dead. But at this moment, at the thought of him getting his fangs into my precious girl, I am again bent on murder.

He could not have my mother, so he settled for me. Now he cannot have me, so he wants my daughter. The monster! "You don't have to write to him."

"Of course I do. He is the emperor and if it appeases him, it may protect us here in Mauretania."

"It's not your place to protect us, Isidora."

At this, she sits straighter. "I *know* what he is to me."

She can't know. She can't see into the past. She can't see what he did.

"He is nothing to you, Isidora."

"Now who is the bad liar?" she asks tartly. "In the Rivers of Time, I saw a future where Ptolemy didn't die in those stables, and he grew into a young man, and the emperor claimed him as a son and made him Pharaoh of Egypt. In that vision, the emperor claimed me as his daughter too."

So there was some possibility that the emperor would do what he said he would do. Perhaps it was not all lies just to toy with me. Perhaps I was not a fool to believe him . . .

None of it matters now. What matters is that I don't know how to defend myself or comfort her. "I say again, you don't need to protect us, Isidora. That's not your place. It's mine."

"What if you aren't here to do it?" she asks softly.

I've always assumed I would outlive my enemies as the emperor has outlived his. Still, even *he* has considered how to defend his family and his legacy after he's gone. He has made all the wrong choices, but he has made an effort. Looking now into the eyes of my frightened daughter, I see that I must also prepare for a time when my magic fails me or my death leaves my kingdom and my family at risk. "You have seen me die in childbirth . . ."

"Sometimes," she replies, letting a curtain of her fair hair shield her face. "I have seen all of us die. We all do. Everyone does. I cannot be sure of when or how."

Tell me how I will die, I once commanded my mage.

He refused, saying only, *Yours will not be, cannot be, an ordinary death.*

Now I take my daughter's cold fingers into mine. "What have you seen, Isidora? I'm not afraid."

"I am," she whispers, her lower lip trembling. "Because I've seen that I am the one who kills you."

Forty-two

AT her confession, she begins to cry, trembling so violently that her teeth chatter. What words she gets out are not all intelligible. "Why would you kill me?" I ask, trying to soothe her.

She will not be soothed. "Sometimes . . . I don't mean to do it. I try to help you with your birth, but it goes wrong. I'm studying midwifery, but you cannot have me at your side when you give birth."

I would not have her there. I would not have my daughter see me in the throes of agony. I am still too prideful a queen to allow it and tell her so. "So you need not fear an accident."

"But it's not *always* an accident," she cries, her voice near hysterical. "You should imprison me. Call Iacentus to put me in chains so I can do no harm!"

I hold her tight against my pregnant belly to keep her from rushing to my guards and proclaiming herself a criminal. "Isidora, you see only possibilities. I've never met a mage in whom Isis has vested perfect knowledge. I don't fear you."

In this, I am telling the truth. The emperor may have abused his family until it is nothing but a mass of festering wounds and Herod may have twisted his family into a knot of plotting, suspicion, and dread. But in spite of all we've suffered and all the ways we have found ourselves at odds, *my* family holds strong. At our worst, Juba and I have never schemed to ruin each other. We have never pitted our favorites against each other. Nor have we tolerated the sort of factional rivalry that leads to so many deadly power games in other royal courts.

My family is not without its troubles, my court is not without its squabbles, and my kingdom is not without ambitious men and strife, but we have built a place like no other. Our court is diverse, scholarly, and civilized. Our king is both wise and just. Our family is bound by love. And I will not trade what we have for suspicion or fear no matter what Isidora sees in her visions.

"*Forget*," I whisper against her temple where I can still catch the scent of her as it was when she was a babe. "Forget what you've seen, my love. *Forget* . . . because we're going to be happy here. That is what I want and I am the queen and I mean to have my way."

AUGUSTUS does not want us to be happy.

"Do not upset yourself so near to your time of birth," Juba says, at my side, laying a gentling hand over my belly to feel the kick of his son in my womb.

Letting Pythia's letter fall to the side of the bed, I protest, "How can I not be upset when he is now preying on my niece?"

My poor niece has been left a widow and now the emperor insists that she remarry immediately, giving her no time to indulge her sentiments—or respectful tradition—with a period of mourning. He is forcing her, as he forced Julia, as he forced me . . .

"Selene, this new marriage will make your niece the Queen of Pontus, the Bosporus, Cilicia, and Cappadocia besides."

"Only through the husband Augustus is foisting upon her."

"Pythia will benefit from King Archelaus's experience and protection. I thought you liked him."

"Friendship with Archelaus be damned. Pythia doesn't need another old man to rule over her."

With wry amusement, Juba says, "I doubt any girl who looks to you for an example finds herself ruled by her king. This marriage mends any hard feelings Archelaus might have toward us. He wanted Isidora for a bride and now he will have your niece instead.

Cappadocia becomes a powerful alliance for us. Not everything Augustus does is done just to vex you."

I think he is wrong. I think Augustus means to provoke me into a reply. Or perhaps to provoke me into returning to Rome. If he cannot provoke me through Isidora, he will do it with Pythia, who is so very far away and out of the reach of my protective arms. "Everything he does *is* to vex me."

Juba presses a soft kiss to my cheek. "Perhaps you are right. Perhaps Pythia's new marriage has nothing to do with the fact that the empire needs a strong power in the East to keep the Parthians and the Sarmatians at bay . . ."

I sulk at his sarcasm. At least until the next day, when another letter comes from Julia.

To My Friend, the Most Royal Queen of Mauretania,

Never has anyone died with such impeccable good timing as Nero Claudius Drusus Germanicus. Drusus will always be young and handsome and virtuous and perfect. He will forever be a golden hero. And I cannot even resent him for it because I am sad that he is dead and grateful too because he has deprived Livia of her best weapon.

Now all she has left is Tiberius, who is so destroyed by grief that he shuns even his friends. By contrast, Livia is remarkably composed. Ovid mused that he would write a poem calling for her to reveal her sorrow, but Livia insists that she does not weep because her son wouldn't want her to.

Good Drusus, so considerate of his mother right to the end!

Too bad he did not think more about his wife before riding out so recklessly. The emperor insists that your half sister must have a new husband. But in her bereavement, Minora fled into Livia's bedroom and found shelter there. The poor girl does not seem to realize that Livia is no true ally.

Livia has already convinced your half sister that her youngest is some sort of drooling idiot, and must, therefore, be surrendered into his grandmother's care. Livia has baby Claudius in her nursery now. Little Germanicus and Livilla are sure to be next.

It is all quite a mess and my father seems at a loss as to how to put it right again. I think you had better come back to Rome, even if you must come without your husband . . .

I will never return to Rome. Not with Juba, and certainly not without him. And it would have to be without him because Juba receives no invitation to return home for Drusus's funeral. The client kings and queens in the empire will use the excuse of the funeral to descend upon Rome to settle debts and press their cases for grants of land and authority. Our absence will be noticed and remarked upon.

I wonder if, even now, gleeful letters are floating across the sea, proclaiming to our rivals that we are *ruined* and if such news is received with the same rejoicing I once felt at learning of Herod's troubles. There is little doubt that our courtiers are wondering the same thing. There was a time when disgruntled merchants and petitioners would not dare appeal our judgments to Rome, but there has been a subtle shift. An erosion of both our authority and our court. Our fall from favor portends abortive careers for our retainers, the more ambitious of whom will abandon us.

I spread Julia's letter upon my writing table. Though our citruswood tables must be polished with wax and wheat to maintain their delicate luster, they are prized for their fiery color and complex grain. The pattern is like a consuming inferno, with spirals and waves and spots of burning black coals. In the surface of this table, I see the fire that killed my son and struggle against an explosion of rage.

I will not be persuaded to return out of love for Julia or fear of the emperor or even for the good of my kingdom. Never again will I be dragged back. Not in chains made of metal, ambition, or affinity. Yet I must acknowledge that it will not serve to remain estranged from the powers in Rome.

Who are our allies there? Julia, certainly. And Iullus too. He has taken my advice. He acquitted himself well as consul, making powerful friends in the Senate. Now my Roman half brother is preparing for his command as the proconsul of Asia. Iullus is becoming powerful. And I *want* him to be. If the emperor should die next week, next month, next year . . . only my Roman half brother will stand in Livia's way.

So whenever Iullus asks my help by way of letters of introduction or money or favors that may be called on his behalf, I do what he asks. Still, it is not enough. I cannot rely on these efforts alone to defend my family . . .

Juba must be reconciled with Augustus.

"NO," the king says, stubbornly and with a vicious swat at the bees trailing us through the gardens.

"But you have not even let me finish explaining—"

"Selene, did we not agree that we must keep apart from Caesar, lest he ruin us? Is that not what you said? Did we not agree that we will have nothing to do with him now?"

Because I am so heavy with child, I cannot match my husband's angry strides, so I sit beneath a grape arbor, forcing him to circle back. I speak only when I see that he has taken a few calming breaths. Then I say, "I am not suggesting that you go to Rome and clasp hands and reminisce about your days fighting Egyptians and Spaniards. I am suggesting that you remind the emperor how powerful and influential a king you are, by *being* a powerful and influential king. You should make a trip East to remind the emperor that your gift at diplomacy outstrips that of most men and that you have been vital to the advancement of his regime."

"I don't care what Caesar thinks of me."

My husband wishes he did not care, but he does. He always has and he always will. But it will do no good to argue the point. "If Herod executes his sons and Princess Glaphyra with them, war may break out between Cappadocia and Judea. Prevent that and the emperor may take it as an apology . . ."

"An *apology*?" Juba snaps, eyes bulging with rage. "I'm not at all sorry. If I regret anything, it's that I didn't bloody Caesar. And I'm not going to Beirut to preside over another trial of Herod's sons. I'm not leaving when you are so soon to give birth."

Men do not arrange their affairs to be near their wives in childbirth. It is my husband's eagerness for another baby—or perhaps his terror for me—that makes him want to stay, so I do not fight him on this. "Wait until I have delivered. Then go East for the Olympic Games, for Pythia's wedding, and to sit in judgment over Herod's beleaguered sons."

He notices my careful wording. "You're suggesting I make the trip without you?"

"I'll have a new baby to care for," I say to excuse myself. But in truth, my presence would undermine him. Augustus must see Juba on his own merits—as a valuable piece upon his game board that he cannot afford to lose.

Alas, the reminder of our forthcoming child only sets Juba's mind firmer against the idea. "No, Selene. You and I have spent enough years apart."

He is right about that. "I would not part with you either. I swear I would not, except for a greater cause. It is only a summer, and with Herod's treasury empty, his family at war, and his kingdom in disarray, this is our opportunity to rise in prominence."

The king sits beside me, plucking an unripe grape from a vine, rolling it between his fingers. "Will you make me say it? I don't want to be without you. When I married you, I vowed, *When and where you are Gaia, I then and there am Gaius.* It means where you go, I go. Where you stay, I stay."

His beautiful sentiments, spoken so earnestly, make my heart ache. I lace my arm in the crook of his elbow and say, "I too made that vow. But I think it means wherever you are, I am also. Wherever I am, you are there too. Whether we are sitting beside each other under a grape arbor or separated by a sea, we are together. That is the strength of marriage. That *is* marriage."

Juba peers down at me. "Do you mean it or is it something you are saying to have your way?"

"I mean it," I reply, resting my head on his shoulder. Time has tested our vows. Defined them. Made them real. Again, we are together beneath a grape arbor, but this time we need no priests or contracts. *"When and where you are Gaius, I then and there am Gaia."*

He softens, threading his fingers through mine. "What would you have of me?"

Never have I hesitated to offer an insincere apology when it would suit me, but where my husband's love for Augustus is genuine, his anger is too. So I must appeal to his heart, not his head. "We can both well imagine if we had allowed Isidora to marry Herod. We would be desperate for someone to help us now. And the man I love, the man I call *husband*, is not a man who abandons a desperate princess to her fate . . ."

I'M excited for the coming of my child. Restless in my own skin. But I know something else is coming too. I taste the spice of the cinnamon desert on the wind. I sense it days before the dry heat descends. I feel the crackle of magic lift the hair on my nape at least a week before the giant wall of red haze rolls in from the desert.

It is the sirocco in all its majesty.

My Berbers know this violent storm. They rush to draw water from the wells into sealed amphora and water skins. The merchants pull down a rainbow of carpets and awnings from the marketplace and load their wares into bundles and barrels. The tribesmen hurry their shaggy goats and bleating sheep up into the hills. Their women shutter up their brick houses, scurrying to cover any crack that lets daylight in.

All the city of Iol-Caesaria makes ready against the strengthening winds. My own women sweep through the palace, taking down precious artwork from the walls and hauling statues in from the gardens, for the open design of our palace invites the wind to howl down its pillared corridors.

Her eyes on the darkening skies, Isidora asks, "Is it true you once swallowed a storm like this one?"

Before I can answer, my poet says, "It is true enough."

I smile, remembering that it was in that storm I found Helios. It was in that storm I found myself. I did not know then that the land of the sirocco would become as much a part of me as my own flesh, and that these winds would become as my own breath. But now I know.

I was saved by a storm like this one, and that is why I am not distressed when I awaken that night to a rush of water and blood between my legs. The contractions come swiftly after that and my ladies rush to me. The drowsy palace comes wide-awake, whispering the news that their queen is laboring to bring forth another babe.

As I am hurried to the birthing room, Isidora peeks out of her bedchamber and goes white to the tip of her nose. I know she is fearful of her vision that she will be the death of me, and so I command her not to follow. I do not want her to see me sweating and panting and writhing in agony should this birth go badly . . .

And yet my daughter seems frozen, grasping at my hands as if she will never be able to hold them again. Like a startled bird that cannot remember it has wings to fly away, she goes rigid. I must command my ladies to remove her, threatening to have them exiled or sold into slavery until they obey me.

"Mama!" Isidora calls after me, but there is another child I must think of now.

It is the third time for me. I know what to expect. But the pains, when they come, are severe. In the birthing room, the ladies light incense, which lends the room a soothing fragrance. Both the midwife and the physician are sent for. Chryssa too, for I need her as I have not in quite some time.

In spite of all the vows I make to myself not to cry out, a wave of agony rolls from my back to my front, sweeping away the foundation of my courage. I scream. Then I scream again because I'm angry at myself for having done so.

The physician arrives and does nothing. The midwife insists that I drink some herbal infusion. Certain it will make me vomit, I shove it away. Then a pain closes over me as if my belly were caught in the maw of a hippopotamus. The contractions go on and on, until the midwife decides I must be strapped into the chair, saying that the pull of the earth should help me birth the child.

Squatting over the opening, I push fruitlessly, until I am shaking with exhaustion.

Chryssa presses a wet cloth to my face, sponging the sweat from my cheeks.

Again and again, I try to dislodge the child from my womb. The pressure of the midwife's hands comes down on my middle as if to position the child, to push it from the outside. But it will not come.

I push and push, screaming until I am hoarse.

Hours pass and I cannot tell whether the sun has risen or set again because of the storm. The wind howls, the sand it carries scrapes at the stone walls and threatens to slip past the coverings on the windows. A forgotten chime in my gardens rings madly. But for it, the wind, and my cries of pain, the world seems empty.

I am half-hysterical with agony when I hear a pounding that is louder than my own heart. It carries up to my room, shakes the floor, and dances on my sweaty skin. "What is that sound?"

Chryssa grimly mops at my brow. "It is the war drums, to heal and trance you. Maysar has the tribesmen gathered in your throne room below. The Berbers remember how you fought a storm before and they will not let their queen fight alone . . ."

They know it is a battle, then. I battle for my baby's life.

And it goes on, and on.

I push until my muscles fail. I push until I can push no more. I wilt against the girls who hold my arms, limp and half-asleep, moaning softly. And when the world begins to blur to nothing, I hear the king's voice at the door.

Husbands do not attend their wives in the birthing chamber. It is not done. Moreover, I do not want the king here. I cannot bear for him to see me like this—to see more blood, more pain, more suffering.

Thankfully, Chryssa hurries to block his way. In wildly flickering lamplight, I see her silhouetted in the doorway like a praetorian, commanding the king to go.

"I will have you whipped," he snarls at her.

Still she will not give way. "Flog me, then, Majesty. You will not be the first."

This is my battle and she *is* my soldier, my brave general. Blinking through half-lidded eyes, I see the Greek physician push forward to whisper something to the king. Whatever it is, my husband does not want to hear it. Even over the roar of the storm, I hear the king bellow, "You bloody butcher!"

I know what the physician must be saying. He is telling my husband that if the baby does not come soon, it will die. The physician can take his sharp instruments and cut my baby out of me. But there is no way to do it that would spare us both. This I know. And Juba must know it too.

Though I would happily give my life that my child should draw breath, I will not suffer as Livia once suffered, knowing her husband would not have minded her death. No, *my* husband smashes the physician against the door with a promise of more violence. "Get out or I'll have your head."

It is not the physician's fault; it is mine. I must bring this babe into the world. This little miracle, this child conceived wholly in love. What must be done is beyond mortal strength, but there has always been within me a divine spark. My magic will consume me—it will tear its way out of me with the baby and take with it my life. But it is mine to use. Mine to choose. Magic carves its way out. This is what my mage taught me. What I taught my daughter in turn.

Even if you can't see the wounds, the magic does cut you.

Juba will not let the physician cut me, so I must cut myself.

Somewhere in the palace, I hear my son's dog barking. Outside, there is the crack and splinter of wood, the clatter of debris as it flies into the air, and the roar of the sand as the storm bears down on us.

Gathering the *heka* in my blood, I call on it now, using the strength of the one who dwells inside me. Helios was always strong, so very strong. He left bruises without meaning to. He broke benches with bare hands. If he is with me now, I call on his strength.

I bear down. With all my strength. With all my will. With every part of my soul. The frog amulet at my throat burns hot with the magic I cannot tame as it tears through me. My scream is something outside of myself. Something raw and jagged and sharp that exposes all the wounds inside me.

But the baby moves. The midwife gets a grip on his little head and pulls. Then my magic and the babe all tear themselves out of me together. I look down to see blood flow down my thighs, bright red, vivid as the fatal spray in an arena. The midwife draws back with my babe, her hands and arms covered in bright blood.

There is so much blood. Too much blood. Salty, tangy, iron blood, an endless River of Time flowing away from me . . .

Struck with terror at the sight, Chryssa sinks to her knees. I do not know if her horror is for me or for the child. Is it malformed? Why does he not cry? These are my fears as a warm river of red rushes from betwixt my legs. Why does my baby not cry?

"My baby," I rasp. "My son . . ."

I want to hear my baby cry. As my own heartbeat pounds fainter and fainter in my ears, that is all I want. Then he does cry. A little bleat of outrage that makes me smile. And as the bowl beneath my birthing chair flows over with my blood, I think I will not have much time now.

Forty-three

THEY cannot stop my blood from flowing. They unstrap me and put me on a bed where the midwife massages my womb to make it close. She holds my head up so that I can swallow a draught of fenugreek and Cretan oregano. I shiver, but it is not a fever that keeps me in a drifting state of listlessness. It is that I am an empty sack, drained and thirsty. I suffer greatly from *heka* sickness, as if it has leeched the life force from the marrow of my bones.

And the bleeding will not stop.

"The baby," I whisper, and they put the little swaddled bundle to my breast, though I am too weak to hold him. *Praise Isis*, my baby is a perfect little boy, pink from head to toe. There is nothing wrong with him. Nothing at all. His hair is dark and his eyes are blue. I wonder if they will turn green like mine or a warm amber like Juba's. I want to hold him in my arms and kiss his tiny nose and the furrowed little brow, but I am too dizzy even to lift my head.

The king is near but Chryssa is gone. He must have vanquished her somehow. Driven her off or had her carried off by his praetorians in his unseemly, and un-Roman, insistence upon entry to my birthing chamber. But I am so tired, I do not mind that he has won the battle.

"Open the doors to the terrace," I whisper.

The midwife says gently, "There is a storm raging. You don't know what you are saying because you are so near to the veil. Rest easy and go peacefully."

She has given up all hope—as if she has glimpsed the carnage from the inside. As if she has seen the hacks and slashes and chunks that have been torn out of me by curses and magic beyond that which one mortal body can endure.

"Open the doors," I say again.

The midwife glances at the king, fearful to let in the storm that rages outside. But Juba, face shadowed and tortured, says, "We commanded you to open the doors."

The midwife moves to obey, but is not fast enough for the king. He goes himself to tear down the coverings from the doorway. Little puffs of sand cloud up by his feet, but it doesn't stop him. Then my ladies rush to help. Pulling rugs from where they are piled at the door, yanking draperies out of the way, and throwing the doors wide.

A great gust of air blows in, showering us with sand. It is the king who lifts me up and carries me out onto the terrace, where his purple cloak billows up around us. With the wind whipping into my face, I take in the view of the sprawling city under siege. In our harbor, the waves froth and churn in the ocean, plucking fishing boats from their lines on the pier only to smash them to splinters.

I want to save my kingdom from this, but I cannot battle every storm. I cannot battle this one. It is too big for me to swallow. I am ravaged by childbirth, too weakened to serve as a vessel for all the desert's rage. Still, the storm and I are kin, so I surrender to its *heka*.

This storm and I, we are both of the desert. We are both of Mauretania. I have given of myself, of my magic, and all of my strength to make this land prosper. I cannot take it all inside myself, but neither does it take me.

The land gives back to me again. The Romans sometimes say of my lands that they are too close to the sun. That it is so hot here that it will set a man's blood boiling. It is true. The heat of the sirocco is like a furnace. It sets fire to my blood. But then, I am part fire now, so I welcome it.

It burns away bile and bloat and phlegm. It cauterizes my

wounds. The hot desert preserves me as it does a mummy, bandaging what has been cut open inside me and drying up the flow of blood betwixt my legs, just as it dries up riverbeds at the end of a season.

And I know it is the sirocco that heals me, because as I cling to Juba, blood rain begins to fall.

"IT is some manner of miracle that you are alive," the physician says while my servants collect silver pots of red rain and the wet nurse drapes my baby's cradle in a transparent purple veil with beaded fringe. "You lost more blood than I have ever known any person to lose and survive to tell the tale."

"I am not *any* person," I reply. "As you can see, I am recovered."

The physician puts his tools back into a small chest designed just for such instruments of torture, then gives a long-suffering sigh. "You may think so, but the body cannot recover from such a loss of blood. Eventually, your blood will pump slower and slower. You will find yourself dizzied and you may swoon away at the smallest provocation. Any exertion will cause exhaustion and you will find it more difficult to breathe. You are very frail."

Frail, am I? He does not know that I have been bleeding most of my life. He has not seen my goddess work her magic through me. What does he know? My women hang extra lanterns and stack coals in the brazier in case I am chilled, but I am sweating through my linen shift, for the sirocco inside me is hot. Gloriously hot. So hot that it has boiled the lethargy from my bones.

And I do not want to spend another moment abed.

Especially since the king is coming to call.

My ladies wash me, comb my hair, and fill the room with sweet-smelling herbs to chase away any lingering odors. Then they put my baby into my arms, though I have no milk for him, for that has dried up with my blood.

The king refuses to be kept away another moment, and when he strides in, my husband's eyes are still shadowed, as if he has not slept at all since the moment of my first birth pang. Perching at the edge of my couch, he says, "You gave me such a fright!"

"I would never die in childbirth," I whisper, as if I had never been afraid. "That is an ordinary death. Besides, Isis favors mothers above all." Then I put my infant into my husband's arms. "I deliver to you a baby boy, King Juba. You're the father of a healthy little prince."

Cradling the bundle, my husband is deeply affected, and I am glad I did not wait to put this baby at the foot of his throne. This moment is meant only for us to share.

"Hello, little prince . . ." Juba's eyes glisten, then flash as a crack of lightning splits open the sky. Our son does not even cry as the storm loudly boasts of its power. And Juba says, "You will make a fine leader of men, for the red rain has frightened many grown men in our court who see ill omens in every bolt from the sky."

"The blood rain is not an ill omen," I insist.

"Blood rain has been witnessed in the islands and across the narrow strait. But here?" Juba peers down at his son. "It is your mother's doing. If it *is* blood, it is the queen's blood, for she battled the sirocco to bring you into the world."

That is not how it happened, but I do not interrupt him, because Juba is in tears, bowing his head as his emotions pour forth. "I am . . . I am . . . I don't even know what I feel."

"Is it joy?" I ask, my own lashes wet with it.

He glances up. "Is it right to feel such a thing again?"

"It is, for if we do not take joy in the good things we are given, do we not invite only evil?"

At my words, I think he will let himself smile.

Instead, he weeps.

He weeps without shame. My husband is weeping over a babe in his arms, and he is weeping with happiness. Moved by his emotions, I weep too. And when we are sniffling, wet and red-nosed, chuckling with embarrassment at our overwrought state, I ask, "What should we name him? You choose this time."

"I would name him Ptolemy. To honor our lost boy and . . . as an act of . . ."

He struggles for his explanation, so I suggest one. "Defiance."

His breath of relief surprises me. Is it possible, after all these years, we finally think the same thoughts? To name our son Ptolemy is to defy the forces—mortal or divine—that took our elder son from us. It is to defy those who would see an end to my family dynasty. It is also to defy the emperor's belief that I would never have a child with another man.

There is no question this time, no doubt that this is the king's son. The months add up in such a way as to frustrate even the delusions of Augustus. This baby belongs to us and only us, no matter what his name. And I am so very glad of it. "Ptolemy the Younger," I say softly. "Prince Ptolemy of Mauretania."

Juba smiles. "The tribesmen are already calling him T'amT'am, the little drum."

I soften, remembering how our Berbers pounded their instruments to encourage me. "Ptolemy. Our tiny T'amT'am, then."

Our little war drum. Our little heart, pumping hot new blood into our legacy. He is also the pulse that beats inside us both. The breath of new life into our kingdom and our dreams.

"YOU are such a *peacock*," Crinagoras accuses from my window seat, where we watch the remaining red drops splash on the stones, evaporating almost instantly into a pink mist. "You cannot even birth a baby without drawing a tempest to our door!"

Sighing, I say, "You last complained I had become domesticated. It seems I can do nothing to please you, court poet."

"Oh, I'm not complaining," Crinagoras assures me. "I'm a great admirer of showy exhibition. But you've terrified the Romans with this bloodred rain. Iacentus cannot step out of the barracks without trembling beneath his praetorian's helm."

We both laugh, then I ask, "Is that why you're the only courtier to call on me? Are they all so afraid? Where is Chryssa?"

"Your freedwoman quit the palace after her quarrel with the king . . . she is with Maysar somewhere in the hills, counting their gold and their big brood of children."

Juba would forgive my freedwoman, I think, for her defiance in my birthing room, but Chryssa has reason to be wary of men who threaten to flog her. "I'll call her back when the king leaves on his trip for the East. What of my daughter?"

"Princess Isidora has not come?" he asks with a raised brow. "I know she visited your babe in the nursery. Perhaps she is distracted . . ."

"Perhaps . . ."

"In any case, you've inspired another marvelous poem, but I dare not read it to you because your physician warns that you're not recovered. My dazzling talent might strike such awe into your heart that you fall ill again."

Fie on the physician! He knows nothing. The scent of iron in the air strengthens me. I am invigorated by the storm and the scorching summer sun that emerges after it to dry up all the rain, leaving the world stained red. I bled. Mauretania bled. Now that is done.

To be sure, I force myself to eat shellfish and generously salted meats, even though I have little appetite. And I decide to make strolling the garden with my son's hound at my heel a morning ritual.

On my first turn around the lavender, I find myself a bit breathless, but that is to be expected. And if my bones ache and I walk like a crone, well, it is still better than being idle in bed. I am quite exhausted when I catch a glance of my daughter's fair hair.

"Isidora?" When she doesn't answer, I say, "I see you there . . ."

Shamefaced, she peeks from behind a hulking statue of Hercules. "I didn't mean to disturb you."

"Why are you skulking about like a criminal?" When she presses her lips together, I know. "Oh, come and see with your own eyes that I am alive and well and that not all visions come true."

With a wary smile, she rustles through the bushes to join me. "But . . . but I was *sure* that I would send you into the afterworld . . ."

I clasp her hands. "You are fifteen years old, Isidora. Trust me, when I was fifteen years old, I was sure of a good many things too. Now the only thing of which I am certain is the world's uncertainty."

Shyly fingering the collar of gold amulet at her throat, she says, "The storm saved you. I didn't know it could."

"We're always saved or lost in the center of a storm. It's the only time we can ever truly know ourselves . . ."

"You sound like a philosopher now."

"Do I? Well, you'll have to compare my wisdom to that of the scholars in Greece . . . I want you to go with the king on his trip. You'll enjoy being feted in the East as the granddaughter of Cleopatra."

She blanches. "I have already done it, and know I wouldn't enjoy it at all."

She is remembering her girlhood, when we rode together with the emperor into Athens and the crowd stomped and roared in welcome such that the earth trembled beneath our feet. "Everyone loves to be feted," I insist. "The Greeks want to see Ptolemaic glamour and you shall stand in my stead."

Panic flares in her eyes. "Mother, I can last no more than two hours in a pleated gown before it is all wrinkled and unpleated and I am pulling the ribbons from my hair and fleeing a social gathering!"

It's true that my daughter seems to have taken her sense of fashion from Lady Lasthenia and the Pythagoreans, but this will be a good lesson for her. "In the East, you'll learn the importance of appearance, the influence of a well-spoken word, and the power of reputation in the Greek world."

She sputters in protest, then crosses her arms. "You're sending me because you don't want me to receive any more letters from the emperor, aren't you?"

"That is not the only reason."

"But—"

"Don't you want to see Pythia?"

At the mention of my niece, her resistance melts away. For all the love I bear Pythia, I think my daughter loves her even better.

And it is only because they were as sisters to each other that I can bear to let Isidora attend the royal wedding in my stead. I am reluctant to part with my daughter even for a few weeks, a few days, a few hours. But the thought of my girls reunited together makes me smile.

"I will watch over Papa for you," my daughter promises.

I smile again, drawing her into my arms. "You'll have a grand adventure. On the first clear sunny day, I'll kiss your cheeks and send you off on a ship laden with gifts for Pythia. Then I'll cry myself to sleep every night and look for a letter from you every morning . . ."

IN the years that Amphio has been building my Iseum, hundreds of workshops have sprung up near the harbor. Stonecutters, carpenters, smiths, and other skilled tradesmen have profited handsomely. Now they must make way for the finer artists. Sculptors to carve cornices and pillars from marble. Painters to color the walls with murals. Tile layers who will cover the floors in mosaic designs that call Egypt to mind. And masters of statuary to render my lovely Isis in ivory and gold.

It is a very great expense, but our amber, our purple dye, our citrus-wood furniture, the pearls from our sea, and even our *garum* sauce will pay for it. Especially if Juba is able to secure trade alliances on his journey.

Days before the king and his entourage are to depart, I call Amphio to account. "Why haven't you removed the centerings from the dome?"

"There was a small matter of a storm," the architect replies archly. "And we have been delayed by the need to scrub everything clean of the red rain."

"Tell me, do you fear the blood rain was a bad omen?" I ask with raised brow. "Or are you now convinced of the miraculous power of my goddess in this land?"

Amphio throws up his hands. "It was neither an omen nor a miracle nor blood! It was merely the red sand of the storm mixed with rain. Cicero wrote that the red rains were born of some *earthly* contagion. Certainly there's nothing divine about the ungodly mess it left behind."

Amused at his effrontery, I say, "The dome in my Iseum had better hold."

The dome holds.

Good thing too, because Amphio is standing under it when its supports are removed . . . just as he promised. I don't think he ever had a moment's doubt, but he makes a great show if it nonetheless, holding his arms up as if his strength alone kept the dome in place.

Let him mock magic if he wishes. I will always know that a true wizard gave his essence to bless this place. And the nearer the temple is to completion, the more grateful I am for it. My temple is already a shining beacon to Isis worshippers who flock to our shores. Surely my goddess will be pleased and give her blessing and protection to my husband and daughter on their quest across the sea . . .

Forty-four

❀

IOL-CAESARIA, THE KINGDOM OF MAURETANIA
SUMMER 8 B.C.

Dearest Mother and Queen,

Have you been taking the tonics of herbs that I advised for you to balance your humors? My snake is very much concerned you will forget . . .

We are missing your company here in Greece where we toured the buildings dedicated to our ancestors in Olympia. I made a rubbing for you of the names of Ptolemy II and his sister, wife, and queen, Arsinoe II, the first female pharaoh of our line, but I continue to guess at the real reason you wished for me to travel with the king in your place.

Was it because you knew married women are not allowed to attend the Olympic Games, but as a maiden, I could sit beside the king and watch the athletes compete?

The champion runner of the stadion was Artemidoros of Thyateira, should you care to know his name. Papa said that you would enjoy watching men race for the glory of it, but I suspect you would consider quite dull a sport in which men are neither running from anything nor to anything. In any case, I liked the boxing. Do you know that a physician must set a broken nose immediately, or the swelling will make it impossible to do it right? Perhaps this explains Amphio's crooked nose.

* * *

HERE I pause in my reading to laugh at my own folly. I sent my daughter to see all the splendor of Greece only to have her take away from it a new knowledge of broken noses! This is the longest that I have ever been apart from Isidora, and the separation gives me keen anxiety, but while she is away, I burn every letter that comes to her under the emperor's seal. Eventually, word must reach him that she is traveling in Greece, because the letters stop. Then, at the height of summer, a dispatch from Rome informs me that the month of *Sextilius* is now to be called *August*, after the emperor.

He has not chosen for his own the month of his birth. Oh, no. He has chosen for himself the month in which he conquered my mother and saw her dead. And though this makes me burn, I will not be goaded into a response.

I miss my husband's arms and my daughter's laughter. I still mourn my eldest son. I ache upon waking and still tire easily. And yet, there is true joy at my hearth. By day, I do my best to rule justly and patiently. Sometimes I even succeed. At night, I cradle my son and sing him little songs to lull him to sleep.

No two children are the same. You love them differently. This little boy is not the same as my first Ptolemy, but he is already his own little person. He does not know anything of the past. There are no scars on him, and I mean to keep it that way.

Dearest Queen and Wife,

The giant statue of Zeus in Olympia is rendered in gold and ivory. Ebony makes up his fierce black eyes. Dust of gold shines in the creases of his strong, muscled chest. And he sits upon an enormous seat of cedar, his throne studded with glittering emeralds and rubies and sapphires. They call it a wonder of the world, and I know you would think so. Even the Romans say that it moves them to believe they are staring at the god himself. And yet I think it no greater or more beautiful than the statue your artists are making for Isis.

All right. Enough of that. I will try not to chronicle our journey like a geographer or point out all the customs that I find unusual here in the East. I will save all that for my next treatise.

Instead, I will tell you how I settled an old score on your behalf.

It has long been my policy to deny the pleas and extortions for money from Greece because we have both seen how Herod's subjects hate him for spending their taxes in places they will never see. But I have decided to make one notable exception. I have given over treasure to rebuild the gymnasium of your ancestors in Athens. We will have statues dedicated to us in thanks not only on the Acropolis, but inside the building itself. It is as plain a statement as we can make that your Ptolemaic dynasty will endure.

Isidora wished to make her own tribute. From her own savings she purchased a small plaque to remember Memnon and your Berber woman, Tala, who I think would be amused to be honored so far from her home.

I smile at the memory of my faithful friends. I think Tala *would* be amused to know she has been honored this way—no simple serving woman, indeed. And though Juba said he would not drone on like a geographer, he proceeds to do just that, filling several scrolls' worth of details about his journey to mountainous Cappadocia, where stones rise up from the ground like dragon's teeth. It makes me sigh with affection, for my husband can never resist an opportunity to lecture. Still, I skip ahead to the part about Pythia's wedding . . .

Your niece came to her new husband wearing a soaring crown of hammered gold and a saffron veil. Pythia did not go shyly to her groom, but with the full majesty of a queen with a cadre of guards at her back. I had the opportunity to speak with Pythia both before and after the wedding, and she bade me to reassure you that she is neither disappointed nor overjoyed by this marriage.

She views it as a political advantage.

How like you she has become.

The reminder leaves me to wish fervently for our reunion. I have taken Isidora to see plays and to hear poets and to debate philosophers. She has tried to make of herself a fine companion for me, but there is nothing we see but that we wish you were here to see it with us. I do not like this separation and I cannot imagine how I let you convince me it was a good idea. You are never long from my thoughts and I would, even now, be on the deck of a ship straining for the sight of our lighthouse were it not for the matter of Herod's trial . . .

Another letter comes from Juba a few weeks later, and this one is written in Latin.

Salve Selene,

As it is now autumn and we have still not returned home to you, I am sure you have surmised that all is not well. We were forced to celebrate Isidora's sixteenth birthday in Beirut.

The happy occasion was ruined by the trial of Herod's sons.

You will have heard by now that the trial was a mockery of justice. I tried to persuade Herod that executing his sons would not gain him favor with the emperor—a sentiment echoed by the Roman magistrates—to no avail. The vast majority of the judges were beholden to Herod. They voted for guilt.

The princes were condemned to be strangled to death.

I fear that I proved unequal to my mission. We will not stay to witness the executions as even the shame of my failure cannot dissuade me from returning home to you. Herod has robbed us of enough time!

*   *   *

THE king's ship sails into our harbor only days after I read this letter. Oh, how I curse the eager crowd of courtiers in our entryway who prevent me from rushing to my loved ones in unseemly haste. The king and Princess Isidora stride into the palace with their servants and baggage close behind. I grasp my daughter by the hands and pinch at her cheeks as if she were still a small girl and not a woman of sixteen.

How could my daughter have become more beautiful? Oh, but she is. With pink cheeks and bright eyes she chatters excitedly about her travels. Then Juba calls my name and I turn. With a courtly bow of his head, he says, "You are looking very well, Queen Selene."

And he—well, how can I describe him without sounding like a lovesick poet? He is a tall king in his own hall, and I am so glad to have him home that I forget all our disappointments.

When I make ready to receive him in my chambers that night, the mirror tells me that he is a flatterer. My skin is not as smooth as it used to be and I spy two gray hairs that I pluck out with my own fingers. I am still tall and regal, but there is a heaviness in my face that was not there before. I have my ladies dress me in my finery, because I find that I am nervous to be alone with the king. In truth, I am as anxious as the day we married, when he took hold of the bed linens and unmasked me by wiping my face clean of the powders and rouge and kohl.

Then he asked me for love and I spurned him.

Now I want nothing more than to be beautiful in his eyes.

We break bread together that night for his homecoming. It is a spicy dish of root vegetables stewed in a clay pot and I worry it will be too hot for the king's tongue. But he does not seem to notice this, or my anxiety.

"Have you heard what the emperor said of it?" Juba asks, rubbing the back of his neck with one hand. "He said it was better to be Herod's pig than one of his sons."

The witty comment does not amuse me. "Augustus is every bit as guilty. He might have put a stop to it if he cared to."

Juba does not reply but encourages me to try some of the wine he brought back from the East. An expensive Falernian that is said to have no peer. "Glaphyra was pardoned. At least I accomplished that before leaving Beirut. Or, I should say, Isidora accomplished it . . ."

This makes me gasp. "You involved Isidora?"

"Not intentionally. One glimpse at Isidora with that snake on her arm and Herod went white with fear."

It should not give me pleasure to imagine it, but it does. "You shouldn't have let him see her."

"She came to my side without my bidding," Juba protests. "And she informed Herod that he was suffering from worm-eaten genitals, an ailment already blinding him and putting a fever into his brain."

I stop eating. "I think I'm going to gag . . ."

Juba lifts his cup as if to bolster my appetite. "She offered a treatment, which, of course, Herod refused. Deep in his cups, he began muttering about how Cleopatra was a witch, how you and Isidora were witches, how even his dead wife was a witch. So I seized upon this to convince him it was the curse of Mariamne that ailed him. I said that being married to you, I'd learned that killing a woman always risks such magical vengeance and that it would be safer to send Glaphyra away. So Herod cast her out. Sent her back to Cappadocia with her dowry besides."

I marvel at him. "Then your mission was no failure, Juba. You saved Glaphyra's life!"

"She was not glad of it," Juba says, head bowed as he dips his bread into his stew. "Herod took her children and she said she'd rather have died than leave without them."

I palm his cheek. "You did more than anyone else could."

Juba's eyes remain downcast. "Evidently, Augustus agrees. His legates in Syria sent word to him commending my conduct." I exhale, relieved, for this is exactly what I hoped for. Then Juba adds, "As reward, the emperor's secretary has informed me that I have permission to style myself as King Juba *Philokaiser*."

At this I wince, for we have never before needed such an appel-
lation to boast that we were *friends of Caesar*, but I must keep up
my husband's spirits. "Augustus is softening, then. It's an opportunity to appease him, and we *must* appease him. Not for our sake,
but for the sake of our children."

"For the sake of our children?" Juba asks, slamming down his
goblet to punctuate his sudden, violent anger. "You know that he
has been writing to Isidora. Caesar will not put a drop of ink to
paper in addressing me, but he sends letters to a girl of sixteen. He
will take her from us . . . I tell you, he will claim her as his daughter
and he will take her!"

"He will not," I say, for though I worry about all the ways in
which the emperor might twist and manipulate my daughter, I will
never let him have her. More importantly, neither will my enemies.
"Livia will poison Augustus before she would allow him to claim
Isidora as his daughter and he knows it."

Juba uses a napkin to wipe up the wine he has sloshed onto his
hand. "Then why is he writing to her?"

"Because he wants me to tell him to stop." When Juba glances
up at me, I vow, "I will not do it. I swear to you that Augustus has
heard the last words from me he will ever hear. But you must be
reconciled with him and I think I know a way. Every other kingdom
in the empire now has a temple for Augustus. Perhaps it is time that
you founded a cult to the divine emperor."

Juba narrows his eyes. "You want the man worshipped here in
our kingdom?"

"Of course not. But he will take it as adoration, and that is what
he needs from you."

"Selene, have you seen such cult temples to him? I saw them in
Greece. He is carved with a breastplate that depicts his victory over
your parents at Actium. Do not tell me that it would not sicken you
to see such a thing here . . ."

"It *will* sicken me. It will be galling beyond compare. But I have
endured galling things before and I can endure this for you, and for
our family."

My husband stares at me in such a way that I cannot tell whether he thinks me a genius or a madwoman. "Where did you even get such an idea?"

"From you. When we first came to Mauretania, you thought to build such a monstrosity, so you should be the high priest now. Pour spoiled milk for his libations and burn gristle and bone for his sacrifices and spit on his statue every day, for all I care. Or do whatever you would have done, when you first thought to build a temple for Augustus."

He seems surprised that I know about the designs he made so long ago. "I had an architect sketch such a temple years ago, but my scribe mislaid the plans. Many things have changed since then."

"Let the emperor forgive you," I say.

My husband shakes his head. "How can you ask that of me?"

"Because I know how much vengeance and spite have taken from us. The emperor has destroyed his family. Don't let him destroy ours."

Juba is silent a good while, staring into the fire.

I break the silence with a confession. "And you should know that your scribe did not mislay the plans. Years ago, when you were away exploring the wilds of Mauretania with your *hetaera*, I found the plans in your study and burned them."

His head jerks up. "You *burned* them?"

"To ash and with great satisfaction. But my rebellion serves no purpose now."

My husband rises from his chair to hover over me. "Do I understand you to say . . . that you burned scrolls you found in the king's study?"

His censure makes me sheepish.

When I can only press my lips together in guilty confession, he says, "I would have a man flogged for such a thing."

To ease his temper, I murmur, "Good fortune that I am not a man."

He smirks, in spite of himself, his anger melting into something else. "Good fortune, indeed. Still, I intend to exact a price."

"What would you have of me, Your Majesty?"

"I would have you stay the night with me in my chambers. The *whole* night."

My cheeks go hot at the suggestion. It is not done. The king visits the queen's chambers and leaves before daybreak. The queen does not go to the king's chambers like some *hetaera*. She certainly does not stay the night. It is not *done*. It will be remarked upon. Our courtiers will gossip.

And I find that I do not care in the slightest.

Forty-five

"IT'S wonderful," I say from the warm confines of the king's bed, the last scroll of his work spread over my bare knees like a blanket.

In the year since Juba's return, we have scandalized our court with vulgar displays of public affection such as holding hands and exchanging kisses in the banquet hall. There are also persistent rumors that we sleep together in the same chambers almost every night.

My Greeks fear I have truly become a barbarian. Perhaps they are right. After these many years of marriage to the king, it is as if I have only begun to discover him. I've learned that he wakes from slumber at the slightest provocation, only to rush from the bed to scribble down some note before returning to sleep again. I've also learned that he can be extraordinarily sensitive when it comes to his writing. "Do you truly think it will be well reccived?" Juba asks, his lips against my shoulder, making no attempt whatsoever to pretend he isn't hovering.

I laugh, stroking my fingertips over his careful lettering, for he does not use a scribe for his scholarship. "I said it was wonderful! It will become an essential volume in every library in the world. There has never been such a comprehensive study of our kingdom. You have cataloged everything, from plants to purple dye, maps of islands and characteristics of our hunting dogs to the source of the Nile.

Why, you even managed to slip in that story about Tala and the lion!"

The king's valet knocks at the door, but we ignore it like petulant children, snuggling down in our nest of lavender-scented bed linens and warm skin.

"I ought to take it out. My fellow scholars think me a credulous fool . . ."

"Let them think what they like. Far more miraculous things have happened here than a merciful lion . . ."

The king takes my palm in his hand and kisses it with a promise of intimacy in his eyes. "Indeed. Perhaps miraculous things shall happen again, right now."

The mischief in his gaze heats my loins, but again the valet knocks.

"Go away!" the king shouts. "Or I'll send the executioner for your head."

I throw my head back in laughter. "Tyrant! You'll terrify the poor boy. Besides, we must get up or we'll be late for our son's birthday games."

"Let the world wait," Juba says, nuzzling my hair.

"But I have a surprise for you."

The king tugs me closer. "All the more reason to let them wait."

"Not here," I say, trying to smother my grin. "In your study."

With mussed hair and desire in his eyes, he says, "My study? I confess I am not very particular about where. Beds, couches, or tents are all the same to me. So I will not argue against the study, though it's rather cluttered and I cannot speak for its comfort . . ."

Again he makes me laugh and I have to thwart him with both hands on his chest. "Careful. You are crushing your scroll between us . . ."

That makes him release me, as I knew it would, and I take the opportunity to roll from his bed and find my own robe. With a growl of frustration, he yanks a tunic over his head, then follows me into the hall, where some servants scatter and others turn to stone, none of them certain how to behave in the presence of the king and queen in dishabille. Together in bare feet, we sweep into his study, where I proudly unveil a brand-new water clock that I had designed by one of the scholars at our university.

With great showmanship, I snap off the coverings, explaining, "At each hour, a little mechanical animal performs some little trick!"

"Fascinating," Juba says, stooping to examine each metal part, entranced by the intricacy of the automata in the form of lions, elephants, monkeys, and other creatures from our lands. Then the hour changes and a little mechanized spearman prompts the metal lion to attack with an accompanying chime.

Juba startles with delight. "How splendid!"

I am even more delighted. "The designer says it's similar to one in Rhodes, where they're experts in making such mechanized things. Do you like it?"

"I like it very much . . . except . . ."

Watching his smile slowly fade, I am deflated. "What is it? I know it is a whimsical gift not in keeping with the serious bearing of a king . . . but I hoped to impress you with the genius of the thing."

"I am impressed. Quite pleased by the gift, Selene. It is only that I already have a water clock."

"The old one is broken," I protest.

"Yes, but I intend to fix it."

I reach for his cheek with my left hand, where our amethyst betrothal ring gleams in the light. "Juba, you have been trying to fix that old clock for as long as we have been married. After nineteen years, don't you think it's time we start everything anew?"

CHARIOTS race to honor the birthday of my two-year-old prince, who sits upon my lap with pink apple cheeks and fat little fists that thump on my thighs when he is excited. Victory wreaths are awarded to our athletes and we pardon many lesser criminals that day.

Then we are treated to a tribute of musicians. We hear the soaring voices of altos, the hollow notes of pipers, and a *kithara* player I find fault with, on account of the fact I have played that song better. I am tempted to call for my own instrument to demonstrate, when a certain besotted soldier offers a basket filled with roses and wildflowers into my daughter's lap.

The love-struck soldier is none other than Tacfarinas, no longer a boy but a man of twenty with a brawny sword arm and piercing eagle eyes. Some fool centurion apparently admired his fighting spirit and made Tacfarinas an *optio*, giving him actual rank and responsibility in the cohort we have stationed in the city. Tacfarinas is very young to hold such a position but has not made a mess of it so far.

At least until he decided to approach the princess so boldly and in front of the king . . .

Juba sees the flowers, then leans over to murmur to me with a violent sparkle in his eye. "I'm going to start a distant war just so that I can send Tacfarinas away to fight it."

I laugh only because I know he will not really do it.

Now that we have a prince to rule the kingdom, some say we ought to send Isidora to a marriage bed in some far away kingdom. But we have decided to let Dora remain unmarried in keeping with her wishes to stay in Mauretania, and our wishes to have her near. I hate to think that my daughter may never have a child of her own, but she says she does not need one, for she has little T'amT'am. And it is true that she treats him as if he were her own child. He is a little boy with two mothers, for Isidora has her baby brother always in her arms. Perhaps that is best, for so long as she bears no sons of her own—boys the emperor might claim as his own descendants—it may keep her from his clutches.

Like me, Isidora has suffered the grievous loss of a brother. Like me, she will never marry the boy who first captured her heart. Like me, she will live under the shadow of the emperor's desire to possess her. But unlike me, she must also live with the burden of what she sees that ordinary mortals cannot see.

And yet, like a cherry tree that must suffer the touch of frost before it can bear sweet fruit, she has blossomed in this adversity. There is no plant in our kingdom that she cannot identify in a glance or find a use for. Lady Lasthenia insists that she is knowledgeable enough to lecture in our university. People seek Dora out for remedies, and though the king *says* he finds this to be an entirely inappropriate vocation for a princess, Juba boasts about her discoveries and the new center of healing she has established adjacent to my temple.

Only a king such as Juba would allow his daughter such leniency, but I do not like it. I cringe every time a dirty peasant rushes upon my daughter begging for her advice on lancing a boil or curing a crusty rash. I seethe that any daughter of mine should pay more attention to someone's earache than she does to the happenings in our council chambers.

But just as I was called to something different than my mother was, I fear Dora has her own calling. Or at least, a very good excuse to keep from marrying anyone other than her Berber boy. I muse to the king, "I don't suppose there are many other men who aren't dissuaded in their affections by a girl who keeps a snake for a friend . . ."

Juba furrows his brow. "You don't think they find ways to meet in secret, do you?"

"Would you want to know if they did?"

As he contemplates the risks our headstrong daughter might take, the king pushes his fingers through his hair, which is turning silver in a way I find most comely. But in the end, he says, "No, I suppose not. I have learned to let every woman have at least one mystery."

LATER that night, I ponder his words, wondering at any hidden bitterness. I will always be a creature who harbors secrets—otherwise, I would not be myself. Even my goddess keeps her mysteries. But there can be no danger now in telling the truth. No painful choices for Juba to make. No risk that he will betray me. So, in the shadow of lamplight, cradled in my husband's arms, I force myself to say, "I once asked you to let me keep a secret . . ."

He hushes me with one long finger atop my lips. "I already know."

"You can't."

Juba insists, "I have suspected for a long time. When they said your twin was killed in Egypt, I told you I would send for the body to bury. And yet you never asked after the corpse again. Never once. *You*, who will wait seventy days for an embalming to be done properly. You built a tomb for Alexander Helios on that hill, but never performed rites for him there. So he must be alive somewhere . . ."

I shake my head, wondering how I will explain that if Helios is alive he is only alive in me. That he is here with us even now, but no longer *between* us.

As I search for the words, Juba whispers, "It took me some time to work out, but then I remembered. You once asked me to swear that I would never help the emperor harm your brothers. I would not make that promise. I would not give you what you needed to put your trust in me. I did not understand, then, that I could not love you and still deny you the one thing you needed most. But I understand it now, and I vow to you I will never tell Augustus. I will never cause harm to your twin or anyone you love. I vow this on my life."

Swallowing, I turn to face him, realizing that he has finally chosen me. He has chosen *me* over the emperor and I am dizzied with love for him. Clutching him, I start to speak, but it comes out only as a sob.

"No tears, Selene," he pleads with me. "I did not say it to make you sad . . ."

"I am not sad," I croak against the wet pillow. But tears wash over me, soaking my cheeks, my shoulders, my bare breasts. Tears flow until I am shaking.

He holds me tight, trying to hush me, begging me between kisses to be content. "Why do you cry?"

I gasp in astonishment that he does not know it. That he cannot see it or feel it. "I am crying because I love you and because I am so sorry for every moment I did not know it . . . and I'm so grateful that I know it now. I love you. I love you."

He smiles tenderly, using his thumbs to wipe away my tears. "That is no reason to cry . . ."

"How did I never know the man you are? You don't know how much I regret."

Where might I even begin to list all the ways in which I wish I'd loved him better?

He tilts my chin so that I must look at him. "Regret nothing. I am only the man you made me, Selene . . . You are loved and you are forgiven all. As I hope I am."

"You are," I say, with a violent intensity. "You are loved, Gaius Julius Juba. You are loved and you are forgiven everything."

THESE are happy years in Mauretania.

The happiest, I think.

And filled with delightful surprises. One sun-drenched afternoon, some commotion erupts in the archway to our throne room, and Juba exclaims, "Aha! Here it is at last . . ."

With great fanfare, a long wooden cage is wheeled into my tiled palace to the frightened and astonished gasps of our courtiers. "Good gods!" Crinagoras exclaims at the sight of the beast inside. "Majesties, are we not even *pretending* at civilization anymore?"

That is when I see a beautiful crocodile inside the cage. She is a massive specimen with rows of gleaming teeth and scales banded with olive and brown. Her spiked tail is as long as the rest of her and she gapes open her mouth to show me her pink, well-fed gullet. Consumed with wonder, I stand up from my throne and ask, "Wherever did she come from?"

"From Lake Nilidis," Juba says, puffed up with pride. "I sent an expedition into the wilds to capture this creature for your temple, Selene, as I know they are sacred to your goddess."

My smile widens until my cheeks ache with it. I am nearly quivering with delight. No one else would have cause to know what this means to me. Why this crocodile is better than any jewels or scrolls or riches I have ever received. Heedless of the scandal, I throw my arms around his neck. "Oh, Juba!"

He embraces me, well pleased by my reaction, murmuring into my ear, "And you think Isidora is strange to squeal when someone gives her a box of dried herbs?"

Our open affection makes the stiff-necked Romans of our court very uncomfortable . . . which makes it all the more enjoyable. But eventually I become aware that one courtier in particular is more distressed than the others.

With a rumble of disapproval, Amphio asks, "You mean to keep this crocodile in my temple?"

I want to remind him that it is *my* temple, but I should not begrudge him. He prides himself on every detail of the Iseum. Every lily pattern in the stonework, every elegant curve in the bronze doors, every plank of wood for the throne of Isis, and every drop of gold paint on the shining dome. And so I take Amphio aside to explain to him why he must now pride himself on a crocodile pool.

"Ridiculous!" Amphio blusters. "How am I to convince workers to put the finishing touches on the Iseum when they are afraid to drop a hammer too near your new pet's snapping jaws?"

I merely lift a brow and say, "I'm sure you will manage it somehow."

"Why not?" he asks in high pique, arms folded over his chest, as if daring me to throw yet another challenge in his way. "What next? An altar for shit-throwing monkeys?"

Not a bad guess, I muse to myself. "We would like you to begin a temple for the divine Augustus."

Since my architect is Roman, I think he should relish this idea. But Amphio snorts in such a way that makes me think it is more than his usual irreverence that gives him a loathing for the idea. His disdain reminds me that in Rome, Augustus is no god but must cloak himself in false humility, calling himself the *First Citizen*. And

Amphio says sourly, "I cannot do better than I have done with your Iseum, Majesty."

"Good."

"To be more exact . . . I have no desire to build another temple. This temple is my mark on the world. *This* one."

I cannot blame him for feeling this way. Amphio is a bald, twitchy shadow of himself. Ten years more, he said it would take, and yet he has nearly completed the Iseum in half that time. And so allowances must be made. "Very well, Amphio. Then set an apprentice to the task of a temple for Augustus. Only see to it that the cult statue is wearing sandals; I will not have Augustus barefoot like some Homeric hero from the *Iliad* or like some god in flight. There is only one winged deity in my lands. And speaking of Isis, I am told the Iseum will be ready to dedicate soon?"

"This spring," he promises.

"You have worked a miracle to get it done."

Amphio does not blush; it is not his way. "I don't believe in miracles, Majesty."

I smile and say, "One day, you will."

COME spring, we are drowned in a deluge of letters. The most notable missive comes for my husband, written in the emperor's own hand, praising Juba's newest geographical treatise. Reminiscing at length about their long-standing friendship and how glad he is to be served by King Juba II, *Rex Literatissimus*, Augustus makes it plain that he has decided to reconcile with my husband, or at least pretend that he has . . .

I am glad of it. "So he has heard about the temple we are building for him."

"Of course he has," the king replies. "No doubt he imagines that you will tend to him as his high priestess, bathing and dressing his statue every day like a humble wife."

"If spitting upon his statue counts as bathing it . . ."

The king is not amused. In a huff, he leaves me to dress for a musical competition at which we are to choose the victor. I sit at my dressing table making ready, dabbing perfumed oil at my wrists, when a servant delivers to me a letter of my own.

This one is from Julia, and her letter explains the emperor's new conciliatory attitude far better than our cult to the divine Augustus.

To My Friend, the Most Royal Queen of Mauretania,

I will send another letter shortly inquiring as to your health and asking after your baby boy and your daughter, who I am told is the incarnation of Asclepius in a frock! But enough about you and yours, for I have excellent news.

Tiberius has finally done something to make me love him.

He has sailed away!

Yes, that's right. I am nearly free of Tiberius.

And good riddance to him.

According to Julia, her husband grew so jealous of the popularity of her sons in Rome that he threw a fit, announced he was retiring from public life, and sailed off to Rhodes. In so doing, he has abandoned Augustus, Livia, and all the power over the empire he had been offered.

Which means that the emperor has one less man upon which he can rely . . .

I read the breathless details in Julia's scrawl, frowning. This is a careless letter, one that she would never dare put to paper if she were not flush with victory. She has been fighting a war in Rome with Livia, each of them maneuvering the strongest men left in the Republic. Julia has won this battle, and I will do anything she asks to help her win the next one, but I will also have to remind her that it is only a battle. A battle for her sons—and my heart aches for my Ptolemy, who would be almost old enough now to take the *toga virilis* and be counted a man.

I am still thinking of my eldest son, tracing his image on the portrait cameo I wear around my neck in remembrance, when Isidora comes to the door of my chambers, her baby brother in her arms. "Mother! Everyone is waiting for you at the music festival. Aren't you coming with us?"

"Yes, of course, I am coming with you."

Glancing one last time at Julia's letter, I set it aside. For this is Julia's war now.

Not mine. Not anymore.

Forty-six

IN the twentieth year of my reign, I am tired by many things I used to do with ease. These days I cannot walk far without gasping for breath. I blame it on the fact that I have grown a little plumper, but some mornings my hands are swollen like they were when the Greek physician told me I had lost too much blood and would never recover.

It is my daughter who first notices. "Why are you panting?" she asks while I play with T'amT'am, rolling a ball back and forth on the beach while Luna barks happily in encouragement.

"It is only that I am not as young as when you were a babe and we played together."

But a few days later, when I accompany the king on a hunting trip, I feel light-headed. Watching Luna chase down a hare, her silver fur nothing but a flash against the greenery, I suddenly swoon.

The king catches me at the elbow before I collapse, then rushes me to the palace, where the entire court is in an uproar wondering if I am again with child.

Alas, I am not.

In my chambers, the physician says, "I warned you, madam, yet you foolishly insist upon exerting yourself."

When he pokes hard at my abdomen, my daughter intervenes. "Be gentle! Can you not see my mother wincing when you touch her?"

Startled, the physician straightens to his full height. "Princess, I fear you are too inexperienced to know that sometimes one must cause pain to heal . . ."

"And I fear you have no interest in finding a cure for what ails the queen. Why don't you come back when you do?"

He stares at her in a most intimidating manner, but she gives not an inch. Instead, she glares back, daring him to defy her, all while raising an imperious brow.

Good. I did not think she knew how to be imperious.

I am capable of defending myself against Greek physicians or any number of other petty irritants, but as a mother lion who has just seen her cub learn to bare her teeth, I find it immensely satisfying to watch the princess back him down. He shoves his instruments and tonics into his medicine chest, murmuring under his breath, but obeys her by taking his leave.

Alas, once he is gone, Isidora subjects me to a series of gentler examinations that try my patience beyond endurance. First she makes me drink some tonic of hawthorn, to help the blood move inside me.

Then she fetches her snake.

It has taken all my forbearance to tolerate that creature in the palace—I do not like it so near to me. "Keep it away and do not tell anyone at court that I am ill. I am not going to be like Augustus, sending everyone into a panic every time I get a sniffle."

"It is more than a sniffle."

"I am only tired," I insist. But I am more than tired. My head aches intolerably and I am also freezing. Though it is springtime, I cannot get warm. When the rains come, I shiver even to step outside of my chambers for a moment. It seems there are not enough woven blankets for my bed or a big enough fire to put the heat back in my blood. I cannot draw the flames into me anymore.

The sirocco gifted me with precious time, but every storm eventually quiets.

This is because of the curses, I think. They took years of my life with them. Or perhaps it's because of my baby. The magic I used to birth him—just like the magic I used to make the crops grow—is not without price. But I would do it again for my tiny prince, my precious T'amT'am. The little boy who has finished what his older brother started by helping Juba and me to find each other.

The next time the physician comes to my rooms, I make an effort to rise from my bed. Every day I try and every time I am defeated. My limbs are heavy and weak. Sleep holds great allure. Even when I'm awake, my head feels as if it's been stuffed with cotton.

And on the morning that I am seized with convulsions, the Greek physician insists that I suffer from an excess of black bile. "You are dying, Majesty . . ."

"We are all dying, or so the philosophers say."

He does not know that I once said this to the emperor. Nor is he amused. "The king must be made aware."

"Are you so high in favor that you can tell him without fear of losing your head?" If I enjoy the way he pales at my words, it is only because I don't like him, and not because I am cruel.

No one needs to tell my husband. He hears my panting in the night. He sees my paleness upon waking. We do not speak of it, but in a dozen little ways he shows me that he knows. He brings my robe to me before the slave girls think to do it. He changes the hour of his daily ride so that he is not apart from me unless I am napping. And once, I hear him berate Chryssa to make swifter arrangements for the dedication of the Iseum, as if he too were afraid that I might die before it can be dedicated.

"YOU'RE not with child *again*, are you?" I pose this question to my freedwoman as she eases into the chair beside the sickbed to which I have been confined. Blushing, she rests a hand on her silver girdled belly, and I have my answer. "*Sweet Isis*, do you and Maysar intend to breed a new Berber tribe all by yourselves?"

She pretends to frown, but pleasure shines in her eyes. "I should never have made him promise not to take a second wife. I would welcome a respite from my duties at hearth and home and motherhood."

"Liar," I say.

And she laughs. She, who once knelt before me and asked me to place a blessing on her head, is happy. Is it a vanity to hope that I saved the slave girl who once called me savior? Or perhaps she saved me, for she helped make possible everything I take pride in.

When her laughter subsides, she ruins my moment of pride by saying, "I must speak to you about Master Gnaios. He came to me with concerns about the latest coin you have made him fashion. Concerns I share."

I give a haughty shake of my head. Or at least as haughty as I can make it, given that I am unable to get out of bed. "If the king does not object to my new coin, why should you?"

"Because the king will forbid you nothing, so it falls to me to warn you that Augustus will not like this new coin."

She holds a prototype of the coin out to me, but I already have one cradled in my palm. I have been sleeping with it. It is reminiscent of one minted years ago by Agrippa and Augustus, proclaiming that Rome had conquered Egypt. *Their* coin shows a crocodile in chains. But the crocodile stamped on *my* coin is free, just as Chryssa is free, just as I am soon to be . . .

"Augustus will think it is a message just for him," I say. "A reminder that he may have conquered my mother, but he has never conquered me . . ."

That is the truth of it. Egypt is not conquered and neither am I. The spirit of Isis has spread the world over. She can be found in my kingdom, in my daughter, and in all the people everywhere who understand her promise. Perhaps I will endure in just the same way.

A crease of worry splits Chryssa's brow. "Majesty, what if the emperor thinks you mean to reignite the old battle?"

"He probably will, but it is too late for that. This coin may be the last thing I ever say to the world. So spend the coins and let the blame fall on me."

For a moment, I think she will comfort me with platitudes about how I will get better soon, but she lowers her eyes. "As you wish, my beloved queen."

She understands that I am dying, and that is a relief to me. I will not entrust my last wishes to the Vestals who were such poor guardians of my father's. Instead, I tell Chryssa what I want done, because

I know she will see to it that everything is as it should be. Silent tears wet her cheeks even as she nods her head to reassure me that my instructions will be followed to the letter.

And I hate to see her sad for my sake. "Be brave, Chryssa. Think how far we have come from the frightened girls we were together in Rome."

She tilts her head, wiping her wet cheek with her palm. "You never seemed frightened. I always thought you were very brave."

"No. I was a good actress. It was Helios who was brave."

She sighs for the master she loved. And she *did* love him. I always knew it. Perhaps she loved him as much as I did. Perhaps she wanted him for her lover; maybe she sensed him inside me before I did. Perhaps that is why she has stayed with me all these years, held only by the bonds of loyalty.

I dare to say it aloud. "I think he died, Chryssa. Helios died some time ago. Perhaps in Thebes when they told us he did. You knew it before anyone did. His spirit found me in the storm so that we could become one *akh*."

"Then he is not dead," Chryssa says, lacing her fingers through mine. "He is here with us now."

SWEET Isis, I am here to do you glory.

The tall bronze doors carved with lotuses and *ankhs* and the story of Osiris open to reveal the glow of a thousand candles on your altar. Clouds of sweet-smelling blue smoke rise up from the braziers where we burn precious amber for you. And while the crowd of priestesses shake their sistrum rattles and your young acolytes drop lilies into the reflecting pool, my daughter helps me to rise up to my feet and walk with shaky steps into the Iseum I have built for you.

How lovely you are. How the sight of your beautiful graven image fills my heart. In all my darkest hours, through all my losses, in the times I have abandoned you or thought you abandoned me, you have always been with me. Here you are now, at the end, with a forgiving gaze, the sacred *tiet* knot between your breasts and bounty in your outstretched hands.

And how much you have given me!

Egypt was taken from me, but you saw me to a new land. My family was taken from me, but you gave me another. I lost my child, but it was you who gave him to me in the first place. You gave me my strength as a woman, as a mother, as a queen. And you taught me forgiveness that I might know love.

Yes, you gave me even that . . .

There, bathed in the light of dusk streaming down from the oculus, is my husband. A man I have forgiven; a man who has forgiven me. A king who showed me the true source of the Nile. A king who now humbles himself before my goddess with a censer of incense in his hand to make fragrant the steps I take today.

Someday, the priests and priestesses of this temple will call worshippers to find solace here in Lamentations. They will lead the faithful in a Path of Tears, to unbind their hair, streak their faces with ash, and confess to one another what they weep for. But as I consecrate this temple, my tears are not for sadness but for a wild, *defiant* pride.

There, beneath the statue, is my chained crocodile. In the hour of judgment, Anubis weighs our hearts upon a scale. And if our hearts are black and heavy with sin in the hour of judgment, it will go to the crocodiles. So I will my crocodile to judge me. If my acts have been wicked, let her eat my heart. And if my heart is light, let it be saved.

I haven't the strength to run to the dangerous beast with her rows of sharp teeth, but I make my way, purposefully, such that I hear gasps go up from the crowd. Amphio surges forward to stop me, but the king bars his way with one outstretched hand, for he has faith in my miracles . . .

Barefoot, I take one step down into the pool, luxuriating in the feel of the Nile water on my feet and legs. Glancing up at Amphio, who stares at me slack-jawed, I splash into the pool to the waist, my gown floating behind me as I open my arms to the crocodile.

I am filled with the magic of Africa—the desert storms, ancient prayers, and life-giving rains. They were never mine to keep, only mine to hold. As I did on the long-ago day my mage and I first consecrated the ground beneath this temple, I make of the bones in my feet hollow things through which my *heka* can flow. I let it seep through the bare soles of my feet into the little bits of colored glass and tile that make glorious mosaic designs upon the floor of the pool. The *heka* flows into the pool beneath me, spreading like a river on the floor until it is twisting in the grooves between each tile, overflowing onto the floor beneath the crowd's feet, splashing the stone walls, soaking into the mortar.

The sacred beast senses my power and, splashing water with a ferocious snap of her tail, glides majestically into my arms, closing her eyes in bliss as I stroke her snout and run my fingers over the roughness of her olive-brown hide. She absolves me, my crimes washed away by the water she splashes up through her snout, and my heart is safe from her jaws.

You know what you are, you say to me.

And I do know.

I am the Resurrection.

But, my sweet goddess, I can now lay down the burden my mother entrusted to me so many years ago. So when I rise from the pool, Nile water streaming from my hair, my beautiful crocodile swimming in my wake, I take the little jade frog from my neck and I offer it to you to wear with the many jewels with which your worshippers will adorn you.

For I have *been* the Resurrection, but now you have risen again, and it will be through you that we find salvation.

I will live to see my son turn three years old. That much, I am convinced I can do, even though it becomes harder to breathe every day. Though I try to stay awake, I drift in and out of sleep. My memory is clogged and muddy and my vision has become blurry.

I'm so *very* tired, but my heart races erratically, waking me even from the respite of sleep with an incessant pounding in my ears.

It is like the drums, I think.

The war drums I heard when giving birth.

And that was a war that gravely wounded me.

I do not want to be in my chambers any longer. I want to be somewhere high, somewhere that the winds can sustain me. So on the morning of my little T'amT'am's third birthday, I demand we celebrate atop the world.

Perhaps the giant fire they stoke in the lighthouse will put the heat back into my blood, but it is very inconvenient to everyone, since I cannot climb up those stairs by myself. I entrust myself to the palace guard and finally into the arms of my husband, who insists on taking me from Iacentus and carrying me the last bit.

The effort makes the king fractious. He all but gnashes his teeth when he sets me down on the makeshift bed made ready by the keeper of the lighthouse. "I don't know why I am indulging you in this foolhardiness. But then, everyone has always indulged you. Caesar. Octavia. All of us. The spoiled princess of Egypt must have her way!"

Juba is furious with me because I am dying.

In his place, I would feel precisely the same way.

It is with a shaking hand that I reach to stroke his smooth cheek, and my fingertips long to memorize the lines of his handsome face. He will say that he has aged, grown stouter, his good looks marred by an increasingly furrowed brow. But I see the handsome young man with desert skin who offered water to a terrified girl and reminded her of home. I see the young tutor who told stories to children at my first Saturnalia and said that the hue of my dress brought out the green in my eyes. I see the dashing cavalry officer who once lifted me into his arms and carried me, bleeding, from a gladiatorial arena.

The things that happened between then and now, the betrayals and disappointments, they are long forgotten. All I see in him is the happiness he has given me.

Drawing him close so that I do not have to shout to be heard,

I whisper words of love. His lower lip trembles as he puts his hand over mine, pressed tight against his cheek. "I will put no stock in your love for me if you don't recover, Cleopatra Selene."

I am too well trained in lies and artifice. He cannot fool me. So I smile because he knows the truth. Both that I love him and that I will not recover. It will be difficult for him to finish all we have started here. He will have to be mother and father to our children. King and queen to our kingdom. When I am gone, I would have him remember all the joys of the life we made together and none of the sadness.

So we celebrate here, high above our kingdom, bathed in morning light. Little T'amT'am—or Ptolemy, as surely he must be called now that he is a man of three—does not understand that anything is wrong. They know there will be feasting afterward. Crinagoras will recite a new poem. Maysar will lead our Berber tribesmen in a wild drumbeat dance while Tala's son and the other young men of our court will make wagers in a dice game, and Chryssa will chase after their boys.

Meanwhile, my little prince and his playmates are excited by the crashing sea below. They are charmed by the gold-painted dome of my Iseum. They squeal with delight when they are given cakes sprinkled with saffron and other pastries sticky with honey.

Luna's excited bark grates on my nerves, and even my son's beautiful laughter, usually so precious to me, hurts my ears. And I find that I am too weak now to hold him upon my lap while he sips from my cup. The king reaches to take our son from me. "Come, Selene. This has been too much for you. Let us get you back to your bed."

I smile in surrender, pressing my lips against my son's chubby little cheeks and admiring his tiny fingertips with their perfect pink nails and their tiny half-moons. When Juba scoops my baby up from my tired and shaking arms, I say, "The wind soothes me. Can I rest here until you come back for me tonight after the festivities?"

He narrows his eyes, but I can see that he will not refuse me. "I'll stay with you and send the boy with his nurse."

I wheeze, fighting back a cough. "Oh, no, they are waiting for you at the palace. And my son should not be without both his mother and father on his birthday! Look how happy he is in your arms. How he needs you. Come back for me tonight and we can have supper together on pillows and low tables as we used to. I will feel much better by evening."

It is the last lie I will ever tell him, I think, and he must forgive me for it, because I cannot bear to see my king weep in sadness at my bedside. It will break my spirit when I most need my spirit whole. He said once that he could not bear to lose me, so I whisper the only words I know that will make him understand he will never lose me. *"When and where you are Gaius, I then and there am Gaia."*

The words make him smile, and he presses a soft kiss to my cheek. *"When and where you are Gaia, I then and there am Gaius."*

Then Juba hoists my squealing son atop one of his shoulders. Ah. My strong king. My little prince, my little war drum. I close my eyes, carving the sight in my soul so I may always see it.

THE king goes down the stairs followed by servants, a merry group of children, and the dog that watches over them, but my daughter lingers behind with me at the top of the lighthouse. She closes the door and leans her back against it. Taking a deep breath as I struggle for mine, she says, "Papa doesn't know how much you're suffering, does he? None of them know . . ."

I grit my teeth and try to deny it to no avail. I have used up all my strength to hide it, and now I am wrung out, sweating and dizzy. I cough and cough until my throat is raw with it and a sob catches in Dora's throat. "I don't know how to make you better, Mother. I have tried everything. Every potion I know. If I knew a magic spell of healing, I would cast it. But I don't know what else to do."

There is nothing else to do. She cannot turn back this River of Time. Just as all winds must die, so must I. And I try to remember that death, well done, is a gateway from this world into another. It need not be the end of anything.

Dora stays at my side as I try to sleep, but my every breath is agony. My hands do not look like they belong to me—they are dead fish dangling from the ends of my arms, pale and wet. I am a horror to myself; helpless and drowning in my own body.

For many hours or moments—I cannot tell anymore—I gasp, shuddering with pain. Every breath is agony. And when a tear slips from the corner of my eye, it wrecks my daughter.

She knows I am fighting. That I am grappling with death. The moon has risen before the sun has set, and in the strange glow, my daughter's face shines with tears. "Mother, if you—if you cannot bear it . . ."

Isidora cannot finish whatever she was going to say. She is trembling and tortured, her slim shoulders shaking as she reaches for my hand. My daughter's tears fall upon my cheeks as she kisses my fingertips. But when our fingers lace together, something changes in her, as if she has found something inside herself to hold on to. "If the pain is too great . . . there is something I can give you that will take it away . . ." Then she shakes her head back and forth with a wail of dismay. "But you will not wake from it, Mama. You will not wake from it."

She is offering me an easy death. She is offering an escape to me as I so unwillingly offered one to my own mother. But my daughter volunteers it with full understanding and the strength of love. She foresaw that she might bring me death, and it terrified her, and yet she offers it to me now.

There is her inner gift. Compassion and courage. She is better than me. She is stronger than me. Let her save that strength for something greater. I will not place upon her the burden that was put on me. So I gather my words up, one at a time, rasping, "Not in this River of Time, my love."

I swore never to leave her. Anubis may take me, but I will never *leave*. I will fight to the end. And it *is* a fight, each breath a battle. When at last I hear the rattle in my own chest, Isidora says, "We love you and will always love you, but you can go . . . you can go . . ." Wiping the tears that have streaked her cheeks with kohl and salt, she whispers. "You can go home now."

Win or Die. That is the motto of the Ptolemies.

I think I have won.

I am Cleopatra's daughter. I am less than she was, but in some ways greater too. I found the world cut apart and flung into the winds of war. I gathered the pieces that remained. I was a girl weighed down by chains in the dirt who rose again to bind people together with the wrappings of a Golden Age.

I am not my mother. I am less and more. She played for the world with armies and ships, while I have shaped the world in whispers and shadows. She lost Alexandria and I rebuilt it here.

She lost a kingdom and I carved out a new one.

I will live on in my daughter, who loves me, forgives me, releases me. She has given me leave to let go my hold on this world. And I bequeath it to her. I bequeath this world to her and her daughters after her, and all daughters of the Nile.

With the last of my strength, I lift my shaking hands to the heavens as a queen bestowing her majesty. From my fingertips, my winds come like the whisper of feathers, then grow loud like the flapping of wings, and I know I am going to fly away . . .

The happiness inside me becomes luminescent, my skin no barrier to it. I glow like moonlight through pale glass, my soul separating into beautiful pieces like a blooming lily, petals folding away from the center.

The winds grow stronger, blowing at my face, sending my hair whipping up into the night. Yes, the winds come for me and Mauretania, and the fire in the tower burns brighter and hotter, illuminating my kingdom. At the blaze, my daughter's head jerks, her eyes on the window, wide with amazement. "The moon. The moon is going dark . . ."

She breaks off, realizing what she has said, covering her mouth with the back of her hand. But I see it too, as vividly as anything I have ever seen. How lovely is the moon in eclipse? Mantled in shadow. So beautiful. So dark. *So extraordinary.*

And mine will not be an ordinary death after all . . .

* * *

A strong hand stretches out for me. It is a hand I know as well as
my own. It is the hand that took mine when we first stood defiantly
against Agrippa beneath the banner of the Ptolemies. The hand that
lifted me from the ground where I knelt beneath the unbearable
weight of the emperor's chains, unable to breathe.

There is no breath for me now either.

*Shall Pharaoh's son open the mouth? Helios—Horus the Avenger,
open the mouth!*

I clasp this hand. His fingertips dance over mine in gladness,
then grasp me tight. Helios pulls me to him, wrenches me up from
the dark ocean in which I was drowning. He kisses me, breathes for
me, filling my lungs with the sweet fragrant air of a new world.

I have already passed through the Lake of Fire and faced my
own serpent. My heart has already been weighed against a feather
and spared anyway, by the mercy of Isis. How else can I explain that
my twin brother and I are young again and in our power?

On the prow of his warship, we sail into the harbor of Alexandria
in Egypt. There is our lighthouse, a tall white tribute, blazing
orange fire against a clear blue sky. Our people throw flower petals
in the harbor. They greet Helios as their king. And just as he once
promised, he takes me straightaway to the Iseum, where I am
anointed.

He puts the sparkling royal diadem upon my brow and the golden
scepter in my hands—and I hold it fast. We journey up the Nile, all
the way to Aswan, on our luxurious river barge. We see the fields
golden with grain and watch fat little children running on the tow-
paths beside the oxen. We see the pyramids on the purple horizon
and our shining city of Thebes, rebuilt. We sleep upon a perfumed
bed draped in netting with silver stars. And I wear emeralds that
match my eyes.

We swim together in the green Nile, my gown floating ghostly
white. Helios washes my shoulders, my arms, my trembling belly.
He *bathes* me. He runs his hands through my hair, combing his

fingers through it, thumbs massaging my scalp. And stroke by stroke, drop by drop, the salt water of my tears mingle with the sacred Nile water until I am wrung out, rinsed away of life's pains. In this sacred space, he is the youthful god and I am a maiden goddess. My skin glows like the pale moon and he is the golden god.

Just as Osiris then rose from the dead, so too shall the deceased Cleopatra walk in the great company of the gods.

There, in the temples, we find our mother in a pure white robe, her complexion a sun-kissed copper as I remember it, her bare arms outstretched like Isis to welcome us home. Our father stands within the sphere of her ethereal glow—having set aside his warrior's helmet in favor of a simple tunic and a reveler's wreath of grape leaves—raises his glass, and makes a toast, merriment in his eyes. I feel as a girl again, as if I would rush to him and find myself staring up at him like the giant he once seemed to me. Our brothers are here too. Caesarion, Antyllus, and Philadelphus. And we fall into one another's arms and weep for joy.

It is all as Helios once vowed to me it would be.

But just as the Rivers of Time flows before us with slippery possibility, so too does the life after. There is no choice to be made between Egypt and Mauretania.

No choice to be made between the men I have loved.

It is Mauretania where I have left the essence of myself. There that I am buried. There that my beloved husband leaves honey cakes and pours libations for me. There that I will be reunited with Juba. And there that I find Ptolemy, my beautiful boy, riding his prize stallion outside our tomb. He rides in the sunshine under the flinty gaze of Memnon, who is young again and holds a sword in one hand and a round shield painted red with my initials in the other. Tala is there too, mixing her henna, shaking her head at me as if to scold me for being away for so long. My sister Hybrida lifts a hand to wave to me, Bast weaving around her ankles, tail twitching in excitement.

Grabbing hold of my skirt, I run through the golden grain fields to reach them. Ptolemy cries out, leaping off his horse to welcome me. How proud he is! He wants to show me the tall spires of antelope horns he has taken as his prize, and we embrace, my happy tears wetting his straight hair.

We will have roasted antelope for our feast when the king and Isidora and little T'amT'am return home. Our hearts are filled with so much love that we cannot want them to hurry, but we will welcome them with the grandest celebration when they come.

For I know. Now I know the truth of it.

I may crumble away to dust, but my spirit remains. I journey home now, and though my lands fall fallow and my palaces turn to sand, my kingdom lives a million years in me. I do not fear, for death is not the end of all things. I shall again warm myself by a fire, loved by a man, children upon my knee. And in the Nile of Eternity, I shall live forever.

Epilogue

ISIDORA

The moon herself grew dark, rising at sunset,
Covering her suffering in the night,
Because she saw her beautiful namesake, Selene,
Breathless, descending to Hades,
With her she had had the beauty of her light in common,
And mingled her own darkness with her death.

—CRINAGORAS OF MYTILENE

MY mother died with the moon. Her poet wrote it down for the ages. We buried my mother in the Royal Mausoleum on the hill with its *ankh* on the door, in all the traditions she held most sacred. We visit her there often, making offerings and telling her news of her beloved Mauretania.

Did she know she had triumphed and that her death would be followed by the most bountiful harvests we had ever known? I think she did.

My mother's last act was to smile at the shadowed moon. But the men who dominated her life did not meet their fate with such grace. King Herod's last acts included the execution of another son, and an order to murder all little boys in Judea under the age of two so that in them would arise no new savior . . .

As for Augustus, his empire is too small for him without my mother in it. Without her to match him, to test him, to keep him from his most despicable impulses, it all unravels. My mother once warned the emperor that if he did not repent, he would suffer the curse Isis put upon him.

You'll live long enough to watch your heirs fall, one after the other, until your empire rests in the hands of those who despise you.

It is already coming to pass, just that way . . .

I have seen how it will be for him at the end. How, whenever his daughter is mentioned to him, he will call her a cancer and cry, "Would that I were wifeless or had childless died!"

His last words will be spoken beneath paintings of theater masks on his wall and he will say, "If I have played my part well, clap your hands, and dismiss me with applause from the stage."

The lasting legacy of Augustus will be the Golden Age my mother spent her life working to achieve. She is there, in the grain fields that feed the empire. She is there, when just laws are administered and the empire goes on without threat of civil war. She is there on his monument, the *Ara Pacis*, though even now they debate which of the goddesses gave Rome her glory.

It was my mother.

She gave them Isis too. The mother goddess with her virgin-born son in her lap will go and on, and in that way, so does Isis, and Cleopatra Selene. I feel her with me, even now. When Tacfarinas whispers love to me and begs me to run off with him. Go anywhere, be anyone, he says . . . but I think of how she would want me to stay and watch over my baby brother.

I remember too that my mother wanted me to be the Queen of Mauretania. She would have gifted me her crown, if she could have, yet she gave me much greater power and dominion. She loved me and wanted love for me. She forgave me for not being *her* and asked only that I be my best self. She freed me to follow my own river, wherever it might lead.

And she taught me that I am a Daughter of the Nile, as are we all . . .

AUTHOR'S NOTE

Ancient sources mention Cleopatra Selene only in relation to others. She was Cleopatra's daughter, Octavian's hostage, Juba's wife, and Ptolemy's mother. But the archaeological and numismatic evidence of her reign tells a tale of a self-possessed and powerful queen who wished to leave behind a legacy of her very own. In light of that desire, it has been my honor and privilege to write about her extraordinary life.

The historical evidence suggests that Cleopatra Selene was a religious symbol for Isis worshippers and a champion of the cult. Though Isis worship was banned in Rome during her lifetime, adherents of the goddess found sanctuary in Mauretania, where Selene and Juba built an Iseum complete with a sacred crocodile. Both Augustus and his successor were notoriously hostile to the worship of Isis, but thanks in part to Selene's efforts, Isis worship would go on to become the dominant religion of the empire until the rise of Christianity.

That is no small accomplishment.

It is, of course, impossible to discuss Cleopatra Selene as a religious icon without comparing her to Jesus of Nazareth, who was born shortly after her death. As a biblical and historical figure, King Herod intersected both their lives, which is why he is featured prominently in this story. More importantly, the history of Herod's reign as told by Josephus is the only detailed chronicle of a client king in the Augustan Age that survives.

Thus, to understand monarchy as it was experienced by Cleopatra Selene and Juba II, we must look to the reign of Herod. To measure the success of their court, we must compare it to the dysfunction of the Herodian court. And if we want to learn how the Iseum was built in Mauretania, we must look to Herod's Temple of Jerusalem. (The time, resources, and labor required for Herod's project served as a measuring stick for me in writing about Cleopatra Selene's undertaking.)

Though war and rebellion would savage her kingdom after her death, Selene's reign was one of relative peace and prosperity. She and Juba spent their treasure building up two capital cities and providing a plentiful grain tribute to Rome. This is especially significant in light of the way slavery seems to have tapered off in Mauretania. There is little evidence of mass importation of slave labor after the initial establishment of Juba II and Cleopatra Selene's reign, as might be expected in a grain-producing client kingdom, so I portrayed my heroine as ambivalent about the role of slavery. And yet, even without mass importation of slave labor after the initial establishment of their reign, Selene managed to transform the coastal city of Iol-Caesaria into a veritable reproduction of her native Alexandria—one of the many clues we have about both her ambitions and her poignant quest to memorialize everything she'd loved and lost.

Selene and Juba were bound in service to Rome, but it would be wrong to dismiss them as puppet monarchs. Selene was no more deferential to Rome than her colleagues and, in some instances, much less deferential. For example, in sharp contrast to other client monarchs of her day—including her husband, whose coins always featured Latin—Selene's numismatic iconography is decidedly provocative. Selene's coins are always in Greek, often flouting the emperor's official narrative. Her coins sometimes celebrate her dead mother. Her coins also elevate the goddess Isis. Moreover, Selene's coins imply that Egypt would break free of its bonds and that Selene represented the throne of Egypt in exile. In short, Selene's coins are so brazen, so nearly belligerent, that one would expect her to have paid some political price for them.

Instead, Selene appears never to have fallen afoul of Rome. This and her formidable influence as Queen of Mauretania is evidence of an extraordinary relationship with Augustus. Perhaps the emperor indulged Selene because she was no threat or because she was a nominal member of his family and he was fond of her.

In this series of novels, of course, I have imagined a much darker reason: a twisted romantic obsession.

That Augustus was an adulterer is attested to by several sources, and my portrayal of him as a despoiler of virgins comes from Suetonius, who also mentions Livia as a possible partner in her husband's proclivities. With this in mind, I invented the sexual relationship between Augustus and Selene as a consistent rationale for the unexplained turns in her life, and imagined that it stemmed from Augustus's preoccupation with Cleopatra VII as explored by Diana E. E. Kleiner in *Cleopatra and Rome*.

However, it was a footnote about the *Ara Pacis* that is to blame for the liberties I have taken. The footnote in question identified the mysterious prince on the *Ara Pacis* as Juba and Selene's son, Ptolemy. (The most prominent alternative theory is that the mysterious prince is the son of Queen Dynamis of the Bosporus and that she is standing behind him, but she appears to have died the year before the processional depicted.) Assuming the prince on the *Ara Pacis* is Ptolemy, I had to know how such a thing came to pass. That led to my study of the famed Tellus panel with its fertile earth goddess and her accompanying winds . . . and my story was born.

The ancients believed deeply in magic. This view was part of their everyday experience. And given that Cleopatra Selene was a religious figure during her own lifetime, it seemed natural to give her miraculous powers.

IN the end, however, the creative liberties taken in this novel are not half as outrageous as the events based on actual history. The wife-swapping, melodramatic Julia-Claudian family soap opera that dominated imperial politics is well documented. Julia's relationship with Iullus is attested to by the historical record. And in truth, I might have included many more details about the deterioration of Julia and Tiberius's marriage if this were not, at heart, Selene's story.

Still, I included as many too-strange-not-to-be-true elements as I could. It really *was* the emperor's habit to slip into Rome under the cover of darkness. Cleopatra Selene really *is* believed to have died during a lunar eclipse. Juba truly *was* a renowned scholar with a fascination for exploration who claimed he had discovered the source of the Nile in Mauretania. (As a matter of geography he was wrong, but if it was political poetry to woo Cleopatra Selene by tying her new kingdom to Egypt, it must have been very well received. In any case, his theory about the Nile was not definitively disproved for almost two thousand years!)

King Archelaus did try to trick Herod out of his murderous ways, and Crinagoras of Mytilene appears to have been in Herod's court during the time of these intrigues.

More astonishingly, Dio tells us that Drusus retreated from his last campaign after being haunted by a phantasm, and that before he died of a fall from his horse, his men were spooked by visions of boys on horseback and the sounds of a mournful mother wailing. These things are plain in the historical record and I have tried to pepper the manuscript with mentions of actual artifacts—such as the silver platter with Selene in elephant headdress—documented quotes, and anecdotes whenever possible. In fact, the story about the Berber woman and the lion comes from Juba's writings, as does his epigram mocking Leonteus's play.

Nevertheless, there were a surprising number of choices to be made where the historical record is ambiguous. For example, we know that Selene and Juba had at least one son, but his age is in dispute. Some scholars believe Ptolemy was born as late as 1 B.C. Others posit that he was born earlier, pointing to portrait evidence and mentions of his later military service in the rebellion of Tacfarinas.

But if it is true that Ptolemy is portrayed on the *Ara Pacis*, then he would have to have been born before its dedication, which complicates the matter even further. To resolve these questions, it has been suggested that Cleopatra Selene and Juba II had more than one son, both named Ptolemy, and that one died before reaching adulthood. I adopted that theory because it solves the problem quite neatly. Whatever the date of his birth or however many siblings he may have had, Ptolemy of Mauretania became the King of Mauretania. His wife appears to have been Julia Urania of Emesa—one of several indications of strong ties between those two ruling families—a thing that may lend credence to the claims of Queen Zenobia, another bad girl of the ancient world, who held herself out as a descendent of Cleopatra VII of Egypt. And it may be of interest to the reader to note that the black stone worshipped in Emesa is thought to be the same one later set into the wall of the Kaaba by the Islamic prophet Muhammad.

We know nothing about Selene's daughter except that she existed. The evidence is an inscription, most likely dedicated during a visit with Juba to Greece, in which the girl is referred to only as the daughter of the Libyan king. Historians traditionally identify Selene's daughter as Drusilla of Mauretania, but recent scholarship indicates Drusilla is actually Selene's *granddaughter*, the future wife of the procurator Antonius Felix in Judea.

Moreover, the single most telling historical fact that we know about Selene is that she named her son Ptolemy, reaching into her dynastic heritage rather than her husband's. This not only bespeaks of Selene's extraordinary power and prestige, but also tells us that her daughter would almost certainly have been given a dynastic name, and that is why I chose *Cleopatra Isidora*.

As for Pythodorida of Tralles, she does not appear to be one of the children taken in by Octavia or Antonia Minor to be fostered in Rome. And yet as the granddaughter of Marcus Antonius, she was able to secure not just one, but two royal marriages that eventually made her sole ruler of Pontus. Importantly, Pythodorida adopted the titles of the Ptolemaic dynasty. That there was only one living Ptolemaic queen for Pythodorida to emulate gives a clue as to who her patroness might have been. In short, if Pythodorida was not raised in Rome, then her presence at the court of Juba II and Cleopatra Selene is the most probable alternative.

As for Selene's half siblings, more is known. Selene's half brother, Iullus Antonius, appears to have held a number of elective offices, so I filled in the blanks, ensuring that he received the military training that would have qualified him for higher office. Both of Selene's half sisters, Antonia Major and Antonia Minor, would go on to play prominent roles in the Julio-Claudian dynasty. Their descendants would eventually restore Isis to great prominence in Rome and Selene's influence is as likely an explanation for that as any.

The fate of Alexander Helios is lost to us. For all intents and purposes, Selene's twin brother entered the household of Augustus after the Triumph of 29 B.C. and disappeared from the history books. Some historians believe that he must have died of natural causes or been done away with by Augustus, and others theorize that he went to live with Selene in Mauretania. In any case, I decided to embrace the ambiguity surrounding his life and death and adopt it as my own.

Though we know that Mauretania was one of the few parts of his empire in which Augustus never set foot, Rome wasn't a far journey from Iol-Caesaria, and Selene would have assuredly visited the capital. There are several indications that she and Juba owned a house in Rome. Precedence for political visits by sitting monarchs can be found in the doings of King Herod, but Selene had more than political reasons to return to Rome; she had family there.

Due to thousands of years of deforestation and depletion of natural resources, today's growing seasons in North Africa may be slightly different than those enjoyed in the land Juba and Selene settled, but I adopted relatively modern climate patterns.

Other ambiguities in the historical record were more inconvenient. We know Augustus was not able to reach Marcus Vipsanius Agrippa before his mysterious death, but the sequence of events leading to Agrippa's death are a matter of some debate. The common wisdom holds that Agrippa set out to crush the rebellion in Pannonia but the natives settled down upon hearing of his imminent arrival, at which time he retired to Campagna and took ill. Biographer Pat

Southern argues more persuasively, however, that Agrippa took ill before starting the campaign and it was, therefore, aborted. What killed Agrippa, we cannot say. Other than Agrippa's foot ailment, which may have been gout, he was known for good health. Given that he and Lepidus were of the patrician class and in proximity at the time of their demise, it has been theorized that they died of plague.

That Augustus immediately removed himself to Aquileia, ostensibly to take over in Pannonia, is consistent with this theory, so I adopted it.

Similarly, the imprecise chronology of Josephus's account of Herod's ongoing troubles with his sons compelled me to make some educated guesses when it came to the exact dates of torture, trials, and executions.

Then we come to the controversy surrounding Selene's death. Due to the discovery of the mysterious El Ksar hoard of coins depicting Selene without reference to Juba as her coruler, historians have traditionally assumed that Selene was alive as late as A.D. 17. If she did live this long, she would have ruled Mauretania while Juba traveled on an expedition with Gaius Caesar. It would also mean that she was alive when Juba married Glaphyra of Cappadocia between A.D. 1 and 6.

The nearly concurrent uprising in Mauretania with Juba's hasty divorce from Glaphyra raises all manner of questions. Did Juba take Glaphyra as a second wife? Did a resentful Selene allow the political situation to get out of hand so that Juba would be forced to return home? Was he compelled to divorce Glaphyra to keep his throne? If so, was it because Selene wouldn't tolerate a rival or because Augustus worried about an alliance between Juba and the Cappadocian dynasty?

A rift in Selene's marriage has been posited—one that was mended after Juba's return. In fact, Beatrice Chanler points to an inscription on a monument she credits to Selene that welcomes Juba home in A.D. 6. However, modern scholars argue that because Juba was a thoroughly Romanized king, he would not have taken a second wife, and his marriage to Glaphyra is probably the best evidence that Selene was already dead. Then they attempt to pinpoint the year of Selene's death by correlating astronomical data with the eulogy written for Selene by Crinagoras of Mytilene. The lunar eclipse that best fits took place in 5 B.C.

I don't share a certainty that Juba's Romanization or citizenship would have prevented him from taking a second wife. His father is known to have had many wives, in keeping with Numidian custom, and the practice may have been considered a way to strengthen Juba's hand amongst his native Berbers. Moreover, although King Herod held Roman citizenship, he had more wives than he could manage. However, it does seen unlikely that the King of Cappadocia would have allowed his headstrong daughter to become a second wife in any arrangement, much less one involving Cleopatra's daughter. Beyond the Glaphyra problem, I'm loath to ignore the numismatic evidence of the El Ksar coins. I'm also wary of taking Crinagoras too literally. After all, the epigram he wrote upon Selene's marriage to Juba demonstrates that he felt free to take creative license.

Nevertheless, in this matter I bowed in deference to the weight of scholarly opinions more informed than my own.

NOW we come to the things that I simply changed or made up.

Selene and Helios were first introduced in *Lily of the Nile* at the age of ten when they would have actually been nine years old. I did this because I wanted older, more relatable protagonists. In the rest of the series, the children of Cleopatra are all aged accurately. Astute readers might notice that Selene's freedwoman was erroneously called Cleopatra Antonianus in the previous novel, but because I realized my translation error, she is referred to only as Chryssa in this book.

Generally speaking, upper-class women in Roman society left their children in the care of a nursemaid, which minimized attachments during the dangerous early years when child mortality was so high. Tutors were often more influential in the lives of children than parents. Given Selene's history, however, and her desperation to continue her dynasty, I chose to give her a much more modern approach to motherhood. For Selene and Juba's court, I mixed known historical figures with those of my own creation. Leonteus of Argos and Gnaios the gem-cutter are known courtiers. Iacentus was the commander of their guard. Much of the fragmentary literary evidence for Selene's life comes down to us from Crinagoras of Mytilene—both her wedding poem as well as one written at her death—so I adopted the theory that the ambassador was a member of her court at some time. That he seems to have maintained ties to Antonia Minor doesn't argue against this possibility, as Selene and her half sister were almost certainly in frequent contact.

Publius Antius Amphio was the royal architect of Mauretania, but his fraudulent counterpart in the novel, Necho of Alexandria, is a figure I made up to represent the dangers of forgery and deception that Cleopatra Selene and Juba II faced away from the Roman capital.

Euphronius (or Euphronios) is an actual historical figure, referenced in ancient sources as a tutor to Cleopatra's children. Euphorbus Musa was also a historical figure. He was brother to the more famous Antonius Musa and Juba's court physician, after whom the plant family Euphorbia is named. With some regret and great trepidation, I combined the two men because of the similarities of their names and because they would serve essentially the same function in the series.

Lasthenia and Circe are both invented characters, archetypes of women who did exist at the time. The Berber characters of Maysar and Tala are both inventions of mine, but Mazippa is not, and he figures prominently into the later history of the Mauretanian kingdom along with Tacfarinas.

As for what I invented in the story line itself, Agrippa and Augustus painted a picture of harmony, but there is historical evidence of tension between them. First there was Agrippa's self-imposed exile before the death of Marcellus. Then there was the advice given to the emperor that he had made his general so great that he had better marry him to his daughter or kill him. That Augustus felt compelled not only to adopt Agrippa's sons but to secure powers for his son-in-law that made him a virtual coemperor can be explained by a strong trust and friendship between the two men. My choice to infer continued tension in their relationship is plausible, but made for dramatic purposes.

We do not know whether or not Juba was present at the final Herodian trial held in Beirut. What we do know is that Juba and his daughter almost certainly made a trip East, during which they were memorialized. The proximity of the Olympic Games, the wedding of Pythodorida, and the Herodian trial left me with 8 B.C. as a likely and convenient date for such a trip.

We also do not know the cause of Cleopatra Selene's death, though it has been widely posited to have resulted from childbirth so late in life. To that end, I ascribed to her the symptoms of Sheehan's syndrome, which is a complication arising out of childbirth when too much blood is lost.

Though Julia traveled extensively throughout the empire, it is not known whether or not she ever set foot in Mauretania. The trip in which she nearly drowned has no definitive date, but my choice to place it in the summer of 16 B.C. might be too early and the subsequent visit to Judea almost certainly took place in the following year. Julia's Villa Farnesina was indeed painted with exotic Egyptian scenes, including a tribute to both Isis and the goddess Selene, but it was likely furnished upon her wedding to Agrippa in 19 B.C. instead of 13 B.C.

My wish to reproduce the exact sequence of the Secular Games was frustrated by conflicting historical accounts and a need not to overwhelm the reader in banqueting, theater, revelry, and blood sacrifice. So I presented here a condensed and slightly reordered version.

The Roman-era culture of the Berbers in general and the Mauri, Gaetulians, and Musulamii specifically are largely lost to us. Strabo, Herodotus, and other ancient geographers give us little to differentiate the tribes of Mauretania from those in Numidia and elsewhere, but what information they gave, I have incorporated. We know that Garamantes were slave traders, but the Berbers in general declare themselves free people, so it seemed reasonable, especially in light of the tapering off of slavery in the Mauretanian kingdom, to ascribe to them a distaste for slavery. Unfortunately, modern-day examples of Berber culture are of limited utility.

For example, ancient proto-Berber men are often depicted in art as wearing a great deal of jewelry, but modern Berber men largely eschew it. Moreover, because the indigenous Berber culture in modern Algeria has been suppressed, it's difficult to reconstruct what these North African people must have been like before the spread of Islam. Indeed, it's always dangerous to assume that the anthropology of tribes as we observe them now has anything to do with their identity in ancient times. Even so, I decided to risk extrapolating known Berber customs of the Tuaregs, including their jewelry and indigo dye, back through time, though in more modern times, it is the Tuareg men who wear blue veils, not the women.

BEYOND these matters, I have made every attempt to hew to the facts when portraying this fascinating and turbulent time in history. Readers familiar with the Julio-Claudian dynasty know that if Selene died in 5 B.C., then she was mercifully spared from witnessing the escalating tensions between Julia and Tiberius in Rome and the tragic conclusion of their conflict. It would also mean that Selene did not live long enough to see the spectacle of Livia's corpse rotting on its bier when Tiberius refused to attend his mother's funeral.

In life, Cleopatra Selene was a nominal member of the imperial family, at the mercy of Augustus, his family, and their intrigues. But that entanglement lasted beyond her death. If the historical Selene ever had cause to lay a curse on Drusus, then it is a curse that touched off an intimate death spiral between his family and hers. And in the end, Selene's granddaughter would be another Ptolemaic princess held captive in Rome. But that is another story . . .